THE ROOTS
AND THE TREES

THE ROOTS
AND THE TREES

NIZAR SULTAN

Praise for
The Roots and the Trees

THE ROOTS AND THE TREES is a historical novel about one Muslim community in East Africa during British colonial rule and the early years of independent African rule. It describes in insightful detail the departure of Ismaili Muslims from Tanzania and Uganda in the early 1970s and their settlement in Canada. It's a fascinating narrative that provides an evocative history for many Ismailis, their children, and grandchildren. For the wider community, the book is a poignant account of one refugee and immigrant community's arrival, challenges, and effective adaptation to life in Canada.

—Professor Dr. Fariyal Ross-Sheriff

THE ROOTS AND THE TREES is a well-written, highly entertaining, and enlightening novel that gives the reader a sound understanding of the experiences of the Ismailis and other South Asian communities in East Africa, and the challenges they faced coming to, and settling in, Canada. It also provides valuable insights into the Ismaili faith, traditions, and history. I recommend it to anyone interested in learning about the contributions that immigrants make to Canada, and the role and value of pluralism in our society.

—V. Maric

NIZAR SULTAN'S seminal novel, Roots and Trees, is a fascinating, deep, and very real story of Ismaili immigrants. The first part is set in Africa, illuminating the simplicity and innocence of life during those colonial days. It depicts the amazing and genuine relationships between communities, drawing the reader into a complex world making you wonder what comes next.

Revolving predominantly around two families and narrated through their eyes, it is through their conversations and their stories throughout that you learn about the fabric of society to which they belong.

This book is a triumph of transition from colonial life to African independence to final transition to the West. While this book could be any emigrant's story, for me, it was nostalgia captured, as it brought back memories of a life which today, is almost forgotten. Nizar has captured time in a book, relevant today to the Ismaili community and indeed, to every community that has faced transition.

—**ALMAS KABANI**

THE ROOTS AND THE TREES hits all the right notes in a bittersweet melody of nostalgia, childhood innocence, built-in societal bigotry, colonial and post-colonial history, strong family ties, community solidarity and, of course, some Bollywood-type drama. In the context of today's Western societies, values such as boundaries in romance, need for parental approval in decision-making, border on the quaint. The journey of the two principal characters in the book – Rafiq and Anil – is a familiar one to many in the East African Ismaili diaspora. The author's keen eye for detail evokes long-forgotten memories and repressed emotions of one's own journey, at times almost verbatim and interspersed with laugh-out-loud moments. The book underscores the enduring value of friendship, transcending geography, age, culture and societal strata. Through thoughtful prose and lively dialogue, it broaches sensitive societal and cultural issues of the day in all the three countries where Rafiq and Anil lived. All in all, it is a delightful, breezy read.

—**DR. FEROZ KASSAM**

NIZAR SULTAN'S The Roots and the Trees can be a tear-jerker imbued in humility and cosmopolitan genre. It is exceptionally well written and is insightful, entertaining, educational, and thought-provoking. The narrative encompasses an array of characters, settings, and motifs that capture the imagination. It successfully brings out the Islamic ethics and values that community's spiritual leader espouses, and which the book's main characters live by.

—Nasrullah and Mehrun Hassanali

THE MOST POIGNANT moment for me, so far, was how Chelsea forgave Tom and the DC when they went to apologize to her for their discriminatory behaviour of the past. The quiet and subtle way in which this character's strength is built and portrayed is masterful. It is inspiring. The reader's interest in this character is piqued. …. Also, how Chelsea could be so readily forgiving and that forgivingness is a central ethic in Islam is communicated subtly and demonstrated in a powerful way. Passages written with an intent to transform the students always provoke thinking and encourage discussion. A wonderful skill.

—Yasmin Jamal

FITTINGLY, I finished reading *The Roots and the Trees* on Canada Day. It took me down the memory lane from Dar es Salaam to London to Toronto and while I read the book I visited all those places and the times. After starting to read it, I could not put the book down.

Optimism is found in the book on the bedrock of faith, prayers, trust and willingness to work hard. While personal success is converted to a responsibility to help others.

The book is a great service to all of us in recording our history in a real sense and I hope that all Ismailis will read and appreciate it.

—Zool Samji

I FINISHED READING this amazing book a few days ago....
I could not put it down and thoroughly enjoyed it. I liked the
story and the twists and turns, always with many lessons for the
readers -young and old. These lessons and messages are the book's
valuable gems that the author has done a superb job of sharing and
imparting. Simply wonderful.

—KARIM SUNDERJI

THE AUTHOR cleverly weaves into his narrative, the importance
of instilling the ethics of Islam (peace, honesty, generosity, tolerance,
humility, compassion) in children, and that culture and traditions play
a crucial role in building strong characters. He further describes the
parents' role in nurturing these principles that can serve the children
well as they move from childhood to adulthood, and the beliefs
become the guiding principles as the children face the unknown.

—MALI DHANIDINA

Cover Design: Agata Broncel, Bukovero - Book Cover Designer
Layout Design and Formatting: Ruth Dwight Graphics

First Printing: April, 2020
ISBN 978-1-7771443-8-8

This book is dedicated to my wife, Ameena,
who inspired me to write

Foreword

The 1960s were a turbulent time in many parts of the world, not the least in the British East African colonies of Kenya, Tanganyika, and Uganda. The decade opened on a peaceful note, but the seeds of coming change had been sown. By 1970, the African peoples in all three countries had gained independence and were pursuing their own sociopolitical agendas. Many had no love for either their white-skinned former masters or the businessmen, shopkeepers, and traders from South Asia, whom they had always considered an adjunct of their former colonial rulers. Many of those South Asians were members of the Ismaili Muslim community. Ismailis in East Africa were mostly second and third-generation descendants of immigrants from what are now India, Pakistan, and Bangladesh. They are Shia Muslims who follow the teachings and guidance of His Highness Prince Karim Aga Khan, who became their 49th Imam and spiritual leader in 1957.

MY FIRST INTRODUCTION TO the Ismailis and East Africa was in 1968 when I was engaged as a consultant to do a market demand and financial feasibility study of the vision of His Highness for a chain of hotels and game lodges in Kenya, Tanzania (formerly Tanganyika), and Uganda. I spent five weeks in those countries and met with His Highness in Europe both before and after my time on the ground in East Africa. The hotels and lodges that were subsequently built became the nucleus of today's Serena Hotels chain.

THE 1970s BEGAN WITH a series of events in Tanzania that caused considerable anxiety among Ismailis there. This was followed by the expulsion of all Asians from Uganda. Many Ismailis chose to make new lives in Europe and North America. By 1973, I had joined the Aga Khan's organization as an executive in what has evolved over the years to become the Aga Khan Fund for Economic Development. One of my jobs was to implement a plan for providing socio-economic assistance to Ismailis, who had immigrated to Canada, the U.K., and the U.S.A.

IN 1974, WE HIRED Nizar Sultan to open an Ismaili Business Information

Centre (IBIC) in Toronto. The Centre's mission was to provide advice, financial assistance, and practical help to Ismailis wishing to establish businesses in Eastern Canada. Similar Centres were opened in Western Canada, and in the U.K. In 1977, I moved to Toronto to head up the Aga Khan's economic development initiatives in North America. For more than five years, Nizar and I had offices within a few steps of each other, and we worked closely together.

NIZAR SPENT 15 YEARS as the officer in charge of IBIC-Toronto, which supported the establishment of hundreds of Ismaili businesses in Eastern Canada. That was followed by his 20 years as CEO of the Aga Khan Council for Canada. Before migrating to Canada in 1972, Nizar had worked for five years as an executive in the Tanzanian government, specializing in economic development. He has first-hand knowledge of the events and forces that led to the emigration from Tanzania of the majority of Ismailis, who lived there.

NIZAR HAS A DEEP COMMITMENT to his faith, as well as a broad under-standing of the history and lives of Ismailis in Canada and around the world.

IT'S NOW BEEN NEARLY 50 years since the events in East Africa that drove many Ismailis to leave for North America and the U.K. Those original migrants are now outnumbered in their new homeland by their children and grandchil-dren. Nizar knows from personal experience that many second and third-gener-ation Canadian Ismailis have only a hazy idea of what happened to their parents and grandparents in the 60s and 70s. He believes that they also need to know more about the Ismaili faith and how a commitment to its precepts can benefit them in their daily lives. When Nizar first told me that he was writing a book, he said he wanted to take a step toward filling gaps in both those areas. He tells the story using fictional characters, but the events his characters faced happened, and real families did what his characters did.

THE ROOTS AND THE TREES is a labor of love – Nizar Sultan's love of his faith, his love for the Ismailis who make up his community, and his love of Canada, his adopted homeland.

FROM THE BOOK, I learned a lot about the Ismailis that I did not know, even after working with them for 15 years, and I have a better understanding of how their faith inspires them.

Herb Holley
Mercer Island, WA

Author's Note

THE ROOTS AND THE TREES is the story of two boys, Rafiq Abdulla, and Anil Damji, of Ismaili Muslim faith and South Asian heritage. It begins with their high school years in East Africa in 1957 and follows them and their families ultimately to Canada as they navigate the political turmoil in East Africa in the 1960s and 1970s. The characters in the book are fictitious. The significant events that shaped their lives are real.

The book relates the life experiences of Ismailis in Tanzania under British colonial rule, the country's transition to independence in 1961, the Ismaili exodus from Tanzania, Kenya, and Uganda, and the community's establishment in Canada, as seen through the eyes of and experienced by Rafiq, Anil, and their family members.

It describes the social governance institutions and economic support programs His Highness Prince Karim Aga Khan - the community's spiritual leader (*Imam*) - established, and on which Rafiq and Anil got appointed to serve, to facilitate the community's settlement in Canada. It then goes on to relate how, guided and supported by their Imam, within five years of its arrival in Canada, the Canadian Ismaili community came to be well settled and respected, from coast to coast, for its organization, self-reliance, voluntarism, professionalism, business enterprise and philanthropy.

To understand and appreciate THE ROOTS AND THE TREES, the reader must have some understanding of who the Ismailis are, the role of faith and the Imam, who the Ismailis refer to as Hazar Imam (a living Imam), in their lives, and their historical evolution. The below description of the global Ismaili community, the hereditary Ismaili Imam and his organizations and structures is derived from The Institute of Ismaili Studies' website and other publications.

The Shia Imami Ismaili Muslims, generally known as the Ismailis, belong to the Shia branch of Islam. They reside in more than 25 countries, mainly in Central and South Asia, Africa, and the Middle East, as well as in Europe, North America, and Australia.

Like all Muslims, the Ismailis believe that Muhammad (peace be upon him) was the last and final Prophet of Allah (God) and that the Holy Quran, Allah's final message to mankind, was revealed through him. Muslims hold this revelation to be the culmination of messages that had been revealed through other Prophets of the Abrahamic tradition before Muhammad, including Abraham, Moses, and Jesus, all of whom the Muslims revere as Prophets of God.

In common with other Shia Muslims, the Ismailis affirm that after the Prophet's death, Hazrat Ali, the Prophet's cousin and son-in-law, became the first Imam of the Muslim community and that this spiritual leadership (known as Imamat) continues thereafter by hereditary succession through Ali and his wife Fatima, the Prophet's daughter. His Highness Prince Karim Aga Khan is the 49th Imam of the Ismaili Muslims and is a direct descendant of the Prophet Muhammad.

During the course of history, the Ismailis have, under the guidance of their Imams, made significant contributions to Islamic civilizations, influencing the cultural, intellectual, and religious life of Muslims. During the Fatimid Caliphate (10th to 12th century AD), the Ismailis built the cities of Cairo and Mahdiya (Tunisia) and founded various learning centers, including the University of al-Azhar in Cairo.

The Aga Khan has emphasized the view of Islam as an intellectual, thinking, and spiritual faith that teaches peace, compassion, and tolerance, and upholds the dignity of man, God's noblest creation.

The first Ismailis arrived in Canada in the mid-1960s. Political changes in the early 1970s in many Asian and African countries led to the arrival of large numbers of Ismailis in Canada. The community went through another important growth phase when several Ismailis from Central Asia settled in Canada after the fall of the Soviet Union in the early 1990s. Today, nearly 100,000 Ismailis are settled throughout Canada, and occupy senior positions in the professions and government; many are highly successful entrepreneurs.

The Ismailis in Canada are governed by volunteers under the aegis of His Highness Prince Aga Khan Shia Imami Ismaili Council for Canada, headquartered in Toronto. Local Ismaili Councils are based in Vancouver, Calgary, Edmonton, Toronto, Ottawa, and Montreal.

THE COMMUNITY REFERS TO itself as the "Jamat," an Arabic word which means a community, but for the Ismailis, Jamat has come to mean the Ismaili community in a geographic area or a congregation.

1957

One

Upon entering the 10th grade at the new Government Indian Secondary School on January 1st, 1957, in Dodoma, Rafiq Abdulla was confident of one thing. He was going to pass the Grade XII Cambridge University Overseas School Certificate examination (the "Cambridge Exam") in the 1st division, which no Indian student in this town had done before.

He had not quite decided what he wanted to study after graduating from high school. Even at this new school, Physics, Chemistry, and Biology were not offered in his grade. Without these prerequisites, fields such as medicine, dentistry, pharmacy, engineering, and a range of other post-secondary level options would not be available to him; however, that was not of much consequence for Rafiq. His areas of interest were economics and financial management.

In 1957, Dodoma was a mid-sized East African town of around 25,000, in the Central Province of Tanganyika. No one knew the exact population because the British, who ruled Tanganyika as a British Territory, did not conduct censuses.

Arid, with annual average daytime temperature of 75 Fahrenheit, the town had around 1,500 people of Indian origin whose ancestors had migrated from India to the island of Zanzibar on the east coast of Africa and then made their way to the African mainland. In addition, there were around 500 Arabs, who had also migrated via Zanzibar to the mainland, and about 200 Europeans. Most of the latter were British colonial rulers of Tanganyika. The remaining population in Dodoma was indigenous Africans.

The mainland on eastern Africa, after the colonists had divided it up into Kenya, Uganda, and Tanganyika, had come to constitute British East Africa.

Of the approximately 1,500 Indians in Dodoma, 60% were Ismaili Muslims. The rest were Hindus, Sikhs, Punjabis, Bohras, and Ithna Asharis. The latter two, like the Ismaili Muslims, belong to the Shia Muslim interpretation of Islam. Rafiq was an Ismaili.

The diverse Indian community in Dodoma, like in other East African towns and cities, lived in harmony. Hostility between the Hindus and Muslims that had erupted in India during the final phase of the country's independence movement, and had intensified after the subcontinent was split into predominantly Hindu India and almost exclusively Muslim Pakistan, was not evident in the East African Indian community. There was not much social interaction between the communities, but they traded freely and respected one another. In Dodoma, their children attended the same school, and while they, too, did not mingle much socially, they considered themselves one ethnic group and were generally friendly with one another.

The new Government Indian Secondary School was established by the British for Grade IX - XII Indian students. Hitherto, all Indian students had attended Indian Public School, probably built in the time when the Germans had ruled Tanganyika. That school was, at most times, staffed with four or five Indian university graduates; most other teachers had less than a Grade XII education. In the school's entire history, fewer than five students had passed the Cambridge Exam and none in the 1st Division. This school had now been turned into an elementary school.

Several better educated Indian teachers were hired by the British for the new Government Indian Secondary School. A brilliant Englishman was also recruited as the school principal.

Rafiq had not come to the new school from Indian Public School, as practically all other students had. He had begun his education there, but when he had completed Grade VII, his parents had moved to Mpwapwa, one of the six districts in Dodoma Region, some 70 miles to the east of Dodoma, to establish a small business. Rafiq was sent to attend The Aga Khan Boys' School in Dar es Salaam - Tanganyika's Capital city.

Both his father, Salim Abdulla, and his mother, Yasmin Abdulla, had attended Indian Public School in Dodoma and preferred that Rafiq continue his education in a better school when they moved to Mpwapwa. The Aga Khan Boys' School in Dar es Salaam was among the best schools in Tanganyika. There being no friends or relatives with whom Rafiq could stay in Dar es Salaam, he had stayed at The Aga Khan Boarding House. When the Indian Secondary School opened two years later in January 1957, seeing that it was staffed with a British principal and better-educated teachers, Salim and Yasmin had brought their son back to Dodoma.

Accommodation had to be found for Rafiq in Dodoma. Fateh and Almas Damji, parents of Rafiq's childhood friend, Anil, who lived in an Ismaili Housing Scheme home, had offered to take him in. They had agreed to charge 250 Tanganyika Shillings (Shs.) per month for Rafiq's boarding and lodging, which was Shs.50 below the market rate. Fateh had a well-paying job with a sundry goods wholesale firm owned by an Englishman, and Almas worked with a nursery school. Between them, they earned Shs.2,000 a month, which was a good income for a young couple. They could afford to be generous.

In January 1957, both Rafiq and Anil were fifteen years old. Anil had a ten-year-old brother, Zahir, and a seven-year-old sister, Tazim.

Rafiq was his parents' only child. Three years after he was born, his mother, a tall and beautiful woman, had miscarried a baby girl and had been unable to conceive again. Rafiq had inherited his mother's height and good looks.

Having no siblings of his own, after he moved to live with the Damjis, Rafiq had become very close to Anil's younger siblings. He liked to play with Zahir and make sure that he did his homework, and he adored Tazim, who, in turn, was very fond of him. She had become the little sister he had never had. He doted on her and sat down with her patiently every afternoon to go over her school work. When going out, Tazim chose to hold his hand, in preference to her parents' or Anil. Fateh and Almas deeply appreciated Rafiq's care and affection for their little daughter and young son.

Rafiq excelled in all subjects at school and always ensured that Anil had a good understanding of what had been taught that day in mathematics and English Language classes. He was smart and knowledgeable, like both of his parents

- respectful, loving, and considerate. He could, however, be quite assertive and defend his position vigorously, if required.

At Salim and Yasmin's invitation, the Damji household piled up into the family station wagon and drove to Mpwapwa at least once every five or six weeks, spending Saturday nights there and returning on Sunday evening. The two families had become quite close. These excursions were great fun for everyone. In the evening, Salim barbecued chicken and beef marinated in yogurt, garlic, ginger, and other spices. The barbeque smell drove the hyenas on the town's outskirts crazy, and the boys enjoyed hearing them howling, which sounded like human laughter. The two families sat in the fenced backyard until wee hours of the morning, drinking tea, eating cakes and biscuits, cracking jokes, and engaging in benign gossip about the Dodoma Ismailis.

Rafiq's parents came to Dodoma once a month to buy inventory for their store. They typically came early on Sunday mornings. His dad dropped his mom off at the Damji residence and went to do his purchasing from the wholesalers in the town.

After enjoying a cup of tea, the two ladies went "shopping" but usually came home empty-handed because "there was nothing worth buying." The two families often went to see the 6 p.m. show of Indian movies at the local *Rhemsons* or *The Paradise* cinemas. Before the movie, the families treated themselves to snacks, tea, and soft drinks at a local Indian restaurant.

The Abdullas drove back to Mpwapwa after the movie. Rafiq worried and prayed that they would not have a flat tire or some other car problem on the way. He did not like the idea of his dad having to change tires in pitch dark when all kinds of animals may be lurking in the jungle bordering the road.

On each of their trips to Dodoma, Salim brought Rafiq copies of the TIME and Reader's Digest magazines, to which he subscribed, and which Rafiq, like his parents, read cover to cover. He also read as much of The Tanganyika Standard, a daily newspaper of good quality, published in Dar es Salaam that arrived in Dodoma a couple of days later. If he did not have enough time to read everything, he was sure to read the Editorial. As a result, Rafiq had a better knowledge of the global political and economic scene than his classmates, or for that matter, most of his teachers, except the school principal, of course.

The first school term had gone quite smoothly for Rafiq. He liked his teachers and had performed at the top of his class. He loved the new school and the smell of new desks and chairs and he could not have been happier with his home away from home. In addition to Anil, he had other friends in school with whom he played soccer, volleyball, and cricket over the weekends, but the sports were not his forte.

The Government Indian Secondary School was co-ed. Like other fifteen-year-olds, Rafiq and Anil had started to take notice of and talk about the girls in their class and in the higher and lower grades. Gender representation in the school, which had improved over the years in favor of girls, was still about 70% boys and 30% girls.

Most girls had secret admirers, and most boys kept their fancies to themselves. There were some, however, who did not mind telling their classmates and other students that they liked a particular girl.

Though the school was co-ed from Grade I, the Dodoma Indian community in 1957 was a conservative group which did not favor their sons and daughters socializing, or even speaking to one another, so the boys and girls hardly ever talked.

Rafiq had been taking notice of a girl, Salima, in his class. She belonged to the Shia Ithna Ashaeri interpretation of Islam. He sat directly behind her desk. She was beautiful, but that was not all that attracted Rafiq. She was super smart. Graduating from Grade IX in Indian Public School, she had stood 2nd in the class. Her hand was always up when the teachers asked questions. Sometimes, when she leaned back, Rafiq could almost smell her. He wasn't sure if she wore *halud*, an oil-based perfume imported from the Middle East, via Zanzibar, but she sure smelled good. Of course, he did not tell anyone, not even Anil, that he liked her.

Rafiq's typical day started at 6.30 a.m. when the household rose. After a quick breakfast, Rafiq, Anil, and Zahir were on their way to school at 7.30 a.m. The school started at 8.00 a.m. and ended at 1.00 p.m. They ate lunch at 1.30 p.m. This was followed by 30 minutes of relaxation; 2.30 to 5.00 p.m. was "study" time, during which Rafiq and Anil went over what they had learned at school that day and did their homework, and Rafiq supervised Zahir and Tazim's work.

When Fateh arrived home from work at 5.30 p.m., all sat down to have their afternoon tea. This was usually some combination of homemade *nan khatai*, *thepla*, (Indian biscuits and crumpets), *samosas* (pastry filled with spicy minced meat and fried), and *chevdo* (a mix of spicy lentils, nuts, potato chips, and other good-ies). This was followed by getting ready to go to Jamatkhana (the Ismaili Muslim place of congregation and prayer) for the evening prayers. Dodoma had a new Jamatkhana, which was the most imposing building in the town. Rafiq loved to attend Jamatkhana, where the Ismailis could also network and socialize.

Dinner was usually at around 8.00 p.m. After sitting with the family and listen-ing to Indian music on a Kenya radio station and then to BBC World News at 9.00 p.m., Rafiq retreated into the room he shared with Anil at around 9.30 p.m. to read his magazines and The Tanganyika Standard. He was in bed by about 11.00 p.m.

ON APRIL 10TH, THE school broke for three weeks of Easter vacation, and Rafiq had to go home to Mpwapwa. He had vacationed in Mpwapwa during the two years when he had studied in Dar es Salaam. At that time, although there was very little to do in that small town and he was often bored, he was happy to get away from the boarding house in Dar es Salaam where discipline, like at other boarding homes, was strict. Now that he was so happy with the Damjis in Dodoma, even though the periodic excursions to Mpwapwa were fun, the idea of going to that little town again with no other Indian kids of his age and nothing to do was not exciting for Rafiq, but he did not say anything.

Also, he was going to miss seeing Salima.

1957
Two

Rafiq left to vacation in Mpwapwa with his parents when they came for their monthly Sunday trip to buy inventory for their store.

His first morning home, his mom let him sleep until 9.00 a.m. After breakfast, he went into the store. The business, like many Indian owned businesses in East African towns, was located in the front part of the building with the residence at the back, connected by a door. He said hello to his dad, who was busy serving the customers and sat down.

The business (John's General Store) had two divisions. One, which Rafiq's dad managed, sold beer brewed in Dar es Salaam, Coca Cola, Sprite, and Fanta, also bottled in Dar es Salaam, as well as imported cigarettes and pipe tobacco, limited varieties of wines and spirits, canned foods, three types of biscuits (Marie, Nice, Shortcake), and other imported groceries, a small variety of English chocolates and sweets, hardware, and building materials. This division catered to the small European population in the town, some of whom were farmers, and British administrators of the District. The majority (mostly British) were employed with a veterinarian research station and the Teachers' Training College located in the town. The division also served some two hundred Indians and a small number of Africans.

The other half of the approximately 1,000 square feet store, which Rafiq's mom managed, stocked *khangas* (cloth for African women's garments) and other locally made clothes, locally grown tobacco, maize flour, sugar, beans, salt, patent medicines, cooking oil, and other staples for the wider African population.

The store had been established by a British family that had moved from the U.K. to Kongwa, 30 miles away, to work for the British Overseas Food Corporation's multi-million pound East African groundnuts scheme to grow peanuts in Tanganyika and create thousands of jobs, including for the decommissioned World War II British veterans. The project was abandoned four years later, with losses amounting to over £35 million and was a major embarrassment for the then Labour government, which had initiated the ill-conceived scheme.

Most British nationals who had worked for the scheme returned home, but a few, who had enjoyed Central Tanganyika's beautiful weather and comfortable life-style, had stayed behind. John and Grace Buttons were among those who had stayed back and with some support from the departing groundnuts scheme managers, had established John's General Store in nearby Mpwapwa in 1951 in a 2,500 square foot building (of which around 1,000 square feet housed the business, and the rest was residence) which they rented for Shs.500 per month from a local Indian landlord.

After four years of running the business and having made good money, the couple had moved back to the U.K. when John had become diabetic and Salim, who had learned about this business opportunity from an acquaintance in Mpwapwa, had paid the Buttons Shs.25,000 for furniture, fixtures, and goodwill, along with a four-year-old Land Rover in good condition, and an additional Shs.23,000 for inventory. The Buttons also left behind high quality, made in England, furniture that they had brought with them from their house in Kongwa. In addition to the monies that they had transferred home during their stay in Kongwa and Mpwapwa, Shs.48,000, which was £2,400 (East African Shilling was convertible at par to the British Shilling) was a tidy sum with which the Buttons could return home.

The store acquisition was financed with equity of Shs.25,000 and an equivalent low-interest loan from Diamond Jubilee Investment Trust, a bank established by His Highness The Aga Khan, spiritual leader of the Ismaili Muslim community, to make consumer loans and help Ismailis and people of other communities finance small and mid-size businesses and other enterprises.

When the family had decided to purchase the store in Mpwapwa and move there, and send Rafiq to Tanganyika's capital city, Dar es Salaam to study, Rafiq had been unhappy with his parent's move. He was, however, too young and respected his parents too much to question their decision, but on this day, sitting in his dad's store, he could not resist asking the question.

"Dad, you had a good job with *Daresco* power utility, Mom had a good job with the bank, and we were happy in Dodoma, so why did you decide to buy this store in this small place? Aren't Mom and you lonely here?"

Salim looked at Rafiq, thought for a moment, and then replied, "See, Son, after you were born, we both began to think about what would happen if I lost my job. If we lived in Dar es Salaam, I could probably find another job with one of the dozens of businesses or in the British Civil Service there, but in a small town like Dodoma, with my Grade XI education, there would be few prospects. We decided to save money and buy a business where I could be my own boss."

"Couldn't you find something in Dodoma?"

"We hoped to find something in Dodoma to buy, or start a new venture, but nothing came our way. We did not have much money to invest. When we learned that this business was up for sale for much less than its market value, we decided to look into it. It was already quite profitable, but your mom saw the opportunity to introduce all of these new lines and said she could manage this side of the business. We borrowed 25,000 Shillings from Diamond Trust to buy this business, and we have reduced that loan to 6,000 Shillings. As soon as that is paid out, we are planning to start saving money to send you to the U.K. when you pass your Cambridge Exam."

"But, you must be so lonely here?"

"We do miss Dodoma, of course, and our friends and we miss being with you, but we are not lonely. We have a *Jamat* (community) of about 100 people here and a Jamatkhana. In life, you have to make choices and sacrifices. What matters to us most is your future and happiness. We thank God every day that we found Fateh uncle and Almas aunty for you to stay with. We want to work until you have graduated as a doctor or a dentist, or an engineer, and after working for a few years, you can tell us that we can retire and you will look after us in our old age."

Rafiq was touched to hear that his parents had done what they had, in large measure, to secure his future. Yes, he was going to look after his parents when he was established in his career, but it would not be as a doctor, dentist, or engineer. He had read enough about global economics and businesses, the U.N. financial agencies, banks, and multi-national corporations to become very interested in economics, finance, and banking. He could visualize himself working as a senior executive for The IMF or The Word Bank.

"I'm sorry, Dad, that you had to make such sacrifices for me."

"This is no sacrifice, Rafiq; this is our duty. When you bring a new life into this world, your lives don't belong to you anymore. In whatever you do, you must take into account the implications of your actions for your child. Your mom and I understood fully well when you were born that you would always be our priority in life. We have sought to give you the best education we can access. We have tried to teach you right from wrong and will continue to do that. With Allah's grace, we believe we have succeeded in much of what we have sought to do, and we see that you are growing up to become someone we can be very proud of."

The conversation was interrupted when some customers came in, and Salim turned to attend to them.

During his earlier vacations in Mpwapwa, Rafiq had come into the store every day but had taken no interest in how business was done. He usually came in and sat for a while and went back into the residence to read or go out for a walk.

On this occasion, Rafiq watched the dynamics between his dad and the customers. An African man ordered two cases of beer, three cases of Coca Cola, and one bottle of Johny Walker Scotch whiskey, paid for it, and drove his vehicle to the rear of the building to the small warehouse attached to the house and managed by the house servant, Rajabu. Upon presentation of the purchase order to him, the customer loaded up his order and was gone. There was not much conversation with him other than hello and *kwaheri* (bye, have a good day).

Another customer came in and bought two bags of cement. There was no discussion with him, either. Then, an Indian customer came in to buy an electric drill, which was priced at Shs.100. The customer said this was too much. He had seen a similar drill in Dodoma for Shs.60, and the transportation cost from Dodoma to Mpwapwa could not be Shs.40, he argued, to which Salim replied that Shs.60 was less than his cost. They finally settled for Shs.85, and neither looked happy with the deal he had made.

A few customers came to buy small things from his mom's division. They were all native Africans. Mom was cooking lunch and dinner and would not come into the store until noon when more of her customers would start to come in.

His dad's behavior towards these customers was quite different. He greeted most by their names and asked how they, their wives/husbands/children were. He asked them what they were in for and attended to their needs. For some, who bought more than three or four items, he totaled up their order and said, "This is 12 Shillings, but give me 10."

All conversation was in Kiswahili, the local language. He asked one customer if he had a sufficient supply of Aspro (Aspirin) and Quinine (medication for the treatment of malaria). Members of his family seemed to be coming down with malaria all the time. When the customer assured him that he had enough of these medications, Salim spoke to him about the importance of sleeping under mosquito nets during the rainy season and said that he would be happy to order them and sell the nets to him at his cost price. And he meant it.

Another customer came in and said, "*Bwana* (Sir), I will get paid tomorrow, and we have run out of *ugali*," (maize flour), and asked if he could get two lbs of flour for which he could pay the next day. Salim asked him if that would be enough for a week. The customer said no, but he would come for more when he got paid. Salim gave him five lbs of the flour and said, "I will make a note of this, and you can pay me when you get paid."

An African lady came in with a small child in tow. "*Habari, mama?*" (how are you, lady?) Salim greeted her. "I see the little one is better now."

"Yes, he has no fever, but he is not eating anything."

Salim pulled out a tube of *Smarties* and said, "Here, I think he will like this." The child's eyes lit up as he fumbled with the colorful tube's cap.

Rafiq was surprised by this uncharacteristic behavior of an Indian trader towards his African customers.

An African couple came in and just sat down on a small wooden bench at the entrance to the store. They said nothing. They just sat.

"Dad, often, when I go fetch my friends, I wait for them in their dads' *Dukas* (little shops) where practically every customer is African, and they do not speak to them the way that you have been talking to these customers. They are polite to the customers, of course, but formal and businesslike, and what are *those* two here for? Are they customers, or they have just come here to rest?"

Salim smiled and said, "When the Buttons ran this store, the Africans felt intimidated by them because they were white, just as many Indians have an inherent fear of the white people, so they never came into the store. The only African customers they had were people like Mike Msasi, who came in to buy beer, Coke and whiskey for the bar he runs, which is patronized mainly by the locals. They started coming in when we bought the store, and Mom added the new lines, which have now become as profitable as what I sell on my side. We want these new customers to feel welcomed and comfortable. How we interact with them has to do with much more than just generating business, though. Mom can tell you about it after dinner tonight, perhaps?"

"You gave away that tube of Smarties that costs one Shilling. Do you do that often?"

"No, but we do give away much cough syrup, Aspro, Quinine, and Iodine for very little or for free. Often people come in with their kids who are coughing away or burning up with fever, or they have fallen and have an open wound. The cost of medications to treat these illnesses and injuries can pay for two days of meals for these families. Children, and even adults, sometimes die from malaria. When you can potentially save a life by giving away a bottle of Quinine, which costs five Shillings, your mom and I don't think twice before we do that. Sometimes your mom makes the kids swallow Quinine right here, which their mothers would have difficulty administering given how bitter it is, or she wipes a wound clean with Iodine. You know how that burns, and with the kids screaming away, she bandages the wounds which their mothers would not have the heart to do."

The couple sitting on the bench got up and walked out. "So, what were they in here for?"

"They probably had debated what things they should buy and if they should buy them from us and had decided to come into the store, sit and decide. This happens often."

Yasmin came into the store around noon and said to Rafiq, "Lunch is ready. You can go to eat now, or you can wait and eat with your dad, or me, later."

"I'm not hungry now, Mom. Maybe, I'll go read a book I have brought with me."

"What are you reading?" Salim asked.

"*The Grapes of Wrath* by John Steinbeck. Fateh uncle read it and gave it to me."

"What's it about?" Salim asked.

"It's an American novel published in 1939 for which Steinbeck won the Pulitzer Prize. It's set in the Great Depression-era and tells the story of a farming family in Oklahoma that is driven from their home by drought and bank foreclosures. The family sets out for California in search of jobs. It's very sad, and it tells you what unbridled capitalism can do to people. I understand it's been filmed and stars Henry Fonda. I would love to see the movie if it ever makes its way to Dodoma."

"Perhaps I can read it after you have finished?" Yasmin asked.

"Sure, Mom."

Both Yasmin and Salim were avid readers. They read everything that they could find. Moving to Mpwapwa had helped. They had more time, and when their interest in reading had become known to their British customers, they routinely dropped off books that they had ordered from the U.K., after reading them. Each month, one vet received a bundle of the past 30 days' publications of *The Daily Mirror* newspaper from London, which, as he finished reading, he passed on to Yasmin and Salim, and which they read with much amusement. Although the issues were old, they contained exciting news reports and articles about British politics and socialites. Salim, in turn, accumulated the newspapers and took them to Dodoma when he made his monthly trips for Rafiq to read. Rafiq read sections that interested him.

Being such avid readers, both Yasmin and Salim had amassed much knowledge and knew a great deal about what was happening outside their little world. They had a particular interest in Indian and Middle Eastern history and evolution of the three "Abrahamic Tradition" faiths - Judaism, Christianity, and Islam.

All of this reading had also made them very proficient in the English language. They communicated with each other and with Rafiq mostly in English, in preference to their Indian vernacular, *Kutchi*. They conversed with their British customers with ease, using terminology that sometimes surprised the customers. Rafiq felt that it was unfortunate that both of his parents had left school after completing Grade XI, although his dad had stood 1st in his class, because, according to their parents, there was no point in going into Grade XII, where they would need to take the external Cambridge Exam which nobody passed. Rafiq was sure that if they were to sit for the Cambridge English Language exam today, they would both pass with Distinction.

When both Salim and Yasmin were free from serving customers, Rafiq said, "Hey, you know, both *Rhemsons* and *The Paradise* cinemas now have a special English movie show every Saturday at 6.00 p.m. for the students. We can sit anywhere for just one Shilling. Anil and I go practically every Saturday. We love English movies. Fateh uncle says they are educational and help us improve our English. Most movies are American, though – MGM, Universal, Columbia productions, but Almas aunty thinks that we are too young to watch English movies, which can have a bad influence on us. She says there is too much kissing and girls in swimsuits, which she says is not good for us to watch."

"Is that true?" Yasmin asked.

"No, Mom, the only movie I have seen with girls in swimsuits was *Dangerous When Wet*, starring Esther Williams. It was an excellent movie about a bunch of swimmers' attempt to swim the English Channel. Miss Williams was delightful. I hardly noticed her swimsuit, and she did not have any bad influence on me."

His parents laughed.

Rafiq went into the house, picked up his book, and sat in the backyard sun to read.

The family attended Jamatkhana in the evening, as they did practically every evening when Rafiq was there. He was invited on numerous occasions to recite the congregational prayer, which he enjoyed. Although going to Jamatkhana was fun, most of the people there were either older or younger than him, but everybody talked to him and asked what his new school was like. Some lamented that it had not opened earlier; they could have stayed in school, passed the Cambridge Exam, and gone ahead. They wished him luck with his studies.

Rafiq was happy to see that this congregation was like a family, and he was happy that his parents were a part of this family. They were well-liked by all. On some days, someone brought Brooke Bond tea and condensed milk (so sweet, no sugar was required), and, with prior arrangement, his mom brought Marie, Shortcake, and Nice biscuits, and everyone enjoyed tea and biscuits after the prayers.

1957
Three

On the third evening that Rafiq was home, as they sat down for dinner after Jamatkhana, he again raised the question about his parents' kindness towards their African customers. "I just wonder how much it costs us each year to give away or discount our products. It must be a tidy sum." He said.

Salim looked at Yasmin, and she said, "Son, we are Ismaili Muslims. In our tradition of interpretation of Islam, there is as much emphasis on ethics and values as on prayers. Honesty, compassion, tolerance, generosity, and humility are cornerstones of our faith and daily life. These values guide and govern our lives, and should govern our lives. Islam teaches us that if we are blessed with material success, we should keep for ourselves what we need; the rest we should share."

"Most people who come into our store," Yasmin continued, "have little or no education and are poor. Some grow fruit and vegetables; others raise chickens, keep hens that lay eggs and bring their produce into the town to sell, door to door. Others work for the Europeans and people like us. They make very little money. Now, we cannot eradicate poverty with what we make, but we can certainly empathize with them, appreciate their situation, and do what little we can to make their lives a little better. I estimate that an average African adult in this town makes around 100 Shillings a month. Compare that to over 3,000 Shillings we make every month. We should be a little generous."

Salim continued, "Generosity in Islam is not limited to giving alms. You can be generous to people with your words. It costs you nothing to be polite, say a few kind words to people - whoever they are - ask them about their health; how their children are. You can be generous simply by smiling at someone. You can be generous by helping an older man climb up the Jamatkhana stairs in Dodoma. You can be generous, as you are, to your fellow students who have difficulty with their studies."

"But isn't there a dilemma here, Dad? You can be generous in other ways, but you need money to be charitable in a way that you can impact someone's life materially; but as you make money, people despise you for being rich. So the poor may like you for your generosity, but your community people despise you." Rafiq said.

"Why do you say that?" Salim asked.

"Well, in Dodoma, people despise the rich Ismaili families with their fancy American cars."

"Why?" Salim asked.

"Well, I don't know, but most students in my class and their parents don't like them."

"Mom and I don't dislike the rich in Dodoma, and I am sure that Fateh uncle and Almas aunty do not, either. Mom and I admire and respect them for their hard work and enterprise, which has made them rich. I have sometimes felt envious of them, but never jealous. In our eyes, they are good and smart people." Salim said.

"But, they are not charitable."

"We don't know if they are or not. In Islam, we are taught that you should be so discreet when making donations that your left hand should not know what you are giving away with your right hand - so to speak. We should not judge others. Christ said, 'judge not others, lest thee, thyself, be judged,'" Yasmin replied.

"So Mom, we believe in Christ's teachings?"

"Of course we do; he is one of our six prophets in Islam. Prophet Muhammad said, 'a Muslim is not a Muslim who does not accept Christ as God's prophet and believe in his teachings.' Now, we call him Issa, son of Maryam, not Jesus, son of Mary, but I don't think he would have cared much about what we call him or his mother. After Moses, Jesus is the most discussed prophet in the Quran and Mary is the only woman named in the Quran. There is an entire chapter in the Quran dedicated to Mary. Of course, we follow all of Christ's teachings. They are no different from what Prophet Muhammad taught us."

"But aren't Muslims and Christians enemies? What about the Crusades?"

"The Crusades were a series of religious wars sanctioned by the Latin Church with the purported aim of liberating Jerusalem from the Muslim 'infidels' and guarantee access for the pilgrims to the holy sites. There is much disagreement among scholars on whether this was the real motivation for the majority who joined the Crusades. Some historians argue that most participated for adventure or to find economic opportunities, or for political gain. The Crusaders, when they came to the Holy Land, killed far more Christians than Muslims because not all Arabs were Muslims; an equal number were Christians, and for the Crusaders, anyone who looked like an Arab was Muslim. They also murdered thousands of innocent Jews who had lived in peace with Christians and Muslims,"

Salim added, "As Islam spread out of Arabia and thousands accepted the new faith, the Prophet told his people, 'as you spread Islam, you will come across people who call themselves Christians. Do not seek to convert them. They are from among us.' So, yes, there may have been historical conflicts between the Christians and Muslims in the Middle East and elsewhere, but they were never sworn enemies. Most conflicts arose out of political differences and not from the faith. Current hostility and discord between the Muslims and Jews and Muslims and Christians have been created by politicians of all stripes, to serve their political agendas."

"That is very interesting. Thank you for your words of wisdom," Rafiq said, thoughtfully.

"Words of wisdom are just words until you internalize them. We hope that you will reflect upon what we have told you and see merit in it." Yasmin said.

"Sure, Mom."

1957
Four

The next day, Rafiq came into the store after having had lunch with his mom, and he saw a European man enter the store. Salim, who was attending to an Indian customer, immediately turned to serve the European (as the white man expected him to do, and so did the Indian customer) and said, "Good afternoon, Mr. Turnbull."

Mr. Turnbull did not return the greeting and said, "Give me a bottle of Scotch, six bottles of Tusker beer, twelve Cokes, half a dozen eggs, and two pounds of sugar. And the Missus wants some biscuits, but I don't remember which."

Salim wrote down the order, even though it was a short order, in case he forgot any item. The Indian was also making a mental note of what Mr. Turnbull had ordered in case Salim forgot anything, as it would be inappropriate to serve the white man one item less than he had ordered or ask him to repeat any part of his order.

Salim wrapped up the whiskey bottle in some layers of newsprint and placed it in a brown paper bag as he opened the connecting door to the residence and called for Rajabu to put six bottles of beer and 12 Cokes in a cardboard carton and load it into the Bwana's car. Rajabu had done this before.

Salim placed the bottle of Scotch on the counter, weighed out the sugar, and poured it into a paper bag, sealed the bag with gum tape, and placed it on the counter. Rajabu appeared with the beer and Coke bottles. Mr. Turnbull picked up the two items and pointing to the carton in Rajabu's hands, said, "I will load these in the car," and he walked out with Rajabu. As he did, Salim whispered to Rafiq, "He is D.C. - the District Commissioner for Mpwapwa - the most senior British official here."

The D.C. came back into the store, and Salim put a dozen carefully selected eggs into a paper bag.

"These are fresh?" the D.C. asked.

"Yes, Sir, these came in earlier today. The farmer said they have just been laid."

"How many hens does the farmer have, laying eggs?"

"About fifteen, I think."

"And twelve decided to lay eggs on the same day?" The D.C. said with some sarcasm.

Now Salim had to deal with the D.C.'s biscuits order. The fact that he had told Salim that his wife wanted biscuits meant that he expected Salim to give him biscuits even if the D.C. could not remember which kind "the Missus" wanted. He could not say something like, "So what biscuits you would like me to give you, Sir?"

Salim pulled out one packet each of Marie, Nice, and Shortcake biscuits and said, "Mr. Turnbull, why don't you take one of each kind? I will charge you for one, and you or Mrs. Turnbull can bring the other two back."

As he considered this proposition, the D.C. looked at Rafiq looking at him with some fascination, but not with the awe and deference he would expect of a teenage Indian boy.

"Is this your son?" The D.C. asked Salim, pointing at Rafiq.

"Yes, Sir, he is here for his vacation from his school in Dodoma."

"You have a new school in Dodoma for the Indians, right?" the D.C. asked Rafiq.

"Yes, it opened this year." Rafiq replied without adding, "Sir" or "Mr. Turnbull."

"He will learn," the D.C. said to himself, and asked, "What grade are you in?"

"Tenth grade," Rafiq answered, again without Sir or Mr. Turnbull.

Salim and the Indian customer were getting uncomfortable with this conversation and wished the D.C. would just pay up and leave, but he asked, "So are you enjoying your vacation here?"

"Yes, I am enjoying being here with my parents."

"That's a diplomatic answer. I take it to mean you are not enjoying your vacation here. How old are you?"

"Fifteen."

"Well, I have a son who is sixteen and on holiday here from his school in Nairobi. He is not enjoying his stay here, nor does he enjoy being with his parents."

"Maybe, he is missing his friends. I do."

"A diplomatic answer again. Are you fifteen?"

Rafiq nodded and said, "My dad tells me you are the D.C. here. What does a D.C. do?"

Salim could have fainted. A grown Indian could not ask a D.C. such a question. He did not know what would happen next. He just prayed that the D.C. would not be too offended, but the D.C. wanted to converse with Rafiq, so he gave him a little talk on how the British ruled Tanganyika - with a Governor for the country, appointed by the Queen, Provincial Commissioners (PCs) for the Provinces, and D.C.s for the Districts. He did not say what the D.C.s did.

"That's very interesting. It sounds somewhat like the governing structure the British had in India. Do you think Kongwa contributed to the Labour Government's loss in the 1951 election? There is continuing criticism over how badly this project was planned and the huge losses. Do you think they will lose the next election also?"

The D.C. was stunned. He would not have expected an Indian of any age in Tanganyika to ask him this, let alone a kid. His son would not know so much about Kongwa.

"How do you know all this?"

"I read the TIME magazine, and Readers' Digest and The Daily Mirror. I have also been reading The Tanganyika Standard for three years."

The D.C. was at a loss for words for a few seconds. He could not believe he was having this conversation with a fifteen-year-old Indian boy in front of his father, who seemed very uncomfortable.

"I think Kongwa will pass. Nobody is taking the blame for it. The Labour Party is unpopular for more than Kongwa and will probably lose the next election."

As he picked up the biscuits and paid for the order, including for all three biscuit packets, he said to Rafiq, "I think I will ask Robert, my son, to come and meet you. The two of you can hang around together."

He was thinking that Robert could learn something from this Indian kid. With that, he left. He did not need Rafiq to say yes; he would be happy to hang around with his son. If Robert did come around to meet Rafiq, there could be no doubt that Rafiq would hang around with him. His was more of a directive than a suggestion. After all, there probably were no British kids in Tanganyika - or for that matter, in East Africa - socializing with an Indian kid. Rafiq and his father should consider this a rare privilege offered to them by a white man in Africa.

Salim was rattled by what had happened. No doubt that Indian customer was all over the town telling other Indians how Salim's son had "taken on" the D.C. Rafiq had not only engaged in conversation with him; he had told him that his government had made a monumental mess in Kongwa. The D.C. may have been appointed by the Labour government. Salim had read in The Daily Mirror that such appointments were political party hacks, and people with political connections got these plum positions. If he was a Labour government appointee, he must be seething with anger to have been told by an Indian boy that his government was inept. But, then, he had also said that The Labour Party was unpopular for more than Kongwa and would lose the next election, so perhaps he was the previous Conservative government's appointee. If he was, he might be happy to know that even a teenaged British subject did not have much respect for the Labour Party.

Salim did not know what to say to Rafiq. Something had to be said. He did not want to reprimand Rafiq because, truly, he was proud of his son's courage in speaking to the D.C. and the display of his knowledge and intelligence. He attended to a few customers and kept thinking about it. Rafiq could sense that his father was very tense and wished that he would say something. Finally, he did.

"Rafiq, these white people are our masters and rulers. If they come into our store, we should serve them as well as we can, and speak when we are spoken to, but we cannot engage them in conversation. I hope that he doesn't ask his son to come to meet you."

"I did not engage him, Dad. He engaged me, and why do you not want his son to meet me? Why are we so scared of them? You know I study Indian history at school – from prehistoric times to India's independence from the British, and these people may rule East Africa now, but they will get kicked out of here, as they got kicked out of India."

"This is not India! India had a highly advanced civilization – you have read about the Mohenjo Dero in your history course. Two thousand five hundred years before Christ, when the Europeans were running around wearing animal skins, Mohenjo Dero was the most advanced city of its time, with highly sophisticated urban planning, drainage, and sanitation systems. When India became independent, the country had thousands of university graduates – doctors, dentists, engineers, teachers, and lawyers like Gandhi. India was ready to rule itself. In Tanganyika, I doubt if there are more than three African university graduates. It will be at least another ten years before Tanganyika becomes independent."

"No, Dad, it cannot be that long. African countries from Nigeria to Nyasaland are waking up and asserting themselves. Julius Nyerere has formed Tanganyika African National Union - they call it TANU. Anil and I attended one of his rallies. He is astute and charismatic. The Standard said that he is saying all the right things that the British want to hear, and I have no doubt that he will lead Tanganyika to independence in less than five years. You should listen to him speak. Tanganyika, unlike Kenya, has little or no tribalism, and Africans throughout Tanganyika are united behind him."

"True, but independence movements take a long time to realize their objectives. The Indians started fighting for independence exactly a hundred years ago in 1857 when the Indian *sepoys* enlisted by the British, like the African *askaris* here, rebelled against the British. You have studied the brutality with which the British put down the 1857 mutiny, and you have learned in your history lessons about the Jallianwala Bagh massacre of 1919 when the British mowed down a crowd of nonviolent Indian protesters and pilgrims. It took India over ninety years from then to become independent."

"Yes, Dad, but the independence movement in India began in earnest only with Gandhi taking leadership of the Indian National Congress in 1921."

"Yes, but even from that time, it took 27 years for India to become independent. And you have to keep in mind the global political situation at the time of India's independence. Your mom and I have both read your Indian history textbook, and the book does not talk about the context in which India became independent. In 1946, the world was emerging from the most monumental destruction in the history of mankind. When the Second World War started, Indians chose not to take advantage of Britain's vulnerability and scaled-down their demands and activities for independence. Instead, as Britain's colonial subjects, they fought and died by the side of the British."

"So, the Indians actually fought in the 2nd World War, Dad?"

"They did, and they also showed the British that they were as good as, or better soldiers than the British were. When the War was over, the Indians were no longer willing to live under the colonial yoke. They told the British to quit India. The British were worn out from the War and had no appetite for the massive unrest and riots in India, which would have certainly followed if they resisted demands for independence, so in 1947 they finally gave up and appointed Lord Mountbatten, who had much experience of the region, as the last Viceroy to oversee the transition of British India to independence in 1948. You have read this in your history lessons."

"But Dad, Gold Coast became independent just last month and now calls itself Ghana. The Tanganyika Standard said Harold Macmillan has made de-colonization of sub-Saharan Africa a priority so other countries will follow."

"Yes, I read that too. I don't know much about Gold Coast. I don't think there was any gold there, or the British would have never given it up. India was Crown Jewel of the British Empire. It was the second-most populous country in the world. If not for the War, the British would still be ruling India. East Africa is a different situation. Kenya is a British colony with hundreds of white farmers and vested interests. Churchill called Uganda the 'pearl of Africa.' They won't give up easily. They say the Africans are not ready to rule themselves. It will take time."

"But Dad, there are many educated Indians in East Africa who are born and have grown up here. We are Africans, and we can help the Africans become independent."

"True. We should. You may consider yourself an African, but will the Africans consider you an African?"

"Why not? I am born here. You and Mom are born here. None of us have even seen India. This is our country, our home. We love it, and we desire peace, prosperity, and happiness for our fellow Tanganyikans. When I have finished my studies in England, I will come back and offer my services to my fellow Tanganyikans to win independence, if Tanganyika is not already independent by then."

"These are noble thoughts Son, but the Africans see us as an extension of the colonial rulers; second class, but certainly as quasi masters. I don't think they share your sentiments. We do, however, have the opportunity to make them look at us differently. You and I may not agree on how long it will take for Tanganyika to become independent, but one thing is for sure. It will become independent one day, and when it does, how the Africans - who will replace the British as our masters - will treat us, and the whites will depend upon how we treat them now. It is not only humanistic, but it is also in our self-interest to be kind and supportive to the Africans."

"How can we do that, Dad?"

"We have so many whites here, in Mpwapwa, and throughout Tanganyika. They should realize that whether in five or ten years, when Tanganyika becomes independent, it will need educated and experienced people to run the country; it will need people to run the veterinary research station, the bank, the Teacher's Training College, the schools, the railways, and other things right here in Mpwapwa, and the railways, hospitals, water systems, airports, and a whole lot of other services beyond here, that the British manage at this time. Only if the British had sense enough to recognize that if they treat the locals well, be friends with them, train them, they would be invited to stay on and work with the Africans, otherwise, they will get kicked out, and maybe we will, too, and we have nowhere to go. Neither India nor Pakistan are our homes."

Just then, Yasmin walked into the store and asked, "Who will get kicked out?"

"Oh, we were just talking about the British Raj and the whites in East Africa. The D.C. came in, and he talked to Rafiq...."

"What? What did he say?" asked Yasmin with grave concern in her voice.

"Oh, Mom, he just asked me if I would like to hang around with his son, who is about my age."

"And what did you say?"

"I did not say yes or no. Let him come, and I will see if I want to hang around with him."

"Salim, what is this about?" Yasmin asked, raising her voice and her eyes blazing.

"Let's talk about it later. It's nothing to worry about."

Her face still red, Yasmin turned to greet some customers that came in, and Rafiq went into the residence to eat his lunch and read *The Grapes of Wrath*.

LATER THAT EVENING, AS they sat down for dinner, Yasmin said, "Rafiq, Dad told me about the D.C.'s visit today. It appears he was not offended by your comments about the Labour Party's Kongwa fiasco, but we don't discuss such matters with our colonial masters. We have to know our place in this society, and we certainly don't socialize with them, so if his son does come around - I doubt that he will - but if he does, be polite and try to get rid of him as soon as possible."

"Wouldn't that be rude, Mom?"

"You can be polite and not too friendly, and he will go away. We don't want to get into any trouble with the D.C. You can end up saying something that they don't like, and there could be trouble. You know the D.C. can, if he wants to, trump up a charge like 'You sold beer after 6.00 p.m.' which we cannot do because only the bars can sell liquor after 6.00 p.m., and revoke our liquor license and 30% of our income would be gone."

"I'm sorry, Mom; this seems to have been unsettling for Dad and you. I will remember what you have said."

1957
Five

The next day when Salim and Rafiq were eating lunch, a white boy came riding a bicycle, parked it, and came into the store and asked Yasmin in a soft tone, "Good afternoon, Madam, is your son home?"

"Yes, he is having lunch. If you come back in half an hour, he should be done."

"Can I wait for him here?" the boy asked.

"Yes, sure," Yasmin said, and he sat down on the bench at the store entrance. He looked uncomfortable and a bit nervous.

"What is your name?" Yasmin asked.

"Robert, Madam. Everyone calls me Rob."

"Would you like a cold Coke or Sprite, Rob?"

"No, thanks, Madam."

Yasmin felt sorry, looking at him sitting there. Also, a white boy sitting on the bench at the store entrance could make Indian and African customers nervous, and that would not be good for the business. "I will check if Rafiq is done," she said to Robert, and opening the connecting door, she said in loud enough voice to reach the dining room, "Rafiq, have you finished lunch? Rob is here to meet you."

"Yes, I'm done, Mom," Rafiq answered and appeared within a minute. Yasmin gestured towards Rob. "He is the D.C.'s son," Yasmin said, although Rob had not told her who he was.

Rafiq walked up to him and said, "Hello, Rob?" Robert stood up and extended his hand and said, "Hi, my dad said I have to hang out with you."

"Do you want to?" Rafiq asked.

"I don't know; I guess we have to."

"No, your dad suggested that we should meet and spend time together. He did not say that we have to, but why don't you come in and we can sit and talk for a while." Rafiq said, pointing to the connecting door.

Coming to meet an Indian boy had been difficult; Robert did not want to go inside an Indian home. "Why don't we walk up to the Rock instead?" he asked. The Rock was a big boulder on a hill near the town that young boys liked to climb up to and enjoy the view of the little town below.

"Okay," Rafiq replied.

"Is it okay, Madam, if I leave my bike here?" Robert asked.

Yasmin nodded, and the boys were on their way. They were both quiet for a couple of minutes as they walked, then Rafiq asked, "So, I understand you study in Nairobi?"

"Yes, I attend a boarding school there."

"I presume it's for the British only?"

"No, it's an all European school with English, Greek, Italian, and other European students."

"Do you like it there?"

"Yes, I enjoy the school. It's co-ed, so it's fun. I wish that I didn't have to come here for my vacations. I hate it here, but the school closes down for vacations, and all the kids go home, so I have no choice. Last August, my dad let me go to the U.K. My brother Peter lives and works as an ophthalmologist in Cardiff. That's in Wales. He is eight years older than me. I spent the month there and had a great time. I wish we would go back to the U.K. My dad's posting here was for four years. We have been here for seven because he renewed it."

"Why did he do that?"

"My dad is a jerk. See, here, he behaves like he is the king of Mpwapwa, with the British staff, and Indian and African servants, and all. I suspect that he is a patronage appointment. In London, he would have a low-level desk job in some corner of Whitehall."

"What is patronage, and what is Whitehall?"

27

"Patronage is like, you know...someone important who is your friend or relative in a position of power who gets you a job or a posting that you are not qualified for."

"And what's Whitehall?"

"Oh, it's a road in Central London where the government administration offices are located."

"So, is Central London where 10 Downing Street is?

"Yes. I guess they got a house for the Prime Minister in the area so that he could get to work quickly, but I don't know how much work the politicians and civil servants like my dad do. I think that they are all a bunch of losers who are in politics because they can't find anything to do in the real world out there."

"I gather you don't like your dad very much."

"No, I don't."

"How about your mom?"

"Oh, she's really nice."

"Why do you not like your dad?"

"I don't like the way he bosses people and me around, and I hate him for having extended his term in this Godforsaken place."

"Have you asked him why he extended his term?"

"No. My mom says that the Home Office likes the job he is doing here and renewed his term, but I am sure he asked for the extension because he was jumping with joy when it came."

"Perhaps he likes the climate here. Most British love it. Don't you? And as you say, he has a much better job here than he can get in London and he is, probably, paid more too. My dad told me a D.C. has his house, and car and servants all paid for, so he must be saving quite a bit. Maybe he's saving up for his retirement and your education in England. And all people like to be respected, so I'm sure that your dad enjoys the authority he has here. You should not be so hard on him."

Robert was quiet. Rafiq continued. "We often don't realize why our parents do what they do. My parents moved from Dodoma to this little town so that they could establish a business and make some money to send me to the U.K. when I finish high school. I was unhappy that they moved here because I, too, had to go to a boarding school in Dar es Salaam for two years, but now I know why they did it. It was for me."

Robert stayed quiet and did not talk more about his father. As they walked and climbed the hill for the next twenty-five minutes, they talked about the subjects that they were studying at school, the courses they liked and did not like, and the sports in which they participated. Robert was his school's cricket team captain.

When they had climbed the boulder, which had a gentle slope on one side that made it easy to climb, and were seated at the top, Robert talked about the girls in his school. Unlike in Rafiq's school, there were as many girls as boys in his school. Some Greek and Italian girls, he said, were gorgeous. The English girls were okay. He had kissed one Italian girl, but she had stopped talking to him afterward; he didn't know why. The two boys were now conversing comfortably. Both had let their guards down. They realized they had much in common.

"So, do you have a girlfriend?" Robert asked.

"No, but there is this one girl I like in my class. She sits at the desk, immediately ahead of me."

"Have you told her that you like her?"

"No, I have never spoken to her."

"Why not?"

"In our community, boys and girls don't mix much. The parents often arrange marriages. There are some boys and girls who smile at each other openly, and they are considered as good as engaged to be married, and they usually do - eventually."

"Oh, my God! So, will your dad and mom arrange your marriage?"

Rafiq laughed. "I am just fifteen years old, and I don't plan to marry until I am 25, and I will find my girl when I marry."

"Good for you. In England, in the last century, parents decided who their children would marry, and it still happens in some cases, but mostly, boys and girls meet, fall in love, and marry, and that's that."

"Good for you!" said Rafiq approvingly.

"So, will you ever speak to this girl you like? I can give you the script for what to say if you want to tell her you love her." Robert offered.

"You sound like you are an expert. How many girls have you told you love them?"

"Two."

"And?"

"Well, one walked away, and the other told me to get lost."

"I think I can do without your script," Rafiq said, and they both laughed.

The boys sat for almost two hours talking. It was getting hot, and they started to make their way down. As they walked, Rafiq asked, "So, how long do you think you, the British, are going to stay here, ruling East Africa?"

"I don't know. In Kenya, the Africans want to become independent. Kenyatta organized the Mau Mau, and all they did was kill hundreds of Africans working for the British farmers, and now Kenyatta is in jail. My dad says that it will be 25 years before the Africans can rule themselves. He certainly expects to stay here for a long time. The Provincial Commissioner in Dodoma will return to England later this year, and my dad is one of three D.C.s gunning for his job. He thinks that he will get it, but he says that they might appoint some idiot with connections in the U.K. who has never seen Africa. Honestly, though, if they select my dad as the new P.C., their standards must be very low."

"I think the East African countries will become independent in five years. Nyerere has organized the Tanganyika African National Union to fight for independence here. He is saying, 'for people to rule themselves is a human right; for you to say to us, you are not fit to rule yourselves is to tell us, you are not fit to live.' He is saying many wise things, and Macmillan's policy is to de-colonize sub-Saharan Africa. Gold Coast became Ghana last month, you know."

"What does that mean? What is the Gold Coast, and what did it become?"

"Ghana – that is the new name for Gold Coast. It is a country in West Africa which was under British rule. It became independent last month, and Macmillan wants to speed up de-colonization of sub-Saharan Africa."

"Who is Macmillan?"

"That is Harold Macmillan, your British prime minister."

"Oh, yes, I remember, I saw him on T.V. in England. The guy with big front teeth and mustache. I think my dad does not like him."

"You know, I believe Tanganyika will become independent in five years. This Nyerere guy will make it happen. This is the time for the whites - and us Indians also, to start to treat Africans with the respect and compassion that they deserve, like all humans do. When Tanganyika becomes independent, the British will pack up and leave, like they did when India became independent. The Indians did not need the British to help them rule themselves, but the Africans will need the Indians and the whites to help build the infrastructure to run the country, and if you guys like it here and want to stay, you can help with building this country. You should stop acting like our masters and start to get to know the Africans and us – socialize with us, like you are socializing with me, now."

"True, but I don't think my dad would agree with you."

It was almost 5.00 p.m. when they got back. Salim and Yasmin knew where they had gone, but were worried that they were gone so long and what they may have been talking about. They knew that Rafiq was smart enough not to tell Robert what Indians thought of the British, but they had never met this boy and who knew what he might be talking to Rafiq about. They could see the two boys approaching the store, smiling and talking like they had known each other forever.

As they got to the store, Robert picked up his bike and said, "I had a great time. May I come around tomorrow again?"

"Sure, but why don't you come in for a drink? You must be thirsty. I am. Come on in." Rafiq said.

"Are you sure?"

"Yes, of course."

The boys came in. Robert's hesitation for entering an Indian home was gone, but Yasmin did not want him to go inside the residence. She wanted to tidy up the place – even though it was always very tidy, so that the English boy would not think that Indians were messy. She said, "Why don't you boys sit here and have a Coke to cool off, and I will go make some tea for you? Then you can have some tea and biscuits."

"Sounds good, Mom," Rafiq said, and they both sat down on the bench in the storefront. Salim opened two ice-cold Cokes and gave the bottles with straws to the boys. The boys sipped their sodas and continued to talk but in somewhat hushed tones.

Salim could not understand why they had been gone for so long, what the two, coming from two completely alien cultures, could have discussed for almost three hours and why they now seemed thick as thieves. They both looked happy. What had happened?

It was 20 minutes before Yasmin emerged from the residence and said to the boys, "Tea is ready. You can go in." The boys nodded but kept talking for another five minutes before getting up.

The dining table was nicely laid out with a fairly new table cover, three varieties of biscuits, mom's home-baked nankhatai, and cake. The boys were hungry and helped themselves to tea and biscuits.

"What is this?" Robert asked, pointing to nankhatai.

"My mom is a great baker. She bakes biscuits and these cookies, which we call nankhatai. She has baked this cake, too."

Robert picked up one nankhatai, took a bite, and said, "This tastes great!" He finished one and took another, and then another. He also tried a piece of cake and said, "This tastes great, too! Your mom sure knows how to bake."

The two sat and chatted for a while, and then Robert got up and said, "I need to get home for supper, although I don't think I will eat any after all this." And then he said, "Can I take one nankhatai home for my mom to taste?"

"Sure, but you should take a couple for your dad and mom, both," Rafiq said. The plate on the table was empty, save one, so he called his mom and asked if she could get a couple of nankhatais for Robert to take home. He had liked them very much.

"Oh, I am happy you liked it," Yasmin said to Robert, and nicely set out six pieces on a small plate, covered it in paper, and handed it to him.

As he took it and thanked her, Rafiq said, "You are riding a bicycle. How will you carry this?"

They put the plate in a plastic bag that Robert hung up on the bicycle steering, and he was ready to go.

"See you tomorrow?" he said, as he mounted the bike.

"You bet! Two p.m." Rafiq said, and Robert was gone.

"SO, WHAT DID YOU two do?" Yasmin asked as soon as Robert left. She couldn't wait to hear what had happened in the hours that had brought this white boy into her home. This was unreal.

"Robert is friendly. He is like any other boy and has the same interests and ambitions as all boys do. We talked about a lot of things. What we are studying in school, sports… he told me that he went to London last year. He doesn't like it here and doesn't like his father much, but he loves his mom. He told me he plans to take science subjects for his "A" levels and then study engineering in England. We cracked some jokes and laughed. I think that we are becoming friends. And of course, he liked your nankhatai. After eating three, he was still eying them. I'm glad that you gave him six. If we had given him just two, he would have probably eaten them on the way, and his mom would not have tasted any!"

Yasmin laughed. "I am relieved. I was worried when you were gone for so long – worried what you two may be talking about. We have to be careful. He said that he will come back tomorrow?"

"Yes."

"And what have you planned for tomorrow?"

"Nothing. Go back up to the Rock; sit and talk."

"Someone saw a snake there, once. Be careful."

"We will, Mom. Don't worry."

1957
Six

The D.C. returned home at 6.00 p.m., and Mrs. Turnbull announced that dinner was ready. As they sat down to eat, the D.C. asked, "So did you go visit the Indian boy?" half expecting Robert to give some excuse for not having done so.

"Yes, and the boy's name is Rafiq," Robert said with a scowl.

"So?" The D.C. asked.

"Rob had a great time with his new friend." Mrs. Turnbull replied. "They went up to the Rock and sat talking for two hours, and then Rafiq invited Rob to his house for tea. He liked some Indian pastries that Rafiq's mother makes so much that he ate three, and Rafiq's mom gave him six to bring home. I tasted one, and it melts in your mouth. You can try it with tea." Mrs. Turnbull replied, looking at Robert.

"So, you actually went inside his house?" The D.C. asked.

Robert nodded.

"What's it like, inside?"

"It's better furnished than our house and very neat." Perhaps his dad was expecting to be told it was messy and smelled of curry, Robert thought.

"So, what did you two talk about?" The D.C. asked.

"The usual stuff. Girls, sports, school. I told him I'm the school cricket captain. He said he is not much good at sports but is a good swimmer. He loves his new school and is at the top of his class. He likes a girl in his class but has never spoken to her. I offered to provide the script for him to tell her that he loves her, but he declined. He knows a hell of a lot about British politics and what's going on around the world."

"Did he ask or say anything about your mom or me?" The D.C. was more interested in the "me" part.

"Yes, he said we may not always understand our parents, but they do everything for us so that we can get a good education and grow up to be successful; they do it for our happiness and our future, even if we don't like some of what they do."

The D.C. was silent for a few minutes. This is what he should have told his son and now a fifteen-year-old kid, an Indian kid, for God's sake, was telling him this. The kid was smarter than he had thought. How could that be? He was just an *Indian.*

"So, what did you think about what he said, I mean about parents?"

"Well, he made me think – think differently about several things, including how we should relate to the Indians and Africans."

The D.C. did not want to inquire more. He hoped that his son would think about what the Indian boy had told him about his parents and find some merit in it.

"I want to send a thank-you note to Rafiq's mother, but I don't know her name." Mrs. Turnbull said.

"I don't know her or her husband's names, either, Jane, but the store sign, where it's written over for *Proprietor* from the time the Buttons owned it, says, S. Abdulla, so you can address it to Mrs. Abdulla."

"Mom, why do we not socialize with people like Rafiq's mom and dad? I'm sure that you would enjoy spending a Sunday afternoon with Mrs. Abdulla much more than with Mrs. Davis or Mrs. Clark. She is probably a lot smarter than those women, and she is so beautiful."

Jane looked at the D.C. to see if he would answer. When he did not, she said, "Rob, we live in a society where we socialize with our own. I don't think that the Abdullas socialize with the Africans, and I don't think that they would like to socialize with us."

"But why not? I spent the whole afternoon with this Indian kid and enjoyed myself. There's no law against socializing with Indians or Africans. Should we not look to be friends with people who are nice and intelligent?"

"Our socializing with Indians could be misinterpreted by other Europeans here, and by the Indians and Africans, as well. It's simply not done," the D.C. said.

"But Ricardo is married to an African woman."

"She is a Somali. They are Africans, but more like Arabs. And it's so unfair to her. She can neither mix with the Africans, nor with the whites. Ricardo and she are both isolated."

"Ricardo is a smart man. His wife looks smart too. She is a high school teacher. She dresses well, wears high heel shoes, her hair is always neatly tied in a bun, and she walks with her head high wherever she goes. Why can't we invite them into our home?"

"So, you noticed all that about her?" the D.C. asked.

"I notice pretty women, and she is beautiful."

"Well, so much for pretty women. I'll have my tea in the lounge, Jane," the D.C. said and rose from the table.

"I don't know how Ricardo would feel if we invited him and his wife over, Rob. I don't know if his wife would be comfortable coming to our house. After all, they have lived here for two years, and whereas your dad likes to share drinks with Ricardo at the Mpwapwa Club, where his wife has never been, to my knowledge, no white family has invited them to their homes, so we can't just walk over to Ricardo and invite him and his wife to come over for tea or dinner. I don't know what their reaction would be," Jane said.

"You know Mom, we live in Africa. We have been here seven years, and yet all we know are the few whites who are here. Why don't you invite Ricardo and his wife, and the Abdullas to join you for a drink at the Club?"

"Oh, my God, Rob! First, although there is no sign posted outside the Club that it's for the whites-only, I don't think any non-white, except for the people who work there, have been inside the Club. Ricardo's wife and the Abdullas would not feel welcome there. And I don't think the Abdullas drink, although they sell beer and wine."

"They would feel welcome if the D.C. brings them there! And soon, other whites would invite their Indian and African friends."

"I know it's difficult for you to understand this, but as Dad said, it's just not done."

"Yes, it is difficult for me to understand," Robert said, and he got up and went to his room. He had had enough nankhatai, which is what his mom was going to serve with tea now, and he could do without it.

The D.C., who was privy to his wife and son's conversation, said to his wife as they sat down to have their tea, "He went out with the Indian kid for two hours and seems to have become transformed. He has never talked like this before. I don't know what that kid said to him. I hope he and his family are not commies. You know in India, the British socialized with Indians, slept with their pretty girls working in their households and produced so many Anglo-Indian children, and then left the women and their children behind to fend for themselves when the British Raj came to an end. The government frowns upon socializing with the people whom we rule."

"Rob is not talking about that kind of socializing, James. What could be the harm in us socializing with Ricardo and his wife, or the Abdullas?"

"You are not serious, are you, Jane? I hope you're not suggesting that we do this?"

"No, but I am thinking about what Rob said. We have lived here for seven years, and all I have is Barbara and Joan to socialize with. Joan is boring, and Barbara is drunk after two glasses of wine. Would it not be nice if we had more friends? If Mrs. Abdulla or Ricardo's wife socialized with me, I would like that. Isn't it a shame that none of us even know Ricardo's wife's name? Mrs. Abdulla has served me in her store on numerous occasions, and I can tell you, Rob is right - she is much smarter than Barbara or Joan."

The D.C. did not respond. He tasted a nankhatai and said, "This does taste delicious. I wonder what it's made from. I taste some custard in it. It's like a French pastry."

It was evident to Jane that the D.C. was not going to talk more about socializing with Indians and Somalis, but she knew that she had gotten him thinking.

1957
Seven

The next day, as arranged, Robert turned up at 2.00 p.m. bearing a note from his mother for Mrs. Abdulla. He had come walking today.

Rafiq went out to meet him. They talked, and both came into the store. Robert went over to Yasmin and said, "Good afternoon, Mrs. Abdulla," with a broad smile on his face and extended his hand.

Yasmin took his hand and said, "Good afternoon, Rob, how are you today?"

"Oh, fine, just fine, Madam. My mom has sent a note to you." And with that, he produced an envelope which Yasmin took and said, "Thank you."

Rafiq pulled Robert aside and asked, "So, what do you want to do today?"

"Go up to the Rock?"

"Yes, we could do that, or if you like board games, we can play carom."

"Love to do that, but I must warn you, I will beat you flat. I am very good at it."

"Okay, let's go see," Rafiq said, and the two disappeared into the house.

Yasmin had expected a small two-liner from Mrs. Turnbull thanking her for nankhatai. When she opened the envelope, the note was more like a letter. It read:

Dear Mrs. Abdulla:

Thank you very much for inviting Rob into your home, and for the 'nankhatai' that you sent home with him. They were delicious. I will request the recipe from you sometime.

It appears the boys had an enjoyable afternoon yesterday. Vacations in Mpwapwa, since December last year, have been trying for Rob. Until then, he had the company of Mr. and Mrs. Johnson's son, who was also in Nairobi at school with him. The Johnsons, who also shopped in your store and whom you might remember, returned to the U.K. in July last year.

For his August vacation last year, we had sent Rob to the U.K., where his elder brother is living. Rob was miserable being here in December last year and did not want to come back for his Easter vacation this year, but his school closes down for the holidays, and he has nowhere to go but home.

The few days that he has been here have been miserable for him. He got into daily arguments with his father over silly things and wanted to do nothing. Yesterday, though, he came home after spending the afternoon with your son, and for the first time, he was smiling and had a somewhat pleasant dinner time conversation with us.

He told us that Rafiq is brilliant and knowledgeable. He said he has not met another boy Rafiq's age who knows so much about what is going on around the world and especially about the U.K. politics!

The boys have planned to meet again today. My husband and I will be grateful if you will encourage Rafiq to please spend time with Rob. I think, and I hope that they can become friends.

I have come into your store many times, and you have looked after me, but we have never really talked, and I don't know your name. My name is Jane. The next time I am in, I would like to know your name and also your husband's name.

Once again, thank you for being so hospitable to Rob yesterday. With warm regards,
Jane Turnbull

Yasmin passed the letter to Salim. He read it and said, "That's a very nice Thank You note."

"Yes, but I read in it a mother reaching out to another mother. I find that touching, especially coming from a British D.C.'s wife to an Indian woman. I wonder what I should do now. The note is long, and I think I should respond, but I don't want to start a conversation that presumes too much familiarity."

"You know, if I were you, I would just write, 'Dear Mrs. Turnbull,' not Jane, and say, 'thank you for your note. The boys seem to have enjoyed each other's company and, I, too, hope that they can become friends. Rob is a very nice boy. I will keep the nankhatai recipe ready for you the next time you come in. Warm regards', and sign it, Yasmin Abdulla. That way, she will know your name, and if that is how she addresses you if she writes again or when she comes in, then you can call her Jane. I think that will be the first time any Indian woman in Africa will address a grown white woman as anything other than 'Mrs.' or 'Miss,'" Salim said.

"That sounds reasonable," said Yasmin, mulling it over. She drafted up the note and kept it ready for Robert to take home.

At around 4.00 p.m., Yasmin went into the residence and told the boys, who had switched from playing carom to playing cards, and said, "I'm going to fry some samosas. The smell will be strong. You guys may want to go into the backyard."

At the mention of the word "samosas," Robert's eyes lit up. "Oh, I love samosas! I love the smell, too." He said.

"Where did you eat samosas?" Yasmin asked, curious.

"At school, there are three boys and two girls whose parents served with the British Raj in India. When India became independent, they moved back to England but missed the luxurious colonial life, so they took postings in Kenya and Uganda. These kids all eat Indian food. They introduced us to samosas, kabobs, and bujia. Every Sunday, when we go into the city, we go to the Curry Pot Indian restaurant and eat samosas and bujia."

"So did you taste samosas and bhajia and loved them at first bite?" Rafiq asked, also intrigued.

"Not really, but seeing how much the British Indian kids loved them, we continued to try and then developed a real taste for these snacks. They were brought up by Indian nannies, and they learned the Indian language, and two of them, whose parents served in Gujarat, also learned the Gujarat language. Sometimes when we go to Curry Pot and order samosas and kabobs, other Indian customers - most speak the Gujarat language, say to each other, 'These kids don't know what they have ordered. Let them put one kabob in their mouth, and they will be running out of here with their mouths on fire', and they laugh, or when sometimes we put the tamarind or coconut chutney on our kabobs or samosas, they say, 'Look, look, they are eating chutney!' The kids who understand the Gujarat language, translate for us, and when we leave, they will say to these customers, '*Kem chho?*' - How are you, and then say something in the Gujarat language like, 'We love samosas and kabobs here, and we hope you enjoy them too. See you later.' The Indians are just astounded that we understood what they were saying about us. Mind you, nobody ever says anything bad."

"That's amazing! We speak the Gujarati language also. That is what the Gujarat language is called: Gujarati. And what you call bujia, is bhajia" Yasmin said.

"These British Indian kids also eat curries, and they love a dish called biryani. I tried the curries one day, but found them too spicy."

"Do your parents eat any of these things?" Yasmin asked.

"No, but they know that I like them."

"Well, you will get to try my samosas today. I hope you can stay for tea." Yasmin said.

"Now that you have offered samosas, I would stay even if you wanted me to leave," Robert said, and all three laughed.

Robert ate three samosas and wanted to eat a fourth, but seeing that Rafiq had eaten only two and had moved on to eating the cake, he resisted, expecting that Yasmin would give him six to take home, which he could start enjoying on the way as his parents would not eat any, anyway.

Unfortunately for him, Yasmin did not give him any to take home. Making samosas was difficult. She had risen early to roll up and fill the samosa pastry, piece by piece, with specially prepared spiced ground beef and kept them in the refrigerator for frying later. She did not want to give any to Robert to take home for his parents, who would probably not like them, and risk that her hard work may end up in a garbage bin.

Before clearing the table, however, she did ask the boys if either of them wanted any more of the samosas, cake, or cookies, and Robert said, "Can I please have one more samosa?"

Yasmin smiled and lovingly said, "You can have two, Son," which Robert promptly did. Now, he was full.

That evening, around the dinner table, Robert was again full of stories about his afternoon with the Abdullas. Rafiq was good at carom, but not too good with cards. He had quoted Shakespeare and had displayed his command of the English language by using terminology that was not part of Robert's vocabulary. He also noted how good Yasmin's English was, spoken without the Indian accent. And, of course, how beautiful she was. He told them he had eaten five samosas. Jane was worried that he might get sick in the night.

The boys had planned to meet the next day again, but Robert said, "I can't keep going to his house all the time. I would like to bring him here tomorrow, or what I would really like to do is take him to the Club as our guest. We can do all kinds of things there."

"We talked about this last night, Rob. You can't take Rafiq to the Club," the D.C. said.

Ignoring him, Rob retorted, "But Mom, you said that there is no sign outside the Club that says it is for whites only."

"No," the D.C. interjected, "There is no such sign, but it is for the whites only."

THE MPWAPWA CLUB WAS like other Clubs in other towns in East Africa that served the white colonists, settlers, white ex-pats, and their families. The Club was small, but it had a tennis court, table tennis, and snooker tables, a spacious bar and lounge, and a social hall for parties and other events, and which also served as a 60-seat cinema every Saturday night for 15 mm movies that traveled from Club to Club in Tanganyika. Mpwapwa did not have electricity, but it had a phone system. The Club had its own generator, as did the Veterinarian Research Centre and Boma, the government offices. The Club was very clean, with nice polished furniture and was managed by a gregarious white, old man who had been in Africa for longer than anyone could remember. It was rumored that many years back, he had lived with an African girl who had died of typhoid. Everyone called him Henry. Few knew his last name.

THE NEXT MORNING, ROBERT walked over to the Club and found Henry. He asked, "Henry, I have a 15-year old Indian friend. He is the son of the people who own John's General. Can I bring him here as my guest to play table tennis?"

"Did you talk to your dad about this?" Henry asked.

"Yes, I did, and he said that I couldn't, although there is no official rule about the Club being whites only."

"He is right, Son. Any Club member or Supplementary member, like you are, can sign in a guest, but there are rules, and then there are conventions. The convention here is that you sign in people of European origin only. The reason is that if you bring in an African or an Indian, your guests will not feel comfortable because some members will look at them as unwanted, and that would not be fair to your guests. If you ask me who these members are and why we do not get rid of them, to be honest, I will tell you that most like to look at others as the members who will not welcome non-whites."

"So, what you are telling me then is that we are no better than those racist bastards in South Africa."

"Truly, we are not, in some ways, but we do it with much more finesse. Like, we say that one can only become a new Club member if a registered member nominates him/her."

"Why did Ricardo not nominate his Somali wife?"

"He did, but any nomination needs to be seconded by another registered member. The British are very smart."

Robert was angry. "When is the next Members' general meeting?" He asked.

"It's on Saturday, 29th, always on the last Saturday of the month. The notices and menu have gone out. Your parents must have received it."

Robert had attended these meetings. Practically all members participated, mostly because a sumptuous meal was served after the meeting. It was like a party.

"You know, Henry, I am going to come to this meeting and tell the members exactly what I think of these rules and their conventions. I will call them out for the racists they are."

Henry could see that Robert meant what he said. He was fuming. Henry was sorry that he had told the boy about the Club's conventions, which he, himself, deplored. If Robert followed up on his threat, the D.C. would surely find out what the source of his information was, and he would get into serious trouble with the

D.C. and other members.

"Now, let us calm down, Rob," he said. "Maybe we can work out some arrangement for you and your friend. You want to bring this kid to play table tennis during the day, right?"

Robert nodded.

"Well, there is no one here after lunch. You can sign him in after 2.00 p.m., and you guys can play until 5.00 p.m. You can even have afternoon tea here, but you have to stay indoors. You can't go out on the tennis court, for example. How does that sound? I can clear this with your dad."

"That sounds like you want to treat my friend as a second-class citizen. Over the past two days, I have gotten to know his family. I can tell you that he and his parents are much more sophisticated and knowledgeable than the majority of your members here are. They know more about us, about the history and all of the evil things that we, the Brits, have done around the world and are doing here. Yet, they have been very kind to me and treated me with the utmost respect and affection. And now you are telling me that I have to sneak my friend into this Club like he is some filthy rat who will soil your linens?"

Henry was alarmed. This was getting out of hand. This teenager had placed him in a predicament in which he had never found himself before. He should have kept his mouth shut. This could end badly.

"Rob, why don't we go to the lounge and discuss this over a cup of tea?" he said.

As they sat down and Henry ordered tea, he said, "Look, Rob, these matters are not simple. There are some members like Ricardo, who are very broad-minded. I find that the more educated they are, the more liberal they are. I am sure that if those individuals had their way, they would throw open the Club membership to everyone. Then some others are inclined that way, as well, but simply keep quiet about it. And some would never allow this."

"And my dad belongs to this latter group?"

Henry did not answer that, but said, "Any outburst at the Members' meeting will not do any good. It will put your father in a difficult position and create problems between you two, and possibly others. If you speak about the rules and conventions I have told you about, I could get into trouble. You know that I have no one back home. I have worked in Tanganyika for over 20 years. I hardly know anyone in England anymore. I can never go back. And if I get fired, no one would hire me at my age."

Robert calmed down. "I would never do anything to hurt you, Henry," he said.

"Even if you or another member speaks at the meeting to suggest that we allow non-whites as guests, if not as members, the members would come to you and say, 'You know, I support what you have proposed,' but many will not. And if you were to go to each, one by one, they would all say the same, except for maybe three or four who are real diehards. And if you thought that you have a majority and brought a motion before the Members' meeting, your proposal would likely be rejected and, because voting is by secret ballot, you would never know how anyone voted. Now, if someone like your dad were to propose this, perhaps we could get somewhere."

"Not a chance, Henry," Rob sighed, "I'm so sorry for getting angry. Can we keep this between us, please?"

"Sure, Rob. This conversation never took place."

Henry was relieved.

1957
Eight

Later that day, when Robert came around to John's General, Rafiq was waiting for him in the store and greeting him, said, "Come on in."

"No, Rafiq, you've got to come to my place today."

Rafiq looked at his mom and then his dad. The D.C. lived in a spacious stone house built by the Germans in their time, for their D.C., in the *Mzunguni* (Swahili for the whites' colony). Non-whites did not go there unless there was a delivery to be made or they worked for a white family. Neither Salim nor Yasmin were enthusiastic about Robert's invitation.

"Rob, why don't you boys stay here? I am making some bhajia today. You can have that with tea." Yasmin said.

"Thank you, Mrs. Abdulla. Yes, we can do that. Rafiq and I can hang around at my place, and then we will come here for tea and bhajia."

Salim looked at Yasmin and smiled to himself. He felt sorry for Yasmin. Rafiq would have to go to the D.C.'s place, and she would have to make bhajia for Robert, which he knew she had not planned to do. To decline Rob's invitation would be rude, so Salim said, "Sure, Rafiq, you can go to Rob's place, but don't get into any mischief."

For a moment, he had wondered if the D.C. would be upset to have an Indian kid come to his home, but thought, 'Well, your son's been enjoying our hospitality for two days; perhaps it is time that you returned the favor.'

The boys arrived at the D.C.'s home around 2.30 p.m. Robert had told his mom that he would bring Rafiq home and had asked that she bake some cake or make something for tea.

Jane met them at the door. She extended her hand to Rafiq and said, "Welcome, Rafiq. We're so happy to have you here. Please come in," and still holding his hand, she asked, "How are your mom and dad? Rob can't stop talking about how kind and hospitable they have been to him and how smart you are. Please come in."

Rafiq was pleased with his welcome but wondered what the D.C. would have to say when he got home. Would he give him that "What the hell are you doing here," look?

Robert took Rafiq to his room and showed him his magazines. Most were sports magazines, but he also had an old copy of *Playboy*. Rafiq had heard about the Playboy magazine but never seen one. He flipped the pages with some guilt but enjoyed looking at the pictures. Robert snatched the magazine from his hands when he heard his mom near the room and hid it in its safe place. They then went into the lounge and sat and talked in hushed tones about things boys their age talk about and about the pictures in Playboy.

They sat down for tea at around 5.00 p.m. The tea was weak, not the type that his mom made by boiling a generous serving of Brooke Bond tea leaves for some five minutes and then adding sugar and evaporated milk and letting it simmer into a thick, flavourful melange. Jane served some homemade cake (nothing compared to his mom's, Rafiq thought), and some biscuits from his dad's store.

As they sat sipping tea and eating biscuits, the D.C. came in. Seeing Rafiq, he said, "Hello, how are you?" Shifting his gaze to Robert, he said, "Rob, you did not tell me that you were bringing your friend home. I would have picked up something nice from the Club." Looking at Rafiq, he said, "You must stay for dinner."

Rafiq almost choked on his biscuit.

"Oh, that is so nice of you to invite me, but my mom is making an Indian snack that Rob likes, and she is expecting us home."

"Yes, Dad, we have to go," Robert added.

"Well, then, tomorrow – you must come for dinner tomorrow. We will have something nice prepared. What would you like to eat?"

"Oh, I like almost everything, but I don't eat pork."

"No pork, then." And with that, he disappeared into his room to change into his shorts. He wanted to get to know this boy better and decide if he had made the right decision in introducing him to Robert.

An hour later, the boys were enjoying real tea and bhajia. After Robert was gone, Rafiq told his parents about the D.C.'s invitation for dinner the next day, which he had accepted. Salim's jaw dropped, and Yasmin did not know what to say or think. In less than five days, Rafiq had gone from speaking to the D.C. to being invited to his home for dinner.

"This is too much, too soon, Rafiq. You can't go to his place for dinner three days after you met him. This is just not on. We must make an excuse and get out of this." Salim said.

"Maybe Rafiq can say that we are going to Dodoma tomorrow to buy some inventory for the store," Yasmin said.

"Come on, Mom. Rob came here the day we met, and you invited him into our house for tea and he came in without any fear that we might kidnap him. Would you really close the store on a weekday and drive all the way to Dodoma just because you don't want me to go to the D.C.'s place for dinner? What if he says, 'Okay, if you are going to Dodoma tomorrow, then come over on the weekend'? Would we run to Dodoma over the weekend again? Why are you so concerned? Do you think that I could come to some harm in going to his place?"

"No, Son. That's not it, but these things are not supposed to happen here. Not this way. Each new day is bringing new surprises in your friendship with this boy. First, his mother's letter and now, this." Salim said. Looking at Yasmin, he asked, "What do you think?"

Yasmin's face was blank. She did not respond.

"Don't worry, Dad, I can deal with the D.C. You have seen me deal with him."

"That's what I am worried about," Salim said.

SALIM AND YASMIN STAYED up late in bed, talking about the D.C.'s invitation. They couldn't make any sense of it. The D.C. was inviting an Indian boy to have dinner with his family. This was unreal.

As they had arranged to do, Robert and Rafiq met at the store at 2.00 p.m. the next day. Rafiq liked his mornings free to read the TIME magazine, Readers' Digest, and the usually three-day-old copies of The Tanganyika Standard.

"Rafiq, I talked to the manager at the veterinary research station and asked him if we can visit this afternoon. He said he will be happy to organize a tour for us. Students from your Dodoma schools come all the time. Would you like to go?" asked Robert.

Rafiq remembered that kids in Grade XI from his school had gone for this tour. He had always wondered what the station looked like on the inside, and what sort of work was conducted therein.

"That sounds very interesting!" he exclaimed.

Both Yasmin and Salim endorsed the idea enthusiastically.

THE RESEARCH STATION TOUR was indeed impressive. Rafiq had expected to see research on all kinds of animals, but it was primarily livestock that was studied. Several different experiments were being conducted, including studies to assess how various traits conferred greater health and amenability to faster breeding, and how these traits could be selected and emphasized preferentially in subsequent generations. People could also bring their house pets for treatment here, and the staff provided everything from simple medication to complex surgery for animals.

After the tour, the boys headed for Robert's place.

When the D.C. got home, they all sat down for dinner. Jane had prepared roast beef and mashed potatoes for dinner. Robert talked about their visit to the veterinary station. The D.C. told the boys about how Mpwapwa had been selected for the location of the station and the important work being done there. It was undoubtedly a source of pride for the town to have this facility located within its perimeter. The D.C. then asked Rafiq if he liked roast beef. Rafiq replied he had never eaten meat cooked this way. He usually ate beef as barbequed steak or in curries, but he liked what he was eating.

When dinner was over, Jane suggested that they sit in the lounge for dessert and tea.

When they sat down, the D.C. lit up his pipe, and the room became filled with the smell of tobacco. It had a pleasant minty flavor. Rafiq made a note to check if his dad carried this brand of pipe tobacco in his store. He should, if he did not.

Dessert was served, which was crème caramel. As they ate, the D.C. said to Rafiq, "Rob tells me that you know everything about British politics."

"Not everything, Sir, just what I've read in the Standard and in TIME magazine or old issues of The Daily Mirror."

"You read The Mirror? If you are reading the Mirror, you are getting all anti-Conservative government propaganda."

"It is critical of the government, yes. It was very critical of the Conservative government during the Suez crisis."

"And did you believe all that The Mirror said about Suez?"

"No, but TIME was also critical. To be honest, I believe the British made a big blunder and suffered humiliation in Suez. Nasser had the right to nationalize the Suez Canal. It is in his country. Israel, France, and Britain attacked Egypt on the false claim that they wanted to protect the Canal. What they really wanted was to remove Nasser from power because he had stood up to the British and French, and then the U.S.A. Russia, and the U.N. forced the British and French to withdraw. It humiliated the U.K. and France and strengthened Nasser. He is now more popular in the Muslim world than ever before, and your Prime Minister, Eden, had to resign."

This boy is not afraid of anyone, the D.C. thought, and said, "I can understand your bias. Rob tells me that you are a Muslim, but I understand you are not a regular Muslim."

"I don't know any irregular Muslims, Sir. I am a Muslim - an Ismaili Muslim."

"What kind of Muslim is that?"

"Ismailis belong to the Shia branch of Islam. The other branch is Sunni. Somewhat like the Catholics and Protestants in Christianity."

"So, how are these different?"

"According to our scholars, the Shia/Sunni split occurred over who should have succeeded the Prophet after his death. Before his death, the Prophet had appointed Ali, his cousin and son in law, as his successor. However, Ali was rejected by a group of the Prophet's close followers, who elected Abu Bakr, one of the Prophet's close associates, as their Caliph, the political successor to the Prophet. Ali's supporters, who came to be known as the Shia, the party of Ali, claimed that to elect the Prophet's successor, the group had met while Ali was taking care of the Prophet's funeral arrangements. The group had disregarded the Prophets' wishes. They claimed that Ali was not only the legitimate Caliph - the ruler of lands under Muslim control but also that he had the authority to guide the Muslims in the interpretation of Allah's final message, the Quran."

"So, what happened to Ali, then?" asked the D.C.

"Ali did not want Muslims fighting Muslims. In order to keep peace, he did not pursue his claim to the Caliphate, but assumed authority to guide those who followed him in the matters of faith. He was eventually elected as the fourth Caliph, but was always considered the leader (Imam) of the Shia. His assassination and the death of his grandson, Hussein, split the Islamic community permanently into two factions: the Shia and the Sunni." Rafiq explained.

"So, the Sunnis are your enemies, then?"

"Oh, no! No Sunni who is alive today had anything to do with the events of 1,400 years ago. Enlightened Sunnis and Shias understand this. To us, what is important is that we are all Muslims, and therefore brothers and sisters. Islam is a way of life which we are enjoined to live by the fundamental ethics of Islam, which are honesty, generosity, humility, tolerance and compassion. A good Muslim lives by these values. Beyond that, how we practice our faith, how we seek to connect with our creator is not, or should not, be a matter for division between us. In Dodoma, every year, we join with the Sunnis in celebrating the Prophet's birthday, and we pray with them." Rafiq said.

"So, you are now all friends. There is no conflict between the Shia and Sunni?"

"The Shia constitute only some 15% of the global Muslim population. In some countries like Iran and Iraq, they are the majority, but in most other countries where they live, they are a small minority. Some Sunni fundamentalists, who consider Shia infidels because we believe the Imams' interpretation of the Quran, incite violence against the minority. In the media this comes across as all Sunnis are persecuting the Shia. That is not true. The vast majority of the Sunnis are good Muslims who seek nothing more than to live in peace and live by the ethics of Islam."

"But, I understand that your people don't attend their mosque here?"

"We attend our Jamatkhana, our place for congregation and prayer."

"But if you are Muslims, why can you not attend the mosque?"

"We can attend the mosque if we wish to. All Muslims can."

"We had this Muslim guy working at the vet station who told me one day that you Ismailis are not Muslims at all. You don't fast during the month of Ramadhan, and you don't go to Mecca for the pilgrimage. He said that you people are just slightly improved Hindus."

"Only an ignorant person would say something like that. A Muslim is one who acknowledges that there is only one God and that the Prophet is His final messenger. We call this statement *Shahada*. The Prophet did not prescribe any other requirements for one to be a Muslim; he did prescribe how Muslims should conduct themselves in day to day life, but the only requirement for one to be a Muslim is the acknowledgment of the Shahada. We Ismailis recite the Shahada in our daily prayers."

"And about the 'slightly improved Hindus,' let me tell you, Sir," Rafiq continued, "The Hindus require no improvement. Their scriptures and faith are older than the Bible and Quran. They believe in various gods, but all of their deities have taught them the same principles – honesty, generosity, compassion, and humility, that you practice in Christianity, and we observe in Islam. My parents and I believe that Hindus are among the finest and most religious people on earth. I have Hindu friends at school, and I admire them immensely."

The D.C. had expected Rafiq to denigrate the Hindus. After all, they were supposed to be enemies. Muslim Pakistan and Hindu India were adversaries. This boy was not going to say anything bad about Hindus or anyone else, so he changed the subject.

"So, what happened with you guys, the Shias, after Ali?" he asked.

"Ali's successors went on to establish the Fatimid Empire, named after the Prophet's daughter, Fatima and ruled Arabia, Syria, Egypt, and Iran. Islam thrived during the Fatimid rule. They founded the cities of Cairo and Mahdiya (Tunisia). Under their Imams' guidance, the Shia made major contributions to the growth of Islamic civilization. They established the first university in the world, Al Azhar, and the Academy of Science, in Cairo. The Fatimid Empire, like other empires, came to an end one day, but the Ismaili Imamat continued. We, the Shia Ismailis, believe that our Imam must always be a descendant of Ali and that he has the sole authority to interpret the Quran according to the time and place."

"So, you have an Imam now?"

"Yes, His Highness The Aga Khan, who is a direct descendant of the Prophet and Ali, is our 48th Imam."

"Oh, that Maharaja?" the D.C. asked, and looking at Jane, he said, "You know what this Maharaja did? He got his followers in India – many poor, to contribute his weight in gold to him. And he was a big man."

Jane had a look of surprise on her face. She needed to hear Rafiq's answer to that.

Looking at her, Rafiq said, "See, Mrs. Turnbull, in India, there was the practice in the British time, and even before, for a Maharaja, which is a king, to be weighed, usually in food items on his milestone birthdays or other festive occasions. The food against which he was weighed and more, which was contributed by the king, was then distributed to the poor – a noble tradition. When the Aga Khan had been the Imam for fifty years, the leaders in my community went to him and requested that they wanted to celebrate his Golden Jubilee and to do that, they would invite donations from Ismailis all over the world to buy his weight in gold bullion, which they would gift to him to use as he pleased. This was an outpouring of love for the Imam under whose guidance the community had prospered, and who was, by the way, not a Maharaja, but one who was held in high esteem by the British in India and the U.K. and the world over. He became the first President of The League of Nations, which later evolved into The United Nations."

Seeing how interested his audience was, Rafiq continued, "The Imam accepted the request of the leaders, and he was weighed in gold. You may not know this, Mr. Turnbull, but we then also weighed him against diamonds and platinum for his 60th and 70th year of spiritual leadership, or Imamat. You would be interested to know that all of the proceeds from the Jubilees went into the establishment of the Aga Khan schools and hospitals, which are globally ranked and open to all, as well as banks to lend money to Ismailis and others at low-interest rates – my dad's business is financed by Diamond Jubilee Trust - and the Jubilee Insurance company through which you probably insure your car. The proceeds of the Jubilees also financed housing colonies for Ismailis, comprised of thousands of units in India, Pakistan, and Africa, including the one in which I live in Dodoma. It all came out of the proceeds of the Jubilees. The Platinum Jubilee Hospital in Nairobi, which is the finest hospital in East Africa, came out of the Platinum Jubilee proceeds. Of course, the schools and projects require ongoing funding, which The Aga Khan provides directly. For the Aga Khan, the Jubilees were opportunities for redistribution and multiplication of wealth for the benefit of his followers and others, not to make money."

As he said all this, Rafiq felt grateful for his two years at the Aga Khan School in Dar es Salaam, where Shia Ismaili Religion was a compulsory subject for Ismaili students. He had just restated what his religious education teacher had repeated many times in his class about the Jubilees.

"But you also give The Aga Khan a lot of money – that's what this Muslim guy told me," said the D.C.

"Zakat is one of the fundamental "pillars" in Islam. It's a form of contribution out of our income. It is very similar to the tithe in Christianity. Zakat is our unconditional gift to our Imam but the Imam uses the money to improve our lives and the lives of others. See, Mr. Turnbull, an average Ismaili in East Africa is born in Aga Khan Hospital. He or she then attends Aga Khan Nursery, Primary, and Secondary Schools. If they are needy and gain admission into a college in the U.K., they will probably study there with The Aga Khan Scholarship. They play sports in The Aga Khan Club. Their family business is funded by Diamond Jubilee Investment Trust; their lives, business, home, and car are insured with Jubilee Insurance, and they probably live in one of the Ismaili housing complexes supported by the Imam. All of this costs money, and the Imam funds it. He also funds the construction and operation of our places of congregation and worship, and our welfare programs to ensure that none of our community members are without the basic necessities of life, and he funds numerous projects for the improvement of the quality of life of others who are not Ismailis."

"That is very interesting, Rafiq. You are an amazing community," said Mrs. Turnbull.

"If we are, it is because of our Imam's guidance and generosity," Rafiq answered.

The D.C. was stunned again by the intelligence of this fifteen years old boy, which was far beyond his fifteen years. His ability to articulate matters candidly - with respect and in detail, and his knowledge, were astounding, more than many full-grown adults'. He was now convinced that Robert could benefit from the friendship of this boy in ways that he had not initially imagined. He would have to think of ways to get the two boys to spend as much time together as possible.

"So, how does The Aga Khan - your Imam - guide you?" he asked.

"Well, he travels to meet with Ismailis all over the world, and he addresses them in huge congregations. For his Diamond Jubilee in Dar es Salaam, there were over 50,000 people gathered in one place. He guides his followers not only in matters of faith, but also in the conduct of their daily lives," Rafiq said, and then he had to pause to recall his teachings, to say the right thing.

"We call his guidance Farmans, which are transcribed and sent all over the world to be read to his followers. We have to obey his guidance in matters of faith; we don't need to follow his guidance in worldly matters, but if the community has prospered, it is because we follow his guidance in totality."

"So, are you two planning to do something together tomorrow?" the D.C. asked, changing the subject.

Robert looked at Rafiq and said, "You know, I thought we could climb up to the Lookout Point on *Kiboriani.* This was one mountain surrounding Mpwapwa.

"I have not done that before, but it sounds like fun," Rafiq answered.

"How would you get there? It's two miles to the base of Kiboriani, and do you know the mountain is over 5,000 feet in height?" the D.C. asked

"We can walk up to the mountain, but I didn't know it's that high," Robert replied.

"If you walk to the base, you will be tired before you start to climb. I will send a Land Rover to take you there. There is a road going up the mountain up to a point. You can get the driver to take you as far up as the road goes, and from there, you will have to climb on foot and then climb down. You are looking at more than five hours, up and down," said the D.C. He was now prepared to break his own rules regarding the use of government vehicles for private purposes.

"Thanks, Dad. Can you send the Rover at 12 noon.? Rafiq, is that okay for you?"

Rafiq nodded, and the D.C. confirmed the arrangement.

They sat and talked until 10.00 p.m. when Rafiq got up and said that he had to call his dad to come and pick him up.

"Don't bother them, Rob and I will drop you," said the D.C., and soon they were on their way.

SALIM AND YASMIN WERE sitting up, going through the anxiety of parents whose teenage daughter is out on her first date, waiting for Rafiq to call for them to pick him up. They were speculating over what could be happening at the D.C.'s home when they heard a knock on the door and were surprised. Who could it be at this hour? Rafiq had his house keys.

Salim opened the door, and when he saw the D.C., for a second, he thought Rafiq must have said something horrible, and the D.C. had come personally to complain, but he saw that the D.C. was smiling broadly.

"Good evening," said the D.C., cordially. "We had a wonderful evening with Rafiq. I wanted to come by and thank you and Mrs. Abdulla personally for allowing him to have dinner with us. My wife…" (not Mrs. Turnbull, which is how he would have generally referred to her, officially) "…also wants to thank you and sends you her regards. Your son is a very smart boy. We really enjoyed his company. Thank you, again."

"Oh, thank you for inviting him, Sir. It was very kind of Mrs. Turnbull and you to invite him." Salim said.

"Won't you come in, Mr. Turnbull?" Yasmin said although she was a little uncomfortable inviting him because she was in her nightgown.

"No, thank you, Mrs. Abdulla, we should be on our way. It's late. Good night."

"Good night and goodnight to you, Rob. Will we see you tomorrow?" Yasmin asked.

"Yes, Mrs. Abdulla, good night."

"SO, WHAT HAPPENED?" YASMIN and Salim asked at the same time.

"Well, we had a nice dinner. Roast beef and mashed potatoes. It tasted nice. Not as good as dad's barbequed steaks, though. For dessert, we had caramel pudding, which was also very nice "

"We are not interested in your dinner menu, Rafiq; what happened there? Why did the D.C. come here?" Salim asked, impatiently.

"Well, we talked. He wanted to know what kind of Muslims we are. Some Muslim guy who worked at the vet station had said disparaging things about Ismailis and Hindus to him. I corrected that. The D.C. thought that Hazar Imam's Golden Jubilee was about making money from poor Ismailis. I told him what the Golden, Diamond, and Platinum Jubilees were all about and how the community and others have benefited, and continue to do so, from the Jubilee projects."

"I presume you learned this in Dar es Salaam?" Salim asked.

"Yes, I relayed everything I had learned from our Religion teacher and written in my Imam's Jubilees assignment papers in Dar es Salaam. I think that they were impressed. I told them about our interpretation of the Shia, Sunni split, and the hereditary position of the Imam. Thank God, I learnt all that at The Aga Khan School. Sadly, we have no religious education for secondary level students in Dodoma. I always got As in my assignments in Dar es Salaam."

"You said all of that?" Yasmin asked, somewhat flabbergasted.

"Well, maybe, you can go over the Jubilees with Mom and me one day. I don't think that we know all this that well. We would also like to know what you learned in Dar es Salaam." Salim laughed and shook his head.

1957
Nine

When the D.C. got home the next day, he told Jane that The Governor's Conference in Dar es Salaam, which was usually held in May of each year and in which all P.C.s and D.C.s were invited to participate with their spouses, was being brought forward to start on Monday, April 24th. All invitees were required to report in Dar es Salaam on Sunday, April 23rd. The New Africa Hotel, the largest and most prestigious hotel in the capital city, had a large event cancellation and had offered accommodation and facilities at a discount. He had already booked two first-class cabins on the train to Dar es Salaam leaving on Saturday the 22nd. Robert would take the flight from Dar es Salaam to Nairobi on the 29th to get back to school on May 1st. They would take the train back on the same day.

"But we can't do that, James. We can't take Rob with us. Remember that one time we took him? No kids came, and he had to hang around with me the whole time. I couldn't do what the other women did. I had to look after him, and we were both miserable. We can't take him!" Jane protested.

"Well, what do you suggest? Leave him here? If you want, we can do that. You will have to cook and leave one week's food for him in the freezer. He will be fine alone."

"What if he forgets to fill kerosene in the fridge? It would go off, and all the food would go bad. And I don't trust him lighting the petromax and lantern at night. He might set the house on fire."

"Oh, come on, Jane! I will teach him tonight how to light the petromax and lantern, and we will fill up the fridge before we leave. It usually lasts a week, doesn't it?" the D.C. asked.

"Yes, but I just don't want him to stay alone here or come there for me to babysit him. Let's ask him when he gets home if he wants to come."

When they talked to Rob that evening about the trip, he said, "No way. I am not coming with you folks. I can stay here." He was excited at the prospect of being alone, but Jane was not agreeable to this arrangement. If it came to that, she would not go, although the Governor's conference was the biggest perk of being a D.C.'s wife.

The next morning as they sat down for breakfast and while Robert was still in bed, the D.C. said to Jane, "I have been thinking about the trip, and I have an idea. Why don't we invite Rafiq to come with us? He and Rob can have a fun time in Dar es Salaam together. Rafiq has lived there for two years and knows the place well. They can go to the movies, swim in the ocean, and walk down Acacia Avenue. I am sure that Rafiq will like that. I have booked two cabins on the train. Each has two berths. The boys can share one cabin and share the room at New Africa. It will cost Rafiq nothing, except for whatever he spends on himself." He was excited by the idea of Robert benefitting from Rafiq's whole week of company.

"That sounds great, James, but that will also be Rafiq's last week of vacation and his parents will probably want him here with them. I don't think that they will let him come with us. And are you comfortable taking an Indian boy to The Governor's Conference? What will the other D.C.s and P.C.s think, and more particularly, what will their wives think?"

"I couldn't care less what those ignorant fools think. Wake Rob up, and let's ask him if he wants to do this."

What a difference a week can make. Less than six days ago, he was the captain of the ignorant, and now he was prepared to take an Indian boy to The Governor's Conference, Jane thought, as she walked to Robert's room.

Robert appeared with sleepy eyes, but as soon as the D.C. told him of his idea, all sleep departed his eyes. "Yes, let me get dressed and go and invite Rafiq." He said, getting up to go.

"Not so fast. Jane, are you comfortable with the idea? If you are, you should speak with Mrs. Abdulla and tell her that we would be delighted if they let Rafiq come with us. Tell her it will not cost Rafiq anything. And Rob, don't say a word to Rafiq until your mom has talked to Mrs. Abdulla."

Jane agreed.

For the next hour, Robert could not stop talking about all of the things he and Rafiq would do in Dar es Salaam. Jane became concerned about how disappointed he would be if the Abdullas did not agree to let Rafiq go or if Rafiq, himself, refused to come. So, although it was early, she decided to call Yasmin. She looked up the number in the local phone directory and called the operator to put her through to that number. Yasmin picked up the phone. Jane identified herself as Rob's mother and said, "Yasmin, would it be okay if I drop in to see you and Mr. Abdulla for 10 minutes today?"

Yasmin could not imagine what Jane would want to come over and talk to her about. It couldn't be the nankhatai recipe. She was tempted to ask what she wanted to talk about but considering that Jane wasn't telling her, she simply said, "Sure, Jane. I don't go into the store until noon. Can you come around 11.00 a.m.? "

"Thank you very much. I will see you at 11.00."

Yasmin quickly got dressed, opened up the windows to get rid of the curry smell from her morning's cooking, and waited for Jane in the store. She told Rafiq that Jane was coming over to talk about something, and he should stay in the store or make himself scarce, which he did by going for a walk around town, although his legs were still aching from the Kiboriani climb the previous day.

When Jane came, Yasmin shook hands with her, welcomed her, and led her inside.

These people do live better than we do, Jane thought as she sat down. Yasmin offered her tea, which Jane accepted. Yasmin made the weak English tea with fresh milk and sugar to add, as she thought Jane would like it. She made a cup for herself, as well.

As they sipped tea, after telling Yasmin what a pleasure it was to have her son for dinner and how smart he was, Jane told her all about the Governor's conference - who attended, what happened there, how it had been brought forward for this year and how nice it would be if Rafiq could join them. The boys would have a great time together in Dar es Salaam. They would travel first class and stay at The New Africa, and whether Rafiq came or not, they would still incur the cost for the train ride and hotel room for Robert, so it would cost Rafiq nothing.

"Jane, I am so touched by you coming here to invite Rafiq. I don't know what to say. You are so generous. I will have to speak to Rafiq about this. I am sure he will be very excited. But Jane," Yasmin said, putting her hand on Jane's, "are you sure you can do this? What would the other delegates say about you taking an Indian boy there? Have you thought about that? Will they resent Rafiq being there?"

"My husband and I have talked about this. We will introduce Rafiq as Rob's friend and create the opportunity to speak with some of them, and they will soon know what an Indian boy can be like. He will astound them with his impeccable manners, finesse, and knowledge, as he has astounded us. They will be eating out of his hands by the time we leave. I wouldn't mind introducing him to the Governor as one of his most enlightened subjects!"

Yasmin did not know what 'eating out of his hands' meant, but she assumed that it meant something good.

"Okay, Jane, let me speak to my husband and Rafiq, and get back to you in the evening."

"I will be happy to speak to your husband if that would be more appropriate," Jane said.

"Don't worry, Jane. I will speak to him."

"Thank you, Yasmin. Please give me a ring when you have decided," said Jane. Yasmin did not know what 'give me a ring' meant either, but she was sure Jane did not expect her to give her a ring to wear.

"I will," she said with a smile.

Yasmin led her into the store, where Jane stopped to thank Salim for sending Rafiq for dinner and said, "You have a delightful wife, Mr. Abdulla."

"Please, call me Salim, and my wife has a delightful husband too."

They all laughed, and leaving, Jane said, "Well, we will have to get together and know you better to validate your claim, Salim."

WHEN YASMIN TOLD SALIM about the invitation, he was happy but skeptical.

The boys could indeed have a great time, but this was the top government officials' conference, with no less than the Governor himself attending. He did not need to be told how arrogant and rude these officials could be to an Indian or African. To send a young Indian boy to their gathering would be like throwing a rabbit to a pack of wolves. "I don't know if we can do this, Yasmin. I don't know if we should even tell Rafiq about the invitation."

"He is bound to ask why Jane was here," Yasmin said and told Salim about the assurances Jane had given, and how confident she was that Rafiq would be fine.

"So, do you think we should let him go?" Salim asked.

"Let's ask Rafiq if he wants to, and if he does, then maybe, we should let him go. I am inclined to agree with Jane."

What a difference a week makes, Yasmin thought. It was only six days ago that the D.C. came into the store and now the boys had become close friends, Robert was eating her nankhatai, samosas, and bhajia, and Rafiq had been to his place and tried roast beef. And now the Turnbulls wanted to take him to the Governor's Conference.

Jane updated Robert on her meeting with Yasmin and called the D.C. and updated him, as well, and said that she expected to hear from the Abdullas by the end of the day.

The D.C. said, "I thought I should inform the P.C. that we have invited an Indian boy. You know he is backing my application for his job when he retires, and I did not want him to be surprised to see us bring an Indian boy there. He told me, for all he cares, I can bring my mother in law and the housekeeper too, so long as Rob and the Indian boy pay for their room and meals and, of course, they can't come to the Governor's Ball."

"Of course, they can't come to the Ball, but the last time Rob came, all his meals were paid for."

"The P.C. was clear. The conference is for the P.Cs and D.C.s and their spouses. We can bring whomever else we choose to bring, but we have to pay for their meals and room."

"Did he say anything about the boy being an Indian?"

"No. Surprisingly, he didn't care."

"Okay, so let's wait and see what Yasmin comes back with."

WHEN RAFIQ GOT BACK, Salim told him about the invitation. He was happy, but not sure if he should go. Later, when Robert came around, and they went for a walk, Robert campaigned hard to convince him to go with him. When he informed his parents of his decision, they agreed but insisted that they would pay for half of the rail cabin and half of the hotel room costs, and all of his meals on the train and in Dar es Salaam.

Later in the day, Yasmin called and thanked Jane again for her invitation and told her that Rafiq would be delighted to go with them, but that they would need to insist upon paying 50% of the boys' travel and accommodation costs, and for all of Rafiq's meals. Jane protested but eventually agreed.

THE TURNBULLS AND RAFIQ boarded the train from Gulwe, some 15 miles from Mpwapwa, at 4.00 p.m. on Saturday. Robert and Rafiq's cabin was two cabins away from the Turnbulls'. The other cabins in the car were occupied, in the main, by other D.C.s and P.C.s and their spouses coming from the west - from Mwanza, Kigoma, Tabora, Singida, Dodoma, and everything in between. Except for a couple of toddlers, there were no children in the compartment.

This train journey was a novel experience for Rafiq. The first-class cabin was more opulent than the second class in which he had always traveled. The berths were more expansive, and there was a washbasin in the cabin. The most unusual experience for Rafiq was going to the dining car to eat dinner. Whenever Rafiq had traveled with his parents or on his own, his mom had packed a tiffin with curry, rice, and chapatti for lunch or dinner.

Robert had checked the time when his parents wanted to go for dinner and had planned to be there a full 45 minutes earlier. As they entered the dining car, they were greeted and seated by the head waiter, an African in a crisp white uniform, and a colorful tie bearing the East African Railways logo. The other waiters wore similar outfits, minus the tie, and all wore Fez caps.

As they sat, the boys could see that they were being observed by the other, mostly white, patrons because they were too young to be in the dining car on their own, and here was this white boy with an Indian boy chatting like they were friends. There were also some Indians in the dining car who were similarly intrigued.

Soup and dinner rolls were served as the first of a four-course dinner. Rafiq wondered if that would be all that they would get for dinner in this fancy rolling restaurant, but as soon as the soup bowls were cleared, fish was served. Rafiq enjoyed the fish, which was served with a small cup of some white sauce that he had not eaten before, but seeing that Robert had spread all of the sauce on his fish, he proceeded to do the same. With the sauce, the fish tasted great. The serving, however, was small, and Rafiq was still hungry.

Eating dinner on the train, as he looked out of the window, enjoying the changing landscape, was fun for Rafiq.

The third course was roast beef and baked potatoes served with another small cup of some white, coarse paste, a little thicker than the sauce served with the fish. As he had done with the fish, Rafiq applied a generous portion of the paste to his first bite of roast beef and almost choked on it. He wanted to cough and sneeze at the same time. His face turned red, and his eyes filled up with tears. His throat was on fire. This was not the kind of fire that the chilies would light in your mouth; this was different.

Seeing his discomfort, Robert said, "Oh my God, did you eat all of that horseradish? This is not the tartar sauce that you ate with your fish. This, you take just a pinch with each bite."

Rafiq gulped down his glass of water, which brought some relief as he finished his third course without touching the horseradish again. His chest was still burning. For what conceivable reason would the English associate the name of a noble animal like the horse with this awful condiment, he wondered. At some point, he must find out why this was called horseradish.

For dessert, the choice was between ice cream and fresh fruit in jello and custard. Rafiq quickly opted for ice cream to cool his innards. Robert asked the waiter to give Rafiq two servings. Coming from a white boy, the waiter was not going to ask why. Rafiq was grateful for the second serving as the first had just served to cool his throat and chest. He enjoyed the second serving. It was a delicious flavor that he had not tasted before.

Robert waived at the waiter and asked for the bill. It was Shs.20. Rafiq pulled out Shs.25 from his pocket and handed the money to the waiter. He was aware of the European custom of tipping for good service, and this waiter had been much better than good. As the waiter accepted the money, he asked the boys if they wanted tea. The boys nodded, and the waiter soon returned with tea for two.

"Rafiq, the arrangement is for us to share the cost of our meals. If you want, you can pay for all the meals and keep an account, and we can settle at the end of the trip." Robert said.

"I have a better idea. I am deeply grateful to your parents and you for inviting me on this trip and to show some appreciation, I would like to pay for all our meals. It will be my pleasure." Rafiq replied.

"I am not sure if my parents will agree."

"You don't have to mention anything to them. You can keep your share and use it in Nairobi to take your friends to Curry Pot for samosas and kabobs or to spend as you please. Speaking of samosas and kabobs, in Dar es Salaam, I am going to take you to a restaurant called NAAZ. You will eat the best samosas, kabobs, and bhajia you've ever had in your life! Even better than my mom's!"

"That sounds amazing, but I doubt whether anyone can make better samosas than your mom."

Just then, the D.C. and Jane entered the dining car and walked over to the boys.

"Did you finish dinner?" Jane asked.

The boys nodded, and, looking at Rafiq, she asked, "Did you enjoy your dinner, Rafiq?"

"Yes, he did, Mom, but he almost choked on the horseradish that they served with the roast beef."

"Oh, Rob, you should have warned him," said Jane, running her hand affectionately over Rafiq's head. "Are you okay, Son?"

"Yes, Mrs. Turnbull. The two servings of ice cream that Rob ordered for me have cooled my mouth and chest," Rafiq said, smiling, "I am fine."

The boys returned to their cabin. Rafiq pulled out his Grapes of Wrath to finish reading the last few pages. Robert read his magazines.

EARLY THE NEXT MORNING, the boys were back in the dining car for breakfast.

"Please warn me of any landmines in this breakfast, Rob," said Rafiq.

"Relax; the breakfast will be the usual, cereal, eggs, and toast."

Breakfast was as elaborate as the dinner the previous night.

It started with a glass of freshly squeezed orange juice and a small fruit plate, followed by cereals and milk, a choice of fried or poached eggs, or omelet, toast, butter, marmalade, jam, and cheese. It was a hearty breakfast which the boys enjoyed thoroughly.

The train arrived in Dar es Salaam at 10.00 a.m. A white man and some Indian government officials were at the train station to receive the conference delegates and transport them to the New Africa Hotel. As they checked in, the receptionist advised them that breakfast would be served each day between 7.00 a.m. and 9.30 a.m., lunch between 12.00 p.m. and 2.00 p.m., afternoon tea between 3.00 p.m. and 4.30 p.m. and dinner between 6.30 p.m. and 8.30 p.m.

After checking into their well-appointed room, the boys went for a walk around the Dar es Salaam harbor, almost opposite the hotel. They returned an hour later, had sandwiches for lunch, packed their towels and swimming trunks, and were on their way to Oysterbay.

Oysterbay was the mzunguni (the whites) area. Except for some affluent Indian families that lived there, it was a European enclave. The beautiful Oysterbay beach with its high waves at high tide, while open to all, was also where, mostly, the whites went swimming. The boys had confirmed that high tide would be at 2.00 p.m. and wanted to be there to jump into the cresting waves.

Salim had given Rafiq Shs.1,000 to pay for his share of six nights of accommodation and meals, leaving a generous balance of over Shs.500 for his other expenses. He did not want Rafiq to run out of money in the company of a white family.

Rafiq had planned to enjoy this trip thoroughly, and that was one reason why he had offered to pay for Robert's share of meals. He did not want to eat all of his meals at the New Africa, which was where Robert was supposed to eat and charge his meals to his room for his dad to pay. He wanted to go to all of the fancy restaurants that he had heard older boys talk about when he was at the boarding house in

Dar es Salaam for two years but had never visited.

To get to Oysterbay, which was three miles from the hotel, the boys hopped into a taxi, for which Rafiq told Robert he would pay, as he would for all taxi rides during the trip.

The turquoise Indian Ocean was warm. Being Sunday, the beach was busy with mainly white swimmers. When the boys went into the ocean, the tide was at its highest level for the day, and the waves were high. The boys dived in, played in the waves and swam for two hours. The smell of salty ocean air on a warm, sunny day, as Rafiq dried himself on the white sandy beach, was a heavenly experience for him.

After the swim, the boys sat in the shadow of a coconut tree and enjoyed the cool breeze from the ocean, eyeing some of the girls their age who were also enjoying the afternoon swim, before taking the taxi back to town.

They were hungry now. Rafiq suggested that they go to the NAAZ. At 4.00 p.m., the restaurant was beginning to get busy. As they sat down, freshly fried samosas, kabobs, and bhajia were coming out of the kitchen for the late afternoon/early evening clientele. Rafiq ordered six samosas and kabobs for them to share. He warned Robert that these would be spicier than his mom's, and what he had eaten at Curry Pot. Robert did not find them hotter than the Curry Pot samosas, but they were tastier than the samosas he had eaten before.

The boys walked around town, up the trendy Acacia Avenue and back to the hotel, showered, and were ready to go out again.

Every Sunday, starting at 6.00 p.m., the Indians in Dar es Salaam liked to go for a walk on the harbor front. Those who owned cars drove along the harbor front and onwards on Ocean Road towards Oysterbay. They parked their cars all along the Ocean Road, sat and walked on the beach, and enjoyed the ocean breeze. They started to return to town at dusk and most headed for the NAAZ or CITY restaurants - the latter for vegetarian snacks. Sunday from 6.30 - 8.00 p.m. was the busiest time of the week for the two restaurants. Finding parking was a challenge. NAAZ was a "drive-in" restaurant. People could park directly facing the restaurant and be served in their cars.

That Sunday evening, Rafiq had told Robert that driving along Ocean Road and Oysterbay was an experience they should not miss. At 6.30 p.m., they hopped into a taxi and asked the driver to take them on a leisurely drive along the ocean to Oysterbay and back.

Robert was amused by the number of Indians in colorful outfits sitting and walking along the miles of white sandy beach. At the end of the drive, Rafiq said that they must go back to NAAZ, although they were done eating samosas and kabobs for the day, to enjoy the Sunday evening experience at the restaurant, where the taxi driver was able to deftly maneuver into a "drive-in" parking spot being vacated. Rafiq ordered one plate each of samosas and kabobs for the driver to eat or take home, and a large Coke for him to enjoy. He ordered two ice creams for themselves, which he had told Robert, was unique. The driver was happy and grateful as he enjoyed his samosas and kabobs. He did not get many customers who were this generous.

True to Rafiq's word, the ice cream was heavenly. It was none of the usual vanilla, chocolate, strawberry, or mint flavors that he had eaten. It was something else. What even Rafiq did not know was that it was *mava* ice cream. Mava was made by boiling milk, continuously stirring it as it boiled until all of the fluid in the milk had evaporated, leaving a solid mass of pure cream. This was a key ingredient, in addition to ground almonds and unique essences, in the NAAZ ice cream.

The boys returned to the hotel around 8.00 p.m., sat in the hotel courtyard under the stars and ate late dinner as a band played, and then walked over to The Empress cinema, just around the corner from the hotel, to see a movie.

FOR THE NEXT FIVE days, Rafiq and Robert explored the city. They went to the Kariakoo market and bought some papayas to eat after dinner; walked down the Jamat Street (named after the Ismaili Jamatkhana on that street) where Rafiq proudly showed Robert the principal Ismaili Jamatkhana in Dar es Salaam, which, like in other towns and cities in East Africa, was the most prominent building in the city; visited Indian stores on India Street and on Acacia Avenue where they did some shopping and visited The Aga Khan Boys' School and Boarding House where Rafiq had spent two years. Both were closed for the vacation.

In the town and on the streets, as they walked, they met boys Rafiq had been in school with and who had become his friends. They also saw some pretty Indian girls, who Rafiq said were Ismailis. Robert saw them looking at them, but Rafiq did not look back at them.

"How do you know they are Ismailis? Do you know these girls?" Robert asked.

"No, but I can tell by looking at them that they are Ismailis."

"And they can tell by looking at you that you are Ismaili?"

"Yes."

"Well, I think they want to speak to you. Look at how they are looking at you. They have not seen any Ismaili boy as handsome as you."

"Rob, can you please stop looking at them? They are looking at us because they are wondering what an Ismaili boy is doing, walking around with a white boy!"

SWIMMING AND VISITS TO NAAZ were a daily must. Rafiq sometimes invited friends whom he met to join them for samosas at NAAZ. They were surprised that Rafiq had a European friend and were even more surprised when Robert casually chatted and joked with them and ate samosas and kabobs with coconut chutney, like an Indian boy.

Robert and Rafiq ate their dinners at fancy restaurants in the town and in Oysterbay and went to the movies most evenings. This was an amazing experience for Robert, as it was for Rafiq.

On Friday, the last day of their holiday in Dar es Salaam, they took Jane with them to walk down Acacia Avenue, Jamat, and India Streets, and then to the Kariakoo market, by taxi, where Jane bought a whole lot of fruit and fresh fish (which she later asked the hotel chef to salt and freeze for her to take home) and ended up at NAAZ. Jane ventured to taste samosas and kabobs. She found both quite spicy but said she enjoyed them. She found the ice cream, "unlike anything she had tasted before."

The restaurant owner was intrigued to see this white boy come into their restaurant and eat samosas and kabobs with their hot coconut chutney every day, and now he had come with this white woman who must be his mother.

Not able to contain his curiosity, the owner walked over to the boys' table, identified himself as the owner, and asked the guests if they were enjoying their food and if they lived in Dar es Salaam. Rafiq replied that they were from Nairobi, Dodoma, and Mpwapwa, visiting Dar es Salaam and that they loved the NAAZ kabobs and samosas. Jane said that the ice cream was unlike anything she had tasted before. The owner asked Robert where they had learned to eat samosas and kabobs. Robert told him that he ate this good stuff at the Curry Pot in Nairobi regularly, but his mother had tasted samosas for the first time that day and had liked them very much.

The owner said this was also the first time that a white lady had come into his restaurant, and he was happy that she had enjoyed the kabobs, samosas, and ice cream, and asked them to come again. Rafiq told him that they were leaving the next day, but would return to enjoy the NAAZ food when they came back to Dar es Salaam.

THAT EVENING, RAFIQ ASKED to be excused as he wanted to attend the Friday prayers at the Jamatkhana, but would be back in time for dinner. At Rafiq's request, the D.C., Jane, and the boys were to dine together that evening at a fancy restaurant nearby. This was to be Rafiq's parent's treat, which the Turnbulls had accepted gratefully.

As they sat down for dinner, Robert told his father everything that they had done during the past six days and the fantastic time he had had with Rafiq. This was his best vacation ever. Rafiq said that it had been an excellent vacation for him too, and thanked the Turnbulls for bringing him along.

Then he asked, "Mrs. Turnbull, did my presence here raise any eyebrows? Were your friends and colleagues surprised that you had brought along an Indian boy?"

Jane noted the expression, "raise any eyebrows?" and said to herself that this boy could select the most diplomatic words to say things. She replied truthfully, "Not really, because you two have spent so little time here, you were hardly seen, but yes, a couple of ladies asked me who you are, and I told them that you are a dear friend of Rob's and that you are brilliant and we are very happy that Rob has you as his friend."

Rafiq was both touched and flattered to hear this and said, "And you could have also told them how happy and grateful my parents and I are to have Rob as my friend."

After dinner, it was time to pack up for the return trip. Rafiq and the Turnbulls were taking the 12.00-noon train back to Mpwapwa and Dodoma. Robert's flight to

Nairobi was departing at 2.00 p.m. the next day, and he needed to be at the airport an hour earlier. Transport had been arranged for him at the front desk.

The boys sat up late into the night talking. Both were surprised by how close they had become in these few short days. They exchanged addresses and promised to write weekly. They spoke about what they would do for their August vacation. They could not stay in Mpwapwa for a whole month, but coming back to Dar es Salaam for the kind of holiday they had just enjoyed would be too expensive. They could not agree on anything final but decided to think and talk more about it. Robert again offered to write the script for Rafiq to confess his love for Salima, and Rafiq again declined, politely.

After breakfast the next morning, the boys decided that they had enough time for one more stroll up and down Acacia Avenue. They returned to the hotel at around 10.30 a.m., Rafiq got his suitcase from the room, and after an emotional goodbye to Robert, the Turnbulls and Rafiq got into the taxi and headed for the railway station.

The journey back was miserable. Rafiq missed Robert and stayed in his cabin most of the time. When Jane asked him to join them for lunch in the dining car, he declined, saying that he was too full from the New Africa breakfast, but would join them for dinner, which he did, carefully avoiding anything that looked like horseradish.

Over dinner, the D.C. asked Rafiq, "What do the Indians think of the British in East Africa?"

Rafiq replied, "Well, the Indians' perceptions of the whites in Africa were formed, first under the pre-World War I German rule when they were terrified of the haughty Germans, and later when the British took over East Africa, by the experiences of the Indians arriving in Africa from India, with the British Raj. The Indians particularly despised Churchill for his treatment of Gandhi. Most older folks today are intimidated by the British and all whites, but younger people like me who are studying history and are aware of what is happening around the world do not see the British or any Europeans as superior to us and my generation will not want to be ruled by the whites."

The D.C. asked, "So, how would you feel about being ruled by the Africans when independence comes?"

Rafiq replied, "I think that most of us would feel more comfortable. In the hierarchical 'whites at the top, Indians in the middle and Africans at the bottom' system you have created here, some Africans look at the Indians as a somewhat degraded extension, but an extension nonetheless, of the British, and to be despised. Still, most Indians relate to the Africans differently from how most whites do, and many Africans consider the Indians sympathetic to their plight and even as friends. If Tanganyika becomes independent, I do not doubt that the Africans would invite the Indians to stay and support them in building this country, which they will not do for the whites, unless the whites change their behavior now."

"What do you mean by 'change their behavior'?"

"The whites have to work their way down. They first have to change how they relate to and treat the Indians, and get the Indians, who understand the Africans better than the whites do, to work with them to understand the Africans' issues and aspirations; become friends with them; offer help in addressing their problems, and convince them that you will help accelerate their independence, and after independence, will stay, if invited to do so, to help the Africans run Tanganyika as a multi-racial society in which all can live in peace and prosper together. You like the good life here. You can continue to enjoy this if you change."

The D.C. had never heard anything like this before.

"This is a tall order, Son. You know that in addition to Mrs. Turnbull and me, there are thousands of whites in East Africa, and they are not all British. They are Italian, German, Greek, French, and many other European nationalities. Almost all consider the Indians and Africans to be inferior to them. Some are here for the good life and to simply make money and go away when the going gets tough, but many want to stay. To change their thinking, to change the thinking of the British in the White Highlands in Kenya, I cannot imagine how we could do that. And after all these years of bad behavior, I don't know if it would do any good, anyway."

He is acknowledging their bad behavior, Rafiq thought.

"You can always start in your backyard, Mr. Turnbull, and see how that spreads. Good things are infectious. It is in your and our - the Indians' interest also to do this, but the better reason to do it is that it is the right and moral thing to do. Even if it bears no fruit, you will have done the right thing for the people you have ruled with such little regard for their wellbeing."

Seeing that the D.C. was interested, Rafiq continued. "And it's not only you, the whites, who must change. Many of the Indians here seem to be living in this la-la land illusion that the British rule will continue forever and that they will continue to eat the crumbs that fall off the British tables; they need to change and see the light. It's time, Sir, that we all change and do the right thing."

The D.C. thought, and after a few moments, looking at his wife, he said to Rafiq, "You know, I see merit in what you say. I would like to invite you to come and speak to our Club membership one day. Would you do that?"

"Oh, Sir, I don't know if I would be qualified to speak to your members. I don't know if my parents would permit me to do that!"

"Rob said that you visit them once every four to six weeks, right?"

Rafiq nodded. "Well, on one of your trips, you and your parents can come over for dinner, and we can talk more."

"Yes, perhaps, we can do that," Rafiq said with some trepidation.

THEY REACHED GULWE THE next day at noon. The Turnbulls had eaten breakfast earlier, so Rafiq had the pleasure of eating alone in the dining car. As the other passengers had grown accustomed to seeing him, by now, he did not attract too many wayward glances.

As previously arranged, Salim and Yasmin were at the train station to say hello and goodbye to Rafiq - as the train stopped at this small station for twenty minutes only, and give a ride home to the Turnbulls. En route, the Turnbulls told Salim and Yasmin about all of the things that the boys had done during the trip, and how much they had enjoyed Dar es Salaam. They thanked them profusely for permitting Rafiq to go with them.

Two hours later, Rafiq arrived in Dodoma. Fateh and Almas, whom Yasmin had advised of Rafiq's arrival that day, and their children were at the train station to receive him. It was a happy reunion, as all had missed one another.

1957
Ten

Anil and his family were aware that Rafiq had made an English friend, and also that he had gone with this friend and his family to Dar es Salaam and stayed at the New Africa Hotel. They could not wait to hear how that had come to pass. Rafiq related to them every detail of the D.C. coming to the store and what had followed. They could not believe that so much could have happened between Rafiq and the D.C.'s family in three short weeks, and some of the things Rafiq had told the D.C.

"And he just accepted this?" Fateh asked.

"Well, as I said, he was testy and asked difficult questions, but like I told him, kids of Anil's and my generation are not scared of the whites anymore."

"And after you said all this, he invited you to speak to his Club members?" Fateh asked.

"You know, if you do that, I am sure that you will really impress them," interjected Almas, "and if the word spreads, they might even invite you to speak at the Dodoma Club!"

"That will be the day, Aunty. His Club members will laugh him out the door if he suggests that they invite an Indian kid to speak to them. But you know what; I think that I got him thinking. I was able to do that because of what you and my parents have taught us."

"You are very kind, Rafiq. I am not surprised that you could communicate with the D.C. and his wife so well," Fateh said with a smile.

The second term at the school was not unlike the first, except that Rafiq's class had a new English Literature teacher from Kerala who was much better than the previous one. She made reading *Julius Caesar* much more interesting.

Rafiq was happy to see Salima again. She looked prettier than before, but perhaps that was just his imagination. He thought about what Robert had suggested – giving him the script to tell her that he loved her, but if he did, then what? Would she just walk away or ask him to get lost, like the girls whom Rob had approached had done? And what if she smiled and was shy and happy? What next? Would they just smile at each other every day? That would be like they were engaged, and rumors would start swirling. What would her two brothers do to him, an Ismaili boy fancying their pretty Ithna Ashari sister? What would his Ismaili friends say about him being "in love" with an Ithna Ashari girl? Would he meet Salima somewhere in secret and hold hands, perhaps kiss? "Oh, God," Rafiq thought, "If she smells so nice, how nice would she be to kiss?"

As these thoughts ran through his head, he finally concluded that looking at her and admiring her was all that was in his destiny; anything beyond that was too complicated and perilous. Perhaps when he graduated from a university in the U.K. and returned to Tanganyika in all his glory, and if Salima was still around, he would tell his parents that he wanted to marry this girl and deal with the firestorm that his proposal would unleash. Perhaps he would just go up to Salima and tell her that he loved her and if she agreed, run away with her and get married.

Within a week of his return, Rafiq received an Air Mail letter from Robert. He had arrived safely in Nairobi; the school was fun, and the Italian and Greek girls were as pretty as he had left them; the first cricket game was scheduled for the coming weekend. But he missed Rafiq and the time they had spent together. He could not believe that he was looking forward to returning to Mpwapwa.

Rafiq wrote back to him, expressing similar sentiments. Salima was still oblivious to his attention; perhaps he would ask Robert for the script he had offered if she would just smile at him once, but that seemed unlikely. The school was fun; he was happy to be back.

Anil had told their other friends in the school about Rafiq having made a white friend with whose family he had spent a week in Dar es Salaam at the New Africa

Hotel. The boys were intrigued, and everyone was curious to know everything about this white boy (who was no less than a D.C.'s son). When in his Commerce class, the teacher asked if they had spent any time studying during the Easter vacation or had just wasted time lazing around and playing games, one boy blurted out, "Sir, Rafiq became friends with the Mpwapwa's D.C.'s English son who is schooling in Nairobi; he got invited to the D.C.'s house for dinner and at the D.C.'s invitation, spent a whole week with his English friend and his parents in Dar es Salaam at the New Africa Hotel."

"Is that true, Rafiq? How did this happen? Do you want to come here and tell us all how you got invited for dinner and spend a week with a D.C.'s family?"

Rafiq went to the front of his class and casually related how the D.C. had come into his dad's store, talked to him and suggested that he meet his son; how he and the D.C.'s son had become friends and all the things that they had done together; how he had eaten this horrible substance that the English called "horseradish" on the train and made everyone laugh; how Robert was just like any Indian boy with the same interests and aspirations. He left out the testy discussions he had with the D.C. and carefully looked for a reaction from the students, but mainly from Salima. She was listening intently to what he was saying and smiled demurely when everyone laughed out loud over his horseradish experience.

ROBERT AND RAFIQ REGULARLY wrote to each other, sharing experiences, what they were learning in school, their sports activities, and what their plans for the following week were. On his six weekly trips to Mpwapwa, Rafiq always made it a point to call on the Turnbulls, inquire if they were well, tell them that he and Robert were in constant communication, and how well Robert was doing at school and in his cricket games. When he wrote to Robert, he told him about his trips to Mpwapwa and his conversations with his parents.

What the Turnbulls did not tell Rafiq was that Robert was calling them every other week, which he had never done before, and was telling them almost everything he was writing to Rafiq. The D.C. repeatedly said to Jane that boy had changed; it was Rafiq's influence on him and how smart he had been to see in his brief exchange with Rafiq that Robert would benefit from being friends with Rafiq. Jane, of course, agreed with the D.C.

One evening as they sat chatting after dinner, Rafiq said, "Fateh Uncle, you know, when we went to Dar es Salaam, Robert and I spent practically all the time by ourselves; we hardly saw his parents. Anil and I are both over fifteen. Would you allow us to go on vacation by ourselves?"

"What place did you have in mind?" Fateh asked.

"I don't know. Anil and I have not talked about this, but we could go to a place like Mwanza on Lake Victoria or Kampala and go see Murchison Falls."

"And what would your parents say about that?"

"I would have to ask them; I think they would be okay, but if you say yes, they will surely agree."

Fateh realized the game Rafiq was playing: You say yes, and I will tell my folks, Fateh uncle and Almas aunty are okay, so you should be okay too.

"We would have to look at what it would cost, how long you want to go for, where you would stay, etc. If you went to some place where you could stay with some friends or relatives, or in an Ismaili guest house, we would feel more comfortable than if you wanted to stay in a hotel. We certainly cannot afford the New Africa standards." Fateh said.

"Well, something for us to think about, Anil," Rafiq said, looking at Anil.

HAVING HEARD ABOUT RAFIQ'S vacation with Robert in Dar es Salaam, Anil was interested in traveling. The boys had many discussions about where they could go for a couple of weeks during their full month vacation in August. Of course, Rafiq wanted to spend a couple of weeks with Robert in Mpwapwa (Robert had promised to bring more copies of Playboy), but he also wanted to vacation with Anil. He had over Shs.200 of the Shs.500 that his dad had given him for his Dar es Salaam vacation left over, and if he was going on another vacation, his dad would surely top that up to Shs.500.

1957
Eleven

After Rafiq's vacation with the Turnbulls, Salim and Yasmin had talked about what they could do to show their appreciation for them. They considered inviting them home for dinner but decided against it. The D.C. and his wife may not like the idea of going to an Indian's house for dinner; they may even be offended to be invited, although they were very friendly when they came into the store. Jane was coming in more often than before to make small purchases.

They considered giving them a nice and expensive gift but decided against it. That may seem like a "payment." Whereas it would have been perfectly acceptable to give them a bottle of *Black Label Johnny Walker* at Christmas time, it would not be nice to just turn up at their doorstep with a bottle of Scotch. They even considered sending the Turnbulls a large plate of nankhatai and another of samosas, but they asked themselves what the D.C. and Jane would do with all that food. They couldn't eat them all at once, and samosas needed to be eaten the day they were fried to be truly enjoyed. So, they did nothing, but always felt like they should do something.

While the Abdullas talked about what they could do to show their gratitude for the Turnbulls, the latter talked about what they could do to advance their relationship with the Abdullas. Could they invite them home for dinner? No, the Abdullas may not be comfortable in their home and may not like their food.

On one of her visits to John's General, Yasmin had told Jane that they were going to Dodoma to see the 1956 Academy Award-winning movie *Marty* the next day, and Jane had said, "Oh, that would be so interesting. It will be a long time

78

before the movie makes its way to the Club here."

"Would you like to join us? We can go in one car," Yasmin had asked. If they came, they could plan to have dinner at East African Railway's newly built posh Dodoma Hotel before the movie. That would be a nice way to show appreciation for the Turnbulls, she had thought, but Jane, having quickly considered what the D.C. would feel about being seen at the movie in the company of an Indian couple by the Dodoma whites (who would undoubtedly be there to watch Marty) had replied, "Oh, Yasmin, that is so nice of you, but I believe James has a social evening planned with some friends at the Club tomorrow."

When Jane told the D.C. that evening about Yasmin's invitation and her reply, he agreed that she had done the right thing and said, "But you know, Jane, it would be nice to invite them to a movie at the Club. We can always sign in guests. Then again, they may not be able to decline out of courtesy, but they may not be comfortable being with people who may not appreciate them being at the Club. You know, I have been thinking about addressing the Club membership at the meeting on Saturday, week, and conveying to them some of what Rafiq told us on the train. I want to suggest we open up the Club membership to everyone."

"You mean that? Would you do that, James?"

"Of course. Why not?"

"That would be a perfect thing to do. Coming from you, it would carry weight, but you would need to plan out what to say. You don't want the members to think that your son has become friends with an Indian boy, and now you want everyone to be friends with the Indians."

"I have been thinking about what I should say, and it's not just Indians I want to suggest we open up membership to. It should include the Africans. I know the educated guys working for the vet station, and Teachers' Training College will be supportive."

"That, James, would be revolutionary. Let's do that. It's about time."

AFTER DINNER AND THE chairman's remarks about the Club's finances and operations, the D.C. raised his hand and told the chairman that he had something to say. The chairman was happy that someone other than himself was going to talk to the members but wondered what the D.C. would have to say. Nobody ever spoke, except to complain about the Club facilities or services or fees. After dinner, the members wanted to quickly finish up the meeting and go see the movie of the week.

The D.C. came forward and addressed the members.

"My fellow members," the D.C. started, "as most of you are aware, I have served the Mpwapwa region as D.C. for seven years. Over the past weeks, I have been reflecting over what I have done, what the British have done, for this country and its people in the time we have ruled Tanganyika. I am ashamed to say that we have done nothing other than safeguard and enhance Britain's position, power, and influence in East Africa and exploit Kenya, Uganda, and Tanganyika's resources and markets for our motherland.

We recognize that the Indians are our tax base, so from time to time, we throw a bone or two at them, like the new school that we have built for them in Dodoma, but for the Africans, we have done nothing. Other than the Mission schools run by the Catholic Church, they have limited access to education. Without education, they have limited access to economic opportunities.

I must admit that this realization has come to me too late. African countries like Nigeria and British Somaliland are now seeking independence, and so are the East African countries. As you know, Gold Coast just became independent from the British. You also know that Julius Nyerere has formed the Tanganyika African National Union (TANU) to fight for Tanganyika's independence. There is a small TANU office here, in Mpwapwa. If you have heard Nyerere speak or read what he says, you will see that he is very strategic. I believe that he will lead Tanganyika to independence faster than Kenya and Uganda. I think that Tanganyika will be independent in less than five years.

In speaking to my fellow D.C.s and the P.C.s at the Governor's Conference that Jane and I recently attended, although the Governor spoke about Macmillan's push for the decolonization of sub-Saharan Africa, I got the impression that most believe that the East African countries are ten years away from independence.

Unlike other African leaders fighting for independence, who lead their countrymen to believe that the day their country becomes independent, they will take over all properties owned by foreigners in their lands and everyone will be rich and live in nice houses and drive fancy cars, Nyerere has made *Uhuru na Kazi* - Independence and Hard Work - his motto. He is telling his people to prepare to work very hard to build Tanganyika when it becomes independent. He is saying, the Indians and whites are not going to pack up and leave, and the Africans are not going to take over the buildings, houses, and cars that the Indians and the whites own. He is telling them that if they desire such riches, they will have to work hard to earn them.

If that is what Nyerere really means, I see an opportunity for us to do some good. Late as it may be, this would not only be the moral thing for us to do, it would be in our self-interest to do so.

Given that our PM wants to speed up the process for the independence of sub-Saharan African countries, it cannot be treasonous for us to assist TANU in working towards and preparing for independence. We know how to govern; we know how to run banks, schools, hospitals, businesses, and colleges. We can start to engage with TANU to help its leadership prepare for independence. Can you imagine how much they would appreciate this if we did it with some sincerity?

And after Tanganyika becomes independent, it will need people to govern the country; it will need people to run the vet station and the Teacher's College here in Mpwapwa. It will need qualified people to run the hospitals, schools, phone systems, and water and electricity generation and distribution systems that the Indians and we now run. If we build goodwill, if we build trust, we will be invited to stay and work with the Africans to build Tanganyika. Otherwise, we will get kicked out of here, the way we got kicked out of India.

If you find merit in what I say, you might ask: where do we start? Well, as a first step, we can begin to build bridges and relations with the Indians and Africans here in our town. Before we can engage with the Africans, however, we have to know them not as our servants, but as our equals. We can do that right here in this Club by opening up the membership to everyone. If we can sit and share drinks with the Africans and Indians, we will get to know them, and then we can talk about how we can assist; how we can work together. For Jane's and my part, we would like to nominate Mr. and Mrs. Abdulla, the owners of John's General, and Ricardo's wife, Chelsea, for membership in the Club. We are looking for secondments of our nominations, but not one or two secondments. If less than 70% of you second our nominations, we will withdraw them. Now you may ask why we want to nominate Indians? Well, the Africans relate far better to Indians than to us. We can work through the Indians to build relations with the Africans.

I hope we will all take some time to think about what I have said.

Thank you."

The D.C. had expected stunned silence, murmurs, and some hostile stares after he spoke. There was the stunned silence, he expected, but it lasted just a few seconds. Some clapping followed, the D.C. noticed, primarily by the Teachers' Training College and the vet station staff. Soon more joined, and then practically everyone except some ten members were applauding.

When the applause ended, Ricardo got up and said, "I have waited for three years to hear someone say this. It's time to wake up."

"Thank you, D.C., for your wisdom. My husband and I have always felt uncomfortable with how we live and behave, ever since we came to Tanganyika. It would be wonderful if we could do what you say, but I think it may be too late," another member said.

"Better late than never. You have my secondments, D.C.," the Teachers' Training College principal said.

And then there was a chorus of "And mine too."

Now it was the D.C.'s turn to be stunned. Neither he nor Jane had imagined this in their wildest dreams. They had not even asked Salim and Yasmin Abdulla if they wanted to become members.

After the movie, instead of heading home, most members came into the lounge and talked about how they should move ahead. The vet station and Teachers' Training College staff proposed names of their fellow Indian and African staff members who might make good members. Those not supportive of opening up the membership said that the Club would soon be overrun and taken over by Indians and Africans, but they got no support.

The D.C. admitted that he had not asked the Abdullas if they wanted to become members but said, "If Jane and I tell them how enthusiastic you all are about them joining, I am confident that they will join."

"I cannot say the same thing about Chelsea, D.C. She is a proud woman, and she may not want to have anything to do with the Club after years of your rejection," said Ricardo.

"I will be happy to speak to her and apologize for our behavior, Ricardo. Please arrange for me to speak to her," the Club chairman offered.

"Jane and I will be happy to join you," said the D.C.

When they got into the car, Jane said, "That was an excellent speech, James. I can't believe the immediate impact it had on the members!"

"I simply repeated much of what Rafiq had said to us, Jane."

"What we saw tonight was a transformation."

"I hope so, Jane, but at the same time, I think that we should be cautious about believing everything that we saw and heard there. Some of the people who were applauding me are people with whom I work and meet every day, and I know what they think of and call the Indians and Africans. The ones who were genuine in their applause were the more educated ones. When the rest saw that these families were going to second our nominations, they joined in because they did not want to be seen as bigots. We should take it with a grain of salt, but I was heartened to see how many are beginning to see the writing on the wall and believe that this is the way to go. We will get a true measure of how much support there is for change when we bring the Abdullas and Chelsea to the Club for the next general meeting."

"That's if they agree to join, James."

"I will leave the Abdullas to you. I have promised to go with the chairman to talk to Chelsea."

Jane spent all of Sunday thinking about how she would talk to the Abdullas and decided not to make a big deal of inviting them to join the Club. She would just tell Yasmin that they wanted to nominate her and Salim for the Club membership and gauge her reaction.

She waited until the following Saturday afternoon to call Yasmin. They exchanged pleasantries. Jane asked how Rafiq was, and Yasmin, in turn, asked how Robert was doing, and then Jane said, "Yasmin, James and I would like to nominate Salim and you for membership in the Mpwapwa Club. We have several programs and activities there that we think you will enjoy. If you like, we can take Salim and you tomorrow to show you the Club facilities and tell you about the Club programs."

After a brief pause, Yasmin said, "I thought the Club is for the Europeans only."

"Any member can nominate a friend or relative for membership, and if another member seconds the nomination, the nominee can join. Having gotten to know you and Salim, James and I would like to nominate you. We are also nominating Chelsea, Ricardo's wife. I presume you know her - the Somali lady. There was a discussion at our members' meeting last Saturday about increasing the Club membership, and there is a desire for diversity. When James told the members that we wanted to nominate Salim and you, there was overwhelming support for our proposal."

"It is very kind of James and you to want to nominate us. I will talk to Salim and get back to you."

"Please do that, Yasmin. And as I said, we will be happy to give you a tour of the facility and tell you about the Club programs."

AFTER SHE HUNG UP, Jane called the D.C. and told him about her conversation with Yasmin and that she had not sounded very enthusiastic. She had not asked about the Club membership fees or programs or how often they used the Club facilities. She had asked nothing.

"Don't worry, Jane, she was probably just surprised. You offered to give them a tour, so she would not need to ask you about the facilities, and I don't think that they would care what the membership fees are. They have turned John's General into the largest business in town. I'm quite sure that they will come back with a yes, or some questions. They won't decline."

After she hung up, Yasmin told Salim about Jane's proposition and said, "In the time that we have been here, I have never heard anything about the Club opening up its membership. The Club is the bastion of their colonial presence here in Mpwapwa. I haven't seen any white, other than Ricardo, be overly friendly with us, other Indians, or Africans. I am amazed that Ricardo's wife would not be a member. Why would Ricardo not have nominated her? Why would he wait for someone else to nominate her? Perhaps they want us three as token members, or there must be another agenda."

"You are hardly ever wrong in such matters, Yasmin, so they probably do have an agenda, but whereas I don't know about the D.C., I don't think that Jane would bring us in as token members. If they intend to create diversity or increase membership, then that's fine. They are inviting us to join; we are not applying for the membership. Let's take them up on their offer to tour the Club and go and check out what they've got there and ask them all the questions we should ask to decide if we want any part of this. One thing we can ask is if we become members and we nominate another Indian couple for membership, will the D.C. and Jane second our nomination? If they are truly looking for diversity, they will want more than just Ricardo's wife, you, and me."

Yasmin called Jane later that afternoon to say they would be pleased to tour the Club and, at Jane's suggestion, they agreed that they would do it the next day, Sunday, at noon.

1957
Twelve

To Yasmin and Salim's surprise, Tom Williams, the Club chairman, and Henry, the Club manager, in addition to the D.C. and Jane, were there to receive them. After a warm welcome from everyone, Tom suggested that Henry lead the tour. Salim and Yasmin knew Henry well, as he was the one who placed orders for liquor and beverages for the Club and settled the bills at the end of each month. He was a friendly person, who insisted that they call him Henry, as did Ricardo, whom they liked very much.

Henry took them through all areas of the facility, pointing out key features of the lounge, the social hall used for parties and screening movies each Saturday, and the dining room where dinners were served on Wednesdays and Saturdays and lunch on Sundays. He also showed them the meal menus and costs, the tennis courts and table tennis and billiard rooms, the rules for booking the court and the rooms, and the rules for the use of the Club facilities for private parties.

Salim, having been to the Club many times to deliver beer, beverages, wines, and spirits, was familiar with the facility, but Yasmin, who had never been here, was thoroughly impressed. She was the one who asked most of the questions, leading their hosts to believe that she was the one in this family who wore the pants, which was not entirely true. Unless both were convinced that they should join, they would not.

At the end of the tour, which took some 40 minutes, the chairman requested that Salim and Yasmin join them for lunch.

When they had walked through the dining room, several members eating lunch had looked up; some had smiled at them, and both Yasmin and Salim had smelled the tempting aroma coming from the kitchen. They looked at each other, and with a nod from Yasmin, Salim said that they would be happy to join their hosts for lunch.

Over lunch, the group conversed freely about a variety of topics.

It was quite an experience for Tom, as he had never spoken with any Indian in this setting, where they were sitting not as his subordinates, but as his equals. He was also surprised by how intelligent and knowledgeable their guests were, and how good their English was. They asked him where he was from in England, and they knew the general area from where he had come. They knew much more about the failed Kongwa peanuts scheme and its political fallout than he did. They clearly described their ancestral background in India and how they had ended up in Mpwapwa.

Henry, who had chatted with them before in their store, was happy that he was sitting down with them having lunch and how, when he revisited John's General, he would be able to relate to them on a much more personal level. Yasmin asked him what his last name was, and he replied, "I have not used it for so long, I have forgotten what it is!" and then while all laughed, he said that it was Bell, but he never wanted to be called Mr. Bell. He did not like the sound of it.

Yasmin and Salim had not eaten roast beef before, but Rafiq was right, it tasted good, though not as good as the steaks that Salim seasoned and barbequed.

After dessert and coffee, all got up to leave. Yasmin and Salim thanked their hosts for their hospitality and offered special thanks to Henry for the tour. Yasmin walked with Jane and thanked her again for the nomination and the tour, and promised to get back to her the next day. She asked her if Chelsea had taken the tour. Jane said she did not know.

As they drove home, Salim asked, "So, what do you think?"

"I was impressed with the Club facilities. These guys do have it good here, don't they? You could teach me tennis, and it would be nice to be able to see the movies here instead of having to drive to Dodoma, but I don't know what to make of this all. It seems like there is a 180-degree change in their attitude. Why do they want to be so nice to us, suddenly?"

"Maybe it's the D.C.'s doing. He is the boss around here, and he may have suggested that they make us members, and everyone has fallen in line. You are a much better judge of such matters, so why don't you decide if we should join?"

"No, don't lay it on me, Salim. We need to think about what we will do if we become members. Will we use the Club facilities or just go there to see the movies? Will we go there for Sunday lunches? If we do, with whom will we sit? We can't always sit with the D.C. and Jane. Their bar is beautiful but of no use to us. We need to think."

"Okay, sweetheart, let's think."

BEFORE THEY REACHED HOME, Yasmin had done her thinking. "You know, I will call Jane tomorrow and tell her that we are inclined to join, but ask her if we do and then want to nominate another Indian or African couple, will the D.C., and she second our nomination. If she says yes, I will ask what the membership fee is and send her the cheque."

"Done. Do you have someone in mind whom we can nominate?"

"Sunil and Nitika Mehta, who both teach at the Indian Primary school here, may be interested in becoming members. I don't know if Mike is married, I presume he is; we could nominate him. He is a smart businessman, and whereas he uses the credit we extend him quite liberally, his bar is doing well, and he is always buying more and more and paying his bills - eventually. I understand he is also involved with the TANU office and may know people there whom we can nominate."

"Great. You always make good decisions."

WHEN YASMIN CALLED JANE the next day and asked if the D.C. and she would second her and Salim's nominations should they decide to nominate anyone, Jane said, "Of course, we will second your nomination. We'll be delighted to do so. The fees are 50 Shillings per couple per month. If you want family membership, it's 75 Shillings. There are rules relating to the number of family members, for kids under 16 and the facilities the kids can use. Anyone over 21 years of age has to have an individual membership for 25 Shillings a month."

"Sounds good, Jane. I will send you the cheque for one year's family membership."

"No, give it to Henry when he comes into your store."

"Okay. Will do."

1957
Thirteen

On Sunday morning following the Club meeting, Ricardo related to Chelsea in detail D.C.'s address of the previous night and what had followed. He had expected her to get furious when he told her that the D.C. and his wife wanted to nominate her. Instead, she looked passively away for a few seconds and then quietly asked, "Did they just find out you are married to me? They have seen me and met me dozens of times in the streets or at John's General, and they have never said 'hello' to me once. They said nothing when no one seconded your nomination. Now that independence is coming, they are scared and want African friends. Are you actually suggesting that I should become a member, after having been rejected for over three years? Go and show my face there?"

"Chelsea, I would not be talking about this to you if I had not gotten the sense last night that there was some sincerity in what the D.C. said – that it's too late for us to do anything for the Africans' socio-economic wellbeing but at this stage, we should help the Africans work their way towards independence. What he was saying was, in effect, we should speed up independence and not be afraid of it. I think that he meant it. Look, honey, it's entirely up to you to decide if you want to join."

"You understand that this is not an easy decision for me to make? After having been treated the way I have been treated?"

"I understand, but I must tell you something. You know that when no one seconded your nomination, I wanted to cancel my membership, but you forced me to keep it because you didn't want me to become isolated from my social circle. It has been difficult going there without you and seeing all other men with their wives. It was agreed last night that if I cannot get you to accept the nomination, the D.C. and the Club chairman will request to meet with you. They said that they would like personally to apologize to you for their past behavior. Now, you don't have to meet them, but I want to tell you that if we reject their nomination, then you must allow me to cancel my membership. I would be much happier spending every minute that I spend at the Club, with you, instead."

"You hardly go there, Ric. You go there for a drink or two after work and then rush home to me. Other than that, you only attend the members' meeting and dinner once a month at my insistence, and you don't even stay for the movie."

"I play tennis there every Sunday."

"Yes, but you could be playing tennis at another court in the town, and I wouldn't go with you. If I played tennis also, you wouldn't go there to play tennis, either. That I know."

"Will you please think about it, Chelsea? And whatever you decide, I will agree with you."

"Okay, I will."

TWO DAYS LATER, CHELSEA was in John's General in the afternoon to buy some groceries. Salim, who was serving her, could not resist speaking to her, now that he knew her name.

He said, "You have been coming into our store for some three years and my wife - her name is Yasmin, and I found out only two days back that your name is Chelsea. We could not call you Mrs., as we address some of our other female customers, because we don't know your husband's last name either. He has asked us to just call him Ricardo. Now that we know your name, may we call you Chelsea? And we would like you to call us by our first names also —my name is Salim - instead of Mr. or Mrs. Abdulla. "

"That would be lovely, Salim. I would love to have you and your wife call me Chelsea," and extending her hand to Yasmin, she said, "Yasmin, right?"

Yasmin extended her hand and holding Chelsea's hand, said, "We are so happy to know you. Isn't it strange that we are getting to know each other after all this time that you have been shopping here?"

"But you never wanted to talk to me when I came in. I thought that was because I am African." Chelsea said.

"Oh, God, no, Chelsea. We did not engage with you because you are a white man's wife, and we could not treat you any differently from a white woman, with whom we cannot take any liberties. I am surprised that Salim spoke to you today about something other than what you want to buy or what we have to sell to you!" said Yasmin.

"Strange world in which we are living with our strange perceptions of one another," Chelsea said with moist eyes, and although she had some idea, she asked, "So, how did you find out my name?"

"The D.C.'s wife told us that she and her husband want to nominate us for the Mpwapwa Club membership, and they are also nominating you."

"So, are you joining?" Chelsea asked.

"We toured the Club last Sunday, and after ensuring that if we join, we can nominate any Indian or African for membership, we said yes. I hope you are accepting the nomination also?" Yasmin asked.

"I don't think that I will. When Ric and I moved here, someone nominated Ric, but not me. When Ric asked why, this guy said that once Rice became a member, he could nominate me. Ric believed this, and he nominated me, but nobody seconded his nomination."

"Did Ricardo not ask the guy who had nominated him to second your nomination?" Salim asked.

"Yes, he did, and the guy said that if he seconded Ric's nomination, he would be in trouble with the membership, so Ric asked another fellow, and he got the same answer. It became clear that I could not be a member because I am not white. Ric was furious and wanted to cancel his membership, but we had come here from Addis Ababa, and he had no friends; the Club was the only place where he could socialize with his people, so I convinced him to keep his membership, but he has always been very unhappy. Now, after all that, they want me as a member. Can you imagine their audacity?" She was almost in tears.

"Chelsea, we are about to close up. Would you like to come in for a cup of tea with me?" Yasmin asked.

"Are you sure? I don't want to take up your time or cause you inconvenience," Chelsea said, but she really wanted to talk to these folks. She had never spoken to anyone about her Club experience, and she felt that she could talk to these people.

"No, it will be our pleasure to know you better. Please come." And with that, Yasmin led Chelsea into the residence. Salim remained in the store and decided to allow the two women at least 30 minutes to talk in private before joining them - if Chelsea had not left by then. He knew that Yasmin would make her feel better.

As she sat down in the lounge, Chelsea said, "You have a very nice home, Yasmin."

"Thank you. Allow me a few minutes, and I will make some tea."

"While you do that, may I use your phone to call Ric? He might worry where I have gone."

"Please do," Yasmin said, pointing to the phone.

Soon, Yasmin returned with tea and biscuits.

Yasmin asked Chelsea about her background.

Chelsea said her parents were well to do and well educated. She had gone to Leeds University in England and graduated with B.Ed. Degree. Her father was a Muslim, and her mother was Christian. She had two brothers and one sister. They were all raised, in the main, as Muslims, but their mother also took them to church sometimes. She had read the Quran. She and her siblings each had two names – one Muslim and one Christian. Her Muslim name was Shaheeda.

She had met Ricardo in England and married him there. After graduating from the university, she had worked as a secondary school teacher for two years in Leeds, and then a veterinary research company in Ethiopia had hired Ricardo. They had lived in Addis Ababa for another two years. She had loved teaching there, and then Ricardo got a senior position at the vet station in Mpwapwa. After coming here, she had applied for a position at Teachers' Training College, but they did not have any vacancies, so she had gotten a teaching job at the Catholic school. She was happy there, although the pay was much lower than what her qualifications warranted.

"You have an interesting background! So you have never used your Muslim name?" Yasmin asked.

"All my life, I was Shaheeda. You know that means someone who sacrifices herself for God or a noble cause. I loved the name, but when we came here, Ric suggested that I call myself Chelsea. He thought that I would find more acceptance with that name, but to these people, I was just another African, and now they want to make me one of their own and expect me to be grateful for their generosity and jump with joy, because, as an African, they must think I don't have the brains to understand how Ric and I have been humiliated for so long."

"My heart goes out to you, Chelsea. I can imagine the pain that you have suffered these past years. How did you live through this? Other than Ricardo, do you have any support? Do you go to the mosque or the church here? Do you have any friends there?"

"No, Ric does not attend the church, and I have never been to the mosque here. With a name like Chelsea, that would be difficult to do."

"So, you have borne this all by yourself?"

"Yes. I decided that I was not going to make Ric miserable over my misery, so I have always maintained a cheerful disposition and made light of the Club's and the whites' rejection of me. I comforted myself by saying that practically all of these white women in Mpwapwa have no better than a high school education and are sitting at home, having their houseboys and *pishis* (cooks) do their work. I say to myself, they may think me inferior because of the color of my skin, but I am superior to them in knowledge and education, and I don't want to socialize with them, either. Sounds like sour grapes, but that's how I truly feel."

"Don't ever think or say that, Chelsea! The color of your skin does not make you inferior. I am brown, and I don't consider myself superior to you or inferior to the whites. You have read the Quran. Allah says, 'Oh mankind, if we had wanted to, we would have created you all the same. We created you from a single pair of a male and female and made you into nations and tribes so that you may know one another.' Only the intelligent will understand that. We are Allah's creation – his supreme creation, and we should seek to know and respect our fellow human beings and never look up to or down on anyone because of the color of their skin."

"You know in the time that I have been here, Yasmin, I have not had this kind of conversation with anyone. You make me feel so much better."

"Chelsea, I would be happy if you would consider me a friend. In fact, I need one! I left all my friends behind in Dodoma. I would love to have a friend here with whom I can sit and have an intelligent conversation – someone like you!"

"You mean that?"

"Of course, I mean that. Will you be my friend?"

Chelsea got up and hugged Yasmin. Now tears were running down her face. Yasmin held her close and said, "I presume this is 'Yes'?"

"I cannot thank you enough for your kindness. Of course, I will be your friend. Your husband won't mind you being friends with a black woman?"

"My husband will be ecstatic that I have found a beautiful and intelligent friend like you. You know you are very beautiful, don't you?"

"Ric says that I am beautiful, but other than you, no one has said that to me since I left Somaliland."

"Well, you are. But now let's talk about your nomination. Rather than declining, why not let the D.C. and chairman come and apologize to you? You can't get any better than a D.C.'s apology. Next, you can ask for a tour of the Club. Go and see the facilities. I am sure that you will like them and remember nothing is being offered free to you. You will be paying for it, so there are no favors. Once you join, the members will see how educated and intelligent you are. You may not be the only educated person there, but most will be without a university education and not much grey matter between their ears. You would be able to attend events with Ricardo – you know how much he would like that, and like showing off his beautiful and intelligent wife? I would do that, Chelsea, not keep hating them. Hatred hurts the hater more than the hated. And I would love to have you at the Club events with me. Maybe you and I could play tennis. Do you know how to play tennis?"

"I played some with my brothers, so I know the basics."

"So, you can teach me!"

"You think I should do that? Accept the nomination?"

"You should think about it. Talk to Ricardo. By the way, what is his last name? Is it a secret?"

"No, it's Sawyer."

"Well, talk to Mr. Sawyer," Yasmin said with a smile, "and then decide."

"You have given me a whole new perspective to reflect upon."

Yasmin changed the subject. "You don't have any children; don't you want any?"

"When we married, we agreed that we would not bring into this world a child who will not know which race he or she belongs to. Eventually, we have to live in the U.K., and Ric does not want his child to be discriminated against or called a half breed."

Yasmin was at a loss for words. She couldn't think what to say, so she said, "You probably know that I have a son. I miscarried a baby girl and have not been able to conceive again."

"I am so sorry to hear that."

Just then, Salim came in and asked, "Did you ladies leave some tea for me, or do I have to make my own?"

"There is tea in the pot, but it's gone cold. I will make you some fresh tea." Yasmin said.

"No, I will make it. You sit and relax. Would you like another cup, Chelsea? Yasmin?"

"Yes, please make some for us, too." Looking at Chelsea, Yasmin said, "Then you can compare my tea with his. He makes a lousy cup of tea."

"Well, that's what I get for gratitude in my home. I hope you are kinder to Ricardo?"

Chelsea laughed and said, "I am sure your wife is just teasing you."

As they sat enjoying tea, there was a knock on the door. Salim opened the door. It was Ricardo.

"Hello, Salim, I presume my wife is still here?"

"Yes, please come in," Salim said.

"No, I think we should go. It's getting dark, and I did not want Chelsea to walk home alone."

"But please come in and have a cup of tea with us. Actually, it's dinner time. Why don't you stay for dinner?" Yasmin said, getting up.

"That's so very kind of you, but I think we should get going," Chelsea said, getting up.

"Well, some other time, you must come for dinner," Yasmin said, and looking at Chelsea, she added with a smile, "now that we are friends?"

Chelsea hugged Yasmin, and they said goodbye.

WHEN THEY GOT INTO the car, Ricardo asked, "What was that all about?"

Chelsea told him everything that had happened. Ricardo was quiet for a few moments and then said, "You know, Chelsea, I believe that from time to time, God sends his angels down to the earth to help people restore their faith in humanity. Perhaps, Mrs. Abdulla is one such angel."

1957
Fourteen

Three days after Tom Williams had told the D.C. that Ricardo's wife wanted to listen to what they had to say before deciding to accept the nomination and that he had agreed to meet her the following Sunday at 10.00 a.m., the D.C. told his wife, "You know, Jane, for three days I have been agonizing about whether I shouldn't have gotten myself into situation where I have to go and apologize to an African woman, not knowing if she will accept our apology or throw us out of her house. I have been wondering about the ramifications. If they tell people that I had gone to apologize to her and she threw me out, the word will spread very fast. The P.C. might even call me in and ask me to explain what I was thinking. He might see Chelsea's treatment of me as an insult not only to me but to the Crown and British Empire."

"So, it could get serious?" Jane asked.

"Yes, and I would become the laughingstock of the white community, not only in the Dodoma Region but the whole country. I don't think that in the history of the British Empire, a senior official representing the Crown has gone to sincerely apologize to a native. I might make history. I considered making an excuse and asking Tom to go alone, but after much thinking, I have decided to go with him, no matter what the consequences. I want to do that because it is the right thing to do."

"You should do it then. Follow what your heart is telling you."

"Yes, I have been thinking a lot about how we have been treating the non-whites. We have always assumed that anyone with dark skin is inferior to us in intellect and is devoid of all emotions. That's what the slave traders thought when they took Africans into slavery. I am going to go with Tom and beg for Ricardo and Chelsea's forgiveness, and if they throw us out, so be it. That will be a small redemption for me."

"You know, James, I am proud of you. I will stand by you to take the consequences. If they kick you out of the Office, hell, we'll go home. You can tell the British papers why you got kicked out. The press will have a field day. There are enough liberals in the U.K. who will applaud you."

"Thank you, Jane; I will need your support if things go awry. And what I said to the Club, about helping Africans achieve independence and afterward build this country, this cannot happen unless everyone subscribes to the idea and the chances of that happening are less than zero. Still, I will do what I can here."

ON SUNDAY, TOM AND the D.C. approached Ricardo's home with much trepidation. They had agreed that the D.C. would do the talking. Ricardo met them at the door and led them inside to the lounge, where Chelsea greeted them with a polite hello (no handshake), and all sat down.

"Mrs. Sawyer, Mr. Williams, and I thank you for allowing us to come and meet with you. We are here to sincerely apologize for our behavior towards you over the time during which you have been in Mpwapwa. We realize that this is coming far too late and that much water has flowed under the bridge, but there is also a growing realization among us whites that our actions have been shameful. We have treated you and all people of color as less than us when, in fact, many of you are much superior to us. We can understand if you are skeptical about why we are here, but I want to tell you and Ricardo that I am, personally, deeply, deeply ashamed and sorry for our behavior, and I hope that you both can find it in your hearts to forgive us."

Chelsea stared at the D.C. for a few moments. She had not expected this. She had expected some patronizing chit chat and a half-hearted "Sorry, and let's forget about the past, lady. Okay?"

Ricardo looked at Chelsea. She needed to respond.

"Mr. Turnbull, my name is Chelsea, but I was raised as both a Christian child of a Christian mother and a Muslim child of a Muslim father. Islam teaches us that only Allah is perfect. Humans make mistakes. If, when a human has erred and realizes his mistake and asks for forgiveness, it is un-Islamic not to forgive. I can speak for Ric to say that we will not carry this in our hearts. The past is behind us, and today is the first day of a new beginning for us all. Now, can I get you some tea?" And with that, she stood up.

And that was that.

Was this all that this woman is going to say? Was she not going to say what pain they had caused her and her husband, not tell them what evil people they were? God, look at her dignity, her poise, her graciousness, her maturity. A black woman could have so much finesse? This was way more than he would have expected of any white person, the D.C. thought.

"I don't know how to ... how to express our gratitude, Mrs. Sawyer."

"Then, don't, Mr. Turnbull, and please call me Chelsea. Do you take milk and sugar in your tea?" she asked.

"Honey, why don't you sit with our guests and I will make tea," Ricardo said and headed for the kitchen.

Chelsea sat down. Both, the D.C. and Tom wished that she had gone to make tea. Now they would have to talk to her. Neither had much experience talking to a black woman. Each hoped that the other would speak. The D.C. began, "So, Chelsea, I understand that you are a teacher at the Catholic school here?"

"Yes, I am, and I enjoy teaching there."

"Did you go to a Teachers' Training College like the one here?"

"The College here trains teachers for primary school. I got my Bachelor's in Education degree at Leeds University in England."

The D.C. was surprised. He never knew Chelsea had been to a British university. "For how long were you there?" he asked.

"Three years."

"That's a long time. You must have missed home."

"Yes, I did. In my first year, I often cried in bed at night, but on the whole, I was happy at the university. Because I was a foreign student, my fellow students treated me with much consideration and kindness. The faculty treated me like I was a ward of the university. The professors and lecturers were very caring. They smiled warmly at me when I met them in the corridors. They constantly asked me if I needed help with my courses and complimented me generously when I wrote a good paper. They asked me if I was comfortable in my hall of residence, if I liked the food, if I missed home."

"That must have been comforting for you."

"Yes. I experienced the same attitude at other British universities when I participated in inter-university programs. One lecturer and his wife once invited me home to spend Christmas with them. Their kindness touched me, deeply. I came to develop very high respect, and in fact, affection for the university staff and the students. As I interacted with the wider society, I also came to respect the British for their professionalism, their ability to remain calm and focused in times of crisis, and their honesty. I could not reconcile the difference between the British in Britain and the British in Somaliland. I concluded that as colonial rulers, they had to behave the way they did."

"Did you not experience any discrimination?"

"Oh, yes, I did. I could see that sometimes I made some customers uncomfortable when I went with my friends to eat in a restaurant. On occasions, I would be on a transit bus when the only vacant seat was next to me, and some ladies would choose to stand, holding the pole, instead of sitting next to me. I wondered if they were afraid that I might have lice on my head that would crawl over into their hair. Otherwise, there was no reason why they would not sit next to me because I dressed and groomed myself well and wore expensive perfumes."

"You must have hated these women."

"No, I did not feel any anger for them. I just smiled to myself. I felt sorry for them. They usually looked like they were uneducated. Often, some smart woman or man occupied the seat next to me, and, despite the British reserve, they would ask me where I was from, what I was reading at the university, and would wish me well in my studies."

Soon Ricardo appeared with tea and a tray of cakes and cookies. As Chelsea poured tea, Tom asked, "Chelsea, would you like me to arrange a tour of the Club?"

"Ricardo can do that, right, Ric? That way, we can do it at our convenience," Chelsea said.

"Yes, why don't we do the tour this afternoon?" Ricardo asked.

"Why don't you take Chelsea to the Club for the Sunday lunch? Chicken Kiev is on the menu today." Tom said.

"What's that?" Chelsea asked.

"I don't know. I have never eaten it, but that's what it said on the notice board, and it sounds good. Why don't you try it out and tell us if the chef should make it again?"

Ricardo looked at Chelsea, and she said, "Thank you for your kind invitation. We'll try the Chicken Kiev today."

After some casual talk about lack of rain that year, the D.C. and Tom thanked Chelsea for her graciousness and took their leave."

"So?" Ricardo asked.

"So, what?"

"So, what did you think?"

"I appreciated the D.C.'s sincerity."

"Honestly, Chelsea, I was afraid they were going to get hell from you, and I am sure that they expected the same."

"What purpose would that have served? I would have proven them right in their judgment of my character; it would have lowered me in their eyes."

'You are right. You are so right, honey. I cannot imagine anyone who has suffered the humiliation you have suffered in this town to have been so gracious, so dignified. I think that they couldn't have been more surprised by your response."

"Well, let's get ready to eat Chicken Kiev. Will that be with the Club's compliments, or will we have to pay for it? Shall I call Yasmin and ask her and Salim to join us?" Chelsea asked.

"Yes, that would be great."

Chelsea called Yasmin and said, "Ricardo and I are going to the Club for lunch today. Why don't you and Salim join us?"

"Oh, Chelsea, so you accepted? I am so delighted! Of course, we will."

"Well, I have to tour the Club, you know, and I will then decide."

THE CHICKEN KIEV WITH roast potatoes and a tangy sauce was delicious. After desserts and tea, Ricardo called the chef, an African, and asked him to tell them the recipe for the chicken. He said that he had found it in a magazine which some guest had left at the Club. He brought it out for them to read. The batter in which it had to be cooked sounded a little complicated, so no one was interested in trying it out. They complimented the chef for a superb job and asked him to make it more often, which he said he would.

The D.C. and Henry came by to welcome Chelsea. Henry offered to give Chelsea the Club tour.

"Why don't you let Henry take you around, Chelsea?" Ricardo suggested.

"Okay," Chelsea said and got up to tour the facility.

When she returned some 30 minutes later, the Abdullas and Ricardo were sitting in the lounge, talking. This was the first time Ricardo had spent any time talking to Yasmin and Salim, and he could see that they were wonderful people and delightful company.

"So, did you like what you saw?" Ricardo asked.

"I think that I will join," Chelsea replied with a smile.

The next day, Ricardo paid the Club one year's family membership fee.

1957
Fifteen

The note from the Provincial Commissioner in Dodoma addressed to all the D.C.s was short. It read:

This is to inform you that my term as P.C. for the Central Province will expire at the end of this year. His Excellency, the Governor, has advised me that he wishes to appoint Mr. Raymond Jackson from Bristol as the next P.C. Mr. Jackson is a Second World War veteran and has served with Britain's diplomatic missions in Egypt and Southern Rhodesia.

Formal communication from His Excellency will follow in due course.
Yours truly,
Michael Anderson
Provincial Commissioner

The D.C. read the note and passed it on to Jane.

"So, it looks like it did not happen," she said with a mixture of relief and disappointment.

"I know for sure that Michael had put in a good word for me, but we have to admit this Jackson fellow looks like he is better qualified than I am."

"Well, we should start to prepare for our return to England. Maybe we should leave in mid- December to celebrate Christmas with our families in the U.K."

"We'll have to wait to be advised of my successor. My term ends December

31st, but we may not depart until March of next year if the new D.C. is appointed by this year's end. I may have to stay for the new D.C.'s orientation. Remember, my predecessor stayed on for a couple of months?"

"I wish we would know soon so that we can start to pack up to leave."

"We don't have much to pack, Jane. Practically nothing here belongs to us!"

"We'll have to think about Rob and his school."

"I would be inclined to have him stay over for his Grade XII and finish the Cambridge Exam here, then pursue his "A" Levels in the U.K. Let's not get ahead of ourselves, though. Let's talk to Rob."

"Yes, it would make sense to do that, but where will he spend his vacations if he stays at the school in Nairobi?"

"He can come to the U.K. for his August vacation, and he will be done in November, so he would return home in December. The Easter vacation is all we'll need to worry about."

They had expected Robert to be delighted to know when they told him that they would be returning to the U.K., but his response was muted. He felt sorry for his dad. He had known how much he had aspired to the P.C. position. It would have been a significant promotion and allowed him to stay in Tanganyika for at least another four years.

"I am sorry, Dad, that you did not get the position. I am sure that with your background, you will land a fine job in the U.K. We will talk about my education when I'm there for my August vacation. The courses continue from Grades XI to XII. It would be disruptive for me to move to the U.K. after completing XI here at the end of December, and starting "O" Levels in the U.K. in January; it would be the middle of their academic year, but I suppose that it can be done. I would need to work very hard."

The Turnbulls were grateful for such a thoughtful response from Robert.

Two weeks later, he wrote:

....You will recall that we had planned to visit the National Parks before we return home. We cannot go back without seeing the Masai Mara in Kenya and the Serengeti and Ngorongoro in Tanganyika. August is the best time to visit the Parks. That's when 1.5 million wildebeests and 500,000 zebras migrate from the Serengeti to Masai Mara, and the weather is dry. We have to see the Ngorongoro crater; it's a natural wonder, teeming with wildlife.

I have checked with a couple of tour operators here, and they have packages which include two night's stay (1 room) at the Norfolk here in Nairobi and surface travel from Nairobi to Mara, Serengeti and Ngorongoro with two nights (2 rooms) stay and all meals at each of the game park lodges and guided tours of the parks for Shs.3,500 for a party of three. The game park lodges offered are the best accommodation available.

I would very much like Rafiq to come with us. I am sure that he would love to do that, and his parents can afford to pay for his share of the cost. The package for a party of four is Shs. 4,500. If you agree and he agrees to come, you could leave Mpwapwa on August 1st and fly from Dar es Salaam to Nairobi on the 2nd. After two days in Nairobi, we can head out to the game parks. From Ngorongoro, the tour operator would bring us to Arusha, from where we can fly back to Dar es Salaam and take the train to Mpwapwa.

It will be the experience of a lifetime! This is the high tourist season, so we have to book soon. The operators say that the tours are usually sold out by mid-July because accommodation in the parks is limited. It is the end of June, so we should decide in the next few days.

Think about it...

The Turnbulls were intrigued. Robert was right. They had to visit the game parks. They would never be able to afford to return to Africa to see them. The schedule that he was suggesting made sense. The cost was not prohibitive.

"It would be great if Rafiq joined. The boys would have an amazing time, and I would like to take Rob back to the U.K. with wonderful memories of his time in Africa. The parks would give him that." Jane said.

"I agree. All that we need is Rafiq's confirmation. Will you talk to Salim and Yasmin?

"I will do that right away."

THE ABDULLAS WERE, OF course, delighted to hear Jane's proposition. This would be an amazing opportunity for Rafiq. Traveling with white people, he would get the best accommodation, transportation, and service wherever they went, which they, as an Indian family, would never get even if they paid more. They agreed to talk to Rafiq and get back to Jane.

ON THEIR NEXT TRIP to Dodoma, Salim and Yasmin told Rafiq about the D.C. and Jane's invitation. Rafiq was delighted, but he said, "Dad, Anil and I have been talking about going somewhere for two weeks in August. We haven't decided where, yet, and that's why I have not spoken to you about it, but we are inclined to go to Iringa for ten days where Fateh uncle's brother lives, and Anil has a cousin our age. His uncle and aunt passed through Dodoma a couple of weeks back and invited us to go there. As you know, Iringa is in the Southern Highlands province, so it's cold in August, but there are hills and the Ruaha River and a place called Tosamaganga where there is a little waterfall."

"If that's what you have decided, then that's what you should do. Safari would have been very exciting and educational, but we can do that some other time." Salim said.

"As a matter of fact, we had also considered going to Arusha and from there to Lake Manyara National Park and Ngorongoro, as one option. One of our teachers took this tour, and he cannot stop talking about it, but it was too expensive for Anil. The bus ride from Dodoma to Arusha, one night in Arusha at New Safari Hotel, the tour from Arusha in a minibus with four other people, and tent accommodation in Ngorongoro and Manyara was almost 1,800 Shillings for two, which was 400 Shillings more than Damjis can afford for Anil's share. We really wanted to do this, but we just can't. So, attractive as this opportunity with the D.C. family may be, Anil and I have decided to go to Iringa, and although we have no confirmed plans, I can never let him down."

"I am proud of you, Rafiq. It takes some character to turn down an opportunity like this to keep your commitment to your friend. We will thank the D.C. and Jane for their very generous offer and say that you cannot go with them." Salim said.

"I agree. Hopefully, one day, we might be able to take the time from our business to go on the safari Rob and his parents are planning to take, and if we do, we will be sure to take Anil with us." Yasmin said.

"As I think about this, Mom, I can go with Rob and his parents for two weeks and then go for a week to 10 days to Iringa with Anil but having talked as much as we have about the Arusha, Manyara, and Ngorongoro tour which we would have so loved to go on, and deciding against it, I don't know how Anil would feel if I went on a similar safari and first-class, at that, with my new white friend. I simply cannot hurt Anil's feelings."

"You are right, Rafiq. You cannot do this."

"If it's okay with you, when we come to Mpwapwa next weekend, as we have planned to do, I would like to meet with the D.C. and Mrs. Turnbull and express my gratitude and tell them why I cannot go with them. I know that Rob will be disappointed, but that's what I have to do."

"Yes, and that's what we will do. And, Rafiq, if you and Anil want to go to Arusha and the game parks, go ahead and plan. Dad and I will pay for the entire trip for both of you. It will be our treat. We want you to travel. Dad and I cannot close the store and travel with you, but you are now fifteen and can travel alone, and we would be happy if you broaden your horizon by seeing the world. Just look for a package that gives you accommodation in game park lodges, not the tents. We don't want a lion to visit you in the night in your tents."

"You would really do that, Mom? Dad?"

"Of course, we will, but we will want to know much more about the tour, the tour operator, who the other passengers will be with you, etc. Give me the contact, and I will talk to the tour operator. I have seen some tour operators' ads in the Standard that look like respectable outfits. I will talk to them also if they are different from the one you've talked to before I send my son and his friend on their safari." Salim replied.

"Thanks, Dad. Thanks, Mom. Anil will be ecstatic when I tell him this."

ON HIS NEXT WEEKEND trip to Mpwapwa, Rafiq visited the Turnbulls and told them why he could not go with them, and about his and Anil's safari plans. They were disappointed, and they knew that Robert, too, would be very disappointed.

The D.C. asked, "What's this lad, this friend of yours, Anil, like?"

"Well, Sir, he is very smart and friendly. He is actually a lot like Rob; I guess that's why we are friends!"

"I was thinking," the D.C. said, looking at Jane, "why can't this friend, Anil, join us?" Looking at Rafiq, he asked, "The trip you are planning to Manyara and Ngorongoro will cost you money, right? If you and your friend come with us and you three boys share a room, it won't cost much - probably no more than your trip to Manyara and Ngorongoro."

"That would be great! Rafiq, do you think that your friend would want to come with us?" Jane asked.

"I am sure he would love to do that, but are you sure you want to take him with you? You have never met him. And would Rob like that? He has never met him. We two are buddies, but he may not like my friend."

"Well, we can call Rob and ask him," said the D.C.

"I think that before we do that, you should meet Anil. He is here with his family for the weekend. I can bring him over to meet you. That way, you can tell Rob what Anil is like."

"That sounds good, but I don't want you to go home walking and come back walking with your friend. Let's drive down and fetch your friend," said the D.C. "You can give him a call and let him know that we are coming, and why."

Rafiq called home and first told his mother what the D.C. and Jane were proposing. She was delighted and put Anil on the line. While Anil talked to Rafiq, she told the Damjis about the D.C. and Jane's plan, and their offer to take Rafiq and Anil with them.

What Rafiq told Anil was too much for him to absorb. He was nervous about meeting the D.C. and could not believe that this white man and his wife were coming to meet him. "Will they interview me? What should I say?" He asked.

"No, they just want to meet you. I suggested that they should. Just relax and be yourself."

Soon, the D.C.'s car pulled up in front of the store. Yasmin walked up to the car, said hello to the D.C. and Jane, and said, "We very much appreciate your generous offer to take both boys with you. I don't know how to thank you for all this. Instead of taking Anil to your place and then driving him back, why don't you come in and chat with Anil in the house? The rest of us will go sit in the backyard so that you will have privacy." Yasmin said.

"That's kind of you, Yasmin. We can do that." Jane said and opened the car door to get down. The D.C. was hesitant for a moment to go into an Indian's house but got out, and they all went inside. Salim welcomed them and introduced them to his guests. The guests were nervous and felt relieved when Yasmin suggested that they go sit in the backyard. Fateh and Almas were concerned about Anil.

The D.C., Jane, Rafiq, and Anil sat down in the lounge. Rafiq could see that Anil was nervous.

"Anil, we are very pleased to meet you and your parents. As you know, Rafiq and our son Rob are friends. We are planning to go on safari to the game parks in August. We have invited Rafiq to come with us. We would like to invite you also to join us." The D.C. said.

Anil was surprised. They were not interviewing him. They were inviting him.

"That is very kind of you, Sir, Madam, but Rob doesn't know me. He might feel like I am intruding."

A valid concern, the D.C. thought.

"Rafiq says that you are a fine boy, and if you are Rafiq's friend, Rob will know that you are a fine boy," said Jane.

"I am very tempted to say yes, but I wish that I had met Rob, and we had known each other. If I come and he does not like me, or he doesn't want to share Rafiq with me, his safari will be ruined."

"Rafiq has told us that he is not coming with us if you are not. You two have planned a safari together, and he is not going to cancel that," said the D.C. "I do hope that you can come with us."

"Sorry, Sir, I would love to come, but I do not want to put Rob in an uncomfortable position," Anil said.

"You know what, James, why don't we call Rob and see what he says," said Jane.

"That's a good idea, Jane, let's go home and speak with him."

"You can call him from here if you like, Sir. Anil and I can join our folks in the backyard. Take your time." Rafiq said.

"It's long-distance. The call will cost at least 20 Shillings."

"Don't worry, Sir. Come on, Anil; let's go sit in the backyard."

Jane dialed the operator and asked for the Nairobi number. Soon, she was connected. Luckily, Robert was in the residences.

"Hi, Mom, what's up?" He asked.

Jane relayed to him the situation and asked, "What do you think? We are here with the boy. He is polite and smart and is raising a valid concern. He doesn't want to ruin your vacation, but we think that you would all get along quite nicely. What do you think?"

"Rafiq talked a lot about Anil. Honestly, if he is Rafiq's friend, he has to be a nice person. I have no problem with him joining us."

"Are you sure that you won't mind sharing Rafiq with him? We don't want any jealousy. It can also happen that you and Anil may get along so well together, Rafiq may feel Anil is stealing you from him. You have to think about all these things."

"No, Mom, you're making a big deal out of this. We boys are boys. Two together or three together, we can be friends and have fun. You said that Anil is there. Can I talk to him?"

"Yes, if you want to, I can get him."

Jane called Anil. He picked up the phone and said, "Hello, Robert?"

Robert replied, "Hey mate, my parents are telling me they're inviting you to join us on the safari, and you're saying no because I might not like you. Rafiq has told me so much about you, I feel like I know you very well, so just come along, and the three of us will have a swell time."

Anil was touched.

"Thank you, so much, Robert, there is nothing I would like to do more, but are you sure?"

"Absolutely. Just come along. I'd like to hear all the jokes that you make about the British."

"Oh my God, Rafiq didn't tell you those, did he?"

"Some, not all. So, if not for the safari, come and let me hear how you make fun of my people." Robert said, laughing.

"I don't know how to thank you, guys. You and your parents are so kind."

"So, that's settled, then. I will talk to the tour operator to add you to the package. Let me talk to my dad now. It's good talking to you, and please, call me Rob."

"I look forward to meeting you, Rob." Anil passed the phone back to D.C.

"Hey, Dad, it's all settled. Anil will join us." Robert said to the D.C.

"Great!" exclaimed the D.C., "You take care, Son."

"I can assure you, we are going to have a great time," the D.C. said, looking at both Anil and Rafiq.

"Shall we go?" Jane asked, getting up.

"No, you have to wait for my dad and mom and Anil's parents to thank you," Rafiq said and went out to get them.

The Turnbulls chatted with Anil. He was still nervous, but it was evident that he was pleased and excited. He told them that he was an average student, not as smart as Rafiq. He liked English Language and Literature and loved to read Julius Caesar. He enjoyed sports and was good at football and volleyball. He had friends other than Rafiq, but when asked, he said he did not have a girlfriend – nor did Rafiq. Yes, he did like girls, but there was none in particular.

The Turnbulls got the sense that Robert would like him.

When Salim, Yasmin, Almas, and Fateh came in, Jane announced, "We have invited Anil to join us on the safari we're going on in August; Robert and Anil chatted on the phone, and Anil has agreed to come with us, subject to his parent's approval, of course."

"That is so very kind of you. Are you sure that it will not be any trouble for you – Anil coming along, I mean?" Fateh asked.

"Not at all. It will be our pleasure to have your son come with us," The D.C. said, getting up to leave.

"Please stay and have some tea, or better still, Salim is going to barbeque some steaks and chicken. You will love it. It's not spicy. Please stay and taste his cooking." Yasmin said.

"Why don't you spend the evening with your guests, Yasmin, and we will get going," Jane said.

"We would love to have you join us for the barbeque. I can assure you that you'll love Salim's steaks and chicken." Almas said.

"Do you have enough food? I have a healthy appetite," the D.C. asked Salim.

"Yes. Whenever these folks come over for the weekend, I marinate almost twice as much meat as we can eat and freeze the rest for Yasmin and me to barbeque and enjoy until they come back the next time. We have lots of food."

"Shall we?" the D.C. asked Jane.

"Sure, why not?" Jane replied.

"Yasmin, since we are going to have the pleasure of Jane and Mr. Turnbull's company, why don't you check if Chelsea and Ricardo are free to join us, also? You can apologize for the last-minute invitation. Is that okay, Mr. Turnbull?" Salim said.

"It would be great if they could join us, and please, call me James," the D.C. replied.

Yasmin went into the store to call Chelsea and Ricardo and soon emerged to announce that they were happy to be invited and would be on their way shortly.

THE BACKYARD BARBEQUE WAS an evening to remember for everyone. The D.C., Jane, Ricardo, and Chelsea had never dined in an Indian family home. Their hosts had never had the English and an African as their guests.

It was a beautiful moonlit evening. Salim's locally made barbeque grill was efficient. Soon, the air was filled with the savory smell of seasoned meat being barbequed, making everyone hungry. Yasmin offered the D.C., Jane, and Ricardo beer (Chelsea, like her hosts, did not drink); all others enjoyed soft drinks with roasted peanuts while Salim barbequed.

Salim opened a bottle of expensive wine from the store for the D.C., Jane, and Ricardo to enjoy with dinner. The steaks and chicken were served with potatoes cooked in lightly spiced Indian sauce. Everyone ate more than they had wanted to. The meats were so tasty!

Ricardo, Chelsea, the D.C., and Jane were full of compliments for Salim's cooking.

They all sat talking well past midnight. Anil told a few benign jokes about the British and lightened up the atmosphere. The D.C. and Ricardo spoke about life in the U.K. Salim talked about his and Yasmin's grandparents' origins in India, how they had traveled in small dhows to Zanzibar, and then moved inland. Chelsea talked about her homeland and life there. Fateh and Almas were hanging on her every word. They loved to see her smile. She was so charming, smart, and amiable. Rafiq shared with everyone his research into the evolution of the game parks and the animals they would look for in the parks. He told the D.C. and Jane that the Olduvai Gorge was located in the eastern Serengeti on the way to the Ngorongoro and that they should stop to visit the site.

As the evening wore on and the D.C. and Ricardo enjoyed more wine, they became much more talkative. The D.C. berated the British, who had ruled India. No wonder they got kicked out! Jane was amused. He had been no better. Fateh and Almas got more comfortable, and each told jokes about the Indians. Even Zahir and little Tazim told some kiddy jokes. Everyone was so happy and relaxed. No one wanted to leave. Yasmin served tea, coffee, cakes, and nankhatai, which encouraged them to sit back and enjoy talking.

Just before 1.00 a.m., the D.C. said that he had had too much wine, and it was time to go before he was too drunk to drive. All got up to leave, and a wonderful evening ended.

1957
Sixteen

By the end of the first week in July, the D.C. had booked their train and airline tickets, talked to the tour operator in Nairobi, and finalized the safari plan.

The additional cost for the fifth person (Anil), would only be Shs. 500 if he shared the room with the other two boys. The game park lodges would only charge for his meals. The tour operator had booked a long wheelbase Land Rover for them which could accommodate up to six people, if one sat in the front in the passenger seat, which the D.C. decided immediately, he would do, to get the best views.

The package for five would be Shs.5,000, and for two would be Shs. 3,000, so the additional Shs.2,000 would be shared between the three boys, which was an unbelievable deal for Rafiq and Anil, almost Shs.500 less than what they would have paid for their trip to just two game parks in super economy class transport and accommodation. The savings would pay for their train ticket to and from Dar es Salaam, and the plane rides to Nairobi from Dar es Salaam and from Arusha to Dar es Salaam.

ALL COULD HARDLY WAIT for the safari to start. Rafiq and Anil counted the days to August 1st when they would take the train to Dar es Salaam and then board an East African Airways flight to Nairobi. They had never flown before.

A VERY SIGNIFICANT EVENT occurred for the global Ismaili community in July 1957. His Highness The Aga Khan III, who had led the community as the 48th Imam for 72 years, passed away on July 11th. In conformity with his wishes, he was to be succeeded by his 20-year old grandson, Prince Karim Aga Khan, as the 49th Imam of some 15 million Ismailis spread over India, Pakistan, the Middle East, East and Central Africa, and Central Asia. In his Will, the 48th Imam had said that given the great changes which had taken place in the world, he should be succeeded by a young man who had been brought up in the new age and who would bring a new outlook to the office of Ismaili Imam.

Rafiq and his Ismaili friends were aware of the vast array of health, education, financial, and social institutions that the 48th Imam had established. These, too, like the Ismaili community, were spread all over the world. Additionally, there were hundreds of Jamatkhanas that served as more than places of congregation and worship for the community; many had schools, guest houses, and institutional spaces attached to them. Oversight over the operation, funding, and maintenance of all Jamatkhana properties was the Imam's responsibility.

The new Imam was just four years older than Rafiq and his friends and was an undergraduate student at Harvard. They could not imagine how a 20-year old young man must feel to become responsible for 15 million people, spread the world over, nor could they fathom how the young Imam was going to manage all of the institutions that his grandfather had created, guide his Ismaili followers, and study at Harvard, all at the same time. Within days of becoming the new Imam, he had told his followers that he would dedicate his life to the community's wellbeing and development. For the youth in the Ismaili community, this brought realization of the sacrifice the young Imam was making – the loss of his youth, the complete dedication of his time and energy, and the ceding of his personal freedom. All that they would do and enjoy as young boys and young men, he would not be able to do.

Rafiq and Anil so wished that they were older and more educated. In the Ismaili tradition of voluntarism and service, they would have offered their services to their new Imam in whatever capacity the Imam desired. For now, all that they could do was worry about him, pray that their fellow Ismailis would not expect too much from their young Imam, and let him do his work and study in peace. Ismailis – particularly the East African Ismailis, were notorious for harassing their Imam - writing to him for his advice over every small health, business, family relations, and other personal issues.

Anil and Rafiq's parents did not share their concerns. They had full confidence in the Imam that he would be able to manage whatever his office required of him.

In the event, the young Imam took a year off from Harvard to organize his work and meet with his global community, before returning to graduate with a degree in Islamic Studies. The hundreds of Aga Khan schools, health and medical facilities, financial institutions, and Jamatkhanas continued to operate flawlessly, and even grow, under the new Imam`s early direction.

Prince Karim Aga Khan was no stranger to the Ismailis. At his grandfather's behest, he and his younger brother, Prince Amynmohamed, like their father Prince Aly Khan, had traveled to the lands where Ismailis lived and endeared themselves to the community. The community had adored their princes, and now, the Ismailis world over could not wait to see their new Imam.

They did not have to wait too long. The community was soon advised that a formal investiture ceremony called *taktnashini* to install Prince Karim as the 49th Imam would be held in major centers in Africa and the Indian subcontinent before the year-end. Preparations for these grand events, which would bring together tens of thousands of people, began in each of the major centers where the ceremonies were to take place. For Tanganyika, it was announced that the ceremony would take place in Dar es Salaam on October 19th, 1957.

For Anil and Rafiq, this was a most exciting time, as they eagerly anticipated their vacation in the game parks in August and their Imam's taktnashini for which they, and thousands of other Ismailis, would travel to Dar es Salaam in October.

THE SCHOOL TERM ENDED on July 31st, and Anil and Rafiq boarded the train in Dodoma for Dar es Salaam. They arrived in Gulwe two hours later, where the Turnbulls were waiting to join them. Salim and Yasmin were also at the train station to give Rafiq Shs.500 for the trip (even though Rafiq had told them he had Shs.200 leftover from the Dar es Salaam trip) and told him that they had already paid the D.C. for Anil and Rafiq's share of the tour package. The aggregate Shs.700 allowance was for him and Anil to spend as they wished and to make sure that they treated the D.C., Jane, and Robert to at least two nice meals in Dar es Salaam and Nairobi. They knew that they did not need to, but still gave the boys a brief lecture on how to show gratitude and respect for the Turnbulls, help them carry their baggage, and to ensure that the boys behaved themselves.

THEY ARRIVED IN DAR es Salaam the next day at noon and took a taxi to the airport. A new airport had just opened in Dar es Salaam which had a fancy restaurant on its upper level. The flight for Nairobi did not leave until 4.00 p.m., so they had time for a leisurely lunch, for which Rafiq insisted on paying. It was one treat on behalf of Anil, Rafiq, and their parents. Rafiq insisted that the Turnbulls enjoy wine with their lobster lunch.

They boarded the East African Airways Fokker Friendship aircraft at 3.30 p.m. and took off, on time, at 4.00 p.m. Anil and Rafiq could hardly contain their excitement as the plane circled over the city and the ocean, and turned north for Nairobi. Soon the flight attendants served soft drinks and peanuts. The boys ordered Fanta orange, which, although it was the same as what they drank on the ground, tasted much better.

In just over two hours, they were on the ground in Nairobi. Robert was there to receive them, and they were on their way to The Norfolk Hotel. Robert was genuinely happy to meet Anil and could not stop telling everyone about the plans that he had made for Mara, Serengeti, and Ngorongoro. He had talked to some people to whom the tour operator had referred him and who had taken this safari. They had told him what times of the day and evening were best for sighting the "Big Five" – the lion, elephant, rhino, leopard and cape buffalo.

He told Rafiq that a parcel was awaiting him at the hotel. It had been delivered earlier that day from a local store. Rafiq could not imagine what or how anything could have come for him at The Norfolk. All of this excitement was getting to be too much to bear.

The Norfolk was quite different from the New Africa in appearance, and stepping inside it felt much more colonial. Practically everyone in the hotel was white.

The environment was more formal compared to New Africa, which was quite relaxed. When he registered, the receptionist handed Rafiq the parcel. All were eager to see what it was, so they sat down in the lobby, and Rafiq opened the box. It was a Rolleiflex camera with a flash and rolls of film. Rafiq had desperately wanted one to replace the Kodak Box camera that his dad had bought for him when he was 12. There were a dozen rolls of films and an envelope with a note which read:

Our dear Rafiq:

If you are reading this note, you have arrived in Nairobi. We wondered what we could give you to take on safari. You and Anil had already bought sweaters and jackets for the cool evenings in Nairobi and the parks. We decided to give you a Rolleiflex to take lots of pictures for us. We hope that you will like the camera. There should be 12 rolls of film in the package, which will take 12 shots each. That will give you 144 pictures of your safari that Fateh uncle, Almas aunty, Zahir, Tazim, and two of us will want to see when you get back, so don't miss anything you can "shoot" with this camera. Read the manual carefully to get good shots.

Please convey our warm regards to Mr. and Mrs. Turnbull, and our affection to Rob.

Love,

Mom, Dad

Rafiq was overwhelmed. He handed the note to the D.C. and asked that he pass it around.

The camera store had requested that he should call to confirm receipt of the package.

THE HOTEL ROOM WAS not very different from the one in which Robert and Rafiq had stayed at the New Africa, except that there was a phone in the room. Rafiq picked up the phone and asked the hotel operator to connect him to the camera store. He thanked the proprietor, who identified herself as Gulshan Adatia. The name told Rafiq that she was, almost certainly, an Ismaili. He asked how his parents had arranged for him to get the camera. She told him that they had located the store name and telephone number from the Nairobi telephone exchange, had called the store and asked about the various Rollei models in stock, and had selected the top of the line model for him. They had arranged to send by Express Registered Mail an envelope containing the Money Order to pay for their purchases and had provided Rafiq's arrival information, and an envelope addressed to him.

"You are a fortunate young man. Your parents went through so much effort to arrange for this gift to arrive for you before you did. They requested that I should call them collect when the package is delivered to you. If you are in town, please drop in to say hello. We are on Delamere Avenue, and we are also Ismailis. Enjoy the camera, and have a great safari! Don't forget to read the manuals for both the camera and the flash. It's important to do that to get good pictures."

Rafiq mused at the amount of effort that his parents had gone through just to surprise him with such an extravagant gift. Were they spoiling him because he was the only child? Perhaps. He had to tell them how much he appreciated their thoughts and the present, so he asked the hotel operator to connect him to his parent's number. The operator told him Shs.25 would be billed to his room for a five-minute call and connected him to his parents. He thanked them heartily for the camera and told them how much he had wanted this particular model.

THE D.C. AND HIS wife chose to dine at the hotel. Robert took Anil and Rafiq to Curry Pot for a sumptuous Indian meal (although Robert could only eat samosas, kabobs, and bhajias).

THE BOYS SPENT THE next day exploring Nairobi. Rafiq was impressed. The city was much larger than Dar es Salaam. Also, practically all of the white men and many Indians were wearing suits or blazers/sports jackets and slacks and ties, which nobody except the Barclays Bank staff did in Dar es Salaam during the daytime.

Walking down Delamere Avenue, Rafiq spotted the CINEX camera shop. He went in, while Anil and Robert hung around outside, looking at the store windows. Behind the store counter, he spotted a beautiful girl with a ponytail fiddling with a camera. He walked up to her. She looked up and smiled at him. "Can I help you?" She asked.

"Yes, I am here to see Mrs. Adatia. Is she here?"

"Oh, that's my mother; she has just gone next door to get some Cokes. She should be back in two minutes unless she is chatting with the store owner. Take a seat," the girl said, pointing to a chair in the store corner.

Rafiq sat down, surreptitiously eyeing the girl. He caught her watching him a couple of times, as well. Mrs. Adatia was taking a long time getting the Cokes. She was obviously chatting with her next-door neighbor.

After almost 10 minutes, she entered the store with two bottles of Coke and handed one to the girl.

"Mom, this young man is here to see you." She said, pointing to Rafiq, whom Gulshan had not seen sitting in the corner.

"Hello, Aunty, I am Rafiq. We spoke yesterday on the phone. I wanted to come in and thank you for arranging for me to get the camera package," Rafiq said, standing up.

"*Ya Ali Madad*, Rafiq, it's so lovely to meet you! How are you? You're going on safari!"

She had greeted him with the traditional Ismaili greeting, Ya Ali Madad. Rafiq had called her "aunty" because that was the conventional Ismaili way of showing respect for an older lady.

"Yes, Aunty, and I am very much looking forward to that."

"You know, it was such a pleasure speaking to your parents. We talked several times as they decided which camera to buy for you. I also called them yesterday after we talked. They are such wonderful people. I feel like I have met them in person. I am happy that you dropped in. I wanted to see what their son would be like. You are such a handsome young boy."

The "aunty" saying this to him in front of her pretty daughter, made Rafiq blush.

"How long are you staying here? I would love to have you come home for lunch. Are you free for lunch today?"

For a moment, Rafiq wanted to accept. This aunty was so nice and her daughter so pretty, but then he reconsidered; what would he do with Robert and Anil? He couldn't tell them that he had accepted a lunch invitation from this woman in whose store he had just walked in, and he couldn't tell this aunty that he had two friends hanging around outside whom she should also invite.

"Thank you very much, Aunty, that is very kind of you, but my friends and I have a full day of sightseeing planned. This is our first trip to Nairobi." Rafiq said, pointing to Anil and Robert, who had appeared in front of the store entrance.

"Your mother said that you are going on this safari with a white family?" Gulshan asked.

"Yes, their son, who studies here, is a friend of mine. His parents live in the small town where my parents live."

"Hmm.... very unusual for an Indian boy to have a white friend ... and you're staying at the Norfolk! It would have been nice if you could have come home for lunch. My husband and my son would have liked to meet you."

"Thank you very much, Aunty. Perhaps, if I come to Nairobi again, I will drop in to say hello." Rafiq said.

"Well, at least have a Coke before you go." The girl said, offering the Coke in her hand to him and smiling. Oh, God, that smile is so beautiful, Rafiq thought.

"No, thank you very much. My friends are waiting outside. I must go. And thank you, Aunty, once again, for getting me the camera. Ya Ali Madad," he said, nodding at both.

"Ya Ali Madad, Rafiq. Have a great safari."

When he was gone, Gulshan said to her daughter, "What a lovely young man! So handsome and polite."

"Yeah, he was kind of good looking," said the girl, noncommittally.

"Kind of good looking? I saw how you were looking at him. Now that's the kind of boy I would like you to marry."

"Oh, come on, Mom! He's gone, and I'm only 15, so forget about him."

"I will look for him in seven years. I have his parents' phone number. I will track him down and ask him to marry you."

"And what makes you think he doesn't have a girlfriend and that he would want to marry me?"

"Marry you? Which boy would not want to marry you?"

"You think I am descended from heaven?"

"Of course; you are my daughter!"

STEPPING OUT OF THE store, Rafiq wondered if he had been "unfaithful" to Salima by looking so admiringly at the girl in the store. Well, Salima would never know, and if she did, would she even care? To her, I am very likely just another Ismaili boy, he thought to himself.

Meeting up with Robert and Anil, he said, "Guys, there was an amazingly gorgeous girl in that store. Her mother invited me to have lunch with them. I declined, of course."

"I can't believe you did that! Why would you do that?" Robert asked, perplexed.

"What was I supposed to do? Tell her that I have two friends whom she should invite, as well?"

"No, you could have told us you were going to have lunch with the pretty girl. Let's go back; I will pretend to look for something to buy. Anil and I can see the girl, and maybe they will invite you again, or invite us all, and you can accept."

"Rob, you are impossible," laughed Rafiq, "come on, let's get going. We have lots left to cover. You have to show us the 20th Century Fox and Kenya cinemas."

RAFIQ ASKED ROBERT WHICH was the best restaurant in Nairobi.

"Simba Grill. It's right around the corner," Robert replied.

"Can we walk over to the restaurant and book a table for five for tonight? Anil and I would like to treat your parents and you to a nice dinner before we start our safari. Do you think your parents may have other dinner plans?"

"My parents? Dinner plans? No. They will certainly be dining at the Norfolk."

"Okay, then let's go and book."

Simba Grill was at the upper level of a two-story building. They booked a table by the window.

LATER THAT EVENING, AS they placed the orders, Rafiq asked the waiter to bring a bottle of some fine wine.

"Rafiq, you boys are spoiling us too much. You paid for the lunch at the airport in Dar es Salaam and now this? This is a gorgeous place with an amazing menu – and pricy too. And you ordered wine for us again; is alcohol not forbidden in Islam?"

"It's our pleasure to treat you. Our parents will be pleased to know that you accepted our invitation. And yes, we do not consume alcohol, but we don't impose our beliefs on others. We know that you enjoy wine with your dinner, so please make sure that the bottle the waiter brings is of the best quality. If not, we can ask him to bring something better from the cellar."

"From the *cellar?*" This boy's vocabulary just does not cease to amaze me, thought the D.C.

The wine served with dinner, Jane said, was one of the best she had tasted. John's General did not carry that brand. It was too expensive for Mpwapwa. Robert asked if he could try a glass. The D.C. was inclined to say no, but Jane said, "Go ahead, Rob, but just one glass. No refills."

At Rafiq's insistence, they had ordered some starters (shrimp and crab salad), main courses (steaks, salmon), all kinds of desserts (peach melba, crème caramel, crème brûlée), and coffee and tea.

"This is the best meal I have had in Africa. Thank you so much, boys," said Jane.

"I echo that," added the D.C.

"We're so happy that you enjoyed the meal! Did you like it, Rob?"

"Yes, I did, but I enjoyed the wine more," replied Rob as he helped himself to the last half glass of wine in the bottle.

Everyone was in a jovial mood. The D.C. looked at Robert somewhat disapprovingly, but let him enjoy the wine. It was a great evening.

With the tip, the tab was Shs.200. Rafiq's savings from the Dar es Salaam trip were gone. He would have to be more careful, going forward, with his balance of Shs.500. He did not want to run out of cash.

As they approached the door, the manager thanked them for their patronage and asked, "How far are you going? Do you have a car?"

"No, but we are not going far. Just walking over to The Norfolk. My son will get a taxi from there to go to his boarding house."

"I suggest that you take a taxi from here. Tourists can get into trouble walking the Nairobi streets this late at night. Shall I call one?"

"Yes, please. Thank you very much," the D.C. replied.

It was past midnight when they got into their rooms, and they had to be up at the crack of dawn the next morning to depart for Mara. The boys quickly brushed their teeth and went to bed.

1957
Seventeen

After an early breakfast, the party was en route to Masai Mara by 9.00 a.m. It was a long, almost eight-hour journey, part of it on paved roads, and part on rough, dirt roads. The tour operator had provided a fairly new Land Rover with less than 10,000 miles on the odometer. The African driver, Bakari, was also to be their guide throughout the safari. He spoke English well.

He said that he had been driving tourists for close to 14 years, the first five as a hunting safari driver. He had given this up because he could not watch the animals being shot for sport. Survival of the fittest was the law of the jungle; the weakest died, but the hunters were killing the best and the fittest for trophies to be mounted on their cottage walls.

Also, this breed of tourists was usually aggressive and brash. They often forced him to take them into game reserve areas that the tourists or hunters were not permitted to enter.

Yes, it was lucrative for the tour operators. They charged three times or more for a hunting safari than they did for a game drive like the one that they were on. There were few extra costs for the hunting safaris. The hunting licenses did not account for even 20% of the additional charge. In addition to the driver, the party was provided with a "game tracker" who wore a khaki uniform, was usually large in build, and carried a high-powered rifle. His job was to find elephants with large tusks, lions with well-grown manes, young leopards with taut skin and bright spots, and rhinos and cape buffalo with large horns.

This did not require much skill; the game reserves were full of such species, and the fancy game tracker did not get paid much more than the driver - unless he was white. In that case, even though he did nothing different from an African tracker, he was described as the "White Hunter" - a rare breed, and it was a different kind of safari. The hunters, who were usually Americans, paid extra for the privilege. The hunting safaris with a White Hunter cost anywhere from Shs.15,000 to Shs.25,000 more than a game drive. Sometimes there were two or three hunters in the party, each of whom needed their trophies.

Yes, some were generous and left large *bakshish* (tips) in American dollars. He got seven East African Shillings for one American dollar.

To make it feel like an authentic hunting safari with all of its "inherent dangers", the hunters were accommodated in tents instead of lodges. These were actually cheaper for the tour operators. The higher cost was justified by the need to provide overnight security from wild animals, the outdoor meals which had to be cooked on portable grills, and the freshwater which had to be brought along for drinking and washing up. The hunters were on rough and "dangerous" adventures and did not usually bathe.

Yes, he did get paid more for driving the hunters – almost Shs.500 more per month. This was a tidy sum of money for him, but he had no regrets giving it up. He would never go back to doing that kind of work again. As opposed to the game drives – where the tourists were thrilled to see the Big Five, watch the wildebeests and zebras move north to Mara or south back into the Serengeti, observe the Mara river crossings of these large herds, or watch a pride of lions with cubs jumping on their mother's back or nibbling at the ears of the sleeping male – the hunting safaris were tense. The hunters were in a bad mood if they had missed a shot or had wounded an animal that had gotten away, and they had not been able to track it. When this happened, the hunters, technically, had used up one hunting license with nothing to show for it.

Bakari described how a hunting safari was organized – the preparations, orientation of the hunters focussed on dangers for the hunters and the trackers (the hunters were never in any real danger and nor were the trackers) and how ferocious a wounded elephant or lion could be. Some hunters had never shot anything larger than a duck. To Bakari, this was all a lot of nonsense to make the hunters feel like they were getting value for their money.

He told them how the animals were tracked and selected for hunting, the process for retrieving the dead beasts and their transportation to taxidermists in Nairobi, who would have the animal's head ready for a wall mount by the time the hunters got back from their safaris. He suspected that they did not always get the head and/or skin of the animal they had shot. He made it clear that he had no love for this breed of visitors to Africa. When Kenya became independent, he was sure, the new African government would ban hunting safaris.

Robert, Anil, and Rafiq invited Bakari to join them for lunch at a small restaurant where all Mara bound tourists ate. He told them that he could not do this; it was against the company policy for him to eat with the tourists. When he could not give the reason why, and when they asked what he was going to eat and he showed them a dried-up sandwich and a banana, they insisted that he dine with them. He was uncomfortable as they sat down and did not know what or how to order. He was worried the restaurant manager, an Indian, would report him to the tour operator.

Bakari selected the same chicken dish that the boys had chosen. The Turnbulls ordered hamburgers. The manager himself came over to take the order. When placing the order, the D.C. said to him, "The boys will have chicken, my wife and I will have burgers, and my friend here (pointing to Bakari) will also have chicken."

After that, when coming to their table, the manager addressed Bakari as "Sir," which Bakari thought was hilarious. The manager thought Bakari must be a senior official from KANU (Kenya African National Union - a party fighting for Kenya's independence) in the company of a sympathetic white family.

To Bakari, his clients looked like good people, although they seemed somewhat strange. He had never seen a white family traveling with two Indian boys. Seeing what the D.C. had done for him with the manager, he felt courageous enough to ask, "*Bwana*" (Sir), "have you adopted these two boys?" He had taken a Swedish couple on safari once who had adopted two African children.

The D.C. laughed, "I wish that they were my sons, but no, they are my son's friends."

"But white people can have Indian friends? And do you think that the manager believed that I am your friend?"

"Well, seeing us in the company of two Indian boys and an African man, he must have believed we are a different kind of white family, one which could also have an African friend," said the D.C.

THEY ENTERED THE MARA region at around 5.00 p.m. Bakari explained that unlike the Serengeti and Manyara, Masai Mara was not a National Park. It was more of a game sanctuary with limited tourism infrastructure, so it was mostly unspoiled. It was an extension of the Serengeti, north into Kenya from the Tanganyika border. Masai Mara was named after the Masai people who had lived on these plains for generations.

Mara was famous for its cheetahs, lions, elephants, Cape buffalo, giraffes, and leopards. The Mara River was teeming with crocodiles and hippos. Mara was the northern destination for the annual migration of over a million wildebeests, and hundreds of thousands of zebras from the Serengeti every year at this time. They stayed in Mara until October before trekking south, back into the Serengeti. On their migration, they were followed by the predators – lions, leopards, cheetahs, and hyenas. Mara also had hundreds of species of birds.

Wildlife started to appear on the horizon as soon as they entered Mara. By the time they had reached the Mara Game Lodge, they had seen giraffes, herds of zebras and wildebeests, some Cape buffalo, dozens of Tommy gazelles, and elands. The sun was setting on the plains, and the sight of various animals and a majestic giraffe, standing right in the center of the setting sun, was spectacular.

THE LODGE, BUILT ON the crest of a hill, was rustic. Its Main Lodge housed the reception, a lounge with a fireplace, and a dining room for 30. There were 12 freestanding cottages (six on either side of the Main Lodge) designed to look like African huts from the outside, each with a large floor to ceiling window overlooking the plains through which the migration moved. Visible from the window, some 30 feet below the boys' cottage was a waterhole. A couple of Cape buffalo were grazing nearby. Soon, some Tommy gazelles appeared, and before sunset, there were all kinds of animals drinking from the waterhole. There were no lions, leopards, chee-tahs, or hyenas in sight. They were probably drinking from the Mara River.

After a long journey and a hearty meal, the Turnbulls and the boys were ready to retire. By 10.00 p.m., all were in bed and fast asleep.

The boys were awakened at around 1.00 a.m. by the roar of a lion, and screeching hyena calls just outside of their cottage. They pulled the curtains and in the lodge's lighting, they saw a large lion near the waterhole with his kill (an impala), and at least ten hyenas trying to snatch it away from him. The lion was furious and tried to chase the hyenas away, but when he chased one, the others tried to pull his kill away. The lion mauled one hyena and would have killed it, but he had to run back to protect his kill from the others. The mauled hyena limped away, whimpering. After fighting the hyenas for 15 minutes from every side, clawing some and biting others, the lion gave up and stalked away. The hyenas, some bruised and bleeding, sat down to enjoy the lion's kill.

The D.C. and Jane, who were four cottages on the other side, slept through all of this and heard nothing.

The game drive the next day was an experience of a lifetime for the Turnbulls and the boys. There were animals wherever they looked. Soon, they came upon a herd of elephants. They were surprised to see Bakari stop a few yards from the herd, which was moving in their direction. He turned off the engine. The elephants kept sauntering toward the vehicle, some pulling grass out of the ground and munching on it as they passed by, almost brushing the vehicle. The boys, who had climbed up on their seats to look out from the viewing hatch overhead, could see that the elephants were making eye contact with them. Rafiq, who was snapping pictures, was sure that he had caught one elephant looking right into his camera. The boys could even hear the elephants munching grass.

Bakari explained that the elephants were among the smartest and gentlest of the big animals. He would not have stopped in the path of a herd of cape buffa-los. The elephants were aggressive only when they or their young were threatened.

Pointing to one large bull with big tusks, Robert asked if the hunters would select him for hunting. Bakari said, "Yes, this would be a good one to shoot."

"Would they just shoot him as the herd grazes like this?"

"They would avoid herds. They would wait for the selected bull to get a little separated, about 50 feet from the others, and then shoot it."

"But these animals are so peaceful. They aren't threatening anyone. They must trust humans to pass so close by us with their little ones. How would shooting an elephant, which is grazing so peacefully, be as exciting or challenging as people are led to believe hunting an elephant is?"

"It's execution. A high-powered rifle bullet hitting the center of an elephant's head, which is a large target, brings him down screaming in a less than a minute."

"I hope that no hunters are surveying this herd," Robert said with some sadness.

With this kind of spectacle of nature, he would need more film rolls, Rafiq thought.

As they moved on, they saw two giraffes, appearing to be affectionate towards each other, locking their long necks. Bakari explained that these were two males fighting over a female who was standing by. As they approached the giraffes, they could hear the loud thuds of the two necks hitting each other. After exchanging a few blows, one walked away, and the other claimed the female.

Bakari kept looking for lions, leopards, and cheetahs. They found one cheetah mother feasting with her three cubs on a Tommy gazelle that she had brought down. They were on higher ground, from where Rafiq could get some excellent shots.

Later, Bakari was advised by radio that there was a lion in a particular area. By the time they arrived there, three Land Rovers had circled the lion, resting under a tree.

The boys wondered if he was the one from whom the hyenas had stolen his meal.

Bakari said, "Likely not. This one seems well fed. He is resting and does not look like he will hunt until the nightfall. Look at his belly - it's full."

As the other vehicles pulled away, one by one, they drove nearer to the lion until they were less than 10 feet from him. When they got very close, the lion opened his eyes, raised his head, and stared at the vehicle and the passengers for a few minutes. The boys, who were looking at him from the viewing hatch, could look at the lion right in the eye, as they had done with the elephants. His eyes were a stunning golden amber color, and his gaze placid, but he quickly closed his eyes and went back to sleep.

After Rafiq had taken all the pictures that he wanted to capture, Bakari started to pull back to make room for other vehicles that were pulling up behind him.

"Bakari, what do you think the lion was thinking as he was looking at us? Do you think that he was thinking we would make a good meal for him?" Robert asked.

"Lions don't attack or hunt humans unless threatened or sick and cannot hunt their usual prey. I think that he must be thinking, here is another bunch of silly humans coming to look at me, I don't know why they want to look at me and then go away. I will just go back to sleep. And that's what he did – go back to sleep."

"Now, would a hunter shoot this lion, sleeping under a tree?" Rafiq asked.

"Yes, he would."

"Oh my God, this is so different from the Hollywood depiction of a brave white hunter standing in the open savannah, firing at a ferocious lion charging at him at full speed and bringing it down just feet from him. Someone has to be a real coward to shoot a sleeping lion."

"Yes, but that's what they do," Bakari said.

THEY ROAMED THE MARA all day and watched the animals graze, run around, play, and rest. They saw large herds of Cape buffalo grazing or lying down to rest. These, Bakari said, were the most dangerous of the African animals.

"James, if there is paradise on earth, this is it," Jane said with a sigh.

"You know, I could have looked to work in Africa as a park warden if I had some knowledge of the animals. Practically all park wardens in Tanganyika are British. Then we could have lived in one of these parks with all of these beautiful animals. We're truly fortunate to visit this place. We might have missed it if Rob hadn't suggested this trip. We must be among the less than 1% of the British who will lay their eyes on these sights. Thank you, Rob, for bringing us here, and thank you, boys, for being with us," said the D.C.

THEY RETURNED TO THE Lodge around 6.00 p.m. and ate dinner shortly after that. As the weather cooled down after sunset, they sat outside the Main Lodge around a large fire and enjoyed coffee and hot chocolate until 10.00 p.m. The D.C. enjoyed a cognac. Anil told his British jokes and made everyone laugh. None of the D.C. and Jane's concerns about Robert not getting along with Anil or jealousies between the boys had materialized. The three had bonded and were having fun.

The game drive on the next day took them to the Mara River. They had to walk with a ranger carrying a rifle to a location from where they could watch the crocodiles and hippos. Many crocs were lying on the shore, sleeping - some with their mouths wide open. Some could be seen swimming just under the surface. The hippos were mostly bobbing up and down in the water; only a couple were on the shores.

Pointing to the gathered herds of zebras and wildebeests on the other side of the river, Bakari said, "The crocs are waiting for those herds to cross the river. Sometimes the migrating animals will wait for days before crossing. There is never a safe time to cross with so many crocs in the water. Zebras are the leaders. They will decide when to jump into the water, and the wildebeest will follow. All will cross together. There is safety in numbers. Most will get to the other side. Some will be pulled under by the crocs; some will drown. It's a sight to see."

The party sat under a tree and ate their packed lunches, which the Lodge had provided. The ranger stood guard with his gun. He said that the crocs could be very crafty. They could creep upon a party like theirs and easily drag one away.

The boys and the Turnbulls shared their sandwiches, fruits, and drinks with the ranger and Bakari, and even after all had eaten, there was food leftover. The Lodge had packed too much.

Soon after they had departed the Mara River in search of the elusive leopard, Bakari got a radio message from one of his colleagues that the zebras had jumped into the river. The crossing had begun. He sped back to the river for his party to see at least a thousand animals swimming across to their side. Dozens of crocs were waiting for them, and dozens of zebras and wildebeest got pulled under. The boys were sad to see that the crocs were catching the calves with ease. Some were getting swept away by the strong current and would make easy prey for the crocs later.

"Why doesn't the government build a bridge for the migration to cross the river?" Anil asked.

"This is nature. Even the crocodiles are entitled to their meals. They will have their bellyful today and will feed on the carcasses of the drowned wildebeest and zebra for the next few days and then wait for days until the next herd gathers on the shore to cross. You will see that most are getting through. When the rains are over in Mara in October, they will cross the river again to migrate south to the Serengeti."

The entire crossing took almost 30 minutes. Then, the river was quiet. Bakari drove towards the newly arrived, wet animals. There was much running around in the herds. Mothers were looking to reunite with their calves. Some calves would not find their mothers and would become prey to the predators, soon. That was nature on the African plains.

THE NEXT DAY, THE drive to the Serengeti took the better part of the day. The ride was bumpy most of the way. They arrived in the Serengeti after sunset and checked in at the Serengeti Wildlife Lodge, overlooking the migration path. After another hearty dinner, everyone was exhausted and in bed by 11.00 p.m.

The game drive the next day in the Serengeti brought them to the middle of the plains, teeming with wildebeest, zebras, and other herbivores en route north to Mara. At close range, they appeared to be grazing, more than trekking north.

Bakari spotted a lioness in tall grass, stalking a small group of impalas. She got as near the impalas as she could without being seen, and then the chase was on. The impalas scattered, and the lioness selected one to pursue. It outran her, and she sat down panting. She would have to look for other prey. With so many animals on the plains, she should not have much difficulty, but Bakari told them only one in five chases resulted in a kill. They witnessed the birth of a wildebeest baby and saw how quickly it had to get on its feet and walk, or risk being snatched away by the hyenas.

Bakari explained that for the lions to bring down a Cape buffalo, a pride would need to work as a team. It was also difficult for a single lioness to bring down a zebra or a wildebeest. Usually, two or three lionesses hunted such larger animals as a team. It was usually the females who did the hunting. The male lions appeared after the prey had been brought down by females and ate first before the females and the cubs did. The males sometimes participated in the hunt of large quarries like a Cape buffalo. They were forced to hunt when they were alone, separated from the pride.

Later in the day, they saw a pride of lions with two males, four females, and several cubs. They sat and watched the pride dynamics for almost 30 minutes. They visited a hippo pool and later spotted a leopard in a tree. As the sun was about to set, Bakari drove them to an open field from where they could see thousands of wildebeest and zebras walking north in a single file. At the day's end, hyenas, African wild dogs, and other smaller predators started to appear.

THE SECOND DAY'S GAME drive in Serengeti was not too different from the first. They encountered a herd of elephants in the middle of the tracks upon which they were driving. When the elephants continued to "occupy" the road for over 30 minutes, Bakari had to turn around and find another route back to the lodge.

THE NEXT DAY, THEY departed early for the Ngorongoro Crater. On the way, they stopped at the Olduvai Gorge center. They attended a presentation on the research programs and excavation carried out by Mary and Louis Leakey at Olduvai, which have served to significantly advance the knowledge and understanding of early human evolution, and convinced most scientists that humans originated in Africa. The Gorge, located within the Great Rift Valley, is located in the eastern Serengeti Plains. The earliest human species had probably occupied the Olduvai Gorge approximately two million years ago.

They arrived at the Ngorongoro Lodge at dinner time and after checking in, sat down for dinner. Rafiq had almost run out of his 12 rolls of film. He was happy to learn that the hotel's gift shop carried the film that he needed. After dinner, the group sat by a fireplace and chatted for two hours. They talked about their Mara and Serengeti experiences, the sights, and sounds. All marveled at God's creation and were grateful that they had been fortunate to witness it. Everyone was a little sad that at the end of the next day, their safari would be over. They would say goodbye to the parks and the magnificent animals. But everyone looked forward to descending into the Crater, which was planned for early the next morning.

Laying out the maps and pictures, Rafiq reminded everyone that the Crater, which was about 150 square miles in area, was formed over two million years ago when a volcano had exploded and collapsed on itself. It was a renowned natural wonder (one of seven wonders in Africa) in a gorgeous setting, with one of the largest concentrations of animals, including the Big Five. It was home to some of the largest surviving tusker elephants. The Crater also had hundreds of bird species. Lake Magadi, in the center of the Crater, hosted hundreds of flamingos, and there was a hippo pool nearby.

THE PARTY WAS UP early the next day and started their descent into the Crater at 8.00 a.m. They wanted to spend as much time game watching on their last day, as possible. The day was bright and crisp, given the high elevation of the region. Animals appeared on all sides of the vehicle as soon as they reached the crater floor. All had expected the ground to be mainly rocky, given that it was a volcano floor, but were surprised to see vast areas of green grass and vegetation. The animals were grazing peacefully. They came upon a pride of lions with two males, five females, and several cubs. The adults were all resting. The cubs were running around playing, but not bothering the adults. Less than 20 feet away, a herd of impalas was grazing. Robert asked Bakari why the impalas were not fleeing, given that they could easily see the lions close by.

"The grazing animals do not run at the sight of their predators. They do know that the predators represent danger, and if approached by one, they will run, as they would if we got out of the vehicle and approached them. The impalas know that the lions are not hunting at this time. They have probably had their fill last night and represent no danger to them at this time. In the jungle, there are no enemies. Yes, the lions, hyenas, leopards, and cheetahs will hunt the impalas, but they are not the impalas' enemies in the same way as you are not enemies of the chickens or cows that you ate for dinner last night. The predators hunt to survive. They do not kill for fun as humans do. When they are fed, they can live in peace like this herd of impalas and the lions we see here."

Bakari's words prompted a contemplative silence among the group. Early in the morning, Ngorongoro was serene. There was so much peace here. It was like a small slice of paradise. This was different from the tumultuous river crossing in Mara and the frenzied activity on the Serengeti plains.

"I could spend days coming into this Crater to watch these animals. This seems so peaceful, I feel like I could get down and pat the animals," said the D.C.

"You are right, *Bwana*, if we were to all get down and walk around, the animals would take no notice of us, but if we approach those lions or run into a female hyena with young cubs, they could see us as a danger to their young and may attack us. I had brought a priest here not long ago, who very much wanted to get down and pat a lion; he was sure that the lion would not hurt him because he looked so peaceful. The regulations require us to stay in our vehicles, and if the priest had gotten down, he could have come to serious harm. I will take you to an area where we will have lunch and where we can get out of the vehicle if you want."

Bakari spotted three Land Rovers at some distance, parked in a semicircle. This meant that they were looking at one of the Big Five. He drove in their direction, and they saw three rhinos – two adults and a juvenile, grazing and utterly oblivious to the vehicles around them. They looked majestic. Bakari said that their numbers were declining, even in the Crater, because of poaching. There was a high demand for rhino horns in Asia for medicinal purposes, although it was a proven fact that the horn did not have any therapeutic value. They sat and watched the rhinos for 30 minutes. Now they had seen three of the Big Five that day – dozens of Cape buffalo, the pride of lions, and now the rhinos. As they drove away, they spotted a herd of elephants with one tusker. Bakari told them that the tusker was getting old, and his head was bending down because he was finding his huge tusks too heavy to carry.

Now they searched for the elusive leopard but did not see one.

The flamingos on Lake Magadi looked beautiful with their pink colors in the bright sunshine. The hippos in the hippo pool seemed playful. They stopped for lunch not far from the pool. As they sat enjoying their sandwiches, a kite swooped down and snatched the sandwich from the D.C.'s hand. The group erupted in laughter. Bakari suggested that they be careful because the baboons who were watching them from nearby could try to do the same.

After watching the animals, until all were satisfied, they started to head back. The pride of lions that they had seen in the morning was still there but had moved under a tree for shade. They reached the lodge at around 5.00 p.m. They had been in Crater for almost nine hours. They were tired for the day but would have been happy to return the next day. Rafiq had purchased three more rolls of film that morning, but there was so much to photograph, almost all of his film was used up.

The four-hour journey the next day from Ngorongoro to Arusha was uneventful. They saw some animals on the way. They missed the herds that they had seen in the parks. The elephants, lions, rhinos, the one leopard that they had seen, the Cape buffalo, the thousands of wildebeest and zebras, the majestic giraffes, the Tommy gazelles, impalas, the hippos, and of course, the ferocious crocodiles in the Mara, would remain in their memories and captured in Rafiq's Rolleiflex.

THEY ARRIVED AT ARUSHA airport two hours before their flight departure time. After ensuring that the flight was on schedule, Bakari said that it was time for him to say goodbye. Everyone thanked him individually for having been not only an excellent guide but also a wonderful companion. As agreed, the D.C. gave him Shs.300 bakshish. They had decided that the tip amount was to be shared equally between the five of them. This was a very generous tip, the kind that Bakari used to get on rare occasions from the American hunters, never from regular tourists. He was deeply touched and grateful.

Each of the boys gave him a tight hug; he shook hands with the D.C. and Jane and walked to his vehicle.

As the boys watched, the Land Rover drove off and disappeared in a cloud of dust.

The safari was over.

1957
Eighteen

After the excitement of the safari, going to Mpwapwa for Robert and Rafiq was anticlimactic. Suddenly, things were so quiet. They could not wait to see the photos that Rafiq had taken. Anil had taken the film rolls for processing in Dodoma. Mpwapwa did not have a photo shop to do that. Salim and Yasmin had agreed with Anil's parents that they would all come over to Mpwapwa the following weekend and bring the pictures with them for everyone to see.

Now that Rafiq was a member, the boys spent much time at the Club playing table tennis and billiards. They agreed that Robert would buy two tennis rackets when he returned to Nairobi, and bring them back with him to Mpwapwa for the December vacation so they could play tennis. Ricardo had promised that he would teach them to play tennis well.

Saturday night movies at the Club, which their parents also attended, were fun, and so were the Sunday lunches, but Robert and Rafiq still liked to go up to the Rock and enjoy the peace and fresh air.

IN THE DAYS DURING which the Turnbulls and the boys were on safari, Chelsea and Yasmin had spent much time together. They spent some evenings at the Club just sitting in the lounge and talking while Salim and Ricardo played table tennis or sat with other male members in the lounge enjoying drinks and eating the roasted peanuts that came from small patches which the Africans cultivated in

Kongwa. These peanuts, they observed, were their weight in gold, given how much the British had sunk into Kongwa to grow them in the first place.

Few other women came to the Club on weekday evenings. This was just fine with Yasmin and Chelsea; they could sit by themselves instead of having to invite others to join them.

Chelsea loved spending time with Yasmin. She was able to talk to her about things that she had not spoken about for three years. For Ricardo, to see his wife enjoying herself at the Club, munching on the most expensive peanuts in the world, and sipping sodas brought immense happiness. There had been so much change in their lives in so few days. He hoped and prayed this would last. He hoped that Yasmin would not tire of Chelsea. They did not share a cultural background. Every time he looked at the two beautiful women of different colors, it was Chelsea who was talking, but he did not detect any lack of interest on Yasmin's face. He also enjoyed Salim's company. For a man without any college education, he was remarkably knowledgeable, and he was also a shrewd businessman. Could he be the next Club Chairman? Ricardo wondered.

Yasmin had told Jane that Anil and his family were coming to Mpwapwa the next weekend and were going to bring with them the pictures Rafiq had taken on the safari, so she would like the D.C., Jane, and Robert to join them for dinner on Saturday night. She was also going to invite Chelsea and Ricardo to come. Jane was happy and grateful, but had come back and said that she and the D.C. wanted to have everyone at their place for the evening. The D.C. was useless when it came to cooking and entertaining people, but she would cook something everyone could enjoy. Given that there would be eleven of them in all, Yasmin insisted that she would bring some samosas and dessert for everyone.

WHEN JANE CALLED RICARDO to invite him and Chelsea for dinner, Chelsea was not home. Ricardo promised to call back when she returned. At first, Chelsea was uncomfortable about the invitation. No white family had invited her into their home in the time that she had been in Mpwapwa.

"Honey, I understand your sentiments, but you have seen that the majority of the whites did not agree with the Club policies, driven by a few members. Yes, the

D.C. was one of the people who believed in keeping the races segregated, but he has changed. He came and apologized to you in person. You are feeling welcomed by most members at the Club, and they are getting to know you, as well."

"I agree, Ric, but if you had lived through what I have endured for the past three years because of people like the D.C., you would understand my hesitation about going to his place."

"I do understand, sweetheart. I feel for you completely, but holding on to our past hurt feelings will not allow us to embrace the new reality that we see in this little town. This, as you say, Inshallah, God willing, will spread to other parts of Tanganyika as the whites wake up to the reality that all three East African countries will soon be independent. They will start to behave differently if they want to continue to stay and farm or trade in East Africa. Let's go to the D.C.'s home with our heads held high."

After thinking it over, Chelsea agreed.

ROBERT WAS IN CHARGE of dinner arrangements at the D.C.'s place. He welcomed everyone at the door and let his parents, who were standing behind him, extend a secondary welcome.

Yasmin's samosas were served as the starters, followed by roast chicken and potatoes, and Yasmin's fruit pudding for dessert.

After dinner, Robert announced that tea would be served in the living room, where they would look at the safari photos.

Robert had not seen any adult as excited as his dad when they started viewing the images. While Jane, Robert, Anil, and Rafiq each recalled where and when the picture was taken, the D.C. was full of exciting stories of the exact day and the weather, the exact species of the various animals, and what had happened before and after they had encountered those animals or those herds.

It took over two hours to go through the over 200 photos. Anil handed Jane an envelope containing one set of pictures for her to keep. Jane offered to pay for the prints, but Rafiq and Anil politely declined. Anil asked Jane and the D.C. if they wanted another set to share with their families in the U.K., Jane replied, "Thank you, Anil, thank you so much for your kind offer. Yes, we would love to get another set to share with our families, but you must accept payment for that."

"Mrs. Turnbull, it will be our pleasure to get you another set." Rafiq said and turning to Anil, he said, "Anil, let us get two sets printed. That way, both Mr. and Mrs. Turnbull can send one set each to their respective families."

Even after everyone had looked at the pictures more than once, the D.C. could not stop talking about the safari and how great it was to have had the boys with them.

"You have delightful sons," he said to Salim, Yasmin, Fateh, and Almas. "You must be so proud."

"And Rob is equally delightful," replied Yasmin, "We are glad and grateful that he is Anil and Rafiq's friend."

Robert could see that his dad's eyes were moist. At that moment, he felt closer to his father than he had ever felt before.

The entire evening, Jane had gone out of her way to be friendly to Chelsea. While Chelsea was a little tense when they came, by the end of the evening, she was quite comfortable chatting with Jane, and the D.C. Ricardo felt that she was gradually beginning to put her painful past behind her.

AS HAD BEEN ARRANGED earlier, Anil stayed over in Mpwapwa when his family left to go back to Dodoma. The boys spent the balance of their vacation in Mpwapwa going up to the Rock, playing table tennis at the Club, and preparing for the final term of the academic year. Rafiq could not wait to get back to school to see Salima.

1957
Nineteen

The first day at school was exciting for Rafiq and Anil. To Rafiq, Salima looked even more radiant than before. In the way she looked at him, it seemed like she had become aware of his stares and interest in her. Was she flattered or offended? Rafiq wondered.

During the recess at 10.30 a.m., Rafiq and Anil shared their safari pictures with their classmates. The photos started to get circulated between the boys and somehow got into the hands of one girl who started to pass them on to the other girls. The recess ended before all of the students had had an opportunity to view all of the pictures. The students agreed to continue looking at them when school ended at 1.00 p.m.

When the school was over for the day, the class continued to sit. The teacher asked why everyone was staying in their chairs, and one girl told her that they were going to view Anil and Rafiq's safari pictures.

"Really, did you go on a safari?" the teacher asked.

"Yes, we went to Masai Mara, Serengeti, and Ngorongoro," Anil replied.

"Well, we must hear about your trip sometime, and I will look at your pictures tomorrow," said the teacher, rising to leave.

The boys and girls continued to pass around the photos. Rafiq and Anil moved from bench to bench to explain to the boys what was in the pictures and where they were taken. The girls did not ask any questions. It would not have been appropriate for them to talk to the boys.

Rafiq watched Salima intently. She was taking longer than other girls looking at each picture before passing it on. At one point, she glanced at Rafiq with a look in her eyes, which suggested that she wanted to ask or say something to him. This was the first time that she had looked Rafiq in the eye, but she quickly looked away, again gazing intently at the photos. He could see that she was smiling. Was she looking at a picture with him in it? He so wished that she would ask or say something to him, but she said nothing.

The class was intrigued by Anil and Rafiq's experience and stories about their safari. It was almost unbelievable that two of their classmates had gone on this trip with a white family - and not just any white family. They had gone with a District Commissioner, his wife, and their son!

When all of the pictures were returned to Anil and Rafiq, everyone got up to leave. As Salima stood up, she turned around and looked at Rafiq, but said nothing and turned back and walked out. He was convinced that some connection had been established between them. "Why did she not smile? Should I have smiled?" Rafiq thought and decided, no, he could not have done that. That could have been interpreted as him being forward, which could have offended her. He could not risk doing that. Should he wait for her to smile at him? No, a respectable girl would not do that. He had to take the risk. He concluded that if he could even see her eyes smiling at him, he would smile at her, no matter what.

Rafiq stayed awake until late into the night, visualizing the look on Salima's face that day, musing to himself that God must have created her on a day when He had nothing else to do and had all the time in the world to create a masterpiece.

He was up early the next morning and eager to get to school to see if Salima would look at him again as she had done the previous day.

When the class started, Salima came in and took her seat without looking at Rafiq, but when the recess bell rang, and all stood up, she turned around and looked at him for a brief moment. She turned away and walked out of the classroom with the other girls. She did the same thing when school ended for the day and several times during the following weeks. This drove Rafiq crazy. Her look, each time she looked at him, appeared not to invite a smile from him. Was she doing this to check if he was looking at her all the time? He was convinced that she wanted to communicate with him, but perhaps, like him, did not know how to?

He considered passing a note to her, confessing his affection. He crafted a message in his mind, but he did not have the courage to write it down. What if she was offended and showed the note to her brothers? They may not beat him up, but the matter would surely get reported to the Principal. His parents would be called in. There would be a scandal. His parents would be humiliated when it became known in the Ismaili community that their son had sent a love letter to an Ithna Ashari girl. He could not risk this.

1957
Twenty

In early October, the Principal advised the school that to enable the Ismaili students to attend their new spiritual leader's investiture in Dar es Salaam on October 19th, regular teaching would be suspended for the 17th, 18th, 21st, and 22nd of October. Non-Ismaili students would attend school and go over the material covered during the year with their teachers. No new content would be taught during these four days.

Excitement among the Ismaili community had started to build by the beginning of October. Travel and accommodation arrangements had to be made by the community members from all corners of Tanganyika to travel to Dar es Salaam. The Abdullas had decided to drive to Dar es Salaam. It was agreed with the Damjis that Rafiq and Anil would go with the Abdullas. The Damjis would travel by train. Salim had managed to book two hotel rooms at *Chez Margot*, a European-owned hotel. Like most Ismailis going to Dar es Salaam, Anil's family was to stay with relatives.

Given that practically every Ismaili family was going to go to Dar es Salaam for the ceremony, the security of Ismaili homes and businesses, which would be unoccupied while the Ismailis were away, was a concern.

The 48th Ismaili Imam had established Councils for social governance, socio-economic advancement, and religious formation of his followers in Tanganyika, as he had done in other countries where Ismailis lived. The Councils were resourced with well-qualified professionals and businesspersons, appointed by the Imam to serve the community in a voluntary capacity. The British government recognized the Aga Khan Councils as institutions representing the Ismaili Imam and the Ismaili community in the country. At the Tanganyika Council's request, the British administration had agreed to provide security for Ismaili homes and businesses in all towns by deploying extra "askaris" (policemen) to monitor the Ismaili properties for a week.

THE ROAD TRIP TO Dar es Salaam on October 17th, 200 miles of which was on dirt roads, was a memorable experience for Anil and Rafiq. Over two dozen other cars, trucks, and buses carrying Ismailis were making the journey, with very exuberant people.

On the first leg of the journey, they stopped twice to help families having car problems. One had a flat tire. That was easy. The boys helped the family replace the tire and were on their way after enjoying some snacks which the family offered them. Another car belonging to a family they knew from Dodoma, with seating capacity for five, but carrying seven occupants, had a more serious problem. The car's fan belt was broken, causing the vehicle to overheat. They offered to take the owner's eldest son, Shiraz, to the next town – Morogoro - for him to get a new fan belt and return to the vehicle with a mechanic and tools to change the belt.

They reached Morogoro at lunchtime. After ensuring that Shiraz got the fan belt and had found a mechanic to go with him back to the car, they proceeded to a popular Indian restaurant in the town to get lunch. The restaurant was overflowing with Ismailis. It looked like a huge party was underway. The owner, a non-Ismaili, had anticipated being busy, but he had not expected this bonanza.

They arrived in Dar es Salaam in the early evening and headed straight to the NAAZ restaurant for snacks and cold drinks. The NAAZ, also, had never been this busy.

The city was hot and humid, and all roads were congested with dozens of cars from across Tanganyika. The entire city was in a festive mood, and everybody was patient and charitable.

After checking in and freshening up at the hotel, Salim, Yasmin, Rafiq, and Anil drove a few yards down the Ocean Road to the beach to enjoy the ocean breeze.

Dozens of Ismaili cars were parked along the oceanfront, taking in the cool, salty breeze and sipping the fresh coconut water being sold by the locals.

After a leisurely English breakfast the next morning, they drove to the top of Acacia Avenue, parked the Land Rover there, and walked down the avenue to the Ismaili Jamatkhana on Jamat Street. The shops and streets were teeming with Ismailis. They met many whom they knew and exchanged hugs. Everyone was smiling and excited in anticipation of the next day.

FINALLY, OCTOBER 19TH HAD arrived. The Jamat had started to assemble on the open Upanga grounds where the taktnashini was to take place. By 4.00 p.m., thousands had gathered, eagerly awaiting the arrival of their new Imam. They were seated on the ground on woven mats.

Members of the Imam's family arrived first, followed by VIP guests - including the Governor and Lady Twinning, Ambassadors and High Commissioners, Mayor of the City of Dar es Salaam, and the British government's Secretary of State for the Colonies, who had traveled to Dar es Salaam for the event - and were seated on chairs in front of the stage.

The young Imam arrived at 5.00 p.m. and was received by his senior community leaders. The excitement within the congregation was palpable. The Ismailis could not contain their pride and happiness to see their young and handsome Imam. Acknowledging his guests and followers with smiles, the Imam proceeded to take his place on the stage.

Senior Ismaili institutional leaders presented insignia of the office of Ismaili Imam, as well as gifts from the Jamat, and paid homage to the new Imam. Then the Imam rose to speak.

He commenced his address to the over 30,000 people by thanking the City of Dar es Salaam for the warm welcome given to him and the magnificent festivities which had marked this occasion. On behalf of his community and himself, he offered special gratitude to the Governor and his wife for their warm welcome and support and thanked the Dar es Salaam police, who had looked after the huge crowds with so much patience.

He spoke about the technological advances which would affect life in the next half-century, and with which would come many blessings, as well as challenges. He committed to devoting his life to guiding his community in dealing with the problems that these rapid changes would bring.

He emphasized, however, that material progress should not be paramount for his community, and that many advanced nations were finding that individuals' mastery of physical forces had outstripped the mastery of the self. The mind could not always grapple with the complexities that the hands had created. That was why his grandfather had attached so much importance to education. Now, education was more important for his community than ever before to prepare for the future. He said that the younger people in the community must be especially aware of the fact that the principles of the faith by which the community had lived would enable them to surmount problems and live in peace.

After the conclusion of all of the ceremonies and after the Imam, his family members, and the VIP guests had all departed, the congregation rose. The Ismailis could not contain their pride and joy over the young Imam's poise and the confidence with which he had conducted himself, his care and affection for his community, his perception of the future, and his commitment to guide the community, half of which was more than twice his age, or older.

One thing was clear in most minds - the community had entered a new era, and the new Imam would chart their path to a prosperous future within the ethics of Islam. For Rafiq and the youth of his generation, there were some key messages that they would take away from this momentous event and talk about at length in the days to come. They noted that the young Imam had said four significant things: the rapid and significant technological progress would bring positive change, but also create challenges; he would devote his life to guiding his community in dealing with these challenges; education, which the 48th Imam had emphasized for the community, was now more critical than ever before to prepare for the challenges ahead, and living by ethics of Islam and the practice of their faith would be paramount in equipping them to address the future challenges.

In his address, the Imam had already started to guide his community in dealing with the challenges of the atomic age.

In the months following the event, the Imam traveled to all centers with sizeable Jamats in East Africa and globally, and re-emphasized the importance of post-secondary education and adherence to the principles of the faith.

THE IMAM'S MESSAGE HAD the desired impact upon the parents and students. Gradually, they began to situate education within a different context. Finishing Grade XII and getting married (for girls), and joining their father's business or finding some clerical level employment (for boys) were no longer viable options. The narrative was changing to what post-secondary education the students graduating from high school should pursue, where, and how the parents would pay for it. Passing the Cambridge Exam had assumed a different relevance. The students would start to talk about the Cambridge Overseas Higher School Certificate (HSC) and the London University Advanced ("A" Level) programs in Arts and Sciences as the next step in educational advancement after passing the Cambridge Exam. They would start to learn that admissions into these programs would require meritorious performance in the Cambridge Exam.

1957
Twenty-One

During the last week of the term, after the annual exams were over, Rafiq's class was advised that their teacher, Mr. Fernandes, whom the class had adored, was returning to India and would be leaving the school at the end of November when the academic year ended.

This news saddened the class. Anil suggested that they organize a farewell party for the teacher. All boys were in favor and agreed to contribute Shs.5 each. Anil spoke to the girls (not addressing anyone in particular but as a group) about the idea, and the girls agreed to participate. Rafiq and Anil asked Mr. Fernandes if he, Mrs. Fernandes, and their little daughter, Celia, would attend. Mr. Fernandes was touched. It was agreed that the party would be held on the evening of the last day of school.

Rafiq and Anil took responsibility for organizing the party. They requested and received permission from the Head Master to use the school assembly hall and arranged with a local Indian restaurant to cater samosas, kabobs, cakes, Indian sweets, and soft drinks.

There had been some discussion about who would write and deliver a short speech to express their appreciation and affection for Mr. Fernandes. None of the girls wanted to do this, so one student proposed that Rafiq, because he was the top male student in the class, should do this. In the chorus of endorsement, Rafiq could see Salima smiling and nodding her head in agreement. That was enough for Rafiq to agree to make the speech.

On the day of the event, Anil and Rafiq arrived early to ensure that the tables were set correctly. It had been agreed that Rafiq and one girl would sit at the head table with Mr. and Mrs. Fernandes and Celia. It seemed logical to Rafiq that if he had been nominated to make the speech because he was the smartest boy in the class, the girls would undoubtedly select Salima, who was the most intelligent girl in the class, to sit at the head table. He could hardly contain his excitement. They would surely be seated side by side, and they would have to talk. When the class had ended, the girls said that they had still not agreed as to whom from among them would sit at the head table, but the decision would be made by the party time.

As arranged, the restaurant staff had brought in and organized the food in warmers and drinks in coolers on tables along the wall. It had been agreed that all students would be seated by 6.45 p.m. and that the Fernandes family would arrive at 7.00 p.m. All would rise to welcome them.

Rafiq anxiously waited for Salima to come and tell him that she had been selected to sit at the head table, but when she came in at around 6.30 p.m., to his dismay, she proceeded to take a seat with other girls at another table. Instead, Kumud, a smart Hindu girl, walked up to him shortly thereafter and said that she was to join him at the head table. Rafiq did not show his disappointment. He thanked her for agreeing to be at the head table and asked if she would rise to thank Mr. Fernandes after the teacher's address and invite everyone to partake in the refreshments. She agreed to do this.

All rose and clapped to welcome Mr. Fernandes and his family when they arrived. Rafiq and Kumud received them at the door and led them to the head table. When all were seated, Rafiq stood up to speak. The class had expected him to read from a page, but he did not have any paper in his hands.

"Mr. and Mrs. Fernandes, and Celia," he began, "We want to sincerely thank you for accepting our invitation to attend this small farewell party for you. We know that you are packing up to leave for India, and you are very busy. Thank you very much for taking the time from your busy schedule to spend this evening with us.

My classmates, Kumud, and I want to thank you for being our teacher for the past year. I am sure that I speak for my class when I say that you have been a superb teacher."

This was greeted with hearty applause. When the clapping stopped, Rafiq continued, "You have taught us not only what we needed to learn to prepare for the Cambridge Exam in two years, but much more than that. You have taught us how to live a disciplined life, how to respect and cooperate, how to study, and how to talk.

For the boys in your class, you have taught us how to dress smartly. Sir, you have been a role model for us, and we are fortunate to have had you in our lives for a year. We are sorry to see you go, and we will miss you very much, Sir. We wish you and your family a very safe trip back to India. We hope that you will remember us when you are teaching another class somewhere. Please write to us when you can.

Mrs. Fernandes and Celia, we are delighted to meet you and so happy you could join us. We will remember you all and keep you in our prayers. Thank you."

As all started clapping, Mr. Fernandes stood up and motioned for others to stand. The students abided and joined in the standing ovation.

When all were seated, Mr. Fernandes rose to speak.

"Thank you very much, Rafiq, for your kind words. I am very grateful for your warm sentiments.

My dear students: it has been a privilege to teach you for one year. We had planned to be in Tanganyika for five years, but we have to return to India because my brother and his wife, who had cared for my parents, were transferred out of town six months back and my sister, who has looked after my parents after my brother and his family left, is to get married next month. It has been a tough decision, but as a family, we have decided that considering all things, we must return to India to care for my parents. So, we must leave you.

I consider it a gift to have had the opportunity to come to Tanganyika to teach at this school and to have you as my students. It has been a pleasure teaching you. I have never had a class where the students have been so respectful and eager to learn. Sometimes, you tired me out with your questions, but I did not mind that. I was happy to see such a thirst for knowledge. I do not doubt that every one of you will pass the Cambridge Exam in two years. Rafiq, will you take responsibility for writing to me and listing what Division each of you is placed in?"

Rafiq nodded, and Mr. Fernandes continued, "And make sure that there is no name against which there is an 'F.' I want you all to promise me that you will work hard - very hard - so that I do not see any Fs!" The students smiled and nodded.

My dear students, most of you are 15 or 16 years old. Your life is ahead of you. This is the time for you to start to plan your life. Decide what you want to do with yourselves, what you want to become. In whatever you plan, remember that passing the Cambridge Exam will be the first and crucial step. Without this high school certificate, your options in life will be severely limited. So, work hard. I know that not all of you can pass in the 1st Division; some will pass in the 2nd Division, but having known each of you, I am confident that there is no reason for any of you to be placed in the 3rd Division or, God forbid, fail. There is nothing that will sadden me more than to have Rafiq write to me that one or more of you have failed.

My dear students, I want to leave you with one message that I would like you to always carry with you. Remember that money is very important in life. The money will determine the kind of life that you will live, the neighborhood in which you will live, the car you will drive, who your friends will be, the kind of education your children will get, how healthy your lifestyle will be, and how well you will be able to dress. But I want you to remember, and never, ever forget, that there are things in life that are much, much more important than money, things that money cannot buy. Keep the pursuit of wealth and the place of money in your lives in sharp perspective. Beyond a point, money can only buy us momentary joy, not happiness. Happiness is within us. It comes from being at peace with ourselves and with those around us. It comes from giving of ourselves. Being kind and considerate to people; being generous with your money, your deeds, and your words. So, when you work hard to pass the Cambridge Exam, your Higher School Certificate, and college exams, you should do that to acquire knowledge, to equip yourselves to enter whatever profession you choose to enter, with competence, but never with the singular goal of making money. What you decide to do in life should never be driven only by what will earn you the most money.

I wish you all success in your education and your lives. I am leaving my address in India with Kumud and Rafiq. I want each of you to feel completely free to write to me if you ever need my advice or guidance on any matter. I pray that you will each find much success and happiness in your lives. Thank you."

The students erupted in thunderous applause. It did not occur to Rafiq to stand up and motion his fellow students to do the same because he had not understood why Mr. Fernandes had done this after his speech.

Rafiq was riveted. How similar, almost identical, the teacher's guidance was to what his parents were teaching him! Mr. Fernandes was a devout Christian. How much congruity there can be between the principles held by people of different faiths, Rafiq thought.

When Mr. Fernandes sat down, Kumud stood up and said, "Thank you, Sir, for your words of wisdom and encouragement. We will always remember what you have told us today. As Rafiq noted, we will miss you, but will always keep your guidance in our hearts. Thank you again, Sir.

Refreshments are ready to be served. Please help yourselves."

Rafiq was impressed with Kumud's few words. She had spoken confidently, and said the right things in very appropriate words, with far less time to prepare than he had had. The girls were smarter than the boys; he conceded to himself.

As everyone enjoyed refreshments, Mr. Fernandes moved around the hall to speak to the students and say goodbye to each one individually. Those with whom he had spoken returned to their tables to enjoy their refreshments. Neither Kumud nor Rafiq felt comfortable returning to their table without the Fernandes family. They would have to talk to each other, and both were too shy to do that with other students watching them. So, they walked around and mingled with other students.

After eating samosas, kabobs, and other goodies, Rafiq went to the beverage table to pick up a Coke. The restaurant staff had opened up the soft drink bottles and dropped in straws for the students to pick up. As he extended his hand to pick up a Coke bottle, he saw another hand extended to pick up the same bottle. The two hands touched and quickly withdrew. When he looked, it was Salima reaching for the bottle. She smiled broadly at him. It appeared to Rafiq that this smile was a culmination of all of the smiles that she had not given him over the past three months. He was mesmerized. They kept looking at each other and smiling. It seemed to Rafiq that she was unable to contain her happiness. He picked up the Coke bottle and handed it to her, which she took, still looking at him, smiling and taking a sip.

"You made an excellent speech," she said.

After a beat, Rafiq was able to muster up a response. "Thank you, Salima. It was simple and short. I felt it was appropriate for us all to hear Mr. Fernandes, instead of me." He realized as soon as the words were out of his mouth that he had taken her name.

"I liked what you said and how you said it."

"Thank you again, Salima." Now he had said her name twice.

She smiled at him and walked away.

Rafiq forgot about getting the drink for himself and moved back to where Mr. Fernandes was talking to other students. He was surprised by how much the teacher knew about each student, asking one to improve his math skills, encouraging another to improve her writing skills. As the teacher circulated among the students, Rafiq walked with him. Taking his cue, Kumud kept Mrs. Fernandes company and took her around, introducing her to the students.

When Mr. Fernandes had said goodbye to all of the students, he spoke to Kumud and Rafiq and wished them well. It was an emotional moment for both students as the teacher and his family prepared to leave. Kumud announced that they were leaving. All of the students stood up. Kumud and Rafiq led the teacher and his family to the door and said goodbye.

The students were in no hurry to leave. They pulled the chairs from the tables and sat down in a circle and talked about their teacher and his message. Rafiq took his seat directly opposite Salima. She kept smiling at him each time he looked at her, and he smiled back.

Someone suggested that they sing Indian movie songs. The girls urged one from among their ranks to sing, and although she was shy to start, she sang a beautiful song and, when forced to do so, sang two more songs. Now it was the boys' turn. Two were selected. Anil was one of them. They did their part in singing. The class discovered that there were at least three excellent singers among them.

At 10.00 p.m., it was time to vacate the hall. Rafiq suggested that they all walk together and escort the girls home first, after which the boys could disperse and go home. As they did this, each girl thanked the boys for accompanying her home. Salima was the fourth one to get dropped off. When acknowledging the boys, she looked only at Rafiq, smiling happily.

That was the last time he would see her.

1957
Twenty-Two

The next morning, as he lay in bed, Rafiq kept seeing Salima's smiling face and wondered if she was thinking of him, as well.

He sat up in bed, and he saw Anil do the same across the room. As was their routine, they said their morning prayers.

When they had finished, Anil asked, "What's going on between Salima and you? What was all that smiling about?"

Rafiq was surprised that Anil had noticed.

"Oh, she was there when I went to get a drink, and we were both reaching for the same Coke bottle, so we laughed. I picked up the bottle and gave it to her. She smiled and thanked me. She said she liked my speech, and I told her it was nothing special, and that was that."

"From what I saw, it was much more than reaching for a Coke bottle and 'that was that.' You were smiling at each other all evening. When did this start? You know she is an Ithna Ashari from a very traditional and respectable family. You, of all people, should understand the consequences of becoming involved with her. You can ruin her reputation in her community. Don't you care?"

Rafiq was stunned by the sternness of Anil's voice and the finality of his words. Why had he not said anything last night before they went to sleep? Was he too tired to talk about it, or was he agonizing over what to say to him? He could not tell Anil that he would stop smiling at, or talking to Salima, and he also understood how right Anil was in what he had just said. *He is a true friend to tell me this, so* honestly, Rafiq thought. He stayed quiet. Knowing Anil as he did, he knew that he would not say anything more about Salima unless he gave him a reason to do so.

RAFIQ'S PARENTS WERE DUE to arrive that morning, and Rafiq was to go with them to Mpwapwa for his December vacation. Anil had agreed to go with him to spend ten days with Robert and Rafiq.

The time with Robert and Anil in Mpwapwa was fun. Robert had brought two tennis racquets from Nairobi. Ricardo, true to his word, appeared regularly at the Club to teach them to play tennis. The boys took turns playing, as they had only two racquets. Henry had found an old racquet that some member had left at the Club and offered it to the boys, but Ricardo discouraged them from using the racket. It would spoil their game, he said.

The boys loved to play tennis and played several sets each day. Anil emerged as the best player, beating Robert and Rafiq each time. They laughed and joked and reminisced about the safari. They climbed Kiboroiani twice and the Rock practically every other day.

After Anil had returned to Dodoma, Rafiq told Robert about what had happened with Salima and about Anil's warning.

"So, are you sure that she is as in love with you as you are with her?" Robert asked.

"I think that she likes me; I don't know if she loves me, but I love her, yes."

"Well, then, you have to find out if she more than likes you, and if yes, you have to find a way to kiss her – to kind of seal it with a kiss."

"I don't know if I can or should do that, or even talk to her. It can create big problems for her, and also for me. She is not from my community."

"But she is Indian, isn't she? There would be no problem if I had a Greek or Italian girlfriend."

OVER THE REMAINING DAYS in December, Robert asked Rafiq several times to disregard Anil's warning and gave him ideas on how to get Salima to meet him secretly, what he should whisper in her ears, and how he should kiss her.

What Robert was saying was very enticing, but Rafiq was convinced that what

Anil was saying was the sensible thing to do. He cared for Salima too much to create any problems for her or to bring shame to her family. He agonized over what he was going to do as he eagerly counted the days to return to school and see her again. But to what end? Could they just be friends? What would she expect of him after that evening? If he suddenly stopped smiling at her and did not make any attempt to speak to her, how would she feel? Would she be hurt? Insulted? He could never hurt her. Perhaps he should ask his parents or Anil how to deal with this situation but decided against it.

ANIL CALLED MID- DECEMBER to tell Rafiq that the exam results were out. Rafiq fully expected Anil to say that he was #1.

Instead, Anil said, "You came in 2nd."

"Who was 1st?" Rafiq asked, thinking for a second that Anil was pulling his leg.

"Salima," Anil said with seriousness in his voice. "She scored nine marks more than you did, overall."

Rafiq was surprised, but it made sense. Salima was brilliant. "Well, she is a smart girl. She deserved to stand first," said Rafiq. Would this be a good excuse to start up a conversation with her when they returned to school? Say, "Congratulations for standing first?"

"And you, Anil?" Rafiq asked.

"I was 10th."

"That's great. We both move on to Grade XI."

In a class of 30, if Anil had stood 10th, that was a good performance, but for Anil, the gap between him and Rafiq was too large. He had felt embarrassed to tell his parents that he was 10th, and Rafiq was 2nd. He was certain that they were happy with his performance, but they, too, must have thought about the gap. He resolved to work harder next year, to be much closer to Rafiq when they finished Grade XI.

1958
Twenty-Three

Rafiq returned to Dodoma at the end of December and went to school with both excitement and trepidation at the start of January. To his surprise, Salima was not there. Her seat was occupied by an Ismaili girl whose family had moved to Dodoma from Arusha during December. Surely, Salima was unwell and would return in the next day or so. But where would she sit? There was no empty desk in the class. Maybe they would bring one in. In a way, it might be better if she were not sitting right ahead of him. Would she come back and claim her desk?

The entire week went by, and she did not return to school. There was no one whom he could ask. Could she be sick with something more severe than Malaria or the flu? Where was she? Did the other girls know? Surely, his teacher knew. Could he ask Kumud, who had smiled at him on the first day of school? Having talked to her at the party, it would probably be okay to speak to her. She might know, but surely, she would wonder why he was asking, and she might tell the other girls he was asking about Salima.

Rafiq's suspense continued to mount into the second week. Midweek, as the boys stood around the schoolyard during the morning recess, one boy, whose elder sister was friends with Salima's elder sister, told the boys that his sister had said to him that Salima's father had pulled her from the school like he had pulled her two older sisters when they had finished Grade X, and Salima, like her sisters, had gone behind the veil.

Rafiq was stunned. This meant that if she came out of her house, she would be wearing a niqab, and he would never see her face again. How could this happen? Why would her father pull her out of the school when she had stood first in her class, beating all boys? Did she know that she would not be returning to school when she had spoken to him and smiled at him that day? If she did, why did she smile at him and talk to him? Or could it be that one or both of the Ithna Ashari boys in his class had told her family about her "behavior" at Mr. Fernandes' farewell party? If Anil had noticed them smiling at each other, then perhaps they, too, had seen that. Could she have been pulled from the school because her parents did not want to risk her ruining their reputation by being friends with an Ismaili boy? If that was the case, was he to blame for this? She had smiled at him first, after all.

Anil was looking at Rafiq and could see the disappointment in his eyes. He felt sad for Rafiq but was happy that this chapter with Salima was closed. Any furthering of a relationship between Rafiq and her would have ended badly for both of them. He considered talking to Rafiq to console him, if he was hurt but decided that it was best not ever to say anything about Salima to Rafiq again.

FOR DAYS, RAFIQ KEPT thinking about Salima. There were days when he saw women in niqab in the town and wondered if one of them might be her. One day, as he passed by Salima's place, three women wearing niqabs emerged from the house. He was sure that one of them was Salima and that she was looking at him through the eye slit in the niqab. Which of the three was her? What was she thinking? Was she feeling sad? Did she want to run up to him, throw off her niqab and hug him? Was she feeling sorry for him? For herself? Was she feeling anything? How different things could have been if she had come back to school, but if she had, where would have that led the two of them? He would wonder about these things for many years.

RAFIQ AND ANIL WERE now in Grade XI. The class atmosphere had changed. There was a seriousness of purpose among the students. Word of the new Imam's guidance to his community on the importance of post-secondary education had spread within the Indian community in East Arica. The students who had not shown much interest in pursuing post-secondary education and had planned to join their fathers' businesses were becoming increasingly studious and were talking about post-secondary education options.

The British school principal was now teaching Grade XI students English Literature and Language courses. It was difficult at first for the students to understand his strong British accent. All of the teachers that had taught them until then were from India and spoke with Indian accents. Soon, the students got used to listening to the principal, and they wanted to hear every word that he spoke. He was by far the most informed and intelligent teacher they had ever had. In the teaching of Shakespeare's Macbeth, Herman Melville's Moby Dick, or Geoffrey Chaucer's The Canterbury Tales, he was able to provide contexts which the Indian teachers were simply not equipped to do.

Many students had serious concerns about the English Language course because no matter how well they performed in the other five or six subjects, if they failed English Language, they would not qualify for the Cambridge Certificate.

The principal was situating the course differently, saying that if the students read as many of the "approved" English books (with literary merit) as possible and spoke English when communicating between themselves to build vocabulary, they would be well equipped to fully absorb what he was teaching and pass the English Language exam. He was expecting everyone in his class not just to pass the courses that he was teaching; he was expecting all students to excel in the two subjects. If even 10% of the students failed either subject, his reputation would be damaged, he said.

Anil, as he had decided to do, had started to work very hard. He spent as much time as Rafiq did reading books and magazines. Like Rafiq, he now read the TIME magazine, Readers' Digest, and as much of the Tanganyika Standard and old copies of The Daily Mirror newspapers as he could. Like Rafiq, he read up the next act/chapter of Macbeth, Moby Dick, or The Knight's Tale for the next lesson. Together, he and Rafiq read more than the minimum required, discussed what they read, and practiced writing exam questions on the sections that they had studied. If they were given the option to write an essay on one of two topics, they wrote on one and came home after school and wrote the essay on the second topic. Then they read each other's essays and offered improvements and identified strengths.

Anil excelled in Accounting. He never got anything wrong. He had an insight into the course that Rafiq did not have, and Rafiq learned from him. By the end of the first term, Anil, like Rafiq, was now determined to pass his Cambridge Exam in the First Division and was going to do whatever was required to realize his goal.

1958
Twenty-Four

December 1957 had come and gone, and there was still no replacement for the D.C. The Colonial Office had advised the P.C. that Tanganyika could become independent within two years, and the office did not want to appoint a new D.C. for the short term and incur the relocation expenses. The D.C. should continue to stay in his position if he had no objection. To appreciate his acceptance of the extension, the D.C. would receive a 25% increase in his salary. The D.C., of course, had no objection. He was enjoying the good life and wanted to be in Africa for the final year of Robert's high school. The additional 25% would help pay for Robert's post-secondary education in the U.K.

The extension also allowed him to put into practice some of what he had said the British should do for the Africans to help them transition to independence.

The best place to start was the local TANU office. He called the office and asked for the local chairman, John Nkwabi. The woman who answered the phone noted the English accent and asked who was calling. When he identified himself, she asked him to hold while she checked if Mr. Nkwabi was in. She came back on the phone and said that the chairman was not in, but would call him back, which meant that he was in, but did not want to talk to the D.C. at this time. She asked what he was calling about, and the D.C. told her he wanted to arrange to meet the chairman.

Upon learning that the D.C. wanted to meet him, Mr. Nkwabi immediately called the regional TANU chairman in Dodoma, who proceeded to notify the national TANU office in Dar es Salaam of the D.C.'s call.

After deliberating upon the D.C.'s message, the national office advised Mr. Nkwabi that he should accept the D.C.'s invitation to meet him, but not take any nonsense from him. The Mpwapwa TANU office was duly registered with the P.C.'s Office; its charter, aims, and objectives had been filed with the registry and endorsed by the British colonial government, and its activities were in full compliance with its charter. If the D.C. raised any non-compliance issues, or made any threats or insinuated anything, Mr. Nkwabi should not enter into any argument with him but should ask the D.C. to speak to the provincial TANU office in Dodoma.

Mr. Nkwabi returned the D.C.'s call the next day. He stated who he was and that he was returning the D.C.'s call. He did not offer any greetings.

"Good morning, Mr. Nkwabi, and thank you for returning my call. How are you today?"

Mr. Nkwabi was quite surprised by the D.C.'s tone and salutation. "I am fine, Sir. How are you?" He said.

"I am fine. Thank you. I was calling to see if we could meet in your Office sometime this week, at your convenience."

Now Mr. Nkwabi was more surprised. He had never met the D.C., but had heard much about him, not much of which was good. He was also surprised that the D.C. was not summoning him to his office, but instead, he was asking if he could come to the little one-room TANU office to meet him.

"I am relatively free this week, when would you like to come in?" asked Mr. Nkwabi.

"Would Thursday at 2.00 p.m. work for you?"

That was two days hence; sufficient time to check with the Dodoma TANU office.

"Yes, that would be fine, but may I ask you, Sir, what is it that you wish to meet with me about?"

"Do you have some time, Mr. Nkwabi, for me to explain?"

"Yes."

"Mr. Nkwabi, as you would probably know, our prime minister is pushing for the decolonization of sub-Saharan Africa. I, personally, support this policy. I would like you not to quote me, but I believe that in the time during which we have ruled

Tanganyika, we could have done more for the Africans, but we did not. Late as it may be to do some good, I believe that as you prepare for independence, we should assist you to assume power whenever Tanganyika becomes independent. We can do this by familiarising the leaders like you and your colleagues with how we run government affairs, and how we manage the schools, hospitals, and other government services. I wish to meet with you to share my thoughts on how we can do this. I must tell you that this is not the official Tanganyika government's policy. These are my personal thoughts and intentions."

Mr. Nkwabi was flabbergasted. He could have never imagined hearing anything like this from a British D.C. There had always been the fear within TANU that the road to independence could become acrimonious and that the British would up and leave. This was an amazing offer, although it was only from a small town D.C. - a single voice. Was there an agenda here? Were the British trying to get at something or someone higher up in TANU through a small town TANU office?

"These are very noble thoughts, Sir, even if, as you say, this is not the official government policy. Let's meet on Thursday."

Immediately after hanging up the phone, Mr. Nkwabi called and advised the TANU office in Dodoma of the D.C.'s offer.

"Well, let him come in and hear him out. Don't offer any information or make any commitments. Just tell him that you will discuss his offer with your colleagues and get back to him," he was told.

IN THE TWO DAYS leading up to the meeting, the D.C. formulated his thoughts on what he would discuss with Mr. Nkwabi. As he did this, a thought occurred to him. Would it not be a good idea for him to take Chelsea with him to this meeting? Salim would be happy to go with him, but the Africans were not particularly fond of *Wahindis* (Indians). But Chelsea was an African, not an indigenous Tanganyikan, but a pure-blooded Somali African. She could undoubtedly lend credibility to his effort.

He picked up the phone and called Chelsea. He told her about his conversation with Mr. Nkwabi and said, "I believe that there may be much apprehension and suspicion at the TANU office-level about my offer. I assure you that I mean well.

Now, you are a foreigner here, but you are also an African, you teach at an African school, and you have a sound understanding of the education system, which should be one of any independent African government's priorities. May I request you to join me for this meeting? If you feel comfortable, we could go and offer our assistance in governmental affairs, and if – only if - you are comfortable and want to do this, you can offer your assistance in building the education system for the Africans in Tanganyika. You are eminently qualified to do this. What do you think, Chelsea?"

"I know that you had said that you wanted to do this, and I am glad that you are taking steps to do it, but does the P.C. endorse this?" Chelsea asked.

"No, there is no appetite at the P.C. or the other D.C.s' level for anything like this, but I feel that I should do something. It's quite possible that the TANU officials may listen to me and dismiss the idea as silly or disingenuous, but I hope that they choose to work with us, and if they do, you can be a partner with me in this effort."

"I do admire what you are doing, and I hope that they will take you seriously, but I need to think about this. Can I get back to you tomorrow?"

"Absolutely, Chelsea, and if you feel the slightest discomfort, please do not hesitate at all to decline."

CHELSEA DID NOT NEED Ricardo's approval for this, but she would ask for his advice. Ricardo was intrigued. The D.C. really wanted to follow up on his speech to The Mpwapwa Club.

"You know, Chelsea, I have always held the view that we could have been more empathetic to and caring for the Africans. The D.C. is right. Education will be, or should be, the first priority of the independent Tanganyika government. He will go to this meeting, and what will he do? He will say, look, guys, if you nominate your people, we can organize orientation programs for them on how to run schools, hospitals, and banks. He may be more generous and say, come to my Office two hours a day, every weekday, and I will train you to do my work. This will ensure that you will become the first African D.C. for Mpwapwa because no one will be better qualified. But *you* could go and tell the chairman that you can develop a strategic education plan for the country with specific goals and plans for the new government."

Ricardo's sentiments solidified Chelsea's resolve. "You know, Ric, I think that you're right. This could be an excellent opportunity to make a difference on a larger scale. I'm going to go with him."

THE D.C. AND CHELSEA appeared at the TANU offices at 1.50 p.m. on Thursday. The chairman appeared shortly thereafter and led them into his tiny Office. His desk was covered with papers. The first thing that he would need to learn, the D.C. thought, would be to become better organized.

As they sat down, the D.C. introduced Chelsea and said that he had taken the liberty of asking her to join him. The chairman said that he knew Ms. Chelsea. She was a much-admired teacher at the school where he himself had studied many years ago.

The D.C. proceeded to say, "I want to sincerely thank you, Mr. Nkwabi, for making the time to meet us."

"You embarrass me, Sir, when you thank me for this meeting. After all, you have come to offer assistance to us."

"No, it is I who should be embarrassed to have come here five years too late. This is something that I should have done a long time ago."

Mr. Nkwabi was convinced that the D.C. was sincere. Misguided - as the D.C.'s superiors and colleagues may consider him to be - but sincere, for sure.

He laid out his proposal, much as Ricardo had speculated.

"Thank you very much, Sir, for your very kind offer. I will discuss this with our office in Dodoma. Also, it will take us some time to identify candidates for training here, but if Dodoma agrees that I should train with you, I will be happy to start next week."

"Thank you very much, Mr. Nkwabi," the D.C. replied and looked at Chelsea to signal if she wanted to say anything.

"Mr. Nkwabi, when we become independent, we will have three priorities: address poverty, improve health services, and educate our African population."

Mr. Nkwabi noted that although not an indigenous Tanganyikan, Ms. Chelsea was identifying herself as one.

Chelsea proceeded to set out the small number of African primary and secondary schools in Tanganyika, the towns in which they were located, the aggregate number of students enrolled in the schools, and the minuscule number of students completing Grade XI. This, she said, would need to change.

In her opinion, the number of African schools and students enrolled needed to quadruple within three years. That would require money to build new schools and engage additional teachers. Some primary level teachers could be trained locally; others would have to be imported. All secondary school teachers would need to be brought, not from India, as the Indian schools were doing, but from other African countries like Nigeria, Ghana, Somaliland, and Ethiopia.

From what she knew, there was no money in the annual British budget for Tanganyika to do all of this. The independent Tanganyika would need to look for foreign aid money to build and equip schools, and ask the U.K., America, and Canada to include teachers in the aid packages. These countries, she said, did not have money to give away to developing countries, but they would respond to a well thought out and articulated strategic plan. She would be happy to work with a team selected by TANU to spearhead such a project. This was not something to be started after Tanganyika became independent. The work could start the next day. Also, TANU should begin to utilize a portion of the TANU membership fees to place selected students in fee-charging schools in Tanganyika.

The D.C. could have never imagined Chelsea capable of the caliber of discussion that she had just initiated. He could not believe that she had at her fingertips the statistics she had rattled out. She had done her research. He doubted whether the P.C. or even the Governor's Office had these data. He did not doubt that this would get communicated to Mr. Nyerere in short order.

Mr. Nkwabi was similarly astounded. A black African woman could be so smart? This was unbelievable. He could not wait for his guests to leave the Office for him to call the Dodoma office and relay what she had just said.

"I am, Mr. D.C. and Ms. Chelsea, most impressed by your offers to assist and your suggestions. You are very kind. May I speak to my superiors and come back to you?"

"Surely, take your time, Mr. Nkwabi," Chelsea replied, taking the lead, with which the D.C. was perfectly comfortable. What he could offer was insignificant compared to what Chelsea had just proposed. She would have to lead this effort, which could produce real benefits and earn genuine appreciation and trust.

"May I order some tea and biscuits for you?" asked Mr. Nkwabi.

"That would be very nice!" The D.C. took the lead on this.

MR. NKWABI LOST NO time in calling the TANU chairman in his Dodoma office. The chairman was skeptical but more interested in Ms. Chelsea's ideas than the D.C.'s. The conversation lasted over an hour.

Finally, the chairman said, "Look, John, this is too important. I think that I have to arrange for you to speak to *Mwalimu*" ("Teacher," as Mr. Nyerere was addressed by his people, in high esteem) "before we do anything."

WHEN THE TANU CHAIRMAN in Dodoma called back in four days, he asked, "Can you organize for the D.C. and Ms. Chelsea to meet Mwalimu when he next visits Dodoma, which will be in a month?"

"Sure, I will speak to them."

1958
Twenty-Five

Both the D.C. and Chelsea were very surprised to hear that Mr. Nyerere wanted to meet them. The D.C. was quite flattered and proceeded to advise the P.C. of his meeting with the local TANU chairman and Mr. Nyerere's invitation.

The P.C. considered the political opportunities and implications of the D.C.'s proposal. Macmillan had made his desire for the decolonization of sub-Saharan Africa known in no uncertain terms. If he could take the position at some future point in time that he had encouraged the D.C. to help Africans prepare for independence, that could look very good on his political resume; but for him to encourage the D.C. to go ahead and meet with Mr. Nyerere without any specific direction from the Governor could be perilous.

The P.C. chose to be circumspect and said, "James, I know that your heart is in the right place, and the PM does want to decolonize Africa, but there is no official policy or strategy for us to do this. This is your private initiative, and you meeting with Mr. Nyerere could be misinterpreted as part of the British government's official policy. So, whereas I am comfortable with you working with the local TANU people in Mpwapwa, I don't think you should meet with Mr. Nyerere."

The D.C. was disappointed but saw the logic in the P.C.'s argument. When he conveyed this to Chelsea, she was privately happy. This would give her more opportunity to present her ideas to Mr. Nyerere. She would convey the D.C.'s regrets and tell Mr. Nyerere what the D.C. had proposed to do for the local TANU nominees.

While somewhat apprehensive about meeting Mr. Nyerere (she had heard that he was very learned), Chelsea had eagerly looked forward to meeting him. When she was led into the meeting room of the Dodoma Hotel to meet him, he greeted her warmly. He told her how happy he was to hear her proposal to help independent Tanganyika address a key priority. He accepted the D.C.'s regrets and the reasons therefor, listened to Chelsea's ideas with much interest, and was gracious in his appreciation of what she wanted to do.

Two of his six colleagues, all native Tanganyikans, seemed somewhat suspicious of her (after all, she was a foreigner) and asked questions that quickly led her to conclude that while they were knowledgeable in other areas, they did not have much understanding of the education system.

Mr. Nyerere had let his two colleagues speak and was happy with Chelsea's responses, which were polite, but pointed, and he said, "Ms. Chelsea, I am pleased to meet you and hear what you have proposed. I would like to work with you, and I invite you to become a member of the Education Council, which we are in the process of constituting. In fact, I would like you to chair it. Would you do that?"

"What would that involve, Mwalimu? What is the Council's mandate? I don't know if I would be qualified to lead the Council. Perhaps, I could serve as a member?"

"We have not yet defined the mandate or the operating guidelines for the Council. I can tell you that the goal is to accelerate the education of the Tanganyikan African population after independence. That is exactly what you are talking about. The approach that you have proposed could be an excellent methodology. Why don't you take a few days to develop a mandate for the Council for us to look at, Ms. Chelsea?"

"Yes, Mwalimu, I would be honored and happy to do that."

"Good, then we can proceed. Thank you very much for taking the time to come to meet us."

"Thank you for inviting me, Mwalimu."

As Chelsea got up to leave, Mr. Nyerere asked, "Ms. Chelsea, do you speak Swahili?"

"Very little, Mwalimu. Just enough to make out what my students' parents are saying when they meet me."

"I request that you take Swahili lessons. Tanganyika will need you to do much more than lead the Education Council. I can see you being a key member of my team."

Chelsea was struck silent for a beat. Recovering her composure, she said, "I will look into the availability of Swahili lessons in Mpwapwa, Mwalimu."

"If you cannot find any, let me know, and we will arrange to send a tutor out for you. And Ms. Chelsea, please thank the D.C. for his initiative. You are here today because of him. Tell him that I very much appreciate his sentiments and offer to assist, and I understand why he could not be here today. Please tell him I look forward to meeting him one day."

"Thank you very much. I will do that, Mwalimu."

And with that, Chelsea left.

MR. NYERERE'S COLLEAGUES WERE surprised by his invitation to Chelsea to lead the Education Council, his offer to have a tutor go to Mpwapwa to teach her Kiswahili and his statement that he now saw this woman as a critical member of his team. The woman was beautiful, no doubt, but Mwalimu was not one to be influenced by good looks. They had to agree that she was very smart and articulate, but she was a foreigner, for God's sake! Mwalimu had treated her like she was a born Tanganyikan. This was further evidence to some around the table that Mwalimu was a true believer in multiculturalism, and he would have on his team anyone – white, brown, black, or a Somali - who sincerely wanted to assist TANU on its way to independence and in building Tanganyika after independence.

THE D.C. WAS PLEASED to hear how the meeting had gone and what Mr. Nyerere had said about him. Could Mr. Nyerere have invited him also, if he had gone to the meeting, to be a part of his team? After all, he, too, had much to offer. It would have been nice to be the P.C. in Dodoma for the Central Province in an independent Tanganyika, he thought, but quickly dismissed the idea as inconceivable.

He was happy for Chelsea. She was on cloud nine. For the first time, she was feeling genuinely appreciated by people of substance. After all, Mr. Nyerere was widely believed to become the first Prime Minister of independent Tanganyika.

She may not have thought about this, but the D.C. could see her being appointed Education Minister in Mr. Nyerere's first government. He would certainly enjoy being able to tell people how that had come about.

1958
Twenty-Six

Robert arrived in Mpwapwa for his Easter vacation two days after Anil and Rafiq got there. The boys were happy to meet after more than three months of separation.

At the first opportunity to speak alone with Robert, Rafiq told him about Salima. He had not written to him about her because he was afraid that his letter might get lost in the mail and someone may read it.

Robert felt sorry for Rafiq. He didn't know what to say. The poor guy did not get to even kiss the girl, and now he would also not see her again. These people are so funny – wearing niqabs and all of this business about Rafiq not being allowed to be in a relationship with this girl, although both were Muslims and Indians, he thought.

"I'm so sorry, Rafiq. I'm sure that she is missing you, too, but as they say, there are plenty of fish in the sea. Someone smart and good looking like you will have lots to choose from. If you come to Nairobi, I could fix you up with any girl you choose in my school, even if you are not white."

"Thank you, Rob. I just wish that I could have had Salima as my girlfriend, no matter the cost or consequences."

"But you won't even see her again, so let's not talk about her, okay? Just put this behind you. What did Anil have to say?"

"Anil and I have not spoken about Salima after that morning when he blasted me for smiling at her. I think that he is secretly pleased that she disappeared - for good reason. He was genuinely concerned for us both."

The boys reverted to doing the things that they had done in Mpwapwa together before. They played darts, tennis, and billiards at the Club. They spent time sitting on the Rock and climbing Kiboriani. When sitting on the Rock, Robert could see Rafiq gazing out at the horizon, and he knew that he was thinking about Salima. In a way, it's good that she is gone, Robert thought. Rafiq is in Grade XI and needs to concentrate on his studies. If the girl had come back and if a romance had indeed developed between the two, based on what Rafiq had said, there would have been a serious problem that neither Rafiq nor his parents needed in their lives at this time.

On this trip, Robert had brought five old copies of Playboy, and he brought one each time they went up the Rock for Anil and Rafiq to look at. As they gazed at the centerfold together, he could see amusement in Rafiq's eyes, and he hoped this was helping him see "the other fish in the sea" and forget Salima.

FOR CHELSEA, THREE WEEKS of Easter vacation was a good time for her to work on the mandate document for Mwalimu. With the school closed, she had very little to do. As she started to work on it, a thought occurred to her. She had, right here in Mpwapwa, three boys, one of whom was going to an all-European school and the other two to an all-Indian school. To advance Mr. Nyerere's education agenda and implement what she was proposing, all schools would need to become fully integrated to create opportunities for the African students to acquire quality education. She could benefit from talking to the boys and getting their input on such an integration effort.

She called Yasmin to explain to her that she wanted to meet the boys and asked her if she could arrange something.

Robert was happy to know that Chelsea wanted to meet them. It would be nice to observe this beautiful woman up close and talk to her. Anil and Rafiq were impressed to learn that she had met Mr. Nyerere and were eager to know more about it.

Rafiq called Chelsea, thanked her for inviting them to speak with her, and agreed that they would meet the next morning at 11.00 a.m. at the Club.

After they had sat down and Chelsea had ordered tea and biscuits for all, she said, "It's very kind of you boys, to come and meet me. I presume that your parents have told you about my meeting with Mr. Nyerere," she said, looking at Rafiq and Robert, "and what transpired at that meeting?"

"They did, Mrs. Sawyer, but can you please tell us what happened there?" Rafiq asked.

Chelsea related to them the details of the meeting. The boys sat listening to her in rapt attention.

"So, now I am working to develop a draft mandate for the Council for Mr. Nyerere to review, and one proposal I have is that to increase opportunities for the Africans, all schools should become open to all. It will take too long to build new schools. I know, Rob, that you are in an all-European school in Kenya, not here in Tanganyika, but there are all-white schools in Tanganyika also, and what I want to hear from you three is how you and your fellow students would react to Africans appearing in your schools."

Robert and Anil looked at Rafiq for him to answer first.

"At the school which Anil and I attend in Dodoma, there are students from all communities, and we all get along well together. I think that we would be quite comfortable to have African students come to our school."

"I don't know about that in my school," Robert said, with some trepidation, "I can't say that my fellow students would be comfortable with that. To be honest, the boys would be concerned that one of the African students may molest one of our girls. And what would happen at the school dances? Would the white girls dance with African boys? I don't know if any white boy would ask an African girl to dance with him unless she is beautiful like you – then every boy will want to dance with her"

Chelsea smiled at Robert, and he was immediately sorry about what he had just said. He had not wanted to be flippant. What he had said was a statement of fact. He was relieved that Mrs. Sawyer seemed to be looking at it that way also.

"I appreciate your honest comments, Rob. That's why I am asking for your input. Although I don't know if you were being honest about the 'beautiful like you' part," Chelsea said, with a teasing smile. Robert blushed, and Anil and Rafiq laughed.

"So, Rob, if African boys and girls came into your school and you got to know them and learned that they were just like you, there to study and were not going to assault your female classmates, they were intelligent and respectful, would you accept them, or always reject them just because of the color of their skin?"

"Come to think of it, Mrs. Sawyer, if Kenya becomes independent, I think the African government will take over the White Highlands from the white farmers. They will never allow a handful of whites to own 70% of the most fertile lands in Kenya. And they should not allow this. If all of the white farmers leave, half of my school would be empty, and if the Africans came in, the whites that would remain would know that their parents have accepted the African rule and would fall in line. In time, as they would get to know the Africans, they would come to respect them and treat them as their equals. As you know, the three of us went on safari last year, and we got to know our African driver and guide very well. We treated him with respect because he was smart, kind, and a true gentleman. All three of us had tears in our eyes when he said goodbye to us."

"I am happy to hear that Rob, but let's say that the African government does not nationalize the White Highlands, and all of the students remain in your school, and only a few African students come in. What then?"

"I will be honest, Mrs. Sawyer, if the Africans are in the minority, the white students, because now they would be living under African rule, would be scared to discriminate against them and yes, the white girls would dance with African boys if invited to, but would not like to do that; and the white boys would probably not ask to dance with the African girls unless they have been sternly instructed by the principal to do so. I think that it would take some time for us to become friends and truly integrate."

"I admire your courage and appreciate your honesty, Rob. This is the input I am looking for. Thank you," Chelsea said, placing her hand on Robert's hand.

"And what do you think, Anil?" she asked, turning to him.

"I don't agree with Rafiq's assessment. Yes, there are students from many communities in our school, but they are all Indian. We know Africans as people who work for us in our households and as customers in our businesses, subservient to us, not as our equals. I don't think they would be received in our school any differently from how Rob says they would be received in his school."

"Anil is right," Rafiq conceded, "I was overlooking this major consideration – in our school, we are different communities, but we are all Indians. That said, for us Ismailis, who are the majority in our school, our faith teaches us that God said that if He had wanted to, He could have created us all the same, but He created us as tribes and nations..."

"So that we may know one another?" Chelsea completed the sentence for Rafiq.

"Yes, do you know the Quran, Mrs. Sawyer?"

My father is a Muslim, and I have read the Quran. Also, your mom quoted this verse from the Quran for me once."

"We probably need to be reminded of this message of Allah more often, and everyone needs to be educated to understand history. The Africans were enslaved and then colonized and have been maltreated. When I was at school in Dar es Salaam, we had gone on a trip to Bagamoyo, about an hour's drive from Dar es Salaam. Bagamoyo was one of the major slave trading centers in Africa, and we were reminded of what the Africans have endured throughout their history in Africa, and told that we have a collective responsibility to try to make amends."

"Yes, I agree with Rafiq. We need to understand that all humans are created equal, and it is the duty of those that are blessed with more material resources and education to help those that are less fortunate. We will have to educate the Ismaili and non-Ismaili students and their Indian parents that if Tanganyika and its people are becoming independent, we should support them and welcome them in our schools. If they come, they would be there to get an education, like we are, not steal or molest our girls," said Anil.

"That sounds reasonable, but you don't mean that the two of you would educate your fellow students and their parents, do you?" Chelsea asked with a smile.

"No, the two of us can't do that, Mrs. Sawyer," Anil said. "The message would need to go from the leaders in each Indian community across Tanganyika to all Indians. People will, or should, see the wisdom in it and those that do not, well, they should pack their bags and leave. Tanganyika doesn't need them. I know that if you were to speak to our Ismaili leaders in Dar es Salaam, they would be very receptive to your ideas. The Aga Khan schools everywhere have always been open to all. They would not have any issues with the proposal. The word would go out that we have to do what we can to welcome African students and even assist them with fees if they cannot afford to pay."

Rafiq nodded in agreement.

"I am happy to hear that. If my work goes anywhere, I will ask your parents to facilitate a meeting with your leaders. And Rob, we might ask your dad to do the same for us with the whites. But whether I get involved with Mr. Nyerere's Council or not, when Tanganyika becomes independent, things will not be business as usual. You will not have your segregated European and Indian schools. There will be integration. If, as you say, many whites may leave, and if many Indians also leave, the Africans could become the majority in your schools, and you will be there at their pleasure and not them at your pleasure. What do you think we can do to make the change as painless as possible for everyone?"

"Education will be the key," said Robert. If you can get the Indian parents on the side, the children will listen and do the right thing. But educating the white parents well, that may be difficult. Most will leave after independence. They have homelands to which they can go back. As far as the Indians are concerned, the students are third generation Africans. They are born here, and their parents were born here, and some of their grandparents were born here, too. They are Indian, but India is not their country. That's what Anil and Rafiq tell me. They will stay, and it would be wise for them to become educated in the manner that my two friends here are suggesting."

"Boys, you have given me much to consider. I will discuss this with your parents and get their views. I very much appreciate your honest perspectives," said Chelsea.

The boys sat for over an hour and enjoyed tea and biscuits, and chatted with Chelsea. They learned everything about her family and childhood, her days in England, the difficult time that she had endured in Mpwapwa, how things had changed lately, and how much she valued Yasmin's friendship. Chelsea, in turn, learned much more about the delivery of education in the boys' schools. She was convinced that effective integration would require much planning. She hugged all three and said goodbye.

As the boys walked back to spend the afternoon at Rafiq's place, Robert said, "You know, my friends and I always look at girls and women like objects to admire, but we don't always see the person behind the face. It was really nice to have met and talked to Mrs. Sawyer today. I feel like we have had an opportunity to see and appreciate what is behind her beautiful face and her figure. She is so smart, kind, and strong. I will never look at her again the way I did before. I have never learned to respect girls much, but I will have to learn to do so because most are smarter than I am."

"You are right, Rob. I will admit that most of my friends and I look at girls as objects rather than persons – even when they are much smarter than us," said Anil.

Rafiq remained silent. He had never looked at Salima as an object, but now she was gone, and he would never look at her again.

SOON, THE VACATION WAS over, and it was time for the boys to head back to school. It had been a great holiday. Anil, who had come to Mpwapwa with the intent to stay there for ten days, had stayed for the full 20 days. Access to Mpwapwa Club for the boys was a major factor in making their holidays so enjoyable.

The D.C. and Jane could not contain their happiness to see their son come home so happy each day, and actually lamenting that the vacation was ending. Every time that they talked about this, the D.C. was sure to remind Jane that it was he who had perceived, after a brief exchange with Rafiq, that Robert would benefit from socializing with this boy; it had been his idea to take Rafiq with them to Dar es Salaam for the Governor's Conference and to take Anil on the safari which had brought the three boys so close together. It was he who had dared to propose opening up the Club membership to all.

Jane nodded in agreement each time that the D.C. praised himself.

Henry was happy to see the boys come each morning and enjoy the Club facilities, laughing and joking around. They sat with him and asked him about his life experiences, to which they listened with great interest. He would miss them. They represented the future, but not the country's future. He knew that Robert and his parents would return to the U.K. after independence, but he wondered what would happen to the Indians, and what would happen to him.

1958
Twenty-Seven

The second semester at Robert's school had become intense. His class was in the final phase of preparation for the Cambridge Exam. Robert was confident that he would pass in the 2nd Division. He was working for the 1st.

Peter, who was eager to have his younger brother come to Cardiff to continue his studies after finishing high school in Nairobi, had told Robert that for admission into the "A" Level Arts or Science courses at good quality U.K. colleges, students must pass at least six Ordinary ("O") Level courses with a "B" average, or the Cambridge University Overseas School Certificate in 1st or 2nd Division. Based on his performance at school, Robert had assured Peter that he would certainly pass the Cambridge Exam in the 2nd Division and that he working to hard to pass in the 1st Division.

Peter had also advised Robert that his inquiries had revealed that if he wanted to pursue a career in engineering, it would be advisable for him to take Physics, Chemistry, and Mathematics at "A" Levels and pass the courses with a B+ average to be admitted into a good university to become a civil, mechanical, structural, or chemical engineer. For Rafiq, if he wanted to read Economics at an English university, it would be advisable for him to enroll in "A" Level Economics, British Constitution, and British Economic History courses. The Cardiff College of Commerce and Technology was an excellent college for these courses.

Peter had also suggested that if Rafiq was interested in *Economics*, he should start to read *The Economist*, and had gone ahead and paid a year's subscription for.

ANIL HAD MADE UP his mind. He did not want to do "A" Levels. He was interested in Accounting and wanted to become a Chartered Accountant and get the C.A. designation. He could enter the C.A. program without "A" Levels. He had been corresponding with a friend's brother, Karim Alibhai, in the U.K., who had qualified as a C.A. five years back and was employed with a midsized accounting and auditing firm, Rosenberg and Weinstein, in London as a division manager. He had told Anil that if, after passing his Cambridge Exam with good grades, he wanted to enroll in the C.A. program, he could get him placed with his firm as an articling student and enrolled in the C.A. program.

Peter had defined for Robert and Rafiq the next steps in what they wanted to study after Grade XII. All they had to do was to pass the Cambridge exam with good grades. In Robert's school, almost 90% of the students passed the Cambridge Exam in the 1st or 2nd Division. At the Indian Secondary School in Dodoma, the first batch of students who had studied Grade XI and XII at the new school was to sit for the Cambridge Exam this year. Their performance would be an indication of how well Rafiq and his class could expect to do, and there was much trepidation in their class about the exam, even though for them, it was still about 19 months away.

THE D.C. CALLED SALIM at the end of June and asked if the two could meet at the Club one evening. He had a proposal that Salim may be interested in, he said.

When they met, the D.C. told Salim that all supplies – practically everything that the Teachers Training College staff and students, the vet station, and other government staff consumed (except for the wines, spirits, and beverages that Salim supplied) - was acquired from a supplier in Dodoma. He had observed that over the past year and a half, the supplier had been jacking up prices, which had seemed unreasonable to him. Over this time, they had also had problems with the quality of supplies. Bags of rice received from him recently were found to contain insects, sugar was less than fully refined, and cooking oil tins were often damaged in transit and leaking when delivered. The relationship with the supplier had become acrimonious. His attitude was that he was doing Mpwapwa a favor. Nobody would supply them with the high-quality goods at the prices he did.

The D.C. had decided to find another supplier. He provided a listing of all items and quantities being purchased each month and the associated costs to Salim and asked if he could supply those items and at that price.

Salim expressed gratitude to the D.C. for his offer of this significant opportunity and thanked him for his confidence in Yasmin and him to become the new suppliers.

Looking at the information that the D.C. had shared with him, Salim noted that the supplier's total billing was in the order of Shs.15,000 a month. Based on his knowledge of the wholesale price for the listed items and transportation costs, he estimated that the supplier was averaging over Shs.10,000 in gross profit per month. His operating costs could not be more than Shs.1,500 per month. He was netting approximately Shs.8,500 a month. This was excessive – almost Shs.2,000 more than the market rate.

He undertook to look into this and get back to the D.C. in about ten days. The D.C. told him to take his time.

WHEN SALIM DISCUSSED THE proposal with Yasmin, she was ambivalent. The supplier was most probably sourcing the merchandise from wholesalers and importers in Dar es Salaam, which meant that he must be making frequent trips there. Salim could not do this, and whereas the goods shipped from Dar es Salaam by railway could be delivered to the Mpwapwa railway station, she believed that the items would be arriving via several small shipments that would need to be picked up as they arrived. This would mean that Salim would have to make almost daily trips to Gulwe railway station, 10 miles away, which would be too disruptive for their business.

"Think about it, Yasmin, if we discounted these items by, say, 2,000 Shillings a month, which would make the D.C. very happy, we could gross 8,000 Shillings a month. Net of operating expenses, we could make 6,500 Shillings a month, which is about the same as what we make in our business here."

"Yes, but our business is a growing enterprise. Every month we are doing better than in the previous month, and we can rely on this business. If the D.C. leaves and there is another guy in his place, and he takes the contract away, what will you be left with?"

"You are right, Yasmin, but this is too lucrative to just let it go. Let's think about it."

And think about is what Yasmin did. Three days later, she said to Salim, "I have an idea. Fateh earns about 1,500 Shillings a month in his job. We can suggest to him that he leave his job and work for us. If we gross 8,000 Shillings a month out of this venture, we could pay him 3,000 Shillings salary. We would pay rent, say 500 Shillings a month, for any space that we need to rent in Dodoma to store goods, and pay Fateh 1,000 Shillings a month for his travel expenses for his trips to Dar es Salaam, plus gas and depreciation of his station wagon for transporting the supplies to Mpwapwa each week. That would leave us with around 3,500 Shillings for ourselves. That way, Fateh will double his income, and we would add 3,500 a month to our income."

"That's a great idea," agreed Salim, "but what if we lost the contract? Fateh would be out of a job. What would he do then?"

"If we lose the contract, Fateh could look for another job. He is smart. He has three kids to educate; he needs to make more money. He knows a great deal about the merchandising business, and this would be his opportunity to double his income without any investment on his part. This is a risk that he will want to take."

"Just thinking aloud, Yasmin, would Fateh not wonder why we want a cut out of this venture when we are doing so well here? Would he not wonder why we are not offering the whole deal to him?"

"The D.C. does not know Fateh, and he may not want to have anything to do with him. He is offering the contract to you, and you will be responsible for its performance, so we would be fully justified in taking a share of the profits. If we buy 10,000 Shillings worth of merchandise from the importers and wholesalers in Dar es Salaam, we will have to pay cash until we establish credit with them. This working capital will need to come from us."

"True. But will Fateh not wonder why we are not forming a partnership with him? If all we need is 10,000 Shillings working capital, he would have 5,000 to invest with us. Why are we asking him to work for us?"

"The D.C. may not agree to deal with some partner whom we bring in and whom he does not know well. Besides, partnerships can create all kinds of problems. We don't want to lose Fateh and Almas as our friends. We want to keep this clean, and we can do this by having Fateh work for us - plain and simple. I don't think that he will have any problem with that."

"Okay," agreed Salim, "let's speak to Fateh and see what he says."

FATEH WAS DELIGHTED TO hear the proposition. He would love to do this, he said, and he had no difficulty working for Salim and Yasmin. He sincerely appreciated the generous salary and reimbursement package that they were offering him. He knew a great deal about this business, and he would have no difficulty managing it.

Salim told him that he would need to discuss the entire arrangement with the D.C. and come back to him.

After returning from Dodoma, Salim told the D.C. that he and Yasmin were most grateful for his confidence and had decided to take him up on his offer. They would form a new corporation, which he and Yasmin would own 100% and employ Anil's father, Fateh, whom the D.C. had met briefly, as the business manager. He told the D.C. how Fateh was well qualified for the job.

He further advised the D.C. that as a first step, he wanted to arrange for Fateh to meet with the relevant people at the Teachers' College, the vet station, and in the D.C.'s office, to understand their needs, preferences, and expectations. He would then travel to Dar es Salaam to meet with the suppliers and establish the costs and the price at which they could sell to the three agencies. He assured the D.C. that he would see a minimum Shs.2,000 monthly saving in the aggregate costs. Fateh would need to give two months' notice to his employer to leave. For practical purposes, the D.C. could advise the current supplier that they would terminate his supply arrangement with him as of the beginning of October, by which time they would be sufficiently organized to serve the customers.

FATEH TRAVELED TO MPWAPWA to meet with all of his future customers, determine their requirements, and understand their issues with the current supplier and how they would like to be served. They were not asking for anything unreasonable. These were people with whom he would be happy to work.

In July, he traveled to Dar es Salaam to meet with the importers and whole-salers of the items to be purchased. Some of them were the same companies from which his firm purchased merchandise, and with whom he was familiar. With these, he found immediate acceptance, and they offered prices that were somewhat lower than Salim had estimated. They would gross more than Shs.7,000 a month, he esti-mated. All were happy to ship his orders by rail to Dodoma.

Fateh resigned from his firm at the beginning of August, effective as of the last day of September. He informed his employer, Ralph Kirkwood that he was going to work for his friend, who was setting up a wholesale business in Dodoma. He assured Ralph that his new business would not carry any of the items that Ralph's company currently sold.

Ralph was sorry to see Fateh go. Fateh assured him that he would help find another competent person to work for him before he left. Ralph appreciated the fact that Fateh was giving him two months' notice when only one month's notice was required. Fateh also told him that he intended to spend one month with his replacement to train him and ensure that the business did not suffer any disruption. This would mean that Ralph would have to pay two salaries for one month, but he sincerely appreciated Fateh's commitment and said that he would have no problem with that.

As the next step, Fateh looked for premises to rent. He found a neat 500 square foot facility in the Rhemsons Cinema building, partitioned between a small 150 square feet office and 350 square feet of storage space for Shs.500 rent per month, commencing at the beginning of September. Salim looked at the premises and agreed that these were perfect for them.

Now Salim had to form the corporation to own and run the business. They met with a local lawyer to do that.

"And under what name will the corporation operate?" The lawyer asked.

"Almin Enterprises," Salim answered.

Fateh wondered what Almin meant.

"Like, A L M I N?" The lawyer asked.

"Yes, Almin is a combination of the first three letters of Fateh's wife's first name,

Almas, and the last three letters of my wife's first name, Yasmin. These two women have brought much happiness and good fortune into our lives, and we hope that their names will bring success for this corporation."

Fateh smiled to himself. It was perfect.

1958
Twenty-Eight

Now that both Rafiq and Anil were sixteen, they wanted to learn to drive. There were no driving schools in Dodoma, so Fateh started to give them driving lessons.

Each evening, he drove them to the edge of the town and taught them to drive. They each got to practice for 30 minutes. The boys were excited to learn and looked forward eagerly to their driving lessons each day.

After one month of practice, Fateh got an "L" plate for the car and let the boys drive in the town with him by their side. In less than two months, both had passed their driving tests.

THE AUGUST VACATION WAS approaching, and Rafiq had invited Anil to go to Mpwapwa with him again, which Anil was happy to do. The Club was a great attraction for him. There was nowhere in Dodoma where they could play billiards and darts, and access to tennis, table tennis, and board games was limited. In Mpwapwa, they had Ricardo to help them hone their tennis skills, and with whom they could play doubles.

Rafiq had written to Robert and told him about Anil's and his plan for the August vacation and asked him if he had any other travel plans. Robert had replied, "I don't have anywhere else to go, and even if I had, I would want to be with the two of you."

On one of their trips to Dodoma, Rafiq advised his parents that Anil would be joining him again on his vacation to Mpwapwa. Yasmin and Salim were happy. It was great to have Anil with them, but after a moment's thought, Salim said, "Rafiq, we are happy that Anil will spend the August vacation in Mpwapwa, but this is a full month's vacation. Don't you boys want to go somewhere else for a couple of weeks? At one time, you were talking about visiting Anil's cousin in Iringa. Do you want to do that? See more of the country?"

"That sounds like something for us to think about. We'd have to ask Rob, of course; we can't leave him alone in Mpwapwa."

Robert was excited by the idea. With stops, Iringa was a six-hour bus ride from Dodoma. The question was where they would stay. Anil's cousin in Iringa could not accommodate three boys, and even if he could, there was no way that they could take an English boy with them to stay with an Ismaili family in a small town. The family would panic if they even suggested it.

When Robert discussed the idea with his dad, he said, "Why don't you all come here first and spend a week with us and then you can go to Iringa. There is a Railway hotel called The Iringa Hotel there. It's like the Dodoma Hotel, but older. I will arrange for you to stay there."

AFTER SPENDING TEN DAYS in Mpwapwa, the boys boarded an East African Railways bus in Dodoma at 9.00 a.m. for their trip to Iringa. Yasmin had packed a large tiffin for them, as there was no restaurant on the way for them to have lunch.

After the halfway point between Dodoma and Iringa, the landscape started to change. They began to climb hills called Nyangoro. The East African Rift Valley was spread out on the right side of the escarpment. The wind blew faster and colder, the higher they climbed. Eventually, the climb was over, and the flat landscape started to reveal tracts of maize farms owned by the Africans. This is where much of the maize for ugali flour (a staple for the locals) grew, and that is why Iringa was called Tanganyika's breadbasket.

They arrived in Iringa at around 4.00 p.m. Anil's cousin, Hassan, was at the station to receive them. The Iringa Hotel was just a five-minute walk from the station. As they checked in, the Goan manager looked curiously at the trio and wondered why an English boy was in the company of two Indians. Whereas the hotel had hosted Indians from South Africa, traveling with young children on their journey north to Kenya, he had never had any local Indian boys this age stay at the hotel. He gave them a room with three beds and said that their one week's stay would be Shs.175. He was surprised when Rafiq, and not Robert, took the money out of his pocket and put it on the counter for the manager to count.

Hassan offered to take Rafiq and Anil to Jamatkhana that evening, but they decided to stay in. June, July, and August were "winter" months in Southern Highlands and feeling the chill in the air, Rafiq and Anil were more inclined to have a nice dinner and then sit by a large fireplace in the hotel lounge. They decided to meet up with Hassan the next day.

THE NEXT MORNING, THEY walked down with Hassan to Iringa's Jamat Street, named after the beautiful Ismaili Jamatkhana building on this one-way street. They walked up and down the long road, attracting much curiosity among the residents looking at them from the shops lining the street. They wondered what this white boy was doing with Hassan and the two visitors.

Rafiq met some boys in the town who had been with him at the Boarding House in Dar es Salaam. They were happy to meet him again. Over the next two to three days, they came to form a group and met up each day. They climbed down the Ruaha hill and viewed the meandering Ruaha River below from the escarpment. Hassan and his local friends took the visitors to the spot where they went swimming in the river when they could manage to get out of their houses with their swimming trunks and towels, without their parents detecting the swimwear.

All the boys in the town were strictly forbidden to go swimming in the river. It could be treacherous in the rainy season, and people said that there were crocodiles in the river, although no one had ever seen or encountered one in this stretch of the Ruaha. Most boys who went swimming had learned to swim in this river.

The Iringa Hotel had a pool table. Rafiq, Robert, and Anil spent much time playing billiards and reading books. Rafiq and Anil attended Jamatkhana most evenings and enjoyed the experience.

Two days before their departure, Hassan told Rafiq and Anil that his parents wanted them to have dinner with them and wanted to know if it would be appropriate for them to invite Robert, and what they should cook if they did. Rafiq told Hassan that it would be fine for them to invite Robert and that he liked samosas and kabobs. For his main course, it would be nice to make some grilled chicken or beef and roast potatoes.

THE DINNER AT HASSAN'S place was fun. His parents had made samosas, well-spiced chicken curry, rice, and chapattis (whole wheat flatbread) for everyone, and grilled chicken legs, and roast potatoes for Robert. They had searched for and found knives and forks for their guests. Rafiq and Anil had missed Indian food and enjoyed the curry and rice. Robert found the grilled chicken rather bland and wanted to try the curry, but felt that if he did not eat what had been cooked for him, his hosts might feel insulted.

Although Hassan had told his parents that Robert was just like other Ismaili boys and very friendly, his parents and siblings were a little tense when he came into their home, but he soon made them comfortable, complimenting Anil's aunt for her cooking (he said that her samosas were as good as Aunty Yasmin's, which was not true) and making them laugh (he told them about Rafiq's horseradish experience on the train, among other jokes).

The next day, the boys rented a taxi and traveled to Tosamaganga, a small village 12 miles from Iringa. They visited the massive Catholic Church there and sat by the rapids and the small waterfall, where they ate the packed lunches that the hotel had provided.

They headed back to Dodoma the next day.

SALIM HAD TRAVELED FROM Mpwapwa to receive the boys. As they started to drive home, he asked, "So, how was your trip? What did you do in Iringa?"

The boys were silent for a moment, then Robert replied, "It was great. We went to Tosamaganga. It was nice to see the rapids and eat lunch by the waterfall. We descended the Ruaha hill to the river. Oh, and we had dinner at Anil's uncle's place."

"We walked up and down the main street and played billiards at The Iringa Hotel," Rafiq added.

"We attended the beautiful Jamatkhana every day," Anil added.

"Sounds like you guys didn't do very much, so what was great about the trip?"

The boys were silent again. Salim was right, they had done so little, and yet they had enjoyed the trip immensely.

After some moments of silence, Robert replied, "Uncle Salim, it was the experience. The change in climate as we entered the Southern Highlands and climbed the hills, the crisp air - as we have in Nairobi. The hotel was nice; it had a fireplace that we sat around in the evenings and talked for hours; the descent down the Ruaha hill was fun, but the climb back was difficult. The hill is steeper than Kiboriani. We made many new Ismaili friends. I enjoyed the dinner at Anil's uncle's place. They were such simple and nice people. They had a lovely little daughter with rosy cheeks and curious eyes. I wondered how much I would have loved her if she was my little sister. I wanted to pick her up and hug her, but I didn't know if that would have been appropriate. The walk up and down the Jamat Street each day felt to me like a different experience. I looked at the people going about their business and wondering what I was doing with these guys. Hassan told us that there was a rumor in the town that Anil and Rafiq were brothers and that their parents had adopted me from a white family in Kongwa who didn`t want me, but Hassan quickly corrected that."

"Well, I'm glad that you could see beyond sightseeing. In a small place like Iringa, there is little to do. It's the experience you go to such places for, and you boys seem to have experienced Iringa to its full extent."

FOR ROBERT, RAFIQ, AND Anil, September to November was the last school semester. For Robert, it was the last critical semester of his Grade XII. He had worked hard and sat for his Cambridge Exam in November. He told his parents and Rafiq and Anil that he had done well. His results would not come until mid-March 1959.

He had agreed with his parents that he would go from Nairobi directly to Cardiff and stay with his brother until September when he would start his "A" Levels. He would find some work and earn some money between January and August, but he told his parents that he wanted to see them, Anil, and Rafiq before he left for the U.K.

The D.C. and Jane felt that it would be good for him to come to Mpwapwa and spend some relaxing time with them and his two friends, assuming that Anil would go there for his December vacation. Now that they were all Club members, they could enjoy the Christmas programs at the Club.

Rafiq and Anil had also sat for their school's Grade XI exam in November. Their exam results were released in mid-December when they were in Mpwapwa. Rafiq had stood 1st, as expected. Anil's hard work had paid off. He had jumped to #4 from his #10 standing when he had completed Grade X.

Everyone was delighted with their performance. The D.C., Jane, and Robert organized a nice dinner party at the Club one evening for the boys and also invited their parents, Ricardo, and Chelsea. Fateh and Almas, who drove down from Dodoma for the party, had never been prouder of their son. They also agreed to come back to celebrate Christmas with the group.

After one of his happiest vacations (Christmas had never been as enjoyable at the Club as it was this year with his two friends and their parents), Robert said good-bye to his parents and friends and boarded the train for Dar es Salaam on December 30th to fly out from there to London. Rafiq and Anil returned to Dodoma to start their Grade XII.

1959
Twenty-Nine

By October 1958, Almin Enterprises was fully set up to supply Mpwapwa. Fateh had made trips to Dar es Salaam and placed orders for all supplies. He made four deliveries in October and received positive feedback for the timing of his deliveries and the quality of the supplies.

When Fateh and Salim sat down to review the first-quarter results, they noted that they had averaged Shs.13,000 in sales per month. There had not been any reduction in the quantity or quality of the products sold; they had discounted prices by an aggregate of Shs.6,000 for three months, which had made their customers happy.

Despite discounting the prices, the business had generated a net surplus of Shs.11,000, which was about the amount that Salim had estimated.

Salim felt guilty about taking Shs.2,000 more than Fateh for each of the three months. He suggested that going forward, they would divide the operating profit equally between them. When advised of this, Yasmin endorsed the idea.

Fateh told Salim that there was a market in Dodoma for the merchandise that they were supplying to Mpwapwa. He had inquired about the prices at which the retailers in Dodoma acquired their supplies from the local wholesalers or those in Dar es Salaam, and he believed that they could be competitive. He had planned to ask the suppliers in Dar es Salaam for larger volume discounts to be able to supply the locals at more competitive prices.

FATEH'S EXPERIENCE IN THE merchandising business was paying off. When they met to review the second-quarter results, Salim saw that Fateh had increased the sales by Shs. 6,000 from the first quarter. The additional sales had come, in the main, from sales to the traders in Dodoma. The Mpwapwa Club had become a customer, as well, and was making a small contribution to the sales revenue. At the same time, Fateh had increased the gross margin by negotiating volume discounts. Operating profit for these three months had risen to Shs.24,000.

In three months, Fateh had increased their remuneration from Shs.3,000 to Shs.4,000 per month, each. They had the D.C. to thank for this largesse. Salim thought about how much he had disliked this man and how he had, almost overnight, become his friend and benefactor. It was dizzying to think how fast things had happened since the D.C. had come into his store and talked to Rafiq.

Perhaps it was Rafiq to whom they had to be thankful?

RAFIQ AND ANIL WERE all work in 1959. They studied hard to ensure that they passed the Cambridge Exam in the 1st Division. They corresponded regularly with Robert. In late March, he advised that his Cambridge Exam results were out, and he had passed in the 1st Division. They were delighted, and so were the D.C. and Jane.

Robert said that he had settled well in Cardiff and liked the city. Two weeks after arriving in Cardiff, through Peter's girlfriend Margaret's connection, he had found a job at a Barclays Bank branch as a teller. He was making £10 (Shs.200) per week. This was very good money for a high school graduate. He had become friends with a pretty teller in the branch but had not asked her out yet. He was working on it. She was older than him, but he did not discriminate against anyone, particularly a pretty girl, because of her age.

After he had received his Cambridge results, he had met with the Registrar at the Cardiff College of Commerce and Technology and enrolled in London University's "A" Level Physics, Chemistry, and Mathematics courses for the academic year, starting on September 2nd, 1959. He had also spoken to the Registrar about Rafiq and his interest in reading Business Economics at university. The Registrar had told him that if Rafiq passed his Cambridge Exam in 1st or 2nd Division, he would offer him admission into "A" Level Economics, British Constitution, and British Economic History courses - ideal for pursuing Economics at the university level.

WHEN SALIM AND YASMIN discussed Almin's second-quarter results, it seemed to them that the angels were smiling on the Turnbull, Damji, and Abdulla families. So many good things had happened. Their children were all doing well in their studies; the Damjis and Abdullas had hit a bonanza with Almin, with practically no investment of capital; relations with the whites in Mpwapwa had improved dramatically, and Yasmin had found a great friend in Chelsea. Chelsea talked a lot, but Yasmin loved to hear every word that she spoke. There was so much to learn from her. There was no other person whom she knew who had a university education. The D.C. was reaching out to TANU, and Chelsea had met Nyerere, who was now sure to become independent Tanganyika's first prime minister, and he had invited her to be an integral part of his team. She had found a new purpose in life.

As Yasmin continued to think about this, she started to get anxious. This was all too good to be true. Could this be a dream that may suddenly end? She began to worry that someone may be diagnosed with a serious illness, suffer a heart attack, or that there could be an accidental death in one of the families that would shatter this dreamlike reality.

Fateh became the first object of her concerns. He was driving to Dar es Salaam every month. The roads were narrow, two-lane, mostly unpaved, and with the truck traffic on the road, driving could be dangerous.

"Salim, how much is the return plane ticket to Dar es Salaam from Dodoma?" She asked.

"I don't know. I think it's around Shs.200. Why do you ask?"

"Well, we should get Fateh to fly there every month, not drive. It's too dangerous. The business can afford that. I don't want him to drive."

There was some finality in her voice.

"Yes, he can do that, but he needs a car to run around in Dar es Salaam, visiting our suppliers."

"He can rent one, can't he? I just don't want him to drive. I don't want him to drive to Mpwapwa every week, either. We should hire a driver."

"Okay, I will talk to him about flying to Dar es Salaam, but he has to come here personally to meet our suppliers to make sure that they are happy, and it's a short trip."

"Accidents can happen on short trips. His station wagon is getting old. He should not use his car for business. Buy a new Peugeot pick up for the business. How much would that cost?"

"Around 12,000 Shillings. We can pay for it in installments. I agree his car is getting old; we will look into that." Salim could see that she was worried about something. He would have to find out what. Right now, he had to do what she wanted.

A COUPLE OF NIGHTS later, as they lay in bed, Salim asked, "Yasmin, you seem to be in a reflective mood of late. Are you okay? Is there anything troubling you?"

"I am worried. I have just been reflecting on everything that has happened over the last two years. It's nothing bad, but too much good has happened too fast."

"Yes, much has happened in a short time, but does that matter? What are you worried about?

"Think, Salim, if some guy who claimed to be a fortune-teller had come into our store two years back and told you that in the next 24 months, the D.C. would have invited you to dinner at his place and he will have dined at our place, as well; you and I will be members of the Mpwapwa Club; Rafiq will have gone on safari with the D.C. and his family; the D.C. will have handed you a business that would produce Shs.4,000 in its first month of operation, without any real capital investment from us - remember how long and hard we had to work to get to making 4,000 Shillings a month in this business? If he had told you that the D.C. would have gone to the TANU office and humbly offered his services; and Chelsea will have become my best friend and an integral part of Nyerere's team, - would you have let him keep talking or physically thrown him out of the store for talking such nonsense?"

Salim was silent. He did not know where Yasmin was going with this. She continued.

"Do you realize how bizarre all of this is? It's happened in just over two years. I am beginning to worry that this is all too good to be true; that maybe nature is playing some game with us, and all of this may come crashing down."

Salim thought for a few seconds.

"I agree that many good things have happened, and yes, too fast. It's always possible that we may suffer a setback here or there, or even a catastrophe, God forbid, but not because good things have happened to us. There is no force out there seeking to balance our happiness with misery. What is important for us to remember is that success is due to Allah's grace. To the extent that our intelligence contributes to our success, we should thank Allah for blessing us with that intelligence. What is important to remember at such times is that when we are successful, we should keep our feet firmly on the ground and not start to float. The English say, 'pride goes before the fall.' With Allah's grace, we will always be blessed with humility."

Yasmin remained quiet, thinking about what Salim had said.

"When we attend Jamatkhana every evening, I offer our *shukrana* (gratitude) to Allah for his blessings, as I am sure that you do, too. I pray for peace, happiness, and protection for not only us, but for Fateh, Almas, and their kids; for the D.C., Jane, and Robert; for Chelsea and Ricardo; and for many people whom we know here and elsewhere. Beyond that, we submit to Allah's will, whatever it may be." Salim said.

"I offer those prayers also, every day, but I still worry."

"We need to worry when something bad has happened. It is futile to worry when good things are happening. These are Allah's blessings. It does not make sense to worry."

RAFIQ AND ANIL CAME to Mpwapwa for their August vacation but spent most of the time studying. They practiced past exams and felt comfortable that they would do well, but the thought of sitting for the Cambridge exams in late November still caused them anxiety. The principal had told both boys and several other students in the class that they would do very well in their English Language and Literature courses. Before returning to Dodoma, both reminded Yasmin and Salim to pray for them every day.

The exams were quite straightforward for both boys and most students in their class. It was a huge relief to be done with them, and now it was time to relax and have fun. Both Anil and Rafiq were tempted to ask their parents to send them on another exotic vacation, but while they decided where to go and strategized how to bring it up with their parents, Fateh came up with an idea. The boys may enjoy their December vacation in Dodoma and become familiar with the business, clients, and suppliers. As of the start of 1960, they would formally join him in the business. He could use them to make local deliveries and look after the office when he traveled to Dar es Salaam or Mpwapwa. That way, there would be someone to take local orders and answer the phone. He would pay each of them Shs.300 per month. In the excitement of joining the business and getting a paycheck (like Robert was doing in the U.K. at the bank), both soon forgot about their vacation plans.

Salim and Yasmin were delighted with the idea. They had worried about what the boys would do from December until mid-March next year when their exam results would be out. Assuming that they both did well, Anil would be on his way to the U.K. to start his C.A. program in April, but Rafiq's new academic year would not begin until September, if he, too, went to the U.K. to pursue post-secondary education.

1960
Thirty

The Cambridge Exam results were announced in mid-March, 1960. Word went out to the students to gather in the school's assembly room.

The principal read out names of the four students, including Rafiq, Anil, and Kumud, who were placed in the 1st Division, seven placed in the 2nd Division, and thirteen placed in the 3rd Division. Four students had failed. He congratulated those who had passed and commiserated with those who had failed. He said that of the latter, two had done well in other subjects, but failed the English Language course. He invited all four to return to school to repeat Grade XII.

After the certificates were handed out and as the students congratulated one another and expressed sympathy for those who had failed, Rafiq walked over to Kumud and offered his hand to congratulate her warmly. She was the only girl placed in the 1st Division. In Grade XII, much to their parents' chagrin, the boys and girls had started to exchange a few words with one another.

She congratulated him also and said, "It's sad that Salima is not here. She would have been with us in the 1st Division."

Rafiq was surprised that she would talk to him about Salima. There was no doubt that she had known about his attraction for her. Women could be so perceptive.

"Yes, it's unfortunate. She would have certainly passed in 1st Division," he said and wondered if he would have given Salima a big hug if she was there.

201

There was much jubilation in the town. This was the best Cambridge Exam performance the town had seen.

Salim, Yasmin, Fateh, and Almas were ecstatic. The D.C. and Jane called Rafiq and Anil to congratulate them and said that they wanted to celebrate the boys' success with a dinner with them and their families at the Dodoma Hotel, which they would host. They had sent a telegram to Robert to give him the good news.

Upon receiving the telegram, Robert called his friends to congratulate them. A call from the U.K. to Tanganyika was expensive. Rafiq and Anil were deeply touched. Robert asked Rafiq to mail him a copy of his certificate for him to take to his college to secure his admission into the "A" Level program starting in September, which Rafiq promptly did.

In two weeks, Rafiq received a letter from Cardiff College of Commerce and Technology offering him admission into "A" Level courses for the academic year starting on September 2nd, 1960.

The letter brought home the realization for Yasmin that her son would soon go away to a distant place and that she would not see him for long periods for five years. This wasn't very easy to accept. Salim told her that Rafiq could visit them during his summer vacations, or that they could go to the U.K. and tour Europe with Rafiq and Anil, which Yasmin knew was not likely to happen, as they had no one to run their store if they went. They had not taken any vacations since they had started the business five years ago, with the brief exception of their trip to Dar es Salaam for the Imam's taktnashini.

Anil had written to his friend's brother, Karim Alibhai, to advise him that he had passed his Cambridge Exam in the 1st Division. Karim had replied to congratulate him and tell him that he could come over to the U.K. any time by giving him eight weeks' notice for Karim to create an articling position for him at his firm.

For Fateh, the realization that the boys would go to the U.K. had broader implications. Anil and Rafiq had become deeply involved in the business. Anil was keeping meticulous records of all financial transactions and was generating critical client and transactional data to help him steer the business. Rafiq was excellent with customer relations, to the point where some local customers asked to speak to him to place orders. He was developing a good sense of how much discount could be offered to a customer based on whether the customer was paying cash or buying on credit, and the quantity being purchased.

The departure of the two boys would be a blow to the business. Now that he had developed a sizeable local clientele and with a new Peugeot pick up, he was venturing into smaller towns around Dodoma to generate more business; he could not afford to have the store closed every time he went out of town. He would have to discuss this with Salim, but he told Anil that if there was flexibility in when he could go to the U.K. to start his C.A. program, he should plan to go in late August when Rafiq was planning to go. Anil was happy to do that.

ALMIN'S FINANCIAL STATEMENTS FOR the third quarter of 1960 showed operating profit of over Shs.30,000, yielding Salim and Fateh Shs.5,000 each per month.

When Fateh discussed the longer term staffing situation with Salim, after some thought, Salim suggested that he ask Almas if she would like to join the business. They would pay her Shs.1,000 per month, a little more than what she was earning in her job. For accounting, they could hire a part-time bookkeeper.

AS AUGUST ROLLED IN, Anil and Rafiq got ready to leave for the U.K. Their flights were booked to depart Dar es Salaam on Friday, August 19th. They would fly by de Havilland's Comet 4 jet (the first jet engine plane addition to East African Airways' fleet of aircraft), which would take them to London in less than 12 hours with two stops, compared to the propeller aircraft used on the route earlier, which took almost 24 hours, with three stops for refueling.

Robert had advised Anil and Rafiq that he would meet them in London. They would stay in London for ten days, sightseeing and shopping. They would stay at the British Council's hostel for overseas students in Knightsbridge. The Council, with branches in all major U.K. cities and over 100 other countries existed to promote, among other things, a broader knowledge of the U.K. and the English language, and change people's lives through access to the U.K. education and educational facilities. The Council also assisted students from the current and former British colonies and territories in securing admission to colleges and universities. Robert qualified as an international student, although he was British, because his parents lived in Tanganyika.

At his request, the Council had found accommodation with a Welsh family for Rafiq in Cardiff and with a 60-year-old lady for Anil in London. Robert had visited the Cooper family with whom Rafiq was to stay in Cardiff. They were friendly people and had another Indian (Hindu) student from Uganda staying with them. The student was excited to learn that another Indian student would join him. Robert had spoken to the woman in London with whom Anil would stay. She had sounded like a pleasant, but a very businesslike older woman. He had not met her in person.

Fateh and Almas - who had traded in their Peugeot 203 station wagon for a new Peugeot 403 sedan - and Salim and Yasmin decided to drive the boys to Dar es Salaam in Fateh's new car and Salim's old Land Rover to bid farewell to them. Anil's siblings would go with them.

Yasmin and Almas had both started shedding tears two days before the boys were to leave. Rafiq sat down with his parents and, holding his mother's hand, said, "Mom, I know that you will miss me, and I will miss you both very much, but I don't want you to cry. I will write to you every week. I promise that I will work hard and do well in my studies. I will say my prayers every day and will not fall into any bad habits. I love you both too much to do anything to make you unhappy."

Yasmin hugged and kissed Rafiq and did not want to stop hugging him.

Anil had conveyed similar sentiments and made similar promises to his parents.

IT WAS A TEARFUL farewell at the Dar es Salaam airport as the boys walked into the departure lounge. The Damjis and Abdullas ran up to the second level terrace to see the boys walking on the tarmac to board the gleaming Comet 4 aircraft. The boys looked back, spotted their families, and waved goodbye as they climbed into the plane. The jet engines started up. They sounded very different from the propeller engines. The aircraft taxied on the runway, took off and disappeared into the horizon.

1960
Thirty-One

After a stop in Nairobi to take on more passengers, and a refueling stop in Benghazi, the flight arrived in London at 8.00 a.m. the next day, Saturday, August 20th. With proper signage everywhere, navigating the airport and clearing Customs and Immigration was not difficult. As they emerged from the Customs area, Robert spotted them and called out their names. They were a little surprised to see him. He had grown a small, well-trimmed beard. They ran to him and hugged him. They had so much to say to and ask one another. They took the coach to Victoria Station and from there a short cab ride to the British Council's men's hostel in Knightsbridge.

After Rafiq and Anil had checked in, they agreed to meet in the lobby in half an hour. Although the boys had not had much sleep on the plane, they were anxious to get out and explore London.

They grabbed some sandwiches at a nearby café and walked over to the Knightsbridge Tube station to take the Tube to Trafalgar Square. It was a warm and sunny summer's day, and the Square was teeming with people. Robert gave Rafiq and Anil a two-minute historical background of the place. Rafiq snapped pictures of the fountains and monuments and of the hundreds of pigeons in the Square, which, as soon as the boys purchased cups of birdseed from the hawkers, landed on their shoulders and started to eat from their hands.

From Trafalgar Square, they walked down to Westminster and the Houses of Parliament. En route, Robert pointed out to Rafiq Whitehall, about which he had told him when they had first met. They were able to get a tour of the Parliament buildings. It was fascinating. Rafiq and Anil, who had read much about what happened here in the TIME magazine and The Daily Mirror, were fascinated to see the solemnity and grandeur of the place.

When they finished the tour, Robert suggested that they return to British Council, rest up, and then go out for dinner at 8.00 p.m., after which he would take them to see the lights of Piccadilly Circus.

WHEN THEY EMERGED FROM the British Council building at 8.00 p.m. Rafiq and Anil were surprised to see bright daylight. They had expected it to be dark. Robert reminded them of their geography lesson - summer days in the northern hemisphere were long, but it would be dark by 4.00 p.m. in winter.

After a nice dinner in the area, they took the Tube to Piccadilly Circus.

Anil and Rafiq had read much about this London attraction. They were fascinated by the number of people and the activity in the area, the neon signs on the buildings, including one urging people to vote for the U.K.'s membership in the European Common Market, the Shaftesbury memorial fountain and statue, which Robert told them was of Eros. Rafiq snapped more pictures.

They stood around and watched the lights. Robert suggested that they walk towards Leicester Square and he could bring them back to Piccadilly when it was dark for them to really enjoy the neon signs and fully lit up Piccadilly.

As they walked, Robert pointed out the theatres on Shaftesbury Avenue and told them that they would go to see *Mousetrap*, a play that had been running for years.

They walked via the famous Coventry Street to Leicester Square. Robert pointed out to them the nationally recognized cinemas such as the Empire and Odeon Leicester Square, where major film premieres were held, and other world-famous entertainment places were located. The 1960 Academy Award winner *Ben Hur* was running at the Empire cinema, which, Robert said, they were also going to see.

After walking around the Square, they sat in the park in the center of the Square with Shakespeare's statue and fountain and watched the excitement around them. The theatres and other entertainment places were all lit up. Rafiq and Anil were surprised to see a large sign which read, "MECCA Dancing," close to the Empire cinema. Surely, it could not have anything to do with the holy city of Mecca in Saudi Arabia.

Robert told them that MECCA ballrooms were a part of the Mecca Leisure Group's entertainment business. MECCA was likely an acronym for something. He doubted if most British had even heard of the holy city. There was a chain of MECCA ballrooms in larger cities in the U.K., where excellent orchestras played music and where they could go dancing for an admission fee of less than £1.00. When they had found girlfriends, he suggested, Anil and Rafiq should go MECCA dancing.

"What's that place, *Talk of the Town?*" Anil asked, pointing to a well-lit place near MECCA, with much activity around it.

"This is a world-famous nightclub. Famous artists like Shirley Bassey, Frank Sinatra, and Cliff Richard have performed here. Dinner, dancing, and a cabaret show here with your girlfriend will set you back by £30 if you don't order any alcohol."

"Wow, that sounds amazing!" Anil said and decided that he would bring his girlfriend here for her birthday someday when he had found one and learned to dance.

"Well, guys, you have seen too much for one day. Let's head back and we will see more of London in the days to come."

Anil and Rafiq were hungry again. Robert suggested that they get some hot dogs near Piccadilly. After ensuring that the sausages were beef, he ordered three and got them topped up with relish, mustard, and ketchup. Rafiq and Anil loved the hot dogs, which they had never eaten before. They wondered why they were called "hot dogs" when there was nothing doggy about them.

THE NEXT DAY, THE trio rose early and were ready to leave by 10.00 a.m. Robert suggested that they do some sightseeing in the morning and shopping in the afternoon. He had asked Anil and Rafiq to not bring with them any of their light-colored suits and white dress shirts. In the U.K., people wore dark suits and colored shirts. Wide lapels were no longer in fashion. New jacket lapels, pant bottoms, and shirt collars were all narrow. The pants had narrow 14 ½ to 15-inch bottoms, and ties looked more like ribbons to match the narrow lapel and shirt collars. They would have to acquire completely new wardrobes - in addition to winter jackets, coats, cardigans, and pullovers. Anil and Rafiq had therefore arrived with almost empty suitcases and just one dark suit each, which they had worn on the plane.

On their first day in London, Anil, who had always been very fond of smart clothes, had been as interested in the attractions that they had visited as in the show windows of menswear stores called Burton's, John Colliers, Hepworth's, and John Temple that they had passed. Robert told him that all of these were part of nationwide chains of stores and were located on Oxford Street, where they would do most of their shopping. He asked how much allowance they had for clothes and shoes.

"£100," Rafiq said.

"I have £200," Anil said.

"That's a lot of money. £100 is more than enough for what you need to get."

"And what's that?" Anil asked.

"Well, you guys will each need to get a blazer and a sports jacket, some matching pants to wear to work or college, two or three polo necks or turtlenecks that you can also wear to work or college, one or two suits for evening wear, about six dress shirts, some ties, a cardigan and a pullover, socks to match, and black and brown shoes to match your suits and pants. The pointed shoes you are wearing are out of fashion. If you buy shirts with French cuffs, you will have to also buy cufflinks. You will also need to buy good winter coats, which you can buy in October, and jackets for the spring and autumn months. £100 is plenty to get all this. Now, if you want to buy all wool, made to measure suits, and shop at Austin Reed, you would need £200."

"That's the Austin Reed on Regent Street, right? What about Saville Row?" Anil asked.

"You seem to have researched London men's fashion scene," laughed Robert. "Your £200 will buy only one Saville Row suit so you can forget about that. The Saville Row tailors will not even talk to boys like us unless I can introduce you as Arabian or Indian princes, and you don't look like princes. I have never been to Austin Reed, but some claim that their suits are almost as good as Saville Row suits.

Their average all wool suit is £25, compared to £15 at Burton's or Hepworth's."

"Will you take us to Austin Reed?" Anil asked.

"Yes, but after Rafiq and you have shopped on Oxford Street."

They first visited Madame Tussaud's wax museum, a major tourist attraction in London. The brochure said that wax sculptor Marie Tussaud had founded it. As they toured the museum, Anil and Rafiq could recognize the waxworks of many famous and historical people and film stars. Robert told them who the others were. Anil and Rafiq marveled at the likeness of the waxworks to real-life characters.

After the museum visit, they proceeded to Oxford Street. The first menswear place that they went into was a Burton's store. Anil was like a kid in a candy store. He and Rafiq quickly selected identical dark blue wool blazers and grey and fawn pants to go with the blazers. Rafiq also chose a nice sports jacket. Anil tried on a couple and selected one which Robert and Anil said looked good on him. After that, Anil wanted to try practically every suit in his size on the rack and just could not decide which he wanted to buy. Finally, he selected a smart-looking dark blue suit. Rafiq tried on a dark grey suit, in which Robert said he looked smart, and purchased it. He did not like any of the other outfits in his size on the rack at this store.

The trio then proceeded to a Hepworth's store where Rafiq selected, in short order, a dark blue suit, and Anil, after trying on four suits, chose a dark brown one. They also picked up one more pair of pants each to go with the sports jackets that they had bought. Along the way and after shopping at Hepworth's, they had purchased five *Rael-Brooke* (a favored brand according to Robert) shirts, each in various designs, golden and stainless steel cufflinks, ties, and *Dolcis* (another favored brand) black and brown leather shoes. Anil also purchased a pair of brown suede shoes.

Now they were laden with clothes and shoes, but Robert said that they were not done yet. They had to go to a Marks and Spencer store for Anil and Rafiq to buy some pullovers and cardigans, and warmer underwear, which they did, and proceeded to Austin Reed on Regent Street. The store atmosphere and service was very different from the Burton's and Hepworth's that they had been to. It was much more formal.

Anil looked at suits in his size and would have purchased all nine on the rack if he had had the money to do so. He selected one after gazing at himself wearing the suit, from every angle in the mirror for almost 10 minutes. He also picked up a sports jacket, and Rafiq and he purchased two woolen polo necks each. Rafiq was out by £15; Anil left the store with his wallet lighter by £50.

With all of their shopping, it would have been difficult to take the Tube back to the British Council, so they took a taxi. Recognizing that Robert had come to London for them, Rafiq and Anil paid for all of his fares, admissions, and meals, and offered to reimburse him for his train fare to and from London and stay at British Council, but he declined to accept that offer.

It had been a busy day, so after dinner in the British Council caféteria, the boys watched some TV in the students' lounge and retired for the day.

OVER THE NEXT EIGHT days, the trio visited the British Museum, Victoria and Albert Museum, London Bridge, Tower Bridge, Kew Gardens, Marble Arch, Buckingham Palace, and several other London attractions, including the Harrods luxury department store located steps from the British Council hostel. They also saw *Mousetrap*, *My Fair Lady*, and *Ben Hur*. They visited Mrs. Jackson, the woman with whom Anil was to stay in Hammersmith. She served them tea and crumpets and showed Anil his room, which was quite spacious with two beds, two desks, two chairs, and two leather seats. The room was also equipped with a washbasin and a large mirror.

"Will I have a roommate?" Anil asked Mrs. Jackson.

"I used to keep three boarders, but I am getting on, and I can't look after three students, so last year I had only two, and for this year, I asked the British Council to send me only one, but sometimes, demand for accommodation is very high, so if the Council insists, I might take on another student, but if I do, he will stay in the room downstairs; you will have this room to yourself. If you prefer, you can stay in the room downstairs. I had my double bed moved into that room after Mr. Jackson moved away, and I got a new single bed for myself."

Pointing to a telephone set on the bedside table between two beds, she said to Anil, "The student who stayed with me last year had this telephone installed. It is disconnected now but can be activated if you want. It costs £2 Shs.10 per month, and you pay for local and long-distance calls."

Anil asked that she have it activated as of the end of the month, and paid her £10 for his first two weeks' stay and told her that he would move in on August 30th. Mrs. Jackson wrote down the telephone number, which the phone company had said would be held for three months if she wanted the phone to be reactivated.

Before leaving, Anil looked at the room downstairs and decided that he would take the upstairs room offered to him. The ground floor room was nice, but the double bed took up much of the space.

Looking at the Tube system map, he saw that getting to his work in Oxford Circus would not be too far to travel from his residence.

ANIL HAD CONTACTED KARIM Alibhai soon after arriving in London, who had suggested that he and Rafiq meet him at the Ismaili Centre at 5 Palace Gate (which also served as the Ismaili Jamatkhana), off Kensington High Street, after congregational prayers on Friday evening. When Anil told him where they were staying, Karim had given him the directions to the Centre and said to him that Palace Gate was one direct bus ride from Knightsbridge.

For their first meeting with members of their community, Anil and Rafiq wanted to dress well. They did not want to be seen as fresh off the boat hillbillies. Anil decided to wear his Austin Reed suit. Rafiq wore his blue suit.

The congregation was small, with some 150 members in attendance; the majority were young students like them. After the prayers, all poured out into the Centre's lounge to socialize. Anil and Rafiq did not recognize anyone, but practically all in the room identified them as newcomers. Both drew admiring glances from some girls.

They looked for Karim. He had said that he would find them. He did see them but thought that these kids were so well dressed and groomed they had to be long-time U.K. residents, probably visiting from another city. They did not look like they were fresh out of Africa, so he kept looking.

Not knowing anyone, Anil and Rafiq were feeling a little lost, so they asked a young student if he knew Karim Alibhai. He pointed Karim out to them, who saw the young student pointing at him and walked over to them.

"Which of you is Anil?" he asked.

"That's me. And this is my friend, Rafiq," Anil said, extending his hand.

"Welcome to London," Karim said, shaking hands with both. He introduced the boys to a smart-looking young lady, who, he said, was his girlfriend, Zabin, as well as a few students their age and another couple, Azim and Gulnar, and suggested that they go next door for coffee. He invited Azim and Gulnar to join them.

They went to a restaurant adjacent to the Centre called *Number One* (for #1 Palace Gate). Azim and Gulnar were impressed that Anil and Rafiq had both passed their Cambridge Exam in the 1st Division. Gulnar could not resist saying, "You two were the best dressed young men in the Centre this evening."

Anil and Rafiq were happy for the compliment and smiled. Rafiq knew that it was more meant for Anil than for him.

"I will have to introduce you both to some girls I know. I am sure that they would like to meet guys like you," Zabin said, making both boys blush.

"They are here to study, Zabin, so let's not get their minds clouded with girls, so soon," said Karim.

He asked them what they had done since arriving in London. Anil and Rafiq told him about their friend, Robert, how they had become friends and gone on safari with his family and how he had been looking after them in London, and all of the places that they had visited, the shows that they had seen, and how much they had enjoyed London. Rafiq told them about his education plans.

"You boys have done and seen more in London in a week than most people do in a year," said Gulnar.

The boys asked Zabin, Azim, and Gulnar what each of them was doing, and were impressed to learn that Gulnar had graduated from medical school and was interning; Zabin was enrolled in the Masters in Education program at the London University, and Azim was working as a structural engineer with a construction firm to get some experience before returning to Kenya, where he was from. These were smart and successful people to be emulated.

In the course of the conversations, the boys learned that Zabin and Karim were not married, but were living together. Azim and Gulnar were just dating.

Before they got up to leave, Karim gave Anil the address and directions to his office from Hammersmith and said to Rafiq, "I know you have your friend Robert to look after you in Cardiff, but if you need anything at all or you have any trouble, here is my phone number. You can call me at any time."

"And if you are visiting Anil here during your Christmas vacation or any other time, you are welcome to stay with us. We have an extra room," Zabin added.

After chatting for almost two hours, Anil and Rafiq said their goodbyes. Anil promised to turn up for work on September 1st before 9.00 a.m.

The boys were deeply touched by the kindness of these people whom they had just met.

1960
Thirty-Two

Robert and Rafiq took the 9.00 a.m. train on August 30th to Cardiff. Robert took Rafiq to the Cooper family residence on Westbourne Avenue in north Cardiff. The family was expecting the boys and invited Robert to stay for lunch.

Mr. Cooper, who was not working that day, introduced the boys to his wife, Rose, the Indian student residing with them, Mahesh, their 14-year old son, Morris, and nine-year-old daughter, Liz. After introductions were completed, Mr. Cooper asked Mahesh to take Rafiq to his room, which was adjoining Mahesh's room on the lower level of the house.

The room was nice, with a large window facing the street, a small desk and chair, a closet, a wash-basin, a comfortable leather seat, and a small gas fireplace. There was no phone, which Rafiq would soon learn, was a luxury in the U.K.

As Rafiq and Mahesh returned to join the others in the lounge, Mrs. Cooper handed Rafiq two envelopes that had come in the mail for him over the past days. One was from the British Council, inviting him to a welcome session for the new Cardiff College students on August 31st at 6.00 p.m. It included a street map of Cardiff with the British Council location indicated thereon.

Another was a letter from his parents telling him how delighted they were to receive his postcards (which he and Anil had sent to their parents each day that they were in London) and to read about the places that they were visiting and how much fun they were having.

"Do you have a telephone?" Rafiq asked Mrs. Cooper.

"No, we don't, but there is a phone booth just steps from our house on the street corner that you can use."

"Do you know how much a 10-minute call to London would cost?"

"We never make any long-distance calls, so I don't know. Do you?" Mrs. Cooper asked Mahesh.

"When I drop 5.00 Shillings into the coin box, I get a little over five minutes when I call my cousin in Manchester. You need coins to make calls. You can change money at the corner store, but if you do, don't just ask for change. They are not money changers. Buy two packets of chocolate for 1.00 Shilling and hand in a £1.00 bill and ask for change in coins."

After lunch, Robert got up to leave. He gave Rafiq his phone number and asked him to stay in touch. Saying that he would be back soon, Rafiq walked out with Robert, said goodbye to him, and walked over to the corner store.

The elderly couple running the store looked at Rafiq as he placed two chocolate bars on the counter and offered a £1.00 bill.

The wife asked, "Are you the new student the Coopers were expecting?"

Rafiq nodded, and the husband said, "Welcome to Cardiff. I am David Saul, and this is my wife, Belinda."

"Pleased to meet you, Mr. and Mrs. Saul, and thank you for your kind welcome. My name is Rafiq."

"Good to meet you, Son. We wish you success in your studies," Mrs. Saul said.

"Thank you. Thank you for your good wishes."

Rafiq picked up his change, which he had asked for in coins, and walked over to the phone booth at the other end of the short street. The Sauls had a good idea of why Rafiq had made the purchase, but they were okay with it. Their sales were in small amounts, and their cash register was always full of coins which they were happy to get rid of.

Rafiq dropped Shs.5 into the phone box and dialed Anil's number. Anil picked up the phone on the second ring.

"Hi, Anil! I'm here in Cardiff at the Coopers'. Are you settled in?"

"Yes, but there is not enough closet space for all of my suits and jackets and shirts."

"You do realize that the closet you have is for two students? You shouldn't have bought so many clothes."

They chatted as Rafiq looked at his watch. He warned Anil that they would get cut off after five minutes, but after eight minutes, when they had finished talking, they were still not disconnected. The call to London was, obviously, cheaper than a call to Manchester.

THE NEXT MORNING, AFTER breakfast, Mahesh walked Rafiq over to a nearby branch of Barclays Bank, where Rafiq opened a chequing account. He had brought with him £300 in cash and traveler's cheques, of which he had spent £200, and a Barclays Bank (Overseas) draft for £300. He kept the cash balance and deposited the bank draft into his new account. He told the teller who opened the account for him that the bank would receive £50 each month into his account from one of its branches in Tanganyika. The first transfer would come in on September 1st.

Mahesh accompanied Rafiq to the British Council in the evening for the welcome session. There was much for the students to do there. He would wait for Rafiq in the Council library until the welcome session was over. For the occasion, Rafiq wore one of the polo necks he had purchased at Austin Reed and his new sports jacket and matching pants. Mahesh told him that he was appropriately dressed for the event.

Rafiq followed the Cardiff College Students Reception sign to a room at the upper level of the building. Two Council staff welcomed him at the door. The students were sitting on chairs along the wall, around the room. He caught sight of a beautiful girl with a ponytail looking at him. She shifted her gaze when she saw him looking at her. She looked like an Ismaili and somewhat familiar. Was she someone from Dar es Salaam whom he had seen, perhaps?

A tall woman entered the room, smiled, and walked to the podium. She introduced herself as Evelyn Roberts, the Student Relations Director, and welcomed everyone on behalf of the Council Director and management.

She spoke about the British Council facilities and services for the students, and the social events held at the Council during the year and encouraged the students to take maximum advantage of the Council services and amenities. She said that the

Council had arranged accommodation for the students, to the extent possible, to make it convenient for them to commute to and from the College. If they had any problems with their accommodation, they should call her.

She invited all students to introduce themselves: their names, where they were from, the program in which they were enrolled, and what they planned to study after graduating from the College. She pointed at one student and said, "Let us start with you, here, and go around."

The student introduced himself as Haneef Khan from Bangladesh; he was enrolled in the sciences and intended to become a chemist. Rafiq could not wait to hear what the pretty girl would say. She was fifth in line. The four students who preceded her had kept their introductions brief, like Haneef's.

When her turn came, the girl said, "Thank you very much, Ms. Roberts, for your kind welcome and words of support. I have been in Cardiff for a few days and have been feeling somewhat lonely. It is very good to hear comforting words of encouragement and support from you. My accommodation here is quite comfortable, and my landlady is nice. My name is Shameem Adatia. My family and friends call me Shama, spelled as S-h-a-m-a. I am from Kenya and will be studying sciences at the College. My ambition is to become a medical doctor."

'Wow, Ms. Shama sure likes to talk,' Rafiq thought to himself.

When his turn came to speak, he kept his remarks brief. "My name is Rafiq. I am from a small town in Tanganyika in British East Africa. I am enrolled in Economics, British Constitution, and British Economic History courses. I plan to become a Business Economist.

After all had introduced themselves, Ms. Roberts, who had been taking notes, said," We have students from seventeen countries here. Isn't that wonderful? You will see this diversity reflected in the Council's programming."

Looking at the student from India, she said, "We have a celebration every year to mark India's independence, and we arrange for Muslim students to use this room for their Eid prayers and enjoy the snacks that they bring. They have a party not only for themselves but with their Hindu and Christian friends, as well. For those of you who do not know what Eid is, it's a festival marking the end of Ramadhan, a month during which the Muslims fast from dawn to dusk. We seek to create understanding and friendship between cultures and ethnicity. I wish you all a very happy stay in Cardiff and success in your education. Refreshments will now be served. I suggest that you go around and meet with your fellow students. Make sure that you meet each one before you leave."

After picking up his food and briefly chatting with two Iraqi and one West Indian student who were enrolled in the same courses as he was, Rafiq headed towards Shameem, who had picked up her food and was chatting with another girl. She smiled broadly at Rafiq when she saw him walking towards her. Before he could say anything to her, she held out her hand and said, "Hello, how are you? Meet Josephine. She is from Nigeria and will be in my class."

"Hello, Josephine," Rafiq said, shaking hands with her. He was surprised that the girl had not formally introduced herself to him and, instead, had introduced Josephine. Did she expect him to know her?

An African student came to introduce himself to Josephine, and she excused herself.

"I presume you are Ismaili," Rafiq said.

"And you are too," Shameem replied. She wasn't asking.

"Unless there are Ismaili students in the second year "A" Level or other programs and are not here, you and I may be the only Ismailis in the College."

"Well, in that case, we will have to do with each other's company. I hope you will tolerate me," Shameem said, smiling.

"How long have you been in Cardiff?" Rafiq asked.

"I have been here for over ten days. I wanted to spend some time familiarizing myself with the city before College started, so I came here straight after arriving in London; took the train the same day. When did you come?"

"A friend of mine and I came to London 10 days back. A British friend of ours from Tanganyika, who lives here in Cardiff, met us in London and took us sightseeing and shopping for over a week before he and I came here."

"Wow! What did you see?"

"A lot. Trafalgar Square, Piccadilly Circus, Westminster, Leicester Square, Buckingham Palace, Madame Tussaud's, Kew Gardens, theatre shows and movies, parks, and a lot more. We also attended Jamatkhana last Friday."

"I wish that I could have done all this and been with you guys, but I know no one in London who could have taken me around. Now that you know all of these places and how to get around, maybe you can show me London next summer."

'This girl is very forward,' Rafiq thought. "Sure. It would be my pleasure."

"You know, I have been so touched by everyone's kindness here. The British here are so different from the colonial British in Kenya. The British Council staff is just amazing. A representative met me when I arrived in London and put me on the train to Cardiff. Have you experienced that?"

"Absolutely! We did a lot of shopping in London, and the store staff treated us with so much respect and courtesy. They addressed us as 'Sirs' and were so helpful with the selections. The people whom we asked for directions seemed to go out of their way to be helpful. I wonder what happens to the British when they come to the countries that they rule."

Rafiq and Shameem talked for the next half hour, to everyone else's exclusion. He asked her if she knew what the word "shama" meant in Hindi and Gujarati. She did not. She had not studied Gujarati at school. He told her it meant "the beloved," the opposite was "parvana," which meant "the lover."

"I presume you are somebody's shama?" he asked.

Shameem just smiled and did not respond.

When the room was emptying, Rafiq asked, "Are you taking the bus home?"

"Yes, No. 15 The Heath bus."

"Oh, that's the one that we are taking. There is a student staying with the family I am with, and because I don't know Cardiff, he came with me - very kind of him. He is in the library. We can get him and take the bus home together."

Rafiq and Shameem sat together on the bus; Mahesh occupied a nearby seat. As they approached their stop, Mahesh got up and said to Rafiq, "This is our stop."

"It's also mine," Shameem said and stood up.

As they stepped off the bus, Rafiq asked, "So, where is your place?"

"It's No.11 Earl Street."

"Oh, that's the next street south of us," said Mahesh. "It's a short street like ours. Her place would be less than five minutes' walk from our place. There are usually quite a few Cardiff College students placed in this area because it's relatively easy to get to the College from here."

They walked Shameem over to her place and then walked home. Rafiq went into the house, collected his change, headed for the phone booth, and dialed Anil's number.

Before Anil had finished saying hello, Rafiq launched in with, "Hey, I just came back from the British Council reception, and guess what? I met a gorgeous Ismaili girl! We talked a lot, and she is delightful. She is in the sciences program and wants to become a doctor. She looks familiar, but I can't place her."

"You seem very excited."

"Her nickname is Shama. I told her Shama means a 'beloved' in Gujarati and Hindi, and the opposite parvana means the lover. She didn't know that."

"And you hope to become her parvana?" Anil asked.

Rafiq ignored the question. "You know, when I told her about all of the places we visited in London and how I have gotten to know the city, she asked if I would take her around London next summer. And she lives right here, on the next street."

"Well, it seems you are set, buddy, unless she is someone's shama already," Anil teased.

"Can't wait to see her tomorrow. But you know, I think I have seen her. You remember there was this girl who came to Dodoma once for her vacation from Arusha, and we all fell in love with her? I don't know if she is that girl, but come to think of it she doesn't look like that girl. She is taller. I just can't remember where I have seen her."

"Whoever she is, it will be good to have a friend. And if she is nice, I hope you can be more than friends with her, but remember we are here to study, so keep your head straight and your heart in neutral. I would hate to see you get lovesick."

Rafiq laughed. They chatted for a while and hung up.

Rafiq sat in his room late into the night thinking about Shameem, and if and where he had seen her. And then it struck him. She was the girl in the CINEX camera store in Nairobi! It was so obviously her! Why did she say that she was from Kenya and not Nairobi? People could not have recognized the name of his little town in Tanganyika, but all would have known Nairobi. If she had said that, he would have recognized her. Could she have recognized him? Probably not. He was in her store for less than 10 minutes. He got up, took his change, and walked over to the phone booth and dialed Anil's number.

Anil answered after three rings. Rafiq asked, "Are you still up?"

"I am now! It's past midnight, Rafiq. What's the matter? Is everything okay back home?"

"The girl! She is the girl in the camera store!"

"What girl? What camera store? What are you talking about?"

"The girl I saw in the camera store in Nairobi. That's her - Shama. I am sure of it. I'm absolutely certain that it's her."

"Well, there is nothing we can do about it at this time of the night if she is, so please go to sleep and let me sleep. I have to start work early tomorrow."

"Okay, but she is the girl, Anil!. I know that."

"Okay, she is. Now can I go to sleep?"

"Sorry, I woke you up, but I had to tell you. Shameem is the girl I met in the camera shop."

"So, now that you have told me this go to sleep. Please!"

"Goodnight, Anil," Rafiq said and hung up.

1960
Thirty-Three

Mahesh and Rafiq were on the bus early for the college on Thursday morning. Rafiq was hoping that Shameem would be on their bus as well, but she wasn't.

Once at the college, as he had been instructed to do, Rafiq proceeded to the Registrar's office, paid his fees, and confirmed his courses. He received the lecture schedule, the number and key for his locker, and a map of the college indicating the rooms in which the courses he had registered for would be delivered. The secretary asked him to be in that room by 9.00 a.m.

Rafiq proceeded to the designated room and selected a seat after nodding hello to everyone in the class. There were five rows of four desks each in the room. He recognized four students, all boys, who had been at the British Council event the previous night. Of the remaining fifteen, eight were girls, of whom one was a Chinese girl from Hong Kong, and another was from India. The remaining students were all British.

A lecturer entered the room at 9.00 a.m. and introduced himself as Mr. Honeywell, their Economics lecturer.

"Congratulations to you all for being accepted in this college. We have high standards, and we work very hard here. You will have to study hard and hand in your assignment on time and pass our internal qualifying exams to qualify to write the London University "A" Level exams." Mr. Honeywell announced.

He then distributed the list of recommended textbooks for purchase and other reading material. After some discussions about the course, the college rating of assignments and exams, and course material, the lecturer said, "Our first class, as you will have seen on the timetable you have received, is at 2.00 p.m. today. I will see you then."

The next lecturer to enter the room introduced herself as Mrs. Bartley. She would be the British Economic History lecturer. She repeated much of what Mr. Honeywell had said and distributed the textbooks and reading lists for her course. Her class was scheduled for 4.00 p.m. that day.

Mr. Norton, the British Constitution lecturer, followed and did the same. His class was scheduled for 3.00 p.m.

The morning introduction session was over around 11.30 a.m.

Rafiq headed for the college bookshop and purchased the recommended textbooks for the three courses. He checked if the shop had the other material that was not recommended for purchase but was available in the college library as reference material. Much of it was available, and he purchased it all.

He deposited his purchases in the locker and proceeded to the college cafeteria, where he lined up for food. He picked the items that he wanted for lunch, paid, and looked around to see if Shameem was there. She had not arrived yet, so he took a seat at a table for two and sat facing the cafeteria entrance. He soon spotted Shameem entering. She proceeded to pick up her tray and food, paid for it, and started to walk in his direction. Rafiq waved at her, but she had already seen him.

She sat down and smiling, asked, "How are you? How was your morning session?"

"Fine. And yours?"

"Oh, it was fine. The lecturers came and talked mostly about the college standards, how hard we will have to work to do well to go to university. Is your British friend not here?"

"He said he usually has classes until 1.00 p.m. Shama, may I ask you something? When you said last night you are from Kenya, are you from Nairobi?"

"Yes."

"And does your family own a camera shop in Nairobi?"

"It took you all night to figure that out?"

"I thought that I had seen you before, but I could not place you! If you had said that you were from Nairobi, I would have guessed it. But you obviously remember me coming into your store and meeting your mother and you. How do you remember me? You must have hundreds of customers coming to your store, and I was there for less than 10 minutes."

"My mom talked about you many times afterward. I called you the Rolleiflex boy. She said that you were the most handsome and cultured Ismaili boy she had ever met. She hoped to meet you one day again when you were around 25 and ask you to marry me."

Rafiq almost chocked on his food. He did not know how to respond.

"So, you would have?" Shameem asked.

"Would I have, what?"

"Married me - if my mother asked you to?"

Rafiq realized that she was playing games with him.

"So, after seeing me for just 10 minutes, you decided that you would marry me?"

Now she was in trouble. She thought for a second and said, "I didn't say that I wanted to marry you. I said that my mother wanted to ask you to marry me."

"Yes, but your mom could not have asked me to marry you if you had not first agreed that she should ask me to marry you, right?"

"No, in fact, I told my mother that I did not want to marry a country boy from some village in Tanganyika."

"Hmmm.... I wonder what I would have said to your mother if she had asked me to marry you. I would have probably told her, 'Sorry, Aunty, I am just a simple country boy; I can't marry some big city girl. She is probably a spoiled brat if she is your only daughter.' Would I have been correct in my answer?"

There was no playing games with this country boy. He was smart. Shameem gave in.

"Yes, you would have been right, but if my mom had come and told me that this is what you said, I would have come to you and said, "Oh, I will be a good wife to you, please, please marry me."

"And why would you have done that?"

"Because you are smart, and you were so respectful to my mom. After all, you wouldn't be here if you weren't smart. In what Division did you pass your Cambridge Exam?" Shameem asked, changing the narrative.

"1st Division. And you?"

"In 2nd. Not as smart as you."

"So, how did you hear about Cardiff?"

"A distant cousin came here and told me that I should apply to this college. This is one of the best colleges in the country. I got admission almost at the last moment. I was all set to go to Bristol, otherwise."

"Well, I'm glad that you are here. It will be good to have a pretty Ismaili girl to see and talk to every day."

"Now, you are making fun of me, right? I'm sorry that I teased you."

"Are you fishing for compliments? You are beautiful, and you know that. That's what I told my friends the day that I saw you."

"Did you? What did you tell them?"

"I told them there is a gorgeous girl in that store. She looks a little mean, but she is beautiful."

"Really? Why did you say I was mean looking?"

"Well, maybe I didn't say that..." Rafiq smiled. "I just told them you were the most beautiful Ismaili girl I had seen."

Shameem blushed, and they proceeded to eat their lunches.

"You know, I was a little upset with you last night for not recognizing me," Shameem said.

"I had not been able to look at you long enough when I came into your store to remember your face perfectly. While we waited for your mother to return, you made me sit in a corner and did not say anything to me. I thought that was not very nice."

"Honestly? I didn't say anything because I felt shy. I was wondering if you had a girlfriend and wished you didn't and was hoping that you would be staying in Nairobi for a few days, and I might get to meet you again. I was hoping that you would say something to me - ask me something, but you did not. You just sat there. I was disappointed when you didn't accept my mom's lunch invitation."

"Well, here we are, three years later, being open and honest with each other. I like that."

"Me, too."

"My last lecture is from 4.00 p.m. to 5.00 p.m. What time is yours?" Rafiq asked.

"4.00 p.m. Do you want to take the bus home together?"

"Yes, why don't we meet in the reception area?"

"Sure."

ON THE RIDE HOME, Rafiq and Shameem talked about their first classes. Both had recognized that their lecturers would only provide an overview of the course content for each section, and the students would have to learn the details from the textbooks and recommended readings. For Shameem, there would also be the exercises and formulae to practice and learn. They could only keep up with the courses if they remained on track. Rafiq suggested that to get the maximum benefit from the lectures, they should read up in advance what was to be taught in the next class.

They coordinated their timing and rode the bus together again the next day, and practically all days for the rest of their two years at the college. On the ride home, Rafiq asked Shameem if she had any plans for the upcoming Labour Day long weekend.

"Not really. My landlady spends her Saturdays with her son and his family. Last Saturday, her son picked her up in the afternoon and dropped her back after 11.00 p.m. I presume she will do the same tomorrow. If you have no plans and want to come over and watch TV in the evening, I can ask her if I can invite you."

"I would love to do that."

"Okay, I will ask her. I plan to look at my course material all day tomorrow. If you come by around noontime, I can tell you what she says."

"Sure, I will do that. If she is not comfortable with me coming over, we can go see a movie. There is a nice Paul Newman movie, *From the Terrace*, running at a cinema near us. We can go see that if you'd like to do that."

1960
Thirty-Four

Rafiq called Anil on Saturday morning and updated him on his classes and the developing friendship with Shameem and asked, "So, how have your first two days been?"

"Well, I went in on Thursday, and Karim introduced me to the two senior Partners. He then introduced me to my supervisor and asked me to meet him in the reception area at 1.00 p.m. and to go out for lunch."

"Nice of Karim to do that."

"The supervisor, Ron Sinclair, told me that mine was an 'irregular' hire. Supervisors interview students who apply and those who make the shortlist are recommended for meetings with Division Heads. In my case, a Division Head had interviewed and hired me. He seemed somewhat irritated to have been bypassed. He said he had to know me to assign me work, so he talked to me for over 30 minutes. He asked difficult questions and seemed to make light of my achievements. He said, passing the Cambridge Exam is one thing. Passing the CA exams is the true test of mettle."

"And this guy is going to be your supervisor? What else did he say?"

"Not much. He gave me the letter confirming my employment for me to register with the CA program, and a list of books that I should purchase, and said that given that I had Cambridge level accounting knowledge, I would start in his Division, which keeps books and prepares accounts for firms with less than £25,000 in annual sales and 15 employees. He then asked me if I had any questions. I asked him how the firm was organized – how many people and at what level. This irked him. He asked me why I had not asked Karim this in my interview with him, implying that there was no interview. He said that there are two Partners, five Division Managers and five Supervisors at the management level, and there are 35 staff and articling students."

"Seems like a large outfit," Rafiq said.

"It's a medium-size firm, as accounting firms go in the U.K."

"I then asked him what the firm's long-term vision and short-term objectives were and how the firm was structured to realize those objectives. There was an interesting article I had read in The Economist, which said that except for the top five, most British CA firms operate without a long-term vision and objectives. That question surprised him. He said that in all the years he had been interviewing students, none had asked him - or to his knowledge, any of his associates - for the firm's organization chart or vision. He then started to treat me with some respect."

"Good for you, Anil."

"When I met Karim for lunch, he said, 'I understand that you asked Ron for the firm's organogram and long-term vision.'"

I said I hoped that I did not do anything wrong.

Karim said that I did not do anything wrong. He said he would tell the Partners at their next meeting that a rookie was asking if the firm has a long-term vision and a strategic plan and maybe, they should start to develop one."

"Wow, Anil, you seem to have made an impression."

"Well, the work has started well. People in my group are friendly. There is one guy from India. He appears to be the smartest of all. At first, he thought I was Hindu and was friendly. Anil is also a Hindu name, but when he found out I am Muslim, he started to distance himself."

"That's unfortunate."

"I invited him to go to lunch with me, and he said, rather tersely, that he does not eat meat. I suggested we go for pizza, so he came, rather reluctantly. I talked to him about our Indian school, all the Hindu friends we had, and how there was never any acrimony between Hindus and Muslims in East Africa, and how we used to participate in Hindu festivals with our Hindu friends. I asked him if he speaks

Gujarati. He said he is from Gujarat, so I started to talk to him in Gujarati, and then he seemed to relax and smile."

"Good for you."

"I think things will work out well. Word has spread that I am Karim's protégé, and Karim is very well respected and very close to the two senior Partners."

RAFIQ THEN CALLED ROBERT and updated him also on his classes and said, "Rob, you remember that girl I had seen in the camera shop in Nairobi?"

"Yes, the one whose mother's invitation for lunch you foolishly turned down?"

"Yes. Her. Guess what? She's here, at our college and we have become friends. She lives five minutes from my place. In fact, I am going to see her after talking to you."

"Good for you, buddy! Have you kissed her yet?"

"No, no. Not yet.

"Well, don't wait too long or she will find someone else to kiss."

Rafiq laughed. "How are your classes going?"

"Well. But the second year is going to be hard work."

"Any pretty girls in your classes?"

"Some."

"Well, find a nice girl, and then, maybe, we can all four go out for dinner."

"If you want to make it a foursome, you remember that girl at the bank I had written to you about, the one older than me? Well, she agreed to come out with me. We went MECCA dancing and had a great time, but then I came to London to meet you guys, and since coming back, I have been busy at the college. I can call her, though, and I'm not sure she will join us."

"So, when you went out with her, did you kiss her?"

"Of course, I did. She would have been offended if I did not, after having known her for some months and dancing all night with her."

"I just want to know at what point I can try to kiss this girl."

"The sooner, the better. That reminds me. You've got to learn to dance. There is a good dancing school on Queen Street. You should enroll. They have one class a week for the starters. They have classes on Saturdays also."

"I do want to learn to dance …… I'll look into it. Shameem's and my lunches are at noon. We will wait for you on Monday in the cafeteria after finishing our lunch. I want you to meet her."

"Sounds good, mate."

WHEN RAFIQ WALKED OVER to Shameem's place at noon, she asked him in and introduced him to her landlady, Mrs. Bowes, who had a spacious house with a relatively large eat-in kitchen, a spacious living room with a fireplace, a dining room with seating for six, and three bedrooms at the upper level.

Mrs. Bowes asked Rafiq about Tanganyika, his parents and their business, what he was studying and wanted to pursue at the university, what foods he liked, and if, like Shameem, he did not eat pork.

Rafiq did his best to answer all of her questions and complimented her on how nicely she was dressed for her outing with her son's family and her hairdo. He asked about her son and his family.

She said that she had a daughter in Swansea, a city some 70 miles away. Her husband, who was a supervisor in a coal mine, had died five years back of lung disease. He had left her a mortgage-free house, and she had received a reasonable sum of money from his insurance policy. She had wanted to keep the house but did not want to be alone. She knew that the demand for student accommodation in the area was high, so she had asked the British Council to send her female students. She had room for three but had not kept more than two at any time. She had been lucky with girls. They had been good boarders and good company for her.

When they had finished talking, Mrs. Bowes said to Rafiq, "Shama tells me that she wants to invite you over to watch TV tonight. You are welcome here anytime, lad."

"Thank you very much, Mrs. Bowes. That's very kind of you," Rafiq said.

Winking and smiling at Rafiq, Mrs. Bowes added, "But you stay down here. No tiptoeing up to Shama's room!"

SHAMEEM WALKED RAFIQ OUTSIDE the house and said, "You've got her eating out of your hand. You are one smooth talker."

"Why don't you walk with me to my place; I will show you where I live and then we can walk back here."

"Okay."

As they started walking, Rafiq said, "I did want to make a good impression with Mrs. Bowes, but my compliments were genuine. She lost her husband five years ago when she would have been only 55. Obviously, she is lonely - that's why she has you - and I asked myself why she would dress up so well to go play with her grandson? Perhaps this is the only occasion when she can go out and can dress up? If it is, and she dresses up so smartly for the occasion, would there be anyone to compliment her? Maybe her daughter-in-law does that, but if she does not, there might not be anyone to compliment her - make her happy."

"So, you did just that — made her happy. How thoughtful of you! What made you think that?"

Rafiq mulled it over for a moment and said, "I guess that it's because generosity is a fundamental principle in our faith. We live by the ethics of our faith every day. You do not need to have money to be generous. My parents taught me that you can be generous with your words, with your acts, and even with just your smile. If what I told Mrs. Bowes made her happy, then that makes me happy, and it cost me nothing."

"So true. In the time that I have been with her, she has not gone to church or a bingo game or anywhere in the evenings. She said that they had friends, but after her husband died, they have drifted away. Her only joy on most days is to watch a TV program called *Coronation Street*. She told me that she would not miss an episode for anything."

"I wonder why she doesn't go out to work," mused Rafiq. She seems smart and could probably find a good job. She could go to work and still have boarders. If they are girls, they can always help her cook and help out."

"And why can't boys do that?"

"Oh, they can too, but she doesn't want boys," Rafiq replied quickly

He realized that he had touched a nerve with his comment, and decided that he should be more careful with what he said to this girl.

"I told Mrs. Bowes to not cook anything for me for dinner. I told her we might go out and then come back and watch TV. Is that okay? She told me that there is a

Fish and Chips shop near here. We can bring it home to eat and then watch TV."

"Good idea. I will ask Mahesh where the fish and chips place is. I'll go buy some and come to your place around 6.00 p.m."

WHEN SHAMEEM RETURNED HOME, Mrs. Bowes said, "You've got a very nice boyfriend. And you've been together for three years? You must have been sixteen when you started dating. Is that normal in your community? It's unusual for kids here to go steady at that age."

Shameem had told her that she had met Rafiq three years ago (which was true) and wanted Mrs. Bowes to believe that she had been friends with him for that long. She did not want her to think that she wanted to invite someone she had just met three days back into her house to be with her alone.

"Well, you hang onto him, girl. The boy is so handsome and smart. You are both tall and good looking. You will make a very fine couple."

"Thank you, Mrs. Bowes," Shameem said with a broad smile.

ON HIS WAY HOME, on a whim, Rafiq decided to visit the Sauls. As he entered their store, Mrs. Saul said, "Hello, how are you, Son? You need some change?"

"No, I just dropped in to say hello and see how you are doing. Are you well?"

The Sauls looked at each other, and Rafiq thought something was wrong.

"I am sorry. I am not familiar with British customs. When I came here three days back, you wished me success in my studies, which was very kind of you, and I thought I would come by and say hello to you. Sorry. Is this not appropriate?"

"We are pleased that you have come," said Mrs. Saul, "It's just that in all the years we have operated this store, friends come in to say hello, but no customer has come in to just inquire about us. That's why we are a little surprised."

"Well, how are you?"

"We are doing very well," she replied. "And how are you? How is college?"

Rafiq told them about his first days at the college and asked them about their business and their health.

After this day, he began to visit them regularly. He found out that they were both interested in politics, and he enjoyed talking and debating politics with them.

The Sauls eagerly looked forward to his visits.

RAFIQ TURNED UP AT the Bowes residence carrying fish and chips wrapped in newsprint, just after 6.00 p.m. The smell was appetizing. Rafiq had generously poured white vinegar on the fish and had brought ketchup for the chips. Shameen had set the table, so they sat down to eat.

After a leisurely dinner, Shameem got up and said, "You go sit in the lounge, and I will clear up."

"No, let me help you. I'm good at washing dishes, and you can wipe them dry."

As they did the dishes, Rafiq wondered if, when they went into the lounge, he should sit on the sofa facing the TV or on one of the two side chairs. If he sat on the sofa, which was not very wide, Shameem may think he was being presumptuous in thinking that she would sit next to him, or that he expected her to sit on the chair; and if he sat on the chair, she might think that he didn't want to sit next to her on the sofa. It was a dilemma.

Shameem made it easy for him. As they walked into the lounge, she sat on the sofa and motioned Rafiq to sit next to her.

Their TV viewing choices were between BBC and ITV. They selected ITV and watched *The Avengers*, which neither had seen before, followed by *Top of the Pops* on BBC, which Shameem had watched with Mrs. Bowes the previous Sunday.

During the shows, both wanted to hold hands. Shameem so wished Rafiq would take her hand. She would hug him if he did and even kiss him back if he kissed her. Although she had met him just three days back, she and her mother had talked so often and so much about him since the day he came into the store, that she felt she knew him well.

Rafiq was not sure if he should try to touch her hand on their first "date."

When Top of the Pops was over, Shameem asked, "Would you like some tea and biscuits? Mrs. Bowes said to help ourselves."

"Let me help you," Rafiq said.

"No, there's nothing much to do. I will just put the kettle on."

Soon she was back with two cups of tea and a plate of biscuits.

Rafiq turned the TV off, and they talked and enjoyed the tea and biscuits.

Shameem asked him about the safari they had gone on. He described it to her in great detail and told her that he would ask his parents to send him a set of the safari pictures he had taken for her to see.

"You know, we've lived in Kenya all our lives and never gone on a safari. You should take me to Mara, Serengeti, and Ngorongoro when we go back."

Rafiq mulled this over. Was Shameen expecting him to be in her life five years from now? Was she thinking of him only as a good friend? Was it something more?

"I would love to do that," he said.

"What do you want to do tomorrow? The weather forecast is good. It will be sunny and warm."

"Do you want to go and see the Paul Newman movie?" Rafiq asked.

"A guy in my class said that there is a park called 'Roath Park' near our home. Why don't we go there? We may not get many more sunny and warm days."

"That sounds good. I'll check with Mahesh where the park is and come get you after lunch, say at around 2.00 p.m.? You can tell Mrs. Bowes that you won't come home for dinner. Mahesh said that there is a very good Indian restaurant near the bus depot downtown called *The Rose of India*. We could go there for dinner if you'd like to do that."

"Sure!" exclaimed Shameem. "After two weeks of eating English food, I'm craving Indian food."

They sat talking until Mrs. Bowes returned home at close to midnight. She asked if they had a good time. They said they had fish and chips for dinner, watched two TV programs, and talked. It had been an enjoyable evening.

Shameem walked Rafiq to the door. He said goodnight and left.

ROATH PARK WAS JUST one bus ride from their home. It was full of people enjoying the last days of warm weather. There was a small lake in the park on which some people were rowing. Rafiq had his camera with him, and he took lots of pictures with Shameen in each one. As they walked around the park, Rafiq spotted a girl from his class waving at him from some distance. He grabbed Shameem's hand to stop her and waved back. He noted that she continued to hold on to his hand as they walked towards the girl and her friends.

Rafiq introduced the girl to Shameem as Angela and Shameem to Angela as his friend from Africa. Shameem let go of Rafiq's hand to shake hands with Angela.

"You have a beautiful girlfriend, Rafiq," Angela said, admiring Shameem.

Rafiq just smiled and did not say anything, but Shameem, retaking hold of Rafiq's hand, said, "Thank you, Angela."

She had not said, "Thank you, Angela, but we are just friends." To Rafiq, this seemed like official confirmation that Shameem was his girlfriend. In four days after "really" meeting him, had she become his girlfriend? Did she not want to know if he wanted to be her boyfriend? Rafiq wondered. Perhaps she knew how much he liked her and did not need to ask him.

They roamed the park, admiring the flowers and butterflies and the lake, the ducks and a pair of swans on the water, and the small children running around. They asked a couple to take their pictures together. They put their arms behind each other's backs and tilted their heads to touch as they posed for the photos. Rafiq took some close-ups of Shameem, which turned out looking like portraits. He would have one framed and place it on his desk in his room.

They took the bus to downtown Cardiff around 6.00 p.m. and found the restaurant easily. They enjoyed samosas, spicy chicken curry, and rice. After walking around on the lively Queen Street, they took the bus home.

When they got off the bus, it was dark. They held hands as they walked to Shameem's place. She invited him to come in for a few minutes. It was okay to ask him because Mrs. Bowes, who was asleep upstairs, had said that he could come over any time.

As they went into the lounge, Rafiq took Shameem in his arms. She wrapped her arms around him and laid her head on his shoulder. Rafiq held her and gently stroked her hair. Shameem looked up, and Rafiq took her face in his hands. They looked into each other's eyes. Holding her face, Rafiq gently kissed her forehead and then her face, and she kissed him back. Their lips met and held, and they kissed each other passionately.

"Shama, I love you," Rafiq said. He was surprised that he was saying this to a girl he had met just four days back, but he had no doubts about what he was saying.

"I love you too, Rafiq. I have loved you since the day you came into my store, and fate has brought us together again. I can't tell you how happy I am."

After holding each other for a few minutes, Rafiq released Shameem and running his hands gently over her face, and in her hair, said, "I am so happy I have found you."

"I can't believe that after thinking about you for three years and never expecting to see you again, I found you, and four days later, you are holding me in your arms and kissing me. I never want to wake up from this dream."

"I should leave now. Do you want to meet tomorrow? We can go see the movie," Rafiq said.

"That would be nice, but I will need to spend the day studying."

"Me too. I've not studied much this long weekend. Shall I come around 7.00 p.m. after dinner? The movie starts at 8.00 p.m."

"That sounds good."

AS SHAMEEM LAY IN bed that night thinking about Rafiq, she could feel his gentle hands holding her face, his tender kisses on her forehead and her face, his hands stroking her hair. Even when their lips were touching, he had not kissed her lips until he could feel her pressing her lips against his, and he knew she wanted him to kiss her. That was the mark of this man.

"This man?" She asked herself. This was the first time she had thought of him as a man and not a boy. She must ask him how old he was.

WHEN RAFIQ CAME AROUND the next evening, and they walked to the bus stop and boarded the bus, Shameem asked, "Rafiq, how old are you?"

"I will be 19 on January 2nd next year."

"So you were born in...1942?"

"Yes, and you?"

"My birthday is on December 24."

"Which year?"

"You shouldn't ask a girl her age."

"But you just asked me mine!"

Smiling, Shameem said, "I will tell you. I am older than you. I was born on

December 24, 1941. That makes me one week older than you. So, both our birthdays are coming up."

"My friend, Anil's birthday, is February 15, 1942. He is one month and two weeks younger than me, and you are one week older than me. We will have a big celebration for your birthday."

"And what about your birthday?"

"We'll see. Maybe we will go out for dinner and dance. Do you dance?"

"Not really. We kind of danced at school social events but I never really learned to dance. There was this Ismaili band called *The Flames*, in Nairobi. They played amazing music, and all the kids loved to dance to their music, but my parents were strict, and other than the school socials, I was not allowed to go dancing. My brother Adil, who is five years older than me, could go, but I couldn't. My mom said that I could go dancing when I am 21."

"I was speaking to Robert, and he said there is a dancing school downtown. We should enroll, and then we can go out dancing with him and his girlfriend. They have classes on Saturday also. Shall we join?"

"Yes, but what will that cost?"

"Don't worry about the cost. Before coming here, my friend Anil and I worked in my father's business for seven months, and we got paid. I saved practically everything we earned. When I came here, my dad topped up my savings to cover my fees and buy clothes, shoes, books, etc. I've got £375 leftover, and I should have received my monthly allowance on September 1st."

"Yes, but I can't let you pay for my expenses. You paid for everything last night."

"Shama, my parents make good money, and if I pay for your dancing lessons, it will be because I want to dance with you. So you will be doing me a favor," he said.

"Well, if you put it that way, okay. I will accept it."

She had heard Rafiq describe his parents' businesses to Mrs. Bowes, and it sounded like they were profitable. Her parents' business made good money also, but after paying for her brother's three years of education in the U.K., they had told Shameem that their savings were depleted, and she must live within a £35 monthly allowance, which was just enough for her. She had come with £100 for clothes, shoes, winter wear, college fees, and books, which she had spent entirely.

1960
Thirty-Five

When Shameem and Rafiq returned to college after the Labour Day weekend, everything started to move rapidly. They quickly became immersed in studying for their courses, researching reference material, and working on their assignments. Their lives soon fell into a routine.

On weekdays, Rafiq walked over to Shameem's place at 8.00 a.m., and they took the bus to the college and went to their classes. They met up for lunch at noon and went back to their classes or to the library to study. When their lecturers ended at 5.00 p.m., both went back to the library to study until 6.00 p.m. and then took the bus home.

Their evening routines were similar. After eating dinner, both said their prayers and sat down to study until 9.00 p.m. when they came down to watch BBC or ITV News until 10.00 p.m. and another program like *Panorama* or a current affairs program until 11.00 p.m. and then went to bed. Mrs. Bowes was partial to BBC. The Coopers watched more of ITV.

Rafiq found his Economics and Economic History courses relatively simple. Both courses required much reading but were not onerous. He did quite well in his assignments, scoring more than 85% in Economic History and 80% in Economics. He found the British Constitution course fascinating. He was intrigued by the British parliamentary system and party politics and devoured all of the reading material he could find on British Constitutional Law. The failed Kongwa peanuts scheme came up as a case study in his course. Rafiq knew more about it than the lecturer and told his class how his family had benefited from the scheme's failure. He scored over 85% in each of his assignments for this course.

For Shameem, her Science courses were challenging, as they were for everyone else in her class. She averaged 75% in Physics and 80% in Biology and Chemistry assignments. At that rating, she was near the top of her class.

On Saturdays, Rafiq came to fetch Shameem at around 11.00 a.m., and they went to Queen Street in the city center, to window shop. Whenever Rafiq saw a nice dress or another outfit on a female mannequin in better quality women's stores, he insisted that they go in and look at the items. He encouraged Shameem to try on the dresses, skirts, blouses, suits, and pants and to buy the outfits that she liked. He insisted that he pay for the purchases using the argument that it was he who wanted to see her in that dress or another outfit, and therefore, he should pay for it. He also made her buy matching shoes, handbags, and other accessories and paid for it.

Sometimes, if he detected her looking at items other than the one he had liked and if, when she tried them on, Shameem liked them, he would buy the items for her and say they were gifts from him for her.

Rafiq could afford to be generous. After making all of the purchases for Shameem, he still had over £250 in his account.

They attended their dancing classes from noon to 2.00 p.m. They were enrolled in four weeks' of Fox Trot, Quick-Step, and Rock' n' Roll dancing lessons, starting in the middle of October.

Soon, Shameem had a wardrobe filled with beautiful dresses, smart suits, skirts, blouses, and pants. As they walked down Queen Street one day, Shameem said, "Do you realize Rafiq, that I have all these nice outfits, shoes, handbags, and costume jewelry that are just hanging in my closet, as I have nowhere to go wearing them? It's all just lying there."

"Let's finish our dancing classes, and then we will go out for dinner and dancing – you will be able to wear your new outfits then! We can go to London for the Christmas holidays, and you can dress up to go to The Ismaili Centre and the theatre and all kinds of places," Rafiq replied.

"Okay, but you have to promise me that you will not take me into one of these stores again until I can wear each of the items you have bought for me at least five times!"

"Well, there is just this amazing black dress I saw in Joey's Fashion store that I want you to look at."

"Rafiq, do you hear me? No more going into ladies' wear stores. Do you understand that?"

"So, you won't even look at this black dress?"

"No. I won't, and that's that."

Rafiq could see that for the first time, she was upset.

"Okay, I won't ask you to purchase anything until next year."

"I just told you…"

"But next year, you will need some summer outfits."

"I will buy what I want for summer with my money," she said with finality.

"I'm sorry, Shama. When you put these outfits on, you look so beautiful that I just want to admire you, and that's why I push you to buy, hoping that you will wear them someday."

"Okay, but no more pushing me to try this stuff," Shameem said and gave Rafiq a peck on his cheek.

THEY EITHER SPENT THE Saturday evenings watching TV at Shameem's place or went to the movies. Some evenings, Rob and his girlfriend, Bernice, joined them. The four enjoyed being together. Both Rob and Bernice had grown fond of Shameem.

Their Sundays were for studying until 6.00 p.m., after which Rafiq and Shameem went to the Indian restaurant downtown for dinner.

Rafiq, Anil, and Shameem all made the time each week to write to their parents, telling them about the week's events and eagerly awaiting their replies telling them that they were well and providing updates on their lives and businesses in Tanganyika and Kenya. Rafiq's dad's businesses were thriving.

Salim, Yasmin, Fateh, and Almas had been delighted to see the boys' London pictures and to learn that Rafiq's studies and Anil's articling and C.A. courses were going well. The parents desired, and so did the D.C. and Jane, that Anil, Rob, and

Rafiq should stay connected and were happy to know that Anil and Rafiq communicated regularly and Rafiq also met Rob at the college all the time, and that they often went out together.

Rafiq had told his parents that there was an Ismaili girl in his college he had become close friends with. She was the daughter of the people in Nairobi from whom they had bought the Rolleiflex camera, and he had met her when he had gone to say hello to her mom. The girl's name was Shameem, but everyone called her Shama. He had sent them Shameem's pictures he had taken in Roath Park, including the close-ups, but not the ones with their heads touching. They had commented that the girl was beautiful, and they were happy that he had an Ismaili friend.

Upon looking at the pictures, Salim had said, "You know, Yasmin, I had read somewhere that men like to marry women who are like their mothers. This Shameem is tall and beautiful like you. Your son seems to have found a girl who is very much like his mother."

"Let's not get carried away with these pictures. This is no time for Rafiq to be finding a wife. They are just friends."

"I hope so. Girls can be mean. Tomorrow, he might come to us crying and say, 'She has dumped me'."

"How many mean girls do you know? I know men who have been so unfair to their women."

"I was just kidding. I hope for both their sakes that they focus on their studies and do not become emotionally attached. They are too young."

1960
Thirty-Six

By the end of November, Shameem and Rafiq had graduated from their dancing school and could dance reasonably well. Shameem had agreed with Rob and Bernice that they would go out for a nice dinner at a restaurant Bernice had been to and liked very much, and then go MECCA dancing on the first Saturday in December. It would be Shameem's treat. Rafiq was touched when Shameem told him this, but he said that it would cost her too much.

"Don't worry, I have been saving up for this, and I am going to wear the red dress that you bought for me. I am also going to get my hair done for the occasion at the place where Mrs. Bowes goes.

Rafiq could hardly wait. When he got to Shameem's place that evening, and she opened the door, he was stunned by how beautiful she looked in her red dress. She was wearing light makeup and lipstick. The hairstylist had done a great job. She was wearing matching shoes and carrying a matching handbag. For jewelry, she was wearing a necklace, bracelet, and earrings, all studded with ruby-colored stones.

"Shama, you look gorgeous!" he exclaimed.

Mrs. Bowes standing behind Shameem in the doorway, said, "She's dressed to kill, Rafiq. Be careful. And you look very smart too. Have fun, love."

"Thank you, Mrs. Bowes," Rafiq said with a smile that he could not suppress.

"Rafiq, why don't you come here for lunch with us tomorrow? I would like to make something nice for you."

"Oh, Mrs. Bowes, that is so very kind of you, but I don't want to be any trouble."

"It's no trouble at all. It will be my pleasure. Say 1.00 p.m.?"

"Thank you, Mrs. Bowes. I'll be here."

"Shall we go?" Shameem asked.

"No, you cannot get on a bus dressed like this. I have called a taxi. It should be here shortly."

As they chatted with Mrs. Bowes, the taxi arrived, and they departed.

AFTER DINNER AT A nice downtown restaurant, the two couples walked down to the MECCA dance hall. It was everything that it was billed to be. The lighting and decor were stunning. The orchestra played all kinds of tunes from the 40s and 50s, as well as the contemporary pop music making the charts. The two couples laughed and danced. As they sat down to enjoy their drinks between dances, Bernice whispered to Rob, "Look around, Rob. There could be a hundred girls and women here, and Shameem is the most beautiful female in this place."

"And she is with the most handsome man in the hall, and his friend is the second most handsome man here," Rob replied.

"True for the first part; the second is debatable," Bernice said.

They danced until 1.00 a.m. when the music stopped, and they took taxis home. It had been a wonderful evening.

THE NEXT DAY, AS they enjoyed the chicken lunch Mrs. Bowes had prepared, Rafiq asked, "Mrs. Bowes, have you ever considered going out to work?"

"Work? Goodness, no! I had worked as a girl before I married, and that was a long time ago. I am too old, and I'm not qualified to do anything."

"That's not true. You are a very smart lady. You can do so many things. Some of the tellers at my bank are your age. They don't have any special skills. They just count money. All of the sales staff at Cecil's department store are your age or older. My Economics lecturer told us that Cecil's is very conscious of customer service, and they like to hire mature people. They don't hire young boys and girls. With Christmas approaching, they must be hiring more staff. If you apply, I think that they would hire you."

"Oh, Rafiq, I don't know. I worked for Woolworths and Marks and Spencer and Denison's General when I was young, but I wouldn't know how to deal with customers today."

"All you need are good communication and interpersonal skills, which you have in spades, Mrs. Bowes. And if you go to work there, they will place you with an experienced employee for a couple of days to train you. Cecil's is one option. We can look for other options if you decide to work."

Mrs. Bowes mulled it over and said, "Let me think about it."

A WEEK LATER, MRS. Bowes said to Rafiq, "I talked to my son, and both he and his wife think it's a good idea for me to go out to work. Cecil's would be a good place to try. I am tempted, but not quite sure if I can do it."

"The important thing is that you want to do it. Whether you can, is something we can only know when you start work. Do you want to work, Mrs. Bowes?"

"I think I do. It will be good to get out of the house, and extra money can't hurt."

"Great! So let's prepare an application."

Shameem produced her writing pad, and a pen and Rafiq started to write:

[Date]
Staff Manager
Cecil's Department Store
771 George Street,
Cardiff

Please accept this letter as my application for a sales staff position with your store.

I am 60 years old, and I have a high school education.

I worked in various positions with Denison's, a general merchandise store, Woolworths and Marks and Spencer when I was in school and after graduating from school. After marrying in 1925, I stayed home to raise my children. I am now ready to return to work.

I have excellent communication and people skills. As a customer, I am aware of the importance of good service, and although it has been many years since I worked at Woolworths and Marks and Spencer, my customer service training is fresh in my mind. I am also aware of the need to dress and present professionally when you are serving customers, particularly customers that come to a high-end store like Cecil's. Even for my regular outings, I like to dress well.

As I am entering the labor market after a long time, I am flexible to work part or full time and in a temporary or permanent position.

I shall be grateful to be given the opportunity to interview with you.

Yours truly,

After reading the letter he had drafted to Mrs. Bowes and Shameem, Rafiq asked, "Mrs. Bowes, what is your first name?"

"Gloria."

Rafiq added the name to the letter and said, "Shama, we need to get this typed up properly. I can mail this to Bernice and ask her if she can get it typed up at her branch."

"I know a couple of Indian girls in the secretarial program at the college. I am sure they will be able to do this for us. I chat with them all the time."

TWO DAYS LATER, SHAMEEM came home with a typed letter on good quality paper and with some improvements to the addressee part. The girls had also given her an addressed envelope.

Rafiq suggested that Mrs. Bowes take the letter to Cecil's in-person instead of mailing it. She might get an interview right away.

SHE DID NOT GET the interview right away. The woman to whom she was asked to hand the letter thanked her for bringing in the application and said, "I will share this with our recruiter. We will write to you if we are interested in your application."

The recruiter, who looked at Mrs. Bowes' letter, passed it to the sales staff HR manager and said, "Look at this letter. It's an unusual application. For 60 years old, this lady writes well. The manager looked at the letter and said, "Call her in and talk to her."

Two days later, when Rafiq and Shameem returned from college, Mrs. Bowes called Rafiq in and showed him the letter from Cecil's. It read:

Dear Mrs. Bowes:

Thank you for your interest in a sales staff position with our store. We invite you to come for an interview on Monday, October 21st, at 2.00 p.m. Please bring any certificates or testimonials you have to support your application.

If you cannot attend for any reason, please call us at the below-listed telephone number.

Yours truly

....

"This is great, Mrs. Bowes."

"But I have no testimonials, and I can't even remember where my school certificate is."

"You are your own testimonial, Mrs. Bowes. Let them meet you, and they will see you don't need any." Shameem said.

ON THEIR WAY HOME from the college on Monday, Rafiq and Shameem prayed that Mrs. Bowes would get the job. When they went into the house, she was sitting in the kitchen, not looking too happy.

Shameem asked, "How did it go?"

"They offered me a job."

"That's great! So why are you looking so glum?" Rafiq asked.

"They offered me the job but said it's from December 15th to January 15th only and for the 2.00 p.m. to 9.00 p.m. shift. They told me to get back to them by tomorrow if I want the job. I am not interested in this kind of work."

"No, no, Mrs. Bowes. This is an excellent opportunity. Remember, you have been out of the labour market for over 40 years. They must have been impressed with you to offer you this work. You have nothing to lose and everything to gain. You will get exposure to today's work environment. They will train you, and you will get to meet so many people in the busy Christmas season. You should accept this offer, Mrs. Bowes. Remember, Cecil's is not the only employer in this city. When you finish here, we will look elsewhere. Please call them tomorrow, first thing, and accept," Rafiq said.

Mrs. Bowes did not respond.

"Mrs. Bowes, Rafiq is right. Please take this job and see how it goes." Shameem said.

"Let me think. If I take the job, I can cook before I go, but you will come home and eat your dinner alone?"

"I will! You just focus on how you will manage your daily schedule, the clothes and shoes you will need to wear to work and how you will serve the customers. Don't worry about me, at all. You know, it may be a good idea for you to go to Cecil's a few times and look at some stuff as if you are interested in buying it and talk to salespeople. See how they talk to you and try to get you to buy," Shameem said.

"Okay, I will, but I am not too sure about how this will work out."

"It will work out fine. Look at this not as a job but as one month's training for which you will get paid," Rafiq said.

"You kids are very persuasive. You really care for me, don't you?" Mrs. Bowes said, taking both of them in her embrace.

1960
Thirty-Seven

When Rafiq called Anil to say hello in early December, Anil asked, "When do your Christmas holidays start? You know you have Zabin's invitation to stay with them if you come here."

"Both Shameem and I are scheduled to finish our first term exams and begin our holidays as of December 19th. We go back on January 2nd."

"That's your birthday!"

"Yes, but there will not be any celebration."

"Too bad, but if you are off from December 19th to January 1st, why don't you come here on December 23rd and be here for Christmas and New Year's Eve? The Ismaili Centre organizes a dinner and dance event for New Year's Eve. I'm told it's very good."

"I would like to come, but I want to bring Shameem with me. I want to take her around some of the places we saw in London. We would have to decide where we would stay. And talking about the dinner dance program, Shameem and I went to a dance studio here last month to take dancing lessons – just the basics, nothing fancy. It's quite easy. You should go to a dancing school and learn to dance."

"But I have no partner," said Anil, gloomily.

"You don't need one. People come on their own and pair up, and you don't need to be stuck with one partner. You can have different partners for different lessons. Learn to dance, and we can go to the Ismaili Centre dance."

"Okay, I'll look into it. But I do want you to come here for Christmas."

"Yes, but where will we stay?"

"Let me look into that. I can check with the British Council to see if they have a girls' hostel in London. YWCA may be an option."

When Rafiq called Anil a week later, Anil said, "I've got your accommodation arranged for Christmas. You remember my landlady telling us about taking on another student who would stay in the room downstairs? Well, she never did, and the room is vacant. It's a nice and cozy room with a washbasin and a small gas fireplace. If you recall, the room has her double bed, which she moved from her room when she kicked Mr. Jackson out. The bed is old but quite comfortable. I asked her if she could let the room to Shameem, and you could stay with me in my room, and we would pay her at the same rate for each of you two as I am paying her per week. It would work out to £12 for the two of you for nine days."

"That sounds great. Did she agree?"

"Yes, she said that you guys can come, and she will give you Christmas dinner, but she can't cook meals for the three of us for the rest of your stay. She's too old to do that. She can only give you breakfast each day. She didn't offer to charge less for not giving you meals, but that's okay. We will be dining out most days, anyway."

"This would be great. We can all stay together."

"She asked me if the girl is your sister. She doesn't like girls. She says she has never had a female boarder; they are just trouble."

"And what did you tell her?"

"I didn't know what to say, so I told her you are cousins and that you are looking after Shameem. I didn't tell her you are 'kissing cousins,' so don't kiss Shameem in front of her."

"You're a crafty one, Anil."

"So, if you come on Friday the 23rd, we can attend Jamatkhana."

"Yes, we can do that. December 24th is Shameem's birthday. I would like to take her to a very special place in London, and I want you to come with us for her birthday celebration. Do you have anyone you can invite to come as your date?"

"I'm working very hard at the office and on my course. I want to ensure that no one ever says to Karim that his protégé is no good, so I don't make it to the Centre for Friday prayers. I go only once a month, so I've not met any Ismaili girls. There is this good looking West Indian lady in my office in the third year of the C.A. program. Her name is Rehana Khan. She is Muslim, but only culturally. She is married, and her husband is in Trinidad. She is three years older than me, but we've become good friends. She doesn't want to fool around with anyone, and I treat her with respect. She invited me out for dinner once. I guess she determined that I am harmless. We had an enjoyable evening. I could ask her."

"Let me check with Shameem if she is okay with this travel arrangement, and then we can firm up the program."

WHEN RAFIQ CAME TO fetch Shameem to go to the Indian restaurant on Sunday, he asked Mrs. Bowes how her first two days at work had been. She said that she had enjoyed the work very much. It felt strange at first, but she soon got settled. Her trainer had told her that she was doing well and would be on her own as of Monday. She was a little worried about that but was looking forward to going back.

On the way to the restaurant, Shameen said, "She came home on Friday and seemed happy, but when she came home yesterday, she was very chirpy. She kept telling me about the customers coming in for different items, and she said that when the counter she is managing did not have the things that they wanted, she suggested alternatives and made sales. She said that it came naturally to her to do this, and her trainer was happy."

"Good. It will be a good experience for her."

As they sat on the bus, Rafiq told Shameem about his conversation with Anil regarding Christmas vacation.

"That sounds interesting, Rafiq, and I know that you want to take me to London, but it would cost a lot of money. London is expensive. We will have to pay Anil's landlady and also here. We can't say to Mrs. Bowes and the Coopers that we will not pay for the time we are away. I can't afford it, and I don't want you to pay for me. It doesn't seem right that you pay for everything."

"Shama, you should stop thinking of me as another person. We are one. What's mine is yours. I wrote to my parents to tell them that we want to go to London for Christmas. I wanted to wait to hear what they had to say before I told you about my conversation with Anil. Even though they would never find out that we went to London and stayed in one house, I wanted to tell them we are going and will stay together."

"And what did they say?"

"They said go and have a wonderful time. They said, 'show Shameem London and take her to a very nice place for her birthday. We will send you £100 instead of £50 for your December transfer to cover the cost of your London trip'."

"They are so kind."

"They now know that we are more than friends. I told them who you are and that we are in love."

"I have to tell you something, Rafiq. I didn't tell you this earlier because I thought you might be upset. My mom wrote to me that she received a call from your mom."

"Oh, my God, what did she say?"

"Your mother reminded my mom that she was the lady who had bought the Rollei from our store for you. My mom, of course, remembered her very well. She asked my mom if she knew we were together in Cardiff and were in a steady relationship. At first, my mom thought that your mom was calling to complain, but she soon realized that your mother was calling because she was worried about us. My mom said that she knew we were dating. I had told her about you, of course. Your mother said that she had not met me, but having read what you are telling your dad and her and looking at my pictures, they like me very much and are very happy that I am in your life. She asked my mom how my parents felt about our relationship."

"What did she say?"

"She said that she and my dad are also pleased that I am dating a nice Ismaili boy. But she told your mom they are worried because we are so young and can get carried away. Your mother told her that you are a very responsible boy, and they know you will always conduct yourself with dignity, but, yes, youngsters can get carried away. Since then, they have talked twice. My mom called once, and your mother called once. Each time, they talked for a long time, and they are kind of becoming friends. My mom says that your mother is a very nice lady, but seems to be worried about us, and so are she and my dad."

"Tell your mom not to worry. I love and respect you, Shama. I would never do anything - we would never do anything - that our parents would be unhappy to hear about."

Shameem sighed. "You know, Rafiq, I love you today, at this moment, more than ever before. Some girls in my classes tell me that all their boyfriends want to do is make love to them. When the girls refuse, the boys say, 'you wouldn't be saying no if you loved me' and want to break off their relationship. You have never done anything like that or suggested anything when we are alone at my place."

"Tell your parents that they have my word. I will not do anything to you that would make them unhappy to learn about. When we break for vacation, let's call our families. My parents have asked me to call and reverse the charges at any time, and that's what I do every time I call them. I will talk to your parents, and you can talk to mine, and we can reassure them together."

"I can't talk to your parents, Rafiq. I wouldn't know what to say to them."

"Don't worry; they will know what to say to you."

1960
Thirty-Eight

By the beginning of December, downtown Cardiff was decorated for Christmas, and everything looked beautiful. The holiday spirit was everywhere. Some snow had fallen. People seemed happy and smiled more.

For Shameem and Rafiq, however, this was a time to study. They spent very little time with each other, focusing mainly on preparing for their first term exams.

After a long period of intense studying, they both wrote their last exams on a Friday in the middle of December. Rafiq was happy with his exams. The science program being as challenging as it was, Shameem had found hers difficult.

As they rode home together, Rafiq put his arms around Shameem's shoulders and said, "Don't look so worried Shama. I'm sure that you've done well. Besides, these are not qualifying exams."

"I know that I will pass, but if I get less than a 60% average in these exams, I don't think that I will be going to the medical school of my choice in two years. I have to get a B+, more than a 70% average."

"And you will. Given how hard both of us have worked and how smart you are, you will average over 70%, I'm sure of it," said Rafiq.

"I am going to go over my exams when I get home and re-do all of my calculations and check my answers," she said, lost in thought.

Rafiq smiled. He knew her well enough by now to know that there would be no arguing about this plan. "Okay, but don't worry too much," he said with a comforting smile.

Before going to Shameem's place on Saturday, Rafiq called Anil and confirmed that he and Shameem were coming to London on the 23rd, and asked him to confirm the arrangement with Mrs. Jackson.

"Great. If you take an early train, we can attend the Jamatkhana together. You can come home and get settled and ready. I'll be there by 5.00 p.m. We can have dinner at *Surma Bleu*, an Indian restaurant in Bayswater, not far from the Ismaili Centre, and be at Jamatkhana by 8.00 p.m."

"There is a train departing here at noon, which arrives in London at 3.00 p.m. I'll buy the tickets."

"Oh, by the way, although you had not confirmed, I asked Rehana if she would come for dinner and dancing with us on Christmas Eve. She said that she would be delighted to come. She loves to dance. I told her that I don't know how to dance and was planning to go to the dancing school, but she said, 'No way! I will teach you to dance and dance right'. So, we've been going MECCA dancing in Hammersmith after work for the past six days, and she has been teaching me to dance. You should see the way she dances! She just glides in perfect rhythm with the music, whatever it is. She says I'm ready to dance on Shameem's birthday, but we're still planning to keep practicing for four more days."

"That's wonderful, Anil. I hope that you're not holding her too close when you dance with her, though!"

"No, I'm behaving myself."

"Good. You don't want any complications with a married woman."

"There won't be any, I can assure you."

"Good. So we will have to find a place to take Shama for her birthday. Do you know any good places?"

"No, Rehana might know some. I'll ask her."

WHEN RAFIQ GOT TO Shameem's place, and she opened the door, she was all smiles. "I went through my exam papers and checked my answers in my texts and earlier assignments, and I think that I will score over 75% in Chemistry and Biology and over 70% in Physics."

"I told you not to worry! I did not doubt that you'd do well. Are you ready to head out?"

"Honestly?" said Shameem, "I'm happy and relaxed, but can we stay home? The last two weeks have been brutal, and I'm just exhausted. We can watch TV and relax together on the sofa."

"Sure."

As they sat down in the lounge, Rafiq told her about having confirmed the vacation arrangement with Anil. They would go to Jamatkhana on Friday, and Anil was going to ask Rehana if she knew of a nice place to go to for her birthday on Saturday.

"Sounds good, but we'll make it a double birthday celebration – yours and mine. Your birthday will be just a week away."

"We'll do that if you say so," Rafiq agreed, knowing better than to argue. After a moment, he added, "Shama, do you remember how I wanted you to look at that black dress when you dropped the injunction on me? I was hoping that you could wear that dress for your birthday."

"But I have other dresses that I can wear."

"I would have loved to see you in that black dress. That would have been my birthday present to you."

"Okay, don't sulk. We'll go downtown on Monday and look for it."

"It's gone. It's not there in the window."

"It's gone from the window. That doesn't mean that it's not in the store. We'll look, okay?"

MRS. BOWES GOT HOME at 10.00 p.m. Shameem had been busy studying over the past week and had not talked to Mrs. Bowe's about her work.

"Did you kids eat anything? I'm starving."

"Rafiq brought some fish and chips. We've eaten, but he brought some for you also. It's in the oven."

Mrs. Bowes thanked Rafiq and went into the kitchen, warmed up her dinner, and said, "Shama, Rafiq, please come, sit with me. I hate to eat alone."

As Rafiq and Shameem joined her at the table, Rafiq asked, "So, Mrs. Bowes, you've been at work for two weeks now. How's it going?"

"I really enjoy it," she said with a smile, "To tell you the truth, in all the time since my husband passed, I've never felt this happy. I know it's short term, but it's good. I just love to interact with people. When I finish here, I will be very grateful if you two could help me find another sales job."

"We are so happy that you're enjoying your work, Mrs. Bowes! Of course, we'll help you find another job. After the Christmas season, things slow down a bit, so we may not be able to find anything until early March, but we'll surely try." Rafiq said.

OVER THE NEXT FIVE days, Shameem and Rafiq went downtown each day.

They went to Joey's to look for the black dress. They didn't have that one but had a new shipment of black dresses for Christmas. Shameem selected one. When she tried it on, Rafiq thought she looked much better in that dress than she would have in the one that he had been admiring in the window.

They went to the railway station and purchased their train tickets to London.

They met up with Rob and Bernice for dinner and went MECCA dancing.

And they called their parents. They had sent telegrams to their parents, giving them the day and the time they would call, just to say hello. Telegrams usually brought bad news, and people were afraid to open them.

After picking up the phone, accepting the charges, and exchanging greetings, Salim said, "How are you, Rafiq? We've been counting down the hours, waiting for your call. Now talk as long as you want. Don't be in a rush to hang up."

Rafiq told his parents how much he missed them every day, about his first term exams, everything that he and Shameem had been doing over their vacation, and their plans to spend time with Anil in London and celebrate Shameem's birthday. He told them that he was in close contact with Rob and asked them to be sure to tell the D.C. and Jane that they had gone out for dinner with Rob and his girlfriend over the past days. It would make them happy to know that Rob's friendship with Rafiq was enduring.

He then said, "Here, Mom, speak to Shameem."

With some trepidation, Shameem took the phone and said, "Hello, Aunty."

"How are you *beta* (my dear child)? Has Rafiq told you how happy we are that you two are friends and that we can't wait to meet you?"

"Yes, Aunty. He always conveys your and Uncle's regards and affection to me. I, too, want to meet you. You and Uncle are very kind. My mom tells me the same thing. Thank you for speaking with my mother. She feels good talking to you."

"And I like talking to her. We've talked so much over the past days – and not only about you two! I think that we now know each other's entire life history. But we worry about you two being so far away from us."

"You don't need to worry, Aunty. We're both studying hard, and Rafiq cares for me a great deal. My mom would have to worry about me if Rafiq was not here! With Rafiq looking after me, there is nothing for her or you to worry about - nothing at all."

"Rafiq tells us that you are the best thing to happen to him in his life. We pray that you remain united and care for each other, always. Study hard. We are praying for your success and happiness. I will pass the phone to Rafiq's dad. He can't wait to speak to you. We love you, beta."

"Thank you, Aunty. I so look forward to meeting you!"

"Shama, before I go, may I ask you if I can write to you?"

"I will be delighted, Aunty, if you do – and I will write back promptly!"

"I've always wished that I had a daughter. I will be so happy if you would keep in touch with me. I will not overwhelm you, I promise!"

"Sure, Aunty, please feel free to write anytime, and I will write back."

"Of course, you know, we live in a small village, so I won't have much to write to you, but you, living in the U.K., will have more to say - I hope."

"Sure, I will tell you all about our college and Rafiq and me, and other things."

"Thank you. I will look forward to that," said Yasmin, before handing the call to Salim.

"Hello, Shama, how are you? Is Rafiq good to you?" Salim asked when he got on the call.

"Oh, Uncle, Rafiq loves and spoils me very much. You have a very nice son. You just have to tell him not to waste money buying me things!"

"You know Shama, when Yasmin and I dated, which means that we smiled at each other and held hands for a few minutes when we met secretly, I wanted to buy so many things for her, but I had no money. Even after we married, I could not give her the things that I wanted to. I'm happy that Rafiq is spoiling you. Let him spoil you. He won't spoil you so much when he is earning his own money!" he laughed, "But focus on your education. That's what you are there for, and we are praying for your happiness and success every day."

"We need your prayers, Uncle. With both our parents' prayers, you won't need to worry about us at all."

"I'm happy to hear that, Shama. I'm sure that your parents will be happy to hear that also. Remember, we may not have met you yet, but we love you very much."

"Thank you, Uncle, and I love Aunty and you, too."

When Shameem passed the phone back to Rafiq, his parents told him how happy they were to speak to Shameem. "Care for her and do all that you can to make her happy. Buy her a nice birthday gift from us. Tell us what it costs, and we will add the amount to your January allowance," Yasmin said.

TO CALL SHAMEEM'S PARENTS, they had to go to the Post Office downtown, where people paid for overseas calls and were asked to go to a phone booth where they were connected to their party.

They paid £10 and gave the number to call. The operator looked up the code and said, "You will get 20 minutes for this. Go to booth #4."

The call with Shameem's parents was very similar to the one with Rafiq's parents.

Shameem's mother picked up the phone.

"Hello, Mom, how are you?" Shameem asked.

"Shama! I'm so happy to hear your voice!"

They chatted for a few minutes, and Shameem's mom passed the phone to her dad.

"How are you, Shama? We miss you so much."

Shameem told him how much she loved and missed them all, and about her exams and how happy she was in Cardiff with Rafiq.

"We are delighted that you've found a nice boyfriend. I wish that I had met him when he came into our store. Your mom says he is a very fine boy."

"He is, Dad. Here, speak to him."

"Hello, Uncle, how are you?" Rafiq said, taking the phone.

"Fine, Son. Thank you for looking after our Shama. We are so happy that she has met you, but you know, parents worry more about their daughters than their sons when they are away."

"Uncle, you should not worry about Shama, at all. She is a very strong and independent person. She is also very precious to me, and I will never let anything happen to her to cause her, or you, any unhappiness. I promise you that."

"It's very comforting to hear you say this. We pray for your and Shama's happiness and wellbeing every day. I will let you talk to Shama's mom."

"Thank you, Uncle."

"Hello, Rafiq. How are you? I wish that you had come home for lunch that day. We could have gotten to know you better, but with everything that Shama's been writing to us, we feel like we know you very well now!"

"Me too, Aunty. I remember how kind you were to me when I came into your store."

"It was lovely to meet you, and we look forward to meeting you again."

"*Inshallah*" (God willing), "it won't be too long before we meet. Perhaps you can come here sometime?"

"That would be difficult. We have no one to look after the store. We wish that we could, though. We miss Shama so much."

"Aunty, I just told my uncle, you never have to worry about Shama. I will always look after her and never let anything happen to her."

"I know you will, Rafiq. I know you are a fine son of very fine parents, and you have been taught good ethics and values."

"Thank you, Aunty. I will let you speak to Shama. We still have five minutes left. And please, don't worry - she will always be safe and happy with me."

Shameem quickly said her goodbyes when the operator interrupted to say, "You have one minute left in the call."

"My mom said to tell you they love you, and what you said to them was mature and comforting for them. They thank Allah every day that you are in my life."

"I hope that our parents feel reassured. I could feel your parents' concern for you. They love you, and they don't want their daughter to get pregnant before she finishes her education and gets married, or to be distracted from her studies."

Shameem was surprised that Rafiq had mentioned her parents' - and his parents' - fears about her becoming pregnant.

"We know that will not happen. I hope that they will stop worrying," she said.

"No, they won't stop worrying, but having talked to us, hopefully, they will worry less."

1960
Thirty-Nine

Before leaving for London, Rafiq called Anil to ask him to inform Mrs. Jackson of their arrival time. He asked if Rehana had found a place for them to go to for Shameem's birthday.

"I asked her, and she said that she doesn't know of any special place. In the time she has been here, she has gone out dancing only once until she started teaching me to dance. She had gone MECCA dancing with a couple of her white girlfriends. Rehana has a nice face and a great figure, but she is of dark complexion. The guys with no partners asked her friends to dance, but no one, except one jerk, asked her for a dance. After two dances, he asked her if she wanted to go home with him for the night."

"So, what will we do? There must be hundreds of places in London we can go to."

"We looked up *What's On in London* – it's a guide to London's entertainment scene. The problem is the timing. December 24th is what they call here Christmas Eve – different from New Year's Eve. This is a special evening when friends and families get together for good food and drinks, and many go out for dinner. Many of the better quality restaurants are fully booked on Christmas Eve and have expensive sct menus. At the upper end, there are places like The Savoy, which is a prestigious hotel in London, where a dinner and dancing package is £12 Shs.10 per person. Drinks are extra. There are also nice places in the West End where Christmas Eve packages are £7 Shs.10 per person."

"Where do you think we should go?"

"Rehana thinks the West End restaurants will be good and we can afford the packages there. She has offered to pay for herself, but I will pay for the two of us, so you are looking at spending around £20 for Shameem and you both."

"This sounds good, but I want to take Shama to a very special place. Please thank Rehana for checking and ask her to check if we can get a reservation at The Savoy. You and Rehana will be my guests."

"Are you sure, Rafiq? You are looking at spending £50 for the four of us."

"My dad is sending me £50 for the London trip. Let's have a great celebration for Shama."

ON FRIDAY, WHEN ANIL came home, Rafiq and Shameem were already there. Rafiq was all ready to go to Jamatkhana. Anil rushed upstairs, hugged Rafiq, and quickly showered and got dressed in one of his smart Austin Reed suits.

When they came down and knocked on Shameem's door, she emerged wearing a beautiful burgundy colored skirt suit. She looked stunning.

Looking at Anil, she said, "Anil?" and without waiting for him to say yes, she hugged him and said, "I'm so happy to meet you! Rafiq loves you like a brother. He has told me so much about you."

"I am delighted to meet you, Shameem."

"Call me Shama, Anil. We are family."

Mrs. Jackson, who had appeared to see them off, said, "Anil, your friend has such a beautiful cousin!"

They quickly said goodbye to her and flagged down a taxi. "What is this cousin business about? I'm not your cousin!" Shameem said to Rafiq.

"Anil had to tell her that you are my cousin, or she might not have allowed you to stay here. So we are cousins, Okay?"

Shameem laughed.

AFTER DINNER AT THE Surma Bleu, they attended Friday prayers at the Centre and went to No. 1 for coffee with Karim and Zabin.

Zabin asked Shameem, "Had you been to the Centre before?"

"No, this was my first time. It's so different from Nairobi Jamatkhanas, but being able to sit down with the congregation in prayers after over three months was a wonderful and peaceful experience for me."

"It was for me, too. You are fortunate to have a Jamatkhana here," said Rafiq.

"Yes, but this friend of yours does not come to Jamatkhana more than once a month," Karim said, poking Anil in the ribs.

"Oh, lay off, Karim. You know that Anil works and studies hard otherwise, you will be on his case. He's a good kid," said Zabin.

They sat and chatted until after 10.00 p.m. and then returned home.

THE NEXT MORNING, AFTER sharing birthday hugs with Shameem and offering prayers for her happiness, giving her birthday cards and gifts, the three had a leisurely breakfast.

Anil stayed home to study, and Rafiq took Shameem to Oxford Street. This was the busiest time of the year for the Street, which was filled with last-minute shoppers. Rafiq wanted to take Shameem into some ladies' wear stores. The merchandise display for Christmas was amazing to look at.

"No, Rafiq, I don't have room in my suitcase for even one more skirt," laughed Shameem.

"Then let's buy another suitcase! My mom told me to get you a special birthday gift from my dad and her. We have to look for something."

"Let's use the money to pay for this evening."

"I have provisions for the evening's costs, and that will be my gift."

"How much can we spend on your parents' gift for me?"

"Will £25 be enough?"

"Enough? That's a lot!"

As they walked, they came to one of several large jewelry stores. Shameem looked at the jewelry in the window and said, "Can we go in?"

She looked at a gold plated necklace, earrings, and bracelet set with shining zircons. Rafiq put the chain around her neck, and when she looked in the mirror, she ran her hand over it and smiled a little. She put on the earrings and liked them too. The price tag read £15.

"Do you have a ring to go with that?" Rafiq asked the lady serving them.

"Not a part of this set, but I can show you some that would match."

As the lady went looking, Shameem asked with a sly smile, "So we are getting engaged now?"

"No, I will buy you the engagement ring with my own money in good time."

Shameem tried some rings and selected one with a large zircon centerpiece for £5.

As they exited the store, Shameem said, "Let's use the £5 balance to call your parents and thank them."

"Sure. Will you wear the set tonight?" Rafiq asked.

"I will. I'll wear my new black dress from the man I love, and I will wear the beautiful jewelry from his parents whom I love, also," she said with a smile.

ANIL CAME DOWN TO get a cup of tea before leaving for The Savoy. He was dressed in an Austin Reed mohair suit he had bought for this occasion.

Mrs. Jackson whispered to him, "Go for your friend's cousin. She won't be able to resist someone as smart as you."

"I think she has a boyfriend, Mrs. Jackson."

"Pity."

Rafiq came down and knocked on Shameem's door.

"One minute." She said and emerged in five. It was worth the wait to see her in her black dress, zircons shining like real diamonds around her neck, on her ears and wrist, and her smart black shoes. For the occasion, Rafiq had worn one of his dark blue suits, a red tie on a white Italian spread collar shirt.

REHANA HAD OFFERED TO make her way, but Rafiq insisted that they pick her up.

They flagged down a cab and picked up Rehana. She, too, was wearing a black dress and looked very elegant. After being introduced to Rafiq and Shameem, she thanked them for inviting her.

"We have to thank you, Rehana, for finding this place and for teaching Anil to dance."

"Anil is a natural! After two lessons, he was good to go, but I kept him coming for more because *I* love to dance!"

THE HOTEL WAS EVEN more plush and opulent than they had imagined. The maître d' led them to their table when they arrived at the Belvedere Room in the hotel. The room had subdued blue lighting, high-quality furniture, linen, china, and silverware. Rehana had booked a table near the dance floor.

As they ordered drinks, Rafiq asked Rehana, "Would you like to order some wine with dinner?"

"I do like wine with my dinner, but Anil told me that you guys don't drink."

"We don't, but you do, and we want you to enjoy your meal." Looking at the waiter, Rafiq asked, "What's your best wine?"

"No, no, not that, Rafiq! That can cost £100 for a bottle!" Rehana interrupted before the waiter could answer. Rafiq obviously did not know much about wines. The waiter nodded in agreement.

"I'll just have a glass of Chardonnay," Rehana said.

They placed their soft drinks and dinner orders – chateaubriand for Shameem and Rafiq, salmon for Rehana, and flank steak for Anil. The band was playing dance music, and some couples were already on the ballroom floor.

"Most of the people here are from the upper echelons of British society. People like us are a rarity here. Also, teenagers like you three don't come here. This place is for the adults. See how well dressed these people are. But then the three of you are just as well or better dressed than some of them." Rehana said.

"You too are dressed like a model, Rehana," Shameem said.

ANIL AND REHANA TOOK to the floor.

"Wow, look at the way she moves. She just flows with the music on fast and slow beats." Rafiq said, pointing to Rehana.

"And look at Anil! How well he is dancing!" exclaimed Shameem.

Rafiq and Shameem joined them on the dance floor. They stayed true to their training but enjoyed dancing to the band's fantastic music.

When they all returned to the table, Rafiq said, "Rehana, you have to teach me to dance like Anil."

"Sure, come on, that's a nice Rumba tune they are playing!" she exclaimed, pulling Rafiq back to the floor. "Anil, please bring Shama."

"But we don't know how to dance to this tune," Rafiq said.

"Now, you do. Get up."

When they got on the dance floor, Rehana said, "Now forget your dancing lessons – there are no set steps for this Latin American beat. You just move with the music."

They started dancing. This was much more fun than their stilted Fox Trot and Quick-Step. After two dances, both Rehana and Anil let go of Rafiq and Shameem's hands and let them dance independently. They were both doing well. Seeing how much fun these two young couples were having, the band played two Latin American numbers ending with a cha cha cha dance. The group took a break, and the four returned to their table.

"Now, you are both good enough to participate in any dancing competition," Rehana said

"Oh, no. But thank you so much for teaching us to dance. I have never enjoyed dancing so much – not that I have done much dancing." Shameem said.

"Me too, I am sweating. I am glad I am wearing my *Old Spice* deodorant."

Dinner was served, followed by desserts. The food was delicious, and the service was flawless. Rehana finished three glasses of wine and was now in a great mood. She was dancing even more freely.

"I have never been happier on my birthday than today, Rafiq. Thank you for doing this for me." Shameem said.

'You are most welcome. And we have to thank Rehana and Anil for bringing us here."

At that moment, two waiters emerged from the kitchen singing 'Happy Birthday' and carrying a large, layered cake on which was written, 'Happy Birthday, Dear Shama'

Some in the room clapped as the cake was placed before Shameem. She was overwhelmed and blushing crimson. Tears ran down her face as she blew out the candles and cut the cake. Two elderly couples dancing nearby came over to wish her happy birthday.

The house photographer was waiting to take pictures. Rafiq gently wiped Shameem's tears, and she posed with the knife in her hand to cut the cake again. The photographer took several pictures of everyone hugging Shameem and Rafiq kissing her.

When things quietened down, Shameem asked the waiter to pass the cake pieces around to the other guests, if they wanted it. Soon, they could see the cake at a few tables. They heard one patron say, "Oh, give me a larger slice. That's too small."

"Whose idea was this?" Rafiq asked.

"Rehana's. She arranged everything as her gift to you."

"Rehana, this is too much. Your good wishes and prayers were enough," Shameem said.

"We wanted to make this a memorable day for you."

"Thank you; thank you both so much for your sentiments and affection," Shameem said, with tears in her eyes.

After dinner, they were back on the dance floor and danced until closing time.

ANIL, RAFIQ, AND SHAMEEM stayed home on Christmas day. Christmas dinner with Mrs. Jackson was a new experience for them. They had never eaten turkey before, and they liked it.

Over the next week, Anil and Rafiq took Shameem around London. They visited some places they had not been to with Robert. They saw the stage production of *My Fair Lady*, for which Shameem wore one of her outfits and attended Jamatkhana at the Ismaili Centre on Friday, for which Shameem could use another of her new dresses. Rafiq took Shameem to see *The Mousetrap*. This was another opportunity to dress up.

After attending evening prayers at The Ismaili Centre, they bought four tickets for the next evening's Ismaili Centre's New Year's Eve dinner dance, which was open to non-Ismaili guests of Ismaili participants. Rehana was to go with them.

The event, for which Shameem had reserved her second favorite outfit, was a delightful experience. Shameem met a few people from Nairobi whom she knew. Anil and Rehana impressed the crowd with their dance moves. Together, they rang in 1961 with laughter and a sense of hope for the future.

1961
Forty

Shameem and Rafiq returned to Cardiff at the beginning of January and celebrated Rafiq's 19th birthday on January 2nd with a quiet dinner at The Rose of India. After all the fun in London, Rafiq did not want any more celebrations.

The start of their second college term forced Rafiq and Shameem back to their books and routine. London was now a happy and somewhat distant memory. On the first day of their term, they were handed back the first term exam papers. Rafiq had scored an A- average. With a B+ average, Shameem was second in her class. Both were delighted with their performance. Rafiq repeatedly told Shameem that the courses he was taking were easier (which was true) than what she was taking.

ANIL FORWARDED TO RAFIQ a letter that he had received from Rehana's husband thanking him and his friends for taking Rehana with them to The Savoy and the Ismaili Centre event. He had not heard of Anil's community, but Rehana had told him how welcome she was made to feel by everyone and the compliments she had received for her dancing. She had told him how much she had enjoyed the two evenings, and he was deeply grateful to them for looking after his wife.

Anil had written back to him to say that it had been their good fortune to know Rehana and that they were grateful for her friendship, mentorship, and company.

Shameem had received a loving letter from Yasmin and had written back telling her everything that they had done in London and how much fun they had.

Mrs. Bowe's work at Cecil's had ended. She missed the job but was happy and grateful for the experience. She had sent applications for sales staff and clerical positions, which Rafiq had prepared for her, to several businesses. Most had responded to say that they were not hiring at this time but would keep her application in their files. And then, at the end of January, she received a letter from Cecil's telling her they had a 10.00 a.m. to 2.00 p.m. opening at the store. The position paid £5 a week, and the letter instructed her to call the store immediately if she was interested. She walked over to the phone booth and accepted the position right away. They asked her to report to work the next day. She could not wait to give Shameem and Rafiq the good news.

"You won't believe this," she said when Shameem walked in. "Ask Rafiq in. Cecil's sent this letter, and I start tomorrow."

Rafiq and Shameem looked at the letter and hugged Mrs. Bowes. "Congratulations. We're so happy for you."

THE FIRST-YEAR COLLEGE INTERNAL exams were set for the last week of June, after which the college would close for two months. Shameem and Rafiq had worked hard and were happy with their performance.

They spent three weeks of their vacation in London, during which time they visited the Lake District and made day trips to seaside resorts of Brighton and Plymouth with Anil. Other than that, they spent the summer lazing around in Cardiff. While in London, Rafiq received a letter from his father, forwarded from Cardiff, which, in part, read:

The date for Tanganyika's independence is set for December 9th . TANU, which had won the election with an overwhelming majority, will form the new government with Julius Nyerere as the Prime Minister. You were right in your assessment of how quickly Tanganyika would become independent. Everyone had expected Kenya and Uganda, both of which have larger populations of educated Africans and are more prosperous, to precede Tanganyika. They are not far behind. I believe that both countries will be independent within two years.

Everything is progressing peacefully. The D.C. and Jane will be returning to the U.K. in early January. They have decided to settle in Cardiff, near their children, instead of in London, as they had planned to do earlier.

You will be pleased to know that Chelsea will become the Principal Secretary of the Education Ministry. This means that she will be the most senior civil servant in the Ministry (like a Deputy Minister in other Commonwealth countries). She believes she could have become a minister if she had been a Tanganyikan. She plans to become a Tanganyika citizen after independence and could, in the future, have a senior political position. She was offered the Ambassadorship to the U.S.A., but she chose to stay with her area of knowledge. She thanks the D.C. for her progress. She is highly respected and has become known all over Tanganyika. Her picture appears in the newspapers regularly. Usually, there is not much of a story to go with the pictures, so I think it is because she looks beautiful on the front pages. She and Ricardo will move to stay in Dar es Salaam. Ricardo will have to find something to do there. I wouldn't be surprised if a position, not related to his work, is found for him in the Civil Service. After all, he is brilliant.

Mr. Nkwabi, whom the D.C. mentored for his position, will, of course, become our new D.C. He has become a good friend and a Club member. We believe he is not going to do anything to take the Mpwapwa government business away from Almin.

I am worried about Mom, though, losing both her friends in Mpwapwa. Chelsea, Jane, and she have become very close and have, of late, spent so much time together that Chelsea and Jane's departure will create a big void in her life.

"So, Tanganyika is becoming independent, and my dad says Kenya and Uganda will soon follow," Rafiq said to Anil and Shameem when he read his dad's letter and passed it on to them to read.

"I worry about what this will mean for our families. What if the transition is not peaceful?" Anil asked.

"From everything I have read and what my dad says, the Tanganyikans are eagerly awaiting independence, but Nyerere has set the right tone. *Uhuru na Kazi*, Freedom and Hard Work, is his motto. People understand that independence will not mean that they can take over our homes and businesses and cars and drive us out. They will have to work hard to build the nation and earn what our parents have worked for, for over a century."

"I don't share your optimism, Rafiq. Sooner or later, the Africans will turn on us in Tanganyika, and also in Uganda and Kenya. I don't mean there will be violence against us, but they will not allow us to maintain our privileged economic status for long."

"Tanganyika is endowed with much fertile land, and there is no tribalism there. The country is blessed with the leadership of illustrious people like Nyerere and Chelsea and vast quantities of natural resources. Our National Parks - the Serengeti, Ngorongoro, and Manyara - are the best in Africa. We have miles of white, sandy beaches. Tanganyika can become the number one tourist destination in Africa. If the country remains peaceful and people get access to education and work hard, there is no reason why there should not be a class of Africans in Tanganyika that is far larger and more prosperous than the Indians in ten years."

"True, but when you can confiscate businesses, property, and wealth from a small privileged group instead of having to work for it, the temptation to do the former is always stronger."

"That would be very unfortunate if that happens in Tanganyika. I doubt it will happen - ever."

"Kenya, you know, is a different story. The Kikuyus and Luos - the two major tribes - have little love for and are deeply suspicious of one another. The Kenyans are much more assertive than the Tanganyikans and Ugandans. I hope and pray that they can unite behind one leader as the Tanganyikans have done after Nyerere. There will be bloodshed, otherwise," Shameem said.

"Don't worry, Shama, Jomo Kenyatta is emerging as that leader in Kenya. Independence will be peaceful," Rafiq said, with certainty.

"Yes, but he is Kikuyu. Will the Luos accept him?" asked Anil.

"After trying and imprisoning Kenyatta for allegedly leading the Mau Mau, the British are now positioning him as the grand old man of Kenya because they have seen the decency and humanity in him and will work to position him to get elected as the first Prime Minister," said Rafiq.

"You can look at everything with rose-colored glasses, Rafiq. I'm not so confident," said Anil.

IN EARLY AUGUST, RAFIQ received a letter from his father asking him to call. Rafiq called at the designated time, and his dad told him that as he had advised him earlier, the country was moving rapidly towards independence. According to Chelsea, the British would soon appoint an "Internally Responsible" government to be led by Nyerere's TANU, and Tanganyika would be independent on December 9th, as planned.

The D.C. had told them that it needed only a small faction left out of power to create serious problems. He had suggested that they should keep their savings in the U.K., just to be safe. They had accumulated Shs.200,000 in cash with which they had planned to buy the property they occupied in Mpwapwa, a rental property in Dodoma, and a new Peugeot 504 sedan. The D.C. had advised that they should postpone the property and automobile purchases until the post-independence period. They had decided to do so and would transfer Shs. 200,000 (£10,000) into his account, which he should deposit into interest-earning savings account with the bank. Additional deposits would follow. In aggregate, the two businesses were generating over Shs.12,000 per month in net income. Their living expenses were less than Shs.3,000 per month, which included the Shs.1,000 allowance that they were sending to Rafiq.

The D.C. had also told them that when Tanganyika became independent, it would likely offer citizenship to all non-Africans who were born in Tanganyika, or who had resided there for a specified period. They, like the majority of the Indians, held passports issued by the British, which classified them as "British Protected Persons". When Tanganyika became independent, these passports would be nullified. Such passport holders would have the option to apply for Tanganyikan or

British citizenship. He had strongly recommended that whereas Salim and Yasmin should apply for the Tanganyikan citizenship because they wanted to stay and do business in Tanganyika, Rafiq should apply for British citizenship. When he graduated, he would not be able to return to Tanganyika and work there, but if he became an economist, he would get a long-term work permit without any difficulty.

The D.C. was knowledgeable in these matters, and Rafiq knew that he should do what he was recommending. When the money came into his account, Rafiq transferred it to the Barclays branch, where Bernice worked. Bernice, who was now Accounts Manager, was able to get Rafiq 0.5% more in annual interest than his branch had offered. He immediately became a preferred customer at the branch, and the deposit served to enhance Bernice's standing for attracting a large deposit. Rafiq maintained the savings account he had opened at his branch, in which he still had over £200.

Rafiq provided the account information (which listed his parents as beneficiaries) to his parents into which they transferred £350 to £400 each month.

OVER THE PAST THREE months, Shameem and Yasmin had exchanged letters regularly. Shameem had told Rafiq that she was corresponding with his mom, but had not told him what they were writing to each other. When he asked, Shameem had replied, "Women just talk. You wouldn't be interested in the specifics."

SHAMEEM AND RAFIQ RETURNED to college at the beginning of September. Their second year at the college was much like their first. They worked hard, went to London for the Christmas vacation, celebrated Shameem's birthday at another fancy place that Rehana had found in the West End, and attended the Ismaili New Year's Eve dinner dance. They celebrated Rafiq's 20th birthday on January 2nd with Bernice and Robert, MECCA dancing.

1962
Forty-One

Rafiq and Anil applied for British citizenship and, in time, received their British passports. Kenya was a British colony, so Shameem was a British subject. On her parents' advice, she, too, applied for and got the British passport.

They sat for their second-semester internal college exams in April and spent the Easter vacation in Cardiff.

When the vacation was over, and they went back to college, they were told the exam results were available in the principal's office, and the students were scheduled alphabetically to go and meet with the principal to get their results.

"You are going to university, Rafiq," said the principal. "You averaged over 85%, that's an A. I presume you have applied to the LSE?"

"Thank you, Sir. Yes, the London School of Economics is my first choice, and Birmingham and Manchester, both are second choices."

Shameem had a similar reception. "You have averaged 80%, young lady. Where have you applied?"

"To The Westminster College of London University as my first choice, and Birmingham and Manchester as my second choice."

"That's smart. I saw another student earlier today who is doing the same thing – indicating all other universities as his second choice. No university listed as a student's fourth choice will be interested in looking at his or her application. "

"Thank you, Sir."

"You are London University material. Keep up the hard work."

THIS WAS AN OCCASION to celebrate with a good dinner with Robert and Bernice. Robert also had sat for his first-year university qualifying exams and had done very well.

The third college term for Rafiq and Shameem was, for the most part, practicing past exams. This made the "A" level exams in late June, easier for them. Now they had almost 12 weeks of summer vacation. The results would not come out until the end of July. Rafiq had a conditional acceptance from the LSE to take him if he graduated with at least one A, one B, and one C. Shameem had also received acceptance from Westminster College conditional upon scoring one A, and one B. Grade for the third subject did not matter so long as she passed.

Anil, who had written his second part C.A. exam, was not concerned. He had done well and did not need to get any specific grades to move to the next level. He just needed to pass, which he had with flying colors.

Rafiq and Shameem spent much time with Robert, who was also on vacation, making day trips to places near Cardiff. They visited Swansea, a city by the sea, where they dropped in to say hello to Mrs. Bowes' daughter living there. With Bernice, they visited Barrie, a seaside resort, just a short drive from Cardiff. They watched Wimbledon on TV and explored more of the city's parks.

The London University "A" Level results for Shameem and Rafiq arrived in the mail at the end of July.

Rafiq saw his first. He had scored two As and one B. He ran over to Shameem's place. She had not checked her mail yet. She opened the London University envelope with much trepidation. She had passed with two As and a B, as well. Both jumped with joy, hugged, and kissed. They were going to the universities of their choice.

"Let's call home!"

They first called Rafiq's parents from the corner phone booth.

"Dad, we passed! We are both going to London University next year!" Rafiq shouted as soon as he heard his father accept the charges and before he could say hello.

"That's wonderful! Congratulations to Shama and you. We have been praying for you every day. Here, talk to your mom."

"Mom, we both passed with excellent grades! We will be accepted into the colleges of our choice."

"*Mubaraki* (congratulations) to you both! We have been praying for you."

"Shama wants to speak with you, Mom."

"Hello, Aunty!"

"Mubaraki, Shama. Our heartiest mubaraki. We knew that you would pass, but we were praying for good grades."

"Your prayers paid off, Aunty, thank you so much! We love you both. We're going to call my parents. And please, Aunty, keep writing to me. I love to read your letters."

"I will, Shama, and I, too, eagerly look forward to receiving your letters. When I write to you, I truly feel I am writing to my daughter. Please give your parents the good news and convey our regards to them. We love you."

WHEN THE OPERATOR AT the downtown post office connected them, Shameem gave her mom and dad the good news.

Then they called Robert. "I will let Bernice know and we'll take you out for dinner on Saturday. We will celebrate."

Anil could hardly contain his happiness when they called him. Rafiq and Shameem had the grades to come to London. They would all be together.

"Look, after the exams, you guys were too tense for me to suggest that we go on a summer holiday. I can take two weeks of vacation. Now that you have your results, you want to come over to London, and we can go somewhere?"

"Are you suggesting we do what we did last year - trips to Brighton and Eastbourne, or are you thinking of going to Scotland as you were suggesting at one time?" Rafiq asked.

"No, I was thinking of something more exciting. I've been looking into conducted coach tours to Europe. There is one 14-day tour leaving London on August 12th. It would take us to Paris, Venice, Rome, and Barcelona. From Barcelona, the coach can bring us back via the French countryside to Paris and then to London. This, return trip, is a two and a half-day journey. We will have the option if we do not take the coach back to London, to stay on at the Barcelona hotel for one more night as part of the tour package, and then make our way back to London."

"Wow! That sounds exciting. How much would the tour cost?"

"Travel is by luxury coaches, and meals and accommodation are A-class, so it's expensive - £35 per person, double occupancy. The tour operator offers discounted Barcelona to London flights for £7.Shs.10 per person and the visas will cost another £7.Shs.10 per person. You're looking at spending around £50 per person, excluding whatever we spend on personal purchases and other expenses. If you're interested, I can ask Rehana. She has wanted to see Europe before she goes home next year, but she didn't have anyone to go with. Single occupancy is £75, which she can't afford. If we go, Shama and Rehana can share a room, and you and I can share one if that's okay with everyone."

"You check with Rehana, and I'll talk to Shama."

Rafiq knew that Shameem did not have £50, but he had over £200 in his savings account, and if he told his dad that they wanted to see Europe, he would chip in something.

Shameem was excited by the idea, but she did not know how her parents would react to her taking a 14-day tour with Rafiq that he would pay for. Also, they would worry that it would not be Rehana she would be sharing the rooms with for the full fourteen days.

"I know you have over £200 in your account, and I am comfortable with you paying for me, but what do I tell my parents? They will be offended if I say you will pay for me. I know they will not want it to look like I am taking charity."

"Let's think it through, and then we can talk to them together," he said.

"I'm sorry, Rafiq, I just don't think that I can suggest something like this to them. They will also worry about our being together for two weeks. They may think we'll end up sharing rooms."

"But we can't do that. For us to share a room, Anil would have to sleep in Rehana's room, and he certainly can't do that."

"Yes, but my parents, and yours too, they don't know this. I don't think that we can do this at this time. We will Inshallah go to Europe for our honeymoon when we are married."

Rafiq was disappointed. At the same time, he appreciated Shameem's position. He wished that Anil had not suggested this idea. He had wanted to see Paris, Rome, Florence, Lisbon, Venice, Madrid, Barcelona, and other European cities and had written to his parents about traveling there at some point during his stay in the U.K., but had not contemplated doing this during his second summer vacation. Anil had come up with this proposal, and they had nothing to do for at least ten weeks of summer. This was so tempting.

HE KEPT THINKING ABOUT it all day. He did not want to say anything more to Shameem. He called Robert in the evening to tell him what Anil had suggested and hear his thoughts.

"That sounds exciting. So, are you going?"

"We have a problem - two problems, actually. One is that Shama can't afford to spend £50; I have the money to pay for her, but her parents will be offended if we suggest that I will pay for her trip. The second is that they will worry that Shama and I may end up sharing rooms on the tour."

"You don't have to tell them you will share rooms."

"But we *won't* share rooms, Rob! She'll share her accommodation with Anil's friend, Rehana."

"But you're both nearly 20 years old and in love!" protested Robert.

"Rob, can we please focus on my problem? Do you have any ideas about what we can do, and if we do go, do you and Bernice want to come with us?"

"I have a summer job, and I don't think that Bernice can afford it, but why don't you talk to your dad about your plan? He's smart, and maybe he can find a way."

"What can he do?"

"I don't know, but he may have some ideas."

RAFIQ THOUGHT ABOUT ROBERT'S suggestion all night and called his dad in the morning, not really knowing what to expect.

He told his dad about Anil's European vacation idea and that he could pay for Shameem, but that this would not be acceptable to her parents and they may also be afraid that he and Shameem may share rooms.

"Shama is right. I have to talk to your mom about this, Rafiq. I, personally, believe that traveling is an education and should be a part of your life. I would like very much for you both to see Europe. I want you to see the world, but you are talking about a 14-day tour. You are saying Shama will share rooms with Anil's friend, Rehana, and nothing is going on between Anil and Rehana. Can you assure me, before I talk to your mom, that there will be nothing for us to be concerned about if you and Shama go on this tour?"

"Dad, there is nothing Shama and I can do on the tour that we could not have already done here. We spend many evenings together alone at her place when her landlady is gone for hours. You have my word. Nothing will happen."

"Okay, your mom and I may be okay, but I don't know what we can do about Shama's parents."

"But mom has become friends with Gulshan aunty, hasn't she? Can she not talk to her?"

"This is a delicate matter. I don't know if she will want to do that. Let me talk to her. Call me tomorrow."

WHEN SALIM TALKED TO Yasmin about his call with Rafiq, she said, "I can't ask Gulshan to allow our son to take their daughter to Europe for two weeks and pay for her! How would you like it if you had a daughter and someone proposed this to you?"

"You can tell them what Rafiq told me. There's nothing they can do on the tour that they could not have done already in Cardiff."

"Good Lord! And what about the money part? How do you expect they will react if I imply to her mother that they can't pay for Shama's trip, and our son will pay for their daughter?"

"Well, that's true. That's the difficult part."

"It's too bad. You will have to tell Rafiq that he should forget about this and not come up with such irresponsible requests."

LATER THAT EVENING, AS Yasmin and Salim sat down for dinner, Yasmin said, "I have this one thought. I can call Gulshan and congratulate her on Shama's success in her exams and say that Rafiq has called to say that his friend Anil has suggested to him that the four of them go on a two-week coach tour of France, Italy, and Spain. Shama will share rooms with Anil's friend Rehana, and the two boys will share rooms. We are fine with the idea. I can say that we had wanted to give Rafiq and Shama a nice gift for passing their exams and since Rafiq has told us about something they would really like to do if it's okay for Gulshan and Bahadur, you and I would like to pay for their tour package and that would be our gift to the kids."

"A good idea, Yasmin, but that would not be entirely honest…"

"Which part of it would not be honest? We had talked about giving them gifts. I thought we would send them £10 each and ask them to buy something they liked. And it would become honest if we actually pay for the tour for both of them instead of Rafiq paying for Shama. All I would be asking Gulshan is if they are okay with us giving their daughter this gift."

"That just might work, Yasmin. But Anil doesn't know yet if his friend, Rehana, can go with them."

"Let's worry about her later. Maybe, Rafiq can subsidize Rehana's expenses if she can't afford the full cost. Tell Rafiq when he calls tomorrow that the tour will be a gift for both of them from us, and he should speak to Shama. He can tell her what assurance he has given us and get her consent for me to speak to her mother."

WHEN RAFIQ CALLED THE next day, Salim told him what his mother had offered to do and that she wanted Shameem's consent for her to do this. Rafiq was happy. "I will speak to Shama and call you back."

Shameem didn't appreciate Rafiq talking to his dad without speaking to her first.

"I'm sorry, Shama, I should have talked to you first. I called him because Rob suggested it. I didn't ask him to pay for our trips. This is their idea - honestly."

"I don't know if it's a good idea for your mom to talk to my mother about this. They have established a good relationship. My mom may be offended by what your mother would say to her, and it may damage their relationship. Is it worth the risk?"

"I know the risk, but my mom is very diplomatic. She will minimize the risk."

"Let me think."

"Okay, Shama. The tour leaves in less than two weeks, and it's selling out, so we will need to decide soon."

SHAMEEM THOUGHT FOR TWO days and then said to Rafiq, "I have misgivings about this, but tell your mom that she can talk to my mother. If she senses any resistance on my mother's part, she should back off immediately, change the subject and talk about other things."

YASMIN WAS NERVOUS AS the phone rang in the CINEX camera store. Bahadur picked it up. After exchanging pleasantries, he put Gulshan on the line.

"Hello, Gulshan, how are you?"

"What a pleasant surprise, Yasmin. I've been meaning to call you to congratulate you on Rafiq and Shama's success. We are delighted."

"Mubaraki to Bahadur, Adil, and you, too. Did Shama tell you that she scored the highest grades in her class?"

"She told me her grades, but did not say that she was at the top of her class."

"We thank Allah for our children's success. Salim and I were thinking of sending them some gifts for their success and admission into universities, but before we could decide on what, Rafiq called and said that his friend Anil is suggesting that they go on a European coach tour. Anil has a friend named Rehana who may be interested in going with them. She is older and married and treats Anil like her younger brother. Her husband is in Trinidad. Anil says that if she comes, Shama and Rehana can share rooms, and Anil and Rafiq will share rooms. The tour would take them to Paris, Rome, Venice, and Barcelona. Salim and I think this would be a great experience for our children and it would be a perfect gift for us to give them. I wanted to check with you that you are comfortable with us giving this tour gift to Shama."

"Wow! I have always dreamt of seeing London, Paris, and Rome. Surely, this would be a great opportunity for our children, but Shama has not called to say anything about this, and do you feel comfortable sending our children together to Europe for two weeks?"

"I think that we need to treat our children as responsible adults. They have demonstrated discipline and maturity in achieving their scores at the college. I think that it speaks to their sense of responsibility. After all, what is it that Shama and Rafiq can do in Europe that they could not have already done in Cardiff? Both have given us assurances, and Salim and I have decided not to worry about those things anymore."

"Bahadur also tells me the same thing. I would be delighted for them to go on the tour and I am sure Bahadur will be too. Thank you so much for offering to pay for the tour. What will it cost?"

"£50 per person."

"£50? That's 1,000 Shillings! My God, that's a lot of money. We can't accept such a large gift for Shama. No, Yasmin, we can't do that. Bahadur will never agree."

"Gulshan, the way we look at it, we are giving £100 to both our children. Shama is very dear to us, and we see her as our child also. If going on this tour will be beneficial for her and makes her happy, it will give us as much happiness as Rafiq enjoying it and benefitting from it. We see this as an educational experience for them. But I will respect your wishes. If you are uncomfortable with this gift idea, we can think of something smaller."

"Let me speak to Bahadur and call you back."

"THAT DIDN'T GO TOO well. I wish I had not done it." Yasmin said to Salim as she hung up.

"What did she say?" asked Salim.

"She was all excited and happy to accept our gift, but balked when I told her how much it would be."

"So she said 'No'?"

"She's going to talk to Bahadur and call me back. I doubt that they will agree. I think this was a bad idea ... "

"THE PHONE RANG THE next morning, and the operator said, "Hold for a call from Nairobi."

Yasmin's hands were sweating as she held the phone to hear Gulshan. Instead, it was Bahadur on the line.

"Yasmin, Gulshan and I are really grateful to you for the gift you want to give to Rafiq and Shama. You do think of Shama as your child, don't you?"

"Yes, Shama is becoming for me the girl that I never had. Salim and I think she is a gift from heaven for us. We pray for her every day, and if we could close the store, we would be on the next flight to the U.K. to meet her."

"Shama has shared some letters you have written to her with Gulshan, and they made her cry. There is so much affection in your words. You talk to her like she is your flesh and blood."

"She is a lovely child. I always wished for a daughter, and now I feel that I have the chance to have one. I'm dying to see her and hold her in my arms."

"That's what I told Gulshan – that you are not looking at Shama as Rafiq's girl-friend. You are looking at her as your daughter. Let's do this, Yasmin, let's share the gift. We can contribute £50, and you add £50."

"That would be fair, but then you would be gifting £50 to Shama, and we would be gifting £50 to Rafiq. Where is our gift for Shama in this? We want to give one gift of £100 to them, both. We will be very happy if you allow us to do this. You can give your gifts to the kids. It doesn't have to be £100. It can be whatever amount if it is wrapped in your love and prayers."

"I cannot argue with that. You know, you can go ahead and gift them the tour and please accept our deepest gratitude for your affection for our daughter."

"THAT WAS A LONG 'No'," Salim said, as Yasmin hung up.

"No, it was a 'Yes.' Send a telegram to Rafiq and ask him to book the tour if Rehana can go with them. Also, ask him to call, and you can tell him about my conversation with Shama's parents and tell him to subsidize Rehana's cost for up to £25 if she can't afford it all. I want them to go see Europe."

1962
Forty-Two

Rafiq called Anil to tell him that he and Shameem were ready to book the tour if seats were still available.

"When I suggested the idea to Rehana, she was very excited, but she had two concerns. She wondered if Shameem would be okay sharing rooms with her and, of course, if she could afford it. After much thinking and communicating with her husband, she has decided to come if Shama will not mind sharing rooms with her."

"Shama is fine sharing rooms with Rehana. Can we book?"

"Let me check with the tour operators and get back to you."

ANIL CALLED THE NEXT day and said, "We've got the seats. These were the last four of the 30 seats. In fact, they had only two left and today, one couple cancelled so we got four. Now that we're just a week from departure, they need non-refundable 50% deposits by tomorrow. I have to pay them £70, or we may lose the seats."

"Please get me their bank information, and I will get my bank to transfer £35 to them today. Are you okay with your £35?"

"Yes, we are. I'm so excited!"

"Me, too," said Rafiq, with a happy smile.

THE COACH WAS LUXURIOUS with reclining seats, air conditioning, and a bathroom.

They arrived in Paris on Saturday afternoon. After dinner at a nearby restaurant (part of the package), the tour group was taken to the world-famous Moulin Rouge cabaret show. It was unlike anything anyone in the group had seen. This was followed by a late evening tour of the Eiffel Tower. Looking down on Paris from the Tower was indeed a thrill of a lifetime.

After the Eiffel Tower tour, the group was brought back to the hotel, which was in proximity to the Tower. Rehana suggested that they walk around and explore Paris by night. They made their way to the world-famous Champs Élysées and walked up and down the mile-long avenue running between the Place de la Concorde and the Place Charles de Gaulle, where the Arc de Triomphe is located. Well past midnight, the Champs Élysées was still lively with its theatres, cafés, and restaurants. They decided to have a late-night snack in one of the bistros and were a little surprised to see the prices. Rafiq had given Anil £50 to pay for any meals not covered by the tour package and all other incidentals so that he could keep an account of their expenses. They would divide up the cost at the end of the tour. He told Anil, Rehana, and Shameem to not worry about the prices, and that if the expenses added up to more than £10 per person, the additional amounts would be his treat. He wanted everyone to enjoy the tour.

Over the next two days, the tour took them to Notre Dame Cathedral, the Basilica of Sacré-Coeur on the Rue Montmartre, the Louvre museum, Eiffel Tower (by the day) and the Arc de Triomphe. The tour guide was highly knowledgeable and patient, and it was a pleasure to hear her speak. She had made it her business to get to know everyone in the group and sought feedback on the tour and her commentary whenever she had the opportunity to sit or walk with the group members individually or in small groups.

The group was given two hours to walk up and down the Champs Élysées, where most of them had their lunches at the sidewalk cafés. The evenings were free. They spent most of their time just walking around the city center. This city of lights was dazzling at night. Dinners were included in the package, and they were given a choice of three restaurants. They tried a different one on each of the three nights and got a real taste of French cuisine.

THE TOUR DEPARTED PARIS on August 15th, and after a very long drive with stops for lunch and an overnight stop for dinner in Milan, they arrived in Venice the following evening.

The accommodation was adjacent to St. Mark's Square ("the Square"). Most of the group retired to their rooms after dinner, but Rafiq insisted that they walk over to the Square, which, with "the little Square" of Venice, forms the social, religious, and political center of the city.

The Square was lively and filled with people. Just being in St. Mark's Square was exciting. Café orchestras played a variety of tunes. They could move from one café to another when the musicians took a break. Listening to the dancing music, all of Rehana's and Anil's fatigue was gone. They joined the happy crowds to dance to Italian music and pulled Rafiq and Shameem on the floor.

They danced, walked, sat, sipped coffee, and watched the crowds until past midnight, and then returned to their hotel.

Over the next two days, they visited Saint Mark's Basilica (the most famous of the city's churches, nicknamed the Church of Gold for its opulent design and gold ground mosaics), the Rialto Bridge (the oldest and one of the four bridges spanning the Grand Canal), the white limestone enclosed Bridge of Sighs, St Mark's Campanile, and the Doge's Palace with its opulent public chambers adorned with masterpieces of Renaissance art. They explored the Grand Canal, Venice's major traffic corridor by gondola, and other significant symbols of the city, including the Venetian Lagoon. And, of course, they enjoyed the Italian cuisine.

They departed Venice in the early morning on August 18th and arrived in Rome six hours later in the afternoon. The evening was free for the group to walk around Rome. They joined some in the group who were taking a walking tour of the city that brought them to places not listed in the top ten attractions of Rome, but gave them a good taste of the town.

On the first day of their official tour, they visited the Roman Forum, which the tour guide said had served as the site for gladiatorial contests, victory celebrations, public speeches, and trials of prominent people. From there, they moved to the Coliseum, the oval amphitheater in the center of the city, which the tour guide said could accommodate around 70,000 spectators and was used for gladiatorial fights and other spectacles, including re-enactments of victories in major battles, and theatrical performances.

They ended the day at the Trevi Fountain, one of the most famous fountains in the world, and like all tourists, threw coins in the fountain for good luck. They spent the entire evening sitting and walking around the fountain. It was an exciting experience for them to watch the hundreds of tourists and locals gather around the fountain and enjoy the sounds of water and the magnificent sculptures of the fountains.

The next day, they visited the awe-inspiring St. Peter's Basilica in Vatican City, adjacent to the Pope's residence, and generally considered the home of the Roman Catholic Church. The tour then moved to the Sistine Chapel, the official residence of the Pope, famous for the frescos that decorate the interior, and most notably the Chapel's ceiling and *The Last Judgment* by Michelangelo. They could not stop admiring the frescos and wished that more time had been allocated to this part of the tour.

They then proceeded to the Capitoline Hill, one of the Seven Hills of Rome, after which the Capitol Hill in Washington, D.C. is believed to have been named, and visited the Piazza di Spagna, one of the most famous squares in Rome. They ended the day at the nearby Column of the Immaculate Conception of the Blessed Virgin Mary.

On the morning of their third day in Rome, they toured the Borghese Gallery, which houses a substantial part of the Borghese collection of paintings, sculptures, and antiquities. The Gallery collection was unlike they had seen anywhere, and they would have happily spent the entire day looking at the paintings and sculptures, but it was time to leave. After a sidewalk lunch, they departed for Barcelona.

Rome to Barcelona was 800 miles, with short stops in Florence, Pisa, Monaco, and an overnight stop in Cannes. They arrived in Barcelona in the evening on August 22nd. After dining at the hotel, they retired to their rooms.

Their first day in Barcelona began with a tour of La Sagrada Família, Spain's most famous attraction. Rising high into the sky in Barcelona's center, La Sagrada has been a "work in progress" for more than 130 years. The church's organic forms, ornately carved portals, and sky-scraping towers were designed by the modernist architect Antonin Gaudí, who drew inspiration from nature and left an indelible mark on the city where he was born.

The group took the lifts to the towers of each facade and looked down over the splendid architecture below and the city around it.

After a quick lunch, they proceeded to the Gothic Quarter of Barcelona, where they wandered around the winding streets of the Quarter, visited its 600-year old Gothic cathedral, and spent the afternoon visiting Gaudí's most famous works and learning more about his architecture. The tour then moved to Passeig de Gràcia, Barcelona's most expensive shopping street. They looked at and admired the merchandise in the stores but, of course, did not buy anything.

The evening was free. The tour guide had recommended that among other activities, the group should visit La Rambla, the tree-lined pedestrian boulevard. This was a stage for flamenco dancers, fire-eaters, musicians, and other performers. The boulevard was teeming with people. This was one of the most exciting evenings of their entire tour.

On their second day in Barcelona, they visited the National Museum of Catalan Art, which houses church frescos designed by Gaudí and the Romanesque art collection, and the Picasso Museum, which houses over 4,000 works of Pablo Picasso.

The tour then moved to Barcelona's beaches area. The group had the rest of the afternoon and evening free to walk around and enjoy the beaches. Dinner at a designated restaurant in the area was at 9.00 p.m.

It had been two beautiful and exciting days in Barcelona.

REHANA, SHAMEEM, RAFIQ, AND Anil came down into the hotel lobby early the next morning to say goodbye to their fellow tourists. Most were older than them, but they had become friends with many of them. The tour departed on its long journey to Paris, and the four of them were on their own for their additional, third day in Barcelona.

On the hotel concierge's recommendation, they visited the Boqueria Market, one of the world's most famous food markets, took a trip to Montserrat and visited the 11th-century monastery, the holiest site in Catalonia with its Black Virgin of Montserrat, and enjoyed the region and its amazing views before returning to the beaches. They spent the evening walking around the beaches, enjoying drinks and a late dinner, and returned to La Rambla for another evening of flamenco dancers and other performers.

THEY DEPARTED THE HOTEL early the next morning for their flight to London at 10.00 a.m.

As they sat in the departures lounge, Rehana asked, "Well, guys, it's over. How did you enjoy Europe?"

"Oh, it was simply amazing," Shameem replied.

"It was worth every minute and every penny that we spent, and much more," Rafiq added.

"You know, I am so awed by the splendor of Europe, the history and culture and the monuments and the people, not to mention the fantastic restaurants and sidewalk cafés, I can't believe that we saw and enjoyed all this in just two weeks," Rehana said.

Everyone looked at Anil.

"So, what did you think, Anil?" Rehana asked.

"Oh, it was an amazing trip, an experience of a lifetime. The Eifel Tower, Champs Élysées and Notre Dame in Paris, St Mark's and the Grand Canal in Venice, the Coliseum, Trevi Fountain, and the Sistine Chapel in Rome, they were all breathtaking. And Barcelona! Barcelona is something else. La Sagrada, the Gothic Quarter, La Rambla, and the beaches, they were beyond anything that I could have imagined, even after seeing what we had already seen in Paris, Rome, and Venice."

"But ... ?" Rehana asked.

"But ... you know what? We saw all this and marvelled at what we saw, but did not truly *experience* anything. We could have spent 10 days in Barcelona or a whole week in Rome and another week in Paris to see and take in everything. Except for our last day, we were rushing –keeping up with the tour schedule. I'm not saying that I didn't enjoy the trip. I had the time of my life, but to truly enjoy these places, we should come back - perhaps visit just one country at a time and take it all in."

"You're so right, Anil. That would be the way to see Europe or any other country, for that matter. You guys can do it. When I go back to Trinidad, there is no coming back for me, "said Rehana.

"Never say, 'Never,' Rehana. As we say, Inshallah, one day your husband and you, Rafiq and me, and Anil and his wife will meet up in London and tour Europe," Shameem said.

"Inshallah," Rehana said. She had learned to use and admire this terminology of her forefathers' faith. It was so beautiful - Inshallah - "God Willing." The Muslims partnered in humility with God in everything that they did, or aspired to do, she thought.

"Something is missing in this equation, Shama. Anil does not have a wife. He doesn't even have a girlfriend," Rafiq said, teasingly.

"We'll have to correct that situation when we move to London," Shameem replied.

1962
Forty-Three

Rafiq and Shameem returned to Cardiff at the end of August. While Shameem searched her handbag for the house key, Rafiq rang the doorbell, and Mrs. Bowes opened the door.

She hugged them both and said that she was delighted to see them back home. "Come on in. I want you to meet someone," she said, and looking up, shouted, "Sophia, can you come down?"

A petite girl appeared at the top of the stairs and came down smiling.

Mrs. Bowes said, "This is Sophia. She is from Iraq," and looking at Shameem, said, "the British Council sent her to me as your replacement. She has been here for one week."

Shameem extended her hand to Sophia and said, "Welcome, Sophia. My name is Shameem, and this is Rafiq. The Council could not have found you a better person to stay with."

Rafiq extended his hand to Sophia and said, "Very pleased to meet you, Sophia."

As they sat down in the lounge, Shameem asked, "What are you here to study, Sophia?"

"I am enrolled in the three-year Nursing program at the university."

"That's wonderful! We wish you an enjoyable stay in Cardiff and success in your studies. We have a friend at the university. We'll introduce you to him."

"That would be nice. Thank you very much."

"I'm dying to hear all about your vacation," said Mrs. Bowes. "Thank you for all of the postcards! I hope that you've not eaten. I've cooked dinner for all of us. I hope that you can stay, Rafiq."

"I sure can, Mrs. Bowes. I'm starving."

Over dinner, Rafiq and Shameem related to Mrs. Bowes and Sophia their tour experiences. Mrs. Bowes was fascinated, and so was Sophia, who had once traveled with her family to Italy, but had not been to Paris, Venice, or Barcelona. Her father was a senior engineer with an Italian oil company in Iraq and often traveled to Rome on business.

Shameem and Sophia got along well, and after Rafiq left to go home, they sat up late into the night, talking. Shameem asked Sophia her age, and if she had a boyfriend. Sophia said that she was 20 and had a boyfriend some time back, but he was Sunni (she was Shia), and her parents had made her break off the relationship.

"I'm so sorry to hear that, Sophia. I'm sure that a pretty girl like you must also have many Shia admirers."

"I'm no Elizabeth Taylor, I know, but thank you for the compliment, all the same," laughed Sophia. "Yes, I had some Shia friends in school who, I believe, liked me, but in our society, marriages are arranged by parents so the boys, in general, do not seek to date girls. There are some, like my ex-boyfriend and me, who ignore these traditions. Even if both are Shia or Sunni, it usually does not end well for them because the parents can make different choices. I'm glad that my parents made me end the relationship before it got serious."

"Is there hostility between the Shias and Sunnis in Iraq?" Shameem asked.

"There is the historical sense of grievance for the murders of our first and second Imams by people who were associated with what later evolved as the Sunni interpretation of Islam. In essence, these were political rather than religious differences. Enlightened Shia, like my parents, say that we cannot hold the Sunni community of today responsible for the deeds of a few of their ancestors 1400 years back. The majority of the Sunnis all over the world are good Muslims who live by the ethics of Islam. Fundamentalists on both sides often ferment divisions between the Shia and Sunnis, and the politicians do that for political gain. My parents say that we all, Shia and Sunni, recite the *Shahada - There is no God but Allah, and Muhammad is his messenger* - so we are all brothers and sisters, and there should be no discord between us."

"Then why did your parents ask you to break up with your Sunni boyfriend?"

"That's a good question. A Shia family may welcome a Sunni boy, but a Shia girl may not be acceptable to a Sunni family. It works the other way, too. There is always the fear amongst the Shia and Sunnis about what strife such unions can create if the marriage does not work out. This does not mean that there are no marriages between the Shias and Sunnis in Iraq. They are just not that common."

"Sophia, you speak English very well. Some Iraqi students with me in college were very good at maths and sciences, but could not speak or write English well."

"I attended the American school in Baghdad. That was one of the perks for my dad for working with a foreign oil company. I spent 13 years in the school, where all teachers were British or American. My high school diploma is equivalent to the "A" Levels here."

OVER THE NEXT THREE days, Shameem and Rafiq took Sophia downtown, familiarized her with the bus routes, helped her shop for winter clothing, introduced her to the Barclays Bank branch where they had their accounts and where she opened one and introduced her to Robert and Bernice, who promised to look after her after Rafiq and Shameem left for London. They gave Sophia their coordinates and asked her to call them anytime she needed any assistance.

SHAMEEM AND RAFIQ HAD seen Iraq on the map but did not know much about the country. Sophia told them that Iraq was a country of some 25 million people. Arabs and Kurds were the main ethnic groups. Over 90% of the people were Muslims, with the Shias in the majority, but a Sunni dominated dictatorship ruled the country. Baghdad was the capital city. Much of the country was dry, but the two rivers - the Tigris and Euphrates - running through Iraq, provided the country with a fair amount of cultivable land. The region between the rivers, known as Mesopotamia, was often referred to as the cradle of civilization. It was here that human civilizations had first begun to read, write, create laws, and live in cities under an organized government. Iraq also had a rich cultural heritage and produced high-quality hand-woven rugs and carpets.

"We are Shias like you, but we are Shia Ismailis. Are there are any Shia Ismailis in Iraq?" Rafiq asked Sophia one evening as they sat sipping tea after dinner at a restaurant.

"Practically all Shia in Iraq and Iran are Ithna Asharis, *The Twelvers*. I've studied a fair bit about Islam, and I know a little about the Ismailis. I know that there are significant numbers of Shia Ismailis in Syria, Iran, and Afghanistan, but I don't think that there are any in Iraq. I had never met one until I met you."

"There were Shia Ithna Ashari students in my school who, like us, were of Indian origin," said Rafiq. "They attended a separate mosque. I know that the Ithna Asharis parted company with the Ismailis after the fifth Imam over succession and I have some understanding of the succession issue, but irrespective of whom we each accepted as our sixth Imam, how did the Shia Ithna Ashari practice of faith come to be different from ours?"

"For that, we have to go back into history. You've read the Quran, of course?"

"To be honest, no, I have not, and neither has Shameem."

Sophia looked quizzically at both and said, "But you do have the historical context for the Shia and Sunni evolution?"

"I do, but I would like to know more," said Rafiq.

"Well, you know that all Shias believe that the Prophet, when returning from his last pilgrimage to Mecca, appointed Ali, his cousin, and son in law, as his successor when he told his followers, 'Of whomsoever, I am the Master (*Mawla*), Ali is the Master.' Two months after that, the Prophet suddenly fell ill and died."

"Yes, we know that, but I can't understand why, given what the Prophet had proclaimed, everyone did not accept Ali as the Prophet's successor. Why did the Shia Sunni split occur over that period of our early history? Did the Sunnis dispute what the Prophet had proclaimed?" Shameem asked.

"No, they did not dispute the Prophet's proclamation, but their interpretation is that the word *Mawla* can also mean "a friend," and that Ali was not the designated successor to the Prophet. When the Prophet died, they said that his followers should determine his succession. After his passing, the majority of the Muslim leaders elected Hazrat Abu Bakr, a close associate of the Prophet, as the first *Caliph*.

This was not acceptable to Ali's supporters, who came to be known as *Shiatu Ali* – the party of Ali."

"And those who did not accept Ali as the Prophet's successor called themselves Sunnis?" Rafiq asked.

"No, Ali's followers came to be known as Shiatu Ali, but they were part of the Muslim community. The Sunnis did not emerge as a distinct group until many decades later. The Shia also believe that during his lifetime, the Prophet had told his followers that he would leave behind him the Quran and his progeny for the Muslims to follow, and they maintained that the progeny of Ali and Fatima (the Prophet's daughter) were his legitimate successors. Ali, however, did not want conflict between Muslims and renounced his claim to the political leadership of the Muslims. The Shia acknowledged Ali as their first Imam, or guide, to guide them in all spiritual matters."

"Were the Sunnis okay with this - Ali guiding the Shias on spiritual matters?"

"The Caliph, in a literal sense, is the supreme religious and political leader of an Islamic state known as the *Caliphate*, but Abu Bakr assumed the title of Caliph as the political successor to the Prophet."

"What happened next?"

"Abu Bakr's tenure as Caliph was short. He died two years later, and Omar, another of the Prophet's close associates, became the second Caliph who ruled for about a decade. He was succeeded by Othman, who ruled for about 12 years. Thus, despite the Prophet's proclamation, Ali, had been passed over three times, but after Othman's death, and some 25 years after the Prophet's death, Ali was elected as the fourth Caliph. During this period, Islam had spread from its roots in Arabia to Syria, Lebanon, Iraq, Iran, Egypt, Palestine, Morocco, and southern Spain."

"Was Islam spread by the sword? My Indian history teacher taught us that after the Prophet's death, the Muslims conquered all these countries and forced the populations to convert to Islam. Those that did not convert, they killed. Is this true?" Shameem asked.

"That's simply nonsense. Yes, the Muslim Empire grew by political conquests, but the growth was not accompanied by the spread of Islam. The Quran says that there is no compulsion in religion, and the Prophet said that Muslims should live in brotherhood with others of the Abrahamic faiths – Judaism and Christianity. The Prophet had encouraged the Christians and the Jews, the two groups with established religions and who also believed in one God, to continue to practice their religions. The Caliphs also permitted the Jews and Christians to continue to practice their own faiths in the conquered lands. The Caliphs wanted to conquer and rule countries and expand the empire, not convert people to Islam."

"So how did the majority of these countries come to be Muslim nations?" Rafiq asked.

"It was an attraction to Islam's simplicity and its message of peace, honesty, generosity, and equality. No Muslim sword or soldier ever entered Malaysia or Indonesia, and yet Indonesia is the largest Muslim country in the world. Here, as elsewhere, those that converted to Islam were converted by the spreading message of Islam, not by any armies. As people in the conquered lands heard and understood the message of Islam, they, too, converted. This occurred over centuries. The Ottomans ruled much of Eastern Europe for decades, but they never forced its Christian population to convert to Islam."

"This is very enlightening, Sophia, but I still want to know how your and our practices of faith became different when we are both Shia?" Rafiq asked.

Smiling, Sophia said, "We believe, as you do, that our fifth Imam, Jafar Sadiq, nominated his eldest son, Ismail, as his successor, but we believe that Ismail predeceased his father and we accepted Imam Jafar Sadiq's eldest son, Musa Kazim, as the sixth Imam and followed him and his successors. You believe that Ismail did not predecease his father, but fearing persecution by the Sunni Caliph, Imam Jafar Sadiq sent Ismail into hiding for his safety. You believe that he was the legitimate successor to Imam Jafar Sadiq, and you followed his lineage. That's why you came to be known as *Ismailis*. In all, we had four Imams after Ali and seven after Jafar Sadiq –twelve in all. We believe that our twelfth Imam, also fearing persecution, went into hiding and will reappear one day to guide us and all humanity. You believe that the Imam must be present at all times to guide his followers. You believe in a living Imam and follow the teachings of your 49th Imam, The Aga Khan, and his interpretations of the Quran. You call him *Hazar Imam*, or the Living Guide. We follow the teachings of our twelve Imams and the Quran, as it was written. That's how our beliefs and practices of faith differ."

"I wish that we had all stayed together. We would all have been happy and united," Shameem said.

"I, too, wish that we had stayed together, but we did not. You do know that you Ismailis went on to split again?"

"Yes, we know that. There was another succession issue, and we followed Nizar as our 19th Imam, who was challenged by his brother, Mustali, who claimed to be the next Imam. His followers came to be known as Bohras, but their line of Imams also ended," Shameem said.

"Sophia, can you tell us something about the Fatimid Empire? We know that our Ismaili Imams established the empire, but how did it come into being, and how did it end?" Rafiq asked.

"The Imams' lineage from the Prophet was always a problem for the Sunni Caliphs. Persecution of the Shia Imams intensified after our first split. This forced the Shia and their Imams into seclusion, but the Ismaili interpretation of Islam went on to spread throughout the Islamic world. Ismaili *Dais*, appointed by the Imam, conducted missionary work to lead others to recognize and give allegiance to the Imam of the Time. By the ninth century, these groups were strong enough to launch a revolt in North Africa and Eastern Arabia, which resulted in the formation of the Ismaili-led Fatimid Empire in Egypt. The dynasty of the Ismaili Imams came to be known as the Fatimid era, after the Prophet's daughter, Fatima."

"I understand that the Fatimids did some great things," Rafiq said.

"The Fatimids founded and established Cairo as their new capital. From here, they ruled over vast stretches of the Muslim world for over 250 years. Under the Fatimids, the Christians, Jews, and Muslims lived in peace and prospered. The Fatimids sought out the best scholars, regardless of their race or religion, to come together and explore mathematics, astrology, science, and medicine. This was the most glorious period of commercial, artistic, and intellectual development in Muslim history."

"This is so very interesting, and you learned all this in the American School?" Shameem asked.

"Oh no, we had Muslim scholars come to our home every day after school to tutor my brother and me in our faith. They first taught us the Quran and about the life of the Prophet, and then Shia history. Do you know how your Indian ancestors came to be Shia Ismaili Muslims?"

"We know that Shia missionaries – the *Pirs*, converted our forefathers, who were Hindus, to Islam," said Shameem.

"Do you know where those missionaries came from?"

"That I don't know. Do you, Rafiq?" Shameem asked.

"No, I don't, either. We did not have the benefit of the kind of education you got."

"Before the end of the Fatimid era, a Dai by the name Hasan i Sabbah established an Ismaili stronghold in the mountains of Northern Iran. During the time of the last two Ismaili Fatimid Imams, Sabbah started a *Dawa*, or proselytizing, called, 'The New Preaching.' A son of the Imam Nizar was smuggled out of Egypt and kept concealed at the fortress of Alamut. From Alamut, the Ismaili missionaries spread Ismailism throughout the Middle East, and Central and South Asia. They were very successful in South Asia, where several Hindu castes converted en masse to the new faith. In 1256, the Mongolian army destroyed the Ismaili state at Alamut, and the Ismaili Imams and their followers thereafter maintained a low profile. Guised as Sufi leaders, the Ismaili Imams lived there for many centuries until the first Aga Khan left Iran in 1841 and came into contact with his Indian Ismaili followers – your ancestors – in South Asia."

"Now you've connected all the dots for us. Thank you very much for educating us about our history, but tell me, Sophia, if the Shia are the majority in Iraq, why do Sunnis rule the country?" Rafiq asked.

"It's because my country is cursed with oil," Sophia replied.

"Cursed? I would think that oil would be a blessing for a country with little fertile land and not much of an industrial base," Shameem said.

"It should be, but oil has brought Western interests into Iraq, as it has done in Saudi Arabia, Syria, Iran, Kuwait, Libya, and other Middle Eastern countries. The Americans and Europeans, above all else, want to ensure a steady supply of oil at dirt-cheap prices for their countries. To do this, they create fear and hostility amongst people within and between the countries in the Middle East. This helps them sell arms to these countries with which they can fight one another, and in the guise of offering protection to regimes like the one that rules Iraq, they extract concessions and use our countries as military bases."

"That is very unfortunate. Do you see all Muslims in the Middle East coming together one day to form a united nation?" Rafiq asked.

"I've heard my parents talk about how great it would be if only the Shia Iran and majority Shia Iraq were to form an economic union that could later lead to a political union, but this can never happen as long as there are external forces working to keep the Muslims divided. It's the divide and rule policy."

"The Prophet was able to unite the warring tribes in Arabia. Perhaps a charismatic leader with the vision for a united Muslim nation in the Middle East will emerge one day and galvanize people in Egypt, Syria, Saudi Arabia, Jordan, Iran, Iraq … and other countries to come together and usher in a new Fatimid period," said Shameem.

"You will wait a long time – a very long time, for that to happen, Shama. Don't hold your breath."

ALTHOUGH SHAMEEM AND RAFIQ had lived in Cardiff for just two years, they had developed a strong affinity for the city. They had come to love the city, its geography, and its people. They had enjoyed the college and the many friends they had made, who were all now moving in different directions.

The Coopers had been kind to Rafiq and had taken good care of him. His relationship with David and Belinda Saul had been very special. They had given him much affection in return for his genuine concern for them. They had treated him as an adult for his knowledge and intelligence but had also imparted much knowledge to him that would serve him well in his future life. They were going to miss Rafiq's visits and the lively discussions they had had with him, as would Rafiq.

They invited Shameem and Rafiq for dinner before they left for London. They sat late into the night talking. As they did this, Rafiq thought to himself that there were no adults in his life, other than his and Anil's parents, that he felt so close to and admired as much as this old couple. The Sauls had taught Rafiq a lot about the history and persecution of the Jewish people, including their own family experiences during the Second World War. Despite the hardships that their families and their people had endured, the Sauls harbored no malice against anyone – not even the people who had persecuted the Jews throughout the centuries. They always maintained a cheerful disposition and wished everyone well. They supported the creation of the state of Israel, yet grieved for the plight of the Palestinians. "No people should be dispossessed of their lands, and we hope and pray that a Palestinian state will be created within the boundaries proposed by the United Nations earlier," they said. Rafiq felt that the world would have been a much happier place if God had created more people like the Sauls. He promised to call them regularly after moving to London.

They had known Sophia for only one month, but Shameem and Rafiq had become so close to her, and she to them, that saying goodbye to her was difficult. They so wished that she had come a year earlier. They had learned so much about the Middle East and Islam from her that they felt like they had become experts in these fields. They promised to stay in touch.

The most difficult goodbye was to Mrs. Bowes. She had tears in her eyes the entire morning of their departure. She had come to love Shameem and Rafiq as her own children. She had never felt remotely as close to any student who had stayed with her before. They had brought so much happiness in her life – not just with placing her in employment, but with their care and affection for her, and the many interesting conversations they had with her. They had filled a void in her life. They promised to stay in contact with her, as well.

A phase in their life during which Rafiq and Shameem had rediscovered each other and fallen in love, the two had come into a new land with very different culture and where they had acquired education to qualify them to enter the universities of their choice, where they had made new friends – young and old – and during which time, they had toured Europe, was behind them.

A new and exciting phase in their lives was about to begin.

1962
Forty-Four

Rafiq and Shameem departed Cardiff for London at the end of September. Their first semesters were to commence at the start of October.

After arriving in London, Rafiq and Shameem stayed with Anil and Mrs. Jackson for two nights and then moved into their respective student halls of residence. Mrs. Jackson had offered to take them in as boarders, and Anil very much wanted them to do that, but both had said that they wanted to minimize travel time to and from college and therefore wanted to stay in the students' residences. Additionally, Rafiq did not want Shameem's and his parents to worry about them living together in one house. Also, not tippy-toeing, as Mrs. Bowes had said to him once, to Shameem's room and spending the night with her, would have been very difficult for him. Shameem shared similar concerns.

THE FIRST SEMESTER STARTED well, and soon they established a routine. They attended college Monday to Thursday, spoke to each other by phone every evening, said their prayers, and studied until 9.00 p.m., after which they joined the other students to watch BBC News and then returned to their rooms to study until exhaustion set in.

After college on Fridays, they moved to Mrs. Jackson's for the weekend, where they kept all of their formalwear and full sets of other clothes and toiletries and went directly to college from there on Monday mornings.

They attended the Ismaili Jamatkhana at Palace Gate on Fridays and spent

Saturdays shopping, going to movies, or dancing with Rehana and Anil. On Sundays, they just relaxed at home and studied. Anil did not make it to Jamatkhana on most Fridays. He usually returned late from work, arriving home when Rafiq and Shameem were leaving, but he made it a point to come home early and attend Jamatkhana on the day of the new moon, which has religious significance for Ismailis, and on other festive occasions.

The weekends cost Rafiq extra money because they did not get any refunds from the college residences for not being there. He had over £15,000 accumulated in the savings account he had opened for his parents and £200 in his personal account.

The weekends were enjoyable for Rafiq and Shameem. Anil loved to have them over, and so did Mrs. Jackson, who charged them the full rate, but other than three breakfasts, she did not have to serve them any meals as all three chose to go out to restaurants for lunches and dinners.

Their first semester ended in mid-December. Shameem asked that they should celebrate her birthday this year with a quiet dinner at a newly opened Chinese restaurant in Earl's Court and go to some nicer place to celebrate Rafiq's 21st birthday on New Year's Eve, two days in advance of his birthday on January 2nd. Anil and Rehana endorsed the idea and so it was decided that they would skip the Ismaili New Year's Eve event this year and go someplace else, which Rehana undertook to identify.

1962
Forty-Five

As they sat down for dinner one evening, Yasmin asked, "Salim, in my last couple of phone calls, Almas has been somewhat distant. Would you know what might be bothering her?"

Salim mulled over the question for a few moments before saying, "You've not accompanied me on my last few trips to Dodoma; perhaps she might be feeling that now that Rafiq is no longer there, you have no interest in visiting them. You know she used to enjoy very much spending those Sundays with you. I am sure she is missing you and is, perhaps, feeling hurt."

"I think that you might be right. I should have realized that. Yes, Rafiq was the motivation for me to accompany you to Dodoma every month, but then I did not have Chelsea and Jane in my life. My weekends with them at the Club here are a wonderful time for me that I look forward to each week. The movies in Dodoma were another attraction for us, but we can now watch movies at the Club. I admit I've been selfish. I will come with you to Dodoma on your next trip."

"Now that we are talking about this, Fateh has also been quite subdued in his telephone conversations with me. You know those two weeks when Almas was away from work because, as Fateh said she was under the weather, I told him that we wanted to drive up to see her and he was quite insistent that there was no need for us to do so. It sounded like he really didn't want us to go. I was surprised. I didn't tell you about this conversation because I did not want you to be concerned."

"So, it looks like both are not happy with us?"

"Well, I was wondering why Fateh was acting that way. One thought that crossed my mind was that Almin is now producing close to 14,000 Shillings in profits per month. Mpwapwa accounts for less than 40% of its sales. The rest is all what Fateh has generated locally. Fateh and Almas may be feeling that it's their hard work that is producing this huge profit, and we comfortably take away 7,000 Shillings – that's 235 Shillings a day - every month for doing nothing. You remember we invested only 10,000 Shillings in this business, and we are racking in 7,000 Shillings every month for doing no work. Some of the richer families in Dodoma are not making this kind of money. This may be the cause of their unhappiness. It's human nature to feel that way when you are putting in all the effort."

"I would be very disappointed if that's the case. If we had not come up with this opportunity, Fateh would still be working for 1,500 Shillings a month. Although he is an employee, we are sharing 50% of the net profits with him. Almin is also paying Almas more than she was earning in her job."

"Look at it this way, Yasmin, Fateh could leave us today and take 60% of the business – the business that he has generated, and leave us with Mpwapwa. What would we do? Move to Dodoma to run Almin for 5,000 Shillings a month? Who knows if Mpwapwa sales will remain with us after Independence?"

"So, what are you suggesting? Are you saying we should offer them 60%? 70%? If this is what they are unhappy about, I would be very disappointed. They should be looking at where we have brought them from where they were. How many families in Dodoma earn Shs.7,000 a month? They could afford a Mercedes with this kind of money."

"True, but let's not get carried away with our speculations. We don't know what they are unhappy about, if they are, indeed, unhappy. One thing I had already decided to do was to increase Almas' salary by 1,000 Shillings a month, subject to your approval, of course. She's doing an excellent job. If we do this, 500 Shillings will be coming out of their share of profits, so her net gain will only be 500 Shillings, but I think that she will appreciate it."

"Well, call Fateh and tell him to do this as of this month and also tell him we are going to Dodoma this Sunday. I don't want this to fester. Whatever it is, let's deal with it."

When Salim called Fateh to tell him about their proposed increase in Almas' pay, he said, "That would make her very happy, but that would be a doubling of her salary. Are you sure you want to do this?"

"Yes, she deserves every bit of it. And Fateh, we are coming to Dodoma this Sunday. Let's plan to have a nice dinner. We will stay the night at the Dodoma Hotel and come back early on Monday morning."

"Okay, we will look forward to that. We've not seen Yasmin in a long time."

Was there a message in this? Salim wondered.

YASMIN AND SALIM WERE surprised to see Almas when she opened the door. She looked like she had lost 15 lbs. She had dark circles around her eyes. After welcoming them and seating them in the lounge, she excused herself to go make tea.

"She looks completely drained. No flu can do this to her," Salim whispered.

After a cup of tea with the ladies, Salim left to make his purchases, and Yasmin, holding Almas' hand, asked, "What's happened to you, Almas? What kind of flu did you have? You look so frail. Why are you going to work when you are this weak?"

Almas' eyes welled up, and she broke down crying. Yasmin took her in her arms and asked, "Almas, what's the matter? What happened? Please tell me what's happened? Is there any problem with Fateh and you? With the children?"

Almas kept sobbing and holding on to Yasmin. Yasmin let her cry, running her hand over her hair and whispering comforting words. Finally, Almas faced Yasmin, said, "You know those two weeks I was away from work, and you guys wanted to come to see me? Fateh asked you not to come because I was not here. I was in Dar es Salaam."

"Why?"

"A couple of months back, a young girl's elbow hit me in my right breast as we stood in line in Jamatkhana, and it caused severe pain. It hurt much more than it should have because she didn't hit me hard at all, and I thought it would go away. When it did not, I saw the doctor at The Aga Khan Health Centre, and he prescribed some anti-inflammatories and pain-killers, but that didn't help. When I saw him again, he spoke to a women's specialist at the Dodoma Hospital and sent me to see her. The doctor examined my breast and found a lump, which I had felt

305

also. She said this was not the swelling from the hit. She immediately called a doctor at the Ocean Road Hospital in Dar es Salaam and asked me to go there the next day, which I did."

"You went alone? Why didn't you let me know?"

"I didn't know what it was, and I didn't want to cause any alarm. My brother received me at the airport and took me straight to the hospital. They performed a biopsy and kept me in the hospital. The next day, they told me the lump was cancerous, and they needed to remove my breast."

"Oh, my God, Almas, why didn't you call me? I would have come to be with you!"

"I did think of you, and I really wanted Fateh to be with me, but I felt that I had to let them do what was needed to be done without waiting. They operated on me and told me that it looked like the cancer had not spread, but, of course, they can't be 100% certain. After a week in the hospital, I was released. I stayed for two days with my family in Dar es Salaam and then flew back."

"Oh, my dear Almas, I am so sorry to hear this. But listen, they told you that there is no sign of the cancer having spread. That is comforting, so let's simply hope and pray that this is it. We have our Jamatkhana and our prayers. The prayers bring peace, and socializing with the Jamat brings us happiness. Have you been going to Jamatkhana regularly?"

"Not since I came back from Dar es Salaam. I've been so worried and miserable; I have not gone anywhere other than to work."

"Have you told anyone about this?"

"Only Fateh and my siblings in Dar es Salaam know."

"Okay, Almas, we are going to go to Jamatkhana this evening, and you are going to attend Jamatkhana every day. And you know what? Tell your friends about what you went through, and they will pray for you. Never underestimate the power of prayer. You will always be in Salim's and my prayers."

"Please don't say anything to Rafiq. I don't want Anil to know this and worry."

"Of course, I won't. Other than Salim, I will not say a word to anyone you have not already told."

"Thank you, Yasmin, for your support. You and Salim have been so kind to us."

"Almas, there is something I want to ask you. Will you please be honest and tell me the truth? Whatever you say will not offend me in any way. I promise you."

"There is nothing more I can tell you about my health situation. Do you want to ask me something else?"

"Yes. Salim tells me that Almin is now making over 14,000 Shillings a month. You get half, and we take half. Salim also tells me that Mpwapwa now accounts for less than 50% of the business. The rest is all that you and Fateh have worked hard to generate. Do you or Fateh feel that what we are taking for doing nothing is too much, and you deserve more? I will understand if you do."

"Whatever would make you think that?" exclaimed Almas. "Whenever Fateh and I talk about the business, we say how lucky we are to have friends like you. You could have just hired us both to work for you, and we would have been pleased if you paid us 3,500 Shillings a month between the two of us. Instead, you are treating us like your partners and giving us 50% of the profits. We thank you and pray for you every day. Neither Fateh nor I would ever think that we want more from this business. We could not be happier with what we are getting. But what made you ask me this? Is that why you doubled my salary? Did Fateh say anything? Ask for more?"

"No, Fateh, bless his soul, has not said a word. It's just that the business is making so much money, and it's all because of Fateh's and your hard work, and I wanted to make sure that we are being fair. As for your salary, Salim said that you are doing such a fine job, you should get paid more. It has nothing to do with what my concern was."

"Without you coming up with this opportunity, Fateh and I would still be working in our old jobs. We are more grateful than I can tell you for transforming our lives in such a short period."

"I'm sorry, I asked, Almas, but I had to know."

"Please, don't ever think that way about us, Yasmin."

"I promise you, I won't. I am truly sorry."

1963
Forty-Six

By mid-April of 1963, Rafiq and Shameem had become busy preparing for their first-year exams in June and spent the weekends at their residences. They missed Anil and being with each other. They did continue to meet for dinner on Sunday evenings.

After completing their exams in June, they now had another long summer vacation ahead of them. They decided to look for work to gain some British experience and to keep them occupied for the summer months.

Through her college, Shameem was able to find work as a support staff member at St. Mary's Hospital for £10 a week. Through his own efforts, Rafiq found a job at a branch of Lloyd's Bank in the city as a Consumer Loans Officer for £7 Shs.10 per week.

Given the proximity of their workplaces to the students' residences and the fact that it was cheaper to stay there than moving to Mrs. Jackson's, and Anil was studying for his exams, both decided to continue to stay in the students' residences while they worked.

They decided to save their earnings to rent a car - Anil had acquired British a driver's license - and visit north England and Scotland for a week before returning to London via Cardiff, in September.

Anil and Rehana sat for their exams in late August and felt positive about their respective performances. Their results would come out in early October.

In late August, Sophia, who also had a summer job in Cardiff until August end, called to say that she wanted to come to London to spend a week with them in September and asked if they could recommend a place for her to stay nearby them.

After discussing it with Anil and Mrs. Jackson, Rafiq and Shameem suggested that they would arrange for her to stay with Mrs. Jackson, where she would share the room and bed with Shameem. Sophia was delighted with the arrangement, as was Mrs. Jackson, for whom this meant extra money.

Shameem also advised Sophia of their plans to tour northern England and Scotland in mid-September and suggested that she come to London at the end of August and join them on their tour. Rehana, about whom they had spoken to Sophia many times, was to join them. They would be five in all. Rafiq and Anil were paying for car rental and petrol. They had planned to stay in bed and breakfast facilities in the places they were visiting. They had checked and ascertained that they could get one room with three beds in each location for the three women to share. The accommodation costs, therefore, would be minimal.

Sophia arrived in London, as planned, on Saturday, August 31st. Anil and Rafiq had rented a car for the Labour Day weekend, and together with Shameem and Rehana, they met her at the train station. After dinner at *The Sahara* (a trendy Middle Eastern food place), which Sophia thoroughly enjoyed, the group went for a walk around Trafalgar Square, Leicester Square, and Piccadilly Circus.

They returned home well past midnight and retired to their rooms.

As they got into the bed, Sophia said, "Shama, I'm sorry you have to send Rafiq upstairs to accommodate me in your room."

"Rafiq always sleeps upstairs when we stay here," said Shameem. "We do not share this room. He comes down in the morning and lies with me in my bed, and we hug and kiss, but that is as far as we go."

"You mean, you have never slept together? Not made love? Is Rafiq okay with that?"

"He is. It's difficult, but we have given assurances to our parents to the effect that I will not get pregnant, and we have to live by our commitments."

"This is unbelievable. You are both almost 22, aren't you? I can't think of any 22-year-old guy who would just come into your bed and hug and kiss you and not want to make love to you."

"Rafiq is disciplined. If he wanted to, I'm not sure if I could or would resist."

"You know, Shama, a variety of contraceptives are available. Making love does not mean getting pregnant."

"Yes, but nothing is 100% safe. They are testing the contraceptive pill, which is supposed to be 100% safe. If and when it's approved, I may take it, and that may change things. We do plan to marry when Rafiq graduates in two years, and I can't see us not making love for another two years."

"I hope that the Pill is approved soon. For two adults your age, your relationship seems unnatural to me!"

"It is."

"Does Anil have a girlfriend? You told me Rehana is not his girlfriend, right?"

"Yes, Rehana is happily married and three years older than Anil. Their relationship is platonic. Anil doesn't have a girlfriend. Why do you ask? Do you like him?"

"He's smart, considerate, and very polished. He treats all of us with so much respect. He insisted on carrying my suitcase."

"You're right. The girl he will marry will be very fortunate."

THEY MADE A DAY trip to Brighton on Sunday and visited Stonehenge on Monday.

Anil and Rehana were back to work on Tuesday. Over the next three days, Rafiq and Shameem took Sophia to see The Westminster Abbey, Houses of Parliament, Tower Bridge, Buckingham Palace, St. James' Park, and Kew Gardens.

At the end of each day, they arranged to meet Anil for dinner at an Indian or Continental restaurant. Sophia requested that they go back to The Sahara for one dinner. She had not eaten Middle Eastern food since she had come to the U.K. and had loved the food there. It would be her treat. For Shameem, Rafiq, and Anil, The Sahara food tasted a little bland, but they had enjoyed it, nonetheless.

Shameem, Rafiq, and Sophia usually got to the restaurant earlier than Anil, and Shameem observed Sophia eagerly looking at the entrance for Anil to come in, but she did not want to say anything to her because Anil, while being friendly and polite with Sophia and holding her hand when she got on or off the transit bus, had not shown any particular interest in her. But the two did enjoy each other's company and often shared animated discussions.

After a busy week in London, Anil and Rafiq left home early on Saturday to pick up the rental car, and the group was soon on its way to Blackpool. Anil had planned out the route. They drove via Oxford to Birmingham, where they stopped for lunch, and then onward to Blackpool, a seaside resort famous for its beaches, illuminations, the Blackpool Tower, and Winter Gardens.

It was around 6.00 p.m. when they got to the Promenade and headed towards the Tower. In the late afternoon, the beaches were deserted, but the Promenade was alive with hundreds of locals and visitors. It was daylight, so the Promenade was not yet lit up. They proceeded to buy the Blackpool Tower Circus tickets for the 8.00 p.m. show and ate dinner at a seaside restaurant nearby. The show was everything that it was billed to be. Rehana had asked Rafiq, Shameem, and Anil not to compare the Tower or the show to anything they had seen in Paris and just enjoy these attractions for what they were.

When they exited the show, the Promenade was all lit up. It looked spectacular. They walked up and down the Promenade and enjoyed the crowds and music, and then made their way to their bed and breakfast place to get there by midnight, the latest check-in time.

After breakfast the next morning, they headed north towards Lake District National Park, the most visited national Park in the U.K. and famous for its forests and mountains. They spent the entire day in the Park enjoying its stunning scenery, abundant wildlife, and clear lakes. They were directed to a cozy lakeside restaurant that advertised homemade celery soup, roast beef, and mashed potatoes, followed by freshly made apple pie a la mode and tea, for lunch, for £1.Shs.10.

The fresh air and long walks in the Park had made them hungry, and it was almost 2.00 p.m. They had not eaten anything since breakfast.

After they had enjoyed their soup and eaten the roast beef entrée, the hostess asked them if they wanted to enjoy their dessert and tea by the fireside, where a sofa and two chairs had just been vacated. Although the day was bright, the air was chilly. They gladly agreed to move. When they were seated, the hostess told them that apple pies were being baked and would be ready in 20 minutes. She hoped that they did not mind waiting. Of course, they did not. They were enjoying the fireplace and the restaurant's ambiance.

The waitress soon appeared with large portions of apple pies topped with vanilla ice cream, and tea. They sat, talked, and slowly enjoyed their desserts until 4.30 p.m. when Rehana reminded everyone that it was time to go and enjoy the Park some more.

They spent the night in Keswick, a small market town in the Park. As they settled into their room, Rafiq asked Anil if he liked Sophia.

"She is delightful to be with. She's good looking and smart. I've observed that unlike some other people who are either always talking or waiting to talk and don't listen to a word anyone is saying, Sophia listens carefully to what we say and then expresses her opinion in a polite, but confident manner. She has impeccable manners. She's the kind of girl I would like to marry, I think."

"So, you like her."

"We could be the best of friends, but I don't think that she would be interested in me, and I can't be interested in her. She is an Ithna Ashari, and we are Ismailis. My mother would faint if I told her I am dating an Ithna Ashari Arab. Imagine the firestorm you would have created if you had become involved with Salima."

Salima! Anil had not mentioned her name since that morning when he had blasted Rafiq for his "irresponsible" behavior the night before.

"But she is a different kind of Ithna Ashari from Salima," Rafiq said.

"How's she different? She is an Arab Twelver. I'm sure she would not want to become involved with an Ismaili boy, either. In any case, she is our guest, so we have to treat her with warmth and respect. I don't want to say or do anything to make her think I'm being forward and make this trip awkward for her. I want her to enjoy the holiday with us."

"What if she were to show interest in you? How would you react?"

"If she were to indicate her interest in me, I might reciprocate. You don't often meet girls with whom you feel comfortable. I would then have to manage my parents, but if I were to marry her, I would certainly not take her with me to Tanganyika to live there. Our lives revolve around Jamatkhanas and the community, and I would not want to subject her to being an outsider for the rest of her life."

"Anil, may I ask you something? You used to be so lively, full of jokes and laughter — teasing me, teasing everybody. I see a different version of you now. You have become quieter, more serious … you hardly ever crack jokes, and you've become very measured in what you say. You come to Jamatkhana only once or twice a month with us. There are many pretty girls there. We both feel that you're not interested in finding a girlfriend. The two girls from the Centre who begged Shama to introduce them to you, you refused to meet. Are you and Rehana in a relationship?"

"I can understand why you would ask this, Rafiq. To your first part, well, I grew up. Do you remember that Indian teacher in Grade XI, Mr. Thakore? He once quoted someone important —can't remember whom, but the quote was: *I slept and dreamt that life was beauty; I woke to find that life is duty.* I think that I've woken up. I'm discovering that life is duty. I have to worry about my parents, Tazim, and Zahir. Sooner or later, they'll have to leave Tanganyika. Where will they go? I know you have a different perspective on our future in Tanganyika, but I worry."

"They'll be okay, Anil."

"Zahir is in Grade XII. Dad says he's not interested in his studies. He's more interested in business. Dad says that he's very business savvy and is a great help doing the kind of work you were doing when we worked for Almin. Be that as it may, he has to pass his Cambridge Exam and pursue post-secondary education. I worry about him and am encouraging him to pay attention to his education. On the other hand, with the foundational work that you did with Tazim, she's at the top of her class. She's taking Sciences and wants to become a chemist. You should read the letters she writes to me. She has an amazing vocabulary. She's in Grade X now; I have to worry about ensuring that she sustains her interest in education and then bring her here to put her through university."

"To your second part, honestly, Rafiq, Rehana, and I are deeply attached emotionally, but there is no physical relationship between us."

"Is that why you don't want to meet Ismaili girls? Because you are so emotion-ally attached to Rehana?"

"Perhaps. She is always there to be my 'date,' so I don't need to find a partner for our foursome. You and Shama like her. The four of us enjoy being together."

"Well, you have to meet some Ismaili girls after Rehana leaves in the coming days. If you don't have a girlfriend, we can't double date," Rafiq teased.

"I will. We'll ask Shama to help me find someone."

SOON AFTER DEPARTING KESWICK the next day, they entered Scotland. This was a land of mountainous wilderness, rolling hills, and highlands, interspersed with beautiful glacial valleys and lakes.

"So this is what the Scottish highlands look like. This is a gorgeous country. It's so peaceful," Shameem said.

"Wait until you meet the people. They are reputed to be gregarious, friendly, and generous." Rehana said.

"And handsome! You know James Bond is Scottish. I wouldn't mind finding one who looks like him for myself," Sophia chimed in.

"You'll find James Bond in Edinburgh - on the screen, that is. His second movie, "*From Russia with Love*," is running in the theatres there. Shall we go see it tonight?" Rafiq asked.

"Sure." All said in the chorus.

"I'm interested in is finding the Loch Ness Monster," said Shameem.

"Well, we'll visit Loch Ness, but we can't promise you the monster. I'm told that in the summer, he's too busy looking for a mate underwater. So, he hardly surfaces," Rafiq teased.

"Ha, ha, ha. Very funny," Shameem replied, rolling her eyes skyward with a smile.

THEY ARRIVED IN EDINBURGH around 5.00 p.m. Given that major Edinburgh attractions are best seen by foot, and most major attractions are within walking distance from one another, Rehana, who had arranged all of the accommodations, had selected an Inn near The Royal Mile for them to stay in. It was rather expensive but very convenient.

After dinner at the Inn, they made their way to The Highlander cinema for the James Bond movie. There was a long line up, and the evening was cool, but they managed to get the tickets and were seated inside the warm theatre 10 minutes before the film started.

After the movie, they debated whether From Russia with Love was as good as, better than, or not as good as Dr. No, the first James Bond blockbuster. After some debate, all agreed that Dr. No was more exciting.

THE DAY WAS SUNNY and fresh when they emerged from the Inn the next morning and visited the attractions on the Royal Mile, the central street that runs from Edinburgh Castle to Holyrood Park.

Over the next three days, they visited the Edinburgh Castle, Scotland's most prominent landmark, St. Giles Cathedral, the Scottish Parliament Building, and other attractions like the Scotch Whisky Experience, Princes Street Gardens, The Meadows, and Holyrood Park and Palace.

They departed Edinburgh for Glasgow on the evening of September 12th and spent two nights there.

In Glasgow, they visited Scotland's oldest museum, the Hunterian Museum, as well as the Glasgow School of Art, Buchanan Street – a shoppers' paradise often compared to London's Oxford Street – and George Square with its trendy restaurants, shops, and hotels.

SCOTLAND HAD BEEN FUN. They began their long trek south to Cardiff on September 14th. Anil and Rehana had not been to Cardiff, and Shameem and Rafiq were dying to see Robert and his parents, Bernice and Mrs. Bowes. And Rafiq wanted to meet Mr. and Mrs. Saul. They spent a night in Manchester and arrived in Cardiff on Sunday evening. Mrs. Bowes had insisted that they all dine with her and that Shameem and Rehana should stay with her. Rafiq had arranged for Anil and him to stay with the Coopers, who had no boarders for the summer.

When they arrived at Mrs. Bowes', she took Rafiq and Shameem in her embrace with tears of happiness streaming down her face. She then welcomed Rehana and Anil and led everyone into the house. Shameem ran up to the room that she had shared with Sophia, and Sophia led Rehana to the room that Mrs. Bowes had prepared for her.

As the group unpacked and freshened up, Rafiq asked Mrs. Bowes to tell him everything happening in her life. She said she was in good health. She was now an old hand at Cecil. She enjoyed her work, and the money, too. She had received a pay raise. Her daughter-in-law had delivered another child, and she was enjoying her grandchildren. She had made new friends. Some were Cecil staff, others, customers. She had been going to a pub downtown once a week with some friends and was enjoying the outing, although she limited herself to just two drinks. She loved Sophia and did not want to take in another girl. Rafiq complimented her on her looks. He said she looked just as young as she did two years back.

When the ladies came down, Mrs. Bowes led everyone to the dining table. They enjoyed her chicken casserole dinner and trifle pudding and sat talking until 10.00 p.m. when Anil and Rafiq said goodnight and headed out to the Coopers residence.

Mr. and Mrs. Cooper and their children were happy to see Rafiq and glad to know that he and Shameem were doing well at the university. Rafiq slept in his old room, and Anil got the room Mahesh used to occupy.

After breakfast the next morning, Anil and Rafiq walked over to Mr. and Mrs. Saul's store. When Mrs. Saul saw Rafiq, she said to the customer she was attending to, "Please excuse me, a very special guest is here after two years," and she ran to take Rafiq in her embrace. Rafiq had a lump in his throat as he ran to Mrs. Saul. He kissed her cheeks and forehead.

"I'm so, so happy to see you, Mrs. Saul! Not a day has gone by when I haven't thought about Mr. Saul and you."

"And we've missed you, too, Son."

Mr. Saul came over and freed Rafiq from Mrs. Saul's embrace to take him into his own. He did not say anything. He just held Rafiq tight.

"Who's that? Can't be a relative. He doesn't look like you people," the customer asked when Mrs. Saul returned to serve her.

"He's like our son. We love him like he is."

Rafiq introduced Anil to the Sauls. Between serving customers, they spent an hour talking to them.

"Are you free for dinner tomorrow night?" Rafiq asked.

"Do you want to come over?" Mrs. Saul asked.

"Actually, our friends and we would like to take Mrs. Bowes and both of you out for dinner."

"We haven't been out for dinner other than fish and chips for so long! I honestly can't remember when we last went out for dinner. I believe we are free?" Mrs. Saul said, looking at Mr. Saul.

"We would be delighted," said Mr. Saul. "What time shall we meet? We close at 7.00 p.m."

"We'll have a cab pick you up at 7.30 p.m. Will that work for you? We can go to The Bavarian Court in Cecil's."

"We've never been there. Is it fancy? Do we have to dress up?" Mr. Saul asked.

"Dress like you are going to the synagogue," suggested Rafiq.

"Oh, we'll so look forward to that!" Mr. Saul said.

They said goodbye to the Sauls, and as they walked out, Anil asked, "And when did you decide all this?"

"Right now," said Rafiq, somewhat sheepishly. "I want to spend time talking to them, but you saw how disruptive it is for their business for them to be engaged with us while the customers are coming in. So, I decided that we should take them out. Shama will also want to see them. It'll be my treat."

"Sounds good. They are lovely people," Anil conceded.

"You know we've arranged to meet Rob and Bernice, but I think that we should invite the D.C. and Mrs. Turnbull, and take them out for dinner on Tuesday. We should take them to a fancy place. You know that D.C. gave your dad and my dad the Almin business, which is generating 15,000 Shillings a month. That is £750. For all that they've done for us, the least that we can do is take them out for a nice dinner."

"You're absolutely right. I've never forgotten how kind they've been to us, and that they took us on the safari. Yes, let's take them out, but that will be our shared treat."

They walked over to the corner phone booth and called Robert.

"Hey, Rob, we're here in Cardiff. How are you?"

"Just fine, Rafiq. My parents have been waiting for your visit. They're excited to see you."

"We're so excited to see you all, too. Listen, Rob, Anil, Shama, and I would like to take Bernice and you, Peter, Margaret, and your parents out for dinner on Tuesday. We can go to *The Marlborough*. It's a weekday so it won't be too busy. Can you organize that?"

"Geez, that would be nice, but are you sure you want to go to the Marlborough? It's expensive, you, know!"

"The Marlborough, it is. Please check with your parents and Peter, Margaret, and Bernice. I'll go ahead and book a table. We'll have Rehana and Sophia with us, as well. I think I've mentioned Rehana to you. Can I call you at 2.00 p.m.? Will that be enough time for you to check with everyone?"

"Sure. I'll check. I think it should work."

They then walked over to Mrs. Bowes' place. She was getting ready to go to work.

"Mrs. Bowes, we'd like to take you and the Sauls to dinner at The Bavarian Court tomorrow. Are you free?"

"What's the occasion, Rafiq?"

"It's to celebrate our return to Cardiff and to be in the Sauls' and your company."

"That sounds lovely, my dear. Let me make the reservation. As Cecil's staff member, I get a 15% discount at The Bavarian Court!"

"That sounds great, Mrs. Bowes, thank you."

"Consider it done. What time?"

"8.00 p.m."

"In that case, I won't come home. I'm working until 6.30 p.m. tomorrow. I'll go for a walk on Queen Street and be back by 8.00 p.m."

"So when did you decide this?" Shameem asked when Mrs. Bowes left.

"We were at the Sauls,' and I thought it would be nice to take them out for dinner and to invite Mrs. Bowes, as well. Do you remember she always used to talk about The Bavarian Court? I thought it would be nice to take them there. It'll be my treat."

"Trust you to think of something like that," Shameem chided lovingly. "They'll be so happy. Thank you for doing this, Rafiq."

"There's more. I spoke to Rob and suggested that we take him, Bernice, his parents, his brother and his brother's girlfriend to dinner on Tuesday at The Marlborough."

"The Marlborough? That will be expensive!"

"Anil and I owe a debt of gratitude to Rob's parents. Peter got me admission into the college here, and Rob and Bernice are dear friends. This will be Anil's and my treat."

"Wow! It looks like we're going to be having some nice dinners here! Shama had promised us the fish and chips and the Rose of India," Rehana said, laughing.

"This is our last vacation together, Rehana. You'll be leaving soon, so let's have some fun," Anil said.

They spent the afternoon sightseeing in Cardiff. Rafiq talked to Rob, who said that Bernice, his parents, and Peter and Margaret were all delighted to accept their dinner invitation and were eagerly looking forward to meeting everyone.

THE BAVARIAN COURT WAS located at the top level of Cecil's. Mrs. Bowes had selected a large round table near the center of the restaurant. Rafiq was surprised to learn that the Sauls did not drink. Rehana ordered one bottle of wine for Mrs. Bowes and herself. They sat and ate and enjoyed desserts and tea until the closing time. Sophia was surprised to see the affection between the Sauls and Rafiq. How could two Jews love a Muslim so much, she wondered.

DINNER THE NEXT DAY with the D.C.'s family was an emotional event for Rafiq and Anil. The D.C. and Jane hugged them and were clearly delighted to see them. After all introductions, they took their seats. Surprisingly, the place was busier and noisier than Rafiq had expected. Rafiq told everyone the dinner was being hosted by his and Anil's parents, who wanted everyone to enjoy themselves. He asked Robert and Bernice to select the wines and made sure that everyone ordered starters.

Looking at the D.C., Rafiq remembered the day he had come into his dad's store and engaged him. He recalled how much his parents had disliked the D.C. and how in a short period, he had become a close friend and benefactor.

"So, where did you meet this gorgeous girl, Rafiq?" Jane asked.

"I first saw her when I went to her parents' camera store in Nairobi to meet her mom, as she had asked me to do in the note she sent with the camera package. I would not have met her and perhaps not have her as my girlfriend now if you had not taken me on safari with you. When I saw her first, she was quite mean to me, but she is a little kinder now," he teased.

"Liar, liar!" Shameem protested.

Everyone laughed.

"She looks like an angel to me." The D.C. said.

Over the course of the evening, the D.C. and Jane updated Rafiq about all of the changes in their lives. They said that they were happy in Cardiff. Being near Rob and Peter who took good care of them (which was evident) was nice, but they missed Tanganyika, the Club, and his parents. Whereas all appeared to have gone well after independence, the D.C. was worried. As he had seen in so many former British, French, and Portuguese colonies, the privileged minorities would come under attack. He had asked Rafiq's parents to accumulate their savings in the U.K. and was happy to know that money was coming into Rafiq's account every month. He had been offered a couple of Civil Service jobs but had not taken them. His pension income and their savings from Tanganyika were enough for them to maintain a comfortable standard of living. They were delighted that they had come to Cardiff and not gone to London. He was contemplating writing a book about his experiences in Tanganyika and the foolish behavior of the colonists. Jane said that he would never do that, as he was too lazy. He had gotten accustomed to sleeping in, reading, going for long walks, and going to the local pub two evenings a week. She was attending a Secretarial college and was planning to go to work when she finished. They were genuinely interested in what Rafiq was studying at the university and what he planned to do, going forward. They were delighted with Robert's progress in his education. They liked Bernice, but Jane wondered if Rob should marry an older woman.

While Rafiq talked with the D.C. and Jane, the others were joking, laughing, and enjoying their food and drinks. Rehana had liked Robert's wine selection, and Anil could see that she was very happy and verbose.

After a joyful and memorable evening, everyone rose to go home. Rafiq had spent all of his time talking to the D.C. and Jane and had not exchanged more than a few words with Robert and Bernice. He asked Robert and Bernice if Shameem, Anil, Rehana, and he could meet them for lunch the next day before they left for

London. Bernice suggested a café near her work where they could get good soup and sandwiches. The Marlborough bill was £52, and Rafiq had money left over to take them to a better place, but Bernice could take only an hour for lunch, so the café, it would have to be.

THE NEXT DAY, THEY shared tearful goodbyes with Sophia and Mrs. Bowes, and Rafiq went over to the Sauls' place to say goodbye to them and get some change to call his bank in Cardiff. He needed to check the balance in the savings account, which he had not transferred to his London bank.

LUNCH WITH BERNICE AND Robert was fun. The boys reminisced about their time in Tanganyika, the safari, and their time together in Cardiff.

Bernice said, "Rob has asked me to marry him when he graduates in two years. I've told him that I'd marry him if he graduates. I don't know why he had to ask me so far in advance."

"I did that to 'book' her, so she doesn't go and find another boyfriend."

Bernice discretely kept herself out of the conversation that followed.

THEY DEPARTED FOR LONDON that afternoon and arrived home in the evening.

1963
Forty-Seven

Shameem and Rafiq were back at the university by the beginning of October. Rehana and Anil received their exam results during the second week of school. Both had done exceptionally well. Rehana was now anxious to return to Trinidad. She had been away from her husband and family for five years and was counting down the days until she could return home to be with them. She booked her flight to leave on October 20th.

Anil, Rafiq, and Shameem took Rehana out for dinner two nights before she left. Rafiq could see the sadness in Anil's eyes. Rehana was also very sorry to have to say goodbye. She did not think that she would ever see them again. Although they were younger than her, they had become the closest friends she had ever had.

They went to see her off at Heathrow airport. It was an emotional goodbye. Anil and Rehana held each other in a tight embrace and kissed each other on the cheeks. Rehana's eyes welled up as she waved goodbye to them and went into the departure lounge.

"WOULD YOU HAVE PREFERRED not to have had us here with you so that you could say a proper goodbye to Rehana?" Rafiq asked when he was alone with Anil.

"By a proper goodbye, you mean to kiss her on her lips?"

"Not necessarily, but be alone, hold her, hold her hand … you know what I mean. You're in love with her, aren't you?"

"Our relationship was supposed to be platonic, but it was difficult not to fall in love with her, and I know she loved me. Love is something that's born inside your heart and grows within you. At times when we had gone dancing and held each other close, I could see in her eyes that she wanted me to kiss her, and it took all of my self-restraint not to do that. I didn't want to violate her husband's trust or the sanctity of her marriage. Perhaps by holding her close when we danced, I did violate the sanctity of her marriage, I don't know. I hope not."

"There are few people in the world with your scruples and who can be as prin-cipled as you are, Anil. I can't think of anyone who would have been as restrained if they were in the kind of relationship that you've had with her. But you did the right thing. She had to return to her husband, and if you had slept with her, I am sure she could not have picked up with him where she had left off. Who knows, her husband may ask her about her relationship with you – how intimate it was - and she will be able to answer with a straight face that you were very close friends and nothing more."

"I will miss her. I hope and pray that she finds the happiness she deserves in her life."

RAFIQ AND SHAMEEM QUICKLY settled into their routine. They attended Jamatkhana every Friday and encouraged Anil to join them, but his attendance did not improve much.

One evening in mid-December when they were socializing with Karim, Zabin, Azim, and Gulnar after the congregational prayers, a young, well-dressed girl whom Shameem had seen many times at the Centre, came over and asked her if she could talk to her, motioning to indicate that she wanted to speak to her alone. When they moved a few feet away, holding her hand out, she said, "May I introduce myself to you? I'm Jenny."

"My name is Shameem."

"Yes, I know your name and your boyfriend's name and where you're from and what you're studying and where."

"Wow! Have you been researching us?"

"Well, a little. Firstly, because you are a very handsome couple and everybody at the Centre talks about you two, and secondly because I'm interested in meeting your friend Anil – the one who comes here with you sometimes."

"I see ..."

"Does he have a girlfriend?"

"No."

"Then, will you introduce me to him?"

"I'll be happy to do that, but I must tell you that he refused to meet the last two girls who asked to be introduced to him. Of course, they were not as good looking as you are."

"Thank you for the compliment, Shameem. Nonetheless, will you introduce him to me?"

"Yes, I will, but can you tell me why you're interested in him? How much do you know about him?"

"I know that he's in the C.A. program. He's the smartest dressed guy when he comes here. He wears expensive clothes so he must be rich. I know that he can't afford to dress like that on an articling clerk's salary, so I suspect that he comes from a rich family, and I'm told he's brilliant."

"What can I tell him about you? Where are you from? What are you studying here?"

"I'm from Kisumu. I completed the Chartered Institute of Secretaries course last year, and I'm working for an insurance company. I don't need to tell you my age, do I?"

"No, you can tell Anil if and when you meet him."

"But you will put in a good word for me, right?"

"I don't know what more I can say about you than what you've told me."

"You can tell him I'm fun to be with."

"Okay, I will."

"Can you bring him here next Friday?"

"I don't know if we can. He usually works late and can't make it on Fridays, but Tuesday week is Chand Raat. He comes for Chand Raat. I will tell you next Friday if he's interested in meeting you, and if he is, I will introduce you to him on the following Tuesday."

"Thank you very much." And with that, Jenny turned around, and walked away.

On the way home, Shameem told Rafiq about her conversation with Jenny.

"I know her by face. She is a vivacious girl and popular – she's always surrounded by boys. Do you think she's Anil's type?"

"Only Anil knows what Anil's type is. She is certainly no Rehana and was being quite pushy. I'm sure he's seen her before. Let him decide if he wants to meet her."

"I KNOW WHO YOU'RE talking about. She has many admirers. I wonder why she wants to meet me," Anil said when Shameem told him about Jenny.

"She said that you're the smartest dressed guy in the Centre – that is when you're there. She also said to tell you that she's fun to be with - whatever that means."

"What do you think, Rafiq?"

"I don't know her, Anil. Why don't you meet her on Chand Raat? We can take her out for coffee. If you like her, you can invite her to the Ismaili New Year's Eve event."

"Okay. No harm in meeting her."

SHAMEEM INTRODUCED JENNY TO Anil on Chand Raat, and as they got talking, she excused herself and joined Rafiq at the other end of the Centre's lounge.

They walked over to Jenny and Anil 15 minutes later, and Shameem introduced Rafiq to Jenny.

"Can you join us for coffee, Jenny?" Rafiq asked.

"Yes, I'd love to."

As they sat down at Number One and ordered tea and snacks, Jenny told them about herself. Her name was Zainab, but everyone called her Jenny. Her parents had a business in Kisumu, Kenya. She had two brothers, both older than her. One was working as an accountant in Nairobi, and another was helping her father in his business. She had one older sister who was married. She was the youngest sibling. She had been in England for three years. She had gone to college in Birmingham, where she had gotten her Corporation Secretary certificate. She had then moved to London and found a job with Global Mutual Insurance Company. She planned to stay in England for some time to get experience and then go to Nairobi, where she expected to find a good job.

"I understand your parents are in business together in Tanganyika. What kind of business is that?" Jenny asked.

Rafiq and Anil looked at each other. "It's a merchandising business," Anil replied.

That was not too illuminating for Jenny. "It's a large business?" she asked.

"As businesses go in a small town, it's a large business," Rafiq replied.

"And very profitable, I presume."

"It generates enough to fund our education here," Rafiq answered. He was tempted to ask her what kind of business her father had in Kisumu but did not.

"So, what do you do in your leisure time?" Jenny asked, looking at Anil.

"There's not too much of it, but over the weekends, we go to movies, out for dinners and dancing sometimes," he replied.

"Oh, I love to dance. Where do you go dancing?"

"Different places. We love to go MECCA dancing," Shameem replied.

"I should take you to this place in Soho. It's very intimate."

She is already thinking about going out with us, Shameem thought.

"Do you have plans for New Year's Eve?" Anil asked.

"A couple of friends have asked me out, but I'm not committed. What did you have in mind?"

"The Ismaili Centre dinner and dance. Would you like to come with us?" Anil asked.

"That's over two weeks from now. Can I let you know sometime next week? Do you have a phone number I can call you at?"

Anil gave her his number, which she wrote down in a small book and put it back in her purse.

After talking for another half hour, they rose to go home.

As they got on the bus, Rafiq asked Anil, "So, what did you think of her? I'm surprised that you asked her out so quickly after meeting her."

"She's kind of interesting. She's vivacious and bubbly. She could be, as she said, fun to be with. I weighed my options. I could have said, 'Good to meet you and look forward to seeing you again.' Or I could have asked her out for dinner, but I'm not ready for that, or I could ask her to join us on New Year's Eve, where we would be in a group. Less personal, and I need a date, anyway."

Rafiq smiled at the pragmatism of Anil's answer. "Makes sense. You can spend New Year's Eve together and decide if you want to spend more time with her."

BEFORE GOING TO BED, Rafiq went into Shameem's room to kiss her goodnight.

"What did you think of Ms. Jenny?" he asked.

"I wish Anil had not asked her out. I found our conversation with her uncomfortable. To me, she seems like a gold digger. I don't think Anil should get involved with her. Rehana was our kind of person. Jenny's not."

"It's just New Year's Eve – not too much of a commitment. We'll be in a group, and Anil will get to know her better. He he can then decide if he wants to see more of her."

"Why do you think she didn't immediately accept his invitation? She was playing hard to get, and also got Anil's phone number. I know her kind."

"I think you're a bit harsh in your assessment…but do you think I should say something to Anil?"

"No, he's invited her out. There is zero chance that she will not come with us. So, let it be. Let this take its course. Hopefully, it will end there."

AS SHAMEEM HAD PREDICTED, Jenny called within two days to say that she would be delighted to join them for New Year's Eve, but she did not want to wait for two weeks to see Anil again. She had enjoyed meeting him very much and wanted to see him again. Why couldn't they go out for dinner the next Saturday and get to know each other better? She knew of an intimate place where she could get a table for two. She made it clear that this was not to be a foursome.

Anil did not have the experience to respond to an invitation from a girl who was, without doubt, popular at 5 Palace Gate. What reason would he give for not going out with her? So, he agreed.

He told Rafiq and Shameem when they came over the next Friday that he was going out for dinner with Jenny the next day.

"And she called you to invite her out?" Shameem asked.

"Don't you think this may be moving faster than it should?" Rafiq asked.

"This is how things are today. We are, perhaps, a little old fashioned. Young people in my office and the places we go for audits talk all the time about having met someone three weeks back, gone out on two dates, and are not going to see each other again or are sleeping together. I can go out with her and get to know her better. If, after New Year's Eve, we all feel I should not get more involved with her, I will pull myself away. She's a modern girl and will be okay with that, I think."

"You are a smart adult, Anil. You can decide what and who is good for you. We respect your judgment," Shameem said.

JENNY HAD SELECTED A restaurant in Piccadilly Circus overlooking the Eros statue. She was already seated at a table near the floor to ceiling window when Anil got there. On seeing him, she got up and briskly walked towards him. He held out her hand with a "Hi, Jenny." She did not take his hand and instead hugged him. Holding his hand, she led him to the table.

"Like the view? The lights?" she asked.

"Yes, it's nice. You've been here before?"

"Yes." She did not specify with whom.

Looking at the small dance floor and a three-piece band playing *Maria Elena*, Anil said, "You didn't tell me this is a dancing place. I thought we were going for a quiet dinner."

"You don't mind, do you? I like to dance, and you said that you do, too."

"Yes, I do. I had just imagined a different kind of dining environment."

They looked at the menu and ordered the food and drinks. The choice was limited and prices high. When the food arrived, and they started eating, Anil thought to himself, 'The poor quality of food here is exceeded only by its high price.'

As they ate, Jenny was full of questions. "What do you plan to do after you graduate?"

"I plan to work with one of the top five C.A. firms in their tax departments. I plan to become a tax consultant."

"Don't you want to open up your own practice? You can make much more money in your own business and write off all kinds of expenses. You could write off this dinner if you had your own practice."

"I can't become a tax specialist in my one-man practice. I need to work with a large firm that will sponsor me for the courses and will have the clients who need tax consulting services."

"So, you would be helping them evade taxes and paying full taxes on your salary?"

"No, I would be helping them find ways to legally minimize their tax burden, not cheat. I believe that it's the norm of a civilized society that people and businesses that make money should pay taxes."

"How much would you earn working as a tax consultant?"

"I plan to specialize in the U.K., Canada, and the U.S.A. taxation laws, rules, and regulations. I want to become an international tax specialist. If I do, I could earn over £5,000 a year."

"And how long would that take you to do?"

"After graduating, I would say five to seven years."

"That's a long time to work to make that kind of money. You could get there much faster if you were in business for yourself."

"You can also go bankrupt in your own business. I see that happen all the time in my work."

"Well, well, shall we dance? They are playing my favorite tune, *Petite Fleur*."

When he put his arm around her to dance, Jenny came into his embrace and started to dance cheek to cheek with him. She *was* fun to be with.

The band, though small, played good music, mostly soft tunes. Jenny was a good dancer, nowhere as good as Rehana, but good. They danced well past midnight and then took a cab to Jenny's hostel in Bayswater.

"Will you please walk me upstairs, Anil?" she asked.

"Sure," Anil said and paid off the cab.

They walked up to her floor, which had five rooms. The lights had been turned off to save money, and only one small light was on.

"Well, thank you very much for a lovely evening, Jenny," Anil said, extending his hand, but as she had done at the restaurant, Jenny took him in her embrace and kissed him on his cheek and immediately proceeded to kiss him on his lips. Anil had not kissed a girl before. He kissed her back. They hugged and kissed for another five minutes, and then they let each other go and said goodnight.

As usual, Rafiq came down for breakfast early on Sunday morning, and Anil soon joined him.

"So, how was last night?" Rafiq asked.

"You can't tell Shama any of this, but I had a very good time," Anil said and then proceeded to tell Rafiq everything that had happened.

"Oh, my God, she kissed you on your first date?"

"Well, you kissed Shama on the fourth day after you met her - didn't you?"

"Yes, but that was different. I had met her in Nairobi."

"And exchanged ten words! Girls and boys here kiss on their first dates."

"Well, Anil, I can't say much, but I find it a little unusual. I think this girl is too fast."

"Don't worry, Rafiq. I'll be okay."

WHEN SHAMEEM CAME DOWN, she asked, "How was your evening with Jenny, Anil?"

"They went for dinner and dancing at a restaurant in Piccadilly. Anil had a good time," Rafiq answered.

From the looks on their faces, Shameem knew that there was much more to the story than that, but she was not going to ask if they did not want to tell her.

"Good, I'm happy you had fun. Are you going to see her again before December 31st?"

"Yes. Probably."

Shameem left it at that and proceeded to eat her breakfast and talk about getting their laundry done while Rafiq ran some errands. They had not talked about what they were going to do for her birthday on Christmas Eve, but she knew that she did not want to spend it with Jenny.

1963
Forty-Eight

Rafiq and Shameem moved to Mrs. Jackson's on Friday, December 20th, for their Christmas vacation.

When they returned from Jamatkhana, Anil told them that Jenny wanted to take him to a dancing club in Soho for Christmas Eve and had asked that he invite Shama and Rafiq to join them.

"Why don't you and Jenny go to this place by yourselves? Shama wants a quiet birthday celebration this year. We'll probably go out for dinner at Surma Bleu, and then on New Year's Eve, we'll all be together."

"Are you sure? It would be nice if we could all go together to celebrate Shama's birthday."

"No, thank you for inviting us, Anil, but you go ahead with Jenny and enjoy the evening," Shameem said.

AS THEY WERE EATING breakfast on the 24th, Anil came down and wished Shameem happy birthday and many happy returns, offered prayers for her good health and success in her education, and said that Jenny was on the phone and wanted to talk to Rafiq and her. The three climbed upstairs, and Shameem picked up the phone.

"Happy birthday to you and many happy returns, Shama!" Jenny said exuberantly.

"Thank you very much, Jenny, for your kind wishes," Shameem replied.

"I was so hoping that we would celebrate your birthday together. I would be delighted if you would join us."

"That's very kind of you, Jenny, but for this birthday, I think I just want to have a quiet dinner with Rafiq."

"Understood, but if you change your mind, we'd be delighted if you joined us."

"We'll look forward to seeing you on New Year's Eve. That can be a celebration for both Rafiq's and my birthdays."

"Absolutely. May I say hello to Rafiq?"

Shameem passed the telephone receiver to Rafiq, suppressing the urge to roll her eyes.

"Hello, Rafiq, how are you?" Jenny asked when Rafiq picked up the phone.

"I'm fine, Jenny, how are you?"

"I'm fine, but a little disappointed that you and Shama are not joining us tonight."

"As Shama said, she wants a quiet birthday this year. Inshallah, we'll be there with you on New Year's Eve."

"I look forward to that."

RAFIQ AND SHAMEEM HAD dinner at Surma Bleu that evening and returned home early. They watched television until midnight and then got ready to go to sleep. Mrs. Jackson, of course, knew by now that these two were not cousins, and she had no doubt that they were sleeping together, but she figured that they were smart and responsible adults, and besides, they paid her good money.

When Rafiq went into Shameem's room to kiss her goodnight, she asked him to lie in her bed with her as he did every Saturday and Sunday mornings.

As they lay kissing and holding each other, Shameem said, "Sophia told me that for two 22-year-olds, our relationship is unnatural. She couldn't believe that we've not been intimate. She said that if we want to keep our promise to our parents, there are contraceptives available in the stores."

"We know that, but you know, nothing is 100% safe, Shama. Forget about our commitments to our parents. Can you imagine having a child while you're in med school? What a disaster that would be for us!"

"I told her that. I also told her that the Pill is being perfected. Will we make love when the Pill is approved?"

"Yes, we will. I read a report, which said that the U.S.A. regulatory body is expected to approve the Pill early next year. It won't be long after that for it to become available here. We can't remain celibate until we marry."

"When will we marry, Rafiq? You have two years to go before you graduate, and then you want to do two years of M.B.A., and I have four years to go before I become a doctor, and I then want to specialize."

"We'll go home for the summer and get married when I finish my B.Sc., in two years. By that time, the Pill will long have been on the market."

SHAMEEM HAD PROMISED TO help Mrs. Jackson prepare Christmas dinner, so she rose early the next morning, expecting to see her in the kitchen, but she was still sleeping. She decided to bring Rafiq down for the two of them to have breakfast. She quietly walked up to his room and opened the door. Anil was fast asleep, but Rafiq was sitting up, saying his prayers. Sensing movement, he opened his eyes and saw Shameem. She quietly shut the door and went back to the kitchen, and Rafiq soon joined her. Shameem fried two eggs while Rafiq opened a can of baked beans, popped some bread into the toaster, and made tea.

As they sat down to eat breakfast, Rafiq said, "Anil came home at almost 2:00 a.m. this morning."

"Did he wake you when he came in?"

"No, I was up. I had not really gone to sleep. I was waiting for him."

"Why, in God's name would you do that?"

"I was just worried."

"So, are you going to do this every time he goes out on a date?"

"I guess I won't. There are no buses at that time. He must have taken a cab."

"Whatever time he got home at and how is not for us to worry about. He's not a child."

MRS. JACKSON EMERGED FROM her room at almost 9.30 a.m., and they wished each other Merry Christmas.

"You know, if you kids weren't here, I don't know what I would have done. I would probably not have cooked turkey dinner. I might have eaten yesterday's leftovers."

"We're happy to be here to enjoy a traditional British Christmas with you, Mrs. Jackson," Shameem said.

"Thank you very much for the lovely Christmas present. I have small gifts for the three of you under the tree," Mrs. Jackson said.

Rafiq and Shameem were surprised. They had not bought any gift for her. Obviously, Anil had bought one and put three names on the card.

"We hope that you will enjoy it," Rafiq said.

"It was thoughtful of you to get me the mixer. You know I like to make cakes and biscuits, and to whip flour, eggs, and butter is getting difficult for me at my age."

They sat and chatted with Mrs. Jackson while she ate her breakfast. Anil came down, still wearing his pajamas and nightgown at 10.30 a.m., and joined them at the table. The four sat chatting for an hour, and then Mrs. Jackson, who was also in her nightgown, said, "Let me go get dressed, and we can then work on the turkey."

"You didn't tell us you bought her a present, Anil!" Shameem said when Mrs. Jackson left.

"Oh, I bought that before you guys came here. I had heard her complaining a couple of times about the manual mixer."

"How much was it?"

"£7 Shs.10"

"Heavens! We'll divide that three ways."

"If you want, Shama. Let's see what gifts she has for us."

For Anil and Rafiq, there was one set each of Old Spice after-shave and lotion, but for Shameem, there was a beautiful silk *Christian Dior* scarf, which Shameem said was worth at least £5.

"Well, she likes you the most, even though she says she never wants girls living with her. As you know, before you guys moved here from Cardiff, I'd asked her if I could invite you two to stay here instead of at the university residences, and she said, "Absolutely." So I asked her, "But Mrs. Jackson, you don't like girls, and she said, "This, girl, I would pay her to stay with me.""

"Wow! What a compliment!" Rafiq said.

"Jenny missed you two last night. We had a great time. She very much looks forward to being with you on the 31st," Anil said.

"We look forward to that too," Rafiq said. Shameem stayed silent.

The three cleared the table and took out everything required for cooking the turkey dinner. The boys went upstairs to get dressed for the day.

"I'm sorry I woke you up last night when I came in."

"No, I hadn't yet fallen asleep."

"Why were you up so late?"

"Oh, I was just thinking about a conversation Shama and I had about getting married."

"Are you? Getting married? When?"

"Not now. In two years, when I graduate."

"Well, I'm happy you're talking about it."

"How did you enjoy your evening?"

"Very much. You know, going out with Rehana, everything was very restrained, very calculated. We would dance close and then pull back. We would get into very personal discussions and then and then become formal. Hold hands and let go. It was lovely to be with her, but also very taxing. Jenny is uninhibited. She was kissing me on the Tube. At the club, she wanted to dance nonstop. She said she has never danced with anyone as good as me."

"Well, I'm glad you enjoyed yourself."

"She's very much looking forward to celebrating New Year's Eve with Shama and you."

"Why? I would have thought she would want to be alone with you."

"I think that she's grateful to Shama for introducing me to her, and she thinks you have a heart of gold."

"How would she know that? We met just once."

"She'd found out a great deal about all three of us before she approached Shama. She initially thought Shama was my sister."

"Happy to know that she likes us … and you, too! And what about you? Do you like her? You must like her to go out on two dates in ten days."

"She's fun to be with."

ANIL, RAFIQ, AND SHAMEEM were all dressed up for the Ismaili Centre's

New Year's Eve event and did not want to ride the bus and Tube. They took a cab to Jenny's hostel and picked her up. Anil was in the passenger seat and Rafiq and Shameem in the back seat. Rafiq moved over to the center to make room for Jenny. She climbed in, hugged Rafiq, and kissed him on both cheeks, and said, "Happy birthday to you, in advance. My best wishes." She then reached over to Shameem and pulled her to give her a peck on her cheek too. "I'm so happy to meet you both again," she said.

THE NEW YEAR'S EVE Ismaili dinner and dance was the usual affair. Good food, proper venue, and a reasonably good band. The best part was meeting other Ismailis. They rang in the New Year and got up to leave shortly after 1.00 a.m. Rafiq suggested to Anil that he take another cab, as he would need to go up to say good-night to Jenny, and they couldn't keep the taxi waiting for too long. Anil agreed.

1964
Forty-Nine

Rafiq and Shameem returned to their residences and college on Rafiq's birthday. They were both now 22 years old. Some concerns Rafiq had about Jenny had dissipated after spending New Year's Eve with her. She was charming. She had asked to dance with him, and she was a good dancer. She had made him laugh. Shameem had become attached to Anil and loved him like a brother, and perhaps, was being overprotective. Jenny was okay.

THEIR SECOND COLLEGE YEAR was busy for both. They came over to Mrs. Jackson's for the weekend, but their weekends were now increasingly shaped by Jenny. They always met up at the Centre on Fridays and Jenny took it from there. Anil was now attending Jamatkhana almost every Friday. For their third weekend in January, she had bought tickets for *Lawrence of Arabia*, which was running in the West End. Rafiq had been anxiously waiting for the movie to go on general release for them to see it at their local cinema, but that would not happen for another year. Tickets were expensive, but Jenny refused to take any money from them. It was her treat. Shameem said that they were grateful that Jenny had arranged to buy the tickets and paid for them, but hereon, they must share everything. All agreed.

Anil spent most Saturday afternoons with Jenny, and then they met up with Rafiq and Shameem for dinner. Every two months or so, they went to see a play and went dancing on special occasions to new places that Jenny introduced them to.

Whatever they discussed over dinners or coffee, Jenny brought the conversation back to money and business. Once, she asked Rafiq, "Do you know about this Beaconsfield Investments IPO? The IPO last week was at £2 a share. The shares are trading at £2. Shs.10. That's a 25% gain."

"I don't follow the stock market. I will be taking a securities course next year, and I will have to become familiar with the European and North American stock markets, and particularly what's trading on the London and New York Stock Exchanges," Rafiq replied.

"Wow, that will be our opportunity to make big money! Once you become an expert, we can all pool our funds together and buy some winning stocks."

"Predicting the stock market is very difficult, Jenny. Unless you buy blue-chip securities and have the stomach to see the shares go down by 50% and hang on to them for the longer term, you can lose a lot investing in the stock market."

"I read about this guy who invested £500 in a stock which very quickly doubled in price, and he kept investing his profits in new securities, and in few years, he has become a millionaire."

"That's good for him, but not everyone's that lucky - or that savvy."

On another occasion, Jenny said to Anil and Rafiq, "I've been thinking about all the goods we import in East Africa. We know the countries well. Most of the imports come from the U.K. If you two could get your parents to provide working capital, we could establish an export company here and export to Kenya, Uganda, and Tanganyika. We wouldn't have to handle any goods. We would just take orders, pass them to manufacturers and they would ship the goods out. We would get our commission. Once we have traded with the manufacturers long enough, they will supply us on credit, and we wouldn't need any working capital either."

"Who would do this, Jenny? Who would find out who the importers in East Africa are, what they import, what terms they get at this time, and why they would buy from us?" Anil asked.

"I asked my brother to find out what's being imported in Kenya. He got from the Customs Department a complete listing of what Kenya imports, what quantities, and for how much."

"You are really interested in business, aren't you?" Rafiq asked.

"Nothing ventured, nothing gained. We are here. We have the opportunity to make money. You can't make money working for someone."

"I admire your aspirations. I do not doubt that you'll become a very successful businesswoman one day. At this time, Anil, Shama, and I need to concentrate on our studies. Also, I doubt our parents will give us money to invest in a business that can distract us from our studies."

WHEN THEY GOT HOME that evening, Shameem said to Rafiq, "This girl has nothing to talk about other than money. To be honest, I'm getting a little tired of listening to her talk all the time about ways of making money. Why do you indulge her? I can see that Anil doesn't like it, either."

"You have to give it to her, Shama. The girl is ambitious. It's people like her who become wheeler-dealers and make money."

"What will you do with the money when your life is consumed with making money?"

IN DECEMBER 1963, THE British had ended the Protectorate status for Zanzibar and made provision for full self-government. Zanzibar became a constitutional monarchy under the Arab Sultan. Just a month later, the Sultan was overthrown in a violent revolution. The Sultanate was replaced by the People's Republic of Zanzibar and Pemba. Some 20,000 people (mostly Arabs who were seen as the colonists, and many Indians) were killed in the revolution. All were dispossessed of all their assets. The remaining Indian population, which included some 2,000 Ismailis, fled to Tanganyika and Kenya.

The arrival of these Ismaili refugees in Dar es Salaam and Mombasa, where most settled, had been disconcerting for the Ismailis in the two countries. The community came together to support the displaced Ismailis. Under their Imam's guidance and with his support, refugee resettlement programs were formulated and implemented, resulting in a majority of the Zanzibarian Ismailis restarting their lives on the mainland and their children becoming integrated into the education system. But the revolution had raised serious concern in the minds of the Indian community in East Africa: could this happen in Kenya, Uganda, or Tanganyika?

And it did.

Two months after the Zanzibar revolution, the Tanganyikan army mutinied. For two days, the military and mobs of people robbed businesses, practically all of which were Indian owned, and attacked people in Dar es Salaam. Fortunately, this did not spread beyond the capital city. The government called the British for help who arrived promptly, and the mutineers surrendered. Peace was restored. In April 1964, the Zanzibar republic merged with mainland Tanganyika. The United Republic of Tanganyika and Zanzibar was renamed "The United Republic of Tanzania."

"WE ARE NO LONGER Tanganyika. The new name of our country is Tanzania," Salim wrote to Rafiq.

EARLY IN HIS THIRD term of the second university year, Rafiq started to think about going into the third year of university with him and Shameem continuing to live in the students' residences. It was very difficult for him not to see Shameem from Monday to Thursday, and it was even more difficult being at Mrs. Jackson's over the weekends with her and not sleeping in her bed. He knew that this was equally difficult for Shameem. This, he was convinced, could not go on.

The Pill had come on the market in April. Shameem had mentioned this to him and had expected him to tell her to start taking it. He had not. He had begun to think about suggesting to Shameem that they travel to East Africa during their summer vacation and get married. They would both be close to 23 years old in August – a little too young to get married; he had always thought he would marry when he was 25, but he would be the same age his father was when he got married. If they married, when they returned to the U.K., they would stay with Mrs. Jackson until they found a nice apartment to rent, not too far from their colleges. Before speaking to Shameem about this, he decided that he should talk to his parents and get their consent. He did not want to suggest the idea to Shameem and then find that his parents were not supportive.

He called home at a pre-arranged time. Salim picked up the phone and said, "Is everything okay, Son?"

"Yes, Dad, all is well. I'm happy to know that things have settled down after the mutiny, and life is as usual for you guys. How's Mom? Has she gotten over Chelsea and Janet's departure?"

"Mom's fine. Chelsea and Jane left a big void in her life, but she has settled back into her old routine. She's encouraging several Africans to join the Club. Some have, and she is making new friends."

"Good for her. Dad, I want to speak to you about something very important."

"Sure, go on."

"As I've told you, Shameem and I stay in the students' residences and spend the weekends with Anil's landlady. Shameem has her room downstairs, and I stay in Anil's room. We've kept our promise to you, and we don't sleep together, but as you can understand, this is very difficult. Also, I miss Shameem a lot during weekdays and she misses me. I want to suggest to Shameem that we come home during our summer vacation and get married in August. We can then come back, rent a flat, and stay together. The cost will not be much different from what it is now for us. But before I suggest this to Shameem, I wanted to seek Mom's and your consent and blessings."

"You have taken me by surprise, and we'll have to talk to Mom about this, but the thought had crossed my mind. But first, tell me, is there anything forcing this idea of marriage?"

"No, Dad, Shameem is not pregnant."

"Okay. I have not been happy with your current situation and have thought about the possibility of you two getting married, but I don't know if you can handle the responsibilities of married life and your education."

"We'll be just fine, Dad. I have thought a great deal about this, and we'll manage fine. If Mom agrees, Shameem agrees, and her parents agree, we will learn to cook when we are there and organize our lives in a way that it won't affect our studies."

"Marriage is more than cooking dinners, Son, but I'm with you. I agree with your thinking. I think it'll be good for both of you. You are a bit younger than I think you should be to marry but you are a smart and mature person. Here, talk to your mom."

"Congratulations, your son wants to get married," Salim whispered to Yasmin as he passed the phone to her.

"What?" she mouthed silently to Salim as she pressed the receiver to her ear. "Rafiq? Is Shameem pregnant? What is going on?"

"No, Mom, she is *not* pregnant. She doesn't even know I'm having this conversation with you." With that, he repeated to Yasmin what he had told his dad.

"I think I'm comfortable with the idea. You can't go on living the way you are. And yes, why not get married? I would have wanted to if I were Shameem. But you know, marriage has its own challenges. We would not want you to get married and then not be able to pay attention to your studies. What if a baby comes along? Will Shameem give up her education?"

"Mom, we won't have a baby until we have graduated and started working."

"I support your idea, but Dad and I have to talk. Give us a few days. Call us next Sunday."

"Okay, Mom."

"Don't talk to Shameem until we have talked on Sunday."

"I won't, Mom."

BASED ON THEIR INITIAL reactions, Rafiq was not worried that his parents would not agree. They might suggest that they wait for another year, although that would make no sense because nothing would change in a year. All that would happen would be that Shameem and he would suffer for another year. He wondered what they would come back with.

WHEN HE CALLED ON Sunday, Yasmin picked up the phone. "Rafiq, we have thought carefully about your proposition, and we agree that you two should get married this year. Talk to Shameem and see what she says. Tell her that your dad and I endorse the idea and will do whatever is necessary to support you. Here, talk to your dad."

"Rafiq, yes, we want you to get married this summer, but when you speak to Shameem, tell her that for you two to live together after you marry, we will buy a nice flat or a house in London for you. We are not going to waste money on rentals or have you live in poor quality housing. Also, we will buy you a small car. We want you to be happy and comfortable as you study, and she can tell her parents this, if and when she talks to them. She can also tell her parents that when you are married, she will be part of *our* family, and we will pay for education and living expenses for both of you. And you are our only child so we will have a nice wedding."

Rafiq was overwhelmed. He asked, "Can you afford all this, Dad?"

"We clear over 16,000 Shillings per month from our two businesses. After taxes and our religious obligations, we are left with almost 13,000 Shillings. Our living expenses are less than 2,000 Shillings. We send 9,000 Shillings to you and we are still left with over 2,000 Shillings from our income. We have significant accumulated savings here and you should have over £20,000 in our savings account there. So, yes, we can afford this."

"Thank you so much, Dad. I love you both."

"And we love you too, Son. Here, say goodbye to your mom."

"Rafiq, speak to Shameem and then call us and tell us what she says. If she would like us to talk to her parents about this, I'll be happy to do that."

"I love you, Mom. Thank you so much."

"You deserve our love and all we can do for you, Son."

SHAMEEM HAD WONDERED WHAT he wanted to talk to his parents about when Rafiq had told her that he was going to the corner phone booth, instead of using the phone in Anil's room to call them. She had not asked, but when he returned, she could see that he was very happy.

"Shama, let's go out for dinner tonight. Just the two of us."

"Without Anil and Jenny?"

"Yes, I'll tell Anil that we want to be alone tonight."

RAFIQ TOOK SHAMEEM TO a nice, newly opened Indian restaurant in Earl's Court. After eating a delicious dinner and *kulfi* for dessert, Rafiq said, "Shama, we both miss each other so much during the week, and over the weekends, after hugging and kissing you, it's very difficult for me to go back to my bedroom. I've been thinking a lot about our situation, and I propose that we go home for the summer vacation and get married."

"Are you proposing, Rafiq?"

"Yes, but I don't have an engagement ring to give you right now. I'll buy you one that you like."

"That would be wonderful, my love! Nothing could make me happier. But we have to talk to our parents. Where would we live after we marry and can we afford to live together? You know that other than frying an egg, I can't cook anything. What will we eat?"

"I talked to my parents, and they strongly support the idea that we get married. They have also said that they will buy us a house and a car, and after we are married, they will fund your education. You will no longer be your parents' responsibility. You will be part of *my* family."

Shameem looked down at her plate, and when she looked up, tears were rolling down her face. "Your parents are so kind and loving, Rafiq. They must love us both, so much. I would be so happy if we can get married."

"So, let's call your parents tomorrow and see what they say."

"Okay, I will. Shall we tell Anil? And what about Robert and Bernice?"

Rafiq noticed that she had mentioned Bernice, but not Jenny.

"Let's wait until you talk to your parents, and then we can tell them."

AFTER SHAMEEM HAD ASSURED her mother that she was not pregnant (they would be able to see that she was not when she came to Kenya), her parents could not have been happier to hear what she told them. The fact that Rafiq's parents had offered to buy them a house in London and a car, and assume payments for Shameem's education and living costs, was unbelievable. They must be much wealthier than they had thought.

"You and Rafiq have our blessings, Shama. We know that you two will be very happy together. Should we call and say something to Rafiq's parents?" Gulshan asked.

"No, Rafiq said that his parents would call you and formally ask for my hand in marriage. I hope that you will say yes.'"

"Of course, we will!"

RAFIQ INFORMED HIS PARENTS that Shameem and her family were delighted with his proposal and asked them to call her parents to formally ask for Shameem's hand in marriage, which they did.

The following Sunday, Rafiq invited Anil and Jenny out for dinner. They went to the same restaurant in Earl's Court, where he and Shameem had gone to the previous Sunday.

After dinner, Rafiq said, "Shama and I have an announcement to make. We are planning to get married this summer in Nairobi."

"Wow! That's wonderful! Congratulations! I wish I could attend your wedding, but I've used up all my vacation," Jenny said as she hugged and kissed Shameem and Rafiq.

"That's great, Rafiq, Shama. I'm delighted! My best wishes and prayers are with you, always. *I* will, of course, attend your wedding, although you've not yet invited me," Anil said, laughing.

"Of course, you must be there. There would be no wedding without you, Anil," Rafiq said as Anil hugged him and offered more prayers.

1964
Fifty

Like everyone, Robert was delighted to hear Rafiq and Shameem's plans.

"Rob, we would really like you and Bernice to attend our wedding. I would also like your parents to attend and bless our wedding, but I will understand if they don't want to return to Africa so soon after having come back here. You and Bernice can fly straight to Nairobi for a week. Shameem's and my parents will arrange and pay for accommodations for all guests at the Norfolk or New Stanley. Your room and meals will be taken care of. Can you think about it, please? You and Anil are my two closest friends. Anil is planning to come. Shameem and I would be very happy if you and Bernice could be there, also."

"Thank you, Rafiq. I'd love to. Let me speak with Bernice and get back to you. I think Bernice can afford £100 for the airfare. I certainly, can. We've got time. When do you plan to fly out?"

"We're planning to depart for Nairobi on June 27th. I'll stay there for a week and then go to Mpwapwa and spend three weeks at home. My parents and I are planning to arrive in Nairobi on July 26th, and we would like Anil, Bernice, and you to reach there by the 27th if you can. Jenny can't come. She has no vacation left. We would like to set Saturday, August 1st, as the wedding date and depart for our honeymoon on the following Monday. "

"Sounds good. Please convey my congratulations to Shama. Rafiq, may I ask – just curious…"

"Shoot."

"Are you still a virgin?"

"Yes, I am."

"Pity."

ROBERT CALLED A WEEK later to say that Bernice was very excited about going to East Africa. They had decided that if they were going there, he should take her on the safari that they had been on, and then spend a week in Mombasa on the beach. They were looking to take four weeks vacation. They would blow all of their savings, but this would be a vacation of a lifetime for Bernice. The D.C. and Jane were also delighted to hear the news and had conveyed their congratulations and best wishes to Rafiq and Shameem.

"That's wonderful, Rob, that's just wonderful. Shama will be thrilled when I tell her this."

"Sooo…I will be your best man, Rafiq? I'm older than you; Anil is younger."

"I would love for you to be my best man, Rob, but unfortunately, you can't, and Anil can't, either. In my culture, the best man has to be married – not single. Also, I'm sorry to tell you that you and Bernice will not be able to attend the formal wedding ceremony which will be in our Jamatkhana where you cannot come, but it will be a short contract signing ceremony which just the family members attend. This will be followed immediately by a reception at the hotel where we will all stay, and that's where all of our wedding celebrations will be. It might sound crazy to Bernice - and to you too - to be invited to go all the way to East Africa to attend a wedding that you cannot attend, but please explain to her that the real celebration will be the reception. And please tell your mom and dad that when we're back in the U.K., Shameem and I will come and visit them in Cardiff to seek their blessings."

"Totally understood, don't worry. I'll explain the situation to Bernice and give your message to my parents.

SHAMEEM AND RAFIQ NEXT wrote to Mrs. Bowes and Sophia to tell them about their wedding plans and to invite them, as well. Both were delighted to hear the news. Mrs. Bowes replied to thank them for their invitation but said she was too old to undertake such a long journey, and Sophia said that her parents were to visit the U.K. in the summer, and they had planned to go over the Continent.

THE EXCITEMENT STARTED TO build in Kenya and Tanzania as the month of June approached. It was the reverse for Shameem and Rafiq. Their focus had shifted from dreaming about their wedding to preparing for their second-year exams. They had left the excitement to their families, who talked by phone twice or three times a week.

From their side, Yasmin advised Gulshan, they would need 11 hotel rooms – for themselves, Anil's parents, Yasmin's two brothers and their wives (who lived in Tabora), Salim's two sisters and their husbands (who resided in Mwanza), Chelsea and Ricardo, Rob and his wife (not girlfriend), one each for Anil and Tazim, and the bridal suite for Rafiq and Shameem.

On their next phone call, Gulshan told her that they had booked the rooms at the newly built and luxurious New Stanley Hotel at Shs.100 per night per room, including full hot breakfasts. Given the number of rooms they were booking, the hotel would not charge anything for the bridal suite. In the Ismaili tradition, they (the Adatias) would host the groom's family and their guests and would pick up the hotel costs and host all lunches and dinners for everyone for the entire week.

This, Yasmin said, was totally unacceptable. In the Ismaili tradition, the Adatias could host Salim and her, but not all of their guests and, other than one lunch on the day following the wedding that, in the Ismaili tradition, the Adatias could host, the Abdullas would pay for all of the Abdulla family's guests' accommodation and meals for the entire week. This, of course, was not in keeping with Ismaili tradition and not acceptable to Gulshan.

In the Ismaili tradition, there were soft arguments. Proposals and counter-proposals were floated. Finally, it was agreed that the Abdullas would pay for all of their own guests' accommodation; the Adatias would pay for Yasmin and Salim's room, and the two families would split the cost of all meals for all guests of both families for the week.

Having settled, Yasmin was not happy with the settlement. "I don't want Shameem's family to incur large costs. The way that Gulshan has argued about this, I bet that she won't give us the account for our share of the guests' meals. She will tell us to forget about it and won't take the money from us," she said to Salim.

"And you haven't talked about the wedding reception yet, my dear. That will be another interesting conversation."

"Oh, no. We had that conversation already. Do you know what Gulshan was suggesting? She said that because 75% of the guests would be from their side, they will pay 75% of the cost! We are looking at some 150 people at Shs.35 a plate. Seventy-five percent of that would be 4,300 Shillings. After lots of arguments, we agreed to go fifty-fifty."

"Look at it this way, Yasmin, we are fortunate that Rafiq is marrying into a family that is so generous. We could have ended up with a family that could have tried to offload as much on us as possible."

"That, I agree. Throughout these discussions, Gulshan has been so generous, but I don't want them to spend more than us on this wedding, and I don't want Shameem to feel that we did not carry our weight. Thank God, this is over, and we are now at fifty-fifty overall, but I am still concerned that they will not give us the lunch and dinner accounts and let us share that cost."

"Don't worry, when we check-in, I will pay the hotel the full reception cost, and when Gulshan and Bahadur ask why we did that, we'll tell them not to worry. When they send us the guests' lunch and dinner accounts, we will add the numbers to the reception cost and divide the total by two and settle the difference. If they don't give us the costs, we won't take half of the reception cost from them."

"That's smart. I like that."

THE NEXT ORDER OF business for Rafiq and Shameem was to plan for the wedding. Shameem had to prepare the list of her friends in Nairobi to be invited to the wedding and reception, to give to her parents. They would take care of all other invites. For Rafiq, other than Anil, Rob, and Bernice, whom he had already invited, his parents would take care of invitations to their respective relatives, Fateh and Almas, Chelsea and Ricardo, and send "courtesy" invitations to a whole lot of their friends and distant relatives, expecting no one to attend. In the unlikely event that anyone did, they would have to be accommodated in the reception where 25 seats were reserved for the Abdullas.

SHAMEEM SELECTED A DIAMOND engagement ring and a gold wedding band and purchased a tailored white skirt suit for the Jamatkhana wedding ceremony. Her mother had acquired a beautiful white saree for her to wear at the reception. Shameem had such an extensive collection of outfits and matching shoes, handbags, and jewelry from her purchases in Cardiff and London that she did not need to buy anything more. What she could take with her was also limited by the baggage allowance. Both British Airways and East Africa Airways permitted only 44 lbs in checked baggage.

At Anil's insistence, Rafiq purchased a new navy blue suit, a white shirt, and a matching tie from Austin Reed for the wedding and the reception. He, too, had a large collection of smart suits, shirts, shoes, ties, and other accessories and did not require anything more. With that, both were set for their wedding.

"Rafiq, we have decided on the date we will leave for our honeymoon, but we have not decided where we will go and for how long. You had mentioned that we would go to a beach resort in Malindi, near Mombasa, or spend a week in Dar es Salaam. Should I ask my mom to make any reservations?" Shameem asked Rafiq as they waited for their departure date.

"Malindi was my thought. I also want to show you Dar es Salaam, but is that what you would like to do?"

"You know what I would really like to do? I would like you to take me on the safari that you went on – to Mara, Serengeti, and Ngorongoro and then have a beach holiday in Dar es Salaam. Do you remember that you had promised to take me on safari when we first met?"

"That's what Rob and Bernice are planning to do - minus Dar es Salaam."

"Are they? Can we go with them?"

"People don't go on honeymoon with their friends, Shama!"

"Now, that's a stupid notion. If we're with Rob and Bernice, I'm sure that we will all respect one another's privacy and yet have each other's company during sightseeing. Imagine, if we went alone and ran into your or my close friends at a resort, would we run away from them? Not socialize with them? Not have dinners together? Not take game drives with them?"

"Sure, we would."

"So, then why can't we go with Rob and Bernice, unless they want to be alone? Have they booked?"

Rafiq could see that further debate would prove fruitless. He knew that when Shameem said something with that tone in her voice, there would be no point in trying to argue, so he said, "I think that they would love to go with us. I'll call Rob today and check. They're not booked yet, but Rob was saying that he would book with the agent we used the last time."

"ARE YOU SERIOUS? SHAMA wouldn't mind spending her honeymoon in our company?" Rob asked, incredulously. "Look, if you're asking me whether we'd mind you joining us on the safari, I mean, c'mon! That would basically be like redoing the holiday that we took together, only this time, with your wife and my girlfriend! I don't even need to ask Bernice – she'll be thrilled! Are you absolutely sure that Shama doesn't mind?"

"Her take is that you and Bernice will give us our space and privacy and that beyond that, it'll be great to spend time together. We don't even need to call it a honeymoon. We'll just tell everyone that we're going on safari with our friends and will then go on a beach honeymoon to Dar es Salaam to swim and 'honeymoon' for a week after that. From Dar es Salaam, Shameem and I will go to Mpwapwa to spend some time with my parents, and then, before returning to London, we'll spend a week with Shameem's parents in Nairobi."

"I can't tell you how happy I am, Rafiq, and I can't wait to tell Bernice that we'll be on safari together. Will you speak to Anil? Ask him to join? Then it will be like the good old days."

"I sure will."

"NO, RAFIQ," SAID ANIL with finality. "I can't come with you guys. I don't have a wife or a girlfriend, and I don't want to be a fifth wheel. Also, I want to be back at the office when my fourth year C.A. results come out. Depending on how well the articling students do in their courses, they get assigned specific roles for next year, but when more than one student has performed equally well and want to be assigned a specific function, you have to fight for it. Rehana emphasized that

I should be there to make my case for what I want and not return after a leisurely summer vacation to be given whatever is left over."

"I understand," conceded Rafiq. "We'll really miss you, Anil. It would've been like the old times."

IN THE DAYS RAFIQ was free in June, he had studied London's residential market. He had also met with Alan Meadows, a successful realtor who was Karim's client. Meadows familiarized them with London's residential real estate scene. They wanted to be within 30 minutes of their colleges by Tube or car and wanted to live in a good area. Shameem would have been happy to live in a flat, but Rafiq was thinking long term. What if what Anil was saying about how things could turn out in East Africa a few years after independence was correct and his parents had to move out? They would likely come to the U.K. His dad had said that he could buy something for up to £15,000 and with that kind of money, they could buy a large house.

"That's a generous budget. You could be looking at properties in better areas of London." Meadows had said.

"Regent Park?" Rafiq asked.

"Not quite. You would need much more money to go there. But there are other excellent areas that meet your requirements."

Meadows showed them several houses but did not pressure them to put offers on any. He was an ethical person who did not want to take advantage of two students with no knowledge of real estate.

"Look, guys, I'll be happy when you are back from Africa to familiarize you with the options fully, and then you can make an educated decision. London is a big place with many options, and the last thing you want to do is make a decision that you'll come to regret in the future," he had said.

In their viewing of the houses and residential areas, both Shameem and Rafiq had liked Harrow. It was well located and populated, in the main, by upper-middle-class people. It was also well served by transit, shopping, education, health care, and other facilities. Most houses they had seen were spacious, with large and well-maintained lots. And they were priced within their budget. Meadows had also shown them beautiful homes in "nice" outlying areas that they could purchase for less than half of their budget, but their commutes would be longer, and the neighborhoods not as upscale as Harrow.

They agreed to connect with Meadows when they were back.

1964
Fifty-One

Shameem and Rafiq arrived in Nairobi on the morning of 28th June. Shameem's dad and mom were at the airport. Standing in the upper-level terrace of the airport, they watched Shameem and Rafiq emerge from the plane and could not contain their happiness to see the two walking on the tarmac towards them. They spotted and waved vigorously at one another.

Shameem's parents could not wait for her and Rafiq to emerge from the Customs area. They had not seen their daughter for four years and were so looking forward to meeting Rafiq. When they did, they saw how much Shameem had grown, and Gulshan could see the change in the quiet and soft-spoken boy who had come into her store, and she had told her daughter that someday she would ask him to marry her. Now, they were here to marry. Bahadur, although he had seen Rafiq's pictures, was surprised to see how tall and handsome he was. His daughter was fortunate to find him, and Rafiq, too, was lucky to find his daughter.

As they drove home, Shameem and her mom talked endlessly about all kinds of things. Bahadur tried to chat with Rafiq, but after an overnight flight from London during which he had little sleep, he was happy to just eavesdrop on the women's conversation. It appeared to him that they wanted to speak about everything they could have talked about in four years if Shameem had not gone to the U.K.

They drove to Shameem's place in the Parklands suburb. It was a nice, well-furnished three-bedroom flat on the second level in a three-story building. Shameem's room had been prepared as she had left it. Rafiq was booked to stay at the New

Stanley hotel. It would not have been appropriate for him to stay in his girlfriend's place before they were married, and, in any case, there was no room for him in the flat. Adil occupied the third bedroom.

After freshening up and lunch, Rafiq asked that he be dropped off at the hotel for him to rest, and he would take a taxi in the evening to come back.

Bahadur drove Rafiq to the New Stanley, checked him in, and said he would be back at 6.00 p.m. to take him back home for dinner. Some close relatives would join.

THE DINNER THAT EVENING at Shameem's place was a formal affair. Shameem's brother Adil was there, but so were Bahadur's brother and sister and Gulshan's two brothers and two sisters and their respective spouses. There was not enough room for seventeen at the table, so only Rafiq, Shameem, her parents, and Bahadur's brother and the eldest of Gulshan's siblings (a sister) and their respective spouses (eight in all) sat at the table. The rest filled in their plates and sat in the lounge to eat buffet style.

This was, of course, Rafiq's formal introduction to Shameem's family – a large family. Her cousins were not present, and Rafiq wondered how many they would all add up to. As he was introduced to each uncle and aunt, he got warm smiles and approving looks.

After dinner, Rafiq sat next to Adil, who was anxious to check out his brother in law to be and was suitably impressed with Rafiq. He said he had a good job and a girlfriend he would have liked to have invited to this dinner, but whereas she would have been happy to meet Shameem and him, she was not anxious to meet all of his uncles and aunts. He was saving up to buy a flat near his parents' place and then get married. He would arrange for the four of them to spend time together.

Each uncle and aunt took turns sitting with Rafiq. They all said the same things: how happy they were to meet him; they were very much looking forward to the wedding and meeting his parents; their best wishes and prayers were with Rafiq and Shameem; they had heard much about him and were confident that he would make Shameem very happy.

As the evening wore on, Rafiq hoped that the visitors would leave, Shameem's parents would retreat into their bedroom, and he would be able to sit with Shameem and hug and kiss her. At around 9.30 p.m., he took Shameem aside and asked, "When are these people going to leave?"

"Leave? They will stay here long after you leave. They will want to talk about you, so they are waiting for *you* to leave. If you are tired, I can ask Adil to drop you at the hotel."

"Can you meet me tomorrow at the hotel?"

"Yes, I'll come around early with my parents when they go to the store, but I will meet you in the lobby or the restaurant. I can't be seen going up to your room with you."

RAFIQ ENJOYED HIS WEEK in Nairobi. Adil's girlfriend, Narmeen, was a teacher at the Aga Khan School. She was shy and talked little but smiled a lot. Rafiq liked her. She and Adil took Shameem and Rafiq out for lunches and dinners (Rafiq made sure that they went at least twice to Curry Pot that Robert had talked about so much, and he loved the food there) and to the Drive-In to see an Indian movie. They visited the Nairobi National Park with its sizable population of wildlife - but nothing approaching Mara, Serengeti or Ngorongoro - and Thika and Fourteen Falls which were a day trip from Nairobi. Rafiq was surprised by how close the Nairobi National Park was to the city and the Drive-In. He wondered if the lions in the park watched movies on the large Drive-In screen at night after a hearty impala or wildebeest meal. Shameem introduced Rafiq to her friends, and together, they invited them to the wedding and reception.

RAFIQ TOOK THE MORNING one hour flight to Dar es Salaam on 5th July and departed for (Gulwe) Mpwapwa by train the same afternoon and arrived in Mpwapwa the next morning. Salim was at the train station. He spotted Rafiq looking out of the window, they waved at each other, and Salim ran to maintain pace with Rafiq's car as it came to a stop. Rafiq emerged with his suitcase, which he dropped to the ground and hugged his dad. They held each other in an embrace for a long time. When they unlocked, tears were running down both their faces.

"You cannot imagine how much we have missed you, Rafiq, every day, every moment."

"And me, too, Dad. You and Mom have been in my thoughts every day. How are you, Dad? You look fine. You look like you have put on some weight."

"Yes, full 10 lbs. It's the fatty foods and desserts we eat at the Club."

"Has mom put on weight?"

"Not one ounce."

"But she also eats the Club food?"

"Yes, but since Chelsea and Jane's departure, she has been walking a lot. She often makes me climb the Rock, and we go and sit there on the Rock Rob, and you used to sit on."

As they walked out of the train station, Salim said, "Rafiq, I have a surprise for you."

"Yes? What?"

"Look over there," Salim said, pointing to a car.

"Wow, Dad, that's an S Class Mercedes Benz. When did you acquire this?"

"We bought it one month back, and I picked it up from the dealership in Dar es Salaam three weeks ago."

"But Dad, you are not into these frivolities – these status symbols. Why did you buy this?"

As Rafiq admired the beautiful two-tone light gray with dark gray top and leather upholstered German-engineered machine and they both climbed into the car, Salim said, "In the eight years we have been here, we have used the Land Rover the Buttons left us – and it was four years old then. The vehicle served us well, but the odometer now reads 80,000 miles; metal fatigue has set in, and things break down. On rough roads, the car rattles, and on dirt roads, powdery dust gets into the car. The other day, I saw your mom's hair covered with dust when we arrived in Dodoma, and I decided there and then that she deserved something better. As you know, we don't even own the house we live in or the premises we run our business out of, and we have lived a simple life with few acquisitions."

"But isn't an S Class Mercedes an overkill? Where will you go with this car in a small place like Mpwapwa? And where will you carry the inventory you buy for the store every month in Dodoma? The trunk in this car is large but not large enough for you to carry the store merchandise."

"I didn't want to buy this. I wanted to buy a Peugeot 403 station wagon in which, with the second-row seats folded down, you can carry much merchandise, but Fateh uncle said that I shouldn't be going to Dodoma any more to buy inventory. I should send him the list of what we need, and he would make the purchases for us and send them over with the supplies for the Club and the Teacher's college and other operations that Almin supplies to in Mpwapwa. This made sense. He insisted, however, that we should visit them in Dodoma at least twice a month and spend Saturday nights there, and we should get something comfortable to drive."

"When Fateh uncle suggested this, my preference was to get a Peugeot 403 sedan, but Fateh uncle said the price difference between the 403 and top of the line Peugeot 505 was not large and that's what we should get. We looked into it and decided to layout 18,000 Shillings to buy a Peugeot 505. They call it a poor man's Mercedes."

"So how did a Peugeot 505 turn into an S Class Mercedes 220 SE?"

"Well, Fateh uncle called one day and said a Mercedes salesman was visiting him and trying to sell him a new model of Mercedes 190 for around 20,000 Shillings. This was a low introductory offer. He told the agent that he was not in the market for a new car, no matter how attractive the price was, but I was looking to buy a Peugeot 505, and he should talk to me. He said the agent was prepared to drive over to Mpwapwa and suggested we see him. So, we did."

"And he convinced you to lay out another 12,000 Shillings? This must have cost at least 30,000."

"You seem well informed about cars."

"Yes, Dad, Mercedes is the car of my dreams, so I do look at the brochures and prices."

"Okay, hear me out. The agent – his name is Haji - was a nice Ismaili guy and it didn't take him fifteen minutes to convince your mom and me to upgrade to a Mercedes for 2,000 Shillings more but as we selected the color and did the paperwork, he stopped and said that for the past four months, his manager had been driving an S Class 220 SE. It had about 4,000 miles on the clock, and the manager was planning to replace it with a new S Class 350 SE. If he did, they would sell his car as a discounted demonstrator. The new one was ~30,000 Shillings. As a demo, it would be discounted to ~24,000. It was a gorgeous car and still under warranty, which he could probably get for us for ~23,000 Shillings. He asked if we would be interested in this deal. Mom and I talked, and we agreed to upgrade if the price was right, but we said we needed to look at the car."

"So, you looked at this and bought it?"

"Well, finally, we agreed to sign the paperwork for a new Mercedes 190, and Haji said he would go back and check out the demo deal, and if it could not be bought for around 23,000 Shillings then we could pick up the car we had signed up for. If the vehicle was available at the right price, he would tear up the paperwork for the 190, and we could pick up the S Class if we liked it. "

"Wow, Dad, so you moved from wanting to buy a Peugeot 403 for 13,000 Shillings to an S Class Mercedes for 23,000 Shillings. Of course, you and mom sure deserve this, but for Mpwapwa, this may be too pretentious?"

"Well, we paid 23,500 to be exact. When I went to Dar es Salaam, the car had been cleaned, serviced, and polished and was sitting in the showroom with a sticker price of 25,000 Shillings. Haji told me there were already two offers on it for 23,000 Shillings. Both had been signed back for 24,000. If I wanted, he would try an offer of 23,500 Shillings. I had fallen in love with the car and would have paid 24,000 Shillings, but Haji took in my offer and emerged with the manager from his office after talking to him for 10 minutes.

"Haji tells me you have been friends since you were five years old and has convinced me to give you the car for 23,500 Shillings. So, I'm going to give it to you. Haji, do the paperwork, he said, looking at Haji and told me to come back the next day with a certified check."

"Looks like you got a bargain, Dad. What do the people in Mpwapwa think about this?"

"Everyone adores the car, but we did not want it on display every day in front of the store, so we are building a garage at the back of the building and will store it there. Rafiq, we have been sitting here for fifteen minutes talking about this car while your mom is dying to see you. Let's get going but, here, you drive."

They changed seats. Rafiq got into the driver's seat, and they drove off. This was unlike anything Rafiq had driven or sat in. The ride was heavenly.

YASMIN RAN OUT WHEN she saw the car pull up in front of the store. Rafiq jumped out and ran to his mother, and she took him in her arms. Tears of joy ran down Yasmin's cheeks. Rafiq kissed his mom and said, "Mom, your son is back."

"I cannot tell you how I have missed you, Rafiq, my Son. You have been gone for four years."

"But I am back now and will be here for almost three months. You remember I was not supposed to come back for five years?"

Holding Rafiq's hand, Yasmin led him into the store. Rafiq looked around and noticed that the merchandize mix on his dad's side had changed. When he commented, Salim said, "After independence, most British left. Canadians and Americans have replaced them. The Africans call them, '*Wamericanos*,' collectively. They are here under the Canadian International Development Agency, CIDA, and American USAID programs. They are different from the British. They are easy-going, friendly, and big spenders. The new merchandise you see here is what they want. We have got most enrolled in the Club, and they are becoming good friends. They are here to help, and they often touch us deeply with their genuine desire to contribute to building Tanzania and their desire to be friends with Africans and us."

"That's great, Dad. That's good for the country and good for your business."

"Yasmin," Salim said looking at her, "Rafiq and I sat in the car and talked for fifteen minutes at the train station and then talked all the way driving home, so why don't you take him in and spend time with him. I'll look after the store. And, by the way, your son does not approve of our purchase of the Mercedes."

"That's not true, Dad! I said I just think it may be too much for us in a small town, but you and mom certainly deserve to drive a nice car after years of bumping around in a beaten-up Land Rover."

Like Shameem's mom on the way home from Nairobi airport, there was so much Yasmin wanted to talk to Rafiq about which could not wait. How much she had enjoyed communicating with Shameem; she was dying to see her; what university life was like; what the congregation at the Ismaili Centre was like; if they volunteered for any services at the Centre; what life in London was like and where they shopped and what they ate.

She also wanted to tell Rafiq how life had changed after independence, how foreign aid was pouring into the country, and how the people and businesses were benefitting from the use of aid money and how the Club atmosphere had changed with Wamericanos as the new members. They were boisterous but respectful of the locals. They played American football in the field behind the Club. This was some silly game that Salim, she, and no one else could understand, but the Wamericanos certainly enjoyed it. Some guy caught the ball and ran, and then everyone fell on him. They said that in America, the game was played wearing elaborate protective gear, without which their play here was much more restrained.

Rafiq called Shameem to tell her he had arrived safely and how much he was missing her. He asked her to meet with the travel agent and confirm the Mara, Serengeti, and Ngorongoro safari for Rob and Bernice and themselves and also confirm the beach resort in Dar es Salaam for them and in Malindi for Rob and Bernice for the dates planned.

Rafiq spent three weeks in Mpwapwa. After the hectic life in London, he had worried he might get bored, but no amount of time with his parents was enough for him. He just loved to be with them. For them, Rafiq was a boy they had sent to the U.K. four years back, and now he had come back as a grown man. He was reflective and measured in what he said. His voice had deepened, and he was worried about his parents with no young children to look after them when he returned to the U.K. They tried to comfort him by saying things were better than ever, and there was nothing for him to be concerned about.

He spent his early evenings and weekends at the Club, where he made friends with the Wamericanos. All were not CIDA and USAID. Some were Peace Corps volunteers. He conversed with them with ease about the U.S.A. political scene, having learned much about the U.S. political system in his first-year university Political Science course. Like him, they were all admirers of President John F. Kennedy. He also loved to socialize with the CIDA staff. Their outlook on life and approach to work was somewhat different from their American counterparts. Their parliamentary democratic political system bore a close resemblance to the British system, on which it was based.

AT THE END OF his first week, they traveled to Dodoma on Saturday and met with the Damjis at the Almin premises. Fateh and Almas were delighted to see Rafiq. They told him that Anil had planned to travel with them from Nairobi after the wedding and spend five days in Dodoma and how wonderful it would have been if both Rafiq and he could have been with them together, even for two days. It would have felt like old times.

They closed the business at noon and went home for lunch. After lunch, Salim and Yasmin said they wanted to go into the town for Yasmin to buy wedding gifts for the relatives attending the wedding – an Ismaili tradition. Almas told Fateh she would take the afternoon off to spend time with Rafiq.

Zahir and Tazim came home from school at 1.30 p.m. Upon seeing Rafiq, Tazim screamed with joy and ran into his arms. Both Tazim and Zahir had grown up. Zahir had grown facial hair but had not started to shave yet. Tazim was growing up to become a good looking young lady. She did not want to eat her lunch. She sat next to Rafiq, holding his hands and wanted to tell him all about her school, her friends, and her plans for the future.

"I am so looking forward to attending your wedding, Rafiq. Will your fiancé like me? Is she a nice girl? Will she be jealous of me because you love me so much?" She asked.

"Shama is a very nice person. She will like you. She knows that you are as dear to me as you are to Anil. Anil and I missed you very much, and I am happy that we all will be together again soon. I am pleased to know you are doing very well at school."

"I want to pass my Cambridge Exam in the 1st Division, like Anil and you."

Looking at Zahir, Rafiq asked, "Zahir, I expect you will attend my wedding also?"

"No, I have to look after the business when Mom, Dad, and Tazim go to Nairobi."

"I'm sorry you will miss the wedding. I would have been delighted if you could have been there."

"Don't worry, Rafiq, I am fine with that. I love to be in the store, and I am looking forward to being in control of the business for a whole week."

"Anil worries that you are more interested in business than in your studies. You will be sitting for your Cambridge Exam in November?"

"Yes."

"Are you well prepared?"

"Well, I have been doing my homework, and I study for one hour after school every day before I go to the store."

"Zahir, doing homework, and one hour of studying is not enough. You need to work much harder. Anil would like to bring you to the U.K. for a three-year Business Administration diploma course that he has talked to you about. You would find it very interesting, and when you come back with that knowledge, you will be able to bring modern management practices into the business and help the business grow."

"But who will help Mom and Dad in the business if I am gone for three years? The business is not the Mickey Mouse operation it was when you and Anil worked there. It's a huge business now. After all expenses, we clear 20,000 Shillings a month to keep Anil and you in luxury in London. To make that kind of money, you have to work hard. You can't expect hired help to do that for you."

Rafiq was stunned by the tone of Zahir's response. He was sorry he had said what he had. It should have been Anil, not him, having this conversation with Zahir. 'How he has changed from the little boy I used to tickle and tutor every day?' Rafiq thought. He did not want to apologize to Zahir and did not want to respond to him, either. He was saddened to see how he had changed.

Zahir got up and went to eat his lunch in the dining room. Rafiq went back to talking and listening to Tazim.

"Tazim, get off the sofa, and go have your lunch. Rafiq is not going to run away." Almas said to Tazim when she emerged from the kitchen.

"Yes, Tazim, go eat your lunch. Why is she so thin, Aunty?"

"That's because the silly girl doesn't want to eat any good food. She wants to diet and be slim."

"Mom wants to feed me all kinds of fried fatty stuff. I don't want to grow fat. I'll never find a boyfriend."

"Boyfriend, boyfriend, boyfriend! That's all she and her friends talk about. Tell her, Rafiq, she doesn't need to find a boyfriend until she has become a chemist."

"Rafiq and Anil have girlfriends, and they are still studying, Mom."

"They are boys."

"What double standards, Mom? Do you know that their girlfriends are girls? If their girlfriends' parents did not allow them to have boyfriends, both your sons would be without girlfriends."

"This girl is impossible, Rafiq. Can you knock some sense into her head?"

"She's a typical teenager, Aunty. Let her finish her Grade XII, and we will take her to the U.K. You know we are going to buy a house in London? I am planning to buy a four-bedroom house. Anil will stay in one, Tazim in another and Shama and I in the third bedroom. We will keep the fourth bedroom for Fateh uncle and you or Mom and Dad when you visit us. We'll keep this girl under tight control. We'll make sure she finds a good boyfriend when Anil and I think she can have one."

Looking at Tazim, Almas said, "You heard Rafiq? No talking about boyfriends until you graduate as a chemist."

"See, Rafiq, she hears only the parts she wants to hear."

"Now, can you get off the sofa? I want to talk to Rafiq. Go and eat your lunch. And when you finish, go to your bedroom and study for half an hour. Give me some privacy with Rafiq."

Tazim gave Rafiq a peck on his cheek and went into the dining room. Zahir, who had eaten his lunch, said he was going to the store and left.

Almas came and sat next to Rafiq on the sofa.

Rafiq took her hand in his and asked, "Aunty, Mom says you are working too hard in the store. I am very sad to see that you have lost so much weight. You don't look like you did when I left. Zahir said the business is making more money than I thought it did, so why do you have to work so hard? Why can't we hire people to work for us?"

Almas looked at the dining room to ensure that Tazim was not listening to their conversation. Her eyes welling up with tears, she said in a hushed tone, "Rafiq, Anil does not know this, and Tazim and Zahir don't, either, but I am going to tell you. To me, you've always been like my son. To Zahir and Tazim, you have been their brother, sometimes more brother than Anil. And also, you're stronger than Anil is.

So I will tell you, but please keep this to yourself."

"Two years back, I was diagnosed with breast cancer and had a mastectomy. I have been well. I attend Jamatkhana every day, and that gives me much strength. There is no problem, but mastectomy takes its toll on you.

Taking both her hands in his, Rafiq said, "Oh, Almas aunty, I am so sorry to hear that. But you say you are well. If you ever have any problem, just get on a plane and come to London and we'll get you the best medical care. Let's be grateful that two years later, cancer has not come back. Enjoy life. You're making so much money. Enjoy it. Be happy that Anil will be here soon. By being unhappy, you are making Fateh uncle unhappy – I'm sure."

THEY SAT AND TALKED, undisturbed by Tazim, for more than an hour. Tazim knew her mom wanted to speak with Rafiq about Anil's girlfriend. Jenny seemed different to Almas, from Shameem. Unlike Shameem, who had talked to Yasmin many times and was writing to her regularly, Jenny had not sought to establish any contact with her or Fateh. Was she a good girl? Had Rehana returned home? Was there anything between Rehana and Anil? Anil had spoken very fondly about her in his letters to Fateh and Almas, making them wonder if he was in love with her.

"Jenny is a good girl, Aunty. Anil likes to be with her. She attends Jamatkhana on Fridays and festive days. And no, Rehana and Anil were very close friends, but there was nothing more between them."

"But is Jenny interested in Anil's family?" Almas asked.

"I am sure she is. In time she will connect with you."

As he said this, he recalled Anil saying to him once, "I told her I have a brother and a sister, but she was not interested in how old they are, what grades they are in and not even what their names are. She has never asked me about my parents either. She has talked to me about them only in the context of the business they are running."

"But are you sure she's a good girl? I don't want her to bring unhappiness to Anil's life. I am uneasy about her. Anil used to write constantly about Rehana. He doesn't say much about Jenny. All he has written is he has a girlfriend, and her name is Jenny - nothing more. "

"Aunty, these days, if you go out with a girl, it doesn't mean you will marry her, or she will marry you. People move on, sometimes. Anil is smart. He will marry the girl who will be good for him."

"You know Rafiq, I so wish that like you, Anil was also coming home to get married to a girl like Shama, and we were preparing for two weddings. Your mom loves Shama so much. She can never stop talking about her."

"Mom has come to think of Shama as the daughter she lost. I think she believes Shama is her daughter. This is not good. Not good at all. Mom may love Shama as much as she wants to, but Shama is not her daughter. Shama loves her, too, but only as much as you can love a person without having met her. She is worried that she may not meet Mom's expectations when Mom meets her. I hope and pray Mom is happy with Shama when she meets her. At Shama's suggestion, we will spend a week in Mpwapwa before returning to the U.K., and Shama just wants to sit with Mom and try and return her love, the best she can."

"It will all work out. My best wishes and prayers are for you all, beta."

1964
Fifty-Two

They departed Mpwapwa for Nairobi early on August 2nd. The route to Nairobi was via Dodoma on the Great North Road, via Arusha. The plan was for Fateh and Almas to drive in their car, and Tazim would ride in Salim uncle's Mercedes with her "brother" Rafiq. Salim let Rafiq drive. They were in Dodoma in two hours. The Damjis were ready to leave, but Almas insisted they come in for a cup of tea before departing for Arusha. Rafiq was happy. He had woken up early, and a cup of tea would be nice. In the Ismaili tradition, tea was not just tea. The table was covered with cakes, naan khatai, and other goodies.

Finally, they were on their way, with Fateh following them at some distance. Salim knew that Tazim wanted to chat with Rafiq, and it would not work to put her in the back seat with Yasmin, so he had asked her to sit in the front passenger seat, saying, "Rafiq, you drive and Tazim, you sit with him in the front. It's a long trip, so make sure Rafiq doesn't fall asleep at the wheel."

Tazim was on cloud nine. She would get to sit in the front seat of a Mercedes Benz with Rafiq and talk to him as much as she wanted. "Sure, Uncle. I will keep Rafiq talking." She said.

And that's what she did - all the way to Arusha.

Halfway to Arusha, they stopped by the roadside for the sandwich lunch Almas had prepared, washed down by Coca Cola and Fanta.

They spent the night in Arusha at The New Safari Hotel and arrived in Nairobi the next day around 4.00 p.m. They had time, after they checked in, to rest.

Rafiq did not want to take a dusty Mercedes to Shameem's place. He inquired at the Reception where he could get it washed. The concierge told him he could get the car vacuumed inside and out, washed, and polished professionally for Shs.100. He would get it done where the car was sitting in the parking lot. All Rafiq needed to do was unlock the car doors, which he proceeded to do. He also asked for an estimate of the wedding reception, and Salim paid the full amount and got the receipt for Shs.5,250.

DINNER FOR THE GROOM'S party that evening at Shameem's place was at 7.30 p.m. Rafiq called Shameem to tell her they had arrived safely, and they would get to her home by this time, but Shameem said, "No, you can't do that. We have to come and formally welcome you at the hotel and then bring you home."

"Why would you do that? I know the way to your place, and we have two cars. You can welcome us when we get there."

"This is the custom. Don't argue. Don't question anything. Okay?"

"Okay."

When Rafiq expressed frustration over this silly custom, his mother said, "This is the custom. Don't argue. Don't question anything. Okay?"

There had been some discussion at Shameem's place over who should go to welcome and fetch the guests to bring them home. It was decided that Bahadur and Gulshan would go and bring back Salim and Yasmin in their car, and Rafiq would drive with Fateh, Almas, and Tazim.

AS THEY DROVE TO New Stanley, Gulshan, although she had talked to Yasmin many times, was nervous about meeting her.

'I hope I make the right impression on her, or she might judge my daughter by her first impression of me.' She said to herself.

At home, Shameem was equally concerned. Was she dressed right? She was wearing a simple summer dress. She had not worn any makeup, only light lipstick. Should she have worn something more ostentatious? Should she have gone to the beautician to have her hair done and face made up, as her mom had insisted she should do? She had refused to do that and forced her mom also to be casual.

"What if they turn up all dressed up and we are casual? We'll make a bad impression on them. They might be even feel insulted that we are not giving enough importance to our first meeting with them." Gulshan had said to Shameem.

"Mom, my wedding is three days away. They won't wear tuxedos and gowns until then, if then. Rafiq won't let them wear anything formal tonight."

When the two ladies were having a vigorous discussion about what to wear and how much makeup to put on, Bahadur had asked the ladies if he should wear a tie.

This was a mistake.

"Can't you yourself decide if you should wear a tie? Why are you bothering us when you can see we are busy?" Gulshan snapped at him.

Bahadur knew there would be more of these moments over the next week, and he better keep out of these women's way. When he had emerged wearing, what he thought was a nice tie, Gulshan snapped at him again. "Couldn't you wear something better than that gaudy tie?"

"I can change it. Which one would you like me to wear?"

Before Gulshan could answer, Shameem had proceeded to remove his tie, saying, "You don't need to wear one at all, Dad. You look smart without one."

Now, as they drove, Gulshan was thinking, "I should have let him wear that silly tie. At least one of us would have looked a little formal."

AFTER CHECKING IN, AS they were going up, Almas had asked, "How should we dress when we go to Shameem's place, Yasmin?"

Without thinking, Yasmin had replied, "Casual."

BAHADUR AND GULSHAN ARRIVED at the hotel ten minutes before the agreed departure time and sat in the reception area. Their guests emerged from the elevator at 7.00 p.m. Gulshan was relieved to see that all were dressed casually. She and Bahadur rose to walk to them. All her anxiety melted away when Yasmin ran up to her and gave her a big hug and said, "Gulshan, you look exactly like I had imagined you. So happy to meet you."

"And you are just as beautiful as I had heard you are," Gulshan replied.

Rafiq proceeded to introduce everyone to everyone, and they were on their way.

Yasmin sat with Gulshan in the back seat, and the two chatted all the way. It was a continuum of their many telephone discussions.

Word had spread in the Parklands' twenty-five apartment complex of the groom's party's dinner at the Adatia residence that evening. All residents of the complex had been invited to the Jamatkhana wedding ceremony, but only two couples were invited to the wedding reception. Word had also spread that the groom's family was wealthy. This was confirmed when the gleaming S Class Mercedes pulled up behind Bahadur's Peugeot.

When they climbed up, Shameem received Yasmin and Salim at the door. Yasmin took her in her arms, kissed her forehead and cheeks, and held her for full ten seconds. She was too overwhelmed to say anything.

"I have been looking forward to this day for a very long time, Yasmin aunty," Shameem said to her.

"Me, too, sweetheart." Yasmin managed to say.

When Yasmeen let her out of her arms, Shameem shook hands with Salim. Taking her in his embrace, Salim said, "We had been counting days to meet you, Shama. We pray that may Allah always watch over you and keep Rafiq and you happy and united."

"Ameen, Uncle."

As Gulshan led Salim and Yasmin into the apartment and introduced them to Adil and his girlfriend Narmeen, Rafiq introduced Fateh, Almas, and Tazim to Shameem and then to Adil and Narmeen. As he hugged Shameem, she whispered to him, "This is all you do to me. Don't try anything else!"

He had so much wanted to kiss her.

THE DINNER WAS INFORMAL and enjoyable for everyone. Everyone chatted freely with everyone. Yasmin and Gulshan went over the details of the wedding plan. Everything appeared to be in order.

Shameem and Tazim bonded instantly.

"I'm so happy you are in my brother's life, Shama. But you won't be happy that I will be in your life. I am that mean and jealous sister in law who creates problems between her brother and his wife." Tazim said to Shameem.

"I don't believe that. Rafiq has told me everything about you. He said you have become a bit more naughty from when he studied in Dodoma, but you are a good girl."

Shameem thought, 'These people are strange. Rafiq's mom thinks of me as her daughter, and this girl is calling Rafiq her brother when they are not even remotely related.' But as the evening wore on, she could see the warmth between the Abdullas and Damjis. For every wedding detail, Yasmin was asking for Almas' opinion and endorsement. She could also see that Tazim, as Rafiq's "sister," was very interested in logistics and was going to be a huge help to Adil and Narmeen.

BERNICE, ROB, AND ANIL arrived in Nairobi the next day. Fateh, Almas, Tazim, Rafiq, and Shameem met them at the airport. It was an emotional reunion for the Damjis.

By Thursday, August 6th, all out of town guests except Chelsea and Ricardo had arrived. The Meet and Greet dinner was organized at a small banquet hall. There were more people than expected, but that was fine. Gulshan had anticipated this and ordered more food.

CHELSEA AND RICARDO ARRIVED the next day. Rafiq and Shameem received them at the airport.

"You have grown so much, Rafiq. You are a young man. We are delighted to see you again, Son," Ricardo said, giving Rafiq a hug."

"And this lady is more beautiful than I had imagined, Rafiq. And your parents tell me she's as smart as you are," Chelsea said, shaking hands with Shameem when Rafiq introduced her to Shameem.

"A little smarter, Chelsea," Rafiq said.

As they drove from the airport, Chelsea said, "Rafiq, your dad and mom are worried and somewhat embarrassed that we cannot attend the wedding ceremony. They were also concerned that your other guests might wonder why they would invite people who cannot participate in the wedding. We understand the setting in which the ceremony will take place and why we cannot attend. We are not here for the ceremony. We are here to partake in the joy and happiness of your two lives coming together. Can you please tell your parents to stop worrying about this? Our happiness is in seeing you again, meeting your fiancé, and participating in the festivities."

"Thank you so much for your understanding, Chelsea. Rob, – the D.C.'s son, and his girlfriend arrived yesterday, and I had to explain to them also why they cannot attend the wedding they have traveled from the U.K. to attend. Like you, they were very understanding."

"We're completely fine with this," Ricardo added.

CHELSEA AND BERNICE PARTICIPATED in the *Puro*, – the ladies only ceremony, where the groom's female family members present to the bride and her family the groom's dowry (Puro). A different family member presents each item.

Yasmin presented to Shameem a diamond-studded necklace, bracelet, ring, and earrings set, which Rafiq had brought from the U.K.

At Yasmin's request, Chelsea presented a heavy 24 carat (locally made) gold band, and an expensive silk saree to Gulshan and Almas presented an Omega watch, a Van Heusen shirt and a tie for Bahadur, which Rafiq had also brought from the U.K.

It was left to Tazim and Bernice to present the many gifts for Adil and Narmeen and all of Shameem's uncles and aunts.

"I had heard that in the Indian tradition, the bride's family has to give dowry to the groom's family and that, if this is not enough, the groom's family may call off the wedding in the middle of the ceremonies and to avoid humiliation, the bride's family may give away their last possessions. Why are *you* giving all these presents to the bride and her family?" Bernice asked Tazim.

"The dowry works in reverse in Islam. In recognition of the fact that the bride, when getting married, leaves her home and her family and adopts her husband's family and goes to live in his house, which is a supreme sacrifice, we present gifts to the bride and her family to show our appreciation for her sacrifice and to her family for giving their daughter in marriage to the groom and his family."

"Wow! That's amazing. Never heard of anything like this."

"There is more. When they get married tomorrow, Rafiq will have to sign a legally binding contract which will include a clause that will say that he is undertaking to pay Shama an unconditional gift of an amount that will have been agreed upon between the two families, the payment of which will be deferred to the day Shama decides to ask for it. This is called *Mehr*. Mehr is legally binding in a court of law."

"Is this a large amount?"

"Could be. The girl's father has to ask for it, and the groom's father has to agree. This is done in the presence of our community leadership. It's a delicate negotiation. If the girl's father asks for too little, it may seem like he doesn't value his daughter too much, or it may even imply that he thinks the groom's family is poor and can't afford much. He could insult the groom's father if he asks too little. If he asks for too much, he may look greedy. He has to strike the right balance."

"What do you think Shama's dad will ask for?"

"If I were Shama, I would ask him to ask for Shs.100,000 – that's your £5,000. Rafiq's parents can afford that."

"My God, you can buy a house for that much in London, and poor Rafiq is not even earning anything yet. How would they expect him to pay that kind of money if Shama asked for it six months after they marry?"

"Mehr can, but usually does not, come into play until the couple divorces. If they divorce before Rafiq has started to earn and saved up enough, it would be his parent's responsibility to pay the Mehr amount. Shama's parents will likely ask for 50,000 Shillings, and they will settle at around the same amount."

"What happens if a couple divorces? Does the wife get anything more than Mehr?"

"If they divorce, there is an equal distribution of all assets between the parties. Also, the wife is entitled to child support and alimony as required by the law of the land. Mehr is on top of everything."

"And Islam prescribes all this? Seems very unfair to the poor husband."

"This is intended to make the husband behave himself."

AFTER THE PRESENTATION OF the dowry, *sherbet* (an Indian milkshake) and a sumptuous dinner was served. This was followed by the second central part of the ceremony - the application of *mehndi* (henna) on the bride's hands, wrists, and feet by a skilled mehndi applicator, followed by the application of mehndi on all ladies' hands.

The mehndi applicator was highly skilled. It took her less than thirty minutes to apply mehndi, creating all kinds of floral and other patterns, to the bride's hands and feet, and no more than five to seven minutes each to all other ladies' both hands. Both Chelsea and Bernice had their hands done. Mehndi dried quickly on their hands. They had to keep it overnight to get a bright color that would wash off in a few days.

The men were out by themselves. Adil took Rob, Anil, and Rafiq to the casino where he and Rob enjoyed local Tusker beer, and they all ate barbequed steak and fries. Bahadur took Salim to Curry Pot for dinner.

FINALLY, IT WAS AUGUST 8th, the wedding day.

The Jamatkhana wedding ceremony was scheduled at 5.00 p.m. It was a short contract signing ceremony with about 200 people in attendance. This was followed by prayers offered by the Parklands Jamatkhana *Mukhi*, *Kamadia*, and *Mukhiani*, *Kamdiani*, (individuals appointed by the Imam to preside over congregational prayers). The bride and groom and their respective parents and bride's maid and groom's best man lined up to accept congratulations and prayers from all adults in attendance. Cakes, samosas, kebobs, and sherbet were served.

Shameem, who had worn her beige suit for the Jamatkhana wedding, went home with Rafiq, her bride's maid, and Rafiq's best man to change into the saree her mom had bought for her to wear at the reception. Rafiq and his best man waited in the lounge while she did this.

When they arrived at the banquet hall in the New Stanley at 7.00 p.m., all guests were seated. Tazim had reviewed the seating plan Adil and Narmeen had developed. In deference to the groom's family, they had allocated the best tables to the Damjis and Rafiq's aunts and uncles, with the bride's family members seated in the next set of rows down the hall.

"No, this is no good. Let us randomly place one couple or two unmarried adults from each of the groom's and bride's families on each table from first to the last row. They should "anchor" each table and host the guests. So Anil and I could be in the previous row - sitting, welcoming, and socializing with whoever in on our table." Tazim had said, and that's what they had proceeded to do. Bahadur, Gulshan, Salim, and Yasmin had strongly endorsed this arrangement.

The hall was beautifully decorated. Roses had been placed on each table. Adil, Narmeen, Anil, and Tazim, who had worked the entire morning and better part of the afternoon setting up the hall, had seen to that.

In the Ismaili tradition, the bride and groom entering the banquet hall is a symbolic entrance of the bride into the groom's family home. The couple was received at the banquet hall entrance by the groom's mother, who performed two ceremonies. The first was the tossing of four beetle nuts, one in each compass direction, to ward off any evil spirits that may have accompanied the newlyweds into their new home. The evil spirits are expected to cooperate by positioning themselves so that they do get hit. When hit, they evaporate and are gone. Next, she showered them with rice and sweets. The latter symbolizes love (sweetness) and unity between the newlyweds and rice symbolizes fertility and prosperity.

These ceremonies were followed by the *Sapatia* ceremony, where the bride and groom step up on two small stools placed side by side and when given the signal, they step hard on two clay saucers, one inverted over the other, filled with rice and Scotch taped (the Sapatia), placed in front of their respective stools. The belief is, whoever breaks the clay saucers first, would dominate the household. Shameem broke her Sapatia first. Rafiq's foot kept slipping over his Sapatia. It took him three attempts to break them.

The couple then proceeded to take their seats at the head table, with the bride's maid and best man and their respective parents on their respective sides. On behalf of the Abdulla and Adatia families, Adil, who served as the MC, welcomed everyone to the reception and invited the guests to proceed to the buffet tables on each side of the hall. Dinner was served.

When Adil and Narmeen, who were seated with them, explained the meaning of the two ceremonies, Ricardo and Chelsea were fascinated. Showering the newlyweds with rice was a Western custom also, but the tossing of beetle nuts and Sapatia ceremonies were intriguing. Narmeen told them nobody believed in the supposed meaning of the two ceremonies. They were part of their historic Indian culture and caused much hilarity and excitement at the weddings. Adil also told them there were other ceremonies performed at Ismaili and Indian weddings, but Rafiq and

Shameem wanted to keep things simple and did not want them.

After dinner, Adil went to the podium and asked if everyone had enjoyed the dinner. Loud clapping told him everybody had. He then introduced Chelsea, whose Muslim name was Shaheeda, as Tanzania's Education Ministry's Principal Secretary and Abdulla family's close friend, and invited her to speak.

Chelsea, who at Salim's request, had agreed to make the speech and had spent over two hours writing it, rose to speak. Taking her place at the podium, she read:

Our dear friends Yasmin and Salim, the groom's parents who have been a blessing in my life for five years, Shama's parents Bahadur and Gulshan, whom my husband and I met five days back, and we feel like we have known them forever, our dear Rafiq whom we love very much, and Shama, whom we have come to adore in the four days we have been here, all bride and groom's family members and invited guests, welcome to this celebration of Shama and Rafiq's wedding.

I was deeply touched when Yasmin and Salim invited me to speak. My husband, Ricardo, and I are grateful to have been invited to this wedding, and I am honored to have been invited to address you.

It's customary at such wedding celebrations to introduce the bride and the groom and make some jokes. I will abide by that custom, but I first want to introduce the two people who gave birth to a son that they and my husband and I are most proud of.

Rafiq's parents, Yasmin and Salim, live and operate a very successful business in a small town in Tanzania. They have not been to any college or university, but they are highly educated. They always surprise me by their intelligence and breadth of knowledge. They have demonstrated to me that you can live in a small town and yet be aware of the global geopolitical and economic scene and social and cultural issues.

They embody the best in Islam. They are the most honest, compassionate, generous, and humble people I have met. By any standard, they are wealthy, yet their prime virtue is humility. They practice generosity and compassion by tending to the needs of their African customers in ways that I have not seen anywhere in my Somaliland or in Tanzania. Mothers with children burning up with fever come to Yasmin for medication. Mothers with children that have festering wounds go to her to have the wounds cleaned, medicated, and bandaged. If someone comes to them or is brought to them who is very ill or injured and needs to be driven to the hospital, Salim abandons whatever he is doing and drives the person to the nearest hospital, which is twenty miles away. They are admired by one and all in our little town for their humanitarian deeds.

Yasmin and Salim Abdulla have passed these cherished Islamic ethics and values, which they say they are always reminded of by your spiritual leader, His Highness The Aga Khan, to their son. There is no better gift they could have given Rafiq, and I say to you all who have children, give this gift that your Imam espouses, to your children. This will serve them better than any material gifts you can give them.

In introducing me, Adil said I am the Principal Secretary in the Ministry of Education in Tanzania. I am a teacher by profession, and education is a prime focus of my life. Both Shama and Rafiq's parents are giving, what I consider the second most precious gift – the gift of education to their children. Yasmin and Salim tell me that your Imam urges you to educate yourselves and your children. If your children live by ethics and values of Islam, which are central to your and my interpretation of the faith, and have a good education, they will never go astray.

When Rafiq left to study in the U.K. four years back, which is where I also studied, I wondered if, after living in the U.K. for five years, he would become occidentalized and lose his values, as I had seen many Muslim students do in England. My husband and I are delighted to see that in everything Rafiq says and does, he continues to live by the values he was brought up with. When we received our invitation card, we saw the request Shama and Rafiq have made. You have all read it, but I will read it for you if you have not:

"Our dear friends and relatives, after we wed, we will be returning to the U.K. to continue our studies. We cannot carry with us any wedding gifts you may want to give us. We request that if you wish to give us a wedding present, please give us a cheque made payable to The Aga Khan Social Welfare Committee. We will request the Committee to use the funds to support the less privileged high school students in our Jamat."

This reflects the bride and the groom's ethic of compassion and generosity and intelligence in directing their potential gifts to the education of their less privileged brothers and sisters. Imagine if every Ismaili couple getting married made such a request. It could, perhaps, serve to meet all the educational needs of all underprivileged children in the Ismaili community in perpetuity.

So much for my lecturing about ethics and values and education.

Now let me turn to what you expect me to do – introduce and say nice things about newlyweds. I will start with the gorgeous bride, although I don't know why I should introduce you to Shama. You should not be here if you don't know her. But since it's my duty, I will do that. Shameem, whom we lovingly call Shama, is Gulshan and Bahadur Adatia's only daughter. Rafiq tells me that she has been spoilt by her parents and is giving him a hard time. I don't believe that, of course. Shama is a gem, a gift of Allah for her parents, her family, and Rafiq and his family. She is an intelligent, humble, and sweet child. Physical beauty is incidental to her. She is enrolled in her second-year M.B.B.S. program at London University and expects to graduate in three years as a medical doctor. We pray for and wish her success.

Rafiq – I have spoken enough about him, is the son I wish I had. He has completed the second year of B.Sc. (Economics) program at London University. He expects to graduate in one year and then plans to pursue a two year Masters in Business Administration course. Rafiq and Shama and their parents have asked me to express their sincere gratitude to you all for accepting their invitation and gracing this event with your presence.

Shama and Rafiq have told me that as you enjoy your desserts and coffee, they will come around to your tables to speak to you, introduce themselves more fully, and thank you individually.

Pause to read a note handed by Adil

"Adil has just passed me a note," Chelsea continued. "It says that he and Narmeen have been opening up your wedding cards, and with more than two-thirds of the envelopes yet to be opened, they have collected cheques totaling more than 2,000 Shillings. Rafiq and Shama are truly grateful to you for your gifts."

"I convey Ricardo's and my warm congratulations to Shama and Rafiq and their parents. I pray to Allah to bless them with good health, success in education, and a very happy life together."

"Thank you for listening to me. I wish you a delightful evening. Enjoy yourselves."

AFTER CHELSEA HAD SPOKEN, most guests were surprised that a Somali lady had reminded them of their Imam's teachings.

Later in the evening, as Rafiq and Shameem circulated among the guests (none were in a hurry to leave), Adil came to the podium and announced that they had finished counting all the cash gifts. These added up to Shs.5,050. He thanked everyone for their generosity and further announced that the bride and groom's parents and Anil Damji's family had offered to match their gifts. Shs.10,100 would be given to the Welfare Committee the next day. This was their wedding gift for Shameem and Rafiq.

"I doubt if even 10% of this comes from my parents. They just don't have that kind of money to give. It's so kind of your and Anil's parents to include my parents' name in this gifting." Shameem whispered to Rafiq.

In fact, Shameem's parents had contributed Shs.750, and the Abdullas and Damjis had each contributed Shs.2,150.

The traditional bride's family dinner (*Shinda*) at Shameem's place the next day was a more intimate and relaxed event. All were tired after five days of celebrations.

Only the Abdullas and Damjis and Shameem's family members were present. Salim and Yasmin had insisted that Adatias not hire an external facility to accommodate all of the Abdulla relatives who had traveled to Nairobi for the wedding. The latter were just fine with this and were busy exploring Nairobi. The Adatias should only invite the number they could accommodate comfortably in their apartment.

Yasmin could not contain her joy that Shameem now was Shameem Abdulla. For the bride, Shinda marks the formal departure from her home and farewell to her family. She could see the sadness in Gulshan's eyes.

Yasmin took her aside and said, "Gulshan, I know this is a difficult time for you. Saying a formal farewell to your only daughter must be very difficult. I want to assure you that Shama will be happy in our home. Salim, Rafiq, and I will always do everything to keep her happy. They are going on their honeymoon tomorrow and will spend one week with us in Mpwapwa and a week with you here in Nairobi before they return to the U.K. Then they will be away from both of us until we see them again. In the meantime, let us keep them in our prayers."

"Thank you, Yasmin. They will always be in our prayers. We will pray for their peace, success, and happiness."

WHILE SALIM WAS HAVING a similar conversation with Bahadur, he said, "Salim, when I went to the counter at New Stanley to ask for the reception bill, they said you paid it when you checked in. Did you do that? They said there was only an incidental charge of 65 Shillings, which I settled."

"Yes, I paid it so we wouldn't have to worry about it when checking out tomorrow. And that gave them time to clear the cheque with the bank."

"They said the total bill was 5,250 Shillings. Our share should be 2,625 Shillings. I will give you the cheque." Bahadur said and started to walk away to get his chequebook.

"Salim caught his hand and said, "Yes, but we had agreed to split the cost of hosting lunches and dinners for all guests for five days, which you have paid."

"That added up to less than 800 Shillings, so I will give you 2,225 Shillings."

"Listen, Bahadur, please don't misunderstand me. With Allah's grace, Yasmin and I have been successful in business. We are blessed with money. Success, as you know, is due to Allah. It's not our intelligence. When Allah is generous to us, we have to be generous to those around us. Will you be offended if we do not take your share? I know you have paid for your relatives' accommodation. You must have spent a lot of money on Puro and this Shinda and all the other costs you have incurred. We would be grateful if you allow us to pick up the entire reception cost."

"Are you sure you want to do this, Salim?"

"The five days we have been here are among the happiest in our lives. You can make this sixth day even happier if you accept what I am requesting."

"I will get into trouble with Gulshan for this."

"Don't tell her anything. I will get Yasmin to talk to her. Yasmin has ways of sweetening everything."

1964
Fifty-Three

As arranged with the tour operator, the Safari vehicle rolled up in front of New Stanley at 9.00 a.m. Shameem had said a tearful goodbye to her mom, dad, Adil, and Narmeen the previous day. Salim, Yasmin, and the Damjis, who also departed Nairobi shortly afterwards, had woken up early to say goodbye to Rafiq, Shameem, Robert and Bernice.

THE LONG RIDE TO Mara was a little different from the last time. More of the road had been paved. They stopped at the restaurant where they had taken their driver and guide Bakari for lunch with them on their first Safari. They asked their driver/guide, Juma, to go in with them, but he was too scared to do that. The Indian restaurant manager was still there.

Shameem and Bernice felt the thrill Rafiq and Rob had experienced when they entered Mara, and wildlife started to appear on the horizon. Their accommodation in the lodge was adjacent to where Robert, Anil, and Rafiq had stayed the last time.

Shameem had seen some big game in Nairobi National Park, but on the two days of game drives, she saw lions, elephants, cape buffalos, cheetahs, giraffes, and wildebeests at close range. Bernice, who had not seen these animals except in the zoo, was thrilled to see elephants gliding past their vehicles so close that she could see the ticks on one elephant's back. Neither wanted to pull away from the pride of lions with one male, four females, and eight cubs. At the Mara River, they saw the crocodiles and hippos, but there was no gathering on the banks or crossing of the wildebeests and zebras.

"You could come here a dozen times, Rafiq, and still want to come back over and over again, isn't it?" Rob asked.

"This is nature at its best. I hope we, the humans, preserve it for the posterity." Rafiq replied.

THE DRIVE NEXT DAY to Serengeti was as difficult on bumpy roads as five years earlier. Bernice had never experienced anything like this. She would have paid £5.00 for a massage when they got to the Serengeti Wildlife Lodge, but no massages were available. Nobody had even heard about massages. To soothe her muscles, Robert had to massage her back.

As they had done on their first Safari, they sat late into the night around the fire outside the dining room. Rafiq and Shameem enjoyed hot chocolate, and Bernice and Robert enjoyed cognac.

THEY ALL WOKE UP the next day to see the plains below their "cottages," teeming with grazing wildlife. The game drive revealed to Shameem and Bernice the real miracle of Serengeti. It was early for the migration, but there were thousands of wildebeests, zebras, impalas, and other plains animals. To be driving through these herds grazing, running around and playing, was a sight to see for Bernice and Shameem and equally thrilling for Rafiq and Robert. They saw some lions lazing in the shade of a tree. The open plains were not the place for them to hunt in daylight. Not being sprinters like the cheetahs, they needed growth to hide in and get very close to the prey before giving chase. Robert, who now considered himself an expert, told the ladies the lions had probably eaten well the night before and were resting. If they had not hunted the previous night and were hungry, they would be stalking the deer or wildebeest and zebra in broad daylight without any cover.

AFTER TWO DAYS OF exploring the Serengeti, they were on their way to Ngorongoro. En route, they stopped at the Olduvai Gorge. Although Robert had told them all about it, visiting the center and hearing how the man had evolved here in the middle of Africa and proceeded to cover the entire planet was fascinating for the ladies.

Two days in the crater and two nights at the Ngorongoro Lodge were blissful. When they descended into the crater on the first day, Rafiq said, "Rob, it looks like the animals are where we left them. We are encountering the same animals in the same order as we did the last time."

"It's a small crater, Rafiq. There is grass everywhere for the herbivores, and the deer, wildebeests, zebra, and Cape buffalos don't migrate, so the lions, hyenas, leopards, and cheetahs know where their food is, and there is no reason for them to move far."

"Guys, the serenity of this place is amazing. With so many animals around us, there is so much peace. Everyone is doing their own thing quietly. They are so many different species, but they all exist together. We have seen occasional fights between males for dominance and right to mate, and we saw a kill which the carnivores need to make to survive, but the elephants are not fighting the lions, the zebras are not fighting the deer or wildebeests. Why can't we humans be more like these animals?" Bernice asked.

"That was our observation also when we came here. Why can't we humans be more like animals?" Robert replied.

"The way I see it, this is God's creation. He created humans as nations and tribes and gave us brains so that we may know one another and appreciate our human diversity. Instead, we behave worse than these animals who have much less thinking capacity. All we want to do is look for diversity that we can downgrade, vilify, and attack." Shameem said.

"Would it not be nice if the park authorities allowed us to build a house in this crater, and we could live in it?" Rafiq asked.

"Yes, that would be wonderful, but there is no supermarket in the crater and no electricity or water supply or sewage system and no offices for us to go to work in and get a paycheck, so I think we should be content with staying in our houses in the U.K. We can come to visit these creations of God when we can afford to. Rob, I wish you had booked us in each of the lodges for four nights instead of two. I don't want to leave here," Bernice said.

"First, we could not afford the cost, and next, you don't have the vacation time, so enjoy what you are getting, honey," Robert replied.

THEY ARRIVED IN ARUSHA the next day and boarded their respective flights to Mombasa and Dar es Salaam.

As they settled in their seats, Shameem reminded Rafiq, "You know that as of today, we are officially on our honeymoon, so be extra nice to me."

"And you to me, sweetheart," Rafiq replied.

Salim had arranged with Haji to organize for a nice rental car for seven days for Rafiq and Shameem. A Ruby Cabs (a reputable car rental agency) car met them at the airport. As requested by Haji, who did much business with Ruby Cabs, the agency had sent a late model Peugeot 404 for them.

After dropping off the driver at his place of work, Rafiq drove to the NAAZ restaurant and ordered samosas, kebobs, and ice-cold Coca Cola. After enjoying their mid-afternoon snack, they drove to The Seagull Hotel located on a beautiful beach twenty miles north of Dar es Salaam. They went swimming in the turquoise blue ocean, ate dinner, sat in the hotel's front open lounge space, enjoying the cool ocean breeze, and rested for the evening.

Their days in Dar es Salaam started with a late breakfast at 9.30 a.m. After breakfast, they sat in the hotel lounge and read books until noon. They then went swimming in the ocean if the tide was in or the hotel pool for an hour, showered, and got dressed for late lunch. After lunch, they socialized with other guests (there was another honeymoon couple there they enjoyed swimming and playing cards with) or relaxed in their bedroom and enjoyed the ocean view from their large bedroom window until 4.00 p.m.

They then got dressed for the evening and drove to Dar es Salaam. They walked around the city, visited NAAZ, or City Hotel, and attended Jamatkhana. On a couple of evenings, they went to see movies. They missed the dinners included in their hotel package. After their heavy lunch, the snacks at NAAZ and City were sufficient. They ordered some fruit when they returned to their hotel and enjoyed papayas, oranges, and bananas sitting in the open lounge.

It had been a wonderful, relaxing week in Dar es Salaam. Shameem had enjoyed the city and loved the NAAZ snacks and ice cream. In Jamatkhana, she had met some girls from Dar es Salaam who had come to Nairobi to train as nurses at the Aga Khan Platinum Jubilee Hospital. All had invited them to go to their places for lunch/dinner or tea. They had politely declined. One who Shameem had become friends with when she was in Nairobi, had insisted that they go to her place for lunch. They had agreed to go for high tea. It had been a delightful afternoon.

They had enjoyed the Seagull and its superb food, drives along the ocean in Oysterbay, their swims in the ocean, and walks on Dar es Salaam streets, but now it was time to leave. They boarded the train on August 27th at noon for Gulwe (Mpwapwa). As they settled in their cabin, Shameem said, "So, the honeymoon is now over."

"Not yet. We have a full day on this train. That's part of our honeymoon."

"You know, Rafiq, I was very apprehensive about meeting your mom. I was particularly worried about spending a whole week in Mpwapwa with her. I had worried about not meeting her expectations – return her love, but she came at me with no expectations at all. She just wanted to love me like a mother loves her child, expecting nothing in return. It was unconditional love. She never looked into my eyes to search if there was any love there for her. I had formed much affection for her communicating with her from the U.K., but I can't say I love her like I love my mother. In time, maybe, but not right now."

"I was also relieved. I had worried about her writing to you and talking about you to me as if you were her daughter when you are not, and I, too, had worried that she might expect you to show as much love for her as she feels for you. Now I understand better. You have filled a void in her heart. I am sure that when she saw me growing up alone, becoming as attached to Anil and Tazim as I am, she must have yearned for the daughter she lost, although she never said anything. She might have even felt that she had failed in giving me a sibling, and then she found you, and you must have filled that void in her heart."

"I am glad if I did. Now I am not at all concerned about going to Mpwapwa. In fact, I am looking forward to it. In the little time we had together in Nairobi, we had some very pleasant conversations – the kind of conversations I would have with a friend."

"I am happy you feel that way, Shama."

SALIM WAS THERE TO receive them at the Gulwe (Mpwapwa) station. They arrived home in thirty minutes. Shameem suggested they freshen up and rest. They had organized dinner for the entire Ismaili community in Mpwapwa after congregational prayers that evening at the Jamatkhana. It was Friday, so they expected full attendance. This was something that would have been expected of them to celebrate their son's wedding and introduce the bride to the community. They had also organized a dinner the next day at the Club for all their other friends.

While the congregation had met Rafiq when he was there earlier and seen the change in him, most were curious about what his wife, who was not only a big city girl but also bore a "U.K. Returned" stamp, would be like. At her request, Shameem recited the first prayer in Jamatkhana, and when dinner was served, she made it a point to get introduced to every adult and speak to every child, picking up babies and toddlers who were friendly enough for her to do that. She showed genuine interest in every adult and listened carefully to the students about what grades they were in and what their aspirations were, emphasizing the importance of education. She invited three girls in grades X and XI to come to meet her at home to talk about studying in the U.K. Salim and Yasmin could not have been more proud of her.

The dinner at the Club on Saturday was as much fun. Some Ismaili Club members from the night before were there. She received a lot of compliments for her looks from the Wamericano men and women. They were also impressed that she was studying to become a medical doctor. She and Rafiq agreed to meet up with some for lunch at the Club the next day.

By midweek, Shameem was asking Rafiq if they could stay longer in Mpwapwa. She had never imagined she could have so much fun in this small town. She was enjoying meeting with and advising young girls and their mothers (who wanted to know if it was safe for them to send their daughters to the U.K.), spending time with new friends at the Club, going up the Rock (where Rafiq confessed to her he had delightfully watched centerfolds of Playboy magazine that Robert had smuggled in) and spending countless hours chatting with her mother in law.

"The only way we can do that is cut our time in Nairobi, and I don't want your mom and dad to feel that my parents and I kept you here longer and cut into your time with them in Nairobi," Rafiq said.

"We would love you to spend more time here. I have a suggestion. Instead of taking the eighteen-hour train ride to Dar es Salaam on Friday, you can stay here for the day, and I can drive you to Dar es Salaam on Saturday. We can leave early in the morning, and we'll be in Dar es Salaam in six hours, and you can catch your flight to Nairobi in the evening. What do you think, Yasmin? Can I drive them to Dar es Salaam?" Salim asked.

"Sure, you can, but I am not going to let you enjoy our children for an extra day by yourself. We'll close the store for one day, and I will come with you."

"There you go. We can all ride together."

THE DRIVE TO DAR es Salaam in the Mercedes was pleasant. The departure for Nairobi was painful.

"It seems like you just came, and now you are leaving. Can you come back next summer after you graduate, Rafiq?" Yasmin asked.

"No reason why we can't, Mom. Perhaps not for the entire vacation, but for part of it, we can come," Shameem replied.

"Shameem and I would like to explore Europe. The tour we had gone on was great, but we did not spend enough time in any one place. What we would like to do is, say, go to Spain and spend three weeks there, traveling into the interior, off the beaten path to see real Spain and know its people and their culture. We would like to do the same in France, Germany, Italy, Greece, Denmark, and Sweden. So, perhaps we will do that for part of our vacation and come home for the balance of the time," Rafiq said.

"I want you to travel as much as you can while you are there. Once you finish and come home and start work, it would be very difficult to go to Europe again," Salim said.

Before leaving for Dar es Salaam, Salim had given Rafiq two envelopes, each containing Shs.50,000 in Shs.100 bills and suggested that he and Shameem should carry the envelopes in their carry-on baggage. He had saved up the money to buy the building in which their business and residence were located, which he had wanted to do for a long time. Other than the Mercedes and inventory in the store, they owned nothing in Tanzania, and both Yasmin and he had very much wanted to own at least the place in which they lived, but Chelsea had strongly advised against doing that. "Keep yourself liquid, Salim. Send the money to Rafiq to deposit in his bank account in London," she had said.

"Perhaps she knows better, Dad. Perhaps she is thinking of business opportunities down the road that may require cash, and if you have money in London, you can bring it back quickly. Or, she may be worried that the Tanzanian Shilling may be devalued, or perhaps she has some inkling of what Anil says all the time – that the government will turn on us."

"That will never happen in Tanzania," Salim said.

"Let us hope so. With this additional £5,000, we will have close to £25,000 in our Savings account, Dad. That's a lot of money."

"Yes, from this money, you should buy a nice house and a car. Let us have a house of our own in London if we can't have one here in Tanzania. Can you do that for £15,000?"

"That will be plenty, Dad."

"Hereon, I will send you, in addition to £100 for Shama's and your educational and living expenses, £500 a month to deposit into the Savings account."

AFTER A TEARFUL GOODBYE, Rafiq and Shameem arrived in Nairobi at 9.00 p.m.

The week in Nairobi was fun for Shameem, who spent a lot of time with her mother in her store talking about everything under the sun, but quite difficult for Rafiq. They had done and seen everything they wanted to do when they were there earlier. They attended Jamatkhana every day, but other than that and movies at the Drive-In, Rafiq did not want to do anything.

Bahadur had put away the cash they were carrying in a safety deposit box at his bank. They must remember to collect it when they left. Rafiq spent a lot of time walking around the city, going into the stores to make small purchases, but more to chat with the Indian owners to find out how they felt about Kenya's future. Most were optimistic. He kept wondering and worrying why Chelsea would advise his parents against buying property - as the D.C. had done earlier.

Finally, the week was over. Shameem woke up crying on the day of their departure - Saturday, September 12th. Rafiq could understand that she would be sad to say goodbye to her family as he had been when they said goodbye to his parents, but he was delighted to be leaving Nairobi.

THE FIRST ORDER OF business for Rafiq and Shameem after arriving in London was to find a house to buy. His dad had given Rafiq a generous budget, and he had been in communication with Alan Meadows, who had advised that there were some good listings in beautiful neighborhoods in Harrow they could look at in their price range when they were back. After unpacking, Rafiq called Meadows and arranged to see some properties the next day.

Meadows showed them three houses. Both Shameem and Rafiq liked the first one they saw, with asking price of £16,900. It was a fifteen years old, 2,500 square feet house with an attached one-car garage, four bedrooms - three at the upper level and one at the ground floor level - a large living/dining room, a dine-in kitchen with new cabinets and appliances, and a family room with log burning fireplace. The fully finished basement had the laundry room, one bedroom with an attached three-piece bathroom, a kitchenette, and a small lounge/dining area. The large master bedroom at the upper level and the bedroom at the ground floor level were each equipped with three-piece bathrooms. The house had central heating and high-quality carpeting throughout. Meadows told them the home was priced for a quick sale and would likely go for £15,500. This was a little over Rafiq's budgeted amount. They would need an additional £1,000 to furnish the place. He would have to talk to his dad about this. They agreed with Meadows to place an offer for £15,000.

Two days later, Meadows called to say that the owners would take £15,900 if the buyers would close the deal within thirty days. He recommended that they should offer £15,500 with £1,550 deposit and closing in thirty days with no conditions, which Rafiq and Shameem agreed to do.

Rafiq had talked to his father and described the house to him. "This will be the first property we will own anywhere, Rafiq. By Tanzania standard, the home for 300,000 Shillings is hugely expensive, but I understand this is a desirable area in

London and not a property in Mpwapwa or Dodoma. The house is enormous, but I presume you will have Anil stay with you and also Tazim, when she comes there, so you need the space. Don't worry about the price. See if you can get it for £15,500 otherwise pay £15,900. It will be an investment, and you've got another three years to stay there." Salim had said.

The owners accepted the revised offer. Meadows told them that the owners were diplomatic corps, relocating to Australia, and were receptive to selling much of their furniture, blinds and curtains, paintings, area rugs, and light fixtures at attractive prices if Rafiq and Shameem were interested.

Everything they had seen in the house was of very high quality and immaculately maintained. They revisited the house and decided to buy practically everything except the master bedroom furniture and a couple of area rugs. Shameem said that for her first house, she wanted her own new bedroom suite.

In the event, they decided to get the owners to move the ground floor bedroom furniture into the bedroom in the basement, which, like the rest of the basement, except for the kitchenette and laundry room, was unfurnished, and move the master bedroom furniture into the ground floor bedroom. Meadows presented an itemized list of the items Rafiq and Shameem wanted to buy for the owners to price. The owners aggregated the amount at £1,400, including all their linen, a beautiful 72 piece dinner set, crystal glasses, and stainless steel cutlery.

This was a huge relief for Rafiq and Shameem. It had weighed heavily on Shameem's mind and would have taken them months to furnish and equip the place. All they needed to do now was to get their bedroom suite. Shameem had seen one at Selfridges, which they promptly placed the order for.

Anil, who had seen the place before the deal was signed, had assumed that he would occupy the ground floor bedroom (for his privacy and also for Shameem and Rafiq's privacy) and was delighted to get the master bedroom mahogany furniture moved from the upper level.

After they returned to London, and before they had purchased the house, Anil had told Rafiq that Jenny was on the Pill, and they had been intimate. She had been coming to Mrs. Jackson's place for the weekends and sleeping in his room. Mrs. Jackson was okay with this. She liked the money and, she said, she liked Jenny. He had asked Rafiq if she could continue to do that, and Rafiq had said, "Of course. The room is all yours now. Shama and I are downstairs."

When Rafiq had told Shameem about this, she had said, "They are two adults and can do what they want. With the Pill, they don't have to worry about Jenny getting pregnant. You know that she makes me uncomfortable with her money talk all the time, but I can put up with that for a few weekends we are going to be here for. Hopefully, it won't be long before we find and move into our own house."

"What if Anil wants to invite her to come for the weekends to the house?" Rafiq had asked.

"He can't invite her to our house without asking us. We can't have her spending all weekends at our place."

"He might offer to pay - like they pay Mrs. Jackson."

"Rafiq, we will be inviting Anil to move in with us because he is family. That's what your parents, Anil and his parents, would expect us to do. And we will have Tazim come and stay with us, if and when she comes here to study, and that too would be because she is family and you love her even more than you love me. But we are not going to be running a boarding house here. We can't have Jenny spending all weekends with us." Shameem had said with finality.

"Oh, My God, Shama! Are you jealous of Tazim?"

"She was jealous of me. The way she was clinging on to you in Nairobi, she did not want to share her "brother" with me."

"She's just a teenager, Shama. Did she say anything disparaging to you or do anything to upset you?"

"No, I'm sorry. I shouldn't have said what I did. She was always very respectful and was very helpful to Narmeen and Adil. I guess I was overly sensitive to her running to you the moment she saw you, clinging on to you and putting her head on your shoulder when she sat down next to you - which was always. But for sure, she was not happy sharing you with me."

"That's understandable, Shama. Ever since she was a little girl, she always had all my love and attention. Now she has to share that with you. She could have been a little jealous but that you should understand, and not get upset."

"Tazim is a sweet girl. I would have loved her to be my sister. I guess I, too, was jealous of her for all the attention she was getting from you. It's okay, Rafiq, for you to love Tazim. She is your baby sister, and Anil is not as close to her as you are. Anyway, we were talking about Anil and Jenny. She can visit over the weekends but not move in for the weekends and spend nights in our place. "

THEY MOVED INTO THE house on Saturday, October 31st, and were fully settled by the end of the day, on Sunday, November 1st. Mrs. Jackson was disappointed to see them go, but the British Council had offered her three students to choose two from. She had become used to higher income from Rafiq and Shameem staying the weekends with her and had decided to take in 2 boys this year.

All Rafiq now needed to do was to look for a car.

1964
Fifty-Four

The neighbors on both sides of the house were friendly. They were somewhat surprised that a couple of university students had bought an expensive house in their neighborhood, and one boy and the girl were married. They seemed too young.

Their concerns about whether the property would be adequately maintained, - grass would be cut when required, snow would be removed, and the house would continue to remain a dignified and quiet place - dissipated quickly. The property was maintained immaculately. There were no noisy parties at this house. The three students came and went quietly, never failing to say hello to them and befriending their children playing outside. They stopped to chat with the neighbors and told them their backgrounds, what they were studying, and what their aspirations were. Soon the word had spread on the street that these three students were smart and very sophisticated, and their parents in Africa appeared to be wealthy.

BY THE END OF November, the three were comfortably settled. While in Nairobi and Mpwapwa, Shameem had learned from her mother how to make three kinds of curries and boil rice. Anil, in the week he had spent with his parents, had sat down with his mom and written up recipes for several Indian dishes that he loved to eat. He had also brought a supply of spices his mom had told him would be needed for the recipes.

They experimented with these dishes. Shameem had learned from Mrs. Bowes and Mrs. Jackson how to make roast beef, roast chicken, and roast and baked potatoes and boil vegetables. Soon, Anil had emerged as the best cook. He loved to cook, and everyone enjoyed his cooking. He took pride in his work and asked his mother to send him recipes for more exotic Indian dishes, which she did. Rafiq helped with the preparations, and it was his sole duty to do the dishes, including the cooking pots and pans. They cleaned their own bedrooms and attached bathrooms, and all three dusted and vacuumed the house every other Saturday.

The household expense per month, including utilities, was averaging £75. Anil insisted on contributing £35, which was what he earned as an articling C.A. student. His dad sent him an additional £35 per month, which was more than enough for him to live in relative comfort.

TWO WEEKS AFTER THEY moved into the house, Shameem asked Anil to invite Jenny to come home for lunch on Sunday, and she did this practically every Sunday thereafter. After lunch and dishwashing, which Jenny helped with, Shameem and Rafiq sat down in front of the fireplace to watch T.V. and Anil and Jenny went into his room "to watch T.V." and give Rafiq and Shameem privacy. Anil had purchased a T.V. for his room.

When passing by Anil's room, Rafiq and Shameem chuckled to hear sounds coming from the room.

They weren't watching T.V.

Early in December, Rafiq said to Shameem, "Shama, we have not had a housewarming party. We have been busy and not invited our friends for our wedding celebration, either. For your birthday this year, why don't we have your birthday party, our housewarming and also our wedding party on Christmas Eve, here at home?"

That will be a lot of work, Rafiq. I don't want to be working on my birthday."

"We don't need to cook anything. We can have everything catered, including the dishes, cutlery, linen, glasses, and whatever is required, from a catering firm. They have five-course packages ranging from £2.10 per person, which include non-alcoholic punch. Their catering van brings everything hot and ready to serve.

Their people will come in and set up everything quickly, and one girl and one guy will remain to serve and clean up. The van will come back three hours later to take everything away."

"Who will we invite?"

"We will invite Karim and Zabin, Azim and Gulnar, and our immediate neighbors. Including Anil, Jenny, you and I, there would be about eighteen of us. If we take one of their better packages for £3.10 per person, it will come to £70, including tips for the server.

"That's a lot of money."

"My parents will send us at least £25 each for our birthdays. That would cover most of the cost."

"Sounds good, but I thought we would use the money towards the car purchase. The garage is still empty, you know."

"The car can wait. We don't need it till summer."

RAFIQ HAD LOOKED INTO buying a car, but he had noticed that vehicles parked on the street were either Rovers or Jaguars or other higher-priced models. A Ford Anglia would be out of place here, and he could not afford a Rover or Jaguar.

There was one young American diplomat, two houses down the road who had a long and sleek late model Pontiac that he always parked in the driveway. The car took Rafiq's breath away each time he saw it.

One Sunday morning, when Rafiq and Shameem were walking to the bus stop, the owner, standing in his driveway, waved at them and said, "Hi, guys! You are the new couple on the street," and extending his hand, said, "I am Edwin Richards, from the U.S.A."

"Very pleased to meet you, Mr. Richards. We are from Africa," Shameem said, shaking hands with him.

"Mr. Richards is my father. My name is Edwin. Please call me Ed. And my wife - I believe she is somewhere in the house, if she hasn't run away, is Gwen."

"And this is my husband, Rafiq."

"You guys look too young to be married. Are you really married or just living together?" Ed asked, shaking hands with Rafiq.

"We are fully and truly married. We will both be twenty-three in five weeks." Rafiq said.

"That's young. You must have rich parents to buy that house. Must have cost you a pretty penny."

Just then, Gwen emerged from the house.

"Hey, Gwen, meet our new neighbors, – Shameem and Rafiq.

"Hi, guys. I am pleased to meet you. What a handsome couple they are, Ed," Gwen said, shaking hands with both.

ONE DAY WHEN RAFIQ stopped to say hello to Ed, who was cleaning the inside of his car, Ed said, "The silly British can't even design a house properly. This garage is too small for my car. We can drive the car in, but we can't open the doors to get out."

"What you mean, Ed, is the *car is too big* for the garage? I love your car, but why did you bring this gas guzzler to England? It's too big for the roads, and parking must be a problem." Rafiq said.

"The Embassy provides us with cars, and we have to drive American cars. Lee Iacocca at Ford has designed a smaller, sportier car called *Mustang*, which everyone is raving about. The TIME magazine had a cover story on it. I am requesting my boss to get me a Mustang to replace this."

"I read the TIME magazine story. The Mustang is being billed a sports car, but it's not a sports car, is it? It's got a regular six-cylinder engine and is built on *Ford Falcon* chassis."

"No, it's not a sports car, but it's designed to look like one. It's beautiful."

"That, it is. I would get one if I could afford to. I love the convertible model."

ED AND HIS WIFE Gwen had a sense of humor, and over the two months Rafiq, Shameem, and Anil were there, they had become good friends. Gwen had formed a women's "bridge club." Five women got together every Wednesday evening to play bridge at one lady's house, in rotation, from 8.00 p.m. – 10.00 p.m. The hosts served dessert and tea and coffee. She had determined that while Shameem was young, she was smart and mature and had invited her to join her Club.

Shameem was reluctant to join because it was difficult for her to give up one evening of study time to play bridge. Also, she did not know how to play the game, and all other ladies, except for Gwen, who was thirty-five, were her mother's age. But Rafiq had encouraged her strongly to join. The ladies were patient with her. She studied books on how to play bridge and soon became a reasonably good player.

SHAMEEM'S BIRTHDAY PARTY WAS much fun for everyone. Jenny helped Shameem host people. Anil had ordered a two-layer birthday cake for her. The food was delicious. The five-course meal included shrimp cocktail, beef, and fish as main dishes, baked and roast potatoes, sautéed vegetables and caramel, and trifle pudding. Rafiq and Shameem had requested the guests not to bring any housewarming or birthday gifts, but instead, donate the money to their favorite charity. They had also told the guests that in their Islamic tradition, they would not serve alcohol, but the guests were free to bring beer, wines, and spirits to enjoy their dinner with, and they would provide the glasses.

The guests were very complimentary about their choice of furniture and furnishings. Everyone admired the paintings in the lounge and dining room. Gwen told Rafiq that the previous owners were quite snobbish with their own circle of Australian friends and had never invited anyone on the street to their house. Rafiq did not tell them that they had acquired practically everything in the house from the previous owners.

1965
Fifty-Five

One Sunday afternoon, as Anil and Jenny lay in bed, Jenny asked, "Anil, you will finish your C.A. this summer. When will we get married?"

"We talked about this before. We'll do what Rafiq and Shama did. Go home in August and get married there."

"And when we're married, you will put my name on the title?"

"What title?"

"Title to this house."

"Title to this house? Why? How? This is not my house!" Anil said, sitting up.

"You are not on the title?"

"No, how could I be? Rafiq and Shama bought this house - not me."

"But you said your parents are in business together. Didn't the money come from the business?"

"The money came from Rafiq's parents, not from any business."

"So, you're living here as a paying guest?"

"I am here at Rafiq and Shama's invitation as their family member, and I contribute to the household expenses."

"How much do you pay?"

"£35 a month."

"You paid only £25 to Mrs. Jackson. Why are you paying so much more here?"

"Jenny, this room is not the small room I occupied in Mrs. Jackson's place, and this house is not Mrs. Jackson's house. Living in this house costs money, and I am paying my share."

"You never told me this - that you have no ownership in this house. So where are we going to live when we get married? I always believed we would live here."

"I never told you I had any share in this house. I don't know what made you think I had any."

"So, where are we going to live when we marry?"

"We have to decide that. I don't have the money to buy a house. I don't know if I want to buy anything. I may not want to live in the U.K. after I specialize. I may want to go home or move to the U.S.A. We might just want to rent a flat until we know."

"Rent a flat? Where?"

"I have to talk to my parents about this and see what they can contribute if we want to buy a flat. They are doing well financially, but they are not as rich as Rafiq's parents. His dad started sending money to him two years back to save up to buy a house. My parents have my two siblings to educate. They can't be as generous with me as Rafiq's parents are with him."

"I don't want to live in some crummy flat. Why can't we live here and pay them £50 instead of £35 a month?"

"Rafiq and Shama have to invite us to live here. I don't think they will. Two families in one house never work out. In any case, I would want my own place to live in when we are married."

"And what are we going to be able to afford to rent? How much will you earn when you graduate?"

"Around £125 a month. You're making £75. That's a good income for us to live in comfort, -rent something nice."

"Yes, an apartment in some suburb. Not a house like this."

"Jenny, you have to understand, my parents are not as rich as Rafiq's. My parents don't own any part of the business they're running. The business belongs to Rafiq's parents. They're working for Rafiq's dad and mom, who are kind enough to treat my parents like equal partners."

"Oh, my God, so your parents don't even own any business? What you're telling me is that they are living on Rafiq's dad's charity, and you are living here on Rafiq's charity. You've really misled me."

"What do you mean by 'misled' you? I am not living on Rafiq's charity. I pay them good money. I never told you this was my house and never said to you, my father owns any business."

"You told me, 'Rafiq's and my dad are in business together.' Didn't you? I remember that clearly."

"I may have – in a manner of speaking. They run a business together, and while my father has no ownership in the business, he shares 50% of all profits, so he is like a partner."

"I wish you had been honest with me. You have led me down this garden path when you've got nothing. No wonder I can come here only when Shama invites me. You have no right to invite me." Jenny said, getting out of the bed and getting dressed.

"So, what are you saying? You don't want to marry me because I don't own this house?"

"What I am saying is you have been dishonest with me, and I don't know if I want to share my life with you. I'm leaving."

"Don't do this, Jenny. Think about what you are saying. You want to end our relationship because I don't own a part of this house? Nothing else in our relation-ship matters to you?"

"I don't want to be in a relationship based on lies. You've deceived me, and I cannot tolerate that kind of despicable behavior. We're done. I don't ever want to see you again."

"Wait, let me get dressed, and I will walk you to the bus stop."

"Don't bother." And with that, she walked out, slamming the door behind her.

Shameem and Rafiq heard the door bang, and Rafiq got up to see what was happening. He saw Jenny walking out of the house. He went into Anil's room and asked, "What happened, Anil? What did you do to her?"

"Nothing, Rafiq. Nothing. She accused me of leading her to believe that I own this house with you, and she would live here when we marry. I never told her anything like that. She said my dad is living on your dad's charity, and I am living on yours."

"Really?"

"She said she doesn't want to share her life with me and doesn't want to see me again. I don't know if I want to see her again after what she has said to me."

"Anil, relationships take time to build and can be broken in a minute. You don't want to make that mistake. Let things calm down. I have no doubt Jenny will calm down and come and apologize to you. She can't end your relationship for money. She'll call you and apologize when she gets home."

"I don't think she will, and I don't know if I want her to call me. I am worth nothing to her. In all the time we've been together, we have never fought - not once. She fights with me for the first time and walks out of here and says those horrible things to me because she wouldn't get some £4,000 worth of share in this house if I were on the title. Me, my education, my character, who I am, the way I have cared for and loved her, all that is worth less than £4,000 to her."

"Anil, she obviously believed that you and I own this house equally - that your share is 50%, and she would live in this house one day as an equal owner with Shama. Now you've told her that's not true. She's a smart girl and will think about it and realize what she's doing and come back to you. Where is she going to find someone like you? Trust me, she will call you."

Jenny did not call, and she did not come to Jamatkhana for the next four Fridays.

One evening, as they waited for Anil to return from work, Shameem said to Rafiq, "The first time we met her, I said that this girl was a gold digger. Money is all she was interested in. She could not see what a gem Anil is and how much he loved her. I never saw love in her eyes for Anil. All I saw floating in her eyes were £ signs. I doubt if the bitch even knows what love is."

Shocked by what he had just heard, Rafiq said, "Shama, I am surprised to hear you use this kind of language to talk about a friend."

"She is no friend of mine! Never was! You, with all that milk of human kindness in your heart, could not see her for what she is. I hate her for what she has done to Anil and don't want to do anything to bring her back in his life. He is better off without her, and if they do makeup, she is not coming to our place again. Ever."

"Shama, Anil is very dear to you and me, and he worships you, and I can see that it hurts you to see him hurting, but this is not how we behave. If Anil can forgive her and wants to let her back in his life, we'll have to forgive her and welcome her here - for Anil's sake."

"And you would do that after what she said to Anil about him and Fateh uncle living on your and Dad's charity?"

"For Anil, we have to do that."

"Well, you can. I won't. There is no worse thing we can do to Anil than bring this bitch back into his life. She will ruin him."

"Shama, I wish you would not utter such foul words. It's not you. We don't say these things."

"You don't. For her, I will."

RAFIQ COULD SEE THAT Shameem was very angry and sad to see Anil so hurt and sad. She had missed her two bridge sessions and was snappy with him. This had to end.

Against his better judgment, he decided to ask Anil if he should call Jenny and talk to her. Maybe she was waiting for Anil to call her and apologize for having given her the wrong impression, and if Anil did not want to call, he would do that to clear up the misunderstanding.

"Me apologizing to her for giving her any false impression will do nothing for her. And why should I? I never said to her that we own anything jointly. You know, I have gone back in my mind over our relationship, over everything that we said to each other, and did together, from the day we met, and I now realize that for her money was always paramount. I was blind and utterly, utterly stupid not to see that. Her priorities in life, her aspirations in life, were completely different from mine. I think Shama did."

"Is that how you feel, Anil?"

"Yes, if I go and tell her that my dad is giving me £10,000 to buy a house, she will be back in a jiffy. I have seen her for what she is. I am not hurting because she dumped me. I am hurting because of the way she did it and what she said to me, and I am angry with myself because I was so blind and stupid not to see her for what she is. I wouldn't take her if she came crawling back to me."

"If that's how you feel, you should put her behind you. You know Shama is sad and is hurting to see you so sad."

"I know. I know. I will try and cheer up."

OVER THE NEXT FEW weeks, Anil regained his composure and became more himself. He refused, however, to go to Jamatkhana. He did not want to see Jenny.

"Forget her, Anil," Shameem said. "There are dozens of very nice girls I know in Nairobi and Mombasa who will do anything to get a C.A. who is as good a person as you are. At our wedding reception, a couple of beautiful and educated girls were asking me about you – if you were taken. All I'll need to do is introduce you to them, and they will be falling over one another for your attention. Let us go back to Africa this summer."

"Let him catch his breath, Shama. Let him graduate, and then he will find a nice girl without our help." Rafiq said.

"Without the love and support from the two of you, this would have been very difficult. I am so grateful that you are in my life." Anil said.

1965
Fifty-Six

With Anil and Jenny's breakup, the year had started badly. Jenny began to appear in Jamatkhana after a few weeks but did not look at or talk to Rafiq or Shameem.

One evening, a friend of hers came over to Shameem and said, "What you guys did to Jenny was unconscionable. How could you do that?"

"What do you mean? What did we do?" Shameem asked, taken aback.

"You enticed her into this relationship with Anil by telling her lies about him."

"Excuse me? She came to me begging to be introduced to Anil because she thought he was rich. You need some grey matter between your ears to see Anil for what he is. Ask Jenny if we ever said anything to her about how rich or poor Anil is and ask her to come and talk to me if she's got anything to say to me, not send her lackeys."

Shameem was livid. She told Rafiq, but not Anil, about this terse exchange with Jenny's friend.

She was hesitant to go to Jamatkhana for three weeks after that. Jamatkhana was a place to go to seek peace, not a place for people to have fights. She was worried that if Jenny or one of her friends came up to her again to say anything rude, she might end up slapping them, and what a scene that would create!

But time went by, and nothing happened.

What did happen was Rafiq and Shameem started to see Jenny in the company of a young man whom Karim had introduced to Rafiq in Jamatkhana once as an entrepreneur from the Congo who was there to study textile engineering. He had engaged Rosenberg and Weinstein to provide some accounting services for his businesses. His name was Shamshudin, but he called himself Dean.

Dean was a good looking and flamboyant person who dressed well. He wore "made to measure" designer shirts and suits cut in Paris, and *Dior* ties. He drove an E-Type Jaguar and had a spacious flat in Mayfair. He spoke fluent French and English, both without an accent. He had started to throw lavish parties at his flat and built up a circle of Ismaili friends.

Rafiq had learned subsequently that he was not enrolled in any college or educational establishment. His study of "textile engineering" involved him meeting with producers of textile machinery and visiting textile plants. His parents wanted to establish a textile mill in the Congo. It also did not look like he was there for a short period of schooling. He had put down roots and was there to stay. He was rumored to be making frequent trips to Amsterdam, where he was selling diamonds smuggled out of the Congo.

One Friday evening, as they exited the Jamatkhana, Shameem and Rafiq saw Dean holding Jenny by the waist and the two getting into his Jaguar.

"Good for her," Shameem said to Rafiq. "The gold digger has struck gold. No fear of her coming back into Anil's life."

Later in the year, they heard that Dean and Jenny were married and after some six months' stay in London, had settled in the Congo but were making frequent trips to Europe.

IN MARCH, FATEH WROTE to Anil to say that Zahir had passed his Cambridge Exam in Third Division. He had no interest in further studies. He wanted to join Almin on a full-time basis. Almin did need him, or someone like him, badly. After discussing it with Salim, they had "hired" Zahir and put him on the payroll.

Anil was disappointed. He wrote to Zahir and even called him to persuade him to come to the U.K. and enroll in a business administration diploma program, but Zahir flatly refused.

"Let it be, Anil. If he doesn't want to study, you can't make him do that. Maybe in a year or two, he will realize that he needs to get more education and will come around," Rafiq said.

BY APRIL, THINGS HAD settled down. Rafiq and Anil were working hard for their final exams. Anil was in regular communication with Rehana, whom he now missed more than ever. Rehana was guiding him through elements of the C.A. course to prepare for his exams. She said she had found an excellent job with one of the Canadian offshore banks. It paid well, and she was treated with much respect. The bank had provided a furnished oceanfront villa for her to live in. She and her husband were planning a family and were also thinking of moving to Canada at some point in the future. But life in Trinidad was great for the moment. They were not about to trade their beautiful weather and blue ocean for Canada's snow any time soon.

RAFIQ PASSED HIS B.SC. with First Class Honors. He had applied for and been accepted for the MBA program at the LSE. Anil did equally well in his C.A. exams. That earned him a promotion and pay raise at work. Shameem also passed her annual exams with flying colors. Life was good, and the summer was before them. Rafiq and Shameem had ten weeks of vacation. Anil could take three weeks.

"What will we do?" Rafiq asked.

"Now that Anil is a full-fledged C.A. let's go to Nairobi and find him a nice girl. And we promised your parents we would go there for a few weeks," Shameem suggested.

Anil laughed. "Can you imagine, Shama, us going to Nairobi and the word spreads in the community that there's this loser - he's a C.A., but he can't find a girl to marry, and his friend's wife is looking for a bride for him, while he is hiding behind her skirt. Besides, I can't meet a girl and get married to her in three weeks!"

"Anil is right, Shama. He's young, and unlike us, he's in no rush to get married. Let him find his own girlfriend. Perhaps we can go to one of the European countries. Italy would be good to explore for a couple of weeks..." Rafiq said.

"Well, let's think about it," Anil said.

In late July, Sophia called to say that she had completed her Nursing degree program with Upper Second Class Honours. She wanted to spend some time in London before returning to Iraq and wondered whether she could come and stay with them for a couple of weeks.

Shameem had told her that they would be delighted to have her. They had plenty of room in the house. They might travel for a few weeks in the summer, and if they did, Sophia was welcome to join them.

ONE EVENING, SHAMEEM CAME home after her bridge session and told Rafiq that Gwen was all excited about them getting a new car – a Mustang. It was coming just in time for them to tour the U.K. in the summer.

Rafiq walked over to Edwin's place the following Saturday and congratulated him for finally getting a Mustang.

"I hope you'll take me for a ride in your new car?" he said.

"Of course, Rafiq. Of course. I'll let you drive it, too. I would invite Shama and you to drive up with us to Brighton for a day, but although the Mustang has a back seat, it's not designed for adult passengers. You can accommodate a couple of kids, but not any adults."

"And what will happen to the Pontiac?"

"Oh, the Embassy will trade it in – send it to the Ford dealership here. The dealership will credit something against the Mustang. There is no market for big American cars here, so they will probably pay pennies for the trade-in."

"Can you find out how much the dealership will pay? If I can match what they offer, I would like to buy it from you."

"The car's not mine to sell, Rafiq, and the Embassy does not trade with the people in the host countries. But do you really want this? It won't fit in your garage, and its massive eight-cylinder engine uses a lot of petrol. Also, the steering is on the left side, and you drive on the wrong side of the road, so driving the car is a bit difficult."

"I've checked my garage. It's two feet wider than yours. I can get the car in, and if Shama gets out before I drive the car into the garage, I can park it very close to the wall on the right side and get out."

"Well, the car is almost new. I've driven it less than 15,000 miles. It's luxurious and prestigious and has all the options. People stop to look at it when I drive around. If you really want it, I can look into it. The Embassy can sell cars or phased out furniture and other items to its employees. Perhaps I can buy it and sell it to you – that's if you like the price."

EDWIN CAME BACK THE following week and said the car had been brought in duty-free, and any buyer from the dealership would have to pay duty on its selling price. The dealership would credit the Embassy with only £200 against the Mustang. This would also be the price at which they would "get rid of the car," and the buyer would have to pay a £25 duty on it. He had talked to his superior, who had agreed that he could buy it for £200, which was a steal, and then sell it to Rafiq, who would pay the £25 tax when Edwin signed the car over to him.

Rafiq couldn't believe that he could get this gorgeous car for £225. He would have been quite willing to pay £500 for it. When he called his dad to ask for his permission to buy the car, he said, "Dad, this is an almost new Pontiac, driven less than 15,000 miles, for sale for 4,500 Shillings. Can I please buy it?"

"You can't even get a motorbike for that price, Rafiq! Grab it, and when you come home, we can ship it here for you."

Anil and Shameem were equally excited. Rafiq signed the papers and had the car transferred to his name at the beginning of August. When Sophia arrived two days later, Rafiq and Shameem went to pick her up in their new vehicle. Driving the car in London was a little tricky, but Rafiq soon got used to it. It did draw people's attention. When he parked, people asked what make the car was, how much it cost, and if he was an American.

It was wonderful to see Sophia after almost a year. When Anil came home, he and Sophia hugged. They both seemed happy to meet again.

When they sat down for dinner, Anil said, "Now that we have a car, Sophia is here and wants to come with us to Europe, where do you guys want to go?"

"Italy?" Rafiq asked.

"Italy would be good, but it's too far. I would love to go there myself, but petrol is even more expensive in Europe than it is here. Shall we do France instead?"

"What do you think, ladies? Rafiq asked.

"France would be great," said Shameem. It would be nice to travel at our own pace and really enjoy all of the places we saw in Paris. We could spend an entire day at the Louvre. And France is much more than Paris. Sophia, what do you think?"

"I would love to tour France," Sophia said, and it was settled. They would go to France.

THEY DEPARTED LONDON A few days later and, after the short ferry ride from Dover to Calais, arrived in France in the early afternoon. The Pontiac's left-hand drive steering was perfect for driving in France, where people do drive on the "right" right side of the road, and all cars are left-hand drive. But the car's size was a problem. Parking was difficult to find in Paris, and in metered parking areas, they had to find and feed two tandem meters because the car occupied a small portion of the next spot.

After two nights of shows, dining, and sightseeing in Paris, they decided to go dancing. The dance hall was even more elegant than the MECCA dance halls. The orchestra was fantastic. Sophia was a good dancer. Anil enjoyed dancing with her and holding her close. Shameem had told her about Jenny and how it had ended. She had told Shameem that she liked Anil very much, and they grew closer to each other over the seven days they were in Paris. They held hands when the four of them went out walking and walked a few steps behind Rafiq and Shameem.

After a week in Paris, when they got into the car to leave to drive to Lyon, Rafiq could see in his rear view mirror that Sophia and Anil were not sitting at opposite ends of the back seat, but were seated in the middle, close together. He was happy. Later, after their lunch stop, he could see Sophia sleeping on Anil's shoulder.

When they arrived in Lyon and were offloading the luggage, Anil told Rafiq he had called the hotel and canceled the third room. He and Sophia were going to share his room.

"Is Sophia okay with that?"

"We talked, and she wants to."

"Very well, then."

Over dinner, Anil and Sophia looked very happy. It was evident that the two had become more than close friends.

Sophia told Shameem the next morning when they were alone that she had fallen deeply for Anil.

"Are you looking at this as a long-term relationship? You are leaving to go home in a few weeks. What will your parents say?" Shameem asked.

"I don't think my parents will have a problem. After all, you guys are also Shia. Our fundamental interpretation of the faith is the same. Anil is a wonderful man. I fell for him the first time we met and longed to be in his arms when we toured Scotland. I was very sorry when you told me he was dating that girl, and very happy when you told me they had broken up. What I'm concerned about is what your people and Anil's parents will have to say about him dating an Iraqi Arab girl."

"They will be surprised. His mom was not happy about him dating Jenny. When Rafiq and I tell them who you are and how good you are, they will welcome you, I'm sure."

AFTER TOURING THE FRENCH countryside for three days, stopping in towns and villages they had not known about or planned to visit, eating in small restaurants and trying to order food and converse with people who did not speak a word of English, they arrived in Nice.

Nice was fascinating. Their car was an indication to everyone that these were people of means, most likely, from some oil-producing Arab country.

They walked up and down the Promenade des Anglais in Nice and sat on the beach looking out over the Mediterranean. They spent an entire week touring the French Riviera – stopping for two days in Cannes and two days in Monaco – with its paths connecting many coastal villages and towns.

RAFIQ HAD DRIVEN MOST of the way in. On their return trip, he asked Anil to drive. Anil would have liked to sit in the back with Sophia, but he also enjoyed driving the Pontiac.

They arrived in London towards the end of August, and Anil went back to work shortly thereafter. Sophia said that she should return to Cardiff and pack up to leave for home.

"If you go away, what happens to your relationship with Anil?" Shameem asked her.

"Well, I can go home and talk to my parents about Anil. Beyond that, I don't know. Anil hasn't asked me to stay here or marry him or anything like that. If he does, I can come back.....or he can come to Baghdad to marry me there."

"Have you talked to Anil about any of this?"

"He knows I'm going back, but he hasn't said anything about what happens next."

"I guess that's because he hasn't figured out what to say to you."

"I DON'T KNOW WHAT to say to her," Anil said when Shameem asked him what his plans were for Sophia.

"She's due to leave for Iraq in a couple of weeks. I don't want her to, but I can't ask her to stay on and find work here without telling her for how long, and I can't ask her to marry me yet. We spent time together on our trips to Scotland and France, but I would like her to get to know me better before we make any commitments. I don't want her to think later in her life that she made a mistake. And we would have to talk to our parents."

"You can't just let her go back to Iraq, Anil!" Rafiq said. "Not so soon after getting into this relationship with her. Ask her to stay here for all of September and you both can decide if you want to spend your lives together. You say you are absolutely certain about her and if she feels the same way about you, she can find work here in October. She said that she could extend her student visa to do a year's practical, working in a hospital. You're welcome to stay here for as long as you like and take the time to sort everything out with your families and look for a place to live in. I mean, who knows? Maybe we can all go to Baghdad in December, and you two can get married there!"

"Absolutely! That's a brilliant idea," Shameem said.

"One thing at a time, guys. Are you sure you would be comfortable with her staying here for almost four months?"

"Anil, we are family. In East Africa, two brothers who are married often live with their parents in one house with their wives. We would invite you to stay here even after you're married, but you should build your life together in the privacy of your own space," Shameem said.

"There is no end to your generosity, is there?" Anil asked, with tears in his eyes.

"Don't say that, Anil. We've been brothers since we were children in school."

Sophia was ecstatic when Anil told her what Shameem and Rafiq had suggested. She could not believe that they could be so generous and giving. Tears ran down her face, also.

"So we have to plan this out properly. You stay here for September and see how you feel about me. If you feel you want to wake up each morning and look at my face, we can talk to our parents, and perhaps we can plan to get married in December…?" Anil said, nervously.

"And what if you feel at the end of September that you don't want to wake up to see my face every morning? Will you ask me to leave?"

"Sophia, I know today that your face is what I want to see every moment of my life," Anil said, kissing her.

"I feel the same way about you, Anil. I don't need September for me to decide."

"I THINK WE'RE READY to talk to our parents," Anil said to Rafiq and Shameem. How shall I do it? My mom will be so shocked; she'll probably faint when I tell her I want to marry an Iraqi woman."

"I have an idea. Let's do this in two steps. Let me call your mom and lay the groundwork for you to talk to her."

"What will you say to her?"

"I'll say the right things. Trust me."

"Okay, but be ready for her to start to cry. She might say, '*Eh Mawla*' (Oh Lord), what did we do to deserve this?'"

"Don't worry; she won't."

FATEH WAS WORRIED ABOUT receiving a call from Rafiq. Calls from London were expensive. This could be bad news.

"Is everything okay, Rafiq? Is Anil okay? Is Shama okay?"

"We're all fine, Uncle. Enjoying summer and having fun. Let me first speak to my favorite aunty, and then I will talk to you." Fateh passed the phone over to Almas.

"Ya Ali Madad, Almas aunty. How are you?" Rafiq asked.

"I'm fine, how are you, beta?"

"We are all fine, Aunty. I'm calling to give you some good news."

"Is Shama pregnant?"

"No, Aunty, we're not ready for that just yet! But you know you weren't too happy with Jenny? Well, she turned out to be no good, and she and Anil have broken up."

"*Shukhar Mawla*! (Thank Lord). I had a bad feeling about that girl. I was wondering why Anil had not said a word about her for weeks. Did they have a fight? How's Anil taking it?"

"Anil's just fine. But I have more good news. Anil has found another girlfriend. She's been our friend for three years. Her name is Sophia and she is a wonderful person. Fateh uncle, you, Dad, and Mom will love her, I'm sure of it."

"Shukhar! Does she attend Jamatkhana regularly?"

Now, this was out of sequence. This was not how the conversation was supposed to go. Rafiq had planned to move into this area gradually after Almas had said how happy she was and asked other things about Sophia but now had to deal with it. He was not prepared for this turn in the direction of his conversation. Why would she ask this? Was it that important to her? It must be for her to ask, Rafiq thought.

"See, Aunty....uh ...she's ..... not Ismaili. She is an Aithna Ashari...from Iraq. She is an Arab Aithna Ashari."

"Eh, Mawla! An Arab? What did we do to deserve this? You found Shama for yourself, why couldn't you find a nice Ismaili girl for Anil?" Almas was shocked and almost in tears.

"Aunty, she's a very modern and cultured girl. She's a Shia like us, and she prays regularly. She is a wonderful human being and Anil loves her and she adores him. After all, isn't that what we want? For Anil to be happy?"

"Yes, but how will we show our faces in Jamatkhana? How can we tell people our son has an Arab girlfriend or an Arab wife, if he marries her? What about her parents? Do they live in England? And if they marry and come home, what will she do when we all go to Jamatkhana? Will she become an Ismaili? What about the children? Will they be Ismailis?"

"That's too many questions, Aunty. These things will have to be thought through. Her parents are in Iraq. They are also well educated and liberal people. Anil will talk about all this to you when he is ready. I called just because I wanted to give you the good news."

"You call this *good* news?"

"It is good news, Aunty because Anil is happy and you should be happy, too. You remember you told us once that when our first Imam, Hazrat Ali, appointed his associate, Malik, as the governor of Egypt, he wrote to him to say, 'O Malik, remember, people are of two types. They are either your brothers in faith, or they are your equals in humanity.' Sophia is a Muslim and our sister/daughter in faith and she is our equal in humanity. Isn't that what it's all about, Aunty? How can we reject her because she is not Ismaili?"

"Well..." Almas sighed. "If Anil is happy....."

"So will you welcome her like mom welcomed Shama, when you meet her?"

"Yes, I will, but she may not like *us*."

"She will love you, Aunty, because you're so lovable. Who cannot love you? She's like Shama. She'll love you and Fateh uncle. And you will love her."

"Is she beautiful, like Shama?"

"She is good looking and a beautiful human being. You will be proud of her."

"Are you sure about this, Rafiq? If you say we should welcome her, then we will."

"Will you say this to Anil when he calls you? Tell him that you are delighted that he has found someone whom he loves and who loves him, and it does not matter to you at all if she's not Ismaili?"

"I will, but talk to your uncle. He won't be happy." Fateh's voice came onto the line.

"Hello, Rafiq, what's all this your aunty is talking about? What Arab girl?"

Rafiq reiterated everything he had told Almas.

"So she is an Aithna Ashari?"

"Yes, Uncle, quite close to us."

"So, what's the problem?"

"What problem, Uncle?"

"What was your aunty wailing about?"

"Well, she's worried that we may not look good in the community if Anil has a non-Ismaili wife."

"I don't care about what the community may think or say. All I care about is what makes my son happy. If he is happy with this girl, Sophia, nothing will make me happier."

"So Uncle, you'll welcome her?"

"Of course I will, and your aunty will, too. God created us as tribes and nations so we may know one another. If Anil loves Sophia, then we will all welcome and respect her. Why isn't Anil calling to tell us this?"

"Anil will call you, Uncle, when he's ready. I just wanted to give you the good news. I'll tell him what you've said."

"Trust you do that, Son. Send us her picture."

Fateh clearly understood how this was playing out.

"I will. I will, Uncle."

"HOW DID IT GO? How did they take it?" Shameem asked as soon as Rafiq hung up.

"Phew! That was tough. Fateh uncle had no problem at all. Almas aunty was worried, but I think that she came around."

"Tell me everything that they said."

WHEN ANIL RETURNED FROM work that evening, Rafiq relayed to him his conversations with his parents.

"Now, you can talk to them."

"Thank you for doing this, Rafiq. I wouldn't have known what to say if my mom started wailing. Your two-step approach worked. I am not surprised by my dad's reaction, though."

WHEN ANIL CALLED HIS parents a couple of days later, his dad said, "I had always thought it was possible that you might find a non-Ismaili girlfriend in England and want to marry her. I always thought she would be a white girl, and I was fine with that, if you loved her. When you started to write to us about Rehana, I knew you were in love with her and if you had said that she was going to divorce her husband and marry you, I would have been fine with that too, even though she was older than you. You don't need our permission to marry whomever you want to, Son."

"But, I need your blessings, Dad."

"You have my blessings and my prayers too, beta."

His mom was less enthusiastic. "Are you sure about this girl, Anil? Will she make you happy and will *you* be able to make her happy? Nothing will hurt me more than to see my son making any girl or his wife unhappy. How will she integrate into our community here?"

"It will be a long time before we come home, Mom. By that time, she will have become aware of our culture and practices. And Mom, I will never make her unhappy. I promise you that."

"Will she become Ismaili?"

"Mom, people should practice the faith they are comfortable with. You can't ask people to give up the faith they are born in. In time, if she finds merit in our interpretation of Islam, who knows, she might want to become Ismaili, but I would never ask her to do that."

"Well, as your dad said, you have our blessings and our prayers. I pray for you every day. Mawla will watch over you and Sophia."

"Thank you, Mom. I love you."

"And I love you, Son."

ANIL WAS RELIEVED. HE was surprised at how perceptive his father was to have known that he had, indeed, been in love with Rehana.

SOPHIA FIRST CALLED HER mother. She spoke to her regularly by phone, so a call from Sophia was no surprise to her. She told her about Anil and her wanting to marry him.

"You can't do that. How can you marry an Indian? Indians work for us here. Rahmat's father has been asking your dad when you are coming home. He has asked for your hand in marriage for Rahmat, and your dad has said yes, if you agree."

"Well, I don't agree, Mama. And Rahmat is fat."

"Yes, but he is a very nice boy, and his bank account is fatter than he is."

"Mama, I'm not interested in money. Anil is a professional. Rahmat has no education."

"Yes, but his father owns shares in oil wells. How many oil wells does this Anil guy have?"

"Mama, there are no oil wells here, so let's not talk this nonsense. In any case, he and I have been sleeping together, and Rahmat will not accept damaged goods, so it's a done deal."

"Oh, my God, Sophia! What have you done? You will bring disgrace to this family."

"You decide, Mama. I can bring Anil home, and we can marry there, or I'll get married to him here."

"Your father will kill you, you shameless girl!"

HER FATHER CALLED SOPHIA the next day.

"Your mama tells me you want to marry an Ismaili boy? An Indian?"

"Yes, Baba, I do. He's well educated and a thorough gentleman."

"How long have you known him?"

"We met two years ago, but our relationship became cemented in the last month."

"And you love him?"

"Yes, I do. Very much"

"Well, then you will marry him."

"Really, Baba? You would allow me to do that?"

"Why not? He's a Muslim, educated, and you say, he is a gentleman. Why not? He is a Shia like us. You know at times, the Ismaili Imams were in concealment for half a century, but they kept their interpretation of the faith alive and emerged to lead the community. Under the Aga Khans' leadership, the community has prospered. I know these people. I know Ismailis. They are good Muslims. Maybe they followed the right lineage - who knows?"

"Oh, Baba, I love you. You are so understanding! We would like to marry in December."

"Not so fast. I have to go to Rome next month. I will bring your mama with me and we will come over to London and meet your boyfriend. We'll stay at the Hilton. Bring him there. I need to make sure that he will make you happy."

"That would be wonderful. You will like him, and I would love to see Mama and you."

"THEY'RE COMING HERE TO check you out, Anil. Better be on your best behavior," Sophia said when Anil returned home from work that day.

1965
Fifty-Seven

Driving to meet Sophia's parents was a little unnerving for Anil. He did not like to be evaluated.

"My father will be fine, but my mom is the kind of person you don't like – either talking or waiting to talk, never listening. She might be rough and ask you pointed questions. She might tell you, you, Ismailis, followed the wrong lineage. She might ask you if you will renounce your faith and become a true Shia. She will ask you how much money your parents have and what you're earning. Don't let her upset you, okay?" Sophia said to him as they drove to the Hilton.

Her parents met them in the elegant hotel lobby. Anil let Sophia hug and kiss her parents before approaching to greet them.

Her father was a short and burly man with a big mustache and no hair. He was wearing an open-neck shirt and no jacket. Anil wished he had not worn his Austin Reed suit and expensive Italian shoes.

The mother was of medium height and quite good looking. Her hair was done up in the latest "beehive" fashion, and her face had been well attended to by the hotel's beauticians. She was wearing an expensive dress and heavy gold jewelry. She was dressed to impress.

"Baba, this is Anil," Sophia said, leading Anil to him by hand.

Anil extended his hand and said, "I am very pleased to meet you, Baba," as Sophia had instructed him to address her dad.

"You're the man who wants to marry my girl, eh?" Baba said, shaking Anil's hand. "Well, let's go have dinner. I am starving."

"And this is my Mama, Anil."

"Welcome to London, Mama, I am very pleased to meet you."

"And me too." That was all that she said, giving Anil a limp handshake.

AS THEY SAT DOWN for dinner, and the waiter came to take orders for drinks, Baba asked Anil if he had any preference for wine.

"I don't drink, Baba," Anil said.

"Good boy!" Baba exclaimed jovially, squeezing his shoulder. It hurt.

After drinks were served, Baba said, "Sophia tells me you have known each other for two years. She also tells me that you are a C.A. We need C.A.s in my company. When you are married, we will get you the visa to come and work in Baghdad. We'll pay you double what you can earn here and give you a fully furnished villa and a Mercedes."

Sophia almost chocked on her drink. He was not asking or inviting. He was ordering Anil. She looked at Anil nervously to see how he would respond.

To her surprise, Anil smiled and said, "That's so very kind of you, Baba. I would love to work in Iraq. There is so much of our Shia history there. And Sophia tells me there is a need for qualified nurses there. It's right that people who get educated should give the benefit of their education to their communities and their fellow human beings."

"Sophia has become a nurse because she wanted to. She's not going to be wiping people's bums. I want her to take a secretarial course or something like that so that she can work in her father's office. He will take care of her," Mama interjected.

"I did not spend three years at the university to work as a secretary, Mama. Have you visited our hospitals and seen the patients' pain and discomfort when they need help to go to the bathroom, or they want their painkillers, but there is no one to attend to them because there are not enough nurses?"

"So, you are going to solve Iraq's nursing problem?"

"No, Mama, but I can help. More of our girls will go into nursing if they see me, the daughter of a rich and prominent man, working as a nurse."

To lower the temperature, Anil tried to change the subject and said, "You both speak excellent English. Mama has an American accent. She can easily be mistaken for a beautiful American woman."

"Thank you. We both went to the American school, and Sophia did too." Mama said, relaxing a little and taking a big gulp from her wine glass. She was on her second glass. Anil was surprised to see her drink. Sophia never touched alcohol.

"So your parents are in Africa? What do they do?" Mama asked.

"They run a business."

"I know they run a business. What kind of business, what do they earn? What do they have?"

"They make good money. They own the house in which they live and the car that they drive. They funded my education. As good Muslims, they pay zakat, and as Islam teaches us to do, they share much of what they don't need. They give a lot to charity."

"Good Muslims? You Indian Ismailis are no Muslims! The Indian Ismailis working for Baba don't observe Ramadhan, don't say Salat, and you don't go to Mecca for Hajj."

"Lay off, Mama, you're insulting Anil. Eat your dinner!" Sophia said, her blood boiling.

Anil could see that Baba was embarrassed. He kept his cool and said, "Mama, the Prophet said that anyone who says the Shahada, *La Illah ha Illulah, Mohammad Rasulilah*, is a Muslim. We Ismailis, recite the Shahada many times a day; you are correct that many of us do not fast during Ramadhan, but we are required to. We pay zakat, one-eighth of our income; we say Salat, but we call it *D'ua*. Like Namaz, it includes a collection of Quranic verses. We don't go to Mecca for Hajj. Honestly, I don't know why, but it's not part of our tradition. What are part of our tradition, and central to our lives, are the core Islamic ethics of honesty, generosity, peace, compassion, tolerance, inclusiveness, and humility. We live by these ethics. To my knowledge, these are also the ethics by which most Muslims in the Middle East live. Your daughter lives by these ethics, and that's why I love her so much."

Baba listened to Anil attentively and said, "That's an eloquent articulation of true Islam! That's what true Islam is. People who practice these ethics are true Muslims, not the ones that just say Namaz five times a day and fast from dawn to dusk and then go back to their foul ways when Ramadhan is over."

Looking at Mama, he said, "By your definition, I'm not a Muslim either, because I don't observe Ramadhan. I don't fast."

"That's why you are so fat," Mama replied, averting her eyes and taking another sip of her drink.

Baba ignored her and turning to Anil, he said, "At one time, I had five Indian Ismailis working as accountants for my firm; one came, and he brought the others. There are still two working with us. I learned a lot about your people from them."

"What did they tell you?" Anil asked.

"They were scared to speak to me at first, but I befriended them, giving them bonuses for Eid and other occasions to send home to their families. They were all alone in Iraq, living in one little house. I felt sorry for them for having to live and work in a foreign land without their families. They told me about your Aga Khans I and II, how they came to India from Iran, their teachings, and how your people have prospered. They told me that the Aga Khan III sent your ancestors to Africa, where you guys have done very well. They also told me the ethics you talk of are your Imams' teachings. Have you been to India, Anil?"

"No, I have not had the opportunity, Baba."

"Mama and I have been to India. It's a different world. Good people. You should go to India and take my daughter with you. Go there for your honeymoon. It will be our gift for you."

"That's very kind of you, Baba!" exclaimed Anil, turning to look at Sophia. "We'll take you up on your offer."

"Yes, go and see the Taj Mahal and Qutub Minar, and see Bombay," Mama chimed in. "Our host took us to an expensive saree store, and I bought some silk sarees there. I like Indian actresses wearing sarees in Indian movies. A model in the store who was demonstrating different sarees for me taught me how to wear one." Now that she had downed more than two glasses of wine and was on her third, she was becoming more amicable.

"Do you ever wear them? You must look gorgeous in a saree, Mama," Anil said.

"Oh, yes, I wear them all the time. At all of Baba's office parties, I wear sarees. I ordered more after coming back from India. I also taught some of my friends to wear sarees. They're better than cocktail dresses for the parties."

"Sophia, maybe you could wear a saree some time? There are Indian stores here where you can get them," Anil said to Sophia.

"I'm too short to look good in a saree," said Sophia, self-deprecatingly. "Because she's tall, Shama looks gorgeous in sarees. I don't think I would look good."

"You look elegant and beautiful in anything that you wear, Sophia," Anil said, and turning to Mama, he said, "You must wear a saree for Sophia's and my wedding, Mama. My people will think you're an Indian actress."

Mama laughed. "Oh no, I don't look like an Indian actress," she said, but she was flattered, and hoped Anil meant what he said.

He has turned on his charm offensive. Let's see how long that lasts, Sophia wondered.

It lasted the whole evening. Between the two of them, Baba and Mama had almost finished the second bottle of wine, and both were now on a roll, laughing and joking. Anil told them some of his jokes, and each time he did, Baba bent over laughing and punched Anil in his shoulder. By the end of the evening, his shoulder was quite sore.

WHEN THEY SAID GOODBYE, Mama hugged Anil and said, "My daughter is brilliant. She has found a good boy. I am happy she has found you."

"She's right, Son. Will we see you tomorrow?" Baba asked.

"No, Sophia will come and meet you here, but I'm sorry, I have to work. I'm in the middle of a major audit. I'll try and get away early and meet you at the airport to say goodbye."

WHEN THEY GOT INTO the car, Anil exhaled audibly and said, "That was one of the most arduous evenings of my life. I didn't know that marrying you was going to be this difficult!"

"I'm sorry, Anil, but I thought that after my mom thawed out a little, you were enjoying their company. No?"

"Well, let me put it this way – I wouldn't want to live through this again."

"But did you mean what you said, that you would come to work in Iraq?"

"I need to work here for at least two years to specialize. What will my choices be, then? I could continue to work and stay here, but I don't think I want to do that. I could go back to Tanzania and earn, maybe, Shs. 3,000 a month, that's £150 a month. That would be an excellent income for Tanzania, but I don't know how the country will evolve in its post-independence era. I'm not as optimistic as Rafiq is about Tanzania. I don't think I want to go back there. I would like to settle in the U.S.A., but I've not been there. I might not like it. So why not Iraq, if your dad can get me a visa and a job that pays me a good salary and provides a home and a car?"

"Would you not feel isolated there?"

"How could I feel isolated with you by my side?" Anil said, pulling Sophia close to him.

1965
Fifty-Eight

A couple of days later, Rafiq, received a call from his father. The government had instituted Exchange Control. This meant that the Tanzanian currency was no longer convertible into other currencies. Importers would have to apply for import licenses and get foreign exchange from the Central Bank. All remittances for funding the education of Tanzanian students would also have to be approved by the Central Bank. The students would have to get letters from their colleges or universities to confirm that they were enrolled in accredited education programs. Rafiq and Shameem should obtain the letters as soon as possible.

Rafiq was shocked. This meant that there would not be any extra remittances from his dad. After the house purchase, he had just over £12,000 in the savings account and about £250 in his and Shameem's joint personal account. His free-spending days were over. He understood now why Chelsea had stopped his father from buying the property and had encouraged him to send their money out of the country.

Anil was not surprised.

"I knew this would come; this is the shape of things to come. It always happens in developing countries. Now that I've graduated, I can't get a letter from the Association of Chartered Accountants stating that I'm a student. My dad will not be able to transfer the £35 he sends me every month. Sophia and I should be paying you £70 a month. Sophia, you will have to find a job quickly."

"Don't worry about that, Anil. I'll ask my dad to continue to send me the £50 a month. That's no skin off his nose. I'll start to look for work, and we'll be okay," Sophia said.

"There's no need for you to double what you're paying us, Anil. You and Sophia are occupying just one room, and it won't cost us £35 extra to feed Sophia. You can contribute £15 to the household budget to cover her cost. We need to think this through carefully. Anil, have your parents been sending you any extra money to save here?" Rafiq asked.

"I told them to do that several times but, no, they procrastinated and did not. I know they've accumulated upwards of 150,000 Shillings. It would have been £7,500 if they'd sent it here."

"Well, then, if anything goes wrong in Tanzania and they all have to leave the country, all we've got is £12,500 to settle them here or some other place."

RAFIQ THOUGHT ABOUT IT for two days and then told Shameem, "I have to withdraw my application for the M.B.A. program. I should find a job and start earning money."

"What will that do, Rafiq? The government will allow your £50 education allowance to continue, so why would you withdraw?"

"What if my parents have to leave in a year? There wouldn't be any allowance anymore. If I'm in college and they come here, we'll have to fund our education and their living and resettlement costs."

"You're panicking for no reason. All that the government has done is bring in exchange control. Nobody is killing anyone in Tanzania. So, should I also withdraw from my M.B.B.S.?"

"No, I've finished my undergraduate program. You've not got your M.B.B.S. yet. You have to continue. I can do my M.B.A. anytime, in the future."

"You have to continue. There is no need for rash decisions. With appreciation in the housing market, we've got almost £20,000 in this house. We can sell it if need be."

"If we sell the house, where will Anil's family and my parents live, and where will we live if they all have to come here? We can't sell the house."

"There is no need to panic, Rafiq. You can't withdraw from M.B.A."

Two days later, Rafiq withdrew his M.B.A. program application and started to prepare his CV and examine job options.

A gloom had settled over the house. Shameem was very unhappy with Rafiq, but she said to herself, "Maybe he's right. What if something does happen in Tanzania, and they all descend upon us here? We'll need money."

Salim and Yasmin were very disappointed when Rafiq told them that he had withdrawn from the M.B.A. program and was looking for a job.

"What are we making all this money for if we can't educate our son?" Yasmin asked.

"The government is permitting us to send money for education, but Rafiq is now worried about things he shouldn't be worrying about. No one is threatening us or throwing us out of here. He shouldn't have done this without asking us. I cannot understand why Rafiq would act so irresponsibly," Salim said.

WHEN THE UNIVERSITY RESULTS had come out, several large banks, insurance companies, airlines, and manufacturers had come to recruit the new graduates on the L.S.E. campus. Although invited, Rafiq had not attended any interviews.

He now started to send his C.V.s to these companies. Within a week, he received interview invitations from two commercial banks, the civil service, and one large corporation. He also received two firm job offers, subject to a meeting. Of the latter, one was from Robertson Richards Wealth Management (R.R. Wealth Management), an investment banking firm, and one from the New England Insurance Company. Both were attractive.

He met with the human resources staff of both firms. With the insurance company, it was a routine matter of fact meeting. He was a First Class Honors L.S.E. graduate, so they did not want to go through a lengthy interview process. He dressed well and looked impressive. The company would take him on as a Management Trainee and pay him £125 a month in the first year, and increase that to £150 per month in the second year. This was more than he had expected.

The Manager at R.R. Wealth Management, Bill Bannerman, was an American, a tall and muscular man. He told Rafiq that the Bank was American. He engaged Rafiq in conversation about his background in Africa, asked why he had married so young before he had even graduated (did he get his girlfriend into trouble?), and empathized with him over his reasons for his withdrawal from the M.B.A. program.

"Do you know what investment banking is about?"

"Only what I learned in my degree program, that investment banks offer services to corporations issuing securities and investors buying securities. For the corporations, the investment bankers offer information on when and how to place their securities on the open market. This involves research. Investment banking also involves advising organizations on mergers and acquisitions. This involves research and negotiating skills."

"That's a good listing of core activities of the investment banks, but investment banking is much more than that. Corporate finance, which involves helping customers raise funds in capital markets and giving advice on mergers and acquisitions activities, is what we are recruiting for at this time. Does that interest you?"

"When it comes to banking, I believe that corporate finance, mergers, and acquisition will be much more interesting than commercial lending. I had hoped to learn much more about investment banking in my M.B.A. program."

"Listen, Son; if you come here, you will learn much more than in two years of any M.B.A. program, not just about investment banking but everything else that an M.B.A. can teach you. I have an M.B.A., and I know that for a fact."

"For a start, we'll send you to our head office in New York for three months of extensive training and orientation. During your training period, we'll give you a monthly allowance of $750. Your travel costs and hotel accommodations will be paid for. I can arrange for you to go next week if you decide. When you're back, we'll set your salary, in consultation with our head office and their assessment of your performance in training. It will not be less than £125 per month. It could be as high as £200 a month. "

"That sounds good, but Sir, why would I need to take training in America to work in the U.K.? Should I not learn how business is done here?"

"That's a good question. The reason we put all our staff from the U.K. Germany, France, Singapore, Switzerland, or other regional offices through this training in New York is that there are fundamental corporate financing and mergers and acquisitions principles and practices that we apply in every country. We want everyone to become familiar with the R.R. Wealth Management culture and modus operandi."

"Thank you very much, Mr. Bannerman, for inviting me for this interview. What you tell me sounds very interesting. I have to talk to my wife about going away for three months. May I come back to you in a couple of days?"

"You can take her with you to New York. We'll cover her cost."

"That is very kind of you, Mr. Bannerman, but she is in her fourth year of M.B.B.S. program."

"That's the M.D. program?"

"Yes, Mr. Bannerman."

"Quit calling me Mr. Bannerman. Call me Bill. And take a week if you want. We can't have you go for three months' training and come back and say I don't want to do this. If you need to discuss this more, come back, and we'll talk. I will give you some material on investment banking to study and learn more about what it's all about."

"Thank you, Mr. Bannerman, ….. I'm sorry, … Bill. Thank you, Bill."

RAFIQ'S INTERVIEWS WITH THE chartered banks and manufacturers (he decided not to interview with the civil service) were similar to his meeting with the insurance company.

"I find the R.R. Wealth Management offer exciting. What do you think?" Rafiq asked Shameem and Anil.

"I would take that offer if I were you," said Anil.

"You would have to go away for three months? What will I do?" Shameem asked.

"You don't have to worry, Shama; Anil and Sophia are here. It's only for three months. "

"It's *three* months, Rafiq. I don't know if I can live without you for that long!"

"You'll manage just fine, sweetheart."

TWO DAYS LATER, RAFIQ accepted the R.R. Wealth Management offer.

When Rafiq told his parents that he was taking this job, which required him to go to New York, Yasmin was beside herself. "Look what this exchange control is doing. Our son had to give up his education, and now he is going to risk his life in

New York!" she said to Salim.

"Yasmin, millions of people live in New York, and 99% are safe."

"Don't you read the TIME magazine? How many murders there are in New York?" Yasmin was in tears.

"Rafiq is smart. He wouldn't be going to New York if it was dangerous. Yes, he did make a rash decision giving up his M.B.A. spot, but let's have faith in his judgment now. And we will pray for his safety and success."

RAFIQ WAS ON HIS way to New York by the end of September. He reported for work at the R.R. Wealth Management offices on Wall Street at 9.00 a.m. the next day. The Bank occupied the entire 39th floor of the Templeton Tower building.

He was led to the Human Resources Manager's office, who asked how his flight was and if his hotel accommodation was comfortable. He gave him his first month's allowance and introduced him to his supervisor, Albert McKenzie, who led him to his cubicle.

"Call me Al," the supervisor said. He gave Rafiq a copy of R.R. Wealth Management's annual report for 1964 to study and said that he would take him out for lunch at 1.00 p.m. Al did not introduce him to anyone else. A couple of girls stopped to say hello. None of the guys came by. The place was like a beehive. It seemed very impersonal. Everyone was working away; many appeared to be engaged in intense discussions on the phone. Rafiq started to read the annual report.

Before he knew, it was 1.00 p.m., and Al tapped him on his shoulder.

"Hungry?" he asked.

Rafiq got up, and they walked out to the street. New York is so different from London; everything here is massive; the city is pulsating with life, Rafiq thought.

They walked just a few steps, and Al led him into a small sandwich place with only a few seats. They lined up to place orders and pick up their sandwiches. Al ordered a pastrami smoked meat sandwich on rye bread with mustard. Rafiq had never eaten a smoked meat sandwich. He watched the server prepare it.

"Yes, sir?" the server asked Rafiq as he handed the sandwich to Al.

"I'll have the same, please."

They each picked up a Coke bottle from the cooler and placed the trays before the cashier. She rang up the bill, and Al paid it.

They sat down at a small table for two and started eating. Rafiq had expected Al to treat him to a traditional British three-martini lunch that would go on until 3.00 p.m.

"Did you read any of the annual report?" Al asked.

"Yes, almost all of it," Rafiq replied.

"Really? All 50 pages?"

"Well, about 48 pages."

"Did you see anything noteworthy?"

"You mean beyond the asset base and how much money the Bank is making?"

"Yup."

"I note that the U.K. portfolio constitutes a minuscule portion of your global revenue base, but what interested me is the IRR. Your Internal Rate of Return on investment in the U.K. is very high."

"You noted that. Good. That's because of Bannerman. He's a seasoned banker. We're relatively new in the U.K. Until now, we just had our big toe in the water. We've now tested the waters and want to dive in. We have only ten people there, compared to 250 here and over 1500 globally. We have two other guys and one woman, two CAs and one Economics graduate like you, in training here from the U.K. We want to increase the H.R. capacity at our U.K. office by 50%."

"When do I start training?"

"Tomorrow. This will involve training on I.P.O.s, matching investors to a security issuance, coordinating with bidders, negotiating with a merger target, and conducting research. The course will run from 9.00 a.m. to 1.00 p.m. every day. Lunch is from 1.00 to 2.00 p.m. 2.00 to 5.00 p.m. is research and study time. You'll do your assignments, one assignment per week, over the weekends. A passing grade is 75%. Each day, you'll be given your reading material for the next day's training. I'll give you your reading material for tomorrow's training when we get back to the office. The course runs in a circle so you can join at any time."

"That sounds interesting."

"Not overwhelming?"

"No. A lot of work, but not overwhelming."

"Good. Because of Christmas, your course cycle will end on December 15th. That's over two weeks short of our regular cycle. What this means is you'll have to do two more weeks of studying in two and a half months of training. You'll have to study for and complete two assignments, essentially, on your own."

Rafiq was happy that he would be done in two and a half months instead of three. As soon as he received the reading material upon their return to the office, he started studying and making notes. He had studied the entire lesson and completed the multiple-choice questions at the end of the lesson before 4.00 p.m. He had scored 90% on the multiple-choice questions. He went over the lesson once again. Now it was 5.00 p.m. He had expected everyone to get up and leave, but no one moved. People were engrossed in whatever it was that they were doing. It was like they had not seen the clock. He got up and walked over to a young woman in the next cubicle, who had looked at him and smiled earlier.

"Excuse me. I'm sorry to disturb you. My name is Rafiq. I'm a trainee from the U.K. This is my first day. I've finished reading tomorrow's training material. Is there a reference library where I can go to find something else to educate myself?"

"Hi, I'm Carole. I'm from Canada, also here for the training. I am on the sixth segment. I can give you my second segment if you want to study that."

"Oh, that would be so kind of you. I'll return it to you as soon as I've read it."

"There's no rush. I know where to find you if I need it."

RAFIQ SAT DOWN WITH Carole's second segment, which was all marked up. As he read it and saw the questions and comments Carole had written on the pages, he realized she was a very smart lady. She was noting down essential elements of the text and raising sound questions.

He spent the next 90 minutes studying. Some people started to get up at 6.30 p.m. Others were still working away. Carole got up and came over to Rafiq and said, "Well, goodnight. I'm leaving. You can keep the lesson and return it whenever you're done with it."

"Thank you for lending it to me. I see you've made some astute comments and jotted down some good questions. What happens with these questions and comments?"

"You can take them up in your class, but you have to navigate your way carefully through this course."

"What do you mean?"

"Do you have plans for dinner? If you want to come with me, I'll be happy to talk about it."

"I don't know New York at all. Where do the trainees eat?"

"There are several restaurants we can choose from. Of our daily $25 allowance, $15 is for breakfast, lunch, and dinner. If you eat breakfast at the hotel for $2.50 and spend $5 for a nice lunch, you can have a pretty good dinner for $7.50. You want to come with me?"

'Sure," Rafiq said, putting his papers away and locking the cabinet.

AS THEY WALKED TO the restaurant, a large bistro, Carole told him that she was from Toronto. She was married with two children. Her husband was an engineer. After graduating with a B. Comm. degree from the University of Toronto in 1959, she had worked as an accountant for a franchising company. She had married in 1962 and had her first child, a boy, in 1963. She had stayed home to raise her son and had her second child, a girl, born eleven months later. She had continued to stay home, raising her kids until June of this year and had then started to look for work. She had been introduced to R.R. Wealth Management by a friend who worked there and had started her training six weeks back. She had hired a live-in nanny after her daughter was born. The nanny and her husband were looking after the children while she was in New York. She missed them very much and was flying to Toronto every other weekend.

Rafiq told her about him and how he had come to be in New York for the training.

"So, what's the scoop on the course?" Rafiq asked as they sat down and ordered dinner.

"The course material, as you've seen, is not difficult. If you study it properly, you can score 75% and pass. Everyone can do that. But passing is not all there is to it. You need to demonstrate a deeper understanding of the material. You need to ask smart questions, questions that others will not have thought of, questions not directly emanating from the training material but related to the topic. This will go on your record. You said there are four other trainees from the U.K. here? Where you'll get placed in relation to them when you go back will depend on how you perform here."

"That explains your smart annotations."

"To ask smart questions, you need to go to the reference library in the office and do research on whatever topic the lessons cover. In your second month, you'll get into case studies. You'll be given the cases and asked to provide your situational analysis and how you would deal with an I.P.O. or a merger or acquisition. The case studies will test your understanding of the material that is covered to that point. To rise above the average, you will need to study more than the course material. You'll have to read The Wall Street Journal every day and look at case studies in the reference library. Some will be real-life case studies, where you will have to go to business libraries and look at old copies of The New York Times and Financial Post."

"How did you know all this?"

"My friend at R.R. Wealth Management in Toronto educated me. This is hard work, but it will not only influence where you get placed when you start, it will also give you a head start in your work. In this field, you have to be learning all the time, or you'll quickly become outdated."

Each morning, Rafiq woke up at 3.00 a.m. to call Shameem. He had to catch her at 8.00 a.m. her time before she left for her class. By the time his day was done, it was too late in London for him to call her. He told her about Carole, and assured her that she was married, with two children, and five years older than him, so Shameem did not have to worry about her.

IN MID-NOVEMBER, CAROLE TOLD Rafiq that she would be done in four days and would leave for Toronto on the 20th. They promised to stay in touch.

"Have you ever been to London?" Rafiq asked.

"No, but my husband and I have always wanted to visit London, Paris, and Rome. We might do that when the kids are a little older, and we have some money saved up."

"Please do come to London. You and your family can stay with us. My wife and I will be delighted to have you. We have a large house. I mean it."

"That's very kind of you, Rafiq, and if you ever visit Toronto, let me know."

LIFE IN NEW YORK after Carole's departure was lonely for Rafiq. Over the weekends, he and Carole had found time for Carole to take him around New York. They had visited the major tourist attractions, Central Park, and some museums. New York was fascinating. He decided that he must bring Shameem here someday.

RAFIQ COMPLETED HIS TRAINING and returned to London by mid-December, to everyone's delight.

While Rafiq was gone, Sophia had found work with St. Mary's Hospital in Harrow. She was entitled to one year's "practical" at an accredited hospital in the U.K. and did not need a work permit. She would be paid £25 a week.

She and Anil had talked about getting married in December, which is what her parents wanted (her mother did not want her daughter living in sin) but had agreed that December would be too soon. They had much to plan. They had to first find a place to live in and schedule the wedding at a time when Rafiq and Shameem, Anil's and Rafiq's parents, and Tazim would be able to travel to Baghdad. December would have been ideal, weather-wise, but it was too soon. It would have to be in the summer of next year when it would be hot as hell, but that's when it would have to be unless they postponed it to the following December. They had decided to search in earnest for a place to rent in the New Year.

Rafiq asked Shameem if Anil, Sophia, and she had been okay managing the house and finances while he was gone. She told him that Sophia had been a tremendous help. She worked shifts, and if she was working the evening shift, she cleaned the house, cooked, and did the grocery shopping, leaving little for Shameem to do. Anil, too, had been very attentive and ensured that she did not have anything to worry about and could pay full attention to her studies.

She also told him that their usual £100 monthly allowance from his dad had come into their account for October and November, but only £50 had been credited at the beginning of December. Anil and Sophia had paid her £150 for three months, which she had deposited into the account. She estimated that after paying for all household expenses for October, November, and December, they would have some £350 in their account at the end of the month. The £100 net addition into the account from the end of September was the money Rafiq's dad had sent for October and November.

"£50 is what we should expect to receive from Dad hereon. If Anil and Sophia pay another £50, we'll have £100 per month, which should be enough for us to live on comfortably, but not lavishly as we did before. Whatever I earn net of taxes and other contributions, we must save."

AS BANNERMAN HAD ASKED him to do, Rafiq reported for work on Monday, December 20th.

"You did very well in your training, Rafiq. Your report here says: *The candidate performed well above average and demonstrated an aptitude for and knowledge of investment banking, unusual for a trainee.*"

"The course was exciting, and investment banking is fascinating, I wanted to learn as much as I could, Sir."

"You're too modest. This is a British trait. Here's your first lesson. In this field, you can't be modest. You have to be aggressive, or you'll undersell yourself."

"I'll remember that, Sir."

"You'll do well to remember that. Obviously, you worked very hard over the past ten weeks. Nothing much is happening here until the New Year, and I have to spend time with the other new recruits who were in training with you. They did well, but not as well as you did. H.R. has put you on payroll from December 15th. Your training allowance covered you until that date. Your payroll deposits will go into your bank account on the 15th and end of each month."

Rafiq was curious to know his salary; if Bannerman did not tell him what it was, he would have to wait to see his first bank deposit to find out, but then he remembered Bannerman's first lesson and asked, "And how much that will be, Bill?"

"We are starting you at £200 per month."

Rafiq had expected and would have been disappointed if it was less than £175. £200 was very generous.

"Thank you, Bill, that's very generous!"

"It may be generous, but you shouldn't say that. Make it known, without saying it aloud, to whoever is paying you for whatever service you provide, that you deserve what you're being paid, and more. When our clients pay for our services, we make sure they understand that what they get from us is worth much more than what they're paying us. Remember that in life, people don't get what they deserve. They get what they negotiate. That's your lesson number two."

"I'll remember that. But I have to thank you for your confidence in me. I will do all I can to live up to it."

"The Bank will reopen after the Christmas break on January 4th. Come to work then. And have a merry Christmas and a very happy New Year."

"And I wish you the same, Bill. I hope that you and your family will have a very enjoyable Christmas and I look forward to seeing you in the New Year. Are you going away anywhere for Christmas?"

"We're leaving for Connecticut on Saturday. That's where my home is."

"THIS IS WONDERFUL, RAFIQ!" exclaimed Shameem. "That's a lot of money for your first job. We'll have to ask Anil to work out what your take-home pay will be. I presume you will be able to claim me as your dependent for tax purposes while I'm a student?"

"I think that after taxes and our religious contributions, I will be left with around £115 per month. That would be a good amount to save."

"THAT'S GREAT, RAFIQ. CONGRATULATIONS. Your dad and mom will be so happy to hear that. Your take-home will be about £130," Anil said when Rafiq told him and Sophia what his starting salary would be.

SHAMEEM WAS ON CHRISTMAS vacation as of the 20th. Anil's offices were to close as of the 24th until January 4th. Only Sophia had to work the three days between Christmas and New Year.

"If you're okay, Shama, may I suggest that we take it easy and have a quiet Christmas and New Year? Instead of going out for dinner, movies, and to the theatre, can we catch our breath and just relax between now and the New Year?" Rafiq asked Shameem when they were alone one evening.

"Of course. This exchange control and internalization of the fact that we now have to adopt an austere lifestyle, you withdrawing from the M.B.A. program and then going away for two and a half months have been very taxing for me, too. I've been craving some peace and quiet. We can attend Jamatkhana whenever we can and the Ismaili New Year's celebration, but other than that, let's keep things simple."

WHEN RAFIQ TOLD ANIL their plans for the Christmas vacation, Anil said, "The last three months have been very difficult for me, also. I've been burning up with anger over my parents' foolishness in sitting on all of that cash instead of sending it over to me, and I'm now worried about what I'll do with them if they have to leave Tanzania. With £7,500, I could have set them up in a small business and put a down payment on a house here."

"Look, Anil, the imposition of exchange control does not have anything to do with our families being able to stay on in Tanzania. I don't know why you're so worried and keep saying that they won't be able to stay there. When I talk to my dad, he is cheerful as ever. He doesn't see anything on the horizon to make him worry."

"Maybe not, but I'm just not that optimistic. I like your idea of relaxing during the break, though. On the days Sophia is working the evening shifts, I can come to Jamatkhana with you if you're going. And yes, of course, we'll go to the New Year's Eve Ismaili Centre event. I want Sophia to meet and get to know other Ismailis. But we *will* go out for dinner on Shama's birthday to celebrate both your birthdays and the amazing job you have landed. Sophia has been waiting for the right occasion to treat you for your kindness to her. She is off on Christmas Eve and is very much looking forward to it."

1966
Fifty-Nine

In early January, Anil and Sophia started to look for an apartment to rent. Pickings were slim in the area where they wanted to rent, near Shameem and Rafiq. For a charge, they got eight listings from one rental agency. Two had telephone numbers. Anil called and was told, "Sorry, it's gone." They went to the addresses given, and at four of these, they were told, "Oh, it's just gone." They were invited to look at the remaining two. They were not the kind of places in which they wanted to live.

They went back to the rental agency and were told that no new listings had come out and that they should check in a week's time. When Anil did, he saw that five of the six listings he was given earlier were still there.

"They told me these four were rented out," Anil said, pointing to the listings and asked, "How come they're still here?"

"I don't know, Sir. They tell us the flats are still available for rent," replied the lady behind the desk.

"LET'S TALK TO ALAN Meadows," Rafiq suggested when Anil talked to him about this.

When Anil spoke to Meadows, he said, "Those people who told you at the door 'it's gone' don't want to rent to non-whites. You'll find that seven out of ten with good properties to rent will tell you that. If you're calling them, they'll recognize your accent and say, 'it's gone,' and if you turn up at their doors, they'll look at you and say the same thing. To find a nice place, you'll have to check 20 to 30 listings and probably pay much more than what a white family would pay."

In the five years that Anil had been in London, he had not encountered this kind of overt discrimination. There was no option but to continue looking.

AS RAFIQ AND SHAMEEM talked about this, Shameem asked, "Why can't Anil and Sophia just stay here? If they leave, we'll have three bedrooms sitting empty and will have to clean all three. Sophia is a delight for me to have here. We're friends. I love to sit and chat with her. She's a huge help around the house. She and Anil help us dust and vacuum, she does all of the grocery shopping, and Anil always does the dishes and cleans up after dinner. They're both so considerate. They pay us good money, and they're family. Why do they have to go?"

"They don't, Shama. I would welcome them to stay here forever, but I'm sure that they want a place they can call their own, where they can invite their friends for dinner if they want to and have their own life."

"They can do that here. Sophia and Anil are great moral support for us. If they move, they'll have to spend much more than what they're paying us here and will be in a place that's not as nice as this house. And I can tell you, neither Anil's nor your parents will be happy if they move. They'll think that there were problems between us. I don't want them to go unless they want to go."

"You want to talk to them?"

"Yes, we should talk to them together."

THAT EVENING, AFTER DINNER, Rafiq said, "Anil, we had never expected that you and Sophia would encounter this kind of racism looking for a place to rent. Shama and I have been thinking about this. Why do you want to move? We have the room here, and we're happy to have you stay on."

"There's nothing we would like to do more than stay here, and it is very kind of you to invite us to stay, but you need your privacy. You have to live your own life. We can't be a burden on you all your life," Anil replied.

"Privacy? You give us more privacy than we need. After dinner, Sophia goes off to your room, and after we say D'ua, you also go to your room to watch TV there. Honestly, I would like you both to sit and watch TV with us!" said Shameem.

"But you can't have us in your hair all the time, Shama. You need your own space," said Sophia.

"We have all the space and time to do whatever we want to say and do with you living here. Honestly, we would love for you to stay," Shameem replied.

"Really, Shama, we can stay on here? You really mean that? We would be so grateful if we can. Life here with you has been heavenly!" Sophia said, holding Shameem's hand.

"Of course!" Rafiq and Shameem said in unison.

"There's nothing more we would like than for you two to be with us," Shameem said, taking a teary-eyed Sophia in her embrace. She could see that Anil's eyes were moist, also.

1966
Sixty

Rhodesia was a British territory in southern Africa that had governed itself since 1923. In November 1965, the Rhodesian government, mostly comprised of members of the country's white minority, adopted a Unilateral Declaration of Independence (UDI), announcing that it now regarded itself as an independent sovereign state.

The U.K., the Commonwealth, and the United Nations declared Rhodesia's UDI illegal, and economic sanctions were imposed on the breakaway colony. Oil, a prime commodity required for the colony to function, was not included in the sanctions list. The British said that they did not wish to impose "punitive" sanctions on Rhodesia.

The African states demanded that oil be added to the sanctions list and that the British should use force against Prime Minister Ian Smith's breakaway colony. They argued that Britain would not have hesitated to use force against one of its colonies if such a UDI had been declared by a government comprised of black Africans.

At first, Britain declined to include oil on the sanctions list, but as pressure grew for it to use force, it agreed to do so. Rhodesia's oil supply from all Commonwealth nations and UN members was cut off. This would have quickly brought the breakaway regime to its knees, but Rhodesia found its supply of oil from South Africa.

The independent landlocked African country of Zambia, bordering Rhodesia, had received its oil supply via Rhodesia. Being starved for oil, Rhodesia cut off oil supply to Zambia. Zambia's main export of copper, which had also flowed via Rhodesia, came to a halt.

To supply Zambia with oil, the Tanzanian and Zambian governments mounted an oil lift with some 250 FIAT tanker trailers running from the Dar es Salaam port to Lusaka, in Zambia. The governments also invited private transporters to apply for licenses to transport oil to Zambia and bring back copper. Twenty-tonne tanker trailers were the preferred vehicles for oil transport, but owners of smaller tankers could also apply for licenses. All vehicles had to be equipped to carry copper back from Zambia. For a 20-tonne tanker trailer, the governments offered to pay Shs.15,000 per round trip. It was estimated that after operating expenses and debt service, one tanker trailer could generate over Shs.30,000 cash surplus per month. That was a huge sum of money.

In mid-March, Rafiq received a letter from his dad which read:

My dear Rafiq,

This letter is for both Anil and you and from Fateh uncle and me.

We have some bad news and what could be some good news. You and Anil will have to tell us if it's good news and guide us on this.

First, the bad news. Effective March 31st, the government has canceled Almin's Mpwapwa contract. It's setting up a depot to supply Mpwapwa and some other towns around Dodoma. This will result in a Shs.5,000 reduction in Almin's bottom line every month. That's a big blow for us.

Now, for what could be good news.

As you are aware, oil has now been added to Rhodesia's sanctions list. The Zambian and Tanzanian governments have formed a corporation (Zambia-Tanzania Road Services) with some 250 tanker trailers to move oil to Zambia. It appears the governments want to limit their involvement in the oil lift and have invited private transporters to apply for licenses to carry oil to Zambia from Dar es Salaam and bring back Zambia's copper for export.

The government prefers that people applying for licenses buy 20-tonne tanker trailers, although smaller five or ten-tonne tankers are also eligible to apply.

Fateh's uncle's brother, Akbar, in Iringa, has proposed that we buy two FIAT 20-tonne tanker trailers. Each requires a Shs.50,000 down -payment. FIAT Tanzania will carry the balance (around Shs.150,000) at 10% over 30 months. He says that each tanker trailer round trip can generate around Shs.30,000 in cash surplus per month. That's more than three times what Almin produced before the loss of the Mpwapwa contract.

We have looked at Akbar's numbers in detail, and we are comfortable that they are accurate. Fateh uncle has also talked to one Ismaili in Dodoma involved in the oil lift in a big way. He has confirmed Akbar's numbers. Akbar says that he has no money to invest. Iringa has become a significant hub for the oil lift, and he is there. He says that Fateh uncle and I should come up with Shs.100,000 for a down payment for two tanker trailers, and he will manage the vehicles. For this, he wants a monthly salary of Shs.2,500. This is included in his cash flow calculation.

You may ask why the two governments are offering such high transport rates. At the projected income of Shs.60,000 per month, the two tanker trailers could be paid off in seven months. For every month, the vehicles would run after that, would generate Shs.60,000 profit.

The answer is, nobody knows how long the oil lift will last. To make it attractive for the private transporters to take the risk and buy these expensive vehicles, the governments have to pay what they're offering. The tankers have to be paid off before the oil lift ends. If there is a settlement with Ian Smith in three months, we will stand to lose our Shs.100,000 deposit and would be on the hook for another Shs.300,000 in loans.

What we want to know from you is, based on what you see on TV, hear on the radio, and read in British newspapers, do you have any sense of how long the oil lift will last? Is the British government talking about settling this? Please think about this and let us know. This has the potential to be very lucrative... or we could lose our shirts!

Almas aunty and your mom send their love to you both, Sophia, and Shama.

Dad

After reading the letter a couple of times, Anil said, "This thing is not going to end in 10 years. Ian Smith is on TV every day, giving interviews to the British media, saying the British cannot use force against their 'kith and kin'. Public opinion is opposed to the use of force against people who are, mostly, British settlers in Rhodesia. Rhodesia is managing fine with sanctions and can continue forever. Ian Smith will seek accommodation with South Africa and may even try to join South Africa."

"I agree. And if FIAT Tanzania is offering 30-month loans, the Italians obviously know that this is going to last for a while. I think we should tell them to go ahead. With the exchange control, they can't send out the money they're sitting on, and in the current political climate, they don't want to make other large investments for long term returns. This has a short payback period," said Rafiq. Relaying the contents of the letter to Shameem and Sophia, he asked, "What do you think?"

"I've been following Rhodesia. This Ian Smith is a sly fox. He wouldn't have declared UDI if he could not sustain it. I don't think this is going to end anytime soon," Sophia said.

"To be honest, I don't know much about politics. Yes, I see this Ian Smith on TV. He makes my blood boil when I hear him making disparaging remarks about the Africans. How long will this last? I have no idea," said Shameem.

"Before we tell them to rush to FIAT to buy the tanker trailers, we need to get some answers from them so that I can prepare detailed cash forecast. We need to know the round trip mileage, the distance the trucks can travel per day, what the governments are offering to pay per trip, what they will need to pay the drivers, how much fuel the vehicles will consume per trip, the cost per gallon of diesel, where the vehicles will be serviced, and what the service and maintenance will cost per month, per vehicle. Let me respond to your dad. I'll ask him all of this," said Anil.

SALIM CAME BACK WITH responses within a week.

The round trip was 2,330 miles. The trucks would travel 325 miles a day. A round trip would take seven days. With the time required for service and maintenance, the vehicles would make four trips per month. The governments would pay Shs.7.50 per mile. Drivers for tanker trailers required specialized training at FIAT and would earn around Shs.1,500 per month. The trucks would each consume about

Shs.600 worth of diesel per trip. The vehicles would be serviced in Dar es Salaam by the FIAT dealership and in Iringa at Abdulla Motors, an automotive dealership, which had six service bays in its auto garage and equipment and mechanics to do the maintenance and repair work. The cost of four maintenance and service charges would be around Shs.2,000 per truck per month.

"We have some transporters as our clients, so I know a fair bit about this business. Akbar uncle is not taking into account the breakdowns and accidents. We could have a truck break down in Zambia. Who's going to fix it there? We could have one tanker trailer overturn. It may be days before it's running again if it's not damaged beyond repair. These and other things have to be factored into the calculation of profits and cash flow. We can't expect the trucks to average four trips per month. We have to count three. We have to budget for downtime. With all this information your dad has provided, let me work out a detailed cash flow projection," said Anil.

"I'll ask my dad how they will deal with breakdowns and major accidents," Rafiq said.

SALIM CAME BACK TO say that Akbar had advised him that Abdulla Motors expected that with the horrible road conditions and narrow two-lane roads, there would likely be many breakdowns and accidents. They had acquired two high powered tow trucks that would be able to straighten a loaded overturned tanker trailer. They also had trucks that could be loaded with parts and mechanics to travel up or down from Iringa to go and fix broken down vehicles or tow them to Iringa for repairs if the trucks are between Dar es Salaam and Mbeya. The FIAT dealership in Zambia would look after the vehicles' repairs and maintenance south of Mbeya.

Anil reworked the numbers with this updated information and produced a three-year forecast of income, expenses, and cash flow. Net of loan principal, interest payments, and management salary, he projected a Shs.50,000 surplus per month compared to the Shs.60,000 Akbar had projected for two tanker trailers. They could potentially recover their down payment in two months and their entire investment in eight months. There was no possibility whatsoever that the oil lift was ending in eight months.

"Let them proceed, Rafiq."

"Let's do that, but I'm worried that your parents have no money here. You're telling me they have 150,000 Shillings saved up there. If they put in 50,000 Shillings in this, that's one-third of their savings, and then there are the loan obligations. This is very serious. Could you consider flying out to Dar es Salaam for a week, ask Akber uncle to come there and make sure we are minimizing the risk. I can ask my dad to send you a BOAC or EAA plane ticket if you can go."

"I think that's a good idea. This is a 100,000 Shillings investment and another 300,000 Shillings in commitment. Let me check at the office tomorrow. There's not much on my desk at this time. I should be able to go. I should go. The trip cost of 2,000 Shillings will be just 0.5% of the total investment."

TWO DAYS LATER, ANIL was on his way to Tanzania. He returned a week later and said he had met his dad in Dar es Salaam; they had incorporated a new company which their parents wanted to be named ShamaSophia Transport Ltd. and placed the order for two tanker trailers with a Shs.100,000 deposit. He had negotiated the loan rate down to 8%, with no personal guarantees.

"That's amazing, Anil. This means that if the oil lift ends in two months and ShamaSophia defaults on payments, FIAT can seize the vehicles they hold as security against the loans, and we would have no further obligation. It's good that you went and worked all this out. Just the 2% reduction in interest rate will save us about 5,000 Shillings in the first year."

"Neither FIAT Tanzania nor anyone else is talking about the oil lift ending in one year. That said, do you realize that our parents have laid out Shs.100,000 solely on our recommendation?" Anil asked.

"I think we've come of age, brother."

By mid-April, the ShamaSophia wagons were rolling, and the money started to pour in.

"ShamaSophia is netting Shs.2,000 a day! It seems too good to be true. This is more than I made in a month working for Ralph Kirkwood," Fateh wrote to Anil.

Soon after the imposition of exchange control, a black market in foreign currencies had developed in Tanzania. £1 could be purchased for Shs.25 compared to the official exchange rate of Shs.20, and the US$ cost Shs.10 compared to the official Shs.7 rate. The premium was not prohibitive, but there were significant risks in parting with hard-earned Shillings because the black market "Currency Traders" did not issue any receipts, nor was there any guarantee that they would deposit the foreign exchange in the overseas accounts of their "clients." They simply collected wads of Shs.100 bills, took the foreign account information – or they said they would open accounts for their clients in London or Geneva – and promised that the money would be deposited into the accounts in four to eight weeks.

Several fly-by-night Currency Traders had emerged, and some played the usual games to gain people's trust. "Sorry, I can't take more than Shs.25,000 from you because even I have to work through third parties, and if anything goes wrong, I would be morally obliged to pay it back to you," they would say.

People desperately wanting to send money out would beg them to take more from them and less from others. This way, the Traders gained confidence and collected hundreds of thousands of Shillings. Many disappeared without a trace.

Salim and Fateh agreed that they were not going to take such risks. They did not want to get involved in illegal money transfers, either. Exchange control, they believed, was a mistake. The economy was booming. All three key economic sectors - agriculture, industry, and tourism - were growing rapidly. Tanzania was receiving more foreign aid than it could generate projects to use the money for. The Central Bank was flushed with foreign exchange. This must have been a kneejerk reaction to something that someone may have observed, suspected, or feared (such as money going out of the country), which would soon be reversed. The developing countries had learned that the imposition of exchange controls always led to a tripling or quadrupling of the amount of money fleeing a country.

BY THE END OF 1966, Zambia and Tanzania had concluded that Britain was not going to do anything to end the Rhodesian rebellion. They decided that the oil lift was too expensive. It was also dangerous. There were too many accidents on what had come to be known as The Hell Run. They decided to build a pipeline from

Dar es Salaam to Ndola in Zambia. The oil lift would continue until the pipeline was built. They also decided to build a railway line from Dar es Salaam to the town of Kapiri Mposhi in Zambia. China financed and built the railway line, which was completed in 1975.

In December 1966, Fateh wrote to Anil:

The oil lift has had a massive impact on several Ismaili families in Dodoma, Iringa, and Mbeya. Small Ismaili transporters with one five-tonne truck who were eking out a living borrowed Shs.5,000 from The Diamond Trust and equipped their trucks with oil tanks. They have managed to get the oil lift licenses and are running up and down the Tanzania-Zambia route. Suddenly, they have become rich and are rivaling the richest Ismailis in these towns in their earnings. It's heartening to see Ismailis prosper.

There is also a secondary impact. Auto garages in these towns, many owned by Ismailis, are working overtime and can charge what they want. Ismaili mechanics have seen their incomes quadruple. The transporters have hit a bonanza and can afford to pay whatever is necessary to keep their trucks rolling. The auto parts businesses are doing more business in a week than they did in a month and have increased their margins. This is a life-changing event for people involved directly or indirectly in the oil lift.

All they worry about is that the oil lift may end before the pipeline is completed and their dreams of earning and saving enough to fund their children's higher education and owning a flat and a car may be dashed. We are telling them not to worry. The oil lift will run for at least a year. We know this because our sons in England say so. We are also advising them not to waste money. Some people are squandering money on expensive cars and other frivolities.

You will be happy to know that three months back, Salim uncle and Yasmin aunty, mom, and I decided to loan five Ismaili families Shs.5,000 each, interest-free, to equip their trucks with oil tanks. We decided that even if something happens and none of this money comes back, it will be our one month's income from one tanker trailer. We could afford to lose it, but all of the money was paid back to us in two months. We would loan it out again and again, but the governments are not issuing any new licenses. There is enough capacity now within the licensed transporters to carry all the oil and copper to and from Zambia.

1967
Sixty-One

On February 5th, 1967, President Julius Nyerere announced the *Arusha Declaration*, which set out the principles of Ujamaa (African Socialism) for Tanzania. The Declaration, which was in five parts, was a watershed event for Tanzania, which would define the course of its history for the next 25 years and more.

Part I defined the principles of socialism (equality of all human beings, right to dignity and respect, freedom of expression, religious belief and association, protection of life and property, etc.).

The principles further stated, among other things, that the state must have effective control over the principal means of production and intervene actively in the economic life of the nation to ensure the well-being of all citizens, prevent the exploitation of one person by another or one group by another, and prevent the accumulation of wealth to an extent which was inconsistent with the existence of a classless society.

Part II laid out the policy of socialism. In a socialist state, all people were workers. It did not have a lower class composed of people who worked for their living, and an upper class of people who lived on the work of others. The ruling party should be a party of peasants and workers. The government was chosen and led by the peasants and workers.

The successful implementation of socialist objectives depended upon the leaders. Socialism was a belief in a particular system of living, and the leaders could not promote its growth if they did not accept it.

Part III set out the policy of self-reliance. It had been a mistake to rely on money, the primary source for which was taxes when the country was poor, and to believe that the country could rid itself of its poverty through foreign aid, which came in the form of gifts and loans, and private investments. Independence could not be real if a nation was dependent on foreign grants and loans for its development. Tanzania could attract foreign investment, but that would leave the country's economy in the hands of foreigners who would take the profits back to their countries.

The country had also made the mistake in thinking that its development was dependent on industrialization. Tanzania did not have the money or technical know-how to industrialize.

The country's focus on money for development and industrialization had led to concentration on urban development. Most aid money was being spent in urban areas to build schools, hospitals, etc. To repay the loans, the government had to use foreign currency obtained from the sale of its exports. The country did not export its industrial products. The foreign currency to pay back the loans had to come from the villages and agriculture, which meant that the people who benefitted directly from development were not the ones who would repay the loans.

The country had more than 10 million people and was more than 362,000 square miles in area, a significant part of which was fertile land, which received sufficient rain. The country could produce various crops for home consumption and export.

Hard Work was the first requirement for development. The energies of the millions of men in the villages and thousands of women in the towns (if both would work as hard as the women did in the villages) were a great treasure which could contribute more towards Tanzania's development than anything the country could get from wealthy nations.

The country's emphasis should be on land and agriculture, its people, the policy of socialism and self-reliance, and good leadership. The Government had to ensure that land was being used for the benefit of the whole nation and not for one individual or just a few people.

The governing Party, TANU, recognized the urgency and importance of good leadership but had not yet produced systematic training for the country's leaders from the national level to the ten-house cell level - so that every one of them would understand TANU's political and economic policies. The leaders must set a good example for the rest of the people in their lives and all of their activities.

Part IV redefined the TANU Membership. It said there must be more emphasis on the beliefs of the Party and its policies of socialism. Anyone who did not subscribe to these beliefs or did not accept the faith, objects, and rules and regulations of the Party, should not be accepted as a member.

Part V of the Declaration spelled out the Arusha Resolution. It said TANU's National Executive Committee had resolved that every TANU and Government leader must be either a peasant or a worker, and should in no way be associated with the practices of capitalism or feudalism. No TANU or Government leader should:

- hold shares in any company;
- hold directorships in any privately-owned enterprise;
- receive two or more salaries, and/or
- own houses which he rents to others.

For this Resolution, the term "leader" would refer to members of the TANU National Executive Committee, Ministers, Members of Parliament, senior officials of organizations affiliated to TANU, senior officers of parastatal organizations, all those appointed or elected under any clause of the TANU Constitution, councillors, and civil servants in the high and middle cadres. In this context, "leader" meant: a man, or a man and his wife, a woman, or a woman and her husband.

SHORTLY FOLLOWING THE ANNOUNCEMENT of the Arusha Declaration, the government nationalized major commercial banks, insurance companies, and a host of manufacturing, mining, and other large merchandising businesses.

In his address to the nation, talking about the exploitation of one person by another or one group by another, the president shocked Tanzanians of non-African descent by castigating everyone who was not a worker or a peasant - mainly the traders, who were neither peasants nor workers – as *Mrijas* (bloodsucking straws) and *Wabenzis* (owners of Mercedes Benz cars), as the most evil of the exploiters.

Rafiq and Anil studied the Declaration summary as it had appeared in the media.

"This reads like pages from René Dumont's *False Start in Africa*," said Anil.

"Yes. The emphasis on agriculture reflects Dumont's philosophy. I applaud the president for defining the principles of socialism and stating that the government should prevent exploitation, but to say that anyone who is not a worker or a peasant is an exploiter is simply not true," said Rafiq.

"Exactly! What this says is that every trader, including the small *dukawallah*, most of whom barely make ends meet from their small shops, are exploiters. It's also a mistake for the state to take control of major industries in the country. The nationalized Bata Shoes cannot now benefit from the research and development that Bata carries out internationally to reduce costs and improve its products. There is enough evidence to show that state-run businesses are not as efficient as private enterprises. Look at what's happened to the industries nationalized by the Labour government here in the U.K.," lamented Anil.

"The Declaration singles out industries and agriculture as the only engines for development. For Tanzania, this is not true. Yes, agriculture generates foreign currency, but tourism is another sector that generates foreign exchange, and Tanzania is blessed in this sector like no other African country is. In addition to the Serengeti, Manyara, and Ngorongoro, we have Mikumi, Selous, Ruaha, and other game parks and reserves, teeming with wildlife that are not yet developed for tourism. We have miles of gorgeous beaches we could develop for tourism. Unlike the industries in Tanzania which produce goods for import substitution and not for export, investment in tourism can generate foreign exchange, as most tourists to East Africa are Western European and North American," Rafiq added.

"I'm alarmed by the policy that a socialist state is a classless state, where all people are workers and peasants. This is the Sino/Soviet model. Do you think Tanzania can really move that way? The Declaration says that hard work is a premier requirement for such development. In Tanzanian villages, as the Declaration says, women do all the work. Men just laze around. For this policy to succeed, a major societal shift will be required. I can't see what will bring that about," Anil said.

"I can't see such a paradigm shift taking place, either. People will have to be forced to do this, and even the Pharaohs learned thousands of years ago that forced labor is not productive. To me, it looks like the Declaration is aimed as much at the 'privileged' minority – us, the *Wahindis* – as it is aimed at individuals within the government itself that may have capitalistic tendencies and entrepreneurial aspirations. Seems like, *these growing feathers clipped from Caesar's wings will make him fly an ordinary pitch*," said Rafiq.

"In a society where everyone is either a peasant or a worker, there cannot be any self-employed people. This means there cannot be any business owners - large or small. Our parents have no future in Tanzania. I wonder what the government will do next," Anil said sadly.

A week later, Rafiq received a letter from his father which, in part, read:

You have to admire the Declaration's objectives aimed at improving the lives of the indigenous Tanzanians. The Declaration, however, states that the government would facilitate the way to collective ownership of all resources of the country. This sounds like the first step towards communism.

There is talk of the government wanting to establish Ujamaa villages where small African farms will be collectivized and run by Owners' Associations. We are hearing that there is resistance to this idea from small African farmers.

The most unsettling thing for us has been the branding of anyone who runs a shop - anyone who buys goods and sells them for a profit or runs a service business like an auto garage that employs a mechanic, no matter how small - as an exploiter, or a bloodsucker. As you know, over 80% of all retail and service businesses are run by Indians. In one stroke, we have all been branded as exploiters and bloodsuckers, simply because we run commercial operations.

Some people are drawing comfort from the government announcement that no further nationalization is planned, and the TANU Creed incorporated in the Declaration, which says, "...every individual has a right to receive from society, protection of his life and property, according to the law." People see this as an affirmation that our property rights will not be violated - our businesses and assets will not be taken away.

Rafiq, I now realize that it was a big mistake to buy the Mercedes. Mom and I are now "Wabenzis," the worst of those who have accumulated wealth by sucking the poor Africans' blood. We are looking to getting rid of it.

I will write more when the dust settles.

"You were right, Anil. You always said that we have no future in Tanzania. The people and government will turn on us. They just did."

"No, they haven't. Not yet. This is only the groundwork. While saying that every individual has the right to protection of his life and property, the government has nationalized all of these businesses and created hatred towards the Indians. What's there to stop it from nationalizing all Indian-owned businesses and properties?"

"Is it time to pull our families out?"

"No. We have to first tell them to take some risks and get whatever cash they are sitting on out of the country."

"I have agonized over this, Anil. Sending money out of the country is now illegal. Would this be ethical to do?"

"Rafiq, if we take money out of the country, whose money is it? Our parents have taken financial risks and worked hard to earn it - both in colonial and post-colonial times. It's not been given to them under some socialistic redistribution of wealth. This is their hard-earned money. They're not stealing it from anyone. And we have to ask ourselves why we want to take our money out. Our parents would have been happy to stay on and invest in the country's development. It's because the government has turned on us and put our lives in danger by branding us as evil *mrija* targets that we want to leave and take with us what is rightfully ours."

In the days that followed, Fateh told Anil that he and Salim each had Shs.200,000 in cash. They each needed Shs.100,000 for working capital in their

457

businesses but could send out the balance. There was one "Currency Trader" who was taking money from people and promptly depositing British £s in their accounts in London, at the agreed rate. For a Shs.200,000 transaction, he would offer them £1 for Shs.25 (instead of the official Shs.20 rate).

"Do it, Dad, but send 100,000 Shillings between the two," Anil said to his father.

"We may not get the preferential rate he's offering if we send 100,000 Shillings between the two of us."

"Okay, send 100,000 Shillings each."

AFTER SOME ANXIOUS WEEKS, transfers of £4,000 came into each of Anil and Rafiq's accounts.

THE TRADER WAS EXPECTING to return to Tanzania and receive at least Shs.200,000 from each of Fateh and Salim for a second transfer, but neither had that kind of money to transfer. They could manage with Shs.75,000 for working capital and could spare only Shs.25,000 each.

In mid-1967, having built a sound reputation as a reliable Trader, he collected over Shs.2,000,000 from over 50 people and disappeared with the money, never to be seen again. Salim and Fateh were lucky. They each lost only Shs.25,000.

Rafiq and Anil asked their parents that they not send any more money with or through anyone. Rafiq wanted to find out what happened with all of the Tanzanian Shillings the Traders collected from people and brought to Europe. He searched to see whether Tanzanian currency was trading on any international currency markets. After searching through his direct bank sources and indirect sources, he found that often large quantities of Tanzanian Shillings traded in money markets in Zurich and Geneva. He searched and found the sellers and the buyers. The buyers were people, corporations, and countries buying Tanzanian goods or investing in Tanzania, who could pick up Tanzanian Shillings here for less than the official rate.

"We don't need to use the Traders. If our dads can put together large enough sums of money, say Shs.500,000 between them, we can bring the money in ourselves and sell it in the money market," he told Anil.

1967
Sixty-Two

In May, Rafiq read a newspaper article on the 1967 International and Universal Exposition, commonly known as Expo '67, which had opened in Montreal, Quebec, in April. This was a Category One World's Fair scheduled to run until the end of October. Sixty two nations were participating. It had set a single-day attendance record for a world's fair, with some 570,000 visitors.

Expo '67 was Canada's foremost celebration of its centennial year. The organizers had created 17 theme elements, which included Habitat '67, a housing complex built for the Expo, Man and his Health, Man in the Community, Man the Explorer, Man the Creator, Man the Producer, and Man the Provider.

The Expo featured art galleries, opera, ballet, and theatre companies, orchestras, jazz groups, famous Canadian pop musicians, and other cultural attractions. Many pavilions had music and performance stages where visitors could find free concerts and shows. Among others, Diana Ross and the Supremes, The Seekers, and Petula Clark were expected to perform during its run.

The Queen of England, President Lyndon Johnson, Princess Grace of Monaco, Jacqueline Kennedy, and Robert Kennedy were all expected to visit the Expo.

When Rafiq got home, he shared the article with Shameem and said, "Wouldn't it be great to go to the Expo? I would love to go!"

"Me, too, but it would be expensive. Just the flight to Montreal and back would be £250 for the two of us."

"If we go all the way to Montreal, I would certainly want to take you to New

York. Also, if we go to Canada, I would want to see more of it. Carole couldn't stop talking about how beautiful Vancouver is; the scenic drive from Vancouver to Jasper and Banff National Parks and via the Okanagan Valley, about how breathtaking the Jasper, Lake Louise, and Banff National Parks are. We would certainly want to see all that. We would also want to go to Toronto to visit Carole and her family and go to see Niagara Falls."

"Are you joking? Do you know how much all of that would cost? We have around £700 in our account. We can't touch the money in the savings account. Forget about the Expo."

"I guess you're right," sighed Rafiq, but he couldn't stop thinking about it.

He connected with Carole and got some information on the room rates at 3 – 4 Star hotels, midsize car rental costs, gas prices, food costs, and other expenses and started to work out different scenarios for the trip. He finally arrived at a 17-day itinerary that would take them from London to New York, Vancouver, Jasper, Banff, Lake Louise, Calgary, Toronto, Niagara Falls, Ottawa, Montreal, and back to London.

Airfare, accommodations, car rentals, gas, and other incidentals worked out to £800 for Shameem and him. This was equivalent to his six months of net pay. There was no cheaper way of doing this. He was deeply disappointed. Flying to Montreal to just see the Expo was not something he was interested in.

When Rafiq talked to his parents, as he did once a month, he told his dad about Expo '67 and how much he would have liked to go.

"Take the money out of the savings account, Rafiq. You know how much I value learning from travel. Go, see the world and educate yourselves," said Salim.

"No, Dad, the savings account is sacrosanct and not to be touched. You never know when we'll need it."

"I have no reason to believe we'll ever need it. After the Arusha Declaration and the nationalization that followed, things have quietened down. Everything is back to normal. The oil lift is on and there are more Mercedes Benz cars on the road than ever before, and many are being driven by the Africans. The £800 you are talking about for your trip, we make in 10 days just from the oil lift."

"Yes, Dad, but you can't send the oil lift money or any Tanzanian Shillings to me, and you need to read the Arusha Declaration. There will be only two kinds of people in Tanzania, peasants and workers. There's no place for you there. You will have to leave Tanzania, sooner or later."

"Well, other than continuing to call us mrijas, the government isn't doing anything to create a classless society. Things have never been better for us. Here in Mpwapwa, we have close relationships with the Africans and African leaders. Mr. Nkwabi, the D.C., came and apologized to me for how we had been branded. He was truly sorry and felt that it was very unfair what we had been called."

"Don't be fooled, Dad. The writing's on the wall. Our days in Tanzania are numbered. I'm not going to use a penny out of the savings account."

"How much of your travel budget will be airfare?"

"£500."

"Well, we can send you the tickets from here. We sent the ticket for Anil to come to Dar es Salaam, remember?"

"Can you do that? I thought you could send airline tickets for travel only between Tanzania and wherever."

"Let me check. I am sure we will be able to do that."

TWO DAYS LATER, SALIM called to say that he had talked to the travel agent and, yes, he could send them prepaid airline tickets. He should send the itinerary and the flights they wanted to take.

"SHAMA, WE'RE GOING TO the Expo! Dad says that they can send us the airline tickets. That means we need to spend only £300 from our resources!" he said excitedly, as soon as he hung up. "Anil and Sophia can come if Fateh uncle sends them airline tickets, as well. Let's talk to them."

Shameem was not happy about even spending £300 out of their £700 savings, but seeing how excited Rafiq was about going, she said, "That would be great, Rafiq. When would we go?"

"August will work for us. Carole said that they were planning to go to Montreal in August and may accompany us if the timing works out for them. That would be so great!" Rafiq could hardly contain his excitement.

461

Rafiq had talked to Anil and Sophia about Expo '67, but given the high cost, they had not entertained the idea. Anil's eyes lit up when Rafiq told him that their dads could pay for their airfare. Sophia was also delighted.

"You know, what, Anil, if your dad is paying for the airfare, I will get my dad to pay for the balance of our cost," Sophia said, and in short order, obtained her father's confirmation that he would transfer £400 (not £300 she had requested) into her account.

Now the foursome sat down, day after day, discussing the timing, budget, and itinerary for their North American tour. Accommodation in Montreal was at a premium and limited. Their vacation schedules had to be coordinated. They noted that the budget Rafiq had prepared was liberal but fairly accurate.

In consultation with Carole, they agreed to depart London on Saturday, August 12th, to arrive in New York the same day and spend three nights there. They would then fly to Vancouver and spend three nights there, where they would rent a car and drive to Jasper, Lake Louise, and Banff via the Okanagan Valley. They would spend one night in each of the three parks. They would then make their way to Calgary, drop the car off at the airport and fly to Toronto. They would pick up another rental in Toronto and spend three days there (one day with Carole's family, one-day sightseeing, and one day trip to Niagara Falls). They would then drive to Ottawa, where they would spend one night, travel to Montreal for three nights, and then return home.

Reports on Expo '67 continued to appear on TV and in the print media. It was receiving rave reviews.

By the end of July, Rafiq and Anil had received the airline tickets with confirmed travel dates and options to make changes as they desired.

They boarded the BOAC flight at 10.00 a.m., arrived in New York at 2.00 p.m., and were settled in their hotel rooms by 4.00 p.m. All were tired, but Rafiq insisted that they optimize their time in New York to see as much as possible. He took them to Times Square, where they had dinner and spent the evening walking around the Square and Broadway, where they purchased tickets for the next day's showing of *My Fair Lady*.

They took the City tour for the next two days and visited the Statue of Liberty, Greenwich Village, Central Park, Fifth and Park Avenues, and other attractions. Anil, Sophia, and Shameem found New York fascinating; everything was as Rafiq had described.

After two and a half fascinating days in New York, they boarded the flight for Vancouver and arrived there at 12.30 p.m. local time. They had flown over the Rockies on their way in, and now they could see the Pacific spread out in front of them.

They picked up the rental car and equipped with B.C. and Vancouver maps, they started to drive into the city center.

"My God, what a change this place is from New York! The city is calm, almost serene. There are no throngs of people dashing around here. Look at the mountains and the ocean and the beauty of this place. Heaven can't be much better," Sophia sighed.

"True, and we have just three days to soak up this heaven, so let's check-in, grab a quick lunch and head for our first stop, which is Stanley Park. We can walk to the Park from our hotel," said Rafiq.

THEY HAD NEVER SEEN a park as large and beautiful as The Stanley. They spent the entire afternoon and evening in the Park, exploring its every element. Even as it grew dark, they did not want to leave. Finally, they headed towards the English Bay area for dinner and then walked back to the hotel.

Over the next two days, they saw more of Vancouver. When they drove up to the British Properties and looked down on the city and the Pacific Ocean, Sophia said, "God is my witness, I'm going get my father to cough up the money for me to buy a house here. This is where I want to bring up my children."

"Take it easy, Miss Scarlett. We have to get married first and have some children, and what makes you think we'll come to live in Vancouver? I've always thought of New York as the place where I would like to settle," Anil said.

"Sorry, sweetheart, but this is heaven. Why would we not live in heaven?" Sophia asked.

"Well, let's enjoy it while we're here and not get carried away with making a home and raising children," interjected Shameem. "But Rafiq, this is heaven. I, too, would like to live here. Wouldn't you?"

"Of course, I would, but these houses must cost upwards of $200,000. We don't have that kind of money, and I don't know if the Canadians would let us in their country. I understand they are partial to the whites, and if they do, I don't know if we could get jobs here."

"As a doctor, Shama can get a job anywhere and me too, as a nurse. And what advanced industrialized country does not need C.A.s and investment bankers, especially an LSE graduate?" Sophia asked.

"I don't think many Canadians have heard of the LSE, and if they have, I don't think they would care much for it. For us to make careers in North America, both Anil and I would need MBAs. That's what Carole said."

EVERYWHERE THEY WENT – Robson Street, Lions' Gate Bridge, Grouse Mountain, Suspension Bridge, Ambleside, West Vancouver – every step they took, convinced Sophia more and more that she wanted to live here.

In whatever spare time they had, they all wanted to go back to Stanley Park and enjoy its beauty.

FINALLY, IT WAS TIME to leave Vancouver. Sophia and Shameem had left their hearts in this city. The men were equally enchanted with the place but had more practical considerations in their minds.

They departed early, and after a two-hour drive east on the Trans-Canada highway, they entered the Okanagan Valley. The beauty of Lake Okanagan was breathtaking. At whichever lookout point they stopped, it was difficult for Rafiq, who was mindful of the time and distances they had to cover, to get everyone back into the car.

"This is paradise, Rafiq. Can't we stay here a little longer? Who knows if we'll ever come here again?" Shameem pleaded as Rafiq shepherded them back into the car.

"Jasper, Lake Louise, and Banff lie ahead. There's even more beauty there for us to take in. We've got to move, honey. We have to go, please."

"You should have planned more time here!" Shameem protested.

"We didn't have more vacation, Shama. Inshallah, one day, we'll come back here and spend all of our three weeks' vacation in B.C."

THEY STOPPED IN KELOWNA for lunch and then drove north to Vernon. Past Vernon, the drive was scenic, but not spectacular, until they reached Mount Robson, beyond which the Rocky Mountains appeared before them in all their majesty. The journey to Jasper, with its many lookout points, was as breathtaking as the drive through the Okanagan Valley.

"I have a surprise for you, guys. Our budget allowed us to indulge for one night. Since we're in Jasper for one night only, I've booked us at Jasper Park Lodge. This is a luxury hotel situated in Jasper National Park, which wraps around the shores of Lac Beauvert. King George VI and the Queen stayed here. It's surrounded by nature and abundant wildlife," Rafiq announced as they approached Jasper after a 500-mile journey from Vancouver.

"How much will this cost?" Shameem gasped.

"Three times what we paid in Vancouver."

"That's expensive, but what the hell, it's a once in a lifetime opportunity," said Anil.

"Hey, guys, I'll pay the difference from the extra £100 my old man sent me. Jasper will be my treat," Sophia announced.

It was still daylight when they arrived. Jasper Park Lodge, like much of this trip, was unlike anything they had seen before. It was massive. There was wildlife (reindeer, moose, or caribou - they didn't know the difference) right on the property. The Main Lodge was vast and gorgeous. They were given two log cabins overlooking the lake. They agreed to settle in and meet in the restaurant for dinner quickly.

It was when they looked at the menu that Rafiq realized that the extra cost in staying at this paradise would not be limited to the higher room rate. Dinner would cost them at least $20 per person if they made economic choices. 'Thank God, Sophia is paying for this. I have no money to pay for these dinners. I will settle for burger and fries,' he thought.

Sophia looked at the menu and said, "Guys, let this be a celebration of our friendship and our love for one another. Please order whatever you want, and we'll also order the best desserts. I will write to my dad to tell him what we did with the extra money he sent. He will be delighted."

"Can we chip in the amount I had budgeted for the meals here?" Rafiq asked.

"Nope. My dad's treat," Sophia replied.

"THIS SALMON TASTES UNLIKE any I've eaten," said Shameem.

"And the steak! God, I've never eaten steak like this. It's even better than the steaks my dad used to barbeque!" said Rafiq.

They did not know that they were eating the best in the world, Pacific salmon and Alberta beef, cooked in Jasper Park Lodge's kitchen.

"If Vancouver was heaven, this is heaven multiplied by two. We are here only one day, Rafiq?" Sophia asked.

"Yes, we check out tomorrow morning. We all want to swim in that amazing pool overlooking the lake. I suggest we do that at 6.00 a.m. We can then go shower, pack up, and have breakfast and leave here by 8.30 a.m. to take the Jasper tour at 9.00 a.m. The tour finishes at 1.00 p.m. We can have a quick lunch in the town, and leave for Banff at 2.00 p.m. All good?" Rafiq asked.

"Yes, Sir, yes Sir, whatever you say, Sir," Anil said, teasingly.

THE EARLY MORNING MINIBUS tour took them through Jasper's scenic valley, giving them stunning views of the snow-capped mountains and pristine lakes, and the surrounding wilderness. They spotted mountain sheep, elk, deer, bears, wolves, coyotes, moose, and many smaller animals. These were, however, few and far between. Unlike on the Serengeti plains, there were no herds of wildebeests, or zebras here. The beauty of this place was the wildlife in the splendor of the Rockies and the turquoise lakes' setting.

The drive from Jasper to Lake Louise, through the Rockies, was like an extension of the Jasper tour. The road ran through mountains, valleys, and lakes. They encountered vehicles that had stopped to look at bears, mountain goats, and other wildlife by the roadside, and just as they had done on the safari, they joined the game watchers.

They stopped at the Athabasca Falls, some 20 miles south of Jasper Township, known for its force due to the large quantity of water falling into the gorge. They made a detour to visit the Columbia Icefield and take the Glacier tour in an all-terrain vehicle. They walked on the glacier and marveled at the other glaciers perched above, and the spectacular valley spread out below.

Soon after, they arrived in Lake Louise, in Banff National Park, known for its turquoise, glacier-fed lake ringed by high peaks. They rented a canoe and paddled on the pristine lake. They enjoyed lunch at the gorgeous hotel overlooking Lake Louise but stayed the night in more modest accommodations.

Banff was another experience the next day. They visited the gorgeous Banff Springs Hotel, but none cherished aspirations of spending a night here. The hotel they had booked was more of a two-star than the three-star that it had been advertised to be. It was quite a disappointment, but in Banff at this time, this was all that they could get for $25 a night.

They walked down the quaint Banff downtown area and ate their fast-food lunch sitting by the Bowes Falls.

They went horseback riding and took the evening wildlife safari. The next day, they took the Lake Minnewanka cruise with stunning views of the Rockies, and rode the Banff Gondola to the top of Sulphur Mountain, at an elevation of 7,500 feet.

They departed for Calgary the next day, and took the afternoon flight to Toronto, picked up their reserved rental car, and drove to their hotel in downtown Toronto.

As suggested by Carole, they drove to Niagara Falls the next day. It was hot. The 90-minute drive in their rented Chevrolet Impala that did not have air conditioning, was uncomfortable, but their discomfort disappeared as the American Falls, and then the Canadian Horseshoe Falls came into view. They quickly parked the car and joined the hundreds of people viewing the falls. The thunder was exhilarating. The spray rising above the falls cooled their faces. They remained spellbound, gazing at the falls and the rainbows in the spray. They walked up and down the Niagara River, the Clifton Hill area, and ate an early dinner at the Skylon Tower's revolving restaurant, which gave them amazing 360-degree views of the American and Canadian Falls, the Niagara River, and the city of Niagara.

They spent the next day walking around downtown Toronto. There was not much to see in the city center, which was cut off from the lake by an expressway. The main street (Yonge Street) was rather drab, but the city was teeming with people and more energetic than Vancouver.

As they walked downtown, Anil suggested that they go into the head office of one of the five largest commercial banks and see if they could talk to its HR department to find out what their prospects for jobs would be with the bank if they ever came to Canada.

They had expected to either not get anyone to talk to them, or to be received and politely asked to apply when they came to Canada as Permanent Residents. Instead, the woman they met referred them to her supervisor when they told her about their qualifications. The supervisor, in turn, referred them to her two bosses, who took the time to meet with Anil and Rafiq separately. Each spent over half an hour talking to them about their education and experience and, subject to verification of their credentials and references, offered to provide offers of employment to support their applications for migration to Canada. Anil and Rafiq took business cards from the managers with whom they met and said that they would write to them when they decided to come to Canada.

SOPHIA AND SHAMEEM WERE furious with Rafiq and Anil for keeping them waiting for over 45 minutes on the pavement in the hot sun.

"Why didn't you just go in and sit in the bank's reception area?" Anil asked.

"And how were we supposed to know which exit you would come out from in this massive building? You would have come out and started searching for us all over the city!" Sophia replied, still fuming.

"We're very sorry, ladies. We expected to be out in ten minutes, but we got introduced to different divisional HR Managers, and they offered us jobs!"

"What?! Did you accept? Can they give you a job with their Vancouver office?" Sophia asked Anil, her eyes lighting up.

"No, we both got their business cards and told them that we would write to them if and when we decide to come to live in Canada," Rafiq said.

"We are sorry to have kept you waiting in the sun. Let's go into that restaurant and cool off and grab a sandwich." Anil said.

As they sipped on their drinks and ate sandwiches called submarines, which were double the size of sandwiches in the U.K., Rafiq asked Anil, "Why didn't you take the job offer letter?"

"We have to think about this. Sophia and I don't want to make our lives in the U.K., but we have to decide where we want to live - in the U.S.A. if they let us in, or in Canada, if the Canadians let us in, or in Iraq."

"I want to live in Canada in Vancouver. Go back up and get that letter of employment for their Vancouver office!" Sophia said.

"Can't do that, sweetheart. Vancouver has its own requirements. The guy here can't give me an offer for a job in Vancouver - at least I don't think he can."

"Why did you not take up the offer?" Shameem asked Rafiq.

"For the same reason as Anil. We haven't talked about coming to live in Canada. I've always thought that if we move, it would be to the U.S.A. I could get a transfer, but now I think that we should consider Canada because it's so calm and beautiful, and the people here are so nice, and especially because of the reception we just received up there."

"I like Canada. I would like to live here," Shameem said.

"It looks like we're all gravitating towards Canada," Sophia said.

"We're all becoming attracted to Canada, but making your permanent home in another country requires much thought. We must divorce sentiments from reasoning when making such weighty decisions. Let's enjoy Canada while we're here and then go back to the U.K. and think about it. Remember that if we come to live here, we won't be driving through the Okanagan valley and the Rockies, or visiting Niagara Falls every day. It will be going to work and counting down days to the annual vacations during which you can do these things," Rafiq said.

THEY MADE THEIR WAY to the Agincourt address Carole had given them, for dinner with her and her family.

Rafiq was delighted to see Carole again. They hugged each other tightly as Shameem and Carole's husband, Geoff, looked on. As Carole bustled about with dinner preparations, Geoff took the guests into the lounge and offered them drinks.

They opted for juices and made small talk. Soon, the children appeared, dressed for bed. They were adorable and very friendly, but after some brief chatter, Geoff said, "Guys, past your bedtime. Go up to your room and go to sleep. No talking."

The children politely kissed everyone good night and went to bed. The guests marveled at how well behaved these little Canadian children were.

The evening with Carole and Geoff was enjoyable. They told them all about their trip and how much they had enjoyed what they had seen of Canada. Rafiq also told them about their meeting with the bank.

"You should come here and settle in Toronto, Rafiq. This is where the action is. RR Wealth Management will give you a job offer tomorrow, if you want one, I'm sure of it," Carole said.

"We've agreed to think about this when we get home, but when are you guys going to visit us?" Rafiq asked.

"We wanted to talk to you about it. We'd like to visit London, Paris, and Rome in September. We're looking at leaving the children with Geoff's parents. Can we take you up on your offer to stay with you in London?" Carole asked.

"Absolutely!" Rafiq replied.

"We would be delighted to have you," added Shameem. "Please come any time and stay as long as you want. I don't know if Rafiq has told you, but we have an American car you can use to drive around the U.K. if you want to."

"You are very kind," Geoff said.

"Please come and visit, we will be delighted to have you and spend more time with you," Rafiq said.

THEY SPENT THE NEXT day visiting the Ontario Science Centre and Casa Loma, Toronto's version of a Gothic Revival mansion and went to see a play in the evening. With every new sight and experience, the group's affinity towards Canada grew stronger.

THEY DEPARTED FOR MONTREAL early the next morning and arrived there in the early afternoon. After freshening up, they made their way to the Expo. It was everything that they had expected, and more.

Over the three days, they visited pavilion after pavilion and learned about the countries the pavilions represented, tasted varieties of ethnic foods, enjoyed shows and concerts, and soaked up everything the Expo had to offer. They spent their evenings in beautiful Old Montreal.

"This is one hell of a city. It's not just a gorgeous place; it's a place where people seem to be enjoying life. It's different from any place we have seen in the U.S.A. or other parts of Canada. Now, this is where I would like to live!" Shameem said.

"I don't know if you can. They may require you to be bi-lingual to work here." Rafiq said.

THE RED-EYE FLIGHT BACK to London from Montreal was tiring. When they arrived in London the next morning and sat in the cab to go home, each bleary-eyed traveler was lost in memories of the places they had seen and loved and longed to go back.

AS PROMISED, CAROLE AND Geoff visited them in September. They had visited Rome and Paris before coming to London and spent ten days with Rafiq, Shameem, Anil, and Sophia, who took them out every evening to the theatre, trendy restaurants, and sightseeing. Over the two weekends that they were there, they took them to Kew Gardens, Brighton, and Stonehenge.

SOON AFTER THEY HAD returned to the U.K., Sophia's mother had started to insist that Sophia stop living in sin and get married. December would be an ideal time for them to do this, she said. She wanted to develop the wedding program, make hotel bookings for the guests, and draw up the invitation list.

After their North American tour, they were tired. They would also need to arrange for Anil and Rafiq's parents to come to Baghdad, and they, in turn, would need to make arrangements for their businesses to be looked after while they were away and get foreign exchange for their travel. All of this would require more time. Both Anil and Rafiq wanted their parents to visit Europe if they were ever going to travel abroad. They did not want them to go to Iraq.

"Your parents will feel so lost amongst our hundreds of guests, many of whom do not speak English. And I always wanted a quiet wedding by the seaside," Sophia said to Anil.

"This should be the happiest occasion in your life, Sophia. You and Anil should decide when and where you want to get married, and we will work our schedules around whatever you plan," Shameem said.

"We've used up our vacation time. Anil and Rafiq can draw on their 1968 vacation days, and you'll be off for at least two weeks in December, Shama, but all I'll have is just the Christmas and New Year holidays. I could take the three days between Christmas and New Year to make it ten days of vacation, but that's not enough to travel to Iraq, get married, go on a honeymoon, and come back to work. December is just not feasible. It has to be next summer, but we can't go to Iraq in July or August. It's hot as hell. I have to tell my parents the wedding will be here. June would be a good time, after Shama has finished her exams. What do you think, Anil?" Sophia asked.

"I agree. June will give us enough time to plan and accumulate vacation time," Anil said, ever the practical planner.

1968
Sixty-Three

As the New Year rolled in, Shameem started to prepare for her final exams. Sophia got promoted at work but was told that the hospital would not be able to have her work permit extended beyond September. When she told her supervisor about her wedding plans and that Anil would sponsor her, the supervisor suggested that she consider a civil marriage ceremony around March so that Anil could sponsor her for permanent residency status to come through before her work permit expired.

Rafiq's workload increased by the day. Seeing how well he was performing on his projects, Bannerman involved him with higher levels of work. He did not get home until after 7.00 p.m. most nights, but came home excited and could not stop talking about his work.

Anil was now a supervisor with four articling students under him. Rosenberg and Weinstein was continuing to be profitable, but its client base had not grown much in five years. The principals had given a 10% share to Karim, for which he had to pay. This made him the third most senior executive in the firm after the principals, who were happy with their income and status quo. They were both north of 65 and were looking for a buyer to purchase the firm, but were in no hurry to sell. Neither partner's children had any interest in the business.

One day in late January, Anil asked Karim to go for lunch with him. He said that he wanted to update him on his wedding plans and discuss another matter. Karim thought Anil might ask for a raise if he was getting married.

As they sat down to eat, Anil said that he and Sophia had planned to get married on Saturday, June 22nd, in Brighton. It would be a small wedding at the seaside King Edward Hotel. They would be happy if Karim and Zabin, who were now married, would attend. Formal invitations would be sent later in the year. They would also invite Azim and Gulnar, who were also, now married.

Karim congratulated Anil and said, "You've got a good girl there. Are your folks happy with her? We'll certainly attend your wedding."

"Thank you, Karim, and yes, our parents are okay with our plans. It would mean a great deal to us to have Zabin and you there. It was you who launched me in my career, and I've gained so much from your mentorship over the years."

"It's been my pleasure, Anil, and the firm values your work."

"Speaking about the firm, you know it's going nowhere."

"Yes, but the owners are happy with the client base. They don't want to chase new clients. They hope that someone will come along and buy them out for £100,000, which will give them five year's current net income, and they can retire."

"They can't live on that for the rest of their lives."

"No, but they've made a lot of money out of this practice. They must have good savings, and they've also invested in real estate, which is earning them good rental income."

"But they could sell the firm for so much more if they could grow the annual income."

"They're not interested in chasing new clients, Anil."

"They don't have to. They can increase their income by offering new services to their existing clients."

"What services?"

"See, when we go out for audits, we do our work and either give the firms a clean bill of health or point out problems for them to address. We have no part in solving their problems – except some that we can address quickly. In the course of our work, they talk to us about their other issues like recruitment, terminations, succession planning, their plans for growing their business, adding new lines, raising money to do so. Some want to acquire other businesses for horizontal or vertical integration that need to be evaluated and for which money needs to be raised.

Most firms that we have audited do not have a long-term vision or a strategic plan for their development. That's what large, successful corporations have, and if our clients don't have these, they will always remain small."

"Not true. Not all remain small. Many have grown and become very prosperous."

"Yes, I've seen some that have development plans and have grown, but theirs tend to be annual plans; none have a 10-year vision and work-back plan to realize that vision. I've seen some, where the owners have long-term visions for their companies that reside in their brains; they're not documented, not shared with the management and staff, and there is no strategic plan to actualize the vision. I see opportunities for us to establish a consulting division; the top five C.A. firms have robust consulting divisions."

"We're not top five, Anil. We're not even top 100. This would require adding staff, bringing in new talent. I don't think that the bosses will agree to that."

"We could do it with the staff we have. We're equipped to offer our clients a range of services, including the formulation of long-term visions, five-year goals, annual objectives, and strategies, and budgets. For the firms that want to grow, we can offer services to determine the viability of their desired expansions – internal or via acquisitions, and guide them on how they can move forward. We can prepare business plans for them to raise capital. We see in our work how some firms have ingenuously addressed H.R., succession planning, and lack of liquidity issues. We can learn from them. We can offer our clients services in these areas. We can help them with inventory management. The list is endless. And we can do all this with our existing clients; there is no need to chase new ones."

"You've obviously been thinking about this for a while. There is merit in what you propose, but this represents a departure from our core business. I'll tell you what, why don't you put together a proposal? It'll have to be comprehensive. You'll have to list the services that you're proposing we should provide, and prepare five-year projections of the number of clients you estimate will bite and the revenue stream that each service will generate. You'll need to calculate the cost of doing business and put together five-year projections with IRR on the time invested. A sound narrative will need to accompany your financials. You and I can review it, refine it, and I can then arrange for you to present it to the bosses - as your idea, of course.

Now, you can't do this in office time. You'll have to do it in your own time. Are you up to it?"

"I'll do it."

"WHY HAS NO ONE thought of this before? Why is this coming to us now, this late?" Mr. Rosenberg asked when Anil presented his proposal three months later to the two Partners.

"Sir, we've always been focussed on providing accounting and auditing services," Karim replied.

"But this is a logical extension to what we do. Nobody even thought about this before?" Mr. Weinstein asked, looking down the conference table.

"Nobody's articulated it and brought it forward in the way Anil's done, Sir," Karim replied.

"Organize a senior staff meeting next week. Circulate copies of this proposal to everyone. Anil, you make this presentation; don't change a word; present it to the senior management. We should hear what they have to say," Mr. Rosenberg said.

WHEN ANIL PRESENTED THE proposal to the wider group, he did deviate a little from his presentation he had made to Mr. Rosenberg and Mr. Weinstein. He named individuals within the firm who were equipped to provide the various consulting services he was talking about. He spelled out commendable work that they had done in the assignments on which he had worked with them in the various areas, which, in his view, had demonstrated their capabilities to provide the proposed consulting services.

'This guy doesn't need any P.R. lessons', Mr. Rosenberg thought.

There was a vigorous discussion on the proposal. Most staff found the idea intriguing but wondered if the firm was equipped to enter this field. Would the firm expose itself to legal liability issues? Poorly written advice or financial projections leading to failed investments could land the firm in courts.

"What is it that we cannot do? We can prepare sound financial forecasts; we can put together business plans; we can prepare long-term strategic plans. We have extensive knowledge of a range of industries. Yes, we have limited expertise in H.R.

and in designing effective organization and management structures, but we have clients whose models we can emulate, and we don't need to venture into areas where we don't have sound expertise. We can protect the firm with appropriate disclaimers," Anil replied.

"This could be exciting work for us. Of course, larger firms require consulting services. Our clients are mainly small to mid-sized family businesses; would they need such services, and if so, would they be willing to pay for them?" one associate asked.

"That will be our challenge. Get them to see the value in what we are offering," Mr. Rosenberg responded for Anil.

The discussion went on for almost two hours. It was evident to all that the Partners, who were very cautious investors, had discussed the proposal and were sold on it. The majority of the management team members supported the idea. Some old-timers who had no appetite for this new line of work said that the firm should stay with the business that had served it well for over 30 years. They were concerned that venturing into this field, which was occupied more by M.B.A.s than C.A.s, would detract from the firm's core activity and weaken it.

"We can move into this gradually, as Anil has suggested; offer services to some clients and gauge their response. We can bring in M.B.A.s if this is profitable. Anil, please develop a project implementation plan. This must have taken time to conceptualize and articulate it. How long did it take you to put together this proposal?" Mr. Rosenberg asked.

"Sir, I worked 20 hours a week for the last three months. I received much help from a friend of mine who is an L.S.E. graduate in Economics of Industry and Trade and an investment banker."

"Bill it," Mr. Weinstein said.

"Yes, bill your time and, Karim, charge it to the Consulting Division. We have one as of today. Anil, bring your friend in one day for us to take him out to lunch and thank him," Mr. Rosenberg said.

As everyone complimented Anil and he walked back to his office, he did a quick calculation of his billing. It would work out to about £200. He would offer Rafiq half of this.

"We're delighted that it was so well received, Anil, but all I did was to write a few pages. You can't give me £100 for that. That's what I get for three weeks of work. And you'll have to pay taxes on what you get," Rafiq said.

"Let's see the net amount, and we'll share it for sure. Yes, I developed the projections and calculated IRRs, but you spent hours thinking about each element of the proposal and offered ideas and wrote them up. Without your articulation, this would not have happened."

A MEMO CIRCULATED IN Anil's office the following Monday announcing the establishment of the Consulting Division within the firm, with Anil as the Division Head. He would immediately relinquish his other responsibilities to lead the Division. That would mean a Division Head's salary, which was good, but there was no mention of any staff attached to the Division, which meant that he alone would have to solicit business and service the clients until he could justify the need for more staff.

This was going to be a challenge, but Anil felt that he was up to the task.

1968
Sixty-Four

To speed up Sophia's sponsorship process, Anil and Sophia registered for a civil marriage ceremony on March 8th. The Mufti (cleric) at the Shia mosque had told them that he and his counterparts were not authorized to perform marriages. They could conduct the Muslim wedding ceremony to solemnize the marriage only after a couple obtained a marriage certificate.

Only Rafiq and Shameem attended the ceremony. Anil, Sophia, and Rafiq had taken the day off from work, and Shameem had skipped classes for the day. They enjoyed a nice lunch following the ceremony and spent the afternoon relaxing at home.

IN LATE APRIL, THE four sat down to prepare the guest list for the wedding reception in Brighton on Saturday, June 22nd. All invitations were out by the end of the month, and based on the RSVPs, they proceeded to firm up the arrangements.

In addition to themselves, the overnight guests would include their immediate families and Rafiq's parents, their neighbors Ed and Gwen, Robert and Bernice, the D.C. and Jane, Karim and Zabin, and Azim and Gulnar. Anil had invited his bosses to attend, but they had declined, citing other commitments and sent generous gifts and their best wishes.

Some people from Anil's office and two Ismaili couples (friends from the Ismaili Centre) would take the short train ride to Brighton to attend the midday reception and return home the same day.

There would be a Muslim wedding ceremony in the Shia mosque on Friday, June 21st, that only the immediate family would attend.

Like Sophia's parents, who wanted a Muslim wedding in a mosque, Anil's parents also wanted an Ismaili wedding, performed by the Ismaili Centre Jamatkhana Mukhi and Kamadia, but like the Mufti, the Mukhi and Kamadia could only solemnize marriages, and they could not even do that for Anil and Sophia, given that Sophia was not Ismaili. They were, however, very gracious. They agreed to drive up to Brighton with their spouses (who co-officiated the congregational prayers at the Ismaili Centre) for the day and attend the reception where they would offer prayers for the couple. Anil invited them to stay overnight at the hotel as his guests, but they said that they must return to London to preside over the evening prayers at the Centre.

RAFIQ'S AND ANIL'S PARENTS arrived in London by East African Airways V.C. 10 (an upgrade from Comet 4) flight on the morning of Thursday, June 20th. Sophia's family had arrived a day earlier and were checked in at The Ritz.

Almas' anxiety rose as they cleared Immigration and proceeded to the Customs area. She didn't know how she would interact with her new daughter-in-law, or how Sophia would react to her. Yasmin could see that she was tense and told her not to worry.

"I wish Anil had found an Ismaili girl, Yasmin. I wouldn't have had to worry so much about how to communicate with her. We know absolutely nothing about Sophia's family or her culture. In all my life, I have never even talked to an Arab man or woman."

"Look at Sophia like a person and not as an Iraqi or an Aithna Ashari. What was it that Rafiq said to you to remind you of Hazrat Ali's quote? Look at her as our daughter in faith and equal in humanity."

Almas gave the Customs Officer her list of gift items, and when asked, she told her what the items were for. The Officer offered congratulations for the wedding and did not charge any import duties since practically all of the items were for guests from Iraq, who would return to Iraq with the gifts.

When they emerged from the Customs area, Rafiq and Shameem let Anil and Sophia approach them first, and Salim and Yasmin let Fateh and Almas go ahead to meet them. Anil hugged his parents. He wanted to introduce Sophia to them formally, but not waiting for this, Sophia took Almas in her embrace, kissed her on both cheeks and said, "Welcome, Mom, I've been counting the days to meet you. We're very fortunate and grateful that you are here to bless us and our wedding."

Almas' eyes brimmed with tears. "And we are delighted to meet you, Sophia," she said, her heart filling with emotions for this sweet girl.

Sophia let Fateh take her in his embrace, kiss her forehead, and say, "We are so happy to meet you, Sophia."

Sophia proceeded to welcome Salim and Yasmin as Anil introduced her to them.

Embracing Yasmin, she said, "Aunty Yasmin, you are even more beautiful than Anil told me. Thank you. Thank you so much for coming. I know it's been very difficult for you to take time off," and before waiting for Yasmin to respond, she embraced Salim, who also kissed her forehead. She returned to Almas and picked up her suitcase. "Come, Mom, let's go home," she said.

On the ride home in the car that Anil had rented for the week, Sophia sat in the back seat with Almas, and holding her hand, talked to her about the flight, how Tazim was doing at school, would Zahir be stretched managing the business alone and how much she was looking forward to meeting them.

She gave Almas all of the details of their wedding plan and asked for her endorsement of each element. "Does this sound okay to you, Mom? Would you like us to do anything differently?"

She engaged Almas so much, making her laugh at some things she said, that all of Almas' anxiety about meeting her melted away. True, she was just a person. She could just as well have been an Ismaili girl, and it would have felt the same.

"My mother, her name is Fatima, she's something else. She is boisterous (Almas didn't know what that meant), loud and, honestly, a lot to take. I have told her to behave herself, but I'm asking for your forgiveness in advance if she offends you, which she likely will. You will like my father, Malik, and my aunt, Jehan, who is just as nice as you are. You'll meet them all this evening."

Salim, Yasmin, Almas, and Fateh were surprised and happy to see the house. It was much larger than they had imagined and beautifully furnished and decorated.

Rafiq and Shameem had invited Sophia's family over for dinner that evening to meet Anil's and Rafiq's parents.

When all had been introduced to one another, men gravitated towards other men and women towards other women as they sat down in the lounge. After exchanging greetings with Sophia's mother, Almas said, "Fatima, your daughter is as pretty as her mother." She had expected Fatima to respond by thanking her for her compliment. Instead, she said, "She's our only daughter and very precious to us. I hope your son will care for her the way we have."

Smiling, Almas said, "Sophia is equally precious to Anil and us. He worships your daughter, and I do not doubt that he will take good care of her." She then proceeded to greet Sophia's aunt and let Shameem "manage" Fatima.

Anil detailed the program and everyone's role for the next three days.

Sophia's father spent most of his time talking to Fateh and Salim. He complimented Fateh for having raised a wonderful boy. Sophia had told him several times over the past months how happy she was. He expressed sincere gratitude to Salim for letting Rafiq invite Sophia and Anil to stay with them. Salim told him that the boys were like brothers. He had not asked Rafiq and Shameem to invite Anil and Sophia to stay with them, but he would have been very disappointed if they had not.

"Sophia told us that in your culture, you don't expect any dowry from the bride's parents. You shower the bride with gifts. She told us that the bride and groom's parents exchange only small token gifts. Is this true?"

"That's correct. We'll do that when the ladies order us to do so, shortly."

"Fatima's got some gifts for your wives. She expected me to buy gifts for you. I thought she was buying them. She just told me that she has bought nothing for you, so I'm sorry, but I've no gifts for you, gentlemen."

Fateh and Salim laughed, and Fateh said, "So we won't give you the gifts that we've brought for you."

"I have a better idea. You each give me the gifts you've brought for me, and I will wrap them up and give them to each of you, as my gifts," Malik said, pointing to each in turn and laughing gregariously.

After exchanging gifts, they sat up late into the night talking.

THE WEDDING CELEBRATIONS WENT as planned. The ceremony at the mosque was solemn and dignified. The Mufi, who spoke perfect English, read verses of The Quran and offered prayers for the couple, imploring Allah to bless the couple with, among many other things, lots of children. Sophia did not say "amen" to that part.

At the wedding reception at the elegant King Edward in Brighton, Sophia looked radiant in the white saree that Almas had brought, and Shameem had put it on for her, and Anil looked debonair in his dark blue Austin Reed suit. Anil had ensured that Rafiq, who was his Best Man, also wore an Austin Reed suit. Shameem, Sophia's matron of honor, looked gorgeous in the maroon and gold saree that Almas had brought for her.

The Ismaili Mukhi, Kamadia, Mukhiani, and Kamadiani individually offered prayers for the couple. The Mukhi quoted the Prophet's hadith (pronouncements) on the exalted place of women in Islam, and a woman's rights and husband's obligations in marriage. Sophia's parents were deeply touched by the love and sincerity with which the prayers were offered.

Anil, in thanking the guests for attending, announced that this event was also a celebration of Shameem's graduation. She was now a qualified medical doctor. Shameem blushed as the guests applauded her achievements, and Rafiq beamed with pride at his brilliant wife.

Early the next morning, Sophia's father settled the hotel bill for all of the room charges, which he had told Sophia he would do. Fateh had told Anil that he had managed to buy £250 in cash from a "trader" and would pay for the reception, which he did.

The guests joined Anil and Sophia for a celebratory breakfast in the hotel restaurant. Everyone was in a jovial mood. After the breakfast, in a formal setting, the couple approached Anil's parents first and then Sophia's parents, bowing down before them to receive their prayers and blessings, as they had done the previous day. They then approached the D.C. and Jane and bowed down before them. The D.C. was too overwhelmed to say anything, but Jane repeated much of what she had heard Anil and Sophia's parents say. She and the D.C. hugged and kissed the couple as their parents had done.

After saying their goodbyes to all, Anil, Sophia, and Anil's parents rode back to London in Anil's rental car and Rafiq, his parents, Shameem, Bernice, and Rob drove back in Rafiq's car, which could comfortably fit six. Sophia's family rode back in the chauffeur-driven limousine to The Ritz, where they were staying for the duration of their time in London.

When they arrived home, Anil and Sophia had to wait outside for Almas and Yasmin to prepare to welcome the bride into the groom's home in the Indian tradition. Almas showered them at the doorstep with rice and confetti and threw betel nuts in four directions to ward off the evil spirits. She could hardly contain her happiness now.

Sophia's father had booked them into the honeymoon suite at The Ritz for two nights, following which they were to fly to the south of France for their honeymoon. Rob and Bernice were to stay with Rafiq and Shameem for one week, at Anil and Sophia's invitation, in their room.

They again sat up late into the night, talking and reminiscing about their days in Africa. Fateh and Salim told them things had never been better in Tanzania. The oil lift would end in October, but they had already amassed a tidy sum of money. They did not see any need to transfer it out of the country, where there were so many new investment opportunities in the tourism sector. Rafiq told them to sit tight and not invest a cent. In due course, he and Anil would tell them what to do with it.

ANIL AND SOPHIA, SHAMEEM, and Rafiq and the two sets of parents dined together at Surma Bleu Indian restaurant the next day, after which Anil and Sophia drove Fateh and Almas home and said an emotional goodbye to them. They promised to go and spend at least ten days with them in Dodoma in December, after spending a week with Sophia's parents in Baghdad.

Salim, Yasmin, Fateh, and Almas departed London two days later. At Bernice and Robert's insistence, they had toured London's major attractions with them during their short visit. They said that they would see more of London when they would come back someday.

Robert and Bernice returned to Cardiff shortly thereafter.

Two days later, as they awaited Anil and Sophia's return, Shameem said to Rafiq, "I always believed that two families in one household cannot work out. Yet, can you imagine Anil and Sophia not being here? I miss them so much. I cannot wait for them to get back."

"I miss them too, Shameem. But one day they'll move, perhaps when they, or we, have children. The four of us have allowed our lives to become too intertwined. One consequence of that is what we saw when we were drawing up the guest list. None of us really have any other close friends."

"I realized that, too."

"We invited Ed and Gwen, who are our neighbors. We invited Karim, Zabin, Gulnar, and Azim, who we look up to, but we don't really socialize with them, and the two Ismaili couples from the Centre who we talk to when we meet them at the Centre, but have never gone out for dinner with, nor invited over. All four of us need more friends. Anil and Sophia could move away to live in the U.S.A. or Canada, and who would we have then?"

"Never thought about it this way."

"Well, think about it."

1969
Sixty-Five

As they had promised to do, Sophia and Anil traveled to Iraq and Tanzania to visit their parents in December, and returned to London in early January.

"Baghdad was fascinating!" said Anil. "There is so much of our history there, and so much to see. The people were really nice. The food was bland. I would like to visit again, but I don't think I would like to live there, no matter what Sophia's dad pays me."

"He's lying," laughed Sophia. "My mom made him very uncomfortable; she paraded him in front of all of our friends and relatives. She invited people home every day to meet Anil. Only a few of them spoke English. Poor guy! I felt very sorry for him, and so did my dad."

"And how was Tanzania?" Shameem asked.

Sophia replied, "That was altogether different. It was peaceful. I loved Dar es Salaam. I could see a lot of Arab influences there. But we were there for only two days. Anil took me to NAAZ restaurant, and yes, their ice cream was as good as Anil said it would be. I loved the samosas. We went swimming one day. The rest of the time in Dodoma was heavenly. Anil introduced me to his friends. Most treated me like any other girl, and I could converse with them freely. I spent quite a bit of time with a couple of smart girls who want to go into Nursing. I told them they could write to me anytime they decide to come here to study, and I will be happy to help them in any way that I can.

"That's good. Meet any other people?" Rafiq asked.

"The older people - Anil's parents' age, kind of looked at me and didn't seem comfortable speaking with me. I guess they did not know what to say to an Arab wife of one of their own."

"So, what did you do all day?" Shameem asked.

Anil replied, "We woke up late, had a cup of tea, no breakfast, and walked over to Almin. Mom ordered samosas and kebobs from *Dawood* restaurant. That was our breakfast. We walked around the town, chatted with people, came home for lunch and rested, - read mainly, and, you know our routine - tea, get ready for Jamatkhana, come home for dinner, listen to the radio and go to sleep. Spent a lot of time talking to Dad and Mom."

"Did you stay at home alone when everyone went to the Jamatkhana?" Shameem asked Sophia.

"No, Tazim stayed home most days with me. Attending Jamatkhana was something Anil really wanted to do, so Tazim urged him to go, and she kept me company."

"How did Tazim and Zahir relate to you?"

"Tazim wanted to be with me every minute that I was there," she laughed. "She would make me sit with her late into the night, much to Anil's chagrin, and talk to me. I enjoyed talking to her. She is very charming, and she knows it. Zahir, on the other hand, I don't know…I think he didn't like me."

"He doesn't like anyone," said Anil with some irritation. "You would be disappointed in him, Rafiq. I recall the boy he was and how much time you spent with him on his studies; it didn't do him any good. He performed poorly in his Cambridge Exam. He is abrasive and venal. He thinks Almin would collapse in a day if he weren't there."

"How's Tazim done in her Cambridge Exam?" Shameem asked.

"She said that she's done well. She's waiting for her results. She still wants to do Sciences and become a chemist," said Anil.

"She's smart. I'm sure she will pass in 1st Division," Sophia added.

"Dad said that between him and your dad, they've accumulated over 500,000 Shillings. The money's in the bank. I asked him to convert that into cash, which they are doing by paying for all purchases and expenses out of their bank accounts and depositing little of their daily cash sales. It'll take them some time to do this. The big problem was where to store this cash. I said that they should open accounts at Barclays Bank in Nairobi and Mombasa, and deposit the cash there. Our currency is East African, so the Kenyan Shilling is the same as the Tanzanian and Uganda Shillings," Anil said.

"Good idea. What's the political climate there like?" Rafiq asked.

"The economy's booming. The Arusha Declaration seems like a distant memory. Everybody is positive. We spent a delightful day and night in Mpwapwa. Your parents and mine think it's a mistake to hoard all this cash or send it out. They see many opportunities for investing in tourism and agricultural projects. They are buoyed by the oil lift money and are comparing it to what they now think are meager earnings from their shops. They want to do something bigger, and they see a bright future in Tanzania."

"You think they should?"

"My sense is that this is the calm before the storm. Nyerere is going to do what he has said in the Declaration. He is preparing for it, make no mistake. Once we have the money in Kenyan banks, you and I should go, empty the accounts and bring the money here."

"It would be nice if they can stay there, Anil. Wouldn't it? They're so happy. Can you imagine how miserable they would be if we brought them here? What would they do?"

"I agree, Rafiq. But they won't be able to stay there. The Ujamaa concept has not taken root, but the government can target the Indians to advance its Arusha Declaration agenda. We are easy targets. They will take over our businesses. Remember, there will only be peasants and workers in Tanzania. That's what the Declaration says."

"How long do you think it will take them to transfer money into Kenyan banks?"

"A year. Maybe two."

"You think they can stay there for at least two years?"

"I really don't know."

1970
Sixty-Six

In the middle of 1970, the foursome had settled into a comfortable routine in London.

Rafiq's work was going well, and he could see the positive potential for his future there. Shameem was enjoying her work as a resident at St. Clements Hospital. Now that she was no longer a student, the Tanzanian bank had stopped her £50 per month student's allowance.

Anil's Consulting Division was doing better than he had expected. He had been given two staff. Sophia was happy in her work, and her Permanent Residency had come through.

The parents were doing well in Tanzania. Between the two families, they had managed to transfer over Shs.400,000 to the Kenyan banks. Their businesses were continuing to thrive.

Tazim had passed her Cambridge Exam in the 2nd Division, and Sophia had secured admission for her into the "A" Level Sciences program at Hampton College, a short tube ride from home. She was due to come to the U.K. in late August, and at Rafiq and Shameem's insistence, was to stay with them. Anil and Sophia could have financed her education, but Anil had asked his dad to get the students' foreign exchange allowance of £50 per month approved for her to get money out of Tanzania. He had proposed that she would contribute £25 per month towards household expenses (although Shameem and Rafiq wanted none) and could use £25 for her education and personal expenses.

Ed and Gwen dropped in one evening to talk to them. Ed said his term as a diplomat in the U.K. would end in June of the next year. At one time, Anil and Rafiq had expressed interest in moving to the U.S.A. If all four were still interested in migrating, they could apply for permanent residency early next year, and he would make sure that they had their Green Cards before he returned home. the U.S.A. needed doctors, nurses, accountants, and investment bankers.

They expressed gratitude to Ed for his offer and promised to get back to him in a week.

"THERE ARE PLACES LIKE Vancouver in the U.S.A. also," Anil said when Sophia said that her heart was set on going to Canada if they ever moved. "And we don't know if Canada will take us. I hear they have a new Prime Minister, Pierre Trudeau, who is a brilliant and charismatic guy who is moving to open up Canada to non-Europeans, but a bird in hand is worth two in the bush. I say, let's apply for Green Cards."

Shameem said, "I've read about private hospitals in America. They are like luxury hotels, and they have the most advanced medical equipment. They also pay a hell of a lot more than the hospitals here. Sophia and I could perhaps work in the same hospital. I wouldn't mind working there, and you, Rafiq, can get a transfer to your New York office. They may even have a place for Anil!"

"There is much more we need to think about. We need to think what we would do with our parents if they have to leave Tanzania - as Anil is convinced, they will have to. Would we take them to the U.S.A.? There is no community and no Jamatkhanas there. Here we have a community and a Jamatkhana. They would be miserable here, but at least they would have a Jamatkhana to go to," Rafiq said.

"They could come and live in this house when we're gone. We could support them until they find a business to run," Shameem said.

"Shameem, they're not us – they've never lived together! There are also Tazim and Zahir to think about. The fact that we have four large bedrooms here does not mean that two families can move in and live happily ever after," Rafiq said.

"Rafiq is right. These matters need to be thought through. But Ed is essentially offering us permanent residency in the U.S.A. I think that we should take up his offer and weigh the situation when we have the Green Cards. It won't be until next year," said Anil, pragmatically.

"Yes, we should," concurred Shameem. "Your parents told us when they were here that they're happy in Tanzania, and they expect to grow old there."

"They may, but I agree with Anil. We should apply for Green Cards," said Rafiq.

"Can we also apply to go to Canada? I mean, there's no harm, is there, in applying?" Sophia asked.

Looking at her, Rafiq said, "Sure, why not? We will apply for Canadian Permanent Resident status when we apply for Green Cards. Let's see what the Canadians say."

ON AUGUST 12TH, THE phone rang just as they were sitting down for dinner. Shameem picked up the phone. It was Zahir calling from Tanzania. He asked for Anil. From his tone, Shameem knew it was something serious. She passed the phone to Anil.

"I have bad news," he began. Anil took a deep breath and braced himself, as Zahir continued. "Dad suffered a heart attack after dinner tonight, and he has passed away."

"Oh my, God!" exclaimed Anil, as the phone slipped from his hands. The silent room fell all the more silent as everyone held their breath. Rafiq stood up and slowly stepped towards Anil, who had begun to shake as tears filled his eyes. Looking at Rafiq, he whispered, "Dad's gone. He suffered a heart attack."

Rafiq gasped, and the two women sat frozen. "How can this happen?" Rafiq asked, taking the phone from Anil. "What happened, Zahir?" he asked.

Zahir said that his dad had suffered chest pains and slumped over as he sat down in the lounge after dinner. They called the doctor, who came right away, but he was pronounced dead shortly thereafter.

"I need to know if any of you are going to come here for the funeral. We need to plan," Zahir said, abruptly.

"Yes. Anil and I will leave tomorrow. Let me talk to Mom."

"She can't talk to you now."

"Give her the phone! Anil wants to talk to her," Rafiq said in a stern voice.

He could hear Zahir asking Almas to take the phone, and he passed the phone to Anil, saying, "Be strong for Mom. Here, talk to her."

Almas took the phone, but she was sobbing, and now so was Anil. All he could say was, "Mom, I love you. We're coming. We'll leave here by the first flight tomorrow."

Shameem and Sophia, who by now were both crying, consoled Rafiq and Anil.

"This is devastating," said Shameem. "I cannot imagine what Almas aunty must be going through, but we will all have to be brave for her and Tazim and Zahir. Fateh uncle is gone, and all that we can do now is pray for his soul."

"The only flights going to Dar es Salaam leave here in the evening. I'll call the hospital in the morning, and if I can get away for a week, I want to come." Sophia said.

"I want to come, too," said Shameem.

THE FOUR DEPARTED THE next evening and arrived in Dar es Salaam the following morning. Sophia had connected with *Tim-Air*, a small charter firm at the Dar es Salaam airport, and booked a six-seater plane to fly them to Dodoma. The Tim-Air representative was at the airport to receive them, and they were on their way to Dodoma by 11.00 a.m. They arrived there two hours later. Salim and Yasmin were at the airport to receive them. They had organized the funeral for 4.00 p.m.

ALMAS AND TAZIM WERE inconsolable. Anil, too, broke down when he saw his mother and sister. Rafiq and Shameem tried to console them as much as they could and asked Anil to be strong for the funeral ceremony. He was now the head of the household. In the traditional Ismaili custom, the service was primarily comprised of prayers for the departed soul, and condolences offered to the family by members of the community, who attended the ceremony in large numbers.

THEY WERE ABLE TO speak to Almas after they returned home that evening. As Anil and Sophia sat on either side of her holding her hands, she described how Fateh had complained of chest pain, and she had gone and sat next to him. Zahir had called for the doctor. Fateh had taken her hand and holding it tight, had stared deeply into her eyes, and then the light had simply gone out from his eyes, and she knew that he was gone.

SALIM AND YASMIN STAYED the next day in Dodoma to be with Almas and then returned to Mpwapwa with heavy hearts. Rafiq and Shameem stayed in Dodoma for two days and then went and spent four days in Mpwapwa to let the Damjis grieve as a family.

Salim, Rafiq, and Shameem returned to Dodoma on August 21st and spent the day with Almas, Tazim, and Zahir. Salim then drove Anil, Sophia, Rafiq, and Shameem to Dar es Salaam the next day for them to catch the evening flight to London.

It was heart-wrenching for Anil to say goodbye to his mother. Tazim was booked to fly on the same flight, but she and Anil agreed that she should stay with their mother until the following Saturday. Her college was due to start on September 2nd. Before they departed, Salim assured Anil that he and Yasmin would look after his mom.

TAZIM ARRIVED IN LONDON the following Sunday. All of her happiness and excitement over going to London was gone. Her puffed-up eyes showed that she had not slept on the overnight flight and had probably cried the whole way there. She had only one day to shop for some warm clothes before college started. Her purchase of winter clothes and other apparel would have to wait until later.

In the time since Rafiq and Shameem`s wedding in Nairobi, Tazim had matured. She was more measured in her display of affection for Rafiq. Her mother had told her after the wedding that she had observed that she was making Shameem uncomfortable by clinging to Rafiq all the time. Also, she did not want Anil to feel that she loved Rafiq more than her brother. Her display of feelings was now limited to kissing all four after watching News and retiring to her room at 10.00 p.m. to study and then go to sleep.

Tazim said that there was one Ismaili girl, Shahin, from Mwanza, Tanzania, in the second year "A" Levels program at her college. She was friendly and very sympathetic and supportive when Tazim told her about her dad's passing just days before she came to the U.K.

Tazim met Shahin at Jamatkhana on Friday and introduced her to Anil, Rafiq, and Shameem. Shameem asked her if she had any plans for the weekend, and when she said that she did not, she invited her to have dinner with them the next day.

1970
Sixty-Seven

In late October, Rafiq received a long letter from his mother. It read:

Our dear Rafiq and Shameem,

Please keep this completely confidential. Under no circumstances should you say anything to Anil, Sophia, or Tazim, and don't tell your dad that I have written this to you. This has been weighing on me, and I wanted you to know what has happened before Anil or Tazim learn about this and tell you.

Three weeks after Fateh uncle passed away, your dad went to Dodoma to shop for the store, and he visited Almas aunty and Zahir at Almin.

Zahir told him that now that he was managing the business by himself, he should receive the 50% of net proceeds Fateh uncle was getting from Almin. Dad told him he was not managing Almin by himself because his mom (she had not come to the store yet) was equally involved in running the business, and he had already told Almas aunty that he would be issuing the 50% cheque each month in her name. She was his father's beneficiary. Zahir didn't like this but did not say anything.

A week later, he called and said he wanted an increase of Shs.800 in his salary. He was asking for a 50% raise. Dad said that was fine; he would add Shs.800 to his paycheck starting September, which he did.

Dad went to Dodoma again at the end of September and went to say hello to Almas aunty. Zahir was there, but he did not greet Dad. After talking to Almas aunty for about 10 minutes, he asked Zahir how he was and whether he was having any difficulty managing the business. Dad had told me before he went that if Zahir was having any difficulty, he would authorize him to hire someone for up to Shs.1,000 a month.

You won't believe what Zahir did. He said, "Why would I have difficulty running the business? Do you think I'm stupid?"

Dad was stunned. Zahir was furious and started shouting at Dad. He said that we had taken advantage of his father when we hired him. All we had invested in the business was Shs.10,000, and we were shamelessly raking in that amount in every month - money earned by his parents' sweat and labor - and that we had continued to do that even after the Mpwapwa contract was lost.

"What is your contribution to this business? What do you do for this business other than turn up every month to collect the money? What right do you have to draw anything from this business?" He asked and said he was happy to refund Dad the Shs.10,000 that we had invested in Almin and never wanted to see his face again. He said that he could walk out and throw the store keys at Dad and asked him how he would like to move to Dodoma and run Almin.

He said that the business had grown with his dad's ideas and hard work and that we should be ashamed of having fleeced his parents. He said that we had made a fortune out of the Zambian oil lift, which was his uncle's idea, and even when we were making so much money, Dad had not offered 50% of Almin shares to his father.

As he said all this, Almas aunty broke down crying and told Zahir to shut his mouth. She said, "You stupid boy, if it were not for Salim uncle and Yasmin aunty, your dad would have been working for Ralph Kirkwood. Do you have no shame? No gratitude? They are keeping your brother and his wife and your sister in the luxury of their home in London. How can you say such horrible things?" She folded her hands and asked for Dad's forgiveness.

Dad remained calm and told her not to take anything Zahir was saying to heart because *he* was not going to take it to heart. His feelings for her and her family would never change, no matter what this boy said to him.

He told Zahir that he had offered to formally transfer 50% of the shares to Fateh uncle's name twice and when the Mpwapwa contract was lost, he had offered to transfer 75%, but his dad had refused this and had also refused to take 75% of the net profit. He had said that he was grateful for and content with what he was getting.

Zahir replied, "You can say what you want now that my dad is gone. If you offered all this to him, how come he never told me anything?"

Almas aunty said, "He told me! He told me what Salim uncle had offered."

Dad was deeply wounded and said, "You are right, Zahir. We invested very little in this business and took too much. Come with me to the lawyer's office, and I will have him prepare the papers to transfer 100% of the shares to your mom's name. She is the beneficiary of your father's estate."

Zahir said, "I am the one who's slaving here, not her. Transfer them to my name, or I will walk out of here."

When Zahir said this, Dad got furious and said, "So, walk out of here. I will look for someone this afternoon in the town to come work with your mom starting tomorrow." He got mad, not because Zahir had insulted him, but because of how much what he was saying was hurting Almas aunty. She was sobbing and asking for Dad's forgiveness.

Dad told Zahir, "Listen to me carefully if you want to stay here, bring your mom to our lawyer's office at 4 o'clock. I will have him prepare the papers for the transfer of shares to your mom. After we sign, I will take the papers to Mpwapwa for Yasmin aunty to sign and send them back to the lawyer for him to complete the transfer. I will also ask the lawyer to prepare an employment agreement for you to sign, which will state the conditions of your work here and your termination if Mom is not happy with your work. If you are not there at 4 o'clock, don't show your face here tomorrow. Consider yourself fired."

Almas aunty was pleading Dad not to transfer the shares. She said, "I don't want any shares. You know how grateful we are for all you have done for us."

Dad told her not to worry about this at all. Nothing will change between us. He said that he and I should have transferred the shares to Fateh uncle's and her names earlier. He told her he was happy to do this and assured her that I would be happy, too. He said Zahir was right. It was Fateh uncle, her and Zahir's hard work that had built the business. Our contribution was only the Mpwapwa contract, which we lost many months back, and a little bit of start-up money. He asked Almas aunty to come to the lawyer's office to sign the papers.

They signed that evening. Poor Almas aunty was crying the whole time. I signed the papers, and now the shares have been transferred. I called Almas aunty and told her not to worry at all about what has happened. My feelings for her will never change, and I meant that. Now that I think about it, maybe Dad should have insisted on transferring 50% of the shares to Fateh uncle. Dad is very hurt and also sorry that we took so much money out of Almin. He is now counting how much we got and is thinking about returning it all to Almas aunty. I am telling him not to be silly. Without the Mpwapwa contract which the D.C. had offered to us, there would have been no Almin. We could have hired Fateh uncle to simply work for us for a salary, but instead, we gave him 50% of the net profit right from the start. That's where we made a mistake. If he had been on a salary equivalent to 50% of the profits, this would not have happened.

Don't say a word about this to Anil, and don't let your feelings for him or Tazim change. It's not their fault. Love them always as your brother and sister. I am sure Almas aunty will write to them. Let them tell you this.

Please convey my warm regards and much love to Anil, Sophia, and Tazim.

Rafiq's eyes welled up as he passed the letter to Shameem. She read it and said, "Oh my God, Rafiq. How could this happen? This must have hurt Almas aunty so much, and I can't even imagine what this will have done to your parents. You're not going to let your feelings for Anil and Tazim be affected by this, are you?"

"No, of course not. What I'm worried about is what Anil will do if he finds this out. He'll kill Zahir!"

"Well, let's not say a word."

THEY DID NOT HAVE to stay quiet for long. Three days later, Tazim received a letter from her mother telling her everything.

"DO YOU KNOW WHAT Zahir did?" Anil asked Rafiq as he returned home from work. Rafiq froze. Tazim was sitting crying on the sofa holding her mom's letter. Shameem and Sophia were not back yet.

"I'm so ashamed and sorry, Rafiq. I hope that you can forgive us," Tazim said with tears rolling down her face.

"Forgive you for what, Tazim? You've done nothing wrong!"

"I'm so sorry for what that rascal said and did to your dad. You know what he did, Rafiq, don't you?" asked Anil.

"Yes, Shama and I know. Mom wrote to us two days back, but it's got nothing to do with you two or your mom. And let's not get too upset with Zahir. He is family, so let not call him names. He is too young to understand what he's doing."

"You've known this for two days, and you said nothing?!" Anil exclaimed.

"What was there to be gained by telling you, Anil? I was hoping to save you the pain. I wish your mom would not have written to tell you this, but I guess she did it for the same reason my mom wrote to Shama and me. Mom said that we should not say a word to Sophia and you about this."

"I don't even know how to ask for your forgiveness, Rafiq," Anil said.

"Please don't. We're family, and can we agree on one thing? Let's never talk about this again. And you," Rafiq said, pointing to Tazim, "stop crying and come here and give your brother a hug."

Rafiq took Tazim in his embrace, kissed her forehead, and wiped her tears, but tears were now running down Anil's face, as well. This wound was too deep for everyone. It would take a long time to heal.

One Saturday morning in November, as Anil and Rafiq sat alone eating an early breakfast, Anil said, "You know, I've been thinking. Mom had told me when I was there that the Kenya bank accounts are in her and my dad's joint names. She's a signatory on the account and can draw the money out at any time. It's the same with your parents' accounts. Your mom can sign and draw the money. The money, as you know, is not in the chequing accounts at the banks. It's all sitting in safety deposit boxes that your and my moms can access as signatories to the chequing accounts. Zahir does not know about the accounts, but he does know that the oil lift money came in, and it's no longer in the bank in Dodoma. I'm concerned that he may pry that information from Mom, and I don't know what he would do if he finds out about the money in Kenya. Mom's not saying anything to me, but I wouldn't be surprised if he has taken control of all of the income from Almin and is just giving Mom a living allowance. She had told me when I was there that he has started drinking."

"What should we do? Shall we bring Mom here?"

"That's something I'm considering, but to do that, I have to get my own place. For now, I'm thinking that you and I can go to Kenya during the Christmas holidays, ask our moms to come there, draw all the money out and bring it here."

"My dad has not said anything about further deposits into the Kenya accounts - I guess because there's no oil lift money coming in and he has nothing coming from Almin. I've also thought about bringing whatever is there here, but I thought we could do that next summer."

"I think we should do it now. I can't risk Zahir finding out about the accounts."

"How will we get our moms to come to Nairobi? What will your mom say to Zahir?"

"She can say that she needs a break and that she and your mom have decided to take a week's vacation with Shama's parents in Nairobi. Time together for both will be good. There's a daily flight from Dodoma to Dar es Salaam. They can take that flight and then the evening flight to Nairobi and meet us there."

"Seems like a good idea. How will you tell all this to your mom?"

"Can you please ask your mom to do that on her next trip to Dodoma? My mom will need some convincing. Your mom can do that."

Rafiq and Anil arranged to meet their mothers in Nairobi on December 28th. They went to the banks in Nairobi and emptied the safety deposit boxes, flew to Mombasa on the 29th and did the same, and took the return flight to London on the 30th with Shs.200,000 in Shs.100 bills in each of their suitcases.

BEFORE LEAVING FOR KENYA, Rafiq had asked Shameem to buy six tickets for the Ismaili Centre New Year's Eve Dinner Dance. "Laughter has to return to this house, and I want Tazim to have some fun, meet people, and make friends. I don't want her to be insulated like us. The sixth ticket will be for her friend Shahin. Ask Tazim to invite her. In fact, ask Tazim to invite Shahin to come to spend her Christmas break at our place. The girl seems lonely to me."

SOPHIA, SHAMEEM, AND TAZIM were worried half to death about the risk that Anil and Rafiq were taking. There were no departure Customs checks from Kenya, but passengers were randomly selected to have their baggage checked. They could also get inspected by the U.K. Customs. What if they raised any issues?

THEY WERE RELIEVED TO see them return home safely on New Year's Eve.

1971
Sixty-Eight

arly in the New Year, Rafiq connected with the banker in Zurich, who had indicated interest in purchasing Tanzanian Shillings. The banker told him to wait. He would likely have a buyer in the coming days for the amount Rafiq was talking about.

The banker called three weeks later and said that he had a buyer. He would give Rafiq US$0.95 for Shs.10 (against the official rate of US$1 for Shs.7). If this was acceptable, he should bring the money over the next day.

The rate the banker was offering was better than Rafiq and Anil had expected. Rafiq was on a flight to Zurich the next day. He opened two accounts at the bank, one in his and Shameem's names and the other in Anil and Sophia's names, and deposited US$19,000 into each account. He told the banker that Anil, Sophia, and Shameem would come to sign the papers in the next ten days.

AFTER ANIL AND RAFIQ returned from Africa, Anil had been agonizing over what to do with his mother. When he had met her in Nairobi, he was shocked and saddened to see that she had lost even more weight and seemed to be withering away. He had asked if Zahir was treating her well. She had said that he was not very respectful. She was missing Fateh and also Anil and Tazim very much.

On top of the salary Zahir was drawing, she had told Anil that he was getting her to give him Shs. 2,000 from the 7,000, the accountant was telling her that she could draw from the business each month. Sales had fallen after his dad's passing.

"What are you doing with the money, Mom?" Anil had asked.

"I use 2,000 Shillings for household expenses, and other outlays, Zahir takes 2,000, the bank transfers 1,000 Shillings to Tazim`s account, and I deposit 2,000 in my savings account at the bank."

"What does Zahir do with the money he's taking?"

"He tells me he is saving 2,000 a month, but I think he is drinking it away, and he also has developed some other bad habits that I don't want to talk about."

This had been very unsettling for Anil. What could he do? If he brought her to London, they would have to move. Rafiq and Shameem would want her to stay with them, but that would be unfair. It was okay for Sophia and him to stay when they invited them, and also for Tazim, who had always been more Rafiq's sister than his, but he could not now bring his mother into their home.

With the £8,500 he had now, he could buy a house in a London suburb. What if he brought his mother over? What would she do all day sitting at home alone all those gloomy winter days? In Dodoma, she had her friends and Jamatkhana, where she could find peace in prayers and meet with people. He could not decide what to do.

One Saturday in April, Rafiq was up early and eating breakfast alone when he heard on the radio that the Tanzanian government had seized private residential and commercial properties. It had published a list of buildings "nationalized" to "end exploitation by landlords." The president had called this a "mopping up" measure. Compensation would be paid only for buildings less than ten years old, on a sliding scale. The published list of owners' names indicated that people of Indian origin owned practically all of the nationalized buildings.

Rafiq ran up to Anil's room and knocked on the door. Anil emerged, still wearing his pajamas. "What's going on?" He asked with fear and sleep still in his eyes.

"They've done it – done what you always said they would do, but this is much worse. The government has seized private residential and commercial properties to end, what they call, the landlords' exploitation of people. I just heard it on the radio."

"And I always thought that they would take over our businesses. They've gone for assets worth a hundred times more. What does the Guardian say?"

"I haven't looked at it yet. Let's see."

Both ran down and scoured the Guardian. It had only a small write-up that did not say much more than what Rafiq had heard on the radio.

"No compensation for properties more than ten years old. How many buildings in Tanzania are less than ten years old? Five percent? Rafiq asked.

This is not nationalization, Rafiq. This is confiscation."

"Shall we call my dad?" Rafiq asked.

"Yes, please call him. Let's find out more."

Shameem and Sophia joined them, still in their nightgowns. As Rafiq dialed the number, Anil whispered to them, "Tanzania is nationalizing private residential and commercial properties." Their eyes widened in surprise and disbelief.

When Rafiq asked for details, Salim said, "We'll receive the paper tomorrow. I expect it will have more details. All we've heard so far is the radio report, which essentially says the same things as you've heard. Anil was right. It was the calm before the storm. This is the storm. I wonder how many of us will survive it," Salim said.

"I cannot believe this. I doubt if the international community will have anything to say or do about it," Anil said.

"My parents don't own any property. Your mom lives in her own house and is not a landlord, so, I guess, we're not impacted by this," Rafiq said.

"It's the action, Rafiq - the message to our people. They will not be the only ones hurt by this. We have seen the consequences of this kind of action in other countries. This will ruin Tanzania. We have to pull our folks out."

"Let the dust settle, Anil. Let's learn more before we make any moves."

A week later, Rafiq received an envelope from his dad containing newspaper cuttings, which provided more detail. Key elements of the new law were:

All rented properties (office and apartment buildings, or residential structures of any kind) were nationalized. Starting May 1st, tenants would pay rent directly to the government

If even one unit in a multi-unit condominium building was rented, the entire complex was nationalized. There was no explanation for why all unit owners would be punished for the "exploitation of people" by one unit owner.

The unit owners who occupied the units they had owned could stay rent-free in their units, but could not sell them. The units now belonged to the nation. If they vacated them to move elsewhere, the government would take over the units and rent them out

If an individual owned any property which was rented and he/she lived in another property that he/she owned, not only his/her rented property(ies), but also the property in which he/she lived, was nationalized, and he/she must start to pay rent on the property where he/she lived, starting May 1st. For buildings more than ten years old, there would be no compensation no matter what their market values. For buildings less than ten years old, compensation would be paid on a sliding scale. As an example, if a building was nine years old, the owner would receive 10% of its book value, no matter what the market value.

Salim's enclosed letter read:

This is devastating for Ismailis and other Indian communities. As you know, over 75% of the buildings in Tanzania were owned by Ismailis. There were some major Ismaili landlords in places like Dar es Salaam who, in partnership with others, owned anywhere from 5 - 15 buildings, and in places like Dodoma who owned 1 - 5 buildings. Suddenly, their incomes of Shs.10,000 – Shs.50,000 per month are gone. From this income, they had spent a significant portion to maintain the properties. You have to wonder if even one cent will now be spent on maintaining the buildings.

Not all landlords were big. There are widows we know whose husbands had worked hard all their lives to build and pay off a two-family unit where one was rented. The widows were living on the rents that their tenants paid. They will now become destitute. Some Ismaili widows are already applying for welfare from the Council because they have no money to buy food.

Scores of young couples who had worked hard and saved money for down payments on their flats have, essentially, lost them. They can stay rent-free, but they can't sell or move. If one gets transferred to another town, his unit is taken over. Practically every single one of the Aga Khan multi-unit housing projects is gone. The prestigious IPS building which the president opened just six months back is nationalized.

Mortgages on a lot of properties were for 25-year terms. If the buildings are more than ten years old, compensation will be zero. The lenders will get nothing. There is mass confusion on who will service the mortgage.

There's also a lot of confusion on where to pay rents, which came due last week. No systematic apparatus or process has been established. Because of the severe penalties for non-payment, people are desperate to pay rent and are approaching different government offices. In some places, the government officials are taking the money, issuing phony receipts, and pocketing the money.

Our landlord came crying to me and said that he had borrowed money against the property, and the bank (which is government-owned) had called him in because he has defaulted on his mortgage payment and threatened to take action against him. He could go to jail. He asked if I could pay him just the May rent. I told him that would be illegal, but I gave him the money, all the same, and I went and paid the rent amount to a local government office. I have a receipt, but other than the amount I paid and the guy's signature (no name), there is nothing to indicate it's a government receipt.

Everything is in turmoil, and things can only get worse. People are talking about leaving Tanzania. Mom and I want to wait and see. We have lost nothing so far, and don't want to make any rash decisions.

After they had read everything, Rafiq said, "The Arusha Declaration did say that a socialist state cannot have a class of people who worked for their living, and another who lived on the work of others. Maybe, this is to give effect to that principle of socialism. The government must view landlords as living on the work of others."

"But someone who owns a flat in a complex where one tenant rented out his or her unit and the entire building is taken over doesn't live on anyone's income, Rafiq. Now he can live rent-free in the place he owned, but can't sell it if he has to move to another town, or for whatever other reason. Look, if the government had wanted to deal with "exploitation" by landlords – and by the way, 90% of the "exploited" tenants are Indians for whom the government doesn't give a damn – it could have levied a 50% or 75% tax on all rental income and used the money for the welfare of its less privileged people. This is a confiscation of as many properties as possible. And what about every individual's right to receive protection of his life and property enshrined in the Arusha Declaration?" Anil asked.

"You're right, but here is our situation. Your place is not impacted, and my parents now have a new landlord. For us, nothing has changed. They want to wait and see. I say, let them. There's no concern for their safety. I'm not in favor of bringing them here if we don't have to. They'll be miserable here."

"Rafiq is right," Tazim said, looking at Anil. "Let Mom and Zahir stay on."

"Can we move them to Kenya? Set them up in business there?" Shameem asked.

"Why, Shama? They're in no danger in Tanzania. And who knows what will happen in Kenya tomorrow? I think Rafiq and Tazim are right. Let them stay," Anil said, with a sigh.

1971
Sixty-Nine

The impact of seizure of the properties in Tanzania was immediate. Whereas there was much anticipation amongst the Africans who believed that the Indians would soon be evicted from their homes in which they would be able to move and live free, the non-Africans became convinced that this would not end here. They feared the seizure of their businesses and other assets.

The shop shelves started to empty. The Indian jewelers no longer sold gold ornaments. They only worked with gold the customers brought in. All diamonds and other imported jewelry disappeared from the jewelry shops. Importers stopped bringing in merchandise. The Indians stopped spending money, with the intent to send it out of the country, but the black market rate for foreign currency rose sharply. Reliable "Traders" asked Shs.100 for £1 (instead of Shs.30 for £1 they had asked before). They said that demand for Tanzanian Shilling had dried up. No one wanted this currency. The economy started to grind to a halt.

Deterioration in the maintenance of nationalized apartment complexes in Dar es Salaam was also immediate. Garbage started to pile up in the building compounds. Properties served by sewage tanks did not get emptied, causing sewage to overflow onto the streets.

Landlords with pre-nationalization high rental incomes, but small savings, had to modify their lifestyle drastically. Some had one or two children studying abroad (most in the U.K., but some in the U.S.A.). They did not have the income now to send Shs.1,000 or Shs.2,000 every month for their children's education. Some students had to drop out of school or look for part-time work to support themselves and pay for their education.

There was much pain and anxiety in the community, and this increased every time they heard of a family or individual severely impacted by the government's action.

Anil and Rafiq's families had not suffered such financial consequences, but they felt the pain of their fellow Ismailis and other Indians.

Most Ismailis concluded that they could not live under a government that had embarked upon this road to socialism. Some, whose children had settled in Europe or the U.S.A., started to leave the country.

IN NOVEMBER 1971, SALIM wrote to Rafiq to say that he had been advised (by whom, he did not say) that the Canadian High Commission in Dar es Salaam was entertaining applications for permanent residency in Canada from Tanzanian professionals, and entrepreneurs with assets to establish themselves in business in Canada. He had been recommended (again, by whom, he did not say) to apply for Canadian residency in the "Business" category. He had received an application form that he had completed, a copy of which he was sending to Rafiq and Anil to look at. He had also requested and received an application form for Almas, which he had completed for their review. Parents over 65 and children under 21, if still in the education system, would be covered under the applications.

Salim said that it was estimated that approximately 5,000 Ismailis from Tanzania would qualify for Canadian visas in the next six months. They, in turn, could go to Canada and sponsor their children over 21 who were not in the education system and parents under age 65. They could also nominate siblings who did not qualify under the designated categories. It was estimated that over time, up to 10,000 Tanzanian Ismailis would become qualified to move to Canada. Tazim was included in Almas' application, but Zahir could not be, as he was over 21 and not in the school system. Almas could nominate him after coming to Canada.

Rafiq and Anil looked at the applications. The forms were simple and had been completed. well

"He is telling us they have decided to go to Canada. He is not asking us if they should go," said Rafiq.

509

"What options do they have? They can't live in Tanzania. We know how bad the situation is there. If so many Ismailis are applying to go to Canada, why wouldn't our parents apply? Your dad is a smart man. He's not telling us everything, but if he has made this decision, you can be sure that it's based on very sound advice and judgment."

"What will they do there?" Rafiq asked.

"If this number of people move, we can be certain that Hazar Imam will establish the Councils and other institutions to guide and support them in Canada. Our parents are in their mid-50s. They're still young. They are smart business people, and we could set them up in businesses there."

"You have to be there to do that," pointed out Sophia.

"Yes. You can't ship them off to this far off land and expect them to fend for themselves. And Anil and you can't go there for a week or a month and find a business for them and come back. We have to be with them at this stage in their lives. We all have to apply to go to Canada," said Shameem.

"They can come here. Prospects for retail businesses in the U.K. are good, and they can't take Tazim with them to Canada. She's in college here. I don't want her education to be disrupted," Rafiq said.

"Rafiq, I think our parents have decided for us where our future is going to be. Sophia and Shameem are right. We have to leave the U.K. and apply for Canada," Anil said.

"And if these numbers move from Tanzania, there will be Jamatkhanas in Canada. A move of this magnitude does not happen without direction and facilitation," Shameem added.

"Maybe. It's a major decision, though. We'd have to give up our good jobs, sell this beautiful house in which we have been so happy, and go and start from scratch in a new land. We need to think about this. Shama, you have to finish your two-year residency, and what about Tazim – what happens to her education if we go?" Rafiq asked.

"We can sort that out when the time comes. We're very comfortable here, but we've never had a sense of permanency. That's why we told Ed we were interested in applying for Green Cards. It appears that our destiny is in Canada if our parents are going there," Anil said.

"Okay, let's look into applying and see if the Canadians will take us."

Sophia was beaming from ear to ear as she said, "We are going to Canada! If they take hundreds of professionals from Tanzania, why wouldn't they take our two men here, who are professionals and of Tanzanian origin?"

TWO MONTHS LATER, RAFIQ, Shameem, Anil, and Sophia filed their applications after Salim advised that they had attended an interview at the Canadian High Commission in Dar es Salaam and their applications had been approved, subject to medical examinations for infectious diseases and police checks for criminal records. The visas would take up to six months to come, after which they would have six months within which to enter Canada.

IN THEIR APPLICATIONS, ANIL and Rafiq stated the approval of their parents' applications and also that when they had visited Canada, they had been offered jobs by a bank, and provided the names and coordinates of the individuals who had offered them senior positions.

When Shameem called the High Commission to confirm that their applications had been received, the officer who acknowledged receipt said that whereas the applications would have to go through due process, all four appeared well qualified to be admitted to Canada as permanent residents.

1972
Seventy

By February 1972, significant numbers of Ismailis in Tanzania started to receive Canadian visas, and many started leaving. Toronto and Vancouver were the favored destinations - the former for its vibrant economy, job prospects, and its place as Canada's financial center, and the latter for its milder climate and scenic beauty.

Because Salim, Yasmin, and Almas had applied after many others had, they were expecting their visas to come through in May or June. Rafiq, Shameem, Anil, and Sophia were expecting their visas to come through shortly thereafter.

THE TANZANIAN GOVERNMENT HAD become aware of the Ismaili exodus. People leaving the country were applying for "Emigration Treatment" where under, they could take up to Shs.25,000 ($3,750), of which they could take $2,000 with them in cash, and the balance would be transferred to Bank of Tanzania's correspondent bank in Canada one year later.

The first step for people wanting to leave was to get Tanzanian passports. Most did not have one. Hundreds of Indians lined up outside the passport office every morning. Only those willing to bribe the doormen could enter the office. Additional bribes had to be paid to Passport Officers to get the passports issued. This happened in full view of everyone.

The departure of Ismaili professionals was a brain drain for the country, but their departure, and that of the people migrating to Canada as prospective business persons, was resulting in these people vacating their apartments and large houses, which the government could take over.

In early 1972, the government passed a law where under anyone with money outside the country had to declare such assets or face serious consequences. It must have known that people knew the consequences of making such declarations and except for a few with £100 or £200 outside the country for their children's education or other such cause, no one would make such declarations. It was rumored that the move was intended to hasten the departure of the rich who lived in better houses, by creating fear for their safety. The government already had a law in place (Detention Act) where under anyone could be arrested and held indefinitely without charges or trial. Reports had emerged of the treatment of those detained under this law, which included physical violence and threats against their families.

Salim, Yasmin, and Almas' visas came through in April. They had until October 15th to enter Canada. In consultation with Rafiq and Anil, they decided to move to Canada by mid-August. Tazim had applied to Canadian universities, which did not require her to complete her "A" Levels. In fact, one year of "A" Levels in Sciences would be a significant advantage for her. All had offered admission into their Sciences programs starting in early September. She had confirmed acceptance with the University of Toronto.

Salim had to decide what to do with his business. No Indian was interested in buying it, and even if anyone did, and paid him Shs.200,000, all he would get would be £2000 for it on the black currency market. So, he called George Nkwabi, the local D.C., who had been very supportive and comforting for Salim, guaranteeing his safety in Mpwapwa and getting Almas, Salim, and Yasmin's passports renewed without having to bribe anyone. He asked Nkwabi if he knew of any African who could buy his business for much less than its worth. He would give it away for Shs.100,000. Nkwabi said he, himself, was interested in purchasing the business, but under the Arusha Declaration, he could not have income from any source other than his D.C.'s salary. He would, however, find a third party to "own" and run the business for him, which he did. He paid Shs.25,000 in cash and promised to pay the balance over one year. Salim transferred the money to the Aga Khan Council in Dar es Salaam to support the Ismailis hurt by the property seizures and asked Nkwabi to also channel his payments there, which he did diligently, as promised.

ANIL AND SOPHIA'S CANADIAN visas came through in early June, and Rafiq and Shameem received theirs shortly thereafter. The visas were valid for entry into Canada until November 30th.

CHELSEA WROTE TO RAFIQ in May that Ricardo wanted to return to the U.K., and both were giving up their jobs with the government. They would arrive in London on June 10th and travel the same day to Leeds, where they were going to live. Rafiq insisted that they spend at least one week with them in London, which they agreed to do.

Chelsea was delighted to see Rafiq, Shameem, Anil, and Sophia. Anil and Rafiq were at the airport to receive them. Each of them had taken one day off work, in succession, to spend time with their guests.

Chelsea was vague, and there was sadness in her eyes when she talked about why she had decided to give up her prestigious job and the good life in Tanzania, but Ricardo, when Chelsea was not present, told Rafiq that she was shocked by the government's actions. She could not work with a government that had taken such action. She had told him the day the properties were seized that their time in Tanzania was over, but she wanted to make a smooth transition. She did not want the students to suffer. That was the reason they had stayed on for over a year. With the departure of so many Indian and also European teachers who did not want to stay there any longer, the education system was in a mess. There was nothing she could do about that.

Ricardo also told Rafiq that the government was surprised that the Indians were packing up and leaving. It had expected them to stay (where would they go anyway?) and diligently pay rents to create a cash bonanza for the Treasury. The government was also surprised that Canada was interested in taking so many Indians. It should not have been, he said. While countries like Australia and the U.S.A. slept, Canada had scooped up Tanzania's cream of the crop. Having known the Ismailis for their honesty, enterprise, and organization, he knew that they would go on to become highly successful and model citizens for Canada, the U.K. or the U.S.A., or wherever they settled and make significant contributions to the economy and cultural mosaic of the country they settled in.

Rafiq thanked Chelsea for stopping his parents from investing in property and told her how critical her advice had been in allowing them to generate savings for his parents in London and Zurich.

One evening as they sat at dinner, Ricardo said, "I understand that there were approximately 30,000 Ismailis in Tanzania. Chelsea knows from her government sources that around 15,000 have left or are leaving. Those that cannot come to the U.K. or go to Canada are going to India and Pakistan. Some are going to the U.S.A. Chelsea and I are worried about what's going to happen with your people in small places like Mpwapwa and in larger towns, who do not have the money or education to go anywhere. We cannot imagine how miserable their lives are going to be."

"I could have never imagined the government doing this. I had told your dad to be prepared to have his businesses taken over. I never thought the government would take over people's homes," Chelsea said sadly.

Other than these painful discussions, the week with Ricardo and Chelsea was a happy time. Chelsea loved the girls and hugged them often, telling the boys how lucky they were to have these wonderful young women in their lives.

Rafiq and Anil drove Chelsea and Ricardo to Leeds on the following Saturday and returned on Sunday, after having said emotional goodbyes.

1972
Seventy-One

Soon after receiving his Visa in June, Anil had sent his CV to the five large Canadian Chartered Banks, large C.A. firms, and some major corporations in Vancouver. He would have liked to go to Toronto, where Tazim would go to college, but Sophia was set on going to Vancouver. He also knew that his mother would be comfortable being near Yasmin and with Tazim. He, therefore, did not insist that she go with him and Sophia to Vancouver.

Sophia had applied to several hospitals in Vancouver. Two hospitals had indicated interest in her applications. Others had said that they would be happy to meet her when she arrived in Canada. There were no job offers.

Anil had better responses. After telephone discussions, the Bank of Nova Scotia and one C.A. firm had made firm offers. The lower offer was for $15,000, and the higher was for $18,000 per year. Others had indicated interest in meeting him when he arrived there. Anil had shown interest in both offers but had suggested that they meet when he came to Vancouver and take it from there if they could hold the positions for him, which both said they could.

They decided they would leave for Canada at the end of September. Sophia advised the hospital of her plan to leave, but for Anil, telling his employers he wanted to go was more difficult. The Consulting Division he had established was just over three years old. He had four staff working in the Division, but none could assume his role. He decided to first discuss his plans with Karim.

"The bosses won't be happy. The Division has grown more rapidly than anyone, including you, had expected. The availability of this service created its own demand amongst our clients, and through their referrals, you have brought in new clients. The bosses will not be pleased that you want to abandon this nascent Division," Karim said.

"But you do understand my position, Karim. People are leaving Tanzania, and my mom had to leave, and I can't send her off to Canada and stay on here. If this were something we had more time to plan, I would have groomed someone for my job."

"I understand, and the bosses will understand that tending to the Division's growth, you did not have the time to groom anyone for your position. Let me think about how we should approach this."

A WEEK LATER, KARIM told Anil, "I reviewed with the bosses the divisional revenues, and we noted that return on staff time invested in the Consulting Division outstrips returns in other divisions. They are receptive to adding people. I have considered suggesting that I take over the Division when you leave. I do not doubt that they will be happy to let me do that. There are at least three people who can step into my role. I've decided that I will tell them you want to leave and why, and offer to take your job."

"Really, you would do that?"

"Yes, but let me also tell you that my family is going to Canada, too, so don't be surprised if I come there in two years and ask you for help in finding me a job."

"Karim, it would be my privilege to help you, anytime," said Anil.

TO FINALIZE THEIR DEPARTURE, Shameem and Rafiq had to first sell the house and were looking at later departure date. Rafiq had applied for a transfer to the Toronto office. Bannerman was not happy to let Rafiq go, but when he explained what had happened in Tanzania and that his parents were moving to Canada, Bannerman was supportive and arranged the transfer.

In August, Shameem would have finished her first year of residency and not yet qualified to practice medicine. She had been communicating with the Ontario Ministry of Health, the Canadian College of Physicians, the University of Toronto, and some of the larger hospitals in Toronto for accreditation of her M.B.B.S.

and one-year residency to check if she could complete her second year in Canada and qualify as an M.D. She was offered a residency position at Toronto General Hospital, starting in mid-November. She would have to sit for one qualifying exam, but pending its successful completion, she would be able to transfer over.

"WHAT ARE YOU GOING to do with the house?" Ed asked one day as he and Rafiq went for an early morning walk.

"We plan to put it on the market in late July. I understand that the prices have increased substantially."

"And they will rise even more. This is London. It doesn't make sense to sell. The Embassy is looking for a house to rent as of November 1st, not necessarily in this area, but your kind of house. Do you want me to check if they would be interested in renting your place? They are looking at a higher-end area, but if they are receptive to renting here, I would suggest you rent it to us. We'll pay top dollar. "

"That sounds very interesting, but we have to sell; we'll need money to buy a house in Canada."

"Mortgage the house and take the money. You have no debt on the house, so mortgage it to the hilt. If we rent it from you, based on our rental agreement, you'll qualify for a mortgage higher than the price you paid for the house, and the mortgage payments will significantly reduce your tax liability from rental income."

Rafiq mulled it over. "That would be great, Ed! Can you please check?"

"I sure will."

A WEEK LATER, ED told Rafiq that he had convinced the Embassy to rent the place, subject to inspection. It would be a 10-year net lease (the tenant would pay for maintenance, insurance, and taxes) with the option to renew for another ten years. Rent would be adjusted every five years based on market rent for similar properties. Rafiq should have an appraisal done. In Ed's estimate, the house was worth £20,000. If the appraisal came in at this level, he could get the Embassy to pay £1,500 rent per annum. Rafiq should talk to his bank to determine the maximum that the bank would lend and if the rent would cover mortgage payments.

The bank appraised the house at £21,500 and offered to lend £16,000 at 7.5%

with annual mortgage payments of £1,440. At this rate, Rafiq estimated his taxable income would be practically nil. He provided the bank's appraisal to Ed, who came back with the Embassy's standard lease for Rafiq and Shameem to sign.

Having signed the rental agreement, they now had to firm up their departure plans. They decided to leave for Canada on October 15th. Both would end their employment at the end of September. They agreed to ship practically everything in the house in one container, and also the Pontiac, to Canada. This would take time to do.

SALIM, YASMIN, AND ALMAS arrived in London at the beginning of August. They had driven to Nairobi in Salim's Mercedes with just their suitcases to avoid problems at the border. They left the car, which was still like new, with Shameem's parents for them to sell and send the money to the Aga Khan Council in Dar es Salaam for allocation to the Council's welfare fund. After the seizure of the properties, the government had prohibited the sale of used vehicles less than five years old. They had with them their bank drafts for $2,000 from their Emigration Treatment.

A couple of days after they arrived in London, Rafiq sat down with his parents and briefed them on arrangements for their travel and accommodation in Canada.

On money matters, he told them that they had the equivalent of $110,000 in their accounts in London and another $20,000 in Zurich. He would obtain a bank draft for $100,000 to take with them to Toronto. They should open an account with a branch of the Bank of Tanzania's correspondent bank, Canadian Imperial Bank of Commerce (CIBC), where the balance of their "Treatment" money would eventually come, and deposit the funds into an interest-earning account.

From the $2,000 "Treatment" money they were carrying, Rafiq asked them to keep $1,000 in cash to spend and make purchases and deposit the balance into a chequing account with the bank. He would give them another £1,500 in Travellers' Cheques, for which they would get around $3,750, which they should also deposit into their chequing account. He told them that Anil was going to ask Almas to do what he had told them to do with their "Treatment" money, and would give her a bank draft for $35,000 to deposit into an interest-earning account at the CIBC.

For their travel, he told them that they would depart London on August 15th and arrive in Toronto the same day. His friends, Carole and Geoff, would receive them at the airport and take them to a hotel downtown where Carole had booked two rooms for them for two weeks. They could check out earlier if they wanted to, or extend their stay.

For their accommodation, he told them that at his request, Carole had also reserved two large two-bedroom apartments in a new building on Bloor Street (this was a major road running east-west in Toronto with a relatively new transit line running under it), from where it would be an easy commute for Rafiq to his work, for Shameem to the hospital, and Tazim to the university. The apartments had not been lived in and included all appliances and window coverings. Carole had paid $500 to hold the apartments until August 20th, by which date they and Almas should go and sign one-year leases with options to renew for one year at $250 per month for each apartment. The lease on Almas' apartment would commence on September 1st and their apartment on October 1st. They could walk over to the apartment building the day after arriving there and sign the leases and reimburse Carole the $500 when they met her.

For furnishing the apartments, he asked them to walk around and familiarize themselves with the downtown. Carole would give them directions to two department stores (Simpson's and Eaton's) on Yonge Street, where they should go to look at furniture for Almas' apartment. Anil told his mother that she should buy good furniture and a nice color T.V. They should identify the items they liked, and Carole would meet them after work to help them make the purchases.

They should also buy crockery, cutlery, pots and pans and everything required to fully furnish and equip the place from wherever Carole suggested. Salim should pay for all purchases and keep the receipts. Rafiq would sort this out with Anil later. They would stay in Almas' apartment until the container he was going to ship from London arrived, and they could furnish the second apartment. The container and car were expected to arrive at about the time when Rafiq and Shameem would get there. They would stay at the same hotel when they arrived in Toronto and arrange to have the car and container released, and for the movers to set up the furniture in the second apartment for the four of them to move in.

"Will do, Rafiq, but what will it cost us to live each month?"

"Carole tells me that in addition to $250 rent on the apartment, you will need about $100 a month for groceries for two, $25 for telephone and $50 for transit fares. All utilities are included in the rent. One parking spot for each apartment is also included. In addition to the amounts for deposit into the savings accounts, you will have with you $7,500. Almas aunty will have $2,000. That will be enough to pay for everything until we arrive."

"What should we do until you arrive? Should we start to look at businesses? We hear that some who have gone to Canada have bought dry cleaning businesses, convenience stores, and gas stations. Should we look at these?" Yasmin asked.

"Look at those and other businesses. Talk to Ismailis who have bought businesses and familiarize yourself with the economics of retail and service businesses, but we are in no hurry to buy anything."

1972
Seventy-Two

Salim, Yasmin, Tazim, and Almas arrived in Toronto in the evening on August 16th. Carole and Geoff were there to receive them at the airport and drove them to their hotel downtown.

They woke up early the next day, and, as Rafiq had suggested they should do, they walked around and familiarized themselves with the area and then walked up to the apartment building on Bloor Street to sign the leases.

Carole had said they could go to the Simpson's and Eaton's department stores on Friday and Saturday to look at furniture and other items that they needed to buy. She would meet them on Monday after work to look at their selections. They need not be in a rush to buy things. They could continue looking in the days after, if necessary. She would meet them after work each day to help them purchase the right things.

They spent the better part of Friday at Simpson's and Eaton's. The selection was extensive, and it was difficult to decide what to buy. They selected a dining table and chairs for six, matching buffet and hutch, and two sofa sets at Simpsons, for Carole to look at. At Eaton's, they selected the beds, coffee tables, and a T.V. set.

IN AUGUST 1972, THERE were about 300 Ismailis in Toronto. Less than 50 had been there for more than two years. Most had arrived in the last six months from Tanzania. They were gradually falling in love with Canada and Toronto. People were friendly and inviting.

As Ismailis do everywhere they go, they had quickly established their place of congregational prayers - the Jamatkhana - in Toronto. The Ismailis who had been there longer had met for Friday prayers at the residences of the families who could accommodate such gatherings, but later, as the population started to grow, a congregational member who had come to Toronto from India and had been formally appointed as Mukhi to lead the congregation in prayers had secured the gymnasium in a school on Broadway Avenue near Yonge Street and Eglinton Avenue intersection for the community to meet and pray in on Friday evenings. Very few Ismailis owned cars at that time, so the "School Hall Jamatkhana" had to be close to the transit system.

Salim had obtained the location of what they called the "Jamatkhana" from another Ismaili family from Dodoma, and that's where they headed on Friday evening, two days after arriving in Toronto. Prayers were scheduled for 8.00 p.m. They were quickly identified as new members of the congregation and were welcomed.

After the conclusion of the prayer services, the congregation poured out into the schoolyard to socialize. People were generally optimistic. Most were professionals. The women, especially those looking for junior administrative and secretarial positions, were finding jobs very quickly; many men with a college education, however, were having difficulty finding jobs because they did not have "Canadian Experience." Some were seeing this as a polite way of being told, "I can see that with the education and experience you've got, you can do this job with your eyes closed, but we don't like the color of your skin."

Others in the congregation, who had found good jobs in their fields of training, were asking them not to become disheartened by such negative experiences and to keep looking. They said that larger employers would only look at their qualifications and not the color of their skin.

An informal network of professionals was forming to help the newcomers find jobs. A few, with university education, who were running out of the few hundred dollars they had come with, had taken up factory jobs and were living in rooming houses. All who had come from Tanzania in the past weeks had come as Independent Applicants and were not entitled to any government support.

Salim talked to a couple of people who had bought businesses. They said that businesses in Canada were hard work, and one needed to be very cautious in evaluating them. It would be wise to seek professional help. Without an established credit record, it was also difficult to get bank loans to finance businesses, which meant that they could only buy smaller establishments with the money they had. One advised Salim that he may want to find a job as a small business manager and work for six months to a year to get experience before striking out on his own.

Yasmin met with some of the longer-term residents and inquired about who had set up the gym to serve as the "prayer hall." Surely, the school authorities would not bring in carpets and furniture and set up the P.A. system for the Ismailis to pray.

She was told that the hall was set up by the Ismaili volunteers who rushed to the school directly from work every Friday to set up the space. That a school gymnasium could be turned into a solemn space of worship by a small group of volunteers in that little time was mind-boggling.

"So they do not go home to eat dinner before coming here? It's at 9.00 p.m." Yasmin asked.

"No. Most volunteers don't have cars, and there is not enough time for them to take the subway home, eat, and come here by bus or subway and get the place ready for us by 7.30 p.m. They will eat when they go home after we all leave. They will vacuum the carpets, roll them up and store them away. They will leave the gym cleaner than they found it. That will be around 10.00 p.m.," one lady answered.

"Poor volunteers! What would we do without them? Who appoints them?" Yasmin asked.

"No one. Young people come here, see what needs to be done and volunteer their services. Like everywhere, they do this for the love of their Imam and desire to serve the Jamat," the lady replied.

"And it's very kind of the school authorities to allow us the use of these premises," Yasmin said.

"Yes, it is. We searched long and hard for a place for us to get together and pray, and this was what we found. I don't know where we would have gone if the school authorities had not accommodated us, and they charge us nothing for the use of their premises," the lady said.

As they rode the subway to the hotel, Yasmin said, "I am so happy to see that the global spirit of voluntarism in our Jamat lives on here. There would be no Jamatkhana if the volunteers were not here to set and wrap up the place."

"You're right, and I was touched by the fact that people whom we have never seen before were coming up to me and asking when we came here; if we have found a place to stay and if they could be of assistance. Some have been here only two months and have not found jobs yet, but were still offering to assist. If this spirit of voluntarism and brotherhood survives in our Jamat in this new land, I do not doubt that we will thrive in Canada," said Salim.

"I saw a couple of guys talking to you, Tazim. Did you know them?" Salim asked.

"No, I'd never met them before. One came and introduced himself. He will be going to York University in September to study Law. He was nice and quite smart, and there was this other guy who asked me if I wanted to go out for coffee with him."

"Oh my! And what did you say? Have you left a boyfriend behind in London?" Yasmin asked.

"No. No boyfriends. Rafiq wouldn't let me go out on dates in London. No boy who asked me out was ever good enough for Rafiq. I will need to get to know people here a bit better and then decide if I want to go out with anyone. For now, my focus is on school."

"Trust Rafiq to do that," said Yasmin. "You know he loves you dearly, and he's very protective of you, but you are a smart and grown-up girl. He can guide you, but not control your life. I'll talk to him when he gets here. Did Anil not have anything to say about that?" Yasmin asked.

"For Anil, whatever Rafiq says is always right, and whatever Anil says is always right for Rafiq. Whenever I asked Anil if I could go out with any boy, he always said yes, I could, if Rafiq was okay and Rafiq was never okay. Shama and Sophia did not intervene."

Yasmin detected bruised feelings and said, "We'll talk to Rafiq about that."

CAROLE MET THEM ON Saturday morning at Simpson's and gently steered them away from some of the large ticket items that they had selected and suggested other, reasonably priced items, which they liked. The three-piece sofa set they had chosen, she told them, was beautiful to look at, but was not comfortable to sit on for long to watch T.V. or read a book. It would look good in the living room in a house where the family spent the most time in the family room on more casual and comfortable furniture.

In the two days they had been in Toronto, they had visited the City Hall directly behind their hotel, walked up and down University Avenue and Yonge Street to Bloor Street, and twice eaten hamburgers at *Big Boy,* which they had loved. They had been told to be at the apartment for furniture deliveries on specific days and times. Carole had endorsed most of their linen, crockery, cutlery, and other selections, which they purchased and took with them to the apartment.

By the week's end, all major items had been delivered and set up. Bell Canada had installed the phone line. Tazim had selected the trendy Contempra phone units. The 24-inch RCA color T.V. had been connected and was fun to watch. The place was ready for them to move in. All they needed were some groceries, which they could get at the Dominion supermarket on Bloor Street.

They moved in on September 1st, and by mid-month, they were feeling well settled in the spacious apartment. Tazim had started college. Almas, Yasmin, and Salim had busied themselves with opening the boxes, organizing the crockery and cutlery, and neatly storing away the linen and other small items. Salim went grocery shopping and made additional purchases when the ladies asked him to. In his spare time, he looked at Businesses for Sale ads and discussed with Yasmin the businesses that appeared worth exploring further. They had looked at a couple of dry cleaning businesses and gas stations, but these did not interest them.

After breakfast, the three usually went out and walked around town. They went to the Canada Manpower Office on King Street and registered for employment.

As suggested by one Ismaili congregation member, they made their way one day to the famous Honest Ed's department store to make some household purchases. The prices here for pots and pans, crockery, and cutlery and other household items were much lower than what they had paid at the other stores. Carole had probably never shopped at Honest Ed's. It was fascinating to walk around this large department store where, they learned later, most new immigrants shopped.

They saw a "Part-Time Help Wanted." sign in the store. When they inquired, they were told that the store was hiring female cashiers to work from noon to 5.00 p.m., Monday to Saturday. Yasmin suggested to Almas that they should apply and see what happened.

Two days later, Almas got a call and was offered the job, but to everyone's surprise, Yasmin did not get hired.

Almas reported for work the next day and, after two hours of training, was stationed at a checkout counter. She was thrilled to know that she would get paid $85 a week. That would more than pay their rent, and she could be home in time to help cook dinner. She loved her work. Honest Ed's was on Bloor/Danforth Subway line, just a few stations from her place. The customers and other staff were very friendly. Many were new immigrants. She was told that the owner was a kind man who had a soft spot for the poor and new immigrants. Anil could not believe that his mother had found a job in Canada in less than one month and was so happy in her new role.

Yasmin got two referrals from Canada Manpower, but, with less than Grade XII education, did not get hired. Salim had indicated his occupation as "Store Manager." He never heard from Canada Manpower.

As they talked to more people in Jamatkhana, they got more tips. They were advised to subscribe to the *Toronto Star* newspaper, where they would find suitable job ads. They were also asked to register with employment agencies, which they did.

1972
Seventy-Three

Uganda is a landlocked country in East-Central Africa. It takes its name from the Buganda Kingdom, which, until 1966, had encompassed a large portion of the south of the country, including the capital, Kampala. Before independence, together with Kenya and Tanzania, Uganda had constituted the British East Africa.

The British had ruled Uganda as a protectorate starting in 1894. In the 1890s, they recruited some 32,000 laborers from British India to construct the Uganda Railway. Most returned home after the railway was built, but by one count, approximately 6,700 remained in East Africa, and subsequently, many became traders.

Uganda gained independence from Britain in October 1962, with Milton Obote as the Executive Prime Minister and the Buganda Kabaka (King) holding the ceremonial Presidential position. A year later, Uganda became a republic within the Commonwealth.

Managing the Buganda kingdom within the framework of a unitary state had always been a problem for the British. Successive colonial governors had been unable to address the issue, and it remained unresolved when Uganda became independent. In consequence, Uganda's immediate post-independence years were dominated by acrimony between the central government and Buganda.

In March 1966, Obote abolished the President and Vice President offices, effectively dismissing the Kabaka. The Kabaka asked for outside help, and his Buganda parliament demanded that the Ugandan government leave the Buganda territory, including the capital, Kampala. Obote responded by ordering his army commander, Idi Amin, to attack the Kabaka's palace. The Kabaka escaped and found refuge in London. He died three years later.

After the Kabaka's departure from the political scene, things were quiet in Uganda. By 1970, the economy was growing, foreign aid and investment were pouring in, and people were generally optimistic about the country's future. The Asians, who now numbered approximately 80,000, were investing in hospitality, farming, and manufacturing businesses. They accounted for 80% of the country's tax revenue.

ZULFIKAR (ZUL) AND AZIZA Rahim were living a happy life in their apartment in the Kololo Ismaili housing complex in Kampala.

Aziza was 30, and Zul was 29 years old. Their daughter, Nisha, and son Nahid were five and four, respectively. Both were attending half-day nursery school.

Aziza had trained as a hairdresser and beautician in the U.K. She operated her salon on Kampala Road, which her affluent father had financed before she married. She employed two girls, one Hindu Indian and one Ismaili. She cleared between Shs.1,800 and Shs.2,000 per month.

Zul had come from a modest background. He had to leave school after passing his Cambridge Exam. His father could not finance his post-secondary education. He had a sales job with a shirts, socks, and men's undergarment manufacturing business in Kampala. He was an excellent salesman. His work took him all over Uganda, which was challenging to do as accommodation in some smaller towns was of poor quality, but he made more money than some of his friends who had gone on to graduate from the prestigious Makerere University in Kampala, did. His commission averaged Shs.2,500 a month. He had a late model Peugeot 404 company car. He and Aziza could afford a nanny for the children and a house servant. In December 1970, like their fellow Ismailis in Uganda, Zul and Aziza had a good life. They could not have been happier. Their world would soon come crashing down.

In a military coup led by (now General) Idi Amin in January 1971, Obote was deposed from power. He sought refuge in neighboring Tanzania. There was jubilation in the streets of Kampala. People had not liked Obote. Many Asians marched with the Ugandan Africans to show support for Idi Amin.

While in power, Obote's government had pursued a policy of "Africanization." This included policies targeted at Ugandan Asians to restrict the role of non-citizen Indians in economic and professional activities. Idi Amin intensified these policies. In August 1971, he announced a review of the citizenship status awarded to Ugandan Asians. He said that his government would recognize citizenship rights already granted, but all outstanding applications for citizenship (~12,000) would be canceled. This did not impact Zul, Aziza, and their children. They were all born in Uganda and were Ugandan citizens. Amin also accused a minority of the Asian population of disloyalty, non-integration, and commercial malpractice, which the Asians denied.

Life for Ugandan Asians changed after the coup. Travel within the country became dangerous. The army set up road barriers at will and extorted money from Asian travelers. Soldiers, armed with machine guns, stopped and boarded trains and buses and robbed Indian passengers and assaulted Indian women.

On August 4th, 1972, Amin ordered the expulsion of Uganda's Asians, giving them 90 days to leave the country. At this time, of the approximately 80,000 people of South Asian descent in Uganda, 23,000 had had their applications for citizenship, both processed and accepted.

Amin declared that Britain should take responsibility for the 50,000 British subjects of Asian origin, accusing them of "sabotaging Uganda's economy and encouraging corruption." The deadline for British subjects to leave was confirmed as November 8th. Amin defended the expulsion by arguing that he was giving Uganda back to ethnic Ugandans.

Five days later, the policy was expanded to include citizens of India, Pakistan, and Bangladesh. The position of the approximately 23,000 Asians who had been granted Ugandan citizenship was less clear. Hundreds queued up to have their citizenship validated.

Amin's decrees drew global condemnation and sent shockwaves within the Indian community in Kenya. After what had happened in Tanzania and what was now happening in Uganda, they wondered what would happen in Kenya. Some started to leave for Europe and North America.

Rafiq, Shameem, Sophia, and Anil heard about Amin's decree on BBC. They noted that the Asians who were Ugandan citizens were not to be expelled.

"I think most Ismailis in Uganda are Ugandan citizens, like we were in Tanzania," said Anil. "They'll be okay, but I wouldn't stay, even if I were a citizen. This guy has gone beyond what Tanzania did. In one sweep, he's taken away everything from 85% of non-citizen Ugandan Indians and getting rid of them in 90 days. His army is terrorizing people. As we just heard, most of the people with British nationality in Uganda are Hindus, who, economically, are the most dominant economic group in the country; if they go, the country's tax base will collapse, and the economy will be in ruins. I don't think Idi Amin and his cronies can run the businesses that the Indians have established."

"Nothing will happen. The BBC report said that of the 80,000 Asians, 50,000 are British citizens. Britain is not going to allow Amin to rob and impoverish them, and then offload them on the U.K. The Ugandan army is not the 'kith and kin' of the British like the Rhodesian whites were. Britain will teach this idiot a lesson. British boots will be on the ground in Uganda in a couple of weeks, if not days," said Rafiq.

AFTER WAITING IN A line, which stretched outside and around the building, for over two hours, Moez and Rubina Samji, two Ismailis who had traveled from Jinja, a small town in Uganda, to have their citizenship validated, entered the passport office in Kampala. They were relieved to be out of the hot sun and to come inside the building, but Rubina, who was standing ahead of Moez in the queue, immediately got a bad feeling when she saw a small pile of passports near the lone officer who was checking them. There were two Indian men and one woman ahead of them.

They had to stand about three feet away from the officer's desk, so they could not hear everything he was saying to the people seated in front of him. The first one, he seemed to approve, and he stamped and handed back the passport to the man; to the second, Rubina heard him shout, "Your citizenship is canceled. You were not born in Uganda," and he threw the passport onto the pile next to him and asked the man to leave. The guy seemed shocked and started to argue and implore. The armed soldier guarding the place took him tightly by the arm and escorted him out of the building.

Now, the woman in front of Rubina was having her passport looked at. Rubina saw a pile of U.S. dollar bills fall out of the passport document. She and Moez had no U.S. money with them and only a few Ugandan Shillings. They had obtained their citizenship legally, and there was no reason for them to expect any trouble, or to bring much money with them. Quickly realizing that Moez was born in Tanzania, she pushed his passport in his hand and asked him to leave immediately.

"Why?" Moez asked.

"Just go, okay!" Rubina told him sternly, and seeing the fear in her eyes, Moez left.

The officer spent some time smiling and chatting with the woman seated before him before handing her the passport. As she rose to leave, his gaze shifted to Rubina.

"Where did the man who was with you go?" He asked Rubina.

"Oh, that was my husband. He ate something last night and he has bad diarrhea. He had to run to the W.C. He could not hold, and now he will have to line up again."

"So, you've got his passport?"

"He had to go so badly, the *pambhafu* (idiot) forgot to give it to me."

The officer looked at Rubina's passport, which listed her six-month-old daughter and handed it back to her. "You are okay. When you find your husband, don't stand in line, or he will have to run to the toilet again and will never get here. Just come up here, and I will look after you," he said, laughing.

"Thank you very much. You are so very kind *bwana* (Sir)," Rubina said and went out. She spotted Moez some distance away and went to him.

"What was that about? Why did you ask me to leave?" he asked.

"Didn't you see what was happening? He was cancelling citizenships of those not born here and taking away their passports. Let's get out of here. You are technically stateless now, but you have your passport. The Canadian High Commission has our applications. We should get out as soon as our visas come."

When the visas came two weeks later, they were on the first available flight to Toronto.

When they emerged from the Customs area, Moez looked around for ground transportation signs. Arrangements to receive Ugandan refugees had not yet been made, and they were on their own. As he did this, three young boys approached him. One asked, "Are you Ismailis from Uganda?"

"Yes, we are," Moez replied.

"Ya Ali Madad, Uncle. I am Shamsh and my two friends here are Iqbal and Sadru. We are here looking for any Ismailis coming from Uganda to help them if they need help. Is anyone receiving you, or do you know anyone here?"

"No, we know nobody here. My name is Moez, and this is my wife, Rubina, and our daughter, Fahreen."

"Do you have any money?"

"I have only $100, but my wife has a one-carat diamond ring that we plan to sell to get us going."

"You're not going to sell anything," Sadru said, picking up one suitcase as his friends picked up the other luggage. "You are going with us, and you will stay with us until you find jobs and a place of your own. We are from Tanzania. We have a one-bedroom apartment with three beds. We work night shifts in a muffler factory; we sleep part of the day and hang around here to look for Ismailis who need help. You can sleep in our beds. Let's go." And they were on their way.

"Have you eaten anything? What about the baby?" Iqbal asked.

"Yes, we ate on the plane, and Fahreen had her bottle. Do you have any milk at home?" Rubina asked.

"We do, but we'll pick up a new bag on our way, and we'll eat something at home. We have not had our dinner, and we always cook a little more."

The boys had a beaten-up 1965 Chevrolet Impala that they had bought for $500. They had made their way to Canada when their visas had come through while their parents had stayed back to wind up their affairs and follow in two months. Shamsh and Iqbal were 20 years old; Sadru was 19. All three had passed their Cambridge Exam and were planning to go to college when their parents arrived and could support them.

MOEZ, RUBINA, AND FAHREEN stayed with the boys for over two weeks.

533

Iqbal took Moez, who was a computer programmer, to the Canada Manpower office two days after they had arrived, and the Office found him a job with a firm in Don Mills at $185 a week.

When they had attended Jamatkhana on Friday after they arrived, they had met a young couple from Uganda who had moved to Toronto in 1971. The couple offered to find them accommodation in an apartment building at 25 St. Dennis Drive in Don Mills, where the couple lived.

By the end of their third week in Canada, Moez and Rubina were settled in their two-bedroom apartment. With the money the couple advanced them, they had purchased a double bed and linen, a crib, and a small kitchen table with four chairs and a sofa. The boys had taken them to Honest Ed's, where they had bought pots and pans and dinner and cutlery sets. The boys had also introduced them to Almas at the checkout counter.

Almas was delighted to meet new Ismailis from East Africa (for whom Honest Ed was a "must-shop-at" place) coming to re-establish themselves in Canada. Amid all the pain and loss, there was a sense of hope and community amongst the growing number of new Canadian Ismailis in Toronto. The pattern was replicating in Calgary and Vancouver: strangers reaching out to help those coming in after them. A new sense of community and solidarity was growing amongst the displaced peoples, and friendship was being formed amongst the new settlers in their adopted land.

"We don't know how to thank you, boys, for what you've done for us. I will call you for dinner once we are settled. You will have to come," Rubina said, hugging the boys with tears in her eyes.

"You know how we love your cooking. And you don't have to thank us, Aunty. Just pray that we get admitted into college and can get an education," said Shamsh.

Moez held each one in a tight embrace and offered prayers for them. In this strange new land, they had found a new family.

1972
Seventy-Four

During the 90-day expulsion deadline period, the Ugandan soldiers intensified with impunity their thefts, physical assaults, and sexual violence against the Asians.

The sight of army vehicles driving through the Asian residential areas after dark struck terror in the hearts of the residents. If one or more of these vehicles stopped in front of a house or an apartment complex, the residents prayed that the soldiers would stop at robbing them and not beat them up, violate the women, or kill them or their children. The soldiers entered the houses of wealthy Asians, terrorized them, and seized jewelry and cash. They beat up people who could not produce much.

People stopped venturing out after dark. Those with British citizenship and assets overseas, started to flee Uganda.

As Idi Amin's deadline approached, the Indians started to leave Uganda en masse. The 12,000 member Ismaili community, many of whom were Ugandan citizens, looked to their spiritual leader, the Aga Khan, for guidance and support. When Amin's decree came, the Aga Khan called his long-time friend, Canadian Prime Minister Pierre Trudeau, and asked him for help. Trudeau's government agreed to allow thousands of Ismailis to immigrate to Canada. It was the first time in Canadian history that Canada accepted a large group of non-European refugees.

To leave Uganda was a nightmare for the Indians. Extensive and intentionally complex forms had to be filled, and tax clearances had to be obtained from the Tax Office to buy airline tickets. There were long lineups at the Tax Office. People were variously told by the officials that their files were lost, or that they owed hundreds of thousands of Shillings in back taxes, or that their employers had not remitted their taxes to the Revenue Department. All of this meant one thing. Offer Shs.5,000 in a folded application form, and all files and clean tax records would magically materialize.

The airlines could issue tickets only if the buyer could produce evidence of citizenship of the country of his/her final destination, or a visa to enter the country, and a Tax Clearance certificate.

Lineups for entry into the British, Canadian, and Indian High Commissions were a mile long. People had to line up to obtain the forms, line up again to hand in the forms, and then line up yet again to attend for interviews - if they were fortunate to be called for one.

Some Africans in government offices empathized with the Indians and resented what their fellow Ugandans were doing. For them, this was not the Ugandan way; Ugandan Africans were good people. If the Asians were being thrown out and their possessions were being taken away, there was no need to subject them to this treatment. They should be allowed to go peacefully, but no one dared to speak.

The exodus of Ugandan Asians took on a new level of urgency in September, following a telegram from Idi Amin to the UN Secretary-General Kurt Waldheim, in which it appeared that Amin was sympathetic to Hitler's treatment of Jews. An airlift was organized for the stateless and others who had not been accepted by any country.

The Canadian government chartered aircraft to fly those who had been issued Canadian visas to Canada. When Zul and Aziza produced their Canadian Visas and their valid travel documents, they were asked to board a bus the next day at 9.00 a.m. for a Canadian charter flight leaving sometime during the day from the Entebbe airport.

AS THE BUS ROLLED out, Zul and Aziza, and all of the other passengers were anxious. They had heard from people that had left earlier that the ride to Entebbe was dangerous. Soldiers stopped cars and buses, and passengers were roughed up and robbed of their belongings. The children could feel the tension and were quiet.

The adults said hellos to people seated next to them in hushed tones but otherwise remained silent.

Forty-five minutes later, the airport was in sight, and everyone breathed a sigh of relief, but as the bus turned a corner, two soldiers, one with a machine gun pointing at the bus, waved the bus to stop. The driver stopped, and the two boarded the bus.

The soldier with the gun announced that everyone should remove their watches and all other jewelry and take out whatever cash they had to handover to them. The terrified passengers complied and felt grateful that it would end at this. As they walked down the aisle collecting the loot, the soldier with the handgun stopped to gaze at Aziza for a few seconds while Zul handed over the watches to his partner and said they had no other jewelry. A chill ran up Aziza's spine, but the soldiers moved on.

After they had gone to the end of the bus and taken all they could from everyone, the soldiers came back to Zul and Aziza's seats. The one wielding the handgun passed the gun to his partner, asked him to point it at Zul's head and pulled Aziza's high neck blouse from her skirt and shoved his hand up her blouse as his partner laughed out aloud. Before he reached Aziza's breast, however, he felt the gold pendant and the long chain that she was wearing under her blouse. He yanked it. The chain broke and made a long and deep gash in the side of Aziza's neck. Blood started to ooze out.

"You *shenzie* (stupid) woman, you're trying to hide this from me?" He shouted, slapping Aziza hard across her face. She froze in fear and did not utter a sound. Nisha and Nahid started screaming. The passengers wondered what would happen next.

Waving some cash he had pulled out from his sock, a Hindu man seated across the aisle from Zul, said, "Captain, please, Captain, see, here, I have $305. Please take this and let us go."

The soldier snatched the money and stopped to think that if this guy was hiding money, there might be others who were also hiding money. A second check was warranted, but just then, his partner told him there was a car, followed by another bus approaching, and they jumped out to rob their next victims.

The driver took off, and in a few short minutes, they were in the airport and being assisted by the airline personnel. But they still had to go through the departure customs, to be robbed of anything that the soldiers had missed.

A flight crew member examined Aziza, cleaned the wound with what she had in the plane's First Aid Kit, and said that she required stitches, but there was nothing they could do for her there. She asked the pilot to radio Nairobi air traffic control to get a doctor. The flight was to land there in an hour to fuel up, as there was not enough fuel at Entebbe for the long journey.

After the flight was in the air, Zul walked down the aisle to look for the gentleman who had introduced himself as Dinesh when they had boarded the bus, and who had come to their aid.

He located the man seated a few rows behind them, and grasped his hand. "You put your life at risk and gave away all of your money to save us. I don't know how I can ever thank you," Zul said, tears streaming down his face.

"We are all children of the same *Bhagwan* (God) who must care for our fellow human beings. Let's just offer thanks to our Gods that we are safe now. I heard you tell your wife she shouldn't have worn that concealed necklace. You should thank God that she was wearing it. Imagine if he had not found it. She is an attractive lady. He would have pulled her off the bus. They would have raped her; perhaps told the bus to move on and probably killed her," Dinesh said.

"You're right, Dinesh. You saved her and me. If they had started to pull her from the bus, I would have fought them, and they would have certainly shot me."

"Bhagwan saved us. He sent the next bus just in time for them to rob."

AN HOUR LATER, THE flight landed in Nairobi, where a proper passenger list was prepared. The airport had called The Aga Khan Platinum Jubilee Hospital and asked for a doctor for Aziza. The doctor, together with the Aga Khan Council leadership, was at the airport. Aziza required stitches. The leadership comforted her and Zul and gave them the names and coordinates of the Ismaili leaders in Toronto for them to contact for support.

THE FLIGHT ARRIVED IN London the next day. The crew had arranged for a doctor to look at Aziza. She had been in pain all the way, but the doctor who examined her said that the wound had been well attended to in Nairobi and was healing. She could lie down and sleep in Heathrow's medical room for the time the flight was in London, but she should stay awake on the flight to Toronto and not fall asleep, tilting her head on either side.

They arrived in Toronto at around 6.00 p.m. local time. An immigration official, who introduced herself as Susan, welcomed Zul and Aziza and their children and processed their papers. Looking at the bandage on Aziza's neck, Susan asked what had happened to her. Seeing Aziza's eyes welling up, she led the family into a room and sat them down. Zul told her what had happened. When he told her that the wound had been looked at in London, giving him a business card, Susan said, "Okay, but you should go to this doctor who is one block from your hotel on the same street, and have him look at it."

Canada Manpower and Immigration officials took all refugees on that flight into a room for orientation and gave them printed materials to guide their initial days in Canada. They gave each family vouchers for the hotels they were to stay in, and $25 cash allowances. They also provided them with addresses of the office where they should go to collect their weekly $25 allowance and the Canada Manpower center where they should go to register for employment.

THE HOTEL ON CHURCH Street looked simple. The manager, Morris Ford, a bald and old man, said, "Welcome, guys. We're practically full with your people!"

As he checked them in, pointing to the room across the reception area, he said, "Breakfast is in that room from 7.00 to 9.30 a.m. We serve a good hot breakfast. You'll be happy here. You folks will be with us for one month or more, so let me know if there is anything you need for your room, and I will see what I can do."

Zul thanked him for his welcome and offer to help. These Canadians were all so kind!

"Are you hungry? Are the children hungry? I can order some pizza for you," he said.

"Thank you very much, but no; we are exhausted and just want to get some sleep," Zul said gratefully.

"Goodnight, then. We'll see you tomorrow morning."

"What's pizza, Dad?" Nisha asked.

"Must be some kind of food they eat here. Are you hungry, sweetheart?" Zul asked.

Nisha shook her head.

THE ROOM WAS CLEAN, with two double beds and an attached bathroom. It was almost 9.30 p.m. They put the children into bed and got ready to sleep.

Zul took Aziza in his embrace and said, "I'm sorry, I'm so sorry, Aziza, that I could do nothing to stop that animal from doing what he did to you."

Aziza, who had said little throughout the journey, said, "Let's put that ugly incident behind us. Let's just sit for a while and offer *shukhrana* (gratitude) to Allah that our children and we are safe in this country that has welcomed us so warmly. I will never forget Susan's kindness and her face. For me, her face will always symbolize Canada. I will remember her in my prayers every night and pray for her and her loved ones' security and happiness. Today, we have nothing more than what we have in those two suitcases and $25, but I feel rich because we are surrounded by the goodwill of people like Susan and Mr. Ford."

They sat in bed and prayed. There was so much to be thankful for.

THEY WOKE UP THE next morning at 8.00 a.m. The children were still sleeping. Zul shaved and showered, and then woke Naheed, helped him brush his teeth, and gave him a shower and got him dressed. Aziza showered and got Nisha ready, and they went down for breakfast.

Breakfast was good with orange juice, cereals, hot scrambled eggs, baked beans, and toast, butter, and jam. This was the first meal they had had in peace in four days.

They met some people whom they knew from Kampala. One couple came over to talk to them. They introduced themselves as Alnoor and Rozmin Daya from Masaka, a small town in Uganda.

The wife asked Aziza what happened to her neck.

"Oh, it was one of those unfortunate accidents as we prepared to leave. I'm going to see a doctor today," Aziza replied.

"We've been here for two weeks. Manpower found Rozmin a job with Sears, not far from here. She starts Monday. I only have my Cambridge certificate. Manpower said that they are looking for something clerical or a factory job for me. There are some Tanzanians here who are educated, but who were desperate for money and have taken up factory jobs. Poor guys, they have come here as Independent Applicants, and so they don't get free accommodation and allowances as we do. One is looking for a factory job for me. As soon as I find a job, we'll move out of here," Alnoor said.

As they emerged from the breakfast room, Morris called Zul over and said in a quiet tone, "I presume you have no warm clothing. It's sunny outside, but it's chilly. The church down the road has collected and donated used clothing and coats for you guys. See me in an hour if you want any. They've all been dry cleaned."

MORRIS HELPED ZUL AND Aziza select coats. Aziza found a nice winter coat and also a lighter jacket that she could wear in autumn weather. Zul could only find a loose-fitting winter coat that had seen better days. The choice for the children's clothing was wider.

Aziza's neck was still hurting, so they decided to stay in and rest for the day. They met more Ugandans, some of whom they knew, and others they did not.

When they came down the next morning, ready to go out and dressed in their warm clothing, they met an Ismaili family in the lobby who introduced themselves as Shirin and Faizal Rajan. They had three kids with them. Shirin said that she knew Aziza from Kampala and knew that she ran a hair salon. "I didn't come to you because you were too expensive for me," she said, laughing.

"Where are you headed?" Faizal asked.

"We're going to the Manpower office to register," Aziza replied.

Shirin said, "You don't need to take the children there. You'll have to fill up forms and discuss with employment counselors your education and experience and what kind of work you're looking for. It's inconvenient to have children with you. I'm staying in the hotel with our children. Two are about the same age as yours. You can leave them with me if you like."

"Oh, that's very kind of you, but we don't want to trouble you," Zul said.

"It's no trouble at all. I'm heading out for my work, but Shirin's going to be here all day. We have some bread and cheese and a can of soup in the room. She will make sandwiches for lunch for the children," said Faizal.

Zul and Aziza looked at each other. Looking at Nisha and Nahid, Aziza asked, "Would you like to stay here with this nice aunty and her children while Dad and I go get some work done?"

Neither replied, but when Shirin gently pulled them over, they went to her willingly.

"I don't know how to thank you, Shirin," Aziza said.

"No need to thank me. I may have to leave my kids with you tomorrow!"

AS THEY STEPPED OUT of the hotel, Zul said, "Do you realize that we just left our children with people we've never met before?"

"Yes, we did. And they'll be fine," Aziza replied.

THEY FILLED OUT THE forms at the Manpower office and were each given a number when they handed them in. Zul's number got called first. The counselor reviewed his form, made small talk about how bad what was happening in Uganda was and said, "You want a sales job. We can try and place you with a department store or other retail business where you can serve people from behind a counter. It doesn't pay much, and that's not your area of expertise. You were in a commission job, and that's where you can do well if you work hard."

"I'm not afraid of hard work, Sir. What kinds of commission sales jobs are available?" Zul asked.

"Oh, you can sell anything from encyclopaedias and vacuum cleaners door to door, to houses and cars for commission. But it takes time to build experience and make good money. The companies will take you on because they pay only when you sell, which is hard work."

"I need to get a job where it doesn't matter if I earn little, but I want to be employed as soon as I can be. Can you find me something quickly?"

"I can't find you something quickly. It usually takes time, but what's the matter with you people? All of you coming here from Uganda want a job today. We're paying for your accommodation and giving you a living allowance. You're not out on the street. I can understand your Tanzanian cousins who don't get what we're giving you. They can't wait, but why can't you wait until we can find you something good?" the counselor asked. He seemed very irritated.

Zul took a deep breath and said, "See, Sir, back home where we come from, the poor in our community were cared for by our community's welfare program. Some were given accommodation and all received a living allowance to feed and clothe themselves. We felt sorry for most of them and we also donated money to the program, but there were some able-bodied freeloaders whom we despised. They didn't work and collected welfare. I'm able-bodied, and I feel like I will be a free-loader collecting your welfare if I don't start working quickly. I'm sure that's how my fellow Ugandans feel. That's why they all want a job today."

"For God's sake, you arrived here the day before yesterday and have been a *free-loader* for only two days! You people should learn to be a little patient. I'll see what I can find you. We'll call you."

"Thank you, Sir."

"You don't have to call me Sir. Do you have any other suits, other than what you are wearing?"

"No. Anything wrong with what I am wearing?"

"Your jacket lapels and shirt collar are too narrow. They went out of style years ago."

"I'm sorry all of my suits and shirts are in this style."

"Okay. Let me see what we can do for you. And don't wear your winter coat when you go for any interviews."

When Zul went back into the waiting room, Aziza was not there. She emerged 15 minutes later and asked, "How did it go?"

"Badly. He got upset that I want to start working immediately and said that my lapels are too narrow and my coat is shabby. He said he'll look for something. How did it go for you?"

"It went well. She was of British origin and recognized the school I attended in England and arranged two interviews for me. First is with a salon far up north on Yonge Street at 2.00 p.m. We have to take the subway to Eglinton station and then take a bus to Sheppard Avenue and walk over to the salon. The second is with a salon on Danforth Avenue at 4.30 p.m. We have to take the subway to a Pape station and walk from there. She gave me the transit map, addresses and directions, and who to ask for."

"That's wonderful. That also gives us time to see the doctor."

They asked for directions and made their way to the doctor's office that Susan had recommended.

Dr. Henthorn looked at Aziza's wound and said that it was healing well. He cleaned the wound and applied a fresh bandage and asked that she come back in five days to have the stitches removed. He also said that they should register with the Ontario Health Insurance Plan before coming back.

THEY REACHED THE SALON on Yonge Street around 1.50 p.m. They walked around for a few minutes, and then Aziza went in. Zul waited outside. It was chilly, and he hopped from one foot to the other to keep warm.

She emerged in less than ten minutes. "Did you get the job?" He asked.

"The owner, whose name I was given, was eating lunch in the back of the salon when I went in. She took one look at me and asked one of the girls working there to talk to me. This young girl asked me a couple of questions - nothing about my training or work experience, and said they will call me if they are interested. Can you imagine, they brought me all the way here to look at my face and throw me out?"

"Don't worry. You still have your second interview. It's on the subway line, and that could be better for us."

The moment she sat down with the owner at the Danforth salon, Aziza knew that she was not going to get the job. She still kept smiling and told the lady that she had trained at a prestigious school in London, had worked there for six months, and had owned and operated a salon in Uganda for five years.

"Thank you for coming in, but you don't have any Canadian experience. We're interviewing other candidates and will call you if we are interested in you," she said.

"I see that Canadian women have the same hair as the British women, so what

Canadian experience are you talking about? The women here are getting their hair done in styles that I'm an expert on. You may do well to tell Canada Manpower to not send you coloured people. You dragged me out all the way here to tell me you don't like the color of my skin," Aziza replied in a loud enough voice for everyone in the busy salon to hear, and walked out.

Zul, who was waiting around the corner, came over to her. He saw that she had tears in her eyes, her face was red, and she had her hand over her bandage. "What happened, Aziza?" he asked.

"My wound is throbbing. Let's go to that coffee shop and sit down," Aziza said, pointing to the cafe across the road.

"What happened? Did you get hurt in the neck?"

"She was throwing me out the way they did on Yonge Street, but I gave her a piece of my mind," she said and told Zul what had happened.

"That's too bad, but we shouldn't do that, Aziza. We should not say such things to people two days after coming here. She'll report you to Manpower, and that's not good. There is her kind, and then there are people like Susan who welcomed us at the airport. We have to believe that there are more like Susan than the two racists you've encountered today."

WHEN THEY ATTENDED THE "Jamatkhana" that weekend, Zul got introduced to a gentleman, Noordin Merali, from Tanzania. He had been in Canada for 10 months. He had worked as an insurance salesman with Jubilee Insurance Company in Tanzania and was working as a commission agent with Sun Life Insurance Company. After listening to Zul's background, he offered to get him a sales position with Sun Life.

"I'll try and get you a training allowance of $100 a week for three months. If you make any sales and earn commissions, it will be on top of your allowance. You can do well, if you work hard. Training will be provided to you and I will guide you. I've recruited two other Ismailis, and they're doing well," said Noordin.

AFTER DISCUSSING IT WITH Aziza, Zul started working with Noordin at Sun Life's North York branch. In three weeks, he made his first sale to a Hungarian couple and earned $162 in commission. From there, Zul went on to become one of Sun Life's most successful and respected salesmen. Insurance sales to the growing number of Ismailis in Ontario, who had always been very insurance conscious, helped, but he always sought to maintain at least 50% non-Ismaili clientele.

Aziza, after three more unsuccessful interviews, got a job with a salon owned by a Greek woman, Celina Papadapolous, in the Thorncliffe Shopping Centre in East York, a short distance from 25 St. Dennis Drive in Don Mills, where they were now renting a two-bedroom apartment.

The owner looked at Aziza like any other woman walking through her door. She was professional in interviewing her, offered her $100 a week, and said that she could start right away as a customer was waiting for a wash and cut.

When Aziza finished, the customer gave her a hefty $3 tip and asked Celina always to assign her this pretty woman. Looking at the professional job that Aziza had done and the speed with which she had worked, Celina knew that she had hit a bonanza with this Ugandan refugee.

1972
Seventy-Five

A week after Idi Amin issued the expulsion order, Abdul and Zeenat Lakhani were riding with their son Bahadur, and daughter-in-law, Shamira, to the fast emptying supermarket in Kampala to get whatever groceries they could find. They had left their 12-year old daughter Shelina with their neighbors.

Bahadur, who was driving the car, after checking for traffic in all directions at a stop sign, slowly entered the intersection. A fast-approaching motorcycle from his left swerved to avoid hitting his car. The rider, a Ugandan soldier, parked his bike and approached Bahadur with a drawn gun.

"Why did you try to kill me?" he shouted at Bahadur.

"I am very sorry, Captain. As you can see, there is this truck parked near the intersection, and I couldn't see if anything was approaching from your direction. That is why I entered the intersection very slowly. I had no intention to hurt you or anyone else," Bahadur pleaded.

The soldier pressed his gun against Bahadur's head. His parents and Shamira were terrified and prayed, but expected to hear the gunshot any second.

"You bloody *Wahindis* (Indians) think you can kill us all? We're going to kill you, every one of you. Get out of the car!" the soldier shouted.

Bahadur stepped out. One of the dozens of army vehicles running aimlessly around the city all day passed by and stopped. A senior-looking officer approached them and asked, "What's the matter?"

"This bloody Muhindi tried to kill me with his car," the soldier replied, hitting Bahadur hard on his head with his gun handle. Bahadur fell to the ground.

"You go, I will deal with this," the officer ordered the soldier.

The soldier walked away, uttering a string of expletives. The officer had robbed him of his opportunity to terrorize and rob these people.

"What happened?" the officer asked Bahadur, who was dizzy but stood up.

Bahadur explained what had happened, while his mother and father pleaded.

"You stay in the car," the officer shouted at Abdul, seeing that he was reaching for his wallet and wanted to get out of the car. "How much money do you have?" he asked.

"I have Shs.105, but you can take my watch and my son's watch," Abdul said.

"Take off your watches and all the rings you are wearing," he ordered.

The ladies immediately took off their engagement rings and wedding bands and handed them to Abdul with their watches to pass on to the officer. Abdul and Bahadur took their watches and wedding bands off and gave everything to him.

The officer pocketed the loot and said, "Go now!"

THE FAMILY, WHO WERE all Ugandan citizens and had planned to stay on in Uganda, drove straight to the Canadian High Commission, instead of driving to the supermarket and stood in line to get the Canadian residency application forms. The High Commission offices were closed, but the people who had lined up said that they were planning to stand in line all night until the next morning when the offices reopened.

The nightlong wait was tough. People sat down on the pavement and to maintain their place in the queue, took turns going to the washroom in the apartment of one Ismaili family in the area. Out of consideration for the people lining up, the Embassy opened an hour earlier. It had also set up booths where the people could get their medical examinations done, while they waited in line.

THE LAKHANI FAMILY'S VISAS came through in less than ten days. They packed and headed for the airport the next day in their late-model Datsun 1600. They took no jewellery and only Shs.200 in cash. The soldiers stopped them, searched their baggage and allowed them to keep the Shs.200, but took the car from them. One soldier drove them to the airport in their car. Bahadur profusely thanked him for the ride and said he hoped the soldier would enjoy the car and showed him where the Owner's Manual and car's service records were, hoping that the soldier would accompany them into the airport to help them clear Customs. The soldier offered to do no such thing and ordered everyone to get out and drove off.

The Customs searches were rough. The women, including Shelina, were strip-searched. The woman conducting the female searches was very abusive and angry that there was nothing left for her to rob.

AFTER ALMOST A 15-HOUR flight, they arrived in Montreal around noon the next day. They received a warm welcome from the immigration officials but were taken by bus to an army barrack. The sight of soldiers in uniform was unsettling for the refugees. The army officer, seeing the fear in their eyes, gathered the refugees around and said, "Please don't be afraid of the soldiers. They are here to help, not to hurt you. We will look after you and help you get to your destinations. Canada Manpower staff will come later this afternoon to sit with each one of you and tell you where you are designated to go. If you have another preference, like you want to go to Kitchener instead of Hamilton in Ontario where you are designated to go, and if you have a good reason for going to Kitchener, they will consider your request. Please understand that we want you to settle quickly and will work with you to make that happen."

"When will we leave here?" one refugee asked.

"We recognize that you have had a long journey and have had harrowing experiences. We want you to rest here for two days while we process you, and then we'll send you to your destinations," the officer replied.

"Can you imagine? This army officer is here to care for and help us?" another refugee whispered.

The Lakhani family was led to their area to place their baggage. They then proceeded to the mess hall for a hot meal.

The Canada Manpower personnel appeared at 2.30 p.m. and started to process the refugees alphabetically. Each family was given a $25 allowance and warm clothing. The Lakhanis got their turn after 6.00 p.m. They were told that they were designated to go to Winnipeg. Shamira said that she had a sister in Toronto who had offered them accommodation and assistance in settling.

"You understand that if you go to Toronto, you will receive the $25 allowance, but no accommodation. You'll be on your own. Do you all understand this?" the officer asked.

"Yes, we understand," each confirmed as the officer looked at them individually.

Two days later, they were on a train to Toronto. The train ride was pleasant. They watched the foliage in its autumn splendor and enjoyed the views of Lake Ontario and a nice lunch for which they had been given coupons.

Canada Manpower had notified Shamira's sister, Mumtaz, of their arrival time, and she was there to receive them.

Mumtaz and her husband, Zahir, who also lived in the 25 St. Dennis Drive complex, helped Shelina get enrolled at an elementary school, almost directly opposite the building, and helped the adult Lakhanis register with Canada Manpower, employment agencies, and other businesses for employment.

Shamira got three job offers for secretarial positions three days later. She took the job with a firm in downtown Toronto at $80 a week. Canada Manpower found a job for Abdul at a plastics manufacturing factory and a clerical position for Zeenat. Now that his parents and wife were all employed and earning incomes, Bahadur could rent a two-bedroom apartment in 25 St. Dennis Drive. The building now had over a dozen Ugandan Ismaili families, and more were being brought in by those who were already there.

Given his keen eye for detecting defects in manufactured products, Abdul got promoted to Quality Controller position, and Shamira moved on to a better job at the Bank of Montreal for $90 a week, but Bahadur's job search was challenging. There were few jobs for a soil engineer with no Canadian Experience. It took him six months to get placed, but once he did, he quickly advanced in his position. Two years later, his parents moved to Vancouver, and Shamira and Bahadur bought a new townhouse in the east end of Toronto. After much struggle, the family was settled happily.

1972
Seventy-Six

Rafiq and Shameem arrived in Toronto on October 15th and put up at the same downtown hotel where Rafiq's parents, Tazim, and Almas had stayed. Rafiq had provided Almas' apartment address to the shipping company for contact. A letter had come from the company advising that his container would arrive on October 18th, and must be cleared within five days, after which storage charges would apply. He quickly looked up the movers in Toronto and arranged with one to clear the container, bring it to the apartment building, and set everything up.

By October 20th, the apartment was all set up, and they moved in. As it was a Friday, Rafiq and Shameem attended a new School Hall Jamatkhana. The congregation had grown by around 700 Ugandans and 200 Tanzanians to over 1,200 in the month since Salim, Yasmin, Almas, and Tazim had first attended the "Eglinton Jamatkhana". The gym at the Broadway school was no longer adequate. The Jamatkhana had been relocated to another school on Coxwell Avenue in the east, south of Danforth Avenue, which had a much larger gym. The new School Hall Jamatkhana was called the "Coxwell Jamatkhana".

The Jamatkhana atmosphere had changed. The Ugandans, many of whom had just arrived, were telling one another which hotel they had been put up at and exchanging phone numbers, inquiring if their family or friends were on the flight they had come on and if they had found jobs. There was anxiety on their faces. Rafiq and Shameem talked to many people, some of whom Rafiq knew from Tanzania, some who Shameem knew from Kenya, and many Ugandans they just approached and introduced themselves to. Most were professionals, looking for jobs. A few had found work and were getting settled; others were still looking.

Shameem got introduced to Aziza. The bandage and stitches on her neck had come off, but the scar was very visible.

After exchanging pleasantries, Shameem asked, "What happened to your neck?"

Aziza looked at her, wondering what she should tell her. Seeing her hesitation, Shameem added, "I ask because I am a medical doctor."

"On the way to the airport in Kampala, our bus was robbed by two soldiers. One yanked off the chain and pendant I was wearing and cut my neck."

"Oh, my God! That must have been horrible. It looks like this was stitched up well. Was the wound deep?"

"Yes, but I got good care in Nairobi. A doctor from our Platinum Jubilee Hospital came to the airport and stitched me up. She did a good job."

"It may leave a mark, though."

After they chatted a little more and Aziza had told her that both she and her husband had found jobs and were settling in their new apartment, Shameem said, "Aziza, I would like you and your family to come over to our place for dinner tomorrow. Can you do that?"

"That's so kind of you, Shameem, but why do you want to trouble yourself? We can meet for coffee sometime," said Aziza.

"It will be our pleasure to know you and your family. It won't be anything formal. Please come. Do you have a car?"

"We have placed an order for one. We'll get it in two weeks."

"Okay, I don't want you to travel by bus and subway with your children. We have a car. My husband and I will come and pick you up from your place and then drop you back."

"Let me talk to my husband," Aziza said and called Zul over.

Shameem called Rafiq, and all were introduced. "This kind lady, Shameem, is inviting the kids and us for dinner tomorrow at her apartment," Aziza said to Zul.

"That's very kind of you, Shameem. We'll be delighted to come. What time would you like us to come, and where?" Zul asked.

Aziza was surprised by Zul's immediate acceptance. Is it because this lady is so gorgeous? She wondered.

"Shameem says they will come and pick us up and bring us back. They have a car," said Aziza.

"Of course, we will," said Rafiq. "Shama and I have just come to Toronto. We're a new Jamat, and we have to get to know one another. My parents will love to have the kids over."

"Shama? Is that your name, Shameem? Do you know what Shama means in Hindi?" Aziza asked.

"My family and friends call me Shama, and you should also call me Shama. And yes, Rafiq told me what Shama means when we first met and asked me if I would be his Shama."

Looking at Zul and Aziza's kids, Shameem said, "We need to make it early for the children. Shall we pick you up at 6.00 p.m.?"

"That will be lovely, thank you. We'll wait for you in the reception area at six," said Aziza.

HAVING BEEN BUSY SETTING up the apartment all day, Yasmin had not had the time to cook, and they had not eaten dinner, so they went to a Greek restaurant on Danforth Avenue with Almas and Tazim. As they sat down to eat, Salim asked Rafiq and Shameem what they thought of the congregation and their impressions of how the newcomers were settling.

"I saw much optimism among the young Tanzanian professionals," said Shameem. "They appear to see a bright future for themselves in Canada. Many think that they can get work experience here and rise to levels they could have never dreamt of back home. Unfortunately, it seems that the middle-age people who were well established in their professions and enjoyed a level of seniority in Tanzania are having much difficulty getting placed in the role and at the level at which they are equipped, and want to, perform. Some accountants and engineers have found jobs in their fields, but at much lower levels, where they are reporting to 25-year old junior managers."

"The guys I talked to all said that they're having difficulty finding employment," added Rafiq. "In desperation, some are showing lower level education and experience on their resumes, just to get placed. One guy told me he is a B.Ed. Graduate from a U.K. university and a teacher by profession, but he has taken up a job managing a newspaper route that involves overseeing a handful of kids who deliver papers each morning. He likes working with the kids, but he misses teaching and the money that goes with it. His wife is employed. Luckily, he finishes most of his work by 2.00 p.m. and is continuing to look for a teaching job, but he's not having much luck. I heard that the people who have come here in the Business category are having a difficult time getting established in businesses and that they're getting desperate because they're eating up their capital. They might buy bad businesses and lose everything."

"What was your impression of the Ugandans?" asked Salim.

"Many are happy to be here, even though they've lost everything. They're confident they'll do very well here. They're getting government support, so they're not under pressure to find jobs like the Tanzanians are. They don't need to go and work in parking lots. Some Ugandans seem to think that the British will overthrow Amin, and they'll go back to Uganda. This is not happening. If the British had wanted to act, they would have done so by now. Amin's army is not their "kith and kin," but neither are the 50,000 Indian British subjects. The British are not going to put their soldiers in harm's way for the Indians," Rafiq replied.

"I invited a couple from Uganda and their two little children over for dinner tomorrow," said Shameem. "I hope that's alright. Tazim, I hope that you and Mom can come. We can cook the fish that I brought from Kensington Market yesterday and make some chicken for the children."

"I'm delighted that you did that, Shama," said Yasmin. "As I was talking to the Ugandans, I was thinking of reaching out to them in some way, but who do you reach out to? And how? There are so many. I'm pleased that you invited this couple."

Looking at Rafiq and Shameem, Salim said, "It is very kind of you to have invited them over, but I think that we need to look at the issue from a broader lens. You are looking at the Jamat here through your prism of prosperity and comfort. Your privileged backgrounds shape your perception. Your parents had the money to send you to the U.K. to study. When you were married, you had a nice house in which to live, a fancy car, and the opportunity to vacation in Europe and overseas. Money, even after the exchange control, was never a problem for you. This, as you are starting to see, is not the experience of the majority of our Ismaili brothers and sisters from Tanzania and Uganda. Some have come here with less than $200 in their pockets. There was no Carole to meet them at the airport and help them buy furniture. They have rented apartments in the suburbs that cost half of what we are paying downtown. You have come here with jobs waiting for you."

"That's true, Dad. We're blessed, but what are you saying?" Rafiq asked.

"What I am saying is that your circumstances are partly the result of the education and work experience you got in the U.K., but primarily the result of our families' good luck. If there was no Kongwa disaster and no John's General, if there was no D.C. to give us Almin and there was no Zambian oil lift, we could not have offered you anything more to come to Canada with than what most of the other Tanzanians and Ugandans have. Their experience is not your experience. They are struggling. What we suffered in Tanzania getting out was a picnic compared to what the Ugandans have gone through."

"Are you suggesting that we do something for the Ugandans, Dad? What can we do? The Ugandans are getting help from the government," said Shameem.

"Certainly the first thing that we should do is what you did tonight, simply reach out to people. Comfort them. Let them know there is someone who cares for them, someone they can lean on. I am proud of you, Shama, for what you did tonight, just days after arriving here when we are not fully set up in our apartment. But we should also try and understand the pain and anxiety of the 45-year-old C.A. who has come here from Dar es Salaam where he may have been the Chief Accountant for Cooper Motors, who will not have the money to pay rent on his apartment in two weeks unless he finds a job – any job – immediately. We should try and understand the frustration of the teacher who is managing the paper route. I do not doubt that sooner rather than later, professionals in our Jamat will find good jobs, and once they do, they will quickly climb the corporate ladders. They will be recognized and respected for their intelligence, enterprise, honesty, and loyalty. But right now, they need help. We are blessed, and we should help"

"But how?" Rafiq asked.

"In the four weeks we have been attending Jamatkhana here, we have not met any professional who has taken more than three months to find a job, but not all have found good jobs. We can help. Offer your support to the group of professionals who are helping others find jobs. We know of professionals who graduated from a university, and all they had to present was their degree certificate to get hired in Tanzania, Kenya, or Uganda. They never prepared C.V.s or resumes. They can list their education and work experience, but they don't know how to prepare a sleek resume that will land them an interview. You can help. You can look for job opportunities in your workplaces and refer them. Rafiq, you can help people evaluate business propositions."

"We can help the professionals, Dad, but people who have come here in Business category are looking for retail and service businesses. I know nothing about ratios in these businesses or the economics of retail trade in Canada. I'm not equipped to advise people on businesses."

"You know how to read – and read between the lines of - a balance sheet and an income statement. You can guide people on asking the right questions. You can prepare business plans for people to take to the bank so that they can get their loans approved. You can go with people to look at and meet with the owners of the businesses that they want to buy, to assess if the business is properly priced, study the leases, and see if there is security in tenancy."

"And when should I do all of this, Dad? I have my job and responsibilities!" exclaimed Rafiq.

"You have the evenings and weekends. You don't work on Saturdays. And Shama, you can also help people prepare resumes and find them jobs in your hospital. Build a circle of people to help the newcomers find jobs and feel supported."

"Seems like we'll have a lot of work to do, in addition to establishing ourselves in Canada, Dad," Shameem said.

Yasmin replied, "Dad's right. Compare yourselves to the people you met in Jamatkhana. You are established. You've got a beautiful apartment, all setup. You've got good jobs. You have a nice car. What more do you need? If we're equipped to help, it's our moral and religious obligation to help our fellow Ismailis. Since coming here, Dad and I loaned $600 to two couples who had found jobs but were going to run out of money before their first paycheques came in. They have paid back $450. I told them they did not have to pay us back, but they insisted that we take the money. It's easy to dish out money to calm your conscience, but what Dad is asking you to do is to be generous with your time and your knowledge. It's hard work, but it's noble work. It's what our Imam teaches us to do."

"We'll let people know next Friday that we're available to help," Shameem said resolutely.

1972
Seventy-Seven

Salim and Yasmin welcomed Aziza and Zul at the door, and each picked up one child when they arrived.

"We're so happy that you could come. Please come in," said Yasmin.

Rafiq introduced Almas and his parents to Zul and Aziza and putting his arm around Tazim's shoulders, said, "And this is my little sister, Tazim."

That's his problem, Tazim thought. He still sees me as the little sister he has to protect.

"You have a beautiful home," said Aziza, taking in the apartment. "Where did you get all of this furniture from?"

"We brought it with us from the U.K.," Shameem said, somewhat sheepishly, particularly as the conversation from the night before replayed in her mind.

Rafiq offered everyone drinks. Salim and Yasmin sat on the sofa with Nisha and Nahid between them. They started to chat with the kids and did not pay much attention to what the two couples were talking about. As Rafiq had thought, they were delighted to have the children visit, and the children seemed to like them.

Aziza told them about her job search experience and her new role. She offered to do Shameem and Yasmin's hair for free. Shameem said that she would take her up on her offer.

Zul told them about his meeting with the Manpower counselor and his advice about what to wear, which he was following. He had bought a new winter coat. Aziza and the kids were still wearing the coats donated by the church.

He talked about his work and the training he was getting and how happy they were to have moved into their own place. They had bought some furniture from a place called Bad Boy, which they were pleased with. They were still looking for a T.V. He needed a car for his work and had placed an order with an Ismaili salesman to buy a Chevy Impala with automatic transmission, power steering, and power brakes. He seemed very excited about the car.

He was happy to be in an insurance sales job. It was challenging, but he was enjoying it. After dropping Aziza at work and the children at school, he went to the office for training from 9.00 a.m. to 10.30 a.m. and operated out of the office until lunchtime, when he brought the kids home from school. He spent the afternoon working from home, prospecting for clients, and making appointments to see them in the evening.

"It's working out well. We don't need to send the kids any place to be cared for while we are working, although there are some older Ismaili ladies in our apartment building who are babysitting," said Aziza.

"Why are all of the Ugandans in this St. Dennis building?" Rafiq asked.

"There is a young Ismaili couple from Uganda that has been living there since 1971. They helped some Ugandans, who had not yet found jobs, to lease apartments by vouching for them, and as these new tenants went in, they brought more of us. For us, it's worked out very well. My work is less than a 10-minute drive, and Zul can walk to his work. The supermarket is a five-minute walk, and the kids' school is right opposite our building. In fact, that's where the new School Hall Jamatkhana is to open the next couple of weeks, because there are so many of us now in Don Mills," Aziza replied.

The conversation flowed comfortably, and Aziza and Zul felt very much at home. They enjoyed the masala (spicy) fish and potatoes. For the children, Shameem had made Shake 'n Bake chicken and French fries. She had also ordered pizza.

"That's pizza, honey," Aziza said to Nisha.

"It's okay!" Nisha replied, taking another bite.

"You have delightful children. Any evening you want to go out, leave them with us," said Yasmin.

"We'll take you up on your offer, aunty," Aziza replied.

"My parents adore children," said Rafiq.

"Well, I hope they will soon have grandkids to play with," Aziza said.

"Inshallah," Yasmin and Salim said in unison.

"The company you work with - Sun Life, is it a good company?" Rafiq asked Zul.

"It's the largest and best of the Canadian insurance companies," Zul replied.

"Let's plan to meet next week. We need insurance for us all. Shama and I have insurance with a U.K. company, but we need more. Can you put together a proposal?"

"What do I need insurance for, Rafiq?" asked Tazim. "I have no dependents."

"You will, one day, and the sooner we buy it, the less it will cost you each year for the rest of your life."

"Rafiq, if I write you all up, I will fill my two months' quota!" exclaimed Zul.

THEY SAT LATE INTO the night chatting. The children had fallen asleep with their heads on Yasmin and Salim's laps.

"This has been a most wonderful evening, Shama. This is the first time we have felt truly relaxed in almost three months. Thank you all for inviting us. It's so generous of you to invite people you just met into your home and be so kind to them. We'll never forget your kindness."

"Don't thank us. We are all brothers and sisters. And we had a selfish motive in inviting you. We, too, had a wonderful evening chatting with you. Inshallah, we'll get together again soon," said Rafiq.

"At our place ... as soon as our dining table and chairs get delivered!" Zul said.

1972
Seventy-Eight

Almost immediately after spreading the word that they were available to assist, Shameem and Rafiq started receiving calls for assistance. Free advice from an investment banker and a medical doctor was not something people were going to pass up.

Shameem met with the H.R. manager in her hospital and familiarized her with the situation of Ismailis from Tanzania and Uganda and the kinds of jobs they were seeking. The manager was sympathetic and asked Shameem to check with her weekly for the positions the hospital was looking to fill. She had also connected Shameem with two H.R. managers of other major hospitals in Toronto. In two months, Shameem had helped place two young women in secretarial positions, one in her hospital and one at another hospital, and secured an interview for an accounting position for a woman with the equivalent of two years of a recognized accounting program (CGA) at her hospital.

Additionally, she was meeting with several women with university education to help them prepare their resumes. In the process, she was making some good friends. She had started to look forward to getting the calls.

Rafiq had been meeting with people to look at the financial statements of the businesses they wanted to buy. Most could not wait until the weekend; they were scared (unnecessarily, in most cases) that the businesses would get sold, so Rafiq ended up inviting them over in the evenings on weekdays.

He looked at the stated earnings, ratios, and asking prices and either decided to visit the businesses with the prospective buyers or discouraged them from pursuing them. His manager had obtained for him Dun and Bradstreet's "Ratios in Retail Business" publication, which he found of immense value in helping the Ismailis. In the process, he was learning a great deal about small businesses and was able to advise his father, as well.

TWO WEEKS AFTER RAFIQ and Shameem arrived, Yasmin received a call from an employment agency with which she had registered, asking her to come in. The agency was working for James Street Credit Union, located at Yonge at Queen Street, which was looking to hire a couple of tellers. She attended for an interview and was offered the position to start immediately at $100 per week, after one week's unpaid training.

By early December, all in the household, except Salim, were gainfully employed. He had looked at several dry cleaning, gas station, hardware, fast food, and grocery businesses. He had found three interesting, but Rafiq had not approved of any of these. Salim was getting frustrated sitting at home, and also with Rafiq's rejection of all of his business proposals.

One day, as he was scouring business ads in the Toronto Star, an ad in the Help Wanted section for a Hardware Store Manager caught his eye. He remembered the Ismaili telling him on the first evening they had attended Jamatkhana that if he wanted to be in business, he should go work as a store manager to gain experience.

On a whim, he called the number. An old-sounding man answered, and after discussing Salim's background and experience, the man asked if he could go for an interview at 2.00 p.m. The store was located on Yonge Street, north of Lawrence Avenue, and was called Mark's Hardware.

When he got there, he saw one guy helping customers and two young women working at the checkout counters. The store was large and busy, and well-stocked. He was directed to a back office where he met the owner, Mr. Mark Goldman. Mr. Goldman was a short man with round glasses who looked like he was in his late 60s. He asked Salim to take a seat and started chatting.

Before asking Salim anything material, he told Salim all about his youth, how he had saved up money working at different places and how he and his dear wife had started a small men's wear store on Queen Street West and made some money to buy this store. When they first started, it was half of what it was now. He had expanded by renting the adjacent premises and tearing down the dividing wall. He told Salim all about his three children, how well they had done in university, and the senior positions they occupied within the government and with large corporations.

Salim found the old man interesting and asked him more about him and his family. Over an hour passed, and the old man had not asked Salim anything, so he said, "Mr. Goldman, should I tell you something about my background?"

"No, you told me everything that I need to know about you on the phone. I want you to come and meet my wife tomorrow at 10.00 a.m. She drops me off here at that time. Can you do that?"

"Yes, I can," said Salim.

"Okay, we'll see you tomorrow. Do you want some tea before you go? I'm going to have some."

"Tea would be good."

Over tea, Mr. Goldman told him how he had met his wife, Johanna, how he had courted and married her, the places they had traveled together, and how they had named their children.

"I WENT FOR A job interview today," Salim announced as they sat down to have dinner that evening.

"What?" Yasmin asked as Rafiq and Shameem looked up in surprise.

"What job interview, Dad?" Rafiq asked.

"Well, I saw this ad in the paper for a hardware store manager. I called, and the owner asked me to come in for an interview."

"But, Dad, you don't even have a resume! You've never talked about working for someone," Rafiq said, looking perplexed.

"Well, I thought it would be useful to get experience as a store manager before we buy a business for me to run."

"But Dad, you can't apply for jobs like this. You have to prepare yourself to make job applications and present yourself. What did they ask, and what did you tell them?"

"Nothing, really. The owner is an older man, and he spent over an hour talking to me. He told me his whole life history but didn't ask me anything. When I asked if he wanted me to tell him something about myself, he said that he didn't need to know anything more than what I had told him on the phone."

"And what had you told him on the phone?"

"Just that I'm here from Tanzania. He had not heard of Tanzania and asked me if I meant Tasmania, and I said, 'No, Tanzania is in East Africa.' I told him my age and the businesses I had run back home, and that's about all."

"So, did he offer you a job, or did he say that you don't have Canadian experience?"

"No, he asked me to go meet his wife tomorrow at 10.00 a.m."

"I hope the old man wasn't just lonely and looking to chat with someone. Why does he want you to meet his wife?"

"I don't know. Maybe she's the decision-maker."

JOHANNA WAS THE DECISION-MAKER. There was no idle chitchat with her. She was all business. She was there when he arrived at 10.00 a.m., greeted him, and said, "So you're interested in the store manager position?"

"Yes, Madam, I am. I believe that I'm well qualified for the position."

"And what qualifies you? You have no Canadian experience."

"I had a hardware division in my store in Tanzania, and I know how to deal with customers, manage inventory and staff, and keep books."

"Was your hardware division as large as this store? How many items did you carry?"

Salim rattled off a list of the standard hardware items that they had sold in their store.

"We carry over 100 types of items in this store. You have to know what people want when they ask for it. We small businesses compete with large automotive and hardware stores by providing personalized service, attention, and advice to our customers. I'm sorry my husband wasted your time asking you to come here this morning, but I don't think that you have the knowledge and skills for this job," said Johanna.

"But I can learn," said Salim. "Let me come and work here for two months with Mr. Goldman and that gentleman who is serving the customers, without pay, and you can assess me in two months."

"We don't have two months. I'm looking for a store manager because my husband is now 70 years old and I want him to retire. I want him to enjoy life. We want to travel starting next spring."

"Well, you have my offer, Mrs. Goldman. If you take me on, you will not be disappointed. I am an honest and responsible person. I will care for your business the way Mr. Goldman does, and I can't think of anything I can't learn in two months."

"Well enough. We have other applicants we are meeting today. We'll call you if we want to talk more. Did my husband tell you what this job pays?"

"No, he didn't."

"You don't know what the job pays, and you want to work here?"

"This will be my first job, and whatever you pay, I will consider it a training allowance. I enjoyed talking to Mr. Goldman yesterday and would be very happy if I could have someone like him as my employer and trainer."

"Okay, I'll call you if we're interested in you."

AFTER SALIM LEFT, JOHANNA said to Mark, "That was not fair. You shouldn't have asked that poor man to come back."

"But I liked him. Ours is a cash business. I feel that we can trust him. He's smart and personable and, yes, if he is to do my work, he has to know what to order and at what price and how to manage the staff and deal with the customers' complaints, but I will still be here full time until March of next year. I can train him, and he's offering to work for nothing for two months. Added help at Christmastime will be useful."

"I'm not interested in free labor, Mark! Why would you hire him if you can hire someone qualified for the job? A guy is coming in at noon, who has worked with Canadian Tire for five years. Why would we not hire him?"

"Johanna, sometimes you meet a person, and you instinctively know he or she is a good person. That's how I felt about this guy."

"Well, I don't trust your instincts."

That evening, Salim related to his family his morning's experience.

"Dad, you shouldn't do this. You've not come here to work for free. We'll find you a good business. Let's keep looking," said Rafiq.

A WEEK WENT BY, and neither Mr. nor Mrs. Goldman had called. Salim didn't expect them to, but then, early on Sunday morning, the phone rang, and a woman asked for Salim. Shameem gave the phone to him. It was Johanna.

"Can you come and see us in an hour? That is if you're still interested in the job. We have a proposition for you," she said.

"Sure, I'm still interested, and I will be there in an hour," he replied.

"The store is closed. Ring the doorbell," Johanna said and hung up.

"They want to see me in an hour. I need to shower and shave."

"There's no time for a shower, Dad. Just shave and let me drive you there," said Rafiq.

AS THEY DROVE, RAFIQ asked, "Do you have any idea what they will propose to you?"

"No. Let's see what they say. You don't need to wait for me. I'll take the subway home."

"No, I'll park outside and wait for you."

"THANK YOU FOR COMING, Salim. We've finished interviewing people, and we have several well-qualified applicants, but for reasons best known to my husband, he's interested in hiring you. If you're still interested, you can start tomorrow and work until the end of January next year. We will pay you $100 a week as a training allowance, and if we keep you on, we will pay you $200 a week, starting February," said Johanna.

"I'll be happy with that," Salim said with a smile.

"Are you sure about this? This is very important for us. We're making travel plans starting April next year. You're not qualified for the job, but this is a cash business, and my husband trusts you, and that's a critical consideration for us. If you don't work out or you decide that this is not what you want to do after two months, it will seriously disrupt our plans. Can I have your assurance that you will work hard to learn this business, and then if we want you to stay, you will?"

"You have my pledge, Madam."

"Call me, Johanna. And let me tell you, we had planned to pay $300 a week to whomever we hired. I'm not going to pay you that kind of money until I'm satisfied that you're worth it. If that's okay, come and start working with Leo, our customer service guy, and Mark, and start to learn the merchandise we carry and how we run this business. We open at 10.00 a.m. and close at 6.00 p.m., Monday to Saturday."

"I will be here at 10.00 a.m. tomorrow."

"ARE YOU SURE YOU want to do this, Dad? Work for someone?" Rafiq asked when Salim sat in the car and told him that he was getting the job.

"I worked for Daresco in Dodoma, remember? I know how to work for someone. I see here an opportunity to manage a large retail business. I can learn a lot. Mr. Goldman looks like a good man. His wife is stern. I don't think she suffers fools. She had driven up in a shiny new Cadillac and was wearing expensive jewelry. She obviously wants to preserve her lifestyle and capital, as she should. I'll be okay."

"But, Dad, this is at least a two-year commitment. You don't have to do this, you know? I hope you're not doing this because I haven't found you a business, and you're bored sitting at home all day?"

"No, I want to do this, Son."

1972
Seventy-Nine

When Sophia and Anil arrived in Vancouver in early October, they put up at the hotel they had stayed at when they had vacationed there with Rafiq and Shameem. It was raining heavily that day, and they decided to stay in and rest.

Over the next couple of days, Anil connected with Bank of Nova Scotia, and Pratt and Rowley, Chartered Accountants, who had made firm offers, and met with the managers in both places. He decided to take up the bank's Senior Accountant position at $18,000 a year. This was lower than the Pratt and Rowley offer of $20,000, but Anil liked the bank's benefits package and potential opportunities for advancement.

Sophia met with the hospitals that had indicated interest in her. After two interviews, St. Paul's offered her a nursing position at $12,000 a year.

Both agreed to start work at the beginning of November, which gave them three weeks to find a place to live.

After arriving in Vancouver, Anil contacted an Ismaili gentleman, Ramzan Lalani, whose name and coordinates Karim Alibhai had given him. Anil told Ramzan that he wanted to attend Jamatkhana on Friday and asked for the address. Ramzan said the Jamatkhana was on Edmonds Street in Burnaby. There were about 300 Ismailis in Vancouver, most from Tanzania and Uganda, and some from Kenya. The number was growing rapidly with the influx of Ugandan refugees. Arrangements were being made to secure additional premises for the community to meet for congregational prayers. Based on information emanating from Uganda, it was expected that there would be over 3,000 Ismailis in Vancouver by the end of November.

Ramzan said it would take Anil a long time to get to Jamatkhana from the hotel if he took the bus. He and his wife lived downtown and would be happy to give him a ride there and back.

ON THE WAY TO Jamatkhana, Ramzan told Anil he was a mechanical engineer. His wife was a teacher. They had been in Vancouver for three months. His wife had found a substitute teacher position with the local school board. He was still jobless, and they were considering moving to Toronto. They were renting an apartment in a relatively new building on Burrard Street and recommended that Anil rent there. Rent for a one-bedroom apartment was $200 a month. For a single couple, one bedroom was quite spacious. Anil told him that he was married to a non-Ismaili. Ramzan's wife, Rumina, offered to meet Sophia for coffee and familiarize her with the places to shop for linen, kitchenware, and furniture.

In Jamatkhana, he got introduced as a new congregation member to The Aga Khan Council for Canada President. "We are expecting a major influx of Ismailis from Uganda in the coming days. There are only 300 of us here. We'll need all the help we can get. Can we count on your support?" the President asked.

"Absolutely, President Saheb (Sir). You can call me anytime. We don't have a place of our own or a telephone number and are not yet settled, but I will provide you with our contact information as soon as we have it."

"I presume you have not started working yet. What kind of job are you looking for?"

"I have an offer from Bank of Nova Scotia to start in November as a senior accountant."

"Then you are more settled than the people we are expecting from Uganda will be when they arrive here. You can help. Is your wife here? I presume you are married?"

"She's not here, President Saheb. She's not Ismaili, but I know she will be happy to support our work. She is a Registered Nurse and has a job also starting in

November, with St. Paul's Hospital."

The President gave Anil his business card and said, "Call me next week, and maybe we can arrange for you to come to the Council office for us to talk more."

"I will call you, President Saheb. I'm happy to have met you."

"As am I," said the President and rushed off to talk to other people waiting to speak to him.

RAMZAN AND RUMINA AGREED to meet Anil and Sophia the next day, and they drove them around and showed them the best places to shop. They also took them to a Ford dealership and introduced them to an Ismaili salesman. Anil test drove a Ford Mustang and, with Ramzan and Rumina's help, negotiated to buy a well-equipped red Mustang for $2,800 plus taxes. The car would be delivered in three weeks.

To thank them for their help and spending the entire day with them, Anil and Sophia took Ramzan and Rumina to a popular Chinese restaurant that Rumina suggested, for dinner.

VANCOUVER WAS TURNING OUT to be a pleasant experience for Anil and Sophia. They had made two friends. Almas and Tazim had settled well in Toronto. Anil had been introduced to the Council president, and he may have some role in the settlement of Ugandan Ismailis in B.C. They had ordered a Mustang, a car Anil that had dreamed about ever since he had seen Ed get his from the Embassy in London. Their jobs were lined up. Now they had to find a place to live.

"The apartment lease we sign has to depend on how long we want to live in a rental. Is your dad going to send you $250,000 to buy a house in the British Properties, where you had vowed to live if you came to Vancouver?" Anil asked Sophia, laughing.

"Ha, ha! My father doesn't have that kind of money, but I've already written to him about what the houses cost here, including in the British Properties, and I've asked him if he can part with $250,000."

OVER THE NEXT COUPLE of days, they visited apartment buildings in downtown Vancouver and signed a one-year lease for an apartment in the building where the Lalanis lived. The apartment was vacant, and they could move in 10 days before the lease commencement date by paying $60. Now they needed to buy furniture and other household items.

In mid-October, Sophia received a letter from her dad, which, among other things, read:

> Your mother and I are happy to know that you are settling well in Vancouver and want to get your own place. You must think that I am very rich and can afford to send you $250,000 to buy a house in the most expensive area in Vancouver. I don't have that kind of money to give to each of my children.
>
> I know you have to decide whether to buy or rent, and where. So here is what we can do for you. I can send you $10,000 now that you can use for a down payment on a house and make other purchases, or do whatever you want to do with it, and I will send you, over the next four months, $90,000 to use as you please. But understand that this will be your full and final inheritance. Other than any jewelry your mother may leave you, you will get nothing more from us. Let me know if this suits you.

"That sounds final," said Anil.

"It is. That's my dad. He says it like it is. He means it. I won't get a penny more from him."

"$100,000 would be a good down payment on a $250,000 British Properties home, but payments on a $150,000 mortgage and realty taxes would work out to over $1,500 a month. That would be almost 50% of our combined net salaries. You still want to live in British Properties?"

"No, but I do want to get the $100,000 from my old man. We have very little by way of savings. All the money that came from Tanzania, you've given to Mom - as you should have. Let's just move into the apartment with minimal furniture and then study Vancouver and buy a house we can afford."

Sophia talked to her father the next day, and a $10,000 credit appeared in their bank account within five days. Anil could not believe their good fortune. $100,000 was a lot of money, more money than he could have dreamed of having in his account in 20 years. He would have to think about what they would do with so much cash.

1972
Eighty

When Anil met the Council President and seven of his Council members a week later, as expected, over 1,000 Ugandan Ismaili refugees had arrived in Vancouver. They were being looked after by the government. All had been accommodated in downtown hotels and were receiving living allowances and money for warm clothing.

The president told the members and four volunteers (like Anil) who had come to the meeting that all new arrivals should be visited as soon as possible. He wanted their names, their hometowns in Uganda, their education, and work experience. He also wanted to know the resources people had come with (if people were willing to share this information) and what they planned to do in Canada. He asked that each family unit should be given the name and telephone number of at least one Council member or volunteer to call if required.

He asked for someone to volunteer to coordinate this work.

There was a short silence. Everyone understood the magnitude of this work, and 2,000 more were coming in the next 20 days. Most around the table were working. They had little time to take on this demanding responsibility.

Anil thought about it and said, "President Saheb, I'm new to Vancouver. We've been here just over two weeks, and don't have a car yet, but we expect to get one in a few days and also to move into an apartment shortly, so if it's acceptable to you, I can coordinate this exercise. We'll need more people than there are around this table, and I'm assuming that everyone here is ready to contribute to this effort?"

There was a general nodding of heads.

"Thank you, Anil. We appoint you chairman of this Council's Settlement Committee. You can take down the names and telephone numbers of everyone here and add whomever you'd like to join your Committee."

"May I put my wife on the committee? As I'd mentioned, she's not Ismaili. She is an Ithna Ashari from Iraq."

"I don't see why not," replied the president. "We will be grateful for her support."

"May I request all members and volunteers here to stay on after the meeting for us to talk?" Anil asked.

"Thank you, Anil. I have to attend to other matters. You can get on with your work," said the president as he left the room.

Anil introduced himself more fully to the group and told them that both he and his wife would start work at the beginning of November. They had less than two weeks to devote to this work on a full-time basis, but the work would not end in two weeks.

He said, "Ladies and gentlemen, I know you're all working, but this is a critical time in the life of our Jamat. An entire Jamat has been uprooted and become refugees. May I request that we meet here every day, for the next 30 days at least, to coordinate work and review progress? You can go home from work, have dinner, and come here by 8.00 p.m. Can we do that?"

Most agreed.

"Okay, we've all been given names of the hotels where people are and where more will be accommodated. They're all downtown. Can we agree to take on one hotel each to visit people and gather the required information? "

A couple of members said that they did not own cars and wanted the hotels nearest to their residences allocated to them. After all had chosen, Anil took the remaining two hotels.

"I suggest we not meet tomorrow, but the day after, to share the information we've gathered. May I suggest that in addition to the information President Saheb has asked us to gather, we should find out if people have any major issues that need to be addressed immediately. There may be diabetics and heart patients, or people with other ailments. We need to ensure that they get the care and medications they need."

"You know medications are not free here. Healthcare is free, but not prescription drugs," one member said.

"Don't worry. Let's just find out if anyone needs prescription medicines, and then we can figure out how to pay for it. They can't go without their medications," said Anil.

SOPHIA WAS VERY EXCITED when Anil told her about the meeting and their new voluntary appointments. "Wow, Anil, so you're a bona fide chairman, and I'm a member of one of your Council's committees? Congratulations! You're asking if I will be a member? You bet I will! Give me your president's number and I'll call to thank him. We can pay for some of the prescriptions. Although the money my dad will send will be zakat effective, as Dad will have paid zakat on it, I'll want to pay some zakat on the money I get. We can pay for the prescriptions from that money."

"But first, we'll have to get them to see a doctor," said Anil.

"Well, let's start working."

"Okay, bright, and early tomorrow."

"Why not now?" It's only 9.30 p.m. You don't have to wake up early tomorrow. Let's cover one hotel now."

"You mean that?"

"Of course, I do."

THEY LOOKED UP THE two hotel addresses. Sophia called the hotels and determined that the Astoria was farther, but had more Ugandans. They took a cab there. When they entered, they saw at least 15 Ismailis in the small hotel lobby, chatting. Anil walked up to a middle-aged man and said, "I'm Anil Damji, and this is my wife, Sophia. I am chairman of the committee appointed by the Council to assist you in settling in Canada. Sophia is a committee member. We can only imagine the hardships you have suffered, but you're safe now, and we hope and pray that you will become established soon in this beautiful country. We've been asked to create a database of all Ugandan Ismailis coming to Canada, and we need to gather some information from you."

"Happy to meet you, Anil and Sophia," replied the man. "I am Aziz Jamal.

How come you've come here so late in the evening?"

"We just got appointed this evening," said Sophia.

"And you've already started working? That's the Ismaili voluntary spirit!" Aziz said, gregariously. "Well, you can start with me if you'd like."

Sophia looked at a woman sitting across the room and said, "Can I start with you?"

SOON, THEY HAD COVERED four family units. The news had gone up to the rooms that Council people were downstairs, and more people came down. Anil requested that those who had finished talking to them should go up to their rooms so that they could have more privacy when they spoke to people. Most complied. Some were curious about what was happening and stayed on.

In the next five families they interviewed, two people had diabetes, and one had heart problems. One person with diabetes and the heart patient had medication to last two and three weeks, respectively, but Mrs. Kanji, the other diabetic, was almost out of her medication. All had been given doctors' names and coordinates to visit if they needed to for any reason.

When they had covered 13 families, the lobby was empty, but there were at least 15 family units at this hotel yet to be surveyed.

As they rode home, Sophia asked, "I asked the three who need to see doctors to meet us in the lobby at 10.00 a.m. Each has been given a different doctor's name. How will we get them there?"

"We've told people that we will be back to collect information at 2.00 p.m. You take Mrs. Kanji to see her doctor and get a prescription, fill it, and meet me at the hotel around 12.30 p.m. We can eat lunch and meet the group at 2.00 p.m. I'll take the other two. The doctors are nearby, but if you feel that Mrs. Kanji cannot walk – she looked a little frail – then take a cab. I'll do the same for the two men."

WHEN THEY MET THE next day after having gotten their guests registered and seen by the doctors, Sophia said, "The doctor didn't like prescribing for Mrs. Kanji without conducting full tests. He said that for all he knew, she might not have diabetes at all. I have to take her back for bloodwork and urine tests in the afternoon. The results will take time, so I implored the doctor to prescribe a few pills for her. I told him I'm a nurse, and he gave me that 'So, what?' look. Anyway, he prescribed her pills for ten days. She has to see him in five."

"The doctors I took my guests to were also not happy prescribing medications, but they did. I think that they felt sorry for them. They're booking them for tests, and they have to see the doctors again in a week. I'll have to take them."

"We'll have to make them independent quickly. We'll have to show them how to get around. We can't create dependency," Sophia said.

Most of the information that they had to gather was statistical and straight-forward, but work experience and what they planned to do in Canada took time to document. Several people they interviewed asked what the Council was going to do with the information and if there was anything tangible the Council was going to do for them.

Anil responded by saying, "The government is providing you comfortable accommodation, and you're getting winter clothing and living allowances. As a first step, we want to help you find your way around Vancouver and to Jamatkhanas, get you registered with doctors and Canada Manpower to find jobs, and help you find accommodation when you have found jobs. We'll also tell you where to shop for furniture and groceries, if you want. The Council needs the information we are gathering to understand your issues and establish programs to assist you. Also, you have come here in an exodus. Not all your family and friends know who has gone where. The Council will start to get inquiries in the coming days from other Ugandan Ismailis in other centers, asking where their friends and relatives are. The Council can respond to your family and friends if we have this information documented."

"Did the President tell you this is why we are gathering the information, and this is your mandate, or did you just make it up?" Sophia asked Anil when they were alone.

"He told me nothing. I made it up, but isn't that why we should be gathering this information, and isn't that what we should do for them?"

"I don't know, but what I do know is that you and I certainly can't do all of this alone."

"Trust me, Sophia, we'll get help."

THEY STAYED UNTIL 7.00 p.m. that day to complete all of their initial registrations. There were four more that needed to see doctors. Sophia and Anil were tired and got up to leave when a young lady they had talked to earlier approached them and said, "We are meeting in a room the hotel has provided for us to say our prayers. You want to join?"

Sophia gave Anil a "You deal with this," look.

Anil thought for a second and decided that people had to know at some point that Sophia was not Ismaili.

"I can come, but Sophia is not Ismaili," he said.

That drew a gasp. "But she said Ya Ali Madad to me when I met her!"

"Yes, she is married to me, and she knows our Ismaili greeting. Also, she is Ithna Ashari from Iraq, and Ali is her first Imam also."

"Anil, you go join them. I'll wait here," said Sophia.

"Are you sure?" Anil asked.

"Quite sure. We all need prayers right now, and there's something powerful about congregational prayers. Please go and pray with your people; and pray for me too. I'll sit here and pray for everyone in your congregation," she replied.

Anil took a moment to marvel at his kind and generous wife. In his eyes, her outer beauty was surpassed only by the grace of her soul.

ANIL DEPARTED AS SOON as the prayers were said. It took less than 15 minutes.

Word quickly spread that Sophia was an Ithna Ashari, but not the Indian kind in Uganda; she was an Arab.

A couple of people were a little wary about giving personal information to her, but most were full of admiration for her sacrifice of time and energy to help her fellow Muslims and human beings.

"What an amazing girl! I will give her a big hug and kiss when I see her tomorrow," said one of the older women, named Zubeida.

WHEN ANIL AND SOPHIA came the next morning at 10.00 a.m., the lobby was empty, except for Aziz Jamal. He welcomed them and said that he had talked to the hotel manager and gotten a small room with two small tables and chairs placed at two ends of the room for them to speak to people quietly and make their notes. They had 12 families remaining to be interviewed, and whom he had listed alphabetically, but first he wanted them to come to the room where they had said prayers last night and where all had gathered after breakfast.

There was much noise coming from the room, but when they entered, all fell silent. All were seated on the carpet-covered floor, as they had done during the previous evening's prayers.

As they entered, Zubeida approached them, hugged and kissed Sophia on both cheeks, hugged Anil, and said, "We are all gathered here to express our deep gratitude for what you both are doing for us. We have been feeling so lost. Some of us are very scared about what the future may hold for us. Your presence here tells us that we are not alone. We pray that may Allah reward you for your seva (service) and bless you with much peace and barakat (prosperity)."

She paused and then added, "We are truly grateful to you, Sophia, for your care and support. We pray that may Allah always watch over you, keep you happy, and bless you with inspiration to serve your fellow human beings."

In unison, all said, "Ameen."

They got up and started to leave the room. Many stopped to hug and thank Sophia.

When all had left, Aziz took them to the interview room and went to call the first family to be interviewed.

"I'm overwhelmed by their kindness," said Sophia. "I've never gotten so many hugs and kisses from strangers!"

"Yes, everyone wanted to hug you. Except for Zubeida, no one hugged me!" Anil said.

Sophia laughed. "Don't be jealous," she said, pinching his cheek.

1972
Eighty-One

The next two weeks for Sophia and Anil were busier than they could have ever imagined. Over 2,000 Ugandan Ismaili refugees arrived in this short period.

They took possession of their rental apartment and moved in with very basic furniture and other household items; the Mustang was delivered shortly thereafter, which made travel around the city much more relaxed. There were nightly meetings of the Settlement Committee to receive individual reports and document members' perceptions of the Ugandan Ismaili refugees' issues, which were not limited to health problems. The Committee recruited some young Ugandan Ismaili refugees to assist in their work – familiarizing the newcomers with Vancouver's transit system, getting them registered with Canada Manpower, and the provincial health plan. Sophia developed a template to summarize all of the information being gathered, and Zubeida, who was still at the Astoria and was given a typewriter, was transcribing all of the data that the Committee members gathered, on Sophia's template.

Anil had taken it upon himself to review all of the information everyone gathered and produce a weekly report for the Council, detailing the numbers and profiles of the new arrivals, the hotels in which they were accommodated, arrangements made for them to say prayers at the hotels, how many had found jobs and moved out and where they had gone, and the support being provided to help them find jobs, as well as the next bunch of "job-ready" individuals identified for assistance in finding employment. The leadership deeply appreciated Anil's meticulous reports. Sophia was as vocal and directional at the committee meetings as Anil, and quickly emerged as a leader to whom others looked for guidance.

"It seems like we're on a treadmill," Sophia said to Anil. "The more we deal with, the more come and the ones we have dealt with are coming to us now with their personal issues. I had this lady call me yesterday to say that her teenage daughter didn't come back until 1.00 a.m. last night. She was worried, sick. She has no idea who she was with and where she had gone. She wants me to talk to her daughter. I'm meeting the daughter this evening."

"Welcome to Ismaili institutional work, sweetheart," Anil replied with a grin. "The other members and I have also had several health, and social issues brought to us. We have to deal with what we can. It's all to serve the Jamat, without any expectation of reward."

"Speaking of rewards, these three weeks have been a life-changing experience for me. I've never served in a voluntary capacity anywhere. I've never felt so fulfilled, rewarded, and appreciated. I feel like I have a new purpose in life. I shouldn't, but I do feel sad that this will all end soon. I've made so many new friends."

"I've never served in a voluntary capacity, either. I should have, because the ethic of service and voluntarism are a foundational pillar of Ismaili ethics. What I've learned in the past weeks is that when you put your heart and soul into serving a community - any community - you get much more out of it than the effort you put in."

"The kind of happiness I felt when I got Sharmeen hired as a nurse at my hospital cannot be purchased with any amount of money. The prayers that old lady was offering for me holding my hands are priceless, even though I did not understand a word of what she was saying. The warmth in her eyes melted my heart. She made me cry."

"The work won't end when we've documented everyone and identified their issues. It'll shift to the conceptualization of programmatic responses. We'll have to keep at it, but we both start work next Wednesday. We'll have to organize our time to continue to do what we are doing. We'll have to streamline; our mandate was never to find the Ugandan Ismailis jobs or deal with their social issues. People from Tanzania and Kenya are also looking to us to help them with these matters, and we

can't tell them that we won't help because they're not refugees. We'll need to dele-
gate some functions to the new committee members."

BY THE MIDDLE OF December, the flow of refugees had slowed to a trickle.
There were over 4,000 Ismailis in B.C. Over 1,000 had gone to Alberta. Over
1,000 from the Congo and Madagascar had moved to Quebec, following political
problems in those countries. In Ontario, the Jamat had grown to over 6,000. The
Canadian Ismaili landscape had changed. From being a Jamat of less than 1,000 in
June, the community had grown to over 12,000 by December 1972.

THE B.C. JAMAT INCLUDED several Ismailis who had been successful entrepreneurs in Uganda, and who had started to invest in hotels and residential real
estate. There was also a significant number of Ismailis who had been in retail and
service businesses in East Africa and had come to Canada with $25,000 - $50,000
in cash holdings. They wanted to buy small retail or service businesses but were
having difficulty evaluating the businesses being offered for sale. Anil and Rafiq
had been exchanging notes, and Anil had started to help these people using Rafiq's
model. He knew a great deal more than Rafiq about small businesses from having
prepared and, in some cases, audited accounts of many small businesses in the U.K.
He shared his knowledge and experience with Rafiq.

Sophia's frontline volunteer work was essentially over, and she was experiencing
a deep sense of loss, but life had to go on. She had her new Ugandan friends, and she
took every opportunity to socialize with them. Sometimes she received calls from
Ismaili women who wanted to discuss their health issues with her before talking to
their doctors. In some situations, Sophia arranged for them to see specialists at her
hospital. The hospital management had become aware of Sophia's work with the
refugees, and she was looked at with much respect and admiration for her work and
leadership qualities.

She had also received in her account (faster than her dad had said it would come)
the balance of $100,000 he had promised. With the help and advice of some of the
long-time Ismaili residents of Vancouver with whom they had become friends, they
made a $25,000 down payment on a $75,000 house in a new subdivision in North

Vancouver, at the foot of Grouse Mountain. The development was scheduled for completion in September of the next year.

One friend, Akbar Manji, had invited Sophia and Anil to participate with him and two other Ismailis in the purchase of a 30-room motel on Capilano Road for $1,000,000 by investing $50,000 for 25% equity in the project. Anil had studied the project carefully and determined that it would generate enough cash flow to service the debt and pay all operating expenses, but the cash on cash return on investment would not be much higher than what Sophia's money was earning in the bank. There was, however, the potential for long-term appreciation. After much thought, they decided that they should participate in the project, but wanted to limit their investment to $25,000. This, Akbar told him, would not work for him and his partners, who were looking for someone to invest the full $50,000.

"You know, Rafiq has money," said Sophia. "Why don't we ask if he would be interested in investing $25,000 with us in this project? If he is, we can form a single corporation through which we can invest together."

"Good idea. I'll call him this evening," said Anil.

WHEN ANIL BRIEFED HIM on the project, Rafiq said, "$25,000 is a lot of money, Anil. Are you sure that you want to invest Sophia's money in this project? We know so little about the hospitality industry in Canada. If the project fails, her dad will blame you for losing the money he has given her."

"You know, Rafiq, I'm sure about one thing – God has made up his mind that he is not going to create more land on this earth. Capilano is a prominent location for a motel. The land will always retain its value, and over time, it will appreciate."

"But you know partnerships can mean trouble."

"I've developed an investment agreement which spells out how much each party will invest and how many shares they'll get, how the shares will be valued at any point in time if one wants to exit or dies; the rights and obligations of the partners, voting rights, and a process for resolution of disputes or deadlock. I've also developed a management agreement where under the corporation we will form to acquire the project will hire one partner, Akbar, to manage the business. We'll pay him a $1,000 salary per month."

"Trust you to do this!" said Rafiq, marveling at Anil's attention to detail. "Is everyone okay with the agreements?"

"The promoters are happy with the terms. Why don't you and Shama fly out here next weekend, look at the motel, meet the promoters, and then decide? Take the Friday afternoon off. If you arrive here by 5.00 p.m., we can attend Jamatkhana and spend Saturday looking at the project and meeting the promoters."

"Okay, let me talk to Dad and get the ladies' permission."

RAFIQ AND SHAMEEM ARRIVED in Vancouver on Friday afternoon, as planned. Anil had organized a dinner for them at a restaurant to meet with Akbar, his two partners, and their spouses. They socialized and talked mainly about how Ismailis were settling in Canada. There was no talk about the motel project.

From what he was hearing, Rafiq noted that Ismaili professionals in Vancouver were having even more difficulty finding jobs than in Toronto, but by remaining persistent, most were landing on their feet. There was no subway system in Vancouver, and bus transit was not very efficient. Some professionals, to stay in their line of work, were traveling up to two hours to work; some were relocating to Calgary and Edmonton, where job prospects were better, but for many, the lure of Vancouver's mountains and the ocean was too strong to consider moving. Also, in many family units, if one spouse (usually the wife) had found work, they were not willing to give up their job and start over in another city.

As in Toronto, people looking to establish in small retail and service businesses were having problems identifying good businesses and evaluating them. Rafiq also knew from his exchanges with Anil that small businesses were more expensive to buy in Vancouver than in Toronto. Leveraging their equity with bank loans was difficult without established credit records in Canada. This was forcing them into businesses that they could buy with only what they had brought with them, or into factory and parking lot jobs. Four or five of them could put their money together and buy a motel like this group was doing, but this was not practical as each needed a job and income, and one motel could not have five managers.

They met the Ismaili realtor, Shiraz Somani, the next morning, and toured the motel. Shiraz took particular care to point out the design and functionality of the motel and how well the property had been maintained. He provided them with copies of recent sales of similar projects in Vancouver and conveyed how happy the buyers were with their acquisitions. He explained that the reason the motel was up for sale was that the owner, who was 70, had made "a ton of money from the project," lived in British Properties, and wanted to retire.

They met the owner for lunch. It was fascinating to hear him describe how he had come penniless to Canada from Yugoslavia at age 25, had worked on the docks before finding a job with a lumber company where his wife was a secretary, and how he had courted and married her. With their savings, they had bought a convenience store on Capilano Road, which they had expanded as the population in the area grew, and they saved up $50,000 to invest in this motel, which had cost $220,000 to build in 1952 and which they had called, "The Mountain View Inn." The man spoke with passion and excitement about the work that he and his wife had done to build the business.

"I THINK THAT THIS will be a good investment, Anil," said Rafiq as they made their way back home. "Your cash flows and sensitivity analyses show that we can't go wrong. Shama likes the project. Let me talk to Mom and Dad."

When Rafiq called his dad, Salim said, "If you're happy with the project, just go ahead. Mom and I are fine with investing $25,000. We trust your judgment, Son."

RAFIQ, ANIL, SHAMEEM, AND Sophia agreed to invest in the project through a corporation that they would establish, which they would call Almin Investments and in which each of them would own a 25% share. Anil would represent Almin on the project board and would develop an investment agreement for the shareholders to sign.

1972
Eighty-Two

W hen Rafiq and Shameem returned to Toronto, there was a message from Carole to call her.

"Hey, Rafiq, how was your trip?" she asked when Rafiq called.

"Productive – we committed to investing in a motel with Anil and Sophia and three other people if our offer goes through."

"Wow, that's great! You must tell me all about it when we meet. The reason I had called was to ask if Aziza, Zul, Shama, and you have any plans for New Year's Eve. If not, Geoff is suggesting that we go to the Royal York Hotel for its annual New Year's Eve dinner and dance. Tickets are $25 per person. It's pricy, but it's excellent. Only a few seats are left."

"I have to check with Zul and Aziza. Shama and I are free, and we'll also have Tazim join us if we come. Let me get back to you."

After sharing Carole's suggestion with Shameem, he said, "Shama, this is your first birthday in Canada. I was also thinking of inviting Carole, Geoff, Aziza, and Zul for dinner on Christmas Eve to celebrate your birthday."

"And January 2nd will be your birthday. This is the first time we have Mom and Dad and Almas aunty and Tazim with us for our birthdays. I thought that we would have a nice dinner at home on the 24th for my birthday, and for yours, we could all go to this Indian restaurant on the Danforth called Sher-e-Punjab – I heard about it from some ladies in Jamatkhana."

"That's a great idea. Let's do that. I told Carole that Tazim would join us if we go to the Royal York. Do you know if anyone's asked her out? Boys are always hovering around her in Jamatkhana."

"Why don't you ask her?

After confirming that Zul and Aziza were free and would join them on New Year's Eve, he called Tazim and asked her to come down to their apartment. They both gave her a hug when she arrived and told her about the investment with Anil and Sophia. Rafiq then said, "Carole called and wanted to know if we want to celebrate New Year's Eve at the Royal York with her and Geoff. I told her that you would also join. Has anyone asked you out for New Year's Eve?"

"No one who dresses like Anil and is as smart as you are," she replied with sarcasm in her voice.

"Oh, Tazim," Rafiq said, taking her into his arms, "I'm so sorry that I was so difficult. You're an adult now, and I guess I've just been having a hard time accepting it. You're my only sister, and I want nothing but the best for you. I just didn't think anyone was good enough for my beautiful sister."

Shameem looked on with a knowing smile. "Tazim, he got the sharp edge of Mom's tongue for being so strict with you in London. And I'm sorry too. I should have intervened, but I didn't feel right overriding anything that Anil and Rafiq decided. You are dear to me, but you're *their* sister. So, has anyone asked you out for New Year's Eve?"

"The guy I chat with in Jamatkhana, Asif, has asked me out a few times. I've gone out for coffee with him twice; he asked me to go see *The Godfather* with him, but I gave him an excuse. I didn't think Rafiq would approve of him. He's from Mombasa. His parents are in Kitchener. They're both working in a factory. They're not rich, and he is a simple person."

"He's a smart-looking guy. What does he do?" asked Shameem.

"He's enrolled in the first year Law program at Osgoode Hall."

"Has he invited you out for New Year's Eve?"

"No. Not yet."

"Well, introduce him to me on Friday, and I'll invite him to come with us," said Shameem.

"Royal York will be very expensive. I don't think that he can afford it, Shama."

"Don't worry about that. You'll both be our guests," Shameem said

ON FRIDAY, WHEN TAZIM met Asif in Jamatkhana, she said, "I'll introduce you to my sister-in-law today, and she'll invite you to join us for New Year's Eve at the Royal York. Would you like to come?"

"Like to come? I'd love to, but I don't have that kind of money. I was hoping we would go to Swiss Chalet for dinner. We can get two quarter chicken dinners and drinks for $6.50. I love their chicken and sauce."

"Me, too, but my brother will pay for everything. Do you want to come?"

"Of course I want to come. When will I get to go to Royal York with someone as beautiful as you?"

"You don't have to flatter me. Come on, let me introduce you to my sister-in-law and brother."

AFTER TAZIM HAD INTRODUCED Asif to Rafiq and Shameem, and they confirmed the New Year's Eve plan, he pulled Tazim aside and said, "It's funny, I didn't really like your sister-in-law before now. She used to stare at me each time we spoke, like she was sizing me up, but to talk to her, she's really very nice."

"And what did you think of my brother?"

"Oh, he's nice and so smart and very good looking too."

"You know he's not my blood brother. He's my brother's close friend and stayed with us for three years when he was in school in Tanzania. He loves me like a sister. He has no siblings of his own. He cares for me more than any brother can, so he'll be watching you more than my sister-in-law."

"I'll need to buy a suit to wear. All of my clothes are from Tanzania. I think that's why your sister-in-law was looking at me so critically when I was talking to you."

"She wasn't sizing you up for herself. She was doing it for Rafiq, wondering if he'll approve of you and permit me to date you. In England, no one who asked me out was good enough for him. Better be on your best behavior. Buy a dark color suit. Do you have the money?"

"I'll see what I can do."

New Year's Eve at the Royal York, the most prestigious hotel in Toronto, was a fun event for everyone. Asif was nervous at first, but as the evening wore on, he and Tazim got into the swing of things and were dancing away, as were Aziza and Zul. Shameem was happy to see that Aziza was having fun. Obviously, she was putting her trauma behind her, although the scar on her neck was still visible. In time, she would look into plastic surgery options. She did not want this to be a life-long reminder for Aziza of what had happened to her.

After a hearty meal, Geoff, Carole, Shameem, and Rafiq sat and talked more than they danced. They enjoyed watching people dancing and having fun. Rafiq was happy to see Tazim enjoying herself. She had warmed up to him after their talk. She had gone back to hugging him the way she had done before he started managing her life in London. Asif seemed respectful and intelligent, but Rafiq knew that if there was any relationship between Tazim and him, Tazim would dominate him. As he looked at her, he wondered if he would have loved his blood sister, if she had survived, as much as he loved Tazim.

Carole and Geoff wanted to know about the investment Rafiq and Shameem were making in the Vancouver motel. Rafiq told them all about the project and also how well Anil and Sophia were settling in Vancouver. He told them about their involvement with the refugee settlement program and the house they had purchased.

"House prices in Toronto are rising," said Geoff. There's a new subdivision coming up on Huntingwood Avenue in Scarborough, not far from us. The models look beautiful. Your apartment lease will expire in 10 months. I think that you should buy a unit there. It'll be ready just in time for you."

"But our work, Rafiq's parents' work. – we're all downtown," said Shameem.

"And so is Geoff's and my work, but we commute. We stay in the suburb to have a quieter life and live in a larger place with room to bring up children…and also because we could never afford to own the kind of house we live in, downtown!" said Carole.

"The largest 2,600 square foot model in the new development is around $50,000. Why don't you look at the models and put down a $5,000 deposit now and an additional $5,000 on closing for one unit? You'll have almost ten months to decide if you want to move or flip the place. I'm sure you'll make money if you sell," said Geoff.

AS THEY ENTERED INTO the New Year, Shameem and Rafiq mulled over what Geoff and Carole had suggested. After the entire family, Tazim and Almas included, had looked at the models and selected a corner lot, four-bedroom house, they decided to bite the bullet and put down the deposit.

Almas was not happy that the four of them planned to move away. She didn't want to move from where she was. She couldn't have been more comfortable in her work at Honest Ed's, and Tazim didn't want to have a long commute to school every day.

"Almas aunty, you can't live in a rental all your life!" said Rafiq. "You have the money to buy a house. It would be good for you to be near us, where I can keep an eye on Tazim" he said, winking at Tazim.

"Why don't you talk to Anil?" he continued. "If you want to be near your work and Tazim's university, we could get you a condominium apartment down-town for you."

1973
Eighty-Three

January 1973 was cold in Toronto. There was a lot of snow on the ground, driving had become difficult, and the days were shorter.

Salim had gone through the busy Christmas season at the store and had performed well. He was learning about the products in the store and was becoming a skilled salesman. Johanna liked him more with each passing day. She liked his pleasant manners, his quiet way of working, and his attention to detail. She could see that Mark had been right about him.

In the time that Salim had worked at the store, he had discussed with Rafiq and Anil how the company was operated and asked for their advice on what business elements he should focus on. Leo was an excellent salesman. Salim did not want to take over his work. He had been hired as a manager. What should he do as a manager, in addition to learning what items the store was selling, to demonstrate his value at work?

"Salim uncle, you're telling me that there is a continuous flow of customers; this, of course, will end in January, and you will have a quieter three-month period," said Anil. "You say that the store is well stocked, with around $100,000 worth of inventory and annual sales are over $300,000. It appears to me that this is a well-run operation. One element you could look into is inventory management – inventory mix, turnover, what items account for what percentage of sales and contribution to gross margin, and inventory replenishment processes. For a hardware store, inventory should rollover two times. Rollover is the cost of sales divided by average annual inventory level. If you have non-performing inventory, you should look at replacing that with fast-moving inventory items, or if you have enough of those, you could look at introducing new lines."

"What new lines should I look at?"

"Difficult for me to say, Uncle. Visit other large hardware stores and see what they carry."

In whatever free time he had, Salim walked around the store, moved the items around on the shelves, and checked if all had price tags. If he saw anything gathering dust, he asked, "When was the last time we sold one of these?" If the answer was six months or longer and the item was relatively expensive, he made a note of it. He had told Johanna that he had some ideas about more efficient inventory management that he wanted to discuss with her and Mark after Christmas. For a start, he said, he wanted to take inventory count on January 1st, when the store would be closed. He wanted Leo and Sarah (one of the two cashiers) to be there to help him and would need copies of all purchase invoices for the past 18 months. They would start at 6.00 a.m. and go on until whatever time it took them to finish their work."

"Why, Salim? Why do you want to do this on New Year's Day? On January 1st, you should be with your family, relaxing after your New Year's Eve celebrations. We take inventory at the end of June each year for our June 30th year-end."

"In December, we get rid of a lot of inventory. You have in place a reorder system. When an item reaches a certain level, you place orders for more. For one thing, I want to examine the economics of this approach. It may be a good system, but there could be opportunities for improvement."

Johanna considered this and agreed. The plan would move ahead as proposed.

THEY COUNTED INVENTORY ON New Year's Day; it totaled just over $92,000. Salim provided this number to Mark's accountant, who already had the sales figure for 1972 and all of the store's operating expenses. Over the next two weeks, the accountant produced the income statement and balance sheet. The 1972 sales were $325,000. The cost of inventory sold was around $130,000, which yielded an inventory turnover of 1.4 times. This was lower than the industry average Anil had told him it should be for the hardware business. Salim produced an analysis of the items sold during the year. This indicated that about 50% of the inventory items had accounted for approximately 80% of sales, about 40% had accounted for 15% of sales, and the remaining 10% accounted for about 5% of sales.

He presented his analysis to Mark and Johanna and said, "Our inventory turnover ratio, at 1.4 times, is below the industry average of two times. We need to get rid of the 10% of inventory, which accounts for 5% of the sales. It's occupying space on the shelves and doing us no good. Let's mark it down by 90%, put it out in the front, and get rid of it for what we can get. We also need to sell as much as possible of the 40% of the inventory that generated only about 15% of our sales."

"But that's our *filler* stock. If we do what you're suggesting, the shelves will be empty," Mark replied.

"It's better to have empty shelves than inventory gathering dust. We want our store to look spic and span like every item is moving."

"You don't understand this, Salim. We have big-ticket items that may move just three times a year, but they're much more profitable," said Johanna.

"I have been visiting large franchised hardware stores in shopping malls in the evenings after we close. They do carry big-ticket items, but not all that we carry. If you ask for items that they don't carry, they say that they can order it and can get it in less than three days. What they are increasingly carrying, and we are not, is building materials, like ceramic and wooden floor tiles, washbasins and sinks, vanities and mirrors, lighting to go with it, paint, and wallpaper. Some carry catalogs of kitchen cabinets and offer installation services. I looked into this and found that they don't have any contractors on their payroll. They've identified reputable contractors to whom they give out their customers' contracts and take a commission. Other than the catalogs, they carry nothing."

"You're talking about charting a whole new path, Salim. We want to retire; we don't want to venture into and put money in new lines. And where's the space for us to carry this in our store? If we get rid of everything you're saying we should, will there be enough space to carry the building materials?" Johanna asked.

"I know you want to retire and sell the business in five years, but your bottom line will determine what you'll get for it. I'm not suggesting that we carry stocks of all of these items. We can carry samples. Let customers look at them and place orders. We can get the suppliers to deliver the items directly. Now for some items, like sinks, washbasins, toilet seats, paint, and wallpaper, we will have to carry some stocks, but for the most part, we can carry catalogs and samples. In aggregate, we'll not spend more on such inventory than the value of the inventory I'm saying we get rid of."

"Paint is tricky. You can carry stocks of only so many colors. I have gone to buy paint for our house renovation, and they can offer you 50 shades of one color. You select any shade, and they mix it up for you. You need to get a mixer. It's a bit messy, and someone has to become an expert in this area," said Johanna.

"I've looked into it," said Salim. "The line is very profitable. The effort will pay off."

"What do you think, Johanna?" asked Mark.

"How do you want to go about doing this, Salim?" she asked.

"Give me one day a week free for the next two months. I will do my research and come back to you with a plan."

"Okay, you're on," she said, not without a trace of doubt.

RAFIQ GOT HIS MOTHER and Almas registered in a six-month evening secretarial certificate program at George Brown College, starting in January. Both found this exhausting after a day's work, but were willing to work at it and were doing well. Tazim and Shameem had taken over some of the cooking responsibilities when they got home early. On most days, the two households dined together.

THE ISMAILI POPULATION IN Toronto had grown to over 8,000 and was still growing from migration from Tanzania and Kenya. Some Ugandans who had ended up in the U.K., India, and Pakistan, and many who had ended up in refugee camps in Europe, were making their way to Canada after being sponsored or nominated by their families.

Now there were four weekend school hall Jamatkhanas in Toronto. On March 21st, *Navrouz*, (New Year's Day for Shia Muslims), the Aga Khan appointed a National and two Regional (for Eastern and Western Canada) Councils to serve the community for a two-year term. He also established a support program (The Aga Khan Aid Fund) to provide education and hardship loans to Ismailis. Several students whose university educations had been interrupted in Uganda had enrolled in Canadian universities and, like Asif, were struggling financially. The Aid Fund made low-interest education loans to students to supplement family and government sources to make their lives more comfortable and help them advance in their studies. There were also families that were struggling financially while the family heads looked for jobs. Hardship loans were made available to them to help them through this transition period.

Anil was appointed on The Aga Khan Council for Western Canada as a Member for Economic Development. The Western Canada Council's jurisdiction extended from British Columbia to the Manitoba border on the east. Ontario, Quebec, and Maritimes fell under the Eastern Canada Council. As part of his mandate, Anil and his committee, appointed some weeks later, were responsible for designing and implementing programs for effective personal financial management and business investments of the community members.

Before the Councils were appointed, early in 1973, the community had become aware of the proposed appointments, and there was speculation in the community as to who would get appointed, in what position, and on what Council or Board. Everyone had expected Anil to be appointed on the National or Regional Council. Sophia had assumed that she, too, would be appointed (perhaps as Health Member), but she had not said anything to Anil, nor did she say anything to him after he was appointed, and she was not. She learned later that only Ismailis, who took an oath of office and swore allegiance to the Imam, could serve on the Imam's Councils and Boards. She also learned that appointment by the Imam to serve in a voluntary capacity on his Councils and other bodies was a rare privilege which the Ismailis considered an honor and a blessing.

Except in exceptional circumstances, it was restricted to only one family member in any one term. Still, she felt excluded. She had so much wanted to serve this community.

IN EARLY APRIL, SALIM presented his plan, which had been vetted by Anil, to

Johanna and Mark. As a first step, he would mark down half of the 40% of inventory that accounted for 15% of the sales and get rid of it. The 10% of stock accounting for 5% of the sales had already been slashed in price by 80%, and most of it was gone. When sufficient space was created, he would introduce the wooden floor and ceramic title samples and bring in small inventories of the most popular designs. For other models, he would carry samples. He would carry small supplies of kitchen sinks and washbasins. He would then start carrying kitchen cabinet catalogs and take orders. He had established connections with two large and reputable cabinet makers who would take the contracts and give them a 15% commission. Paint and wallpaper would come further down the line.

"You know we're going away for two months next week, Salim. Do you want to wait for us to come back to start this?" asked Mark.

"I could, but I would like to have these lines in place before the summer. Summer and fall are the time for us to sell house renovation items. I would like to start now if that's okay," he replied.

"Let's sleep on it, and we'll let you know," said Johanna. "And Salim, our compliments for your research and a very well thought out plan. Whether your ideas will work, we don't know, but we're happy with your thinking, and irrespective of whether we proceed with your plan, I've instructed the accountant to bring you up to $300 per week starting at the beginning of April."

"Thank you very much, Johanna. I'm very grateful to you and Mark for your confidence and generosity."

"You deserve what we're giving you. You know Mark has grown so fond of you, the one day a week you were away doing your research, he missed you. He likes to see you in the store, even if you're busy and can't chat with him."

"I love to chat with him, too. There's so much that I have yet to learn from him."

1973
Eighty-Four

The appointment of new Councils and committees created stability and a sense of comfort amongst the Canadian Ismailis. The Portfolio members on the new Councils were supported by committees appointed by the respective Councils that mobilized to develop and implement community support programs. The Jamat now numbered close to 13,000 across Canada. As their numbers grew, the professionals reached out to assist new professionals arriving in Canada with advice and support in finding jobs.

By July, one year after the Tanzanian Ismailis had started to arrive in Canada, there was a sense of confidence in the community. Most were optimistic and looking forward to becoming established in Canada. For them, East Africa was a distant past to which they would never return, but there were a significant number of Ugandan Ismailis, particularly those who had lost large businesses and valuable real estate, who believed that Idi Amin could not last. He was a madman and would either be overthrown by his own people, or some western power would engineer his removal. What they had experienced was the work of the army, most of whom were uneducated brutes, suddenly empowered to rob and kill, and a small number of government officials who wanted to get whatever they could get out of the departing Asians. These people were not representative of the Ugandan Africans who were good people, many of whom hated what Amin and his army had done. Uganda had a significant class of well-educated Africans who, they were sure, would not tolerate Amin and would eventually take power, and when they did, they would invite the Indians to return and reclaim their properties and businesses. These Ismailis waited for this to happen, which impeded their effective settlement in Canada.

What they did not know was that Amin also recognized the threat that the educated Ugandans represented for him. After the Asian expulsion, he turned on them and systematically eliminated the educated class and anyone he remotely suspected of posing any threat to his regime. Between 100,000 and 500,000 Ugandans died in the seven years he ruled the country until he was eventually overthrown in 1978 by the invading Tanzanian army.

IN EARLY AUGUST, ANIL called Rafiq to say that he had prepared the Mountain View Inn income statement and balance sheet for six months ended July 31st, and had proposed a board meeting in mid-August to review the performance. Whereas under their agreement, Anil could represent Almin on the board, he felt that Rafiq should attend. The other directors were okay with that. He said that he and Sophia had planned to visit them in September, but if Rafiq would participate in the board meeting, he could bring Shameem, his parents, Tazim, and Almas with him. They could all stay at The Mountain View Inn at a family discount rate. Rafiq's parents, Almas, and Tazim had not seen Vancouver, and Anil felt sure that they would enjoy the place. He and Sophia would take two weeks off, and they could tour the province and drive to Calgary via the Okanagan, Jasper, Lake Louise, and Banff.

Rafiq was excited about the idea and committed to check with the families and circle back. "I'm on vacation, and my summer job at the Shopper's can end on August 10th. Mom can take a vacation any time," Tazim said when Rafiq discussed the idea with her.

"Would you like to take Asif with us? We'll pay for his room and flight, and Anil and Sophia can meet him."

"No, Asif and I are not serious. We date, hug and kiss, but there is no more romance between us."

"Are you bullying him, Tazim?"

"What do you mean by *bullying* him? I don't bully him. Why do you ask?"

"Let me put it this way. Who decides what movie you're going to see when you go out?"

"I do because I read the critiques, and I know what movies have been well rated."

"And who decides which restaurant to go to for dinner?"

"I do because the only place he wants to go is Swiss Chalet."

"What's wrong with Swiss Chalet? I love their chicken."

"What planet are you living on, Rafiq? You can't go there for your dinner dates. Remember the places in London where you used to take Shama for dinner?"

"I guess Asif wants to take you where he can afford to treat you. Who pays when you go to fancier places?"

"He puts some money on the table, but mostly, I pay."

"And who decides what time he will come around to pick you up and what evenings you will go out?"

"Uhm…I do."

"I rest my case, Tazim. Your parents and I have spoilt you, and now you've become a brat. At times, I see you being rough with Mom too, and I don't like that."

"Am I that bad, Rafiq?"

"You're not bad, sweetheart. You just need to be mindful of these things. I know you're frustrated because Dad passed away, Anil is in Vancouver, and Mom is your responsibility but look at her – she's happy here. She's enjoying her work and making friends in the community. She's earning enough money to pay for your education and all other household expenses, and she's giving you a liberal pocket allowance. You know, Anil has been sending $250 a month for Mom and you, and she has asked me to deposit all of it into a savings account for you, and she has not drawn a penny of it, nor of the money, your dad had sent to Anil when we were in the U.K."

"Oh, my God! I feel awful. You're right. I am a bit harsh with her sometimes. I'll watch myself."

"So, how does the future look for you and Asif?"

"I think we both know it's not going to last. I'm too assertive for him."

"You mean you're a *bully*?" Rafiq said, laughing.

"You're really enjoying this, aren't you, Rafiq?"

WHEN RAFIQ DISCUSSED THE Vancouver trip with his dad, Salim said, "You can take Mom, but I can't come. I've introduced all these new lines in the store, and they are moving well. July and August are the months for maximizing our sales of these new items. I have to be here. These two months will determine if my ideas have worked or not."

"Oh, Dad, this would be our first family vacation here! B.C. is so beautiful. Alberta's parks are gorgeous. I'd always dreamt of taking you and Mom on safari, but that never happened. In Vancouver, we'll have a nice hotel to stay in. Anil and Sophia know Vancouver and will show us everything. Can't Mark and Leo manage without you?"

"They can, but it'll look bad if, after introducing these items, I'm gone during the busiest period for marketing and selling them."

"But we want to go for only two weeks, not two months."

"Even two weeks will not look good, and if I come, I'll be thinking about the store and will not be able to relax and enjoy the vacation. Maybe we can go somewhere later in the year. We'll see."

THE PLAN PROCEEDED WITHOUT Salim. Rafiq, Shameem, Yasmin, Almas, and Tazim arrived in Vancouver, and Anil and Sophia received them at the airport. Rafiq picked up a full-size rental car. After checking in at the Mountain View Inn, they walked over to *Earl's* for lunch. They spent the afternoon walking around Stanley Park and explored Robson Street and visited other downtown attractions in the evening. The next day, they followed Anil and Sophia up to the subdivision where the house they had purchased was being built. The area was still a construction site, so they could not enter the house, but they could see it almost completed from a distance.

"The house is beautiful. Vancouver is beautiful. Why didn't we come here with you, Anil?" Tazim asked.

"You got admission into U of T, not here, and Mom wanted to be near Yasmin aunty."

"Yes, but in three years, when I finish, I'm coming here," she said.

"I KNOW YOU DIDN'T see the inside, but did you like the house?" Sophia asked

Almas when they were alone.

"It's a beautiful house, Sophia."

"Would you like to come live with us here? You know Shama, Rafiq, Uncle Salim, and Aunty Yasmin will move away when their house is ready in a couple of months. They won't be in the same building as you anymore. I don't want Tazim and you to be alone."

"Is there an Honest Ed's here? And what about Tazim? She has her school."

"No, Mom, there is no Honest Ed's here, and if you come here, Anil won't let his mother work for anyone, and neither will I. You can retire. Tazim is a big girl now, and she can stay in a university residence or move to live with the Abdullas."

"No, Sophia, I'm grateful that you are asking. I'm very happy with my work. They're so kind to me. We'll stay on in Toronto. I will, however, give up everything and move here if you have a baby."

"Will you, Mom? I would be so happy if you do that."

"Of course! So, when will the baby come?"

"Anil and I have started thinking about it. Hopefully, within the year."

"I will pray for you, beta."

THE BOARD MEETING WENT smoothly. Everything looked positive. Akbar had aggressively marketed the hotel at the airport and with travel agents. He had also placed ads in travel magazines and was getting overseas clients. He had replaced staff at the front counter who, he said, had become complacent, with a new team that was friendlier to customers. Room revenues for the first six months were 10% higher than Anil's conservative projections, and the bottom line was 22% better. Everyone complimented Akbar, who asked Anil to revise his next six-month forecasts by a further 5%. That would be his challenge to realize.

One partner, Rahim Jaffer, invited all of the partners and their families to dinner at his large house in Burnaby that evening. He also announced that his brothers, who had settled in Dallas, were asking him to move there to participate in a large hotel purchase. He wanted to divest his shares. Based on the formula value in their partnership agreement, they were worth around $60,000. According to the agreement, he had to offer the shares first to the existing partners, and if none wanted to buy, he could sell to another investor acceptable to all partners, which he did not plan to do. If no existing partners wanted to buy, he would stay in, but would likely move to Dallas.

"You will have to let us discuss this amongst ourselves after we finish this meeting, Rahim," said Akbar.

"That's perfectly fine," he replied, rising to leave the room.

"Before you leave, Rahim, I want Akbar to give us a few minutes to review his employment agreement," said Anil, who had been leading the meeting.

"Sure," said Akber, and he exited the room.

"Well, as you can see, Akbar has done very well, and he is ambitious. I meet him for lunch every two weeks. He's full of ideas and enthusiasm. Now, he may run out of steam at some point, or he may move the hotel to higher levels. Good performance should be rewarded. I propose we give him a 15% increase in his salary."

"I agree, but would it not be better to offer him a performance bonus at year-end?" Rahim asked.

"You're right, Rahim. That's something we should have built into the employment agreement when we started. Why don't we give him a 10% raise now to reward his first six-month performance, and hereon, we can offer him 5% of pre-tax profits as a performance bonus," suggested Rafiq.

"Sounds good to me," replied Rahim.

"I'm fine with it," said Anil. "Rafiq, of course, does not have a vote, as I vote for Almin. You're okay, Yusuf?" he asked the fourth partner, who was older than the others."

"What do I know? I'm okay with whatever you youngsters decide," said Yusuf with a smile.

They called Akbar in, and Anil said, "We have a majority vote here to increase your salary by 10% per year starting at the beginning of August and to revise your employment agreement to give you a performance bonus of 5% of pre-tax profits going forward. We can make it unanimous if you vote in favor."

"Oh, that's so generous of you guys," said Akbar, becoming a little emotional.

Everyone congratulated Akbar, and Rahim left to go help his wife prepare to host dinner.

"Any takers for Rahim's shares?" Anil asked.

"I'm not comfortable with anyone of us acquiring all 25% of Rahim's shares and becoming a 50% shareholder," said Akbar. "Can we each consider buying 33% of his shares? That way, our shareholding will remain equal."

"I'm happy with that," said Yusuf.

"We should be okay to invest $20,000 between us?" Anil asked Rafiq.

Rafiq nodded.

Speaking to everyone, Anil said, "So, it is hereby recorded that Rahim has offered to sell his shares for the formula value of $60,000, which shares will be acquired equally by Yusuf, Akbar, and Almin as of September 1st, 1973."

The women were all ready to go to Rahim's place for dinner when Anil and Rafiq went to Tazim's room, where they had gathered. They had enjoyed a full day of sightseeing with Sophia.

RAHIM AND HIS WIFE, Nadia, received them at the door of their elegant house. Akbar, Yusuf, and their wives were already there.

This is going to be a difficult evening listening to everyone talk about business, Tazim thought to herself. After all were seated in the lounge, a smartly dressed young man came down the stairs. Rahim introduced him to everyone as his son Shabir.

Shabir said hello to everyone and boldly pulled a chair and parked himself next to Tazim's seat.

"So how do you like Vancouver?" he asked Tazim.

"Hi, I'm Tazim," she said pointedly, extending her hand. He shouldn't be asking how she liked Vancouver without first knowing who she was and properly introducing himself, she thought.

"I know. You're Anil's sister. My dad told me about you. He saw you at the hotel. He said that you're beautiful and that I would like you. That's why I stayed home."

"So, do you think I'm pretty?" she laughed, aware of several pairs of eyes trained upon the two of them.

"You're beautiful, but I have to get to know you better. Why don't we take our drinks to the patio deck and leave the elders here?"

What a pompous brat! But let me take him on, Tazim thought, and picked up her glass and stood up to go out. Everyone looked at the two exiting. Rahim and his wife, Nadia, smiled at each other.

"Do you have any siblings?" Tazim asked as they sat down.

"I'm an only child."

"Don't only children usually grow up to become brats?"

"Are you saying I'm a brat?"

"So far, you're certainly behaving like one, but why don't you convince me that you are not?"

Shabir seemed to revel in the challenge. They sat and talked for a half-hour until dinner was served and returned to the patio deck after filling up their plates.

Shabir was in his fourth year of the B. Comm. program at the UBC. He had his own car - a Pontiac Trans-Am. He was full of hot air, and Tazim thought it would not be at all difficult for her to puncture his balloon and bring him down to earth. He was fun to talk to, and he laughed a lot and made her laugh, too. He did not seem to have a serious view of the world and lacked maturity.

"How long are you here for?" he asked.

"Until Saturday. On Sunday, we plan to drive to Calgary via the Okanagan Valley, Jasper, Lake Louise, and Banff, and return home from Calgary on the 25th ."

"Oh, that's a beautiful drive. I've done it twice. But you can't all fit in one car. Why don't we do this? I can come with you guys. You ride in my car with me, and we'll have a lot of fun."

"Uh, I don't think that my brothers will like that," she laughed. "Anil and my sister-in-law will drive in their car, and the rest of us will ride with Rafiq in our rental."

"That's too bad. We could've stayed at a beautiful lodge I know in Okanagan. You're not leaving until Sunday, and I'm on vacation. Why don't you spend tomorrow with me? I'll take you around and show you Vancouver."

"I've seen most of it."

"Then let me take you to Whistler. If we leave early, we can be back by 9.00 p.m. Will your brothers be okay with that?"

"I've heard about Whistler. I understand it's beautiful. Let me check."

After having spent almost 90 minutes on the patio, Tazim said, "I think we should go in and socialize a little with the adults."

"So, who's here from your family? I can try and make a good impression on them."

"Well, you know, my brother, Anil. Seated next to him is his wife, Sophia."

Pointing at Rafiq and Shameem, she said, "That's Rafiq, my other brother, and that's Shameem, his wife. Then there are my mom and Rafiq's mom over there."

"Hold on a second. Your two brothers have two separate mothers?"

Tazim laughed. "Rafiq is not my biological brother, but we're family. I'll have to get his permission to go to Whistler with you, more so than Anil's. He's the one you have to impress."

"Can I impress his wife instead? She's the most gorgeous Ismaili woman I've ever seen…I mean, other than you, of course."

"Stay away from her. She'll chew you up and spit you out in five minutes. Rafiq is kinder."

When they went in, Shabir sat next to Yasmin. "Aunty, you have a very charming daughter," he said.

"She's her daughter," Yasmin said, pointing to Almas. "I'm Rafiq's mom. And you are a smart-looking young man."

"Thank you, Aunty," he continued glibly. "Is this your first trip to Vancouver?"

"Yes, it's beautiful. We love it."

After watching Shabir talk to Yasmin for a few minutes, Tazim walked over to him and said, "Come over here, I'll introduce you to my brothers and their wives." After some small talk with Anil, Sophia, and Shameem, Tazim introduced him to Rafiq and said, "Shabir wants to take me to Whistler tomorrow."

Without missing a beat, Rafiq said, "That's very nice of you, Shabir. Anil was suggesting that we, too, should go to Whistler, but we don't have two days to go and come back."

"I was proposing a day trip. We can leave early and come back in the evening. Can I please take Tazim there?"

Looking at Tazim, Rafiq said, "Let me talk to Anil to see what he has planned for us for tomorrow, and we can then decide."

ON THE DRIVE BACK to the hotel, Rafiq said, "Almas aunty, our hosts' son invited Tazim to go to Whistler for the day. What do you think?"

"I don't know what Whistler is, but whatever it is, you decide with Anil if she should go. Whatever you two say is fine with me."

Tazim rolled her eyes, and Rafiq took notice.

"Aunty, Tazim is grown up. She's almost 22 years old, and she's smart as a whip. It's not for Anil and me to decide where she can go and with whom."

"Do you want to go, Tazim?" asked Yasmin. "When you guys were out on the patio, his mom sat next to me and said that her son does not have a girlfriend, and they would be very happy if he could find a nice girl. We both knew who she was talking about."

"Well, he's a little childish, but he's harmless. I can go with him."

"Then you go," Rafiq said, not without a little discomfort.

TAZIM'S TRIP WITH SHABIR was fun. The ride in his Trans-Am was a thrill. He got a $20 speeding ticket for driving at 75 m.p.h. in a 60 m.p.h. zone. "Not a problem. I didn't get any demerit points," he laughed.

He took her to the mountains where he said he skied with his friends in winter. "You should come here for Christmas. This place is beautiful in summer, but it's gorgeous in winter. I'll teach you to ski in one day."

After spending the entire afternoon exploring Whistler, Shabir took her to Fairmont Chateau Whistler for an early dinner, and they arrived back in Vancouver by 9.30 p.m. In spite of herself, Tazim had to admit that it had been a fun-filled day.

"My parents said that I should bring you over for them to meet with you before I drive you back to the hotel. Would you mind?" he asked.

"My mom will be worried. I think I should go home."

"We can call the hotel and let your mom know. My dad also has Anil's phone number. We can call him too if you want."

"Okay, but isn't this too late for them?"

"No, they don't go to sleep until midnight."

NADIA GAVE TAZIM A big hug when they arrived and holding her hand, led her into the lounge.

"I'm so glad that you came, beta. Did you have fun in Whistler?" she asked.

"Yes, Shabir showed me around, and we had a great time. The drive was also beautiful."

They sat and talked for about 15 minutes. Nadia told her that they were planning to move to Texas, where it was warmer, but Shabir would stay on in Vancouver, and they would often visit, so they would keep the house. She said that she had always wanted a daughter and hoped that someday Shabir would bring home a wife.

Like Yasmin aunty, she's looking for a Shama to be the daughter she never had, but I don't think I want to be this lady's Shama, thought Tazim, although her affection touched her. They seemed to like her genuinely.

"You kids must be hungry. Let's have something to eat," said Nadia.

"We had dinner before we came," said Tazim.

"Ok, just a small snack then," replied Nadia.

Tazim knew better than to argue with an Ismaili mother about food.

They sat enjoying cakes, cookies, and other goodies and talking until past 11.00 p.m.

"We'll be pleased to see you again before you go, beta," Rahim said as they prepared to leave.

"We leave on Sunday, Uncle, so I don't think we'll have the time, but my family and I have really appreciated your warmth and hospitality."

Hugging him, Tazim added, "I'm very pleased to have met you, and I'm very touched by your affection."

"You're most welcome, beta. Please come again. We are here until the end of the year," said Nadia.

When Shabir dropped her off at the hotel, her family was sitting in the lobby, waiting for her. "So, how was your day?" asked Rafiq.

"A lot of fun; Whistler is beautiful. And Shabir was very gentlemanly. He treated me with respect, opened the car door for me, and he slowed down when I asked him to do so, but he still got a ticket. I think when we met at his house, he was trying to impress me and didn't know how to impress a girl. He was alright. His parents were also very kind to me."

"You know they would like you to be his girlfriend," Yasmin said.

"Yeah, but I don't think I want him to be my boyfriend. He invited me to come here for Christmas and go skiing in Whistler, but I don't think I'll take him up on that."

"Well, they seem like nice people. Why don't you keep in touch by phone and get to know him better? You can always be friends with him," said Shameem.

Tazim laughed. Relationship by committee…it was the Ismaili way.

THEY RETURNED TO TORONTO with beautiful memories of Vancouver, whale watching in Victoria, the ride through Okanagan, and the breathtaking views of Jasper, Lake Louise, and Banff. Salim listened to their stories and wished that he could have been there with them, but he was glad that he had stayed back. The new lines he had introduced were performing better than expected because he was there to push them.

1973
Eighty-Five

S ophia told me that they're planning a family," Shameem told Rafiq two days after their return from Western Canada. "She also said that if they have a baby, Almas aunty will move to Vancouver to care for the child."

"That's great! I wish that we could do that too, but you still need to finish two years of your Neurology specialization."

"In two years, you and I both will be 33 years old. If we want to have children, now is the time. I wish we could have had children when I was 25, but it just wasn't feasible while I was studying and doing my residency and working all kinds of crazy hours. Now I'll have more regular working hours, and if we have a baby, there's the six-month maternity leave. I'm sure that like Almas aunty, Mom will want to look after the child when I go back to work."

"I'm sure she'll be happy to stay home to look after the baby, but I'd like to ask her before we make any plans."

A COUPLE OF DAYS later, when he was alone with his mother, Rafiq asked, "Mom, now that you and Almas aunty have graduated from your secretarial program, do you both want to look for better jobs?"

"Almas aunty doesn't. She took the course because you asked her to, and she wanted to get some higher education, but she's so happy with her work that she will not change jobs for anything. She also told me that Sophia and Anil are planning a family, and if they have children, she will move to Vancouver to look after the kids.

When are you going to have children? You're not getting younger, you know."

Rafiq laughed. "You'll be happy to know that now that Shama has finished her residency, we're also thinking of planning a family."

"If that's the case, there's no point in me looking for another job that I would have to quit when the baby arrives, is there?"

"Would you give up your job if Shama and I have children?"

"Of course! Are you planning for Shama to give up her work and stay home to look after the children?"

"No, she has two more years of specialization to do. She can't stay home."

"Well, then who will look after the baby if I don't? I wouldn't want you to send your baby to daycare if I'm here. I will give up any job and look after my grandchild, but Dad and I talked about something recently that he said I should ask you. The house will be ready in a month; do you want us to move there with you? It was okay for us to be together here for a year, but now that Dad has a good job and we're all settled, we would understand if you and Shama would like to be alone in your own place. Of course, if the baby is born, Dad will drive me over to your place every morning and bring me home in the evening. We might even move into an apartment building near your place."

"Mom, for a start, the house is not mine. We're buying it with your and Dad's money. The Vancouver investment is in Shama's and my name, but the money is yours. It's your investment. Everything in this apartment is what we bought with the money Dad and you sent. But why do you ask, Mom? Did Shama say anything to you or Dad to lead you to believe that she would like us to live separately?"

"No, she hasn't said a word, Rafiq. Dad and I just thought that you may want privacy, like all young couples do. Do you want to at least ask Shama? If we want to all move together into the house in a month, we should be sure that we all want to do that. We can't move and then find out it was a mistake."

"I'll ask her, Mom, but I know what she'll say."

"I'M HURT THAT MOM would think that way," Shameem said when Rafiq relayed to her his conversation with his mother. "Why would she think that we would ever want not to have them in our lives? Or is it that they want to have a place of their own? I find this very disconcerting."

"No, I don't think that they want to be alone. I think it's fair of them to suggest that we should think this through to avoid problems down the road. What you wanted to know, and what she has confirmed, is that she will be there to look after the baby, if and when we have one. They will be delighted to know that we want them to stay with us if I can tell her that."

After remaining silent for a few minutes, Shameem said, "I think you're right that they want us to think this through. I'll speak with Mom tomorrow."

SHAMEEM WOKE UP EARLY the next morning to find Yasmin in the kitchen. Hugging her, she said, "Mom, Rafiq told me about your conversation with him. I told him that we're staying with you for the rest of our lives."

Yasmin smiled and said, "Are you sure, Shama? Nothing would make us happier than to be with our children and grandchildren, but we want you to be certain. It's a big decision."

"You're a blessing in our lives, Mom. You're not just our parents; you're our friends and mentors."

Yasmin smiled and averted her eyes to hide the tears welling up.

THE MOVE INTO THE new house involved a lot of work. Appliances had to be purchased. Drapes and blinds had to be ordered and installed. Carpets and area rugs had to be ordered, and the deliveries coordinated. A lawnmower and snow shovel had to be bought. The move into the apartment had been so easy. All four of them had to take two days off from work. Salim coordinated as much as possible through the hardware store. It took them almost ten days to become fully settled.

One week into the move, they realized that one car for all four of them to travel to and from work was not working out. For Rafiq, making three stops to drop off his parents and Shameem, parking the car in the City Hall parking lot, and walking to his office building took almost two hours.

"You can't keep doing this, Rafiq," said Salim. "Get another car for yourself. The Pontiac is good for me for at least another three years," Salim said.

"I agree, Dad. What car would you like us to buy, Shameem?" Rafiq asked.

"I don't know much about cars, but the other day I drove with a colleague to a meeting in her Ford Thunderbird. I loved the ride."

"That's a sporty two-door car. Looks great. I like it too. Let's look into it. The GM counterpart is Pontiac Grand Prix. I'm partial to the Grand Prix. We can look at that too." Rafiq said.

A week later, an Ismailis agent sold them a well-equipped Thunderbird from a Ford dealership's showroom.

Rafiq and Shameem could now attend the Jamatkhanas that their friends attended and go out afterward. The freedom of independence enabled both generations to settle comfortably into their new shared home.

Five inches of snow came down in the night a month and a half after they moved into the house. In anticipation of the storm, Salim and Rafiq were up early and started shoveling. Rafiq had experience shoveling snow in England, but there, the driveway was small, and so little snow fell. This was backbreaking. Salim wondered if moving into the house was the right decision. Life was so much less work in the apartment.

IN EARLY DECEMBER, ANIL called Rafiq to say that Rehana had invited the four of them to go to Trinidad for the Christmas holidays. It would be nice and warm there. Also, she was five months pregnant.

"That's wonderful, Anil. It's very kind of Rehana to invite us all, but we can't leave Dad and Mom alone during our first winter in the house. Dad and I shovel the snow together. Also, we spent quite a bit on our trip to Vancouver and Alberta in August. We really can't afford to take another holiday until next summer, but you guys should go. You don't move into your house until January, so you don't have to worry about snow removal and pipes bursting when you are not there."

"Sophia and I have been working hard. The Council work has also kept me very busy. A break would be good. Sophia is looking at hotels for us to stay. She doesn't want to impose on Rehana," said Anil.

"That sounds like a good idea. How's your Council work going?" asked Rafiq.

"It's a lot of work. The way I see it, as we approach the year-end, the Jamat here is coalescing into several categories."

"How so?"

"The first are the monied people. There are five to eight families who have come here with $250,000 to $500,000. They're in a class by themselves. I don't know what they're doing, but a couple of them have bought large houses in British Properties. They're less than 1% of the Jamat.

"Wow! Even though the numbers are small, it's good to hear that in less than two years of being here, Ismailis are prospering."

"I, too, am happy for these families, and they're quite generous in their support for Jamati programs and Imamat projects."

"What's the second category?"

"These are a handful of people, maybe 300 families like our partners, who came to Canada with $75,000 to $100,000. They account for about 5% of Jamati households. These people are forming groups and buying hotels and small apartment buildings. Some are even buying these properties on their own. Some are coming to me for help with project evaluation. That's not too difficult for me to do, but many have also heard about the partnership and management agreements our group entered into and want me to draw up similar agreements for them, which, of itself, would also not be difficult, but some don't appreciate the need for the agreement to be fair to everyone and want clauses changed to suit them.

I'm getting drawn into their negotiations and, at times, their arguments. I'm ending up mediating between them. I sometimes return home at 2.00 a.m. on weekdays."

"Oh, my God! Is Sophia okay with this?" "You'd be surprised; all she says when I finish dinner and run out to meet these people is that we must help our fellow Ismailis."

"You're a lucky man, Anil, to have Sophia as your wife. But aren't you getting tired of doing this? Have you thought about the liability issues arising out of your work?"

"To some extent, as a Council Member, I have to do this; it's my mandate. To protect the Council and me from any liability suits, I get everyone to sign a declaration that I got an Ismaili lawyer to prepare, that says that my work is gratis, I'm advising them in my personal capacity and not as a Council member, and they cannot hold the Council or me liable for any work I do for them or advice I give them. All of my work must be reviewed by their accountants and lawyers before they implement anything. This is quite ironclad. I'm not worried about this. People who worry me are the ones who think they're too smart and don't want to ask for my help or their lawyers and accountants' help and believe they don't need any partnership agreements. They're going to get into trouble."

"What's the third group?"

"Well placed professionals. There are many who are well qualified, can present themselves well, and have found good jobs. Mind you, even in this group, many had to search hard before landing good jobs. Their spouses are also, in many cases, professionals. Many are coming here from the U.K. with pre-arranged jobs and moving up the corporate ladders. Many are buying homes. In my estimation, they account for 50% of Ismaili households in Vancouver."

"That's a good number, Anil. Who's next?"

"Professionals who are not well placed. These are people who are well qualified and should be in good jobs, but either due to their inability to market themselves effectively or simply a lack of motivation, have not found jobs in their line of work and have changed careers. There is this Nairobi University graduate who is a structural engineer and who, I think, should have worked harder to find a job in his field here or moved to Calgary or Toronto. He's now enrolled in the C.A. program. It will take him five years to earn the kind of money he would have been earning in his profession right now if he had persevered. This group, in my estimation, is some 10% of Ismaili household heads in Vancouver."

"Who's the fifth group?"

"Professionals who have taken up whatever jobs they could find, - counter sales, commission sales, low-level provincial government administrative jobs, etc. They are not doing anything to advance their career, not moving to Toronto or Alberta for better prospects and have become demotivated and some are struggling. They're making their ends meet. I estimate they're some 5% of Ismaili household here."

"That's around 70%. Who are the rest?"

"Over 20% are people who came here with $35,000 - $45,000 and want to be in business. They're having a difficult time. Good businesses here are expensive, and they don't have enough money to buy. Without established credit records, they can't always borrow from the banks. Some have decided to put their money away and have taken up factory jobs or other labourer positions. Others are buying smaller businesses where they have to work ridiculously long hours to generate any sort of a living wage. This group is a major area of focus for me."

"And the last 10%?"

"People who have come here from the refugee camps in Europe on their family sponsorships; people without much education and with no money. About half of them, - about 5% of all, have found factory jobs or as parking lot attendants. Their spouses are working as housekeeping staff in hotels or cashiers in supermarkets or daycare centers. Some have two jobs. Their kids are delivering newspapers before going to school. They're working their hands to the bone and are focused on their children's education. A small number are going to trade schools to acquire market-able skills. Of all Ismailis here, I hold this group in the highest respect. I believe that they will break their cycle of poverty in one generation."

"And the other half of them?"

"These are people from the same background and in similar jobs, but they have no desire to improve their lot, and some don't even know what grades their children are in. I think they will end up as what I call the 'comfortably poor'. They were poor in Africa and will be poor here."

"I don't know the status of Ismailis in Toronto, but I don't think it would be too different from Vancouver. There are some who, Dad says, just made ends meet in Tanzania, but have found their skills in demand here. These are people who were auto mechanics, plumbers, and carpenters. They're making good money and doing well. Some, like my friend Zul, who has little formal education, are raking in big money as insurance and car salesmen."

"This is a land of opportunity," said Anil. "I am with everyone who wants to work hard and invest time in their own and their children's education. We need a survey of the Jamat to establish some baseline data that we can chart against data we gather in the future. As we come to the end of 1973, we estimate that there are 6,000 of us here in B.C., 1,000 in Alberta 800 in Quebec, and 10,000 in Ontario, but we don't know how many, exactly. We don't know what the male/female breakdown is.

We don't know how many are employed, how many are looking for jobs, how many are in businesses, and who is still searching for a business. We need this information for other jurisdictions, as well. The numbers have grown and are growing rapidly, but we have little granular detail."

"It's good to see the Jamat grow."

"Of course, but we must be able to make sure that the Jamat is successfully settling and integrating into the wider Canadian milieu. For that, we need a comprehensive demographic and socio-economic survey of the Jamat."

LATER THAT MONTH, TAZIM also received a call from Vancouver. Shabir was calling to invite her to go to Vancouver for the Christmas holidays. He had been calling often after she came back from Vancouver, and she found herself enjoying their chats. Her relationship with Asif had all but ended. His mother also got on the phone to invite her.

"I would love to, but I can't, Aunty. My brother and his wife are going to Trinidad for two weeks at Christmastime."

"That's not a problem. You can stay with us, beta."

"See Aunty, the Abdullas have all moved from our building to their house. If I come there, my mom will be alone here, and she won't be able to go to Jamatkhana or grocery shopping without me. But let me check, and I'll get back to Shabir and you."

"I'LL BE ALRIGHT, TAZIM, you should go, if you want to," said Almas, who was eavesdropping.

"I would've gone, but Anil and Sophia are going away, and I don't want to go stay at Shabir's house. Also, I don't want to waste your hard-earned money when I'm not earning anything."

"You don't need to worry about that, Tazim. It would be fine to draw $300 from the funds Anil has been sending. Go and have a nice holiday."

"That's very kind of you, Mom. I do want to learn to ski. Girls in my college talk about how much fun skiing is. I was hoping that I would ask Anil and Sophia to come with us to Whistler and they could learn to ski also. We would have made a nice foursome. But that's fine. We had a great holiday in summer and Anil and

Sophia deserve to take a relaxing vacation. Inshallah, I can do that next year."

"Inshallah. How are your driving lessons going?"

"Well, Mom. The instructor said he will schedule my driving test week after next."

"I hope you pass, and we can then get a car. It's difficult taking buses and subway everywhere. Have you decided what car we will buy?"

"No, Mom. Anil said he will buy and pay for the car in Vancouver and arrange for it to be delivered here."

"I hope he doesn't buy a car like his car. It was so uncomfortable to sit in the back. Why would Anil buy a car like that?"

"He won't buy a car like that for us, Mom. He will buy us one with lots of room and four doors."

ON THEIR RETURN FLIGHT from Trinidad, as the aircraft taxied towards the runway, Anil asked, "So, did you enjoy Trinidad? "

"It was great. In the middle of our winter, it was good to enjoy the island's lush vegetation and the turquoise ocean. I wish the ocean had been a little warmer. It was not comfortable to swim in. How did you enjoy the place?"

"Rehana and Eugene went out of their way to make our stay comfortable. Their villa is beautiful and the room they gave us was well equipped and had such a great view. I'm glad we could stay there instead of in a hotel. They had taken time off from work and took us to the finest restaurants and all of the tourist attractions. I can't imagine what more they could have done for us. I am glad you invited them to visit us in the summer," Anil replied.

"I'm so happy that you could spend time with Rehana again, Anil," said Sophia. "You must have missed her a lot."

"Yes, we had worked and socialized together for over three years. We were close friends, and I did miss her."

"And you had loved each other very much. I could see the affection in your eyes for her and in her eyes for you. Trinidad would not have been my first choice for a vacation. I would have liked to have gone to the Bahamas or Hawaii, but I could see how happy you were when Rehana invited us, and that's why I agreed to go."

Anil was surprised to hear Sophia say this and was quiet for a few moments before asking, "So you knew that I was in love with Rehana, and you still wanted to take me to see her?"

"Anil, the ability to love is Allah's gift. You have that gift. There are people, like your ex-girlfriend Jenny, for whom relationships are purely transactional. They don't know what love is. How could anyone spend as much time as you did with someone like Rehana and not fall in love with her? And how could she not fall in love with you? I'm not jealous of your love for one another. I admire and respect the fact that in spite of loving each other, you both respected the sanctity of her marriage, which you could have so easily violated. This is why she could invite you to go to her place; otherwise she would have never wanted to expose you to her husband. I knew about the purity in your relationship, and that's why I agreed to go to visit her."

"I don't know what to say, Sophia. I cannot imagine another woman being so understanding. I presume you know all this from Shama, right?"

"She had told me this before we got together - and about Jenny too."

"It will be good to have Rehana and Eugene visit Vancouver, but when the baby is born, they will be busy, so I guess we won't see them for a while."

"Probably. Speaking of babies, I'm late this month…"

1974
Eighty-Six

Shortly after moving into the house, Yasmin had seen their neighbors, Drs. Patrick and Lisa Roberts, getting out of their car in their driveway and had walked over to introduce herself. "Hello, neighbors! My name is Yasmin Abdulla. My family and I just moved in. We're from Africa."

"Delighted to meet you, Yasmin," said Lisa. "We were planning to drop in to introduce ourselves to you. My name is Lisa, and this is my husband, Patrick."

Yasmin shook hands with both and said, "Let's plan to get together for coffee at our house, and you can meet my family. Anyone else in your family? Any children?"

"No," said Patrick. "Lisa is an obstetrician, and she's so busy delivering babies, she doesn't have the time to make one for us!"

Lisa added, "Patrick is a cardiologist, and he's so busy listening to people's heartbeats, he doesn't have the time to listen to mine telling him to help me make a baby!"

Yasmin laughed and said, "Inshallah, you will have children soon. My daughter-in-law, Shameem, is a doctor also."

"You're a Muslim. You said *Inshallah*, God willing. I have Muslim friends. My parents told us that our great, great grandparents were Muslims when they were plucked from a place on the East African coast and brought to America as slaves," Patrick said.

"That place could be Bagamoyo in Tanzania," said Yasmin. "I have been there and seen remnants of the slave market. We're from a small town in Tanzania. We are missing our home and our African friends very much. I guess I walked over to say hello to you without hesitation because I felt an affinity for your African origin. I'm happy you will be our neighbors."

The Roberts were surprised that this lady had such warm feelings for people who had not been very nice to them. Both had read about the Asians' property seizure in Tanzania and Idi Amin's expulsion of Asians from Uganda.

THEY CELEBRATED SHAMEEM AND Rafiq's birthdays on New Year's Eve in the new house. They invited over 20 guests, including Patrick and Lisa, Geoff and Carole, Mark and Johanna, Rafiq and Shameem's work colleagues, Zul and Aziza, and some of Tazim's friends.

Much planning had gone into organizing the event, which was intended to also serve as their housewarming party. Tazim and Shameem had coordinated the invitations and decided on the menu, and Yasmin and Almas had taken the lead with the cooking.

It was a lively group. The majority of the guests had never been to an Indian home, nor tasted Indian food. Chicken biryani was the main entrée, but they had also prepared chicken Kiev - for which Yasmin had brought the recipe from Mpwapwa Club - for people who did not want to risk putting hot Indian biryani in their cold Canadian stomachs. Rafiq had purchased some good quality wine for whoever wanted to partake, which most of the non-Ismailis did.

When coffee and tea were being served, all gathered in the lounge. It was a cold evening, and Salim had lit the fireplace. The house was nice and cozy. The conversation soon turned to the Canadian political scene.

The October 1972 general election had resulted in a minority Liberal government with only two more seats than the Conservatives. The Liberals were governing with New Democratic Party (NDP) support.

"Do you think the Liberal-NDP coalition will last?" Aziza asked one of Rafiq's colleagues, Nick Barton.

"I don't think it will last much longer," replied Nick. "The NDP is not supportive of the Liberal measures to control inflation. I doubt that they'll support the next Liberal budget. If they don't, the government will fall and force an election."

"We can't vote because we're not citizens yet, but if I could, I would vote for the

Tories," said Aziza.

"Really? Research shows that immigrants to Canada vote for the party that was in power when they arrived here. Wouldn't you vote for the Liberals? They rescued you from Uganda."

"And for that, I will be eternally grateful to Trudeau and his Liberals. I pray for him and his family every night before I go to sleep, but inflation is a huge issue for Canada, and I don't think that the Liberals will do enough to control inflation. Our exports are becoming expensive, savings are being eroded, and the tourists are staying away."

"I would vote for the Liberals," interjected Zul. "The Tories are talking about controlling wages and prices to curb inflation, but they will probably end up controlling wages only. I don't like that."

"Ah, so you're a house divided when it comes to politics!" said Nick. "Do you argue about it?"

"We argue, yes, but we respect each other's viewpoints," replied Aziza.

"If there's an election, we've agreed to canvass for our respective local candidates. I'll try to convince her to work for the Liberals, but if she wants to drop flyers or go door to door for the Tories, I'll respect that," said Zul.

"And will you campaign for the Liberals because Trudeau brought you here?" Nick asked.

"Yes, and because I like his immigration and multiculturalism policies," Zul replied.

"You know, I personally believe that Trudeau's multiculturalism and open immigration policies are ahead of the Canadian public opinion. There is a segment of people here who are not happy to see so many immigrants from non-European countries coming to Canada. I do not doubt that you've experienced some discrimination in your time here," said Nick.

"I experienced it when I went looking for a job," said Aziza. "It hurt a lot, but we kept reminding ourselves that there are far more people here who are generous and welcoming and see us as fellow human beings, than those that are bigoted."

"This segment of people doesn't like immigrants - any immigrants. We've seen that immigrants, of whatever color, work hard, take jobs that the locals don't want, or want much more money to do. They help our economy grow. Many come here and can't find jobs in their fields of education and training, and they end up driving cabs or working in factories, to build a future for their children. They buy homes, household items, clothes, cars, and create employment. These immigrant haters are now beginning to see brown immigrants, and they don't like it at all. In the main, it's the uneducated ones that are racists," said Nick.

"Not necessarily," said Geoff, who had been listening in. "Carole and I have been to parties where senior-level professionals, after a few drinks, turned to make 'Paki' and Chinese jokes. On both occasions, when this happened, Carole and I left and later told our hosts how offensive their guests were."

"That's sad," said Nick. "I'm sorry to hear that. I would like to believe that as Canadians, we're better than that. The Asians are experiencing the discrimination that the Jews, Italians, Greeks, and East European immigrants suffered when they came here."

"And don't forget the blacks," added Lisa. "What we have suffered – and still suffer – even though we are born here. The other night, a white woman was brought into the Emergency Room because she had gone into early labor with complications. They called me at home, and I got there in 15 minutes. She was having a rough time and screaming in pain, but she took one look at me and started yelling, 'I don't want this n***er to deliver my baby.' I put my hand on her shoulder and sought to comfort her. I told her that she was endangering herself and her baby's life, and no other obstetrician was available. She screamed, 'Take your filthy hands off me. Don't you dare touch me!' I ended up having to guide a white intern on duty to help position the baby for the delivery. The patient was willing to risk injury or even death for herself and her baby rather than let a black doctor touch her."

To move the narrative from the doctor's unfortunate experience, Shameem's friend Sally asked Shameem, "You're very light-skinned, Shama, you could easily pass for a European; have you encountered any discrimination?"

"Not really," replied Shameem, feeling somewhat embarrassed by the question and the attention. "Rafiq and I had jobs lined up when we came here, and Carole and Geoff had rented the apartment for us. Unlike in England, where you would find it very difficult to rent a place if you are colored, I've not heard of any of our people having trouble renting apartments here, but some of the professionals in our community are finding it difficult getting placed in positions for which they are well qualified. In some situations, the employers may truly be looking for people with Canadian work experience, but there are many situations where you can see that their rejection is blatant racism."

"Tazim, tell them what happened to you walking home from the university last summer," said Justin, one of her classmates.

Tazim blanched. She hadn't told her family about what had happened. All eyes were on her, so she took a deep breath and began. "Well, it was scary. I left school at around 10.30 p.m. one evening. It was nice outside, so instead of taking the subway home, I decided to take a leisurely walk along Bloor Street. There was little foot traffic, but I felt completely safe. Then I saw this rusty old two-door car with three boys driving west and slowing down. When they were directly opposite me, the driver rolled down his window and shouted, 'Hey Paki! Why don't you go back to your filthy Punjab? Why are you taking over my country? I hate you. I hate you. We're coming for you. You're dead meat!'

"Luckily, a car drove up behind them and honked, so they drove on, but I had seen the look on their faces, and I knew that they would turn around and come back for me. I ran and ducked into a variety store and asked the owner to call the police."

"A cruiser must have been in the neighborhood and pulled up in less than two minutes. One officer came in and asked what the problem was. I told him what had happened. He said, 'You were right to call us, young lady. Come, let's look for them' and he took me into the cruiser."

"They waited for a while, but the guys didn't come back. The police offered to drive me home, and as we were driving, the hoodlums raced around the corner and overtook the cruiser. 'That's them!' I said, and with the lights flashing, the police drove ahead and stopped them. One went to talk to them and returned after a few minutes and said, 'We can't arrest them or file any charges, but I've taken their names and addresses, and asked them to report to the Police Station tomorrow. They're pretty scared.' I had never been more afraid in my life, and I don't walk alone after sunset anymore."

Rafiq, Shameem, and Salim were speechless. It was a good thing that both mothers were still in the kitchen and out of earshot.

"That's very unfortunate," said Nick. "Things will get better; I believe that it's a matter of time. Ignorance in any society creates fear and suspicion of people who are different. I do not doubt that in time, the white Canadians will get to know you for who you are and will come to respect you."

"Nick is right," piped in Mark. "You need to show people who you are, what your traditions, ethics, and values are, which so resonate with the Canadian ethics and values, how well educated, organized, disciplined, knowledgeable, and sophisticated you are. As Jews, we have suffered similar discrimination, more so when we first started arriving in Canada. I got beaten up in school several times, and there remain clubs and institutions in Toronto where Jews are discriminated against. It's a slow process, but as people come to learn about who you are and how any surface differences are simply just that, attitudes begin to shift."

"I agree, Mark," said Rafiq. "But we believe that pompous self-praise about how good we are and how great we were where we've come from won't get us anywhere. We'll have to earn respect over time with our actions, our professionalism, generosity, engagement in civil society, voluntarism, and contribution to the communities in which we live."

"It's true," added Patrick. "In the few days we have known you as our neighbors, we've come to admire you for your humility, generosity, and friendship. But more people will have to know your people."

The conversation then shifted to life in Uganda before Idi Amin, during the 90-day expulsion period, and the community's escape. Aziza and Zul related their experiences, leaving out the soldier's assault on Aziza.

Jameela and Arif, whom the family knew from Jamatkhana, had a terrifying story. They had been dating for two years when they were at Makerere University in Kampala. After they had graduated - Jameela with a B.A. in Business Administration, and Arif as a medical doctor - they had planned to marry after working for one year to save enough money to rent and furnish a place of their own. Just one month after they graduated, Idi Amin issued the expulsion order. Their departure from Uganda quickly became very complicated.

Arif and his parents were Ugandan citizens. Their citizenship had been validated. They could stay, if they wanted to - at least it appeared so, initially.

Jameela and her two siblings were British and could go to the U.K., but her parents, who lived in Mbale, a small town in Uganda, were Ugandan citizens. Their citizenship had been canceled when they had gone for verification because they were not born in Uganda. That meant that unless Canada or some other country took them, they would end up as refugees in some European country.

Arif wanted Jameela to apply with him to go to Canada. Jameela's parents wanted their daughter to be with them and certainly not go with Arif to Canada when they were not yet married.

Jameela's brother, Alim, wanted to go to the U.K., where he had studied. Her sister, Nooreen, was just 13, and Alim wanted both of his sisters to leave immediately with him and sponsor their parents to join them in the U.K., but Jameela knew that the Ugandan British citizens were themselves having difficulty entering the U.K. Being able to go there and sponsor their parents in short order was wishful thinking.

Arif maintained that Jameela going to Canada with him, was the best option for her family. Alim could go to the U.K. with Nooreen, and then Arif and Jameela would sponsor everyone once they were in Canada.

The arguments dragged on, and in the meantime, the army had become increasingly violent as fewer Indians remained for them to rob. One Ismaili was shot through the head for failing to hand over his car keys to a soldier immediately. There were reports of other killings. Finally, Arif convinced Jameela to apply for Canadian residency. By the time their visas came through, and a flight was designated for them to leave on, Alim and Nooreen had left for the U.K., and only two days remained for all Asians to leave Uganda. The Ismaili leadership had told Jameela that her parents were to leave in the afternoon on charters organized by the Aga Khan Council, to go to a refugee camp in Austria and that she or her brother should sponsor them immediately. Arif's family was already in Canada.

For Jameela, it was an emotional goodbye. She could not imagine what would happen to her parents in a refugee camp.

"I told them, 'As soon as you arrive in Austria, write to us and tell me where you are. We'll be with Arif's family in Toronto. You have their address. I will keep you in my prayers,'" said Jameela as everyone in the room listened in rapt attention to the story. She continued. The bus carrying passengers for the Canadian charter flight departed from The Grand Hotel at 6.00 a.m. It had a Canadian embassy car escort and arrived at Entebbe airport an hour later, without incident. The atmosphere at the airport was tense and chaotic. The Customs officials were searching all baggage and strip-searching everyone. The terminal was filled with machine guns carrying soldiers.

Arif and Jameela were to fly on a Canadian Airlines jet, which the Canadian government had chartered to bring the refugees to Canada.

When the passengers had boarded and the flight was cleared for takeoff, the hydraulics light flickered and then turned solid red. The hydraulics control – among other systems – the landing gear, flaps, and brakes operations, all of which are vital for the aircraft to take off and land safely. This needed to be checked out, but there was no mechanical support available in Entebbe. The aircraft's hydraulics had recently been examined when the warning light had come on, and it was determined that the problem was with the light switch and not the hydraulics system. It could be the light acting up again, or it could be something very serious.

Under normal circumstances, the aircraft would have been grounded until the problem was examined and rectified. The pilot had two options. One was to call for support from Nairobi, which could take up to six hours or more to arrive and another six or twelve to fix. This would require the passengers to deplane. If they did, some might not return alive. The second option was to take off. Whereas he himself was in no danger if he stayed, he did not want to lose any of his passengers. He had seen some passengers holding rosary beads in their hands when they had boarded. This appeared to be a religious group. He decided to level with them and announced, "This is your captain speaking. We have a technical problem with the aircraft, which could be minor or it could be serious and cause us to crash if we take off. There are no aeronautical engineers here who can examine our problem, and it could take up to twelve or more hours to have mechanics brought from Nairobi and the problem fixed. By that time, the deadline for you to leave Uganda will have passed, and I don't know what can happen to you if you are still here. If we decide to call for mechanical support from Nairobi, you will have to disembark. I have seen from the window, and many of you may have also seen, the terminal is not a safe place for you to return to. We are cleared for takeoff now, but with the chaos on the ground, we may be stopped any minute if we don't leave quickly. I have decided to risk the takeoff. Please understand this could be dangerous. If any of you wish to disembark, you have ten minutes in which to do so."

The passengers did not need ten minutes. They started shouting, "Let's go, please! Let's take off."

The pilot came on again, and as the plane started to taxi, he announced, "It looks like we're going. I ask you to pray to whichever God you pray to and keep praying until we land safely in Nairobi. I will be praying with you."

As the jet raced down the runway, all prayed. The takeoff was smooth. The landing gear retracted, and two hours later, as they approached Nairobi, fire engines and ambulances were lined up for a crash landing if the landing gear or the brakes failed.

The pilot, a practicing Catholic, asked the passengers again to pray. The landing gear functioned properly. The brakes engaged when the plane landed, and they came to a steady stop. A loud cheer went up in the cabin.

After hearing their story, the room was silent for a few moments before Nick said, "That must have been a terrifying experience!"

"Yes," replied Jameela. "But we knew that our lives were in the hands of this angel of a pilot who was risking his own life to save ours, and we knew that God would guide him and bring us down safely, which He did. After we arrived here, we asked for his address, and we have been communicating with him. He asked us recently if we could coordinate our messages to him because he certainly cannot respond to all, but he cannot even read everything. It's not just us passengers who are writing to him. Our friends and relatives are also writing to thank him. He is and will remain in our prayers forever."

1974
Eighty-Seven

Salim was up early on January 1st. He had to count inventory for the year-end statements to be prepared. Leo and one of the cashiers assisted, and they were done by 4.00 p.m. Inventory was down by $22,000 from a year earlier and had rolled over 2.1 times compared to the 1.4 times in the previous year.

At Salim's request, the accountant, Ronald Diamond, produced the store's year-end statements by mid-January. Salim requested that Ronald present the accounts to Johanna and Mark, who were eagerly waiting to see the impact of changes Salim had made.

"I have good news all around," said Ronald, as they sat down to review the statements on a Sunday morning. "I hope you have a champagne bottle to break open." He passed a copy of the reports to each of them.

"As you can see, sales increased by $50,000 from last year. Gross profits were up by around $30,000. Operating expenses, including Salim's salary, increased by about $6,000 from a year ago, but operating profit was up by $13,000. This means that Salim paid for himself through the changes he made and increased your net bottom line by $10,000 from last year. He also freed up about $12,000 for you to deploy as you wish by reducing inventory. You can each withdraw $48,000 in management salaries as you did last year. You have a very streamlined operation now."

"That's amazing!" exclaimed Johanna. "I was seeing more cash, but this is more than I'd expected. Congratulations, Salim," she said, hugging him and kissing him on his cheek, leaving a red lipstick stain.

"For God's sake, Johanna, see what you've done now to this poor man!" laughed Mark. "The guy has to go home to his wife."

"I'm sorry," Johanna said, wiping Salim's cheek with a Kleenex. "I'm not just happy about the money you've made for us, Salim. I feel like you're a part of our family. I deeply appreciate the way you look after Mark and care for our business like it's your own. We have never felt so close to anyone outside our immediate family as we do to you."

"Congratulations, Salim," added Mark. "As Johanna says, you're family."

Salim was deeply touched. "That's very generous of you, but I could not have done this without your confidence and guidance," he said.

"Yes, and you listened to us. Now I realize that I stopped you from making certain changes that would have worked well for us." Johanna said.

"True." Mark agreed. "So, what do you want to do this year?"

"Significantly increase our samples and contract business," Salim replied, without missing a beat.

"Can we go easy on that, Salim?" asked Johanna. "I worry about the liability issues if one of our customers is disappointed with the work our contractor does for them. Also, if it's agreeable to you, hereon, I would like Mark to attend here from 2.00 p.m. to 6.00 p.m. only, and not work on Saturdays. To compensate you for Mark's work, we will increase your salary to $1,500 a month. Can we afford that, Ronald?"

"You sure can. Speaking for me, personally, it has been a real pleasure working with Salim," Ronald replied.

"Are you okay with what Johanna is proposing, Salim?" asked Mark.

"I am," replied Salim. "It's time you relaxed, Mark. You have my commitment that the business will continue to run as if you are here. And, Johanna, we'll grow our contract business slowly - at the rate you're comfortable."

SALIM WAS ON CLOUD nine. He could not wait to get home to give the good news to his family and then call Anil and Sophia. He ducked into the washroom to make sure none of Johanna's lipstick remained on his cheek and was on his way home.

Yasmin, Rafiq, and Shameem were still finishing their breakfast when he got home and relayed the good news. "Johanna was so happy, she kissed me!" he said, and added when he saw Yasmin giving him a look, "On my cheek, ... here."

"Congratulations, Dad. I knew that your ideas would work out well!" said Shameem.

"Don't forget that most of what I did was based on Rafiq and Anil's advice. I want to call Anil to thank him."

"They're probably just waking up, Dad. Let's wait until noon their time. So Dad, how much of a raise did they give you?" Rafiq said.

"Let's not count money," Salim said with a laugh. "One thing I want to do as of now is to make the full mortgage payments on this house, although I don't know why you want to carry a mortgage when we have money sitting the bank earning less than what we pay on the mortgage."

"We've got about $50,000 left after the Vancouver investment and the down payment on this house," said Rafiq. "I am constantly reminded of what Anil said when we were considering the motel purchase. He said that property values may go up and down but will always increase in the long term. Now that it looks unlikely that you will go in business for yourself, I think that we should invest in some property here."

"Are you thinking of another motel project? We don't have the $200,000 that the group invested in the Vancouver project, and there is no such group here for us to join," said Salim.

"No, Dad, I was thinking of investing in a couple of new apartments. There is a new development in Don Mills. They are selling for $20,000 - $25,000. If we put down $5,000 on each, a three-bedroom for $25,000 would carry for $300 a month. We could rent out the units for that amount. Almas aunty and Tazim can rent one from us if they decide to move to be nearer to the Jamatkhana and us."

"Shama, Yasmin, what do you think?" Salim asked.

"I don't know, Dad. This is the first time I'm hearing about investing in real estate here," replied Shameem, and looking at Rafiq, said, "Rafiq, you want to become a landlord? You don't know anything about real estate. You've got to find and look after the tenants and collect rent, you know. Do you have the time to do that?"

"I think we should ask for Anil's advice," said Yasmin.

"I wouldn't do it without asking him," Rafiq said, and looking at Shameem, he added, "Shama, this was something I had thought about, but not considered seriously. I'm bringing it up now only because of what Dad just told us. Mark and Johanna are now going to depend on him, and he's not going to be looking for a business for himself. These are new apartments, and if we are selective about tenants, we should not have too many challenges - I think."

ANIL WAS OVERJOYED WHEN Salim told him about the meeting with the accountant. "Anil, any success that I've had in my work is due, in great part, to you. You took as much interest in guiding me as you would have done if it was your dad working here in my place. I'm very grateful to you, Son."

Anil was silent for a moment. He thought of his late father and his immense respect and affection for the Abdullas. "I'm always here, Uncle, to do whatever I can to be of help. We can never repay the debt of gratitude we owe you."

"There are no debts within a family, Son. In our old age, all we need and are just grateful for is your love and prayers."

"You're not old, Uncle! You still have to guide our children and us…and speaking of children, I have some good news for you. Sophia and I are expecting a baby. It was just confirmed yesterday."

"That's wonderful!" exclaimed Salim. "Congratulations! We are delighted." He placed his hand on the receiver and called out to the others.

Everyone was excited to hear the good news and took turns congratulating Anil and Sophia. After expressing his happiness, Yasmin lectured Sophia at length on what she should and should not do during her pregnancy. Rafiq said, "Anil, as Dad told you, he is now committed to the Goldmans. He's not looking for a business for himself. We have some money to invest, but not enough to buy a motel. I was looking at a new development in an area where lots of Ismailis are settling in Toronto. It's a nice area called Don Mills. Three-bedroom units of 1,300 sq. ft. are priced at $25,000. I was thinking of putting down $5,000 on two units. They are almost ready and can be rented for about the same as the PIT and monthly condominium fees. What do you think?"

631

"You want to become a landlord. Rafiq? Tenants will call you in the middle of the night and say the toilet is not flushing or the sink is blocked. You want to deal with that?"

"This is a new building, and I can make it a triple net lease – make the tenants responsible for all maintenance. I think that we'll still be able to find tenants."

"If I had the money - not Sophia's, but my own, I would also invest in real estate. What you want to do maybe one way of doing that. I think it's a great idea to put money into bricks and mortar. If the economics work, go ahead and buy three if you like."

LATER THAT AFTERNOON, RAFIQ took his parents and Shameem to look at the model suites and talk to the sales office. They learned that on their income, they could buy the units with down payments of as little as $2,500 each.

"Rafiq, I suggest that we buy three units, but put down $5,000 on each," said Salim.

"I agree, Dad. These are very well located for access to schools, shopping, banking, medical services, community centers, transit, and weekend Jamatkhanas. We'll find Ismaili tenants easily. Let's buy these in Mom's name."

THE PLAN WENT AHEAD, but the apartments did not get leased as quickly as Rafiq had thought. When they spoke to prospective Ismaili tenants, they looked at the apartments and said that they could rent larger three-bedroom units in rental buildings one block south for $250 a month. Eventually, one unit was rented to an Ismaili family, one to a Tamil family, and one to a Romanian family. Rafiq got them all to sign up for pre-authorized bank payment plans.

IN MARCH, SOPHIA CALLED Shameem to tell her that she had been exchanging letters with Rehana since their return from Trinidad. Rehana had been having problems with her pregnancy and had been hospitalized twice. The doctors were recommending a Caesarian section, but she had opted to attempt a natural birth. Sophia said that Rehana was due in three weeks, and Shameem should pray for her when going to Jamatkhana.

"Oh, dear! I will certainly keep her in my prayers. Our neighbor is an obstetrician. Rehana should come here for the delivery. She would look after Rehana very well, and she could stay with us."

"I suggested that she come here, where I can arrange for her to be cared for by my hospital and stay with us, but she said that the airlines won't take her now that she is over eight months pregnant. How about you? Have you got anything stirring in your belly?"

"Not yet, but hopefully, soon! Please convey our warm regards and prayers to Rehana. I'll tell Rafiq. He will surely want to call her."

WHEN RAFIQ CALLED, REHANA sounded very weak. She said, "I'm tired, Rafiq. I'm drained. I hope that the baby will be born soon. I'm just exhausted."

"Hang in there, Rehana. When the baby is born, Shama and I will come and visit you both. She wants to say hello," he said, as he passed the phone to Shameem.

After a brief conversation, Shameem hung up and said, "She's weak and could not talk more. I'm worried, Rafiq. She didn't sound good. I don't know why she does not want a C-section."

"She's just tired, Shama, and who knows what sort of surgical capacity they have there. Let's just keep her in our prayers. I'm sure that she'll be fine."

TWO WEEKS LATER, THE phone rang at 11.00 p.m. Rafiq picked up the call, and it was Sophia on the line. "I have some horrible news!" she exclaimed, sounding tearful.

Rafiq's heart froze as she continued. "Eugene just called and said that Rehana went into labor, but there were complications, and she lost a lot of blood. The baby died shortly after birth, as it had been severely deprived of oxygen. The hospital gave Rehana a transfusion, but she needed more than they had. It took the hospital some time to find a donor with Rehana's blood type, and by the time they did, Rehana had passed away."

Rafiq's eyes filled with tears. "What? This can't be true! She can't just go like that! We just spoke with her a couple of weeks back! She sounded weak, but this is just horrible. Our dear, dear Rehana."

By this point, Shameem had rushed over, hearing Rafiq's panicked reaction.

"What is it? What happened?" she asked frantically.

"The funeral is scheduled for the day after tomorrow," continued Sophia. "Anil and I are flying out via Toronto tomorrow. If you want to join us, it's Caribbean Airlines Flight 647 departing Toronto at 4.00 p.m."

Rafiq was shaking his head in disbelief as Shameem stared at him imploringly. "I'll check first thing tomorrow morning and book us on that flight, or whichever flight is available."

After ringing off, Rafiq shared the news with Shameem, and both cried as they embraced one another. They informed Yasmin and Salim, who were also devastated to learn of Rehana's passing. They knew how close the children had all been with her, particularly Anil, and it broke their hearts to know that such a lovely young person's life could be cut short so tragically.

SHAMEEM FOUND HERSELF ON the verge of tears throughout the entire flight. She could not believe what had happened. How could Rehana, who was so full of life, be gone, just like that? They had spent so many happy days together. Why did this have to happen? Of all people, to Rehana?"

ANIL AND RAFIQ WERE seated in a different row. Anil tried to control his emotions, but tears were rolling down his face. Every moment he had spent with Rehana was flashing before his eyes. Rafiq could see what he was going through and tried to console him, but each time he tried, he broke down in tears himself. They had imagined that they would go to Trinidad to meet Rehana and play with her baby; instead, they were going there to bury them both.

Eugene was at the airport to receive them with his sister, Dolly. He broke down the moment they emerged from the Customs area. All four embraced him with tears running down their faces. "Thank you for coming. Rehana was closer to you four than she was to anyone outside her immediate family."

"We have no words to express our sorrow, Eugene, and we cannot even imagine the pain you must be feeling," said Anil.

Eugene could see their bloodshot eyes and knew that they were filled with sorrow, as well.

After checking into their hotel, they spent some time with Eugene and Dolly, who told them that in Rehana's family tradition, there would be a Muslim funeral. Approximately 40% of the population in Trinidad was Muslim. Rehana's South Asian ancestors had been brought to Trinidad in the mid-1850s as part of the Indian indenture system to work on sugar cane and cacao plantations.

In the local tradition, the bodies were brought home first and then transported to the local mosque for the prayer service. The service took place first thing the next morning. There were about 100 mourners in attendance, including colleagues, family, and friends. The cleric recited verses of the Quran and offered prayers for the departed souls. The burials were simple but dignified. More prayers were offered after the burial ceremony. The four friends stood close together, united in their grief. The sight of the tiny, baby-sized casket broke everyone's hearts.

After the wake, they spent the afternoon with Eugene and his family and then returned to their hotel. Before departing Trinidad the next day, they met with Eugene to say goodbye.

"I wish you were staying longer. Your presence here was very comforting for me," he said.

"Please stay in touch, Eugene," said Shameem. Rehana will always live in our hearts and memories. Those she has left behind must support one another."

"Thank you again. Thank you so very much for coming, and thank you for being Rehana's friends," he replied.

"We were all blessed to have Rehana in our lives," said Anil, who had been quiet throughout most of the trip.

ON THE FLIGHT HOME, Anil was pensive. "Eugene will have to vacate the villa. He worked so hard for five years in his low-paying job to put Rehana through her C.A. program. He didn't even see her for five years. When she returned and started working with the bank, it was like the doors to heaven had opened up for them. The bank provided the furnished villa and the car and paid her well. All they needed was a baby to complete their lives. Now Rehana is gone, and there's no baby.

Poor Eugene will have to suffer not only Rehana's loss; he'll have to mourn the loss of everything that could have been, and leave behind memories of their life in their beautiful home. They were so happy there. The company car will go too. He does not earn much," he said.

"There must be some life insurance?" asked Sophia.

"I don't know if she had much life insurance. Eugene probably could not afford insurance for either of them while Rehana was studying. My understanding is that the offshore Canadian banks provide up to a maximum of $100,000 life insurance as part of the employees' Group Insurance package. That's a good sum, but not enough to replace Rehana's earnings and the home."

"Let's both stay in contact with Eugene and help out if and where we can, Anil," she said. Anil smiled softly, touched by his wife's kind heart.

1974
Eighty-Eight

The Ismaili population in Canada continued to rise in 1974. By the year-end, it was reaching the 30,000 mark. Around 50% were in Ontario, 10% in Quebec, 25% in B.C., and 15% in Alberta. The professionals were feeling confident and starting to assert themselves in their workplaces. They were moving up the corporate ladders. The newcomers, many of whom were professionals from Kenya, were finding it less difficult to get placed than their earlier counter-parts had. The Ismaili professionals were slowly becoming known within corporate Canada and all levels of government as intelligent, well-educated, hardworking, and loyal people.

Those who had come in the Business category, however, were still struggling. Unable to raise debt financing, some were ending up in small tuck shops where they worked long hours and eked out a living. Most had yet to find businesses and were eroding their capital.

PRIME MINISTER TRUDEAU'S MINORITY Liberal government fell in May 1974 when the NDP withdrew its support and voted with the Conservatives to reject the budget that the Liberals had introduced, which the opposition parties felt did not go far enough to control inflation. The Conservatives had proposed a "90-day wage and price freeze", which Trudeau had rejected.

The campaign was vigorous. Most Ismailis were not yet eligible to vote but followed the campaign carefully. Many, like Aziza and Zul, campaigned for the parties of their choice. In the election held on July 8th, the Liberals were re-elected, going from a minority to a majority government and giving Trudeau his third term as Prime Minister. After having campaigned against the wage and price freeze, Trudeau introduced his own wage and price control system in 1975.

Of the four major party leaders, only Trudeau remained in place to fight the next federal election, five years later. The Tory leader, Robert Stanfield, stepped down in 1976 and was succeeded by Charles Joseph (Joe) Clark. The NDP leader, David Lewis, who had planned to resign for health reasons but had not announced this before the election, lost his own seat and stepped down within a year of the election. Ed Broadbent succeeded him.

South of the border, it was all talk of impeachment of President Richard Nixon. Nixon resigned from the highest office in the world on August 8th when impeachment by the House of Representatives and removal by the Senate became all but certain. He officially became the first American president to resign.

It seemed ridiculous to many Ugandan Asians in Canada that a President could be forced from office because some of his men were caught stealing some information from the opposition Democratic Party's offices, which the president had sanctioned. The Americans would learn to respect their Presidents more if they knew what the leaders in Africa could do every day of the week, they said.

IN JUNE, SHAMEEM TOLD Yasmin that she was two months pregnant. It was confirmed three weeks back. She had not told Rafiq because ever since Rehana's passing, he had stopped talking about babies. "I think he's so shaken by what happened to Rehana, he's terrified about me getting pregnant. Anil told me that Rafiq calls him twice a week to ask how Sophia is doing. He's anxious about her. I don't know how he will react."

"You have to tell him, sweetheart. You can't hide this. Tell him, and tell him not to worry. You are a doctor, and we have a specialist living next door to us."

That evening, when Rafiq and Shameem retired to their room, Shameem said, "Rafiq, I have some very good news. You're going to become a daddy."

Rafiq paused for a beat before saying, "Wow!"

"I'll be honest with you," Shameem continued. "I've known for close to a month, but I didn't want to tell you because what happened to Rehana has been very unsettling for you. Anil told me that you've been very anxious about Sophia. Why? Are you scared that something like what happened to Rehana could happen to her?"

Again, Rafiq was quiet for a moment. "I am worried about her, Shama, and now I'm worried about you."

"Rafiq, you are a rational man; you know that the chances of something like that happening in Canada are minimal. We have all been shaken by Rehana's passing, and we'll always live with the pain of her loss, but that's no reason to live in fear. We have been praying for this for a long time, and we should be jumping for joy right now, but you look almost sad."

"No, please don't feel that way. I'm happy, Shama. I'm delighted, but I'm also very nervous."

"If every man in Toronto whose wife gets pregnant starts panicking, the city would be full of scared men! Can we please celebrate and enjoy this pregnancy?"

"We will, I promise," Rafiq said, taking Shameem in his arms.

ALMAS LEFT HER WORK at the end of July to prepare to move to Vancouver in August. Anil and Sophia had offered to pay for Tazim's living and education expenses as she wanted to stay on in the apartment, but the Abdullas had insisted that Tazim give up the apartment when the lease expired at the end of September and move in with them. Anil had bought her a new Chevy Nova, which she had become very comfortable driving around in Toronto. She could commute to the university, they said.

Tazim had found a summer job with a Shoppers Drug Mart store. She had planned to use the money accumulated in her account to stay on in the apartment, but Shameem talked her out of it.

"I know you'd like to have a place of your own to entertain friends and have your privacy, but think ahead. After you qualify and work for a couple of years, you should aim to be in business for yourself. You'll need money to buy or start a pharmacy. Stay with us and save the money Anil sends every month. You can use what you earn at Shoppers for your pocket expenses. You don't have to pay us a penny."

Shabir visited Toronto in July and spent a fair bit of time with Tazim. Now that he had been living alone, he seemed to have matured a little. He told Tazim that he was very fond of her and wanted her to go to Vancouver with him for the balance of her vacation.

Tazim thought about it and was tempted but said, "I have a summer job until the end of August. I don't want to leave halfway. Maybe I'll come there in December when my mom will be there, and you can take me to Whistler."

THE SUMMER OF 1974 was a wonderful time for the Abdullas, who had formed a tight-knit group with Aziza and Zul, their neighbors Patrick and Lisa Roberts, and Carole and Geoff. They got together practically every weekend and either went to a local park to barbeque on Hibachi grills, or went exploring Ontario, visiting small towns and large lakes in the Muskoka and Haliburton regions, or went to the theatres to watch movies and plays. Some warm weekdays, they enjoyed Salim's marinated steaks and chicken in their backyard where Salim had brought a large propane gas BBQ from The Canadian Tire.

IN LATE AUGUST, ANIL advised Rafiq that the Council was expecting a team of senior Industrial Promotion Services (IPS) executives, led by Prince Amyn Mohamed Aga Khan (the Imam's younger brother), to come to Canada in early fall on a fact-finding mission. Now that the community had grown to over 30,000 and the median timeframe the community had been in Canada was 18 months, the team's mandate was to evaluate how well the community was settling in Canada.

IPS was the business arm of the Aga Khan's organizational network, headquartered in Geneva. The team would first visit Vancouver, meet with the Council leadership there, and then make its way to Toronto.

The news was soon announced to the entire Canadian Jamat. There was much jubilation and anticipation in the Jamat over their Imam's brother's visit to Canada. Surely, he would bring good tidings from the Imam.

After its cross country tour and meetings with the National and Regional Councils, the team determined that those who had been admitted to Canada as "Independent Applicants" (based on their education and professional qualifications) had encountered some initial difficulty in having their qualifications recognized and finding suitable employment, but most had found good jobs, and many were making good progress. On the other hand, those who had come to Canada in the "Business" category were having difficulties in identifying good business opportunities, evaluating businesses being offered for sale/establishment, and financing businesses that they wished to purchase or establish.

The team returned to Europe to present their findings to the Aga Khan and work on a programmatic response for the Canadian Ismaili immigrants in the Business category.

Business information and consulting services and a bank loan guarantee program evolved out of the team's deliberations with the Aga Khan.

"IT'S A STROKE OF genius, Rafiq," said Anil. "The programs will involve the establishment of two business information centers, one in Toronto, which will serve the Jamat in all provinces east of Manitoba, and one in Vancouver, to serve the Jamat in B.C., Alberta, Saskatchewan, and Manitoba. The centres will be named Ismaili Business Information Centres, or IBICs. The centers will be staffed with Business Information Officers and Executive Secretaries who will provide information on doing business in Canada and business consulting services."

"That's great! It kind of sounds like what you and I have been doing. What consulting services will the IBICs provide?"

"They'll assist with the evaluation of existing franchises and other retail, service, or merchandising businesses the Ismailis want to purchase for total costs not exceeding $100,000. Higher limits of up to $250,000 will be considered on a case by case basis. They'll assist with the assessment of business locations, sales, expenses, and cash flows, and will also review purchase/sale agreements, leases for the premises, and franchise agreements, and prepare business plans for presentation to the banks to support their loan applications. For those that want to establish new businesses, the IBICs will help prepare feasibility studies for the businesses to help determine their viability."

"That will cost money. What will IBICs charge for their services?"

"Not a penny, Rafiq. All services will be gratis. Hazar Imam will pay for the entire operation, and IPS is entering into agreements with the Bank of Nova Scotia and Canadian Imperial Bank of Commerce, where under IPS will guarantee up to 33% of loans the banks will make to 'Approved Applicants.' IPS will deposit $1,000,000 with each bank to support the loan guarantees."

"That's amazing. What's an Approved Applicant?"

"Hazar Imam will establish two Approval Committees to look at applications for loan guarantees. The Committees will be chaired by the Eastern and Western Canada Council Presidents. Together with five other members whom Hazar Imam will appoint, my counterpart in Eastern Canada and I will be members in our ex-officio positions on the Councils."

"Congratulations, Anil! So, what will your committee do?"

"We'll determine the eligibility of the applicants for the IPS guarantee."

"And how does one qualify for the guarantee?"

"You need to be an Ismaili, over 21 years of age, resident in Canada for over six months, have 25% of the total project cost to invest in equity and be a person of good moral character."

"So, will you be asking for Police Reports or hiring a P.I. to check people out?"

"No, Rafiq," Anil laughed. "We'll require references from two other Ismailis in Canada."

"It all sounds good, but you and I have both seen that when some people have come to us for our advice on businesses that they want to buy, they don't want to tell us what specific business they want to buy or the location because they're concerned we might divulge that information, and if it's an attractive deal, our friends and relatives might scoop it up. What makes you think that your applicants will be willing to share this detail with your committee?"

"Here's the thing. For the business proposition, they don't need to give us anything more than the project cost, their equity amount, and the nature of business. We'll also determine that the amount the applicants invest in businesses is not less than 40% and not more than 80% of the applicant's readily marketable assets. The program is for the needy, not the greedy, so if someone is buying a business for $100,000 and has that amount sitting in their bank account, they can't get away with investing just $25,000 in equity. They'll have to invest $40,000 and borrow $60,000.

This will reduce the IPS's guarantee exposure to $20,000. At the same time, Hazar Imam wants to ensure that the money people invest is not more than 80% of their readily marketable assets, in case the business fails."

"The Imam has thought through, everything, hasn't he? So, you will ask for people's statements of personal net worth?"

"That, we'll have to do."

"And the committee won't look at bankability of the business?"

"The applicants will bring their proposals to Business Information Officers for evaluation, but unless they consent to have this information presented to the Approval Committee, the Officers will hold the information confidential, even from the Approval Committee. We believe that about 90% will share the information, but in the final analysis, the participating banks will establish the bankability of all projects."

"So if the IBIC Officer deems that a business is not viable, but the applicant satisfies the personal criteria, can they still get the guarantee?"

"Yes. For every dollar that IPS guarantees, the banks will loan two at their own risk, so they'll carefully evaluate the project's viability. The IPS guarantee will make the project more bankable and provide a blue-ribbon introduction for Ismailis who do not have established credit record in Canada."

"It looks like the program will address all of the needs of the Ismailis who've come to Canada in the Business category."

"Yes. The only thing that the program won't do is find businesses for people."

"But won't people need to know about the opportunities and economics of different businesses?"

"The IBICs will set up libraries containing materials on doing business in Canada, ratios in different retail and service businesses, information on franchises, and also economic reports and also provide this information in one on one discussion."

"Sounds really interesting."

"It is," said Anil. He paused before adding, "…and your name is one of a few proposed for appointment on the Approval Committee for Eastern Canada. The voluntary service you've been providing has not gone unnoticed."

IN THE AUTUMN OF 1974, speculation in residential property started to push housing prices up in Toronto and other major cities in Ontario. At one point, the average house prices were rising at $100 an hour. The house which Rafiq and Shameem had bought for $50,000 was now worth about $95,000, and the three apartments that they had acquired in Yasmin's name had risen to around $40,000 each. Finally, the Ontario government slapped on a speculation tax, which stopped the prices from spiraling upwards and, in some cases, brought them down somewhat.

"Mom, if we sell your three condos, we can make $45,000 on your investment of $15,000; this would be a 200% return in less than six months," said Shameem. "Do you want to sell?"

"We're not speculators, Shama. Let's keep them and just be happy with the rent we are getting."

Twenty-five years later, when the family no longer wished to look after the tenants and upkeep anymore and sold the units, each sold for over $150,000, and ten years later, the units were worth $250,000 each. The insatiable demand for residential property in Toronto kept the prices rising.

ANIL CALLED ON SEPTEMBER 15th to say that Sophia had delivered a healthy eight-pound baby girl, whom they had named Naila, which meant a rosebud. Both mom and baby were doing well.

Tazim couldn't wait to see the baby and was on a flight to Vancouver on the first day of her Christmas vacation in December. She spent ten delightful days playing with Naila, and two days with Shabir in Whistler, where she learned how to ski.

1975
Eighty-Nine

The IBIC programs became operational in Canada in January 1975. Over the first 15-years of the program, a third office was established in Calgary in 1979, and some 4,500 in-person business consultations with Business Information Officers were recorded. On average, two consultations were held over the telephone for every in-person meeting. Over the same period, over 750 Ismaili businesses were established or expanded with IPS loan guarantees. Support was also provided to a significant number of businesses in raising debt financing without the benefit of IPS guarantees.

SHAMEEM DELIVERED A HEALTHY baby girl on January 20th. Her pregnancy had been relatively smooth. She had worked until one week before the baby was born. Rafiq chose to be with her in the delivery room. Between contractions, she had smiled at Rafiq, who seemed to be sharing her physical pain. He could not wait to take the baby in his arms when she was born.

When Yasmin and Salim came to see the baby, Shameem asked, "Mom, what shall we call her? Your son was so worried about my pregnancy, we never talked about what we will call the baby."

"Well, now that he's no longer worried, you guys can talk about it and decide," said Yasmin.

"Mom, we would like you to name her," said Rafiq. "We've discussed it already. It would be a blessing for her to have a name that her grandmother has chosen."

"Maybe, her grandfather should name her," Yasmin said, passing the responsibility to Salim.

"Well, the other night, I met this young lady in Jamatkhana whose father I had met some time back. She had a lovely little girl with her and she said that her name is Farrah. I thought it was such a beautiful name. It means happiness. Can we call her Farrah? She has brought so much happiness for us all."

"Farrah, it is Dad. It's Farrah Abdulla," said Shameem.

SHAMEEM HAD SIX MONTHS of maternity leave, so there was no need for Yasmin to leave her work, but Yasmin had resigned as of the end of December and was home to help Shameem look after Farrah. Both she and Salim had insisted that the baby's crib should be in their room until Farrah was old enough for them to move the crib into her own room. They would manage the nighttime bottle feeding so that Shama and Rafiq could sleep. Shameem tried to object but to no avail.

"Farrah will keep Mom and Dad up all night, and Dad has to go to work!" said Shameem.

"Let her do what she wants, Shama," replied Rafiq. "Perhaps she sees in Farrah, the baby girl that she lost all those years ago. This experience is bringing her such joy. You can see it on her face and in her eyes. You can look after Farrah in the daytime and let Mom rest, and Dad is such a sound sleeper, you'd have to beat drums to wake him up."

BETWEEN THE HELP PROVIDED by Yasmin, and by Tazim, Rafiq, and Salim when they got home, Shameem did not have to do much more than feed and play with Farrah, who was growing up to be a delightful little girl. She seemed most comfortable in Yasmin's arms.

One morning, in early February, Rafiq said to Shameem, "I'm worried that Farrah is going to grow up to be as beautiful as you are, and all the boys are going to be after her. We'd better have a boy soon to go to clubs and parties with her and keep all the boys away."

"So, you're not scared about me getting pregnant again?"

"No, it wasn't bad at all."

"And what if the second baby is also a girl?"

"Oh, my God, that would mean double trouble!" he laughed. "Don't misunderstand me, Shama; I'd love to have a second daughter, but can you imagine me at 50, trying to supervise two teenaged girls? You know that they'll be strong-willed and independent, just like you. And we should never let them outnumber us, so we don't want more than two children. It's settled – the second one has to be a boy."

"You mean, *you* don't want more than two children. Maybe I want more."

"Really?"

"No; relax. We should have two to replace us two when we go. If the second is a boy, we will say, Shukhar to God. If it's a girl, we'll still say Shukhar."

"Have you talked to Sophia? Do you know whether they're planning a second baby?"

"They are, indeed. She also said that Almas aunty, like Mom, is monopolizing Naila. When Mom told her that she was going to have the crib in her room, Almas aunty insisted that they move Naila's crib into her room, also. With Almas aunty there, Sophia finds it very easy, like I do, to bring up Naila and wants to have the second child while Almas aunty is still young and can help."

"It's a blessing, isn't it, to have parents with us to love and care for our children?" Rafiq asked.

"I can't even imagine how difficult it would be for me to care for Farrah if Mom wasn't here, and I'm still on mat leave! Can you imagine having to get up in the morning, get the baby fed and clothed, put her in a car seat, drive her to a daycare centre, and still get to work in time? Often, women at the hospital get calls from the daycare centres telling them that their children have a fever or an upset stomach and they should go pick them up. I just can't fathom being able to manage all of the responsibilities without the parents to help."

"We're blessed to have Mom and Dad with us, but all parents may not be as willing or able to help as they are. Also, young couples often want privacy."

"Well, I value their love and support more than I value any notion of privacy. I want your parents here, and when they grow old and need care, we will care for them the way they're caring for our daughter."

SHAMEEM RETURNED TO WORK in July, but she was already pregnant with their second child. She decided that if her pregnancy were as smooth as the first one, she would return to work in three months. She did not want her specialization in Neurology to be dragged out too much.

She delivered another baby girl on December 12th. They decided to call her Rehana. Sophia and Anil had also become parents to their second child, a son, on October 28th. They named him Shaheed.

IN 1975, THE ISMAILI population in Canada grew by another 5,000 to just over 35,000, with roughly the same regional breakdown as before. People had started to acquire homes. Homeownership for the Ismailis was always a priority. By the end of the year, homeownership in the Jamat was estimated at 20%, which is high for an immigrant community in its second median year of settlement.

The Ismaili students were doing well in schools, but the importance of university education, which had been paramount in the Jamat in East Africa, seemed to have receded somewhat from many students' and their parents' minds. No statistics had been compiled, but it was believed that after high school, only two in ten were going to university, and an equal number were going to community colleges.

With the establishment of the IBIC program, the ratio of heads of Ismaili households in business had risen to about 25%. They were acquiring pharmacies, hardware and electronics stores, dry-cleaning plants, gas stations, car rental and fast food franchises, supermarkets, and other retail or service type of businesses with the IBIC support programs. About 40% were employed or self-employed as professionals, around 10% were employed in trades, and approximately 25% were employed in unskilled jobs.

The latter included some with post-secondary education who had not been able to find work in their areas of education and training, many of whom were pursuing continuing education, and would land on their feet eventually.

1976
Ninety

By 1976, most Ismailis who had arrived in Canada in 1972 from Uganda and Tanzania were feeling very much a part of the Canadian milieu and were becoming much more conscious of what was happening around them. The Canadian values were very much aligned with what they had grown up with, and they identified themselves more and more with the Canadians.

1976 was an eventful year for Canada.

On the political front, in February, Joe Clark won the leadership of the Progressive Conservative Party and went on to win the 1979 election, defeating Pierre Trudeau's Liberal government and ending 16 years of continuous Liberal rule. The tenure of Clark's minority government, however, was brief. It was defeated on a motion of non-confidence and lost the 1980 election to Trudeau's Liberals. Most Ismailis, although not yet eligible to vote, closely followed the fortunes of the three major political parties and their leaders. Like many new immigrants who had voted for the party in power when they came to Canada, the majority of Ismailis supported the Liberals; the Ugandans felt sincere gratitude towards Trudeau for offering them asylum when they were expelled from Uganda.

Construction of the CN Tower, a 1,815-foot communications and observation tower, was completed in downtown Toronto. It held the record for the world's tallest free-standing structure for 32 years until 2007 and was the world's tallest tower until 2009 when Dubai's Burj Khalifa overtook it. It continues to be an icon of Toronto's skyline and attracts more than two million international visitors annually.

In May, Anil's favorite team, the Montreal Canadiens, won their 19th Stanley Cup by defeating Rafiq's favorite team, the Philadelphia Flyers, four games to zero.

On June 30th, the Canadian Parliament voted to abolish the death penalty. Most Ismailis who took an interest in politics and were aware of the abolition, supported it. Like all Muslims, they believed that "for he who takes a life, it is as if he has killed the entirety of all humanity, and that for he who saves a life, it is as if he has saved all of humanity." No human had the right to take another human's life.

In July, Canada watched the Opening Ceremony of the Montreal Summer Olympics. For most Ismailis, the games were a novelty. They were familiar with only some of the competitions. For many, the incomplete Olympic Stadium was a greater spectacle.

Rafiq, Shameem, Anil, and Sophia, who like many other Ismailis, had grown fond of ice hockey, loved to watch the NHL games. Tazim found the games boring and hated the fights and body checking in the hockey games. She couldn't stand to watch ice hockey.

The year ended with the unanticipated election of René Lévesque's separatist Parti Québécois (PQ) in November. The PQ victory and the size of the majority vote were a surprise, even for René Lévesque, who immediately set to work to organize a referendum on Quebec's separation from Canada. The PQ victory and the impending referendum were unsettling for the Anglophones in Quebec and the rest of Canada. Many large corporations headquartered in Montreal started to move to Toronto. Quebec also began to suffer from a brain drain. There were many Francophone Ismailis in the Quebec Jamat of around 1,000 who disliked the Anglophone dominance in Quebec and favored separation, but this did not create any rift between the Anglophone and Francophone Ismailis in Quebec.

Shameem returned to work at the beginning of March, over three months before the end of her maternity leave. Sophia also returned to work one month before the end of her maternity leave. She felt incredibly grateful to have her mother-in-law to help her with Naila and Shaheed.

1977
Ninety-One

1 977 marked the fifth year of the Ugandan Asian Exodus. The Ugandan Ismailis were continuing to consolidate themselves and becoming proud Canadians. Immigration from Tanzania and Kenya was continuing. By the year-end, the Ismaili population had grown to over 35,000.

Five years into their settlement in Canada, the Jamatkhanas had remained – and would continue to remain forever – a central element in the life of Canadian Ismailis. The community was now feeling well enough established to transition from the weekend school hall Jamatkhanas to permanent, daily, owned, or rented Jamatkhanas. Also, there were sufficient numbers of Ismaili couples in all major centers of Ismaili settlement in Canada who were self-employed or employed in positions which allowed them the flexibility to be appointed to serve as Mukhi, Mukhiani, Kamadia, Kamadiani and preside over the daily congregational prayers for a full year.

The Jamat in Montreal had established a daily Jamatkhana on the second floor of a leased facility on Van Horne Avenue. In Toronto, a large warehouse facility at Victoria Park and St. Clair Avenues had been leased and converted to serve as Jamatkhana to supplement the several weekend school hall Jamatkhanas. The Jamat in Vancouver had established a daily Jamatkhana on Drake Street in downtown Vancouver in a facility acquired by a group of Ismailis.

These leased and converted Jamatkhanas were a far cry from the palatial Jamatkhanas in which the Ismailis had congregated to pray and socialize in Africa, but they were important milestones for the community. The establishment of daily Jamatkhanas was bringing a sense of permanency to the community in Canada and created spaces where the community could come together every day to assemble and pray, as had been the community's centuries-old tradition.

The process for the establishment of leased Jamatkhanas was also serving to provide valuable experience to the Councils in the establishment and operation of places of worship. They could not merely identify and rent a large warehouse or vacated office space, and have a planner divide up the area into the various Jamatkhana components (prayer hall, anteroom, foyer, social hall, classrooms, cloakrooms, and washrooms) and proceed to rehabilitate, furnish and equip the space to serve as Jamatkhanas.

For a facility to be leased for the purpose, it had to be located on land zoned by municipal authorities for institutional use or for use as a place of worship. If it were not so zoned, a zoning change application had to be made to the appropriate municipality; for minor non-compliance with zoning regulations, an adjustment had to be obtained from the municipalities' Committee of Adjustment. Hearing of applications of both these changes were open for support or opposition from the public. The landlords were usually willing to hold their properties for 60 - 90 days, depending on demand for such spaces in the area, but were not willing to pull their properties from the market for as long as it took the Council's zoning change application to be approved, without any guarantee that it would ever be approved.

If a property was zoned for use as a place of worship, it had to have adequate land for construction of a building of the desired size and onsite parking. Whereas neighborhood street parking could be used, where permitted, for the building permit approval, the prayer hall size was determined by the available and dedicated onsite parking spaces. Next, the rental spaces had to be in the areas where there was a significant Ismaili presence or had to be within easy access to clusters of Ismaili residences.

The re-planning of spaces was often a bigger challenge. In many ideally located and zoned facilities, the Councils ran into difficulties configuring the areas as required. The existence of obstacles such as load-bearing interior walls, inappropriately located or inadequate washroom facilities, inappropriate lighting systems, and inadequate (or non-existent) HVAC systems often made it very difficult or impossible to re-configure the existing spaces for the desired functionality without incurring huge re-definition costs.

The answer was purpose-built Jamatkhanas – facilities that could be designed and built from the ground up to meet the community's requirements, but these would have to wait. In the countries where they had resided, the Imam had granted Ismailis the privilege of contributing up to 50% towards the costs of building Jamatkhanas, and the Imam had funded the rest. In many other countries, the Imam funded 100% of Jamatkhana development costs. The community in prosperous Canada did not want to go to their Imam and ask for purpose-built Jamatkhanas without being able to participate equally. Ever since its arrival in Canada, the community had been making donations to community programs and events and charitable causes but had not yet amassed sufficient wealth to make the substantial contributions that dignified Jamatkhana development would require.

Further, Canada had been plagued, since the mid-70s, by what had come to be known as Stagflation (stagnant economy, coupled with inflation). In 1975, unemployment had risen to almost 7%, and the situation had not improved much in 1977. Like other Canadians, the Ismailis were feeling the pinch.

MANY ISMAILIS HAD BY now become Canadian citizens and were overwhelmed with their pride in having acquired Canadian citizenship. The Ontario provincial election was held in June in which most eligible Ismailis voted; some were voting for the first time in their life. William Davis' Progressive Conservative party won a second consecutive minority government.

ROBERT AND BERNICE, WHO had been living together for the last five years, visited Toronto in early July. Robert, Rafiq, and Anil had communicated regularly and were aware of what was going on in each other's lives. Robert and Bernice were doing well in their careers and had bought a house in Cardiff. They were happy there, but Bernice now wanted to get married and have a baby. Robert was enthusiastic about marrying, but not about babies. This was causing some unhappiness between them.

When they arrived in Toronto, Bernice wanted to spend more time playing with Farrah and Rehana than sightseeing. Robert also warmed up to the girls
quickly, and they were always in Robert and Bernice's arms.

"If I had a daughter like Farrah or Rehana, I guess I could love her," he said
to Rafiq.

"Once you have a child, you'll find out how much happiness they bring in your
life, Rob. And not just in Bernice's and your lives; in your parents' lives also."

"Will you and Shama come to our wedding? We'll probably marry in the
spring of 1979."

"Of course, we'll be there! We'll also bring my parents, and we want to visit
Mrs. Bowes and the Sauls, and show them our children."

ALMAS, ANIL, SOPHIA, AND the children came to Toronto in the summer
to attend Tazim's graduation. Now there were nine adults and four children in the
house, but accommodating everyone was not a problem. Soon after moving into
the house, Rafiq had the basement finished, creating two bedrooms - the larger one
with an attached three-piece bathroom, a second two-piece bathroom, a kitchenette, and a recreation area.

Tazim had secured four convocation seats for herself and a friend from Halifax,
who was not planning to return to Toronto for the ceremony, had given Tazim her
four tickets. It was decided that Almas, Anil, Sophia, Rafiq, Shameem, Rob, and
Bernice would attend; Salim and Yasmin would look after the four kids. At Anil
and Sophia's request, Shameem had organized a graduation dinner at the Simpson's
department store's Arcadian Court restaurant for them to go to after the convocation ceremony.

The day after Tazim's convocation, the Aga Khan Council for Eastern Canada
had organized a Jamati *Jaman* (Ismaili communal feast) for around 15,000 Ismailis
at The Toronto International Centre (TIC) to celebrate the 20th anniversary of the
Aga Khan's Imamat (spiritual leadership). The annual Jaman was a decades-old
Ismaili tradition in Africa, India, and Pakistan and was also being held on the same
day in Montreal, Ottawa, Calgary, Edmonton, and Vancouver.

Massive preparations had been undertaken to organize the event. Space had to be rented; meat, rice, potatoes, spices, oils, and other ingredients to make biryani (a dish rich in spices served on ceremonial occasions), starters and desserts had to be purchased; volunteers needed to be coordinated to manage all aspects of the programming. A commercial kitchen had to be rented for the food preparation committee to prepare and cook the various dishes. Trucks equipped with ovens to keep the food warm had to be rented to transport the food to the TIC from the kitchen. The application had to be made for government health inspectors to inspect the cooking facilities and certify the food.

Spaces in the massive TIC facility had to be divided up into areas and organized for a sit-down lunch for the seniors and buffet-style for the rest of the Jamat. Sufficient numbers of serving stations had to be set up so that people would not have to line up for more than five minutes.

Spaces had to be also allocated for Information, Lost and Found booths and First Aid station, games and other activities for the children, dancing and dandia raas (traditional Indian stick dances) for the youth and other entertainment (Indian music and songs) for those who were that way inclined.

Garbage disposal bins and bags had to be secured, and garbage removal arrangements had to be made. All this had to be done by the volunteers who had started working weeks before the event and had spent the last two nights at the TIC, organizing and equipping the place. The entire event was funded with donations from the community members.

Sophia, as a non-Ismaili spouse, was eligible to attend the Jaman, but Robert and Bernice were not. Anil and Sophia suggested that they would take them sightseeing downtown, and everyone else should go for the Jaman, but Robert and Bernice insisted that they did not need to be looked after. They would visit the CN Tower and walk around downtown Toronto.

The Ismaili Council, concerned with the organization of such a large event and fearing that some outsiders may seek to disrupt a large ethnic gathering, had secured the services of 12 off-duty police officers for the event.

The officers had thought they would be involved with crowd management and could be expected to intervene if there was a scuffle or a disturbance, but when they arrived, they were warmly greeted by the uniformed Ismaili Volunteer Corps (IVC) leaders and three divisional IVC Team Leads, who suggested that three officers position themselves at each of the three TIC entrances, and the remaining three just walk around all areas and keep an eye for any disturbance.

As people began to arrive, they greeted the officers, and there were smiles all around as the guests hugged and kissed others whom they had not seen for some time.

When they had come in, the police officers had seen the IVC directing traffic in the TIC's massive parking lots. It was a hot day. When people came inside, the IVC members were there to guide them to different areas. There were wheelchairs to transport seniors to their designated areas. The IVC was also positioned at the food line-ups to help carry small children while their parents picked up their food on paper plates and collected their plastic cutlery.

When lunch was served, all of the officers were invited to partake in the areas in which they were positioned. For 10 of them, who had indicated that they could not eat spicy food, the IVC had ordered burgers, fried chicken, French fries, and pizzas. Arrangements had been made for different volunteers to pick up the various food items so that they would arrive fresh and warm for the officers to enjoy. The IVC Lead and two Sectoral Leads invited three officers in one area to sit with them to eat.

"May I ask," began one of the officers, "why do you need us here? Everyone is so well behaved. I haven't seen a single person pushing, or arguing, or fighting with anyone; everyone seems to be following your directions with smiles and appreciation. I think we're looking a bit silly just standing around. You know, our security service here costs you guys a lot of money?"

"Yes, and who is paying for all this?" asked another. "I didn't see anyone collecting any tickets at the entrance. It looks like people can just walk in and eat."

One of the Sectoral Leads responded, "This is the first time, so many of us have gathered under one roof in Canada, and we wanted everything to go well. We did not want there to be any pushing or fights. Your presence ensures that."

"But you know your community. These people are highly disciplined. They are all well-dressed. They're not the kind who would push or fight," the officer said.

The Regional Lead smiled sheepishly. "You know, some guy can spill his plate of biryani on someone's wife's nice dress, and tempers can flare. Biryani stains never come off."

"One volunteer told me that there are close to 1,000 of you uniformed volunteers here. Are 1,000 volunteers not enough to break up a fight if there is one? Why do you need us? Anyone carrying guns here?" the officer asked.

The IVC Lead said, "Let me be honest with you, officer. As you might know, there is a small segment of people in Toronto and in Canada, who don't like us being here. We are concerned about the safety of our people and wanted you here to protect us if any such people appeared to make any mischief or hurt anyone."

"I'm truly sorry to hear that," said the officer. "You're right. There are people who may do such things. I believe the guy who got pushed off the subway platform onto the tracks by two ruffians some months back was a member of your community, right?"

"Yes, he was. He suffered severe injuries, but luckily, he survived," replied the IVC Lead, with sadness in his eyes.

"Don't worry," said the officer. "We'll look out for anyone suspicious and take care, but you guys should have told us this upfront, not at lunchtime. Looking at his colleagues, he said, "Let us finish eating and tell others what we are here for."

THE JAMANS WERE JOYOUS events for the Ismailis across Canada. The community members who had settled in Kitchener, London, Hamilton, Oshawa, Kingston, and other smaller towns in southern Ontario had traveled to participate in the Toronto event. People met others whom they had not seen since they had left East Africa, India, and Pakistan. They hugged and exchanged telephone numbers and promised to call one another and remain connected. They learned of family members who had stayed behind in the countries of their origin and those that had passed away, married, and gone to university. There was so much to catch up on.

UPON SEEING THE FIRST Aid station when they entered, Sophia asked, "What's happening there?" When they talked to the people at the station, one of them said, "I'm the only doctor on duty. I wish there were another to help me."

"Do you need nurses? I am one, but I'm not Ismaili," said Sophia.

"Yes, we could surely use another nurse! I don't think our patients will care if you are Ismaili or not. There is only one nurse here. We're expecting one more, but she's not arrived yet. Please join us if you can. I'm Amin Kanani," said the doctor.

"I'm a physician," said Shameem. "I can help, too?"

"Thank you very much. Please join us," the doctor said.

In short order, Anil and Rafiq had lost their wives, and only five of them were left to care for the four children. Tazim had gone off with some guys and girls whom she met when they came in.

The event continued until 4.00 p.m. When they met up with their families again, Shameem said, "We had a patient with severe chest pains. I took his BP and pulse, and Sophia got a volunteer to call 911. Dr. Kanani and I worked to stabilize him until the ambulance came, and Sophia comforted his wife, who was beside herself when she heard our conversation. Other than that, most of the cases were relatively minor, although two volunteers got severe burns on their feet and lower legs when they dropped a percolator filled with hot tea. We sent them to Emergency after administering First Aid."

"There was one lady volunteer who had cut her hand that I looked after. She did not need stitches. Other than that, there were children with small cuts and bruises and one kid who seemed to have had an allergic reaction from nuts in the sherbet. Dr. Kanani had a couple of epi-pens and gave him a shot, and he was okay." Sophia said.

"There was this big man brought in with bad stomach pain. I checked him out and made him sit here for a while to see if his appendix was acting up, in which case we would have called an ambulance. He was okay after a little while. I think he was hurting because he may have eaten too much biryani." Shameem said.

"Did you get to eat?" asked Yasmin worriedly.

"Yes, we did. The biryani was amazing and was served hot," Shameem replied.

"My God, who can cook such tasty biryani for fifteen thousand people? I can't do that for fifteen," Yasmin said.

"You are right. The biryani was amazing and served hot," Almas added.

"Mom, you will be happy to know that they told us that there is biryani leftover, and we, volunteers, can take up to two plates home for $5 each. Between Shameem and I, we've got four plates. They really piled them up for us. It'll be enough for us for dinner tomorrow." Sophia said.

"Is that what it cost? $5 per serving?" Almas asked.

"That's what they said. They estimate the biryani cost was $5, and other foods and drink items were $1.50 per serving."

"So, fifteen thousand people are going home with close to $100,000 worth of food in their stomachs?" Almas asked.

"Mom, that's just the food cost. Someone told me this hall cost $75,000 to rent for two and a half days, plus there are all other costs," Sophia said.

"That must be a ton of money. We don't realize how much a gathering like this can cost. I will double my donation," said Almas.

"And we should do the same," said Salim.

ANIL, SOPHIA, TAZIM, SHAMEEM, Rafiq, Robert, and Bernice spent the entire following week traveling around Ontario and to Montreal. It felt wonderful to be reunited and spend time together.

When the week was over, Anil sat down with Tazim to talk about her future plans.

"I'm planning to work here for a while, but I plan to move to Vancouver eventually," she said.

"Why don't you do that now?" asked Anil. "I would like us all to be together as a family. You'll find a job in Vancouver easily."

"As a family?" she exclaimed. "You do recall that a family member is languishing in Tanzania that neither you nor Mom ever talks about? Like he doesn't even exist?"

Anil was taken aback. While it was true that they had not been in touch with Zahir, he had not forgotten about him for even one day.

"I've been in touch with him," Tazim continued. "I've told him several times that I can nominate him to come to Canada, but he says he doesn't want to come. The truth is that he can't face Salim uncle, Yasmin aunty, and Mom, after what he did."

"Tazim, you have to understand that what he did was unconscionable," said Anil. "The things that he said to Salim uncle are unforgivable. I know that Mom misses him, and I'm sure that she prays for him, but he has never bothered to write to her or Salim uncle to apologize for his actions. I'm happy that you're in touch with him. How is he?"

"He says that after we all left, Tanzania's tax base collapsed and the government started printing money. A loaf of bread we used to buy for 2 Shillings, now costs 200. There are import restrictions, and he can't get the merchandise to sell in the store. Small town officials who can't live on what they earn keep going into Indian homes for "inspection," with a bar of LUX soap – which is an import item – in their pockets. They plant the soap in the house and put the household head in jail until the family pays 5,000 Shillings bribe. Life has become a living hell for the Indians and even for the Africans. The Ujamaa Villages have all collapsed, and the African farms which had fed the country have turned to dust bowls. The business for which Zahir destroyed relationships and caused us all so much pain is now worth nothing. But he still doesn't want to come here and face Salim uncle and Yasmin aunty. He's always asking me to ask for their forgiveness, but he's adamant that he won't come here."

"Have you talked to them about it?"

"Yes. Salim uncle said that Zahir was just a boy and didn't know what he was doing. Maybe he was influenced by some friends to do what he did. He asked me to tell him that they have never held what he did in their hearts, and there is nothing to forgive. He said that I should ask him to come here and that he would give me $1,000 to send to Zahir immediately, and another $500 a month until he can come here."

"Did Yasmin aunty say anything?"

"She said that Zahir has been in her prayers because she has heard how bad things are in Tanzania and that she too wanted him to be brought here. I accepted their money and added $500 of my own, and sent him $1,500. He was very grateful, but he said that he doesn't want any more to be sent. I think that he may have a woman living with him. Anyway, he doesn't want ever to come here."

"You should have told me this, Tazim," sighed Anil.

"Told you? Why? You don't give a hoot if our brother is alive or dead!"

"That's not true! Not a day has gone by when I've not thought about him. Does Rafiq know any of this?"

"And what did you do about it, Anil? Did you ever write to inquire? Our Post Office Box number in Dodoma is still the same, you know! And no, Yasmin aunty asked me not to say anything to Rafiq or Shama."

"I'm sorry. I should have reached out, but..."

"But what? You didn't, and you should be ashamed."

"Tazim, you're angry. Let's talk when we can speak about this in a more civil tone."

"Don't patronize me with your fancy English. There won't be any conversation with you about Zahir in a civil tone. Look at Salim uncle and Yasmin aunty – how gracious they are, and then there's you and Mom who just haven't been able to find it in your hearts to forgive him."

Anil looked away sadly. There was nothing left to say.

ANIL, SOPHIA, ALMAS, AND the children departed for Vancouver the next morning, and Bernice and Rob took an afternoon flight back to London. It had been a wonderful time for everyone, except for Anil, whose last day was marred by his harsh exchange with Tazim. He had much soul searching to do. Biting as it was, Tazim was right about some of what she had said.

IN 1977, SECTIONS OF Toronto's Yonge Street, south of Bloor Street, had turned quite seedy. Several strip joints and massage parlors had sprung up. The latter were fronts for prostitution. Towards the end of July, in the middle of what had been a pleasant summer, a tragic event shook all of Toronto. A 12-year old boy, Emanuel Jacques, was abducted on Yonge Street. Each day the police searched for him, Yasmin, Shameem, and hundreds of other Torontonians prayed for his safe return. Their hearts went out to the boy's mother as they thought about what she must be going through. Emanuel's strangled body was found several days later on the roof of an apartment building. Four men were arrested for the crime. For the East Africans who had come to Canada, this was horrifying. Violence in East Africa was not uncommon, but violence against children was unheard of.

A WEEK AFTER ARRIVING in Vancouver, Anil told Sophia about his conversation with Tazim.

"Look, he's your brother, and you and Mom have essentially, disowned him. How could you spend all these months without talking or inquiring about him? I'm glad Tazim has been communicating with him. Since you guys never talked about him, I didn't say anything, but I've always wondered why you wouldn't reach out to him. I think you should write to him."

Anil was chastened. Before writing to Zahir, he told his mother about his conversations with Tazim and Sophia. Almas' eyes welled up, and she said, "Not a day goes by when I don't think of him. In all the time that we've been here, I have wanted to communicate with him, but I was always scared that you might get upset if I do. I know how angry and bitter you were about what he did. I was hoping that one day you would talk about him and we would decide to connect with him. Now, as I reflect on what Tazim said to you, I think that this was my excuse for doing nothing - for failing my son as his mother. I believe that saying to myself, 'Anil will talk about Zahir one day, and we will decide to phone him' was just a way of avoiding writing to him, which was so difficult and unpleasant to do. For you, it was his behavior towards Salim uncle. For me, it was much more than that. It was what his behavior told me about his character, the bad habits he had formed, and the way he treated me after Dad passed away. But whatever he did, he's still my son, and I should not have failed him."

"We've all failed him. I'll write to him, but I don't want to give him the impression that all he did is forgotten. It is forgiven, but will never be forgotten. We'll turn a new page in our lives if he wants to, but he must understand how much he has hurt us, and particularly you, by what he did."

"But Tazim said he asked for Salim uncle and Yasmin aunty's forgiveness."

"Yes, he did, and they not only forgave him, they sent him money. We haven't inquired about him, but he has not bothered to write to you either, to ask for your forgiveness or ask how you are, so let's not wear all the guilt."

Three days later, he told Sophia and Almas that he had written to Zahir to say that he was happy to know that Tazim was communicating with him. He was sad and disappointed that Zahir had never written to their mother to inquire how she was, and he was sorry for having not written to ask how he was doing, especially at this challenging time in Tanzania. The purpose of his letter was to tell Zahir that bad things may have happened, but he wanted to turn the page. If Zahir was willing to put the past behind, they could all be part of one another's life once again. If Zahir wanted to come to Canada, he and Tazim would work to bring him here. If he needed any financial support, they would support him. He had also told Zahir everything that had happened in their lives since they came to Canada. He had sent a copy of the letter to Tazim.

"Well, you did a good thing. Let's wait and see how he responds," said Sophia.

TEN DAYS LATER, ANIL received a half-page letter in which Zahir said that he was very sorry for everything he had done. He was missing their mom very much, but he was okay, and he did not need any money. He wanted to see his little nephew and niece and asked that Anil send him their pictures, but he did not want to come to Canada.

"What next?" Sophia asked.

"I see on the letterhead that our business phone number has not changed. I'll call him next week."

1978
Ninety-Two

In early 1978, Anil advised Rafiq that the Mountain View Inn, which they had purchased for $1,000,000 in 1972, had appreciated in value by about 20%, and they had also reduced the mortgage by $75,000. The motel's cash flow permitted them to borrow $200,000 against the project. Their partners in the Mountain View, Yusuf, and Akbar, were looking at purchasing another motel in the Richmond area of Vancouver, listed for $1,950,000, with an existing assumable mortgage of $1,500,000. If acquired for $1,850,000, with closing costs and working capital, the project cost was estimated at $2,000,000. Equity of $500,000 was required, of which $200,000 could come from an increase in the mortgage on the Mountain View, leaving a $300,000 funding requirement. Akbar and Yusuf were willing to invest up to $100,000 each. Sophia and Anil would invest $50,000 if the Abdullas were also willing to invest up to that amount in the project.

Rafiq discussed the proposition with his parents and Shameem, and they decided that he should fly out to Vancouver to look at the motel and commit to investing if he liked it.

THE MOTEL, CALLED "THE Valley Inn," had 35 rooms compared to the Mountain View's 30 and was newer and superior in the finish. A 50-year old man, Paul Berger, with education and training in hotel management, had been hired to oversee the hotel operations when it was built. He had done an excellent job of running it. Rafiq noted that he was making more money than they were paying Akbar for managing the Mountain View.

When Rafiq got to Vancouver, Yusuf and Akbar had tied up the purchase for $1.86 million in trust for a corporation and subject to financing and several other conditions. Rafiq confirmed his and Anil's participation via Almin, the corporation through which they had invested in the Mountain View, and suggested to his partners that they should retain Berger as the manager, and raise Akbar's salary from $1,450 to Paul's $1,650 per month level.

That evening, when Rafiq, Anil, and Sophia sat down after dinner, Anil said, "We're very fortunate to have Akbar and Yusuf as our partners. In all my dealings with them, they have been upfront and absolutely honest. I've heard of situations where there are real conflicts between Ismaili partners in projects like ours because one or more has been devious or dishonest. Our investment and employment agreements are of little use where people want to lie and cheat."

"We have situations in Toronto also that worry us," said Rafiq. "There are unscrupulous people in practically all immigrant communities who prey on their own. At the Approval Committee level in Toronto, we see some applications for loan guarantees for purchases of tuck shops. These are not bankable propositions, even with the IPS guarantee, because other than furniture and fixtures worth some $10,000 in a $100,000 project, there is nothing the banks can take as collateral. We're told that some Ismaili realtors had initially sold tuck shops and dry cleaning businesses to some Ismailis that did well, and now everyone wants to buy these businesses. These agents, we are told, are now approaching the owners of Tuck Shops and dry cleaners and asking what they think their business is worth. If an owner says that his business is worth $75,000-$80,000, they tell him that they can get $100,000 for it. They get the listing and then hive it off to some Ismaili for 25% more than what the business is worth. The higher price earns them a higher commission. The buyers invest $30,000 in cash, borrow $15,000 from one of our participating banks with the $5,000 IPS guarantee, and the realtor and seller carry the balance in a mortgage at 10%, secured by the business. "

"Has the Council done anything to warn people of what's happening?"

"No, there's no proof that what we are hearing is true. What the Council has done is to urge the people buying such businesses to consult with the IBIC officer. The Business Information Officer does what he can to dissuade people from buying such businesses with inflated prices if they're brought to him for evaluation, but some Ismailis are so desperate to get into a business, they don't listen. At the same time the unscrupulous realtors dissuade people from consulting with the IBIC officer by telling them if they do, the officer will tell others about this unique opportunity and friends and relatives of the IBIC staff and Jamati leadership will scoop up the business. Where people get into such deals, with or without reference to the IBIC, the families end up working 14 - 16 hours a day to pay the bank loan and mortgages, and earn less than minimum wage."

"We haven't seen much of this in Western Canada, but I wouldn't be surprised if it's happening here, also. It's sad, isn't it? With all of our Imam's emphasis on ethical living, this shouldn't be happening. Unfortunately, we have our share of unethical people, just like any other group," said Anil.

"In Toronto, we have fights erupting between people who had bought businesses in partnership, based only on the goodwill and personal relationships, without any kind of written partnership agreements. They're now approaching the Approval Committee for mediation and resolution of their disputes, some of which are quite bitter. In some situations, it's evident that one partner is dishonest or unreasonable," said Rafiq.

"How do you deal with such issues?" Anil asked.

"It's not our job to mediate, but one of us gets involved in his/her personal capacity, and in some situations, we get them to settle. Some end up going to lawyers, and you know what that entails. On the positive side, I have heard of this one group which has mobilized a large number of Ismailis who have invested small sums - I think it's $7,500 - $10,000 each - to buy an apartment building. I am told the promoters know much about real estate. This one guy, who has participated in this project, told me the project is doing very well, and they will soon have their original investment returned to them and continue to own shares in the project," said Rafiq.

"Good for them!"

Sophia, who had been listening to Anil and Rafiq talk, said, "This is why it's so important for Ismaili parents to take the time to talk to their children about Islamic ethics and values. This is easy to do here in Canada because our ethics and values resonate with the Canadian values of what is right and wrong. You two find such unethical behavior abhorrent because of the ethics our Imam tells us to live by and what your parents have taught you. Your parents served as the roots that nurtured you to grow up to become strong trees and bear healthy fruit. We have to do the same for our children."

Anil and Rafiq both noticed that Sophia had referred to the Imam as "our" Imam and not "your" Imam, as she had always done before.

IN MID-FEBRUARY, AS THEY sat down for breakfast one Sunday morning, Sophia said, "Anil, I've decided to become Ismaili."

Anil froze with his cereal spoon, lifted halfway to his mouth. After a beat, he recovered from his shock enough to sputter, "What? Why? When did you decide to do this? You've never said a word about this before. Why do you suddenly want to become Ismaili?"

"It's not sudden," said Sophia, amused by his reaction. "I've been thinking about this for over a year and talking to my dad for the past six months. Our children, by birthright, are Ismaili. Mom takes them to Jamatkhana all the time. You don't go to Jamatkhana except on festive occasions because you don't want to leave me alone. As you know, I've studied a lot about Islam, and I've also been studying all of the Ismaili literature that you've brought into the house, including all of the Imam's Farmans. Our interpretations of Islam are the same. We both believe in the institution of Imamat and Ali as our first Imam. Somewhere along the line, our sects parted company, but we both believe in the Imam's authority to interpret the Quran, which makes us Shia Muslims."

"But our Indian Ismaili practice has evolved quite differently from the way you pray," said Anil, still somewhat gobsmacked.

"Yes, your rituals and practices have evolved differently from mine, but our central beliefs are the same. I've studied the D'ua that you recite three times a day.

You start with the first Sura from the Quran, Al hamdu li-lahi rab-bil Almin - All praise is due to God, Lord of the universe), and then go on to recite Sura al ikhlas, Kul huw Allahu ahad, Allahu samad - Say, it is Allah who is the one. Allah is absolute, independent. Recitation of these two Suras is central to all Islamic prayers, and I also recite these in my prayers."

"Talked to your dad? What does he say about this?"

"He's just fine. He says that you guys are Shia, as are we. You believe in a living Imam, and as he has said before, maybe, you followed the right lineage because it has continued for 1400 years. He says that if I become Ismaili, I'll still be practicing Islam and its Shia interpretation; I'll just be accepting your 49th Imam as the legitimate Imam descended from the Prophet's family, *ahl al- bayt*, and accepting his interpretations of the Quran. Dad is quite comfortable with that."

"I know you've always wanted to serve on our Councils and committees," said Anil. "You were happy when you got to serve at the First Aid Station in Toronto. You didn't even want to go and eat your lunch. Is that why you want to become Ismaili? Serve on the Council?"

"Don't be silly, Anil. I told you I've been thinking about this for a year. Yes, I did talk to my dad after the Toronto event, which was very gratifying for me, but that's not why I want to become Ismaili. I want you to understand that if I apply, it doesn't mean that I have any difficulty with my Ithna Ashari practice of faith. In addition to saying the daily D'ua and observing your other practices - some of which sound like fun when Mom describes them - I'll continue to pray as I've always done. I grew up with my way of praying, and my prayers give me a sense of peace, as I'm sure I will find in praying with you. I simply see your practice as another way of connecting with God, and I'm comfortable with your belief in your 49th Imam."

"Well, it certainly sounds like you've given this a great deal of thought. If you're certain, then I can inquire about the process for you to apply, but are you sure you want to do this?"

"Yes, I am. I've never attended a mosque here. I don't even know if there is one in Vancouver. I want to participate in congregational prayers, and I want to be a part of the Ismaili community. I think I understand the essence of Ismailism better than you do, Anil."

"You don't have to rub it in, Sophia. I didn't have the benefit of the religious training you received. I just want you to be sure you want to do this. If you want to attend congregational prayers, we can find out if there is an Ithna Ashari mosque here. If not, you can attend a Sunni mosque. I will attend with you. We can attend any mosque with our Muslim brothers and sisters. They will welcome us."

"No, I don't want to remain an outsider when our interpretations of Islam are the same. I have so many Ismaili friends. I like the way your Imam teaches you to be good human beings and to connect with Allah. My Ismaili friends call me an honorary Ismaili, and I already feel like I am a part of the faith."

SOPHIA APPLIED TO BECOME Ismaili the following week and attended Jamatkhana on March 21st, Navrouz, the first day of spring and New Year's Day in the Shia calendar. She was well known within the Vancouver Jamat and Ismaili leadership. The latter wondered why she had waited so long to become Ismaili.

IN MAY, TAZIM TOLD Rafiq that she had applied for jobs with some Vancouver drug stores. She had received two favorable responses, and she was planning to move at the end of June.

"Why do you want to move?" asked Rafiq ruefully. "I know Vancouver is beautiful – the mountains and the ocean and all that – but Toronto is bigger and more vibrant. If you want to be in business for yourself one day, you'll do much better here. Is there anything we can do to convince you to stay?"

"Aww, Rafiq…no one could love me more than you and your family. Neither Anil nor my mom loves me the way that you guys do. If I move, being away from you will be hard. Ever since I was a girl, you've treated me like your little sister, and I cannot even tell you how much that means to me. You've been the brother that Anil and Zahir could never be. But I can't be your baby sister forever. I need to be independent and have my own life."

"You're unfair to Mom and Anil - they love you more than you can realize. They're just not as tolerant of your anger as I am. But you can have your independence here. Get your own place downtown if you want, or you can move into one of our condos in Don Mills when the lease comes up for renewal."

"No, for some reason, I'm drawn to Vancouver. I want to go there."

"Is it Shabir?"

"God, No. He's just a friend."

"He's in love with you, you know?"

Tazim smiled and walked away.

She left at the end of June to start her new life in Vancouver.

1978
Ninety-Three

In September 1978, rumors started swirling within the Ismaili community that the Imam had expressed the desire to visit Canada and meet with his Jamat. There was palpable anticipation in the community. The rumors got stronger when it became known in the Jamat that the Eastern and Western Councils were checking for dates when the Toronto International Centre (TIC) and Pacific National Exhibition (PNE) in Vancouver were available for renting.

The Jamat's suspense and speculation came to an end in late October, when it was announced that the Imam and his wife, *Begum* (Lady) Salimah, would be in Canada from November 12th to 22nd and would visit Ottawa, Vancouver, Calgary, Edmonton, Winnipeg, Montreal, and Toronto.

Whereas the Jamat – which by this time numbered over 40,000 – had settled well, the events in Uganda and Tanzania had left many feeling deeply bruised. For them, the wounds had not yet fully healed. The Imam's visit would serve to ease the pain. He would comfort them and define the path ahead for them. The Jamat could not wait to receive their Imam and the Begum.

Immediately after the visit announcement, preparations went into high gear in all designated centers. The Councils, as the bodies responsible for the organization of the Imam's visit, sought guidance on the nature of the visit. Was it to be a private visit, limited to Imam's meetings with the Jamat, or a public one, involving meetings with government officials and media coverage?

In the time they had been in Canada, Ismailis had been occupied with building and strengthening their administrative structures, and settling in Canada. They had not sought any limelight. In the Canadian government's assessments of the Ugandan refugee settlement program, however, the Ismailis had emerged as a highly educated, entrepreneurial, organized, disciplined, and self-sufficient community that had settled in Canada in record time with minimal government assistance. In 1975, there was only one Ugandan Ismaili in Canada who was receiving government support, and he was blind. The community was mostly unaware of this external perception of it itself.

The Aga Khan Council for Canada (National Council) soon received direction that this would be a public visit. The Imam and Begum would be Prime Minister Trudeau's guests, and the Imam was receptive to giving media interviews. He was also receptive to the National Council's proposal to organize banquets in at least two centers, Vancouver and Toronto, to which the Council wished to invite "Who's Who in Canada."

Under the National Council's direction, the Eastern and Western Canada Councils appointed committees to source facilities in all centers that could accommodate congregations varying in size from 500 in Winnipeg to 20,000 in Toronto, cater meals to feed them for at least two days, and make security arrangements for all events at all venues. In cities like Ottawa, Montreal, Edmonton, and Winnipeg, Local Administrative Committees appointed by the respective Councils were mandated to do all of the planning and implementation work.

Anil was appointed to serve on the Facilities Committee for Western Canada. Like other volunteers with significant responsibilities, Sophia, Anil, and Rafiq (who was appointed onto the Banquet Organization and Facilities Rental and Management committees for Eastern Canada) took a week off from work before the visit.

Accommodation and transportation arrangements for the Imam, Begum, and their entourage had to be made. Offices from which the Imam and his staff could operate upon arrival in any center had to be set up. The Imam's work for his Jamat never stopped.

The planning of gala banquets in Vancouver, Edmonton, and Toronto was a challenging assignment. These events were intended to serve as introductions of the

Imam to the Canadian establishment and had to be of the highest caliber in organization and participation. The theme was to be "Thank you, Canada." Lists had to be developed of all senior politicians and civil servants, top corporate executives, university chancellors, and presidents, school board trustees, hospital board chairs, as well as senior community and multi-faith leaders in each region. All of these people had to be identified and invited to attend banquets that, of necessity, would need to be scheduled on weekdays. It was no small task.

Sophia became heavily involved with the Banquet Committee in developing guest lists, sending out, and following up on, the invitations.

The Ottawa Administrative Committee was advised that no accommodation for the Imam and Begum was required, as they would be Prime Minister Trudeau's guests at the government cottage at Harrington Lake. In Vancouver, the Imam and Begum were to be guests at an Ismaili family's home. In all other centers, presidential suites and additional rooms for the staff and entourage were booked in prestigious hotels.

THE EASTERN CANADA COUNCIL President requested that Rafiq, along with Iqbal Alibhai, a National Council member residing in Toronto, travel to Ottawa and Montreal to meet with the Local Administrative Committees and check out the facilities that the Committees had selected, and all logistics for the Imam to meet with his Jamats.

The Ottawa Committee had selected a banquet hall in the Château Laurier hotel. Little setup was required here. The President had asked that Rafiq and Iqbal look at functionality and the logistics for entry into and exit from the hotel of up to 1,000 people within a short period, and ensure that this would cause no inconvenience to the hotel guests or patrons - although the hotel had made no such request. Additionally, Rafiq and Iqbal were asked to check arrangements for parking cars, the sound system, and cloakrooms.

Montreal was a different situation. The Administrative Committee there had proposed to rent a space in the CEGEP college facilities in Old Montreal for the Imam to meet with his 1,500 Quebec and North Eastern U.S.A. Jamats. This required a set up similar to that of the TIC in Toronto, albeit on a smaller scale.

Rafiq told his parents and Shameem that he and Iqbal planned to travel to Ottawa early on Friday, November 3rd. They had arranged to meet with the Ottawa Administrative Committee Chairman and Honorary Secretary for lunch at 12.30 p.m., and then visit the banquet hall in the Château, and review all arrangements. They planned to attend Jamatkhana in the evening and spend the night in Ottawa, then travel to Montreal on Saturday morning to be there by noon, where they had planned similar arrangements and would return to Toronto on Sunday. He told Shameem that the Ottawa and Montreal Administrative Committee Chairmen had suggested that he and Iqbal should bring their spouses with them if they wished to do so. Arrangements would be made for them to go sightseeing while Rafiq and Iqbal did their work.

"I'm tempted to come. I've met Iqbal's wife, Razia, once. Mom, would you be alright if I went? You won't get your weekend break from the girls."

"You don't have to ask, Shama. Please go. For me, it will be an opportunity to be with Farrah and Rehana over the weekend, not the loss of a weekend break."

"I would like you to come, Shama. These are such exciting times for the Jamat. There is jubilation in all Jamats. It'll be nice to attend Jamatkhanas in Ottawa and Montreal and pray with them," said Rafiq.

AS PLANNED, IQBAL, RAZIA, Rafiq, and Shameem departed for Ottawa on Friday morning. After a short coffee break in Kingston, they arrived at their hotel in Ottawa's famous ByWard Market area at 12.30 p.m. The hotel was just a few minutes walk to the Château Laurier. The Ottawa Administrative Committee Chairman, Honorary Secretary, and their spouses met them at the hotel for lunch. After lunch, Razia and Shameem departed with their hosts' spouses for sightseeing and Rafiq, Iqbal, and the hosts proceeded to the Château Laurier.

Rafiq and Iqbal were impressed with the Committee's attention to detail and meticulous planning. They reviewed each element against a minute to minute program. They identified some small gaps which the Chairman undertook to address. They finished at 5.00 p.m. and walked back to their hotel. The wives arrived shortly after that. For them, even in the cold of an Ottawa November, it had been fun to visit several attractions and do some shopping.

They attended Jamatkhana that evening. Both Rafiq and Shameem met people they knew from back home. After the conclusion of the services, they returned to the ByWard Market with the entire Ottawa Administrative Committee members and their spouses for dinner at an Italian restaurant.

AS ARRANGED, THEY ARRIVED in Montreal the next day and met with the Montreal Administrative Committee Chairman, Honorary Secretary, and their spouses at their hotel on Sherbrooke Avenue. After lunch, the spouses departed for their sightseeing tour, and Rafiq, Iqbal, and their hosts proceeded to the CEGEP to review the proposed facility set up and logistics.

They were equally impressed with the Montreal Administrative Committee's detailed planning and implementation strategy.

THAT EVENING, AFTER DROPPING off Shameem and Razia at the Jamatkhana entrance, Rafiq and Iqbal drove to a nearby street to park the car and returned to the Jamatkhana.

As they reached the top of the stairs at the first-floor level where the prayer hall was located, Rafiq saw a woman with two young children, a boy and a girl, who looked at him, seemed to recognize him and smiled. He smiled back at her but did not have time to speak to her as the recitation of the prayers was commencing, and they rushed into the prayer hall to join the congregation.

A moment later, it dawned on Rafiq that the woman he had seen was Jenny. She had changed. She had lost weight, had worn no makeup, and her hair had looked a bit disheveled. What could have happened to her? Could Dean have left her? When the prayers were over, he looked for her and saw her talking to Shameem. He walked over to them, and she turned and hugged him.

"I'm so happy to see you, Rafiq. It's so good to see you both. I knew that you were in Toronto, and I was hoping you would visit Montreal one day, and here we are. What brings you here in this cold weather?"

"Rafiq had some Council work in town, and I decided to join him," said Shameem. It looked like she did not want Rafiq to speak to her because she knew he would be kind to her, which she did not want to be.

"Do you live here, Jenny?" asked Rafiq.

"Yes, I've been in Montreal for about six years. Are you staying here for a few days?"

"We leave tomorrow," he replied.

"Can you please come home for lunch before you leave? It's what, a five-hour drive to Toronto?"

"That's very kind of you, Jenny," said Shameem. "But we need to get back to Toronto by 5.00 p.m. We have to go to work on Monday."

"Then, for coffee earlier. Can you please come? I would be so happy and grateful if you do. Please come for breakfast. You can come as early as you want to. Please."

"Sorry, Jenny, we have another couple traveling with us," said Shameem. Maybe the next time we're here?"

"Where do you live, Jenny?" asked Rafiq.

"In Mount Royal. It's very near downtown Montreal. Here is my address," she said, as she pulled out a business card and handed it to Rafiq.

"Can we come for breakfast at 8.00 a.m.?" he asked, much to Shameem's chagrin.

"I would be delighted to have you come anytime! Yes, 8.00 a.m. will be perfect. That will give us some time to talk."

"Okay, we'll see you tomorrow. You have lovely children."

Jenny thanked Rafiq and hugged them both. Rafiq saw that her eyes were damp as she did this.

"Why did you do that?" hissed Shameem, as soon as they were out of earshot. "Why would we want to go to her house? And at 8.00 a.m.? That means we have to wake up at 6.00?"

"Shama, she was practically begging us to go over. Did you see the sadness in her eyes? She obviously wants to talk to us. Even after you told her that we're here with another couple, she didn't say, 'Oh, bring them along.' She clearly wants to talk to us alone."

"What will we say to Iqbal and Razia? 'We'll go to Jenny's place, wherever that is, and then come back to pick you up; sorry, you're not invited'?"

"It's alright, Shama. Look at how much happiness there is on everyone's face here and then look at Jenny's face. There's no smile there. She was reaching out to us. Maybe she'll just give us breakfast and send us on our way, or maybe she wants to talk to us. Perhaps she's ill or needs help."

"Ever the Rafiq filled with the milk of human kindness…" Shameem muttered under her breath before saying, "Now you manage Iqbal and Razia, okay?"

"Not a problem. Leave it to me."

THEIR HOSTS TOOK THEM for a nice dinner in Old Montreal. It was 11.00 p.m. when they got back to the hotel.

As they walked towards the hotel elevator, Rafiq said to Iqbal and Razia, "We met an old friend of ours from the U.K. tonight in Jamatkhana. She has invited us to go to her place for an early breakfast tomorrow, so you guys can relax and sleep in. We'll be back by 11.30 so that we can check out and leave before noon. We're sorry to delay our departure, but we really couldn't say no to her."

"That's just fine," said Razia. "There's a boutique on Rue St. Catherine that a friend has recommended to me; I checked with the concierge, and he said it's not far from here. I'll be happy to spend some time shopping tomorrow morning."

"Perfect!" said Rafiq.

When they got to their room, Shameem said, "Rafiq, on the way home, I was thinking about what you said. I think that you may be right. Something was off with Jenny. To be honest, I wanted to get away from her when she first approached me, but I think that she just wanted to connect. I wonder why she wants so much for us to visit her. I truly hope she's not ill. Her children are so young."

"Hopefully, not. For now, let's just commit to listening to her and being support-ive. After all, she did nothing to the two of us, and Anil is happy, so why hold onto small grudges?"

"She did spread lies in London Jamatkhana about us; she told her friends that we had misled her about Anil's wealth."

"Yeah, but so what? That was a long time ago. We can move past ancient history."

They checked out early the next morning and got directions to Jenny's house from the hotel reception. It was less than twenty minutes drive from the hotel. They arrived at Jenny's just after 8.00 a.m. It was a very expensive neighborhood with large homes. They parked in the driveway of her three-car garage. When they got out, Jenny was already at the door to welcome them. She had been waiting for them. She hugged them both and led them inside her majestic home and sat them down in the lounge. Neither Rafiq nor Shameem had been inside a house as large and ornate as this before. There were paintings on the wall that they knew were worth thousands, if not hundreds of thousands of dollars.

"You have a beautiful home, Jenny," said Shameem.

"Thank you, Shama, but it's too much to manage. I have four people working to maintain the property. I would have been much happier in a small subdivision home, but Dean wanted this as an investment."

"Will Dean be joining us?" asked Rafiq.

"No, he's traveling. Can I get you some orange juice? Breakfast will be ready shortly."

"Orange juice will be nice," said Rafiq.

Jenny stepped away for a few seconds and returned to sit with them. Soon, a white lady appeared with orange juice in crystal glasses on a silver tray.

"Where are the children?" asked Shameem.

"The nanny will bring them down later. I wanted to have some adult-time to talk to you. I'm very grateful that you could come."

"We're happy to be here," replied Shameem.

"I understand that you're a doctor now and have two children," she said, looking at Shameem.

"Yes, and we're fortunate to have Rafiq's parents living with us. His mom looks after the children when I'm working."

"How's Anil? I understand that he married an Arabic girl and lives in Vancouver."

Rafiq and Shameem glanced furtively at each other. Obviously, Jenny knew a great deal about them all, but before either could answer, a white gentleman appeared and said something in French to Jenny.

"Breakfast is ready. This is Armand, our chef," she said, and spoke to Armand in French, introducing him to Rafiq and Shameem.

He smiled and nodded at them, said something, and left.

As they walked to the dining room, Shameem said, "Where did you learn to speak French?"

"I learned it in the Congo."

THE LARGE MAHOGANY DINING table for 12 was immaculately laid out with delicate bone China, polished silver cutlery, crystal glasses, and at least seven varieties of breakfast items.

"Goodness! We would have been happy with just cereal and toast, Jenny. You did not have to do all this," said Shameem.

"I didn't do anything. Armand came in early, and he and my housekeeper prepared and set all this up."

"How many people do you have working in the house?" Rafiq asked.

"Three. There's the nanny, the housekeeper who served you orange juice, and Armand."

"So, you're a lady of leisure," Shameem said, smiling.

"I wish that I wasn't. I would like to be able to go to work. I did, briefly, after moving here, but Dean insisted that I resign, as he felt that I was neglecting our children by going to work all day. So here I am, sitting in this house all day, with nothing to do."

Shameem and Rafiq smiled politely and sat down at the table.

As they ate breakfast, they talked about Rafiq's work and Shameem's specialization, what had happened in Tanzania, and how and when they had come to Canada. Jenny told them about the predominantly French-speaking Quebec Jamat. About 50% of them were from the Congo and Madagascar and had come to Canada speaking fluent French.

When they finished eating breakfast and were having tea, Jenny asked, "So, how's Anil? Is he happy?"

After a beat, Shameem spoke. "He's very happy. His wife, Sophia, is now Ismaili, and they have two children. Sophia is a nurse, and Anil has a senior position with a bank. How about you, Jenny? How are you?"

Jenny did not answer. She looked at them, and her eyes filled with tears. She took a sip from her teacup and then looked down to compose herself.

When she looked up, she said, "Look around. This is everything that I ever wanted. Actually, this is much, much more than I ever wanted. This house is worth $500,000, and it's in my name. I have three luxury cars sitting in the garage - all in my name. I have the staff to look after me, the children, and the house. I have over $1,000,000 in the bank here in my name, and I don't know how much more in the banks in Geneva. This is what I wanted, and to get it, I put myself up for sale to a higher bidder. Not a day goes by when I don't think of Anil. How happy my life would have been with him. What a perfect gentleman he was. How cultured and smart he was. How kind and considerate he was."

Tears were now sliding down from her eyes.

Shameem took her hand.

"What happened?" asked Rafiq. "You are living very comfortably. You have two adorable children. What's wrong?"

"Soon after I left Anil, I met Dean and started dating him. He is not a very loveable person, but I loved his money. He invited me to move into his home in Mayfair. He asked me to quit work and began transferring funds into my bank account to use as I pleased. In the five months, I was there, I felt like the world was at my feet. I could buy anything my heart desired. Dean traveled a lot, but when he was in London, he spoilt me. He asked me to take driving lessons and bought me a Rover. I wasn't comfortable driving his Jaguar. I didn't mind Dean being away so much. I enjoyed myself when he was not there. I shopped, went to the theatres and restaurants, and did whatever I had wanted to do. Suddenly I had more friends than before, and life became one glamourous event after another. We stayed in London until the end of 1965. Those were the happiest days of my life."

"But we didn't see you in Jamatkhana," said Rafiq.

"That's because I didn't go. My weekends were too busy. If I wasn't going danc-ing or to the movies or the theatre, I was jetting off to Paris, Rome, and Brussels, and taking my friends with me. Every time Dean came home, he topped up my bank account."

"It sounds like you were happy. What changed?" asked Shameem.

"In early 1966, Dean's father passed away in the Congo. Dean was there at that time. When he came back, he said that we needed to get married and move to Leopoldville - Congo's capital city. A year later, it became Kinshasa. We had a civil marriage ceremony in London and moved shortly after that. I'd expected Dean to have a large business operation and had hoped that I would work with him in the family business, but that didn't happen. They had a massive old mansion in an exclusive area of Kinshasa, where Dean's mother had lived with her husband. When he died, her daughter, who had been living in Belgium for many years, came for the funeral and took her mother back with her to Brussels. We took over the house after that."

"What was life like in Congo?" asked Rafiq.

"I settled in the house. At all times, there were at least 15 people employed there. The house was designed by a Belgian architect and built with every conceivable security feature. It was surrounded by 12-foot concrete walls with electrified gates and fences and closed-circuit TV cameras. There were half a dozen machine-guns wielding Belgians employed as security staff guarding the inside and outside perimeters of the house. These were mercenaries who had fought in the various civil wars in the Congo on different sides and had stayed on."

"Was that the norm there? Were all houses of wealthy people protected that way?" asked Rafiq.

"Most had some security. Our house had the kind of security that the government ministers had. If I wanted to go into the city, I had to be driven and accompanied by these bodyguards. I could never drive alone. They even came with me into the hairdressing salon. Because of the size of tips I left them, the staff never complained, but it was embarrassing for me – I felt like a mobster's wife! I asked Dean why I needed that much security. He said rich people could get kidnapped, and the kidnappers could ask for huge ransoms. He would be happy to pay the ransom for me, but they would probably rape me. After that, I was scared to venture out, but soon I started to fear the security guards. Dean was traveling all the time. They were unruly, and from the way they looked at me, I was afraid one of them might attack me one day. Millions of dollars, gold bars, and uncut diamonds were stored in a large in-ground safe in the house. I worried that someone must have known about the safe when it was brought in and installed. What if the security guards collaborated with someone to come and steal the safe or just its contents? What would they do to me? The house was so cut off from the outside world, they could work for a week to dig up the safe, and no one would know."

"Did you share your fears with Dean?" Shameem asked.

"I did, but he said that I had nothing to fear because his security people were loyal. Their families in Europe depended on him to live in luxury. When Dean was in town, the house was filled with ministers, senior government officials, and mining company executives. They ate and drank and behaved lecherously. I learned to stay away. There were always enough Belgian women there to entertain them. Dean took care of that."

"I can imagine how difficult that must have been for you, Jenny," said Shameem.

"There were some interludes. From time to time, Dean asked me to go with him to Amsterdam and Geneva. We traveled first class and stayed in presidential suites in the most expensive hotels with dedicated staff to serve us. Sometimes, he took an entire floor. In Geneva, we went to the banks where Dean deposited massive sums of money into our joint accounts. He also opened accounts in the names of Congolese ministers, which he managed for them. He moved money around, opening new accounts here, and taking money out of there and getting me to sign for everything. Once, he wanted to open a joint account in a minister's, his, and my names. I asked why my name needed to be included, and he said that we were living in a dangerous place, and one day, the minister and he could both disappear. He wanted me to have control over the money if this happened. I refused. I told him that I didn't want to be involved with whatever he was doing, but I was already involved. When on these trips, I would suggest going to London for a few days, but Dean always found an excuse to return home. I found out later that he had a mistress living in our Mayfair flat. One day, a pretty Belgian girl I met at my hair salon asked me if I knew that Dean had a mistress in Kinshasa, as well. She told me that she had been his mistress at one time, but he had tired of her."

"You must have been furious!" exclaimed Shameem.

"Not really. I had smelled perfume on him before and decided not to confront him, but after three years of imprisonment in Kinshasa, I couldn't take it anymore.

I had a lot of money in my name, and I wanted to run away, but in 1968, I became pregnant. It was a bad pregnancy, and I miscarried in the fourth month. After that, my resolve weakened, and I began to accept that this was my fate."

"Did you not have any contact with the community there? Did you go to Jamatkhana?" asked Shameem.

"I did, and I found out very quickly that Dean and his family were very much despised for their immoral ways and illegal dealings, and for never lifting a finger to help any Ismaili in trouble with the government. People saw me as one of them, and nobody wanted to socialize with me. When I invited some ladies to my place, only two came, and they seemed afraid to be there. They were happy to leave as soon as they could."

"And you stayed there until 1972?" asked Rafiq.

"I got pregnant with my daughter, Sabrina, in 1970. Dean wanted children, and I thought that children might stabilize our lives. After Sabrina was born, Dean wanted another child. I think that he wanted a boy. We had our son in 1971. After the children were born, I became busy raising them, and life became more bearable. They brought some purpose in my life. Dean spent more time at home, but the flow of money had accelerated. By this time, I had learned to read and speak a little French from a tutor who came home every day to teach me the language. One day I heard on the radio that one of the ministers who came to our house regularly had been arrested and thrown in jail. I was terrified that they would come for Dean, but he told me not to worry."

"How did you come here?" asked Rafiq.

"In 1972, following the Asian expulsion from Uganda and the departure of the Ismailis from Tanzania, the Congolese Ismailis started to leave for Canada. Dean said that it was no longer safe for the children and me to be there. He applied for Canadian residency for us all. Given his government connections, he had no problem getting a clean police report, and by revealing only a tiny fraction of the money in his accounts in Geneva, he got approved in the Business category. We came here in November and then bought this place. Dean hired interior designers and decorators and had the place fully renovated and furnished with items from Paris and Brussels. Once we were settled here and the kids were enrolled in a Montessori program, Dean left. He visits from time to time and flies us to Geneva a couple of times a year. He is now in the big league. He has a Lear Jet, which he has never brought here because he says, it does not have the fuel carrying capacity to cross the Atlantic. He adores the children and spends all the time with them when we are together, but the rest of the time, it's just us without him. I think that he's gotten himself caught in a web of theft and deceit from which he cannot extricate himself. I'm certain that he has other women in his life. So, this is my life. I'm all alone, and I have no idea what the future will hold for my children and me."

"I'm so sorry to hear this, Jenny," said Shameem. "Do you have any friends here?"

"Not really. The majority of the Jamat here is from the Congo. They all know Dean, and they have no respect for someone who would marry someone like him. They know where the money they see I'm enjoying comes from. I have some friends who are from Uganda and Tanzania. They, too, have heard all about Dean and his family, but I think that they see me as a victim and feel sorry for me. I feel quite trapped. I could divorce Dean and make a go of things on my own, but then what? Move into another house in Montreal? What about my children's relationship with their father? I'm also scared to take any such action. I don't know how Dean would react. In the final analysis, however, I am happier here than I was in the Congo. I have more freedom to move about. I can take the children for nice holidays. They have given me a reason to live, but still, it's a very lonely and desolate life."

"What about your family? Where are they?" asked Rafiq.

"Still in Kenya. I wanted to sponsor them to come here, but Dean doesn't want them anywhere near me. He met them once, and they didn't get along. We send them money, but he doesn't want them here with the children and me."

"What about the neighbors?"

"They're polite enough. I think that they appreciate that we speak French, but they're not particularly welcoming to a brown-skinned immigrant family with a patriarch who appears infrequently and may be engaged in questionable activities."

"Would it be possible for you to move to Toronto? The Jamat there is large and you can find more anonymity there. You may find people more open-minded and welcoming there," said Shameem.

"I've not considered it, to be honest," replied Jenny. "Dean may be receptive to the idea."

"Think about it. Talk to him and let us know. Here's our contact information," said Shameem, writing quickly on a small pad that she carried in her purse.

"We are here for you, Jenny," said Rafiq. He glanced at his watch. It was time to leave, and they had not seen the children yet.

"I'm truly grateful that you came," said Jenny. "Please, can we stay in contact? I've not been able to talk about all of this to anyone. I know that I can trust you," she said with a soft smile, before abruptly asking, "Has Anil forgiven me?"

After a moment, Shameem smiled and said, "Yes, Anil harbors no ill feelings towards you."

"Will you tell him that we met? That I'm here?"

Shameem looked at Rafiq.

"Would you like us to tell him we met you, Jenny?" he asked.

She paused. "Perhaps, not. He has his own life now. No good can come from him knowing me anymore."

Shameem and Rafiq looked sadly at her before hugging her and saying their goodbyes, with promises to keep in touch.

ON THEIR WAY BACK, Rafiq said, "She's gotten herself into a dangerous mess. This is much more serious than she realizes."

"My heart goes out to her. She couldn't have seen all she was getting into when she got involved with this guy. It's a sad and dangerous situation."

When they got back to the hotel, Iqbal and Razia were not there. Rafiq had checked out in the morning, and their baggage was already in the car, so they sat down in the hotel's reception area to wait for them.

Razia came running in at around 12.30 p.m. She was out of breath and laden with shopping bags. Iqbal, who was also carrying some shopping bags, proceeded to the checkout counter.

"We're so sorry to have kept you waiting for so long, Shama. We were supposed to leave here at noon, and now we'll be almost an hour late. There was so much to see and buy. I got carried away, lost track of time. With all the bags, it also took longer walking back. I'm really sorry," Razia said

"You don't have to apologize, Razia. We have been sitting here, enjoying coffee. After all, you don't come here every week, and it's good you took half an hour more to shop. We're in no hurry to leave."

"Thank you for your understanding, Shama."

On the way back to Toronto, Rafiq and Iqbal went over all of the Ottawa and Montreal arrangements. They agreed that Iqbal would make the presentation to the Council on their findings and recommendations.

1978
Ninety-Four

The Canadian Ismailis waited anxiously for the day of their Imam's arrival in Canada.

The Imam and Begum Salimah arrived in Ottawa on November 12th to commence their first visit with the Canadian Jamat. They were received at the airport by senior government officials, members of the Diplomatic Corps, and the Ismaili institutional leaders. After greeting everyone, the Imam and Begum departed for Harrington Lake with the Chief Protocol Officer, to join the Prime Minister.

The following morning, they met with approximately 800 Ottawa and visiting Jamati members at the Chateau Laurier and later joined the Prime Minister at his 24 Sussex Drive residence for a luncheon.

In the afternoon, the Imam sat down for an interview with CTV Network's nationally televised Canada AM program, which was aired the next morning and was watched by thousands of Ismailis and non-Ismailis. In response to the question, if the Imam, who was educated in the West, spoke like a Westerner and looked like a Westerner, there was not a contradiction between what he represented as a spiritual leader and the lifestyle he lived, the Imam said that he saw no such contradiction. The holy Prophet had been a businessman and had ongoing business activities. He led armies, and yet, that did not stop him from being the Prophet and leading the prayers.

The Imam's words would be a resonant theme in the continued settlement and evolution of the Ismaili community in the western world – a balance between the material and spiritual worlds, and recognition that participation in one should not preclude participation in the other.

In discussing the Ismaili settlement in Canada, the Imam acknowledged with gratitude the Canadian government's remarkable co-operation, understanding, and help in welcoming Ismailis to Canada. His community, he said, had changed psychologically, which was understandable, and very palpable. There was a visible sense of peace and equanimity within the community. They understood that they were in a new country that they were getting to know and one to which they had grown very attached and were loyal. They viewed Canada as a country with excellent prospects, completely different from their countries of origin. It was very exciting for them to be here.

In another interview with the Global Television Network, the Imam said that Canada had one of the most practical and best-founded foreign aid development programs. He had requested that Prime Minister Trudeau and federal officials strengthen Canada's aid program, which was having a significant positive impact in poorer countries.

Asked whether his wealth was a handicap in convincing people in the developing countries that he really wanted to help them, he said the West tended to look at the individual, the Aga Khan, and not the institution of the Ismaili Imamat that he represented. The Ismaili Imamat was very active in economic and social development worldwide.

LATER THAT AFTERNOON, AFTER meeting with the Prime Minister, the Under Secretary of the State for External Affairs, the President of the Canadian International Development Agency (CIDA), and other government officials, the Imam and Begum departed for Vancouver.

Approximately 8,000 Vancouver Ismailis and 1,500 from the U.S.A. anxiously awaited the arrival of their Imam at the Pacific National Exhibition (PNE) on November 14th.

Over his three days of meetings with the Jamat in Vancouver, the Imam asked the Jamat to make Canada their definitive and permanent home and to remain united, and regular in the practice of their faith. He said that they now lived in a country where they could plan for the future without fear and uncertainty. He expressed immense happiness for the lavish praise he had heard the government officials express for the Ismaili community in Canada.

In a separate meeting with the students, the Imam emphasized the importance of post-secondary education and talked about careers for which they would find demand in Canada and elsewhere. He warned them against unhealthy social habits such as smoking, drinking, and drug use, which, he said, would limit their mental and physical capacities. To the younger students, he emphasized the importance of regular attendance in school.

"MAKE CANADA YOUR PERMANENT home," which the Imam emphasized strongly to his Jamat in all of the centers that he visited, sent a clear message to Canadian Ismailis that their future was here. There was no going back to Uganda or Tanzania. It brought to an end any aspirations that some Ugandan Ismailis had cherished of Idi Amin's overthrow and the formation of a new government that would invite them back to claim their businesses and properties.

The Imam's guidance to the youth on facile social habits was no different from what they had heard their parents say countless times, but coming from the Imam, it had a completely different meaning and impact.

The Imam's guidance to the very young students, - there was no reason good enough to miss school, would reverberate through the Ismaili homes for years to come when a child was feigning stomach ache for missing school (when the real reason was he/she had not done his homework).

WHILE IN VANCOUVER, THE Imam approved the construction of a first purpose-built Jamatkhana in Canada, on a parcel of land in Burnaby, B.C. This would be a statement of permanence and presence of Ismailis in Canada.

In banquets hosted by The Aga Khan Council for Canada in Vancouver, Edmonton and Toronto, which were attended by senior government officials, the diplomatic corps, top corporate heads, academia, faith leaders, major media groups (Prime Minister Trudeau had sent a message of regret for not being able to attend), the Imam expressed praise and gratitude for the welcome the Canadians had offered to Ismailis who were expelled from Uganda in 1972. "It was Canada which opened her arms, and none of us will forget that gesture of spontaneous goodwill. All of us are determined to repay the kindness," he said.

Over the next four days, the Imam and Begum Salimah visited the community in Calgary, Edmonton, Winnipeg, and Montreal, and then arrived in Toronto on November 19th. Over 18,000 Ismailis had gathered in the Toronto International Centre to receive them.

In the three days that he spent in Toronto, the Imam repeated his advice to the Jamat to make Canada their permanent home and work to contribute to Canada's well-being. He urged the students to excel in their studies. He expressed the hope that in time, those educated and trained in Canada would offer their knowledge and experience to the Jamats and Imamat institutions in the developing countries.

IN INTRODUCING THE AGA Khan at the banquet in Toronto, the Eastern Canada Council President said that as a community, Ismailis valued the spirit of self-help, discipline, and efficient organization. When admitted to Canada in 1972, they had brought with them their commitment to adapt, integrate, work hard, and fully identify themselves with the Canadian value system. He went on to say that Islam maintains that material progress without spiritual well-being is meaningless and that the Imam, as the community's spiritual leader, placed as much emphasis on progressive spiritual advancement through regular prayer and self-discipline as he did on material progress through purposeful and responsible action. He expressed the hope that under the Imam's guidance, the Canadian Ismailis would develop deep roots in Canada and become known as a progressive, civic-minded community with genuine loyalty to their new country of adoption.

The Honourable Norman Cafik, Minister of State for Multiculturalism, read a letter that the Prime Minister had prepared for this occasion. It read:

"I am most pleased to convey my warmest greetings to all those attending the banquet in honor of His Highness Prince Karim Aga Khan The Fourth and Her Highness Begum Salimah. If Canada is to be thanked tonight by the Ugandans, I am certain that this gratitude is reciprocal – for the members of the Ismaili sect of the Muslim religion have greatly contributed to the cultural richness of our society. Therefore, I would like to join in the homage paid to His Highness Prince Karim Aga Khan The Fourth and Her Highness Begum Salimah and extend to all present my very warmest personal good wishes for a most memorable evening."

After reading the prime minister's letter, Minister Cafik went on to say, "We in Canada appreciate the gesture of gratitude that is being expressed tonight. But a simple fact of the matter is that gratitude is a two-way street. The 6,000 who came to Canada then contributed a great deal more than they ever received."

On behalf of the Government and all Canadians, he thanked the community for all that they had done for Canada. They had shared their culture, background, richness, and traditions that had enriched and benefited all Canadians. He thanked the Aga Khan and his organizations for their contribution to enable the 6,000 new Canadian Ismailis to integrate into Canadian society quickly by providing the financial and other resources to the Ismailis who came to a foreign and strange land to help them integrate and become full and proper Canadians. He also thanked the Aga Khan for encouraging Ismailis in Canada and others who lived in other countries to hold onto their traditions, values, and their cultures, but first and foremost, be true citizens of their newly adopted land. He concluded his remarks by saying, "Your presence in Canada comes at a time of great change, a time of renewal, a time of national reflection, and a time when we as Canadians have got to learn to put our lofty principles into practice, into the practice of tolerance and human understanding between all of our people. It is a great challenge, and I think that the lessons that you have learned in other countries before coming here are lessons that we can learn from. We look forward to you sharing with us those messages, and that lesson of understanding and to share it with all of us so that we may learn from your misfortunes in the past and be richer as a people and more united as a consequence. I want to thank all of you for making this your new home and to say that we are as proud to have you here as you are to be here."

In his address, the Aga Khan said, "I would like to begin by thanking the Prime Minister of Canada and the Premier of Ontario for the extremely kind messages which they have sent this evening. And to thank also the Honourable Lt. Governor of Ontario, the Honourable Minister for Multiculturalism, the Honourable Minister of Intergovernmental Affairs and His Worship, the Mayor of Toronto, for their very generous and their very kind words about the Ismaili community and about my wife and myself."

"For my wife and me, this has been a very memorable evening as well as a most moving one. We are almost at the end of our tour of your country, which has taken us from coast to coast and back again. We have been greeted everywhere with immense kindness and warmth by your government and your civic leaders. This has been our first extensive visit to Canada, and we have enjoyed the experience immensely, and we express to you this evening our deep thanks."

"The tributes which have been paid to the Ismaili Community this evening have been generous indeed, and I am extremely happy to know how well the Ismailis are regarded and how quickly they have established themselves as good citizens of your country."

"You have heard from the first speaker tonight that we take pride in being an organized community. This characteristic has served us well in Canada, where the great majority living here today arrived just six years ago, having been expelled from Uganda almost overnight by President Idi Amin. Most Ismailis came here stateless, destitute, and almost literally with only the clothes they stood up in. Canada was the first of several countries to recognize this as the immense human tragedy it actually represented."

"Spontaneously, you opened up your arms to our people; you welcomed them and made it possible for them to start a new life in a new world. It was a gesture we shall never forget. We are not a large community, but in the six years since the Ismailis left their country on the other side of the world, with a totally different social and economic environment, they have adjusted themselves to new customs, new laws, new institutions, and a new way of life. They have done this in the best of our traditions of self-reliance, free enterprise, and good citizenship."

He went on to say that Ismailis were fortunate because the majority were well-equipped, both physically and intellectually, for such a sudden transformation. In Uganda, as in Pakistan, India, and elsewhere, the Aga Khan schools were among the best. Many of the Ismaili children who had attended these schools in Uganda had gone on to leading universities and colleges in Europe and North America.

They had arrived in Canada with skills to offer, and they could be found in a wide range of businesses and professional activities. They were doctors, lawyers, teachers, accountants, engineers, insurance brokers, pharmacists, and nurses, but not all who came to Canada were university graduates. Some were older, and others were less well-educated. They had a more difficult period of adjustment. Many had started their own businesses. The specialized facilities which Canada was able to offer through private, as well as official channels, married well with the internal community programs. Without the active participation and encouragement of Canadian friends, the community could have never have achieved so much in such a short time. Under the business loan guarantee program for small businesses, established with the assistance of the Bank of Nova Scotia and the Canadian Imperial Bank of Commerce, special loan facilities had been organized. A large number of businesses had been established under these programs, the failure rate for which compared quite favorably with the national average.

He praised Canada by saying, "She is welcomed diplomatically everywhere in the world, and her influence extends far beyond her natural size and wealth. The foreign aid administered by the Canadian International Development Agency illustrates very well what I mean. Canada is not among the largest international donors, but her programs are extremely well administered and reach the ordinary people whom they are intended to benefit. That is a rare accomplishment today. Foreign aid is but one facet of Canada as an international power who takes her responsibilities seriously and whose policies have never in her history been tainted by the cruder forms of colonialism, racialism, or isolationism. I believe it is this great tradition, more than any other, which prompted your country to help my people in their hour of need."

THE IMAM AND BEGUM Salimah departed Toronto on November 22nd.

Over the Christmas holidays, one evening after dinner and putting the girls to bed, Rafiq, Shameem, Yasmin, and Salim sat down in the family room. Rafiq lit the fireplace and said, "For the past month, the Jamat has been basking in the glow of the Imam's visit to Canada. We've been overwhelmed with his affection and concern for the Jamat, and we've been marveling at the praise lavished upon our Imam and on us. We never knew that we were held in such high regard. He told us to make Canada our permanent home. This is where we will live, and this is where our children will make their lives, and he has left us with much guidance on how to build our lives here and be good citizens of Canada."

"Yes, and the Imam also has expectations of his Canadian Jamat," said Shameem. "He has seen the talent in the Jamat. In as much as he expects us to be good Canadians and live by the ethics and values of Islam, he expects us to contribute to the development of the institutional capacity of Imamat institutions in the developing areas of the world in Africa and Asia where the Jamat lives, to improve their lives and the lives of the communities within which they live. That is a call to action for you and me, Rafiq, and all of the other professionals in the Jamat."

"And we shall be ready to answer that call, whenever it comes," said Rafiq.

"We hope that we will live up to our Imam's expectations," said Yasmin. "In five years, we will celebrate his 25th year of accession to the Office of Imamat - his Silver Jubilee. Inshallah, he will visit us again in Canada during the Jubilee year. We should all work to establish ourselves, rooted in the practice of our faith and as good citizens of Canada, so that when he comes back, he sees a stronger Jamat with even greater capacity to contribute to his efforts to improve the lives of those who are less fortunate than us."

"Ameen," Salim, Rafiq, and Shameem said in unison.

Acknowledgments

My sincere gratitude to the following for their contribution and support in the production of *The Roots and the Trees*:

Karim Ladha – my nephew, who read the book as it was written and provided valuable feedback

Almas Kabani – my cousin's wife, who offered early validation of my work and has been an on-going source of inspiration

George Herbert Holley – my former boss, guide and mentor, for his sound endorsement, writing the Foreword, and his guidance throughout the book's production

Professor Azim Nanji – a dear friend who read the entire manuscript and provided valuable feedback on key elements of the book

Professor Dr. Fariyal Ross-Sheriff – a dear friend since 1961, for her review, generous praise of the manuscript and encouragement in taking my work forward

Roxana Sultan – my daughter, who edited the entire manuscript and made outstanding culturally sensitive and content edits

Firoz Abdulla – a dear friend, who had lived in Mpwapwa (the little town in Tanzania where the book's main character's family lived) and provided useful information on the town and its surroundings

Aziz Velji - my former colleague and friend, for his invaluable assistance in the book's publication

Farrah Jinha – my dear niece for designing and leading the implementation of the marketing plan for *The Roots and the Trees*

About the Author

Nizar Sultan was born and raised in British-ruled Tanganyika (now the Republic of Tanzania). After completing high school and a two-year teaching program, Nizar Sultan studied in England for five years and graduated with a degree in Economics. He returned to Tanzania in 1967, where he worked for five years in tourism infrastructure and project development. He and his wife migrated to Canada in 1972.

In Canada, Nizar has worked for 45 years in paid and voluntary capacities for the institutions of His Highness Prince Karim Aga Khan for socio-economic development of the Shia Ismaili Muslim community in Canada, of which His Highness is the spiritual leader. This included 15 years as manager of a business consulting and financing program for Ismailis in Eastern Canada and 20 years as CEO of the Aga Khan Council for Canada.

Nizar's early life and work experience in Tanzania followed by his work for the Ismaili institutions in Canada and beyond, have provided him with a deep and unique insight into the Ismaili community's historical background in East Africa, the events leading up to the community's departure from Kenya, Uganda, and Tanzania, and its settlement in a new land.

THE ROOTS AND THE TREES is Nizar's debut novel. It is a real-life study of an uprooted community's migration and early establishment in Canada, set in a fictional narrative.

Made in the USA
Coppell, TX
13 November 2020